to

Ellen Violett

in remembrance
of the nice hours when
I was painting you —

[signature]

May, 1941, New York

THE END IS NOT YET

The characters of this novel are symbolic. Their resemblance to persons alive or dead is, indeed, a remarkable coincidence.

THE END IS NOT YET

A NOVEL   O<small>F HATRED AND LOVE; OF DARKNESS</small>
<small>AND LIGHT; OF DESPAIR AND HOPE; OF DEATH AND LIFE; OF WAR AND A NEW</small>
<small>courage . . .</small>

FRITZ VON UNRUH

STORM PUBLISHERS · NEW YORK

THIS BOOK
FRIEDERIKE
BELONGS TO YOU

PRELUDE

IN STRASSBURG "THEN YOU'VE REALLY CONSENTED
TO DANCE FOR THAT HENCHMAN OF THE DEVIL'S TONIGHT?" KASPAR FRIED-
rich Uhle looked at the girl reproachfully. And thought: Here she sits
beside me on a bench in Strassburg Cathedral, and she smells of spring.

"Consented!?" Olenka's voice, when it came, was a whisper. "Consented! Olala! I have to! Or do you think that when the lord of the
manor in Obersalzburg decrees: 'That Polish dancer Olschewska is to
dance the "Swan" before me on the twenty-third of August, 1939,'—
do you think I can refuse? But what a gloomy face, my dear and
exiled knight of liberty! Not afraid that . . . Monsieur Adolf might
fall in love with me? Not . . . ?" Her head, with its beautiful, freshly
set curls, came nearer.

"Precisely . . ." Uhle ducked, and then said tonelessly, "The first
time I saw you, in the opera house—wonderful! unforgettable! Such
lightness! And in every movement! And at the end, when you tossed
up that silvery scarf—actually, the material itself seemed to have more
weight than you—"

"Merci! I try to keep in training!"

"What?—And such an Ariel! . . . no! Impossible! I mean, that you
should exhibit yourself before that monster."

"Olala! And was it to tell me *that*, please, that you persuaded me to
come here from Paris?"

"In our struggle against the Beast we cannot forego anyone. Least
of all such a spirit of light as you!"

"Spirit of light?" She smiled, flattered. "Nevertheless, my good sir,
you are not objective! The Beast, as you call him, has been extremely
nice to me. He actually sent me a bunch of orchids worth 5000
marks . . ."

"Five thousand marks? Ah! these eternal realists! they're always the
ones who can pay! They draw salaries from the Devil! And all the

1

while, they have been preparing the world cataclysm, which we idealists foresaw and warned against, day and night, with every ounce of our thought! Oh, they can simply buy anything they want—even the music in those thighs of yours . . ."

"You too have your reward, my dear idealist—'the better world.'"

"Nevertheless," Uhle interrupted her mocking laughter, "once again—and in spite of everything—we Idealists are going to rescue the world from the hellish claws of the archrealist Devil—"

He rose and walked down the side aisle until he came to the so-called "Kaiser Window." As if under a spell, he stared at the long slanting rays of sunlight streaming in through the glass. Myriads of drifting rainbow-hued motes. In imagination, did he see before him something of the unending space of the cosmos, in which God with His all-powerful creating word, "Let there be . . ." had just scattered all His worlds?

Out of her doe-brown eyes Olenka watched him wandering through the cathedral. At that morning hour it was nearly deserted. In the cold high, gray twilight of the multitude of Gothic arches and pillars, the only spot of warm color was the red-lacquered organ, high up on one of the side walls. Then she too rose, thinking at first that she would follow him. Suddenly she danced off in the other direction, past the dusty, dim confessionals—still going away from him—until she came to the font near the entrance door. There she waited. She was wearing a high-crowned felt hat trimmed with a pheasant's feather; she pushed it back, and the chestnut curls fell about her face. Uhle was slowly making his way toward her from the vicinity of the high altar. Suddenly, outside in the street, the "Marseillaise" rang out.

Uhle stopped and stood stock-still, listening. The fiery rhythms of the revolutionary song moved off in the direction of the Rhine. Were they French troops?—From the stained-glass window above him—a bit of turf, St. George with the slain dragon—a red-green light fell on Uhle's straight, combed-back hair. Through the shadow that his bulging forehead threw over his eyes something like a decision suddenly shone. The tanned skin tightened over his broad cheekbones. His head and shoulders forward, his lips pressed together, he looked indomitable, as if he, too, were ready to wrestle a dangerous fall with Lucifer's hosts.

"Come!" Olenka drew him out into the street. "I have to be at the airport in an hour. But before that—oh, I'd love to find some little place where we could taste their famous Strassburg goose liver—"

She had more to say, but Uhle had already crossed to the other side

2

of the street, where a crowd was following the "tarantara" of a military band.

"Hé, Monsieur!" Olenka ran after him and took his arm. Then, fallen silent, she wandered with him through the maze of streets, between the half-timbered medieval houses with their high, pointed gable-roofs. Suddenly Uhle stopped. He stared at Olenka so long that she blushed and blushed again. Then he asked:

"And how does it happen I have not been told why you of all people —a Pole!—should have received this most honorable invitation to his gangster hide-out?"

"Didn't I tell you?" She gnawed her glove, embarrassed. "Quoi? I didn't tell you about Tchechova? About the Russian actress? Olala! The poor thing! A while ago when I was in Budapest she absolutely fell in love with me. You know, as a dancer I have a style of my own! Naturally it's not like Pavlova's . . . not a bit the way they teach you to dance in the Russian ballet. Of course I adore the Russian ballet. But I have my own individual note." She smiled proudly and blew her cigarette smoke through his hair. "So—how I came to receive this most honorable invitation? Is that what you want to know? Écoutez: some weeks ago I was appearing in Warsaw. And—if I may say so—I was marvelous. Right after the performance Tchechova came bursting into my dressing room. 'Darling!' she said, 'tomorrow I'm invited to appear before Him!' (And by 'Him' she meant her Führer against the Bolsheviks.) After she had kissed me enough she told me that she had had a brown taffeta crinoline dress made for her dinner at the Reich Chancellor's Palace. But suddenly she whispered into my ear, 'Child, child! *He* must see you! And I know how it can be done! Göring has ordered a few girls from the Winter Garden to dance after dinner. And instead of Lola—you shall dance!' "

"And you did?" asked Uhle slowly.

"Why not?" Then, seeing Uhle's lips go white, she began to tease him: "So it seems I was right not to tell your highly idealistic self a word about it! You always take things in the funniest way! Uhle . . ." she caressed his shoulder. "Yes! I danced! And it was in his new, huge Mosaic Hall in Berlin. And the crowd of beautiful, silver-laced aides de camp—it made my head swim! And then afterwards in the wonderful suite they'd given me for a dressing room—there I was all alone with the maid—and roses—olala, Uhle—on every table, on every bureau. Roses! yellow roses! red roses! It was simply crazy! Suddenly the door opened. And who appeared?"

"The Realist?"

3

"Quoi?" she burst out laughing. "No—Tchechova! '*He* was enchanted!' she said. 'He really fell in love with you! Did you get a good look at him? I was sitting on his left. On his right, Frau Ribbentrop. But in the middle! In his snow-white uniform! That was *He!*' 'Did I see him?' I pinched Tchechova all over. 'Of course I did! That's why I worked so extra hard.' " She looked at Uhle defiantly. "Yes! . . . I danced! The spotlights were playing on me! The flowers were flying around my legs! Oh! I danced, danced . . ." She spun round once and her curls whirled out. Then, seeing that Uhle became more and more monosyllabic, she cried:

"Mais oui! . . . and now, through their embassy in Paris, he has sent me an enchanting invitation. And a bigger piece of publicity for a dancer than that—there's no such thing in the world today! No, Monsieur!"

Uhle walked slowly on.

"Darling!" she came after him. "Angry?—just because I work at my profession? What's the matter with you? My agent telegraphed me from Munich, expressly to tell me not to miss this plane!"

"Who is to meet you at the airfield in Germany?"

"Who? A Colonel Egath."

"Egath? Not the Chief of Police in Berchtesgaden?"

"Do you know him?"

"In a way," Uhle nodded. "Yes! In 1914 once, in the Ardennes Forest, we were on patrol together, lying side by side in that sweet-smelling moss. My horse had stretched out all four legs like a dog. He was as tired as that. I lay with my head against the saddle, the reins over my arm. Night birds were calling. He kept humming, 'Blow, blow, thou winter wind.' "

"Egath?"

"Do I know him!—In 1919 he was a Spartacist. 'Long live the Russian World Revolution!' Ha-ha! And now he's with the Gestapo. In any case, since then he has several times tried to contact me through questionable intermediaries—"

"He has? Then, Uhle—Or don't you feel any longing for your native land? Hm—why are you breathing so hard?"

". . . Yesterday, when I took the street-car and rode out to the border, all the way to the iron bridge across the Rhine—and on one side I saw the French guardhouse, painted red, white and blue and barricaded with barbed wire, and across on the other side, in Kehl, the German guardhouse, barricaded just the same way! . . . And down under the bridge, the wide, wide, eternal river—" He made a long

4

pause, then added bitterly, "But you—you are willing to go over there today, across the Rhine, to dance for the monster?"

Olenka avoided his eyes.

"No!" He clutched her wrist. "You must not do that!"

"Quoi?" She turned round and looked at him in astonishment. The color rushed to her face; her cheeks trembled. He let her hand go. Then, for many minutes, they stood side by side without a word.

Suddenly the ancient cathedral clock began to strike twelve over the town.

"Olala . . . twelve already!" She shivered in her thin, sand-colored suit. Uhle had started on. In front of the big show window of a Cook's Bureau stood a gaudy colored placard with a picture of a tourist bus, proclaiming its message: the prices of trips to the battlefields around Verdun. Suddenly he disappeared into the office. Olenka's lips curled. Almost at once he came out again with two tickets. One of them he handed to her.

"For me?"

"Yes—because before you go to dance at Obersalzburg—I want very much to show you the mass graves that the 'Realists' dug for the human beings they sacrificed in 1916 . . ."

"Are you mad?" She stared at him. "It's outrageous that you can't shake off your memories of the war."

"Outrageous?!"

"You want to show me graves? Olala, Monsieur! I'm alive. I love life! And I want you to love it too!"

"Come," he said with sudden force, and tried to lead her to the bus, which was already waiting.

"Let me go! . . . I have to get to the airport!"

"And you seriously intend to . . . exhibit yourself in front of that beerhouse bully from Braunau? A girl like you? I could never respect you again."

"Respect?" she giggled, bewildered. Then she opened her handbag and powdered her face, hot from walking, traced the delicate outline of her small mouth with lipstick, and repeated, crossly, "Respect?"

"I have left everything behind, there. My brothers. My people. The bells of home. Yes. Home.—For I could never go back. But along comes a little girl like you—and simply flies quietly over all the barbed-wire-barricaded guardhouses, over the broad Rhine—there. And all to dance for an abortion dropped by an Austrian custom official's widow! To dance!"

"Dancing is my life!" she said wonderingly. "Or what else should

5

my life be, Monsieur—what else?"

"Everything—I have left everything behind there. At night my old mother starts up in her bed, and prays aloud for her son in exile . . ."

"In exile!" She laughed nervously. "And why? Come *with* me! Do come! Olala, I simply don't understand you. Naturally, if a Jew hates him, I understand that. But an Aryan like you! Besides, we Poles too say, 'My country, right or wrong!' "

"Wrong?" He straightened up. "No! if my country does what is wrong, how can I call it 'my country'? No, no!"

"Uhle—" She held the ticket in front of his face. "For me there is only one 'or'. Love *or* fame!"

Uhle remained silent. She waited for a few tense moments, then tore up the ticket. She turned and signaled a taxi. Uhle looked after her, until he could no longer see her in the crowded street. Then he climbed into the bus for Verdun.

BOOK ONE

CHAPTER ONE

STEPPING OUT OF THE CROWDED BUS, UHLE HAD TAKEN A TAXICAB, AND NOW WAS ALONE ON THE WILDER-ness of overgrown desolation that had been the battlefield of Verdun. He had been driven along the so-called Chemin Sacré, the avenue that leads to the tunnel of the Fort de Tavanne. Along this road each mile-stone, capped by a trench-helmet decked with flowers, had reminded him that here at every few steps some soldier had been mowed down by murderous gunfire. At length he had arrived at one of the gigantic mass cemeteries.

Here the fallen of all nations, collected from the vicinity, had been interred, military fashion, in nice, neat ranks of endless graves. Hun-dreds of thousands of precise, short wooden crosses, painted white, had been soberly planted out as far as the eye could see, one after the other, at the head of each dead hero beneath his leveled mound of earth. Roads and paths, indicated by signposts, traversed the vast array of uniform, mass-fabricated crosses, like the streets of a modern city. And round about, mile after mile, stretched the empty, deserted battlefields.

Uhle hesitantly approached the autumn-parched lawns beneath which reposed more than two million broken bodies, the 'human materiel' of war. As he raised his arm to salute his dead comrades, the long, black raincape slipped back, revealing an old field-gray Uhlan jacket from which the silver buttons of the former Imperial German Army had been painstakingly removed. Horn buttons had been sewn in their place. Corduroy breeches, heavy walking shoes, and roll puttees completed his costume. The knapsack on his back was almost empty.

Looking about the cemetery with all its mementos of horrifying mass slaughter, he murmured:

" 'L'Homme Mort' Incline, Hill 304, Bois de Fayette, Death Gorge! Yes—in those days, in 1916, the citizens of the Twentieth Century, eyes frenzied with blood lust, knives clenched in their teeth, hurled

7

hand grenades and drove bayonets at each other, raging, slaying or bleeding."

Uhle walked slowly from grave to grave. He fell to reading the names of the fallen. It was like a melancholy chant as he read aloud in his deep voice: "Born 1887, fallen 1916, before Verdun; born 1896, fallen 1916, before Verdun; born 1893, fallen 1916, before Verdun;— born . . ."

Finally he arrived in front of a wooden torso of the Christ held upright by a few bricks. Apparently the crossfire of artillery had shot the Saviour down from the Crucifix which had once dominated the landscape. Now the legless body, still glossed with the patina of the First World War, wound about to the waist with barbed wire, stood piteously propped up. Of the outstretched arms, torn from the Cross, the right hand had been shot away and three fingers of the left hand were missing. The carved hair fell to the shoulders about the head, bowed with grief. The painted eyes gazed fixedly in the direction of the square-built towers of Verdun Cathedral, faintly discernible on the cloudy horizon. As once with thorns and knotted whips, this body of the Christ had been torn by bullets and shell fragments. At the base of the figure someone had recently placed a board on which was written, in crude capitals traced in red paint:

WAR and LIFE is OVER.

The paint was still wet.

Coming back to the waiting taxicab, Uhle directed the chauffeur to drive along the Route Nationale to the station at Metz. But as he came to the hill leading up to Beaumont, he was suddenly so struck by the remembrance of all the butchery he had seen in these fields, hills, and valleys, that he called to the driver to stop. They got out. Uhle abruptly left the path and cut across the sloping meadow to the left. With a glance of distaste for the wilderness of blackened stumps and charred branches ahead, the chauffeur said: "If you want to go further, go ahead. I'll wait here."

After a long and fatiguing walk, Uhle at last came to a signpost bearing the legend:

HERE FORMERLY STOOD
THE PROSPEROUS, FLOURISHING
VILLAGE OF BEAUMONT.

Up and down the ruined street, now a waste of nettles, all he could discern of the former village were a few stones and fragments of walls.

Here and there he could just make out the charred foundations of houses blasted from the face of the earth by artillery fire. Behind the only church pillar left standing, open graves and family vaults gaped wide—the effect of plowing shells. One of these vaults, about ten feet deep, was now a pool full of croaking frogs. The paths were almost impassable, overgrown with weeds and flowers: cornflowers, geraniums, plantains, forget-me-nots, and hepaticas, their blossoms innocently gay.

At the further end of this scene of horror and devastation, embedded in bittersweet, wild onions, rhubarb, and narcissus, Uhle found an intact skeleton, whose trench helmet had tumbled off the skull through which a bullet had bored clean. To get to it, he had to push aside a roll of rusted barbed wire, tearing his finger in doing so.

He stopped to examine the bones, washed snow white by the elements, as if they had been scoured for a medical classroom.

"I wonder who it could have been? A Frenchman? A German? Or 'the hereditary enemy'?" He heaped bluebells, sorrel, and grasses on the bleached bones until they were completely covered.

The heat of the sun behind a heavy blanket of clouds was so great as nearly to stifle thought. Still he kept his eyes on the flower-covered skeleton before him in the grass. He was thinking how, many years ago, as a soldier among soldiers, in the midst of bombardment and merciless artillery fire, he and many a long-remembered comrade-in-arms, their blood-stained fingers cramped and intertwined, had sworn an oath before Heaven. Had they not sworn, indeed, one to another, that life should be rebuilt on a new and different basis? Had it not then appeared to them, confronted with the insane, macabre laughter of death, that a tiny clump of green earth, not yet destroyed by shellfire, was Paradise itself? Had he not written a field postcard to Irene that he felt an entirely new Love triumphant within himself?

"If every one of us who fought here had kept his oath . . . perhaps . . . But where is there a single one! Where!—"

CHAPTER TWO

THERE WAS A SUDDEN, EAR-SPLIT-TING SHRIEK. THE NEXT INSTANT A GIRL, FOLLOWED BY AN OLD WOMAN, both wearing ragged khaki trousers, scrambled out of a deserted trench.

9

In evident terror of their lives, they ran for their bicycles, propped against a ruined abutment, mounted, and rode off, hell-for-leather, down a narrow pathway along a blackthorn hedge, through the fields, heading for the highway to Verdun. Startled by their cries, Uhle looked toward the trench.

Great cloud shadows swept over him, on and away. Swallows, blue as night, flitted past, skimming the earth. Down below, on the highway, the dust rose and eddied in swirls as if flung up by some ghostly hand. Abruptly an unwieldy fat man clambered out of a concealed hole in the ground. There, in the wilderness of that No Man's Land, he stood, clumsily brushing the burrs off his sleeves. With a handful of blood-red clover blossoms, he swabbed some of the mud and slime from a filth-encrusted uniform. He was a repellent figure, his greasy, parchment-yellow cranium and jowls adorned by a tangled growth of bushy, reddish hair.

Uhle ducked down into the weeds out of sight. Galvanized into extraordinary activity and dragging a dirty brown sack behind him, the corpulent creature scurried along, pouncing now right, now left, as though gathering potatoes. His harvest, however, was of another kind. For as Uhle watched he saw him darting here and there, picking up bones, the bleached and scattered bones of the dead, and, as swiftly, tossing them into his trailing sack, like a miser snatching at stray gold coins. Apparently chilly despite the intense heat, the figure pulled a silk field cap over his bald dome and then dashed on, faster and faster.

"A ghost," muttered Uhle, "in broad daylight!!"

At that instant, the fantastic bone-collector caught sight of him. His revolver swiftly drawn and aimed, he bawled:

"Halt! Who goes there? Advance!"

Confronted by this threat, Uhle went forward cautiously.

"Closer! Damn it!" His watery blue eyes glared fixedly at Uhle. At length, with a grin, and in a rusty voice, he spoke:

"Afraid of me, eh? Come on! I'm flesh and blood!" He saluted Uhle. "Sir, I presume that smartly uniformed chauffeur down there on the highway is yours? I asked the monkey: 'What're you doing around here?' He said you were on your way to the station at Metz. Permit me! You must belong to the Cook's Tour group expected from Verdun about two o'clock? Eh? So you came on ahead of the others, eh? You see that?" He pointed at the sack. "I've just been laying in provisions. . . . But permit me!"

With a brief formal bow, he handed Uhle a soiled visiting card. The latter read aloud: "Captain Hermann!"

"Yes, Monsieur! . . . And since 1916, I have never left this battle-field . . . Ha-ha! Mais oui! And that's how it happens that I know every square inch of the terrain . . . Now, let's see! What would you like to inspect first? Of course, you're an American, mister? . . . You know, the Cook's Tour people won't let you see anything but a lot of old junk. For instance, there's an utterly uninteresting tangle of dead Frenchmen—they'll show you that. But all you can see is a lot of twisted bayonets sticking out of the ground. . . . I, on the other hand, am in a position to show you all sorts of curiosities nobody else has a chance to see.

"You may be sure they'll be weirder and more wonderful than any-thing Cook's could show you. Ha-ha! Am I right, mister? You like to feel your flesh creep, don't you . . . Then, just come along with me!" He made no move to proceed, however, but mopped his brow. "By Christ! . . . It's hot!"

"What was that? Thunder?"

"Yes. Thunder! The Weather Bureau has promised us a storm. But you don't have to worry; unfortunately, the thunder of artillery fire stopped long ago. But once upon a time Death, the Red Knight, his horse shod with flame, used to gallop back and forth through drifting fog across these fields. Indeed! And now his path is bordered with ruins and graves! . . . March!" Abruptly, he motioned downhill, pointing with his revolver toward Haudroumont Quarry. "S'il vous plaît—I live down there!"

There was nothing for it but to humor him as he forced Uhle on ahead. Suddenly Captain Hermann jumped to one side of the pathway, stamping about in the grass and bellowing.

"Kill the dirty swine! Why doesn't that damned piece of carrion give up and croak?"

Returning to the path, he took up his stand, legs widespread, and made water in the infinity of those fields.

Some skylarks were startled into abrupt flight. Grinning amiably, the captain returned, poking Uhle in the ribs with his revolver and grunting:

"Go on."

When they reached the bottom of the quarry, he said to Uhle:

"Careful! . . . Don't step on that misfire! How foolish that fat sugar canister looks there among the forget-me-nots! Yet, mister, the poor thing never reached its destination! Ha-ha! There it lies, hoping against hope that some day it will! So—attention please! Ha-ha! For its time will yet come! Therefore—prenez garde!" Bringing his heels together smartly and saluting with one finger, he declared:

"So! Here we are! By the living God, this is my palace!"

'A dugout!" Uhle inspected what was apparently the entrance to a rude cave.

"Ha-ha! Every time you people from the Land of the Dollar arrive here, you always ask: 'Dugout—what's that?' . . . A dugout is a hole! And in such holes the sons of men dig themselves in as deep as they can—like rats—to find what protection they may from bursting shells . . . S'il vous plaît, this is the entrance to my abode!"

Uhle held his nose. "It smells like death!" He stared into the black aperture. "Down there for four long years soldiers of all races and parties kept house together with rats and corpses! At the bottom of that stinking hole they crouched and cowered, smoked and drank, gobbled their food and played cards, hoping and fearing and every instant praying:

'Peace! Peace! Peace! No matter how or why!
Peace!—peace!—peace! Let only the battle die!' "

"Mon gars," groaned the Captain ominously, "you're not a pacifist? As far as I am concerned, I'd just as soon kill a flea any time, whether he's in your pants or in your shirt! . . . Go on, mister!" He signed to Uhle. "I'll have my stiffs perform for you! . . . Halt! I'll go ahead."

CHAPTER THREE STICKING THE REVOLVER IN ITS HOLSTER, HE BENT OVER ALMOST DOUBLE, HEAD AND SHOULDERS DISAPPEARING in the crumbling entrance to the dugout. Last to disappear was the widespread seat of his grimy trousers. Uhle descended behind him, counting the steps downward in the pestilential murk.

"One! Two! Three!"

"Look out up there!" Captain Hermann's voice re-echoed hollowly as from a cellar. "Those steps are slippery. You'll fall!"

"Thirty-three steps!" Uhle murmured to himself. "Exactly thirty-three steps! This must be the very same dugout! Haudroumont Quarry!" Excitedly he looked about him. "Could it be? . . . Yes! That's the coffering we put up to hold back the clay!"

"Ho-ho! So you're a General Staff Inspector in mufti, are you?"

The Captain glared at him resentfully. "I suppose you're one of those fellows who's determined to hammer it into his brain right here on the spot, that your so-called 'modern' materiel of war is infinitely superior! Well—of course, for the perpetual warfare that is coming you'll have to have all the latest improvements!"

His lighting facilities were primitive. Each time a match was struck, the dripping moisture made short work of it. For a time he led the way by a phosphorescent hand compass.

"Watch out, mister," the Captain called back to Uhle. "The next step is missing!"

"There's a rat!" Uhle called out.

"Ha-ha! You'll find plenty of them rustling about here among the empty tin cans . . ."

Uhle clambered on down through the clutter of cartridge cases and mildewed knapsack leathers, on the heels of the Captain. The latter finally produced and lit a candle stump. In its reddish glow Uhle saw the clay walls, well smoothed, with any number of rifles, bayonets fixed, stacked against them.

"Yes!" exclaimed his guide, holding the candle high, like a torch. "Here primal instincts held sway, but they had the advantage of the most scientific instruments of destruction." In the flickering light, formless shadows came and went.

On a rough wooden table, hammered together out of fragments of discarded packing cases, stood a cooking pot with a ladle in it, and round the table itself sat a group of eight soldiers.

"Come ahead! Step right up! Don't be afraid! These are my pals!"

"But—they're all dead!" Uhle recoiled.

"Don't worry about that, my boy. They were all tee-totally gassed twenty years ago!" Rapidly, in turn, he held the candle before one after the other of the corpses. There were two poilus in sky-blue uniform, an English Tommy in a long khaki cloak, four Germans in field gray, and a Senegalese Negro in the uniform of the French Colonials. There they sat, soldiers all, all wearing trench helmets, their rifles between their knees, like Madame Tussaud's waxworks. Hollow-cheeked as they were, there was no sign of decay about them. Uhle was transfixed at the sight: "And you, Olenka—you dare to think it is *outrageous* that I cannot shake off my memories of the war!"

The old Captain maundered on: "Heavens! I suppose you're wondering why they haven't all putrefied long ago? That's easy. The air-conditioning in this fancy tomb hermetically sealed by the force of an explosion in the bombardment of 1916 has handsomely mummified

13

these fellows! . . . Hey, there!" Captain Hermann taunted them. "So you're playing League of Nations again! The fact is, whenever they're playing League of Nations, you can't get one sensible word out of them. They just sit there, a respectable assembly of corpses, and won't touch their sugar rations!" The table was strewn with lumps of white sugar and, as he held forth, he rolled them to and fro like dice.

"How goes it, Emil!" He nudged the Senegalese so that the corpse swayed slightly. "See that! Every time I wave the candle and he sees the shadows dance, the rascal grins. Just look how he grins! How his teeth shine in that black map! . . . Well—we might as well leave them to their League of Nations game!"

He urged Uhle some ten yards farther on into the darkness. Here the wet, streaming walls formed a sort of niche where he deposited the candle on an empty packing case.

"So-o-o!" he said with some satisfaction. "Just a moment! Whenever I have a guest, I always light my big altar-candles! These five-branched candelabra are a legacy from Major von Schleinitz! When his regiment was fighting up above, he managed to bag them from the Beaumont village church. This little chapel was his brainwave! Allow me!" He lit the thick yellow wax candles in two Baroque candelabra, each a yard high.

"There we are!" he cried. "How's that for the Kingdom and the Glory!" The dull, old-gold finish, richly carved, glowed in the gloom.

Licking his beard, he blinked at Uhle.

"Yes, yes! That beautiful red brocade and the white lace runner—not so white as it used to be!—they're all due to von Schleinitz. You see, he was very devout. So, while his men were in the thick of it, he used to spend his time down here on his knees, praying for them. Ha-ha-ha! The dumb donkey! . . . Praying for them! . . . Take a look; there he is, behind the box!"

"What!" Uhle craned his neck to see. "You don't mean to tell me you've got his corpse down behind that box!"

"Exactly!" Captain Hermann threw back the folds of a coat, and there lay the dead von Schleinitz. "Well!" He hastily covered up that face. "Let's not disturb his eternal rest!" He sat down again. "Yes, sir, you're wondering how I can stand it down here. But just imagine; how could I, after having spent so many cockeyed years down here together with the living and the dead, ever again manage to return to your comfortable bourgeois way of living? Can you see me getting up in the morning, breakfasting on rolls and coffee and, brief case under my arm, punching the clock punctually at 9 a.m. in a life-insurance office, or

14

some such idiotic business? . . . You want to know what time it is?" Uhle was looking at his wristwatch. "There's no such thing down here!"

"I have to be on my way. My taxi is waiting."

"Out of the question! First, we must drink a glass of noble old cognac! . . . For God's sake, what a mess I am! Well, there you have it! To-o-otal war produces to-o-otal filthiness! You'll pardon me! I must make myself presentable. Dear Lord! Now where is my lion skin?"

He turned to a cupboardlike recess in the wall, noisily pulling back a curtain on brass rings and revealing a whole collection of uniforms on clothes-hangers, close-packed in the small space. Evidently, in his business of scavenging on the deserted battlefields he had hoarded this store of virtually every uniform in the fighting forces on both sides. There they hung: French, Austrian, Canadian, American, Serbian, German, Russian and English uniforms, along with Hindu and Spahi outfits.

"So-o-o!" Carefully selecting the uniform of a Prussian General, he removed it from the hanger and put it on. The gold-embroidered collar and epaulettes glittered in the candlelight. He adjusted the "Pour le Mérite" Order on its ribbed, black-and-white silk ribbon about his neck. Between the golden eagles, the lapis-lazuli cross gleamed brightly.

From the depths of his improvised clothespress, Captain Hermann now produced a cooking pot, which he opened as reverently as if it had contained the Holy Sacrament.

He pointed to the fabulous, sparkling pile within. "These are my well-earned decorations! Why should the soldier be deprived of the visible testimonials of his courage? Who would deny the secret desires of his heart, so often leaping for joy amid the voluptuous excitations of battle?"

Ceremoniously he pinned on his left breast the Star of Brabant, the English Star of the Order of the Garter, the pearl-gray Persian Order of the Sun and the Lion, the Russian Cross of St. Andrew, the plaquette of the Légion d'Honneur, the Belgian Order of the Lion. As the space was soon full, he continued setting them forth on his right breast: the Prussian Order of the Black Eagle above the Iron Cross, First Class, the Medal of Honor, the Finnish Cross of Honor, the Italian Order of the Annunciation, the Order of the Prussian Crown, and the bediamonded Chrysanthemum Star of the Emperor of Japan.

The corresponding regalia, ordinarily worn about the neck, he hung from the buttons of his coat and, when there was no more room, from the buttons of his trousers. The Iron Crown of the Habsburgs dangled below the Papal Order of the Spurs of Christ, the Turkish Crescent, and the beflagged Order of Lenin. Since the last was in his way, he removed it and threw it with careful aim at the head of Emil, the Senegalese. Once again the corpse rocked lightly.

Finally satisfied, drawing himself up to his full height in the candle-lit recess, with blue, rheumatic hands Captain Hermann lovingly stroked his startling array of medals and decorations.

Stalking back to the table they had left, he picked up a company daybook, encrusted with blood and filth, opened it, and poked through the pages with the barrel of his revolver. Like a hotel register, it contained the autographs of many visitors who had evidently found their way down to this limbo.

"Please," he grunted throatily. "Will you kindly enter your name here? Whoever descends from the upper regions to this underworld, has to enter his name in my guest book." He handed Uhle a fountain pen.

In the uncertain light he could just make out the signatures: "Mussolini . . . Trotsky . . . Churchill . . . Thyssen . . . Göring . . . Stalin . . . Roosevelt . . ."

"Ha-ha! Yes! Nothing but big shots! And they're all sons of 'The Father of All Things'—whose name is, War! Here you are, now. Can you decipher this handwriting? That sentence was written by the president of the German Academy of Letters: 'When I hear people talking about culture, then I cock my revolver!' Isn't that magnificent? Mark me well—I never carry my revolver any other way!" He shook with laughter. "Yes, we live in a marvelous age! The warrior spirit, in your upstairs world there, will soon replace the scholastic spirit! Certainly! For Prussia is actually drilling and hammering the Manual of Arms into the whole world. On the Thames and on the Hudson the password today is: 'One—two! One—two! Hep!—Hep!—Hep!' . . . They're pounding it in until the skyscrapers wobble: 'Right—about face! Left—turn! One—two! One—two!' Ha-ha!"

"I see you have quite a pile of books there." Uhle pointed to a heap of moldy, tattered volumes.

"Yes! Everything that opposes the warrior spirit! Here!" He stooped down, puffing asthmatically, and pulled out one of the books. He handed it to Uhle.

"Hölderlin's poems!"

"Now I ask you! What do you say to this statement?" He pointed to a page marked with red pencil and Uhle read aloud:

" 'The time shall come when thou, Germania, disarmed, shalt give counsel to the kings and peoples of the earth!' "

"Well, what do you say to that? 'Disarmed,' the idiot says!" He snatched the book out of Uhle's hand. " 'Disarmed,' indeed! Anyhow, the introduction says this so-called poet went mad, and stayed mad for forty-four years. That's what I call Nemesis!" He clenched his fist. "And that's what should happen from now on to anyone who ever dares to babble about 'disarmament'! . . . . But why waste time on such a nincompoop?" And with that he flung the Hölderlin volume back onto the rubbish heap, carefully wiping his fingers as if they had been soiled by their contact with belles lettres. With vigorous tread he trampled on the pile of novels, plays, poems, and philosophical works, and immediately thereafter fell to manicuring his nails.

"Oh, well!" he winked portentously at Uhle. "What do we care— we worshipers of 'Might-is-Right'—for such Pegasus-jockeys, ink-slingers, and brain-athletes? Believe me, my friend, today we're enter-ing upon an era when the telephone book is going to be a whole lot more important than all that childish babble from Socrates to Kant, from Bertha Suttner to the League of Nations! Ha-ha!"

"So you're an enemy of democracy?"

"I'm an enemy of every kind of hokum!"

Suddenly he ducked down in his corner.

"Lay low! Wasn't that shrapnel exploding?" But, at Uhle's reassuring smile, he stood up again, his sudden movement causing the candle flames to flicker. "I've worked up a thirst! You too?"

From behind the altar, he fished out an imposing bottle of brandy, turning it to the light until Uhle could discern through its film of grime the Napoleonic "N." "How's that for a prize, eh? Right out of Napolibum's own cellars! Ha-ha-ha!" Lifting the purple-red altar-cloth, with its brocade angels, he dragged out from beneath it two golden chalices, reverently filling them to the brim with brandy.

"Well, here's to your liver and lights! There's nothing like a chalice if you want to get the real flavor out of a noble old brandy! Ha-ha!" The chalice emptied, he immediately refilled it again. "So! There, now! Bottoms up, my boy, or I'll blow your brains out!" Again he emptied the chalice . . . "As for me, I'm no Christian! My bowels are weather-proof! My appendix of transcendentalism was removed when I was still in the Cadet Corps. Ha-ha! Drink it down! Mud in your eye! No toast to that dwarflike creature, Man! No! I drink to the might of the 'Secret Soldier!' "

Uhle, conscious of Captain Hermann's meaningful gaze fixed upon him, was studying the curious convolutions of a gold-framed mirror above the improvised altar.

"That's a rococo mirror you have there?" he said.

"So you collect antiques, too?" The Captain's face was a twisted mask of distrust as he growled: "Major von Schleinitz 'collected' that neat little piece from the Château of Princess Irene Cagliostro. Not far from here. He used it for shaving. Ha-ha!" Brusquely he changed the subject as if to distract Uhle from his obvious interest in the mirror, the quicksilver surface of which seemed mysteriously disturbed by the shimmering candlelight. Pushing the brandy bottle to one side, Captain Hermann became matter-of-fact:

"Well, I still have to initiate you into the mysteries I celebrate here under the earth in my leisure hours. That is, whenever I get any rest from my heavy duties. Yes!" He watched Uhle suspiciously as the latter never took his eyes from the mirror. "The fact is, I have a hell of a job down here! . . . But, it's time we were getting along. Come on!"

"Just a moment!" Uhle stood stock still. "It looks as if something were moving behind that glass!"

"As if something were moving?" Squinting distrustfully, his host stood up, unbuttoned the two bottom buttons of his military jacket, opened his mouth, and belched with a hiss. "Pardon! Haven't got any thinner since 1916! Anyhow—'Naturalia non sunt turpia!' as the Romans say. I am no Latinist. Only graduated from grade school. You know, I was a cadet, Room 78 . . . However that may be, my good sir, may I now show you the field of my activities?"

Pushing aside a carpet that served as a curtain, he disappeared into the uncertain shadows beyond. His voice dropped as if he had entered a church.

"Turn right!" he cautioned. "Ss-s-sh! We are now within the purlieus of the Cadaver Utilization Factory."

"The what?" Uhle's jaw hung slack.

"Yes—the Cadaver Utilization Factory! . . . Isn't it magnificent?" Sniffing the musty air with satisfaction, he clutched at Uhle's sleeve. "Did you ever see anything so magnificent?"

In the dimness, lit only by the dull light from a single lantern, Uhle gradually perceived that they were now inside extensive, apparently endless, subterranean excavations, like the vaulted spaces of an unlighted metropolitan subway yard. Narrow-gauge tracks ran off in all directions, disappearing into pitch-black tunnels leading to deserted shelters. Probably these caves were formerly used as an artillery munitions depot.

"Attention, please!" Pointing into the heart of the darkness, Captain Hermann continued: "You see, my boy! Instead of the gaudy advertising placards of a metropolitan subway, these walls are lined with mummified corpses, right and left as far as you can see! Isn't it magnificent?" Uhle still could see nothing. The Captain dragged him further on into the gloom.

"Now! Can you make things out better now? You see that marvelous apparatus back there? . . . Those enormous glass containers and retorts are all connected by means of those pipes and tubes with that amazing machine that looks like a huge printing press . . . Sh-s-sh! Just look how those brown-shirted workers halt their labors in silent greeting to me!"

Although Uhle could see nothing but murky clay walls streaked with moisture, the Captain proudly persisted:

"My boy, you are here privileged to behold one of the most inspired inventions of the age, result of the combined researches of distinguished Heidelberg professors, protected by Reichspatent, etc." His breath reeked of alcohol. "Possibly you remember how in the last war, of a sultry summer night on the battlefield, every once in a while there would be the nauseating noise of gas bubbling forth from decaying corpses? Well, we have to thank that very natural phenomenon for the origin of this delightful machine!" He pushed Uhle forward in the darkness.

"You observe how, with astounding rapidity, every ten seconds or so, my people pitch a soldier onto the conveyor belt. Isn't that magnificent? . . . . Now, watch! That moving band feeds the cadavers, one at a time, into a coffinlike recess under the steel press . . . Boom! Gr-r-rack! A nauseating sound, isn't it? The long-sealed lungs and bowels collapse, the escaping gases are caught up and conducted, through those handsome glass tubes and retorts, farther on into the gas-bombs department.

"Just think what that means! The poisons hermetically sealed in such cadavers are so virulent that no human organism can withstand them. Flourishing countrysides, men and mice, just turn up their paws to heaven once this gas is released. On these tracks, the Artillery Command despatches countless express trains loaded with Cadaver Utilization bombs in all directions—to London, Paris, Berlin, Madrid, Moscow, Warsaw, etc. . . . ! Such a pity! Before the battle of Verdun, for instance, we had only five million shells ready for action. But—live and learn! Now, at least, we have several billions in reserve. The world has never seen such a gas! The chemists assure us that this 'Fuma bubonica,' as they call it, will revolutionize modern warfare. We shall save it as a last resort, 'ultima ratio' as it were, when all other arguments fail! Ha-ha-ha! Beware!" Abruptly he pulled Uhle back. " 'Chi tocca—muore!' 'To touch is death!' Beware! Live wires! Contact them and you'll be toast Melba in no time! . . . . Here's where our electricians are working. And when their job is finished, all you'll have to do is just press this button and England will sink under the North Sea. That's the trump card we're saving till the very end, when things get 'pretty bloody,' as the British say. . . . Technical improvements, eh? The march of progress! Ha-ha-ha!" His laughter re-echoed like the death rattle of countless throats in those underground caverns. The hollow, mocking tones were nightmarish. "Yes! The dear, kind human race! . . . Well, now, that's the end of my little tour. If you feel like giving something to the Soldiers Aid Society, of which I am president and treasurer—thank you very much! Now, I'll take you back to your upstairs world."

He lighted the way.

No sooner, however, had they returned to the altar niche than Uhle came to a fresh halt. "Isn't that a radio I hear?"

"Go along, I say!" Captain Hermann's pupils narrowed to pin points. "Get on! There is nothing more to see."

"Oh, but there is! What have you got behind that rococo mirror? There's a light shining through it!"

"Sir!!—I've just told you—!"

"But there's somebody moving in there!" Uhle pressed forward, peering between the altar candles. At that instant, Captain Hermann jammed a battered trench helmet so hastily onto his head that his unkempt red beard was caught in the chin strap. In an instant, he had armed himself as if for battle. Adjusting his equipment, he recited:

"Three pineapple hand grenades on the left; time fuses on the right; right coat pocket, the .08 pistol; right trouser pocket, the little Mauser 800; left coat pocket, five lovely little egg-shaped hand grenades; and in the left trouser pocket—don't forget!—the whistle! So-o-o!" Buckling on his belt and shoulder strap, he pulled on his gloves. The next instant, like a sentry on duty, he had planted himself before the mirror, thundering at Uhle:

"Get the—hell—out—of—here!"

"There!" Paying no attention to his antics, Uhle examined a section of the mirror, where the mercury had been rubbed away. "There's a light burning in there! Somebody's alive and moving around in there!"

CHAPTER FOUR   Lost in contemplation of the
ENIGMA, UHLE STRODE FORWARD DELIBERATELY UNTIL HE CAME FACE TO
face with Captain Hermann. Minutes passed in silence, except for the
sputtering of the candle wicks. Then, as the radio started up behind
the mirror again, Uhle pointed to the damaged surface where the
mercury was missing.

"Who is in there?"

"March! Get the hell out of here! If you don't get going, I'll put a
bullet through your brain!"

"Isn't that a soldier sitting in there? I can barely make out." Uhle
tried in vain to see past the Captain's shoulder. "There—he's moving
now!"

"One—two—three—and out you go! I am not joking!" Captain
Hermann waved his revolver with decision.

"What are all those things around him? Look like piles of magazines.
Are those bundles of newspapers? . . . Optical instruments! There's
a pair of compasses! And that's a battered pair of field glasses!" Uhle
gazed steadily at the Captain. "Who is that in there?"

"Son," suddenly shrugging off his threatening posture, Captain
Hermann gave vent to a deep groan. Filling the chalice, he once more
drained it, his glance wavering from Uhle to the mirror and back
again. "The fact is, nobody knows what superhuman duties I have to
perform down here. . . . My boy, I, too, have spent hours observing
that Diogenes in there, particularly when he's sitting like that, apparently lost to the world in ethereal visions."

"But what is he up to?"

"How the hell should I know! As far as I can see, he spends his
time measuring the radiation of candlelight with that old compass.
He once told me he was studying the Laws of Light! Ha-ha! . . .
Only the other day he said: 'The greatest joy ever experienced by
the human body is the action of light.'"

"Did he say that?" The longer Uhle looked through the mirror at
the strange prisoner, the more he felt a joyous expectancy. It was as
if, as soon as that silently brooding figure should turn his countenance
upon him, he would find himself once more face to face with some
comrade-in-arms he had long believed dead. He felt hot and cold by
turns.

"Are you going to tell me who it is you've got locked in behind that mirror?"

"S-s-s-sh! . . . . The fact is—but can I trust you? Can you keep mum, boy? Above all, Cook's must never find out—"

"Who is it?"

"By the Eternal!" the Captain groaned. "By the living God—it's the Little Jew Jesus!"

"The—who?" Uhle tried to control his own mounting excitement. "You've been guzzling too much brandy!"

"No-o-o! I'm absolutely cold sober. . . . And I'm telling you for your own good, boy, get the hell out of here! The fact is—I have been appointed General in Attendance upon the Little Jew Jesus by the All-Highest Board of Control of the Global Military Command . . . Is that clear enough for you?"

"The All-Highest Board of—!" Uhle began to think he was perhaps confronted by one of those unfortunates, a shell-shocked officer such as he had seen, arms wildly flailing, running down the village street of burning Beaumont in the bombardment of 1916.

"I tell you, it's a superhuman job! So please don't make it any harder for me! Go on! Get out of here!" He trembled as with ague.

But Uhle was lost in what he saw through the damaged mirror. "He's watching a spider spinning its web!"

"Boy!" Nonplussed, Captain Hermann pushed his helmet back off his forehead. "You haven't the faintest idea what a lunatic that is in there! And all the time he has such an unconcerned smile on what's left of his face, just like my hosts of the dead when they're watching us who are alive! . . . . Yes! You see, I've simply got a lunatic on my hands—a danger to the whole community . . . That's why I tell you, keep your hands off the frame of that mirror! If *he* should ever break out—!"

"A lunatic! I'm not so sure. If I could only see his face!"

"You'd only have to ask him, as I did: 'Hey! What's your regiment?' He comes back at you: 'I come from the Seven Planets!' When all the time I know perfectly well he's from the Engineering Corps."

"From the Engineering Corps?" The words came slowly as if some memory were stirring in Uhle. "One of the pioneer troops? . . . Is he a very pale fellow? Gaunt-faced? Deep-set blue eyes? With a black beard?"

"Pale?" Captain Hermann shrugged. "When I first found him twenty years ago, he had a jagged cranial wound. I dressed it for him, but he tore the Red Cross bandage right off again. My uniform

was drenched with such a spurt of blood from his head that I felt
sure he couldn't live. But then he did live after all!"

"And it was *you* who took care of him?"

"Yes! Later on, we even got to be good friends."

"Good friends? Then what do you keep him locked up for?"

"S-s-s-sh! See what he's up to now? That's old von Schleinitz' Bible
he just dragged out from behind the radio. It's a damn shame he doesn't
spend as much time in studying that good old-fashioned and eternally
new Bible of the he-man: 'The Manual of Arms!' I ordered it from
Potsdam especially for him! Not he! He's all the time moping over
that idiotic 'Good Book' that the Jewish Santa Claus dumps under
the Christmas tree as a bait for the poor, suffering human race! And
in spite of the fact that I said to him only the other day, after giving
him an hour's lecture on 'The Heroic'—'You don't suppose the vacant
premises of a vanishing Christianity can afford any kind of shelter
to us soldiers?'"

"And what did he say?"

"He looked at me with those ice-blue eyes of his and had the crust
to tell me that, during his solitary confinement in this hole, he had
rediscovered the Archimedean lever with which he's going to dis-
lodge the present-day world of global military power!"

"What did you say to that?"

"I tried to drive it into his head that the world of military power
is a Juggernaut of such tremendous force—the will of man to kill and
be slain in battle, so without beginning and without end—that only
a soldier can truly understand the thunders of Mount Sinai!"

"He's kneeling down!"

"What! At it again? I suppose he's lost in adoration of that yellow
caterpillar of his he found the other day. For days and days now he's
been philosophizing about the physical structure of that insect as if
the fate of the whole world depended on it . . . Hey, there!" he
suddenly bawled into the mirror, "are you bowing down to your
caterpillar idol again?" The Captain winked at Uhle: "Wait till you
see, my boy! The next thing you know he'll say: 'I kneel before the
Spirit of Life in it!' . . . . Ha-ha! . . . . Just watch!"

Inasmuch, however, as no sound came from the prisoner, the Captain suddenly frothed with rage. His hand shook as if with the palsy;
he seized one of the communion chalices and hurled it with full force
against the rococo mirror. It missed and fell to the floor with a crash.
The next instant his voice rose to a frenzied roar, the zigzag blue
veins in his temples swelling as if they would burst:

23

"You fool! How often have I got to tell you: *To live is to kill!*"

Dumbfounded, Uhle dashed toward the mirror as if to protect the pioneer. But the Captain gave him such a blow on the shoulder that he was thrown off balance and stumbled against the wall. In so doing he knocked something down, apparently a mask of some sort, that rolled and wobbled to his feet. As he stooped to pick it up, his antagonist thrust his head forward threateningly; his lips were drained of blood.

"Leave that alone! . . . Hand it over!"

Disregarding this outburst, Uhle carefully examined the mask. Apparently made of some soft, indestructible plastic, a perfect likeness of the human features, it was pliable between his fingers.

"Hand over that mask! Professor Essex presented it to me when he paid me a visit."

"What a wonderful plastic! I wonder what it is made of?"

"Yes, it's a perfect gem. Of course, it's only one of hundreds of thousands manufactured to specifications of the various supreme general staffs in order to conceal the shell-shattered and flame-eaten faces of such poor devils. The idea is to mask their disfigurement so they won't give the screaming meemies to those who may be under their command or to future soldiers in training." He snatched it out of Uhle's hand.

"The trouble is, every time my Little Jew Jesus catches sight of this mask, we have a life-and-death tussle! He's determined to get hold of it. If only he could cover up that charred and blasted mug of his, he'd like nothing better than to escape from here, clamber upstairs into the outer world and pay a visit to his 'exploited brothers' as he persists in calling the mob you've got up there."

"Is he a communist?"

"No-o-o-o. At least, he's always saying: 'The First and Second Internationals should not have combated capitalism on the same old economic plane alone'."

"What should they have done?"

"He says that they should have fought it on the basis of 'higher and more ethical' principles!" He laughed scornfully. "You know what he confessed to me?—He wants to fulfill 'the yearning which is latent in every human heart!' That's how he put it! Ha-ha! Now can you see why I am held responsible by the combined military powers of the world for the security of this fellow? Under pain of degradation to the ranks, it's my duty to see to it that the Little Jew Jesus never gets out to upset the world again."

24

"Good God! There's a key sticking in the frame of that mirror!"

"I forbid you! Hands off!" With a lightning gesture the Captain whipped out and aimed his revolver. Nothing daunted, Uhle leaned across the altar, grasped the key, and turned it. The ornate, massive frame of the rococo mirror swung wide into the room, and at the same instant Captain Hermann fired. The dugout was shattered by a rending blast.

CHAPTER FIVE OLENKA LANDED IN BERCHTESGA-
DEN AFTER A STORMY FLIGHT FROM METZ. WHILE SHE WAS BEING DRIVEN up to Obersalzberg in one of the Führer's black Mercedes cars, a man in a white summer uniform was already impatiently waiting for her outside the castle enclosure. He was sitting on the grass, caressing a boy member of the Hitler Youth. A cheerful mountain brook murmured silverly over shining pebbles at their feet.

Farther down the meadow children were picking flowers. The rays of the calmly setting sun grew redder and redder. They touched the huge square-hewn walls of the mountain eyrie up on the cliff, warming the granite into gold. Butterflies chased each other, playing and reeling into the grass stems. High in the air danced shimmering swarms of May flies.

"Look! . . . . Isn't that a grasshopper!"

"Where?" Rudolf Hess pressed the nine-year-old Hitler Scout closer to his side. But the child resisted, and began to cry. Blowing coolly from the summits and the broad glistening snowfields of the Alpine world, a breeze swept playfully around the bobbing, downy blond heads of the boys and girls in the freshly mown meadow.

Suddenly a band of young S.S. officers, silver galloons flying, rushed into view, chasing a wolfhound dog with cries of: "Churchill! Churchill! . . . ."

"What now!" The Deputy Führer sprang to his feet. "Isn't that Adolf's Walküre running there, with our Churchill in his teeth?"

The bitch came tearing down the stairs from the castle, her teeth set in a fat rubber doll that was a caricature of the English Prime Minister. Hoping to elude her pursuers she was about to dash across the driveway onto the wide, freshly-sprinkled lawn. But, unfortunately

25

for her, a car raced into the porte-cochere at full speed. She escaped death by a hair's-breadth. Someone screamed. Scattering gravel, the chauffeur braked the car to a halt.

The S.S. officers jerked to attention, arms outstretched—and grinned. From under the left front wheel peered Churchill's head, cigar uptilted at a jaunty angle. Prince Ferdinand, in the black uniform of a Storm Flyer, jumped out of the car and, adjusting his sword, the hilt of which was encrusted with precious stones, assisted Olenka to alight.

Veiled from head to foot, she drifted past the guard of honor as intangibly as a breath of Paris perfume, and on up the steps of the mountain castle. A handsome S.S. Staff Officer, his head bare, hurried to meet her. He introduced himself:

"Colonel Egath. The Führer is still at table. I have orders to conduct you at once to his workroom. . . ." Offering her his arm, he turned to Prince Ferdinand: "The plane was late?"

The slender-built son of the former German Crown Prince smiled. "At your service . . . The lady says there was a thunder-storm over the Rhine. And when they tried to land—clouds. Absolute pea-soup . . ."

Major-Domo Schellbaum swung wide the glass doors of the grand hallway. But Olenka got no farther. A footman in Hitler's livery presented the veiled lady with a much too heavy bouquet of fiery roses, of which Egath at once relieved her. He then addressed a few curses impartially to the four corners of the huge room, where sundry bull-dogs, greyhounds, and smaller watchdogs, egged on by the on-duty officers of the household troops, were tussling with a lion cub belonging to Göring. A Tyrolese golden eagle joined in by fluttering and screaming in his cage.

"Your pardon, Mademoiselle! It's a madhouse again . . ."

One of the bulldogs had caught Wotan the lion cub by a hind knee and was shaking him.

"You can see for yourself . . ." Kicking several dogs out of the way, Prince Ferdinand beckoned a pair of chambermaids, who had just come down, to take charge of the Führer's guest. But at that moment the sharp clicking of dozens of heels drawn together rang out. House porters in green jackets and Tyrolese leather shorts scurried in with brooms and hurriedly swept away the droppings of the menagerie. Behind the porters came towering peasants, in pompous livery, carrying braziers of incense. And now the stone floor again glittered and shone—so much so that a General Staff officer who came hurrying out of the dining room was unable to make his formal bow before the dancer; instead, balancing maps, compasses, and straight-edges in either hand, he slid past like a yokel on the ice in December—and disappeared into the map room.

A drone of voices suddenly came from an anteroom to one side: the dark, excited buzzing of many masculine throats, to an accompaniment of softly clinking silver spurs.

"Fräulein—the Führer! . . ."

His napkin still tucked in between the first and second buttons of his military jacket, Hitler dashed out ahead of his generals. There had obviously been some difference of opinion. His face was lobster-red with rage. He stopped short, stamped and roared.

"Damned blockheads! You imbeciles! What a General Staff! . . . Field Marshal Keitel!"

"Here, my Führer!" A strapping, gray-haired General stood at attention as smartly as his slight obesity permitted.

"Bitt schön,—when I say May 10th, I mean May 10th! and not November! . . . Understand, you towering intellects of my General Staff?"

Outside, on the ramp, a chorus of children began to sing. The Führer listened. Then he strode straight across the hall, without a glance toward the girl sunk in a deep curtsey beside the immobile Colonel Egath.

Before the portico, drawn up in military fashion, a group of about twenty flaxen-haired children between five and seven years old chanted in clear, high voices, heaping handfuls of autumn crocuses about the feet of the Supreme Master of German youth:

> "There is no death more beautiful
> Than to be struck down by the foe . . ."

Picking up the smallest, Hitler kissed the child and accepted from its hand a freshly gathered lilac-tinted chalice. Sniffing at it, he grimaced, murmuring:

"Autumn? What! Is it autumn already?" About-facing, he plunged into the hallway, shouting: "General Halder! Can it really be autumn again? My toes tingle. . . . there'll be snow tonight . . ."

The Generals exchanged glances under raised eyebrows.

"Bitt schön, my Prussian Generals! A winter campaign. . . . that means . . . snow in your boots! I always suffer in freezing weather. You too, Keitel? . . . . This damned tingling in my toes! We'll have to give every soldier his own oven! Well, that's all right. As long as we keep going! Where the hell is Halder?"

"In the map room!" There was a chorus of heel-clicking.

"Ha-ha! Gentlemen! What's a little snow? Nothing but frozen water! Ice-crystals! So they say . . . and there's no reason I can see, my good Keitel, why my tanks shouldn't be able to waltz over ice-crystals. . . . Besides—" he took a map out of an orderly officer's hand and tapped on it—"all the roads beyond Kalinin are concreted. . . . Snow! Snow! . . . This Orel, for instance . . . it's nothing but a little dung heap! Almost on top of Moscow! And besides, as far as the attack goes, except for the Kremlin, all their moujik houses have nothing but garden fences to resist us. As for their idiotic Kremlin that they're so proud of since Napoleon's failure, my poor, dear, weak-minded Brauchitsch, why shouldn't we build ourselves a bonfire there, this time, to warm our hands? What a damned, funny, ticklish feeling in my big toe! No, gentlemen! The sun sets, but it rises again." His face cleared, he bellowed lustily:

"The storms of winter yield to the month of May,
And spring shines clear in the lovely light."

While the castle orchestra on the balcony above caught up the Wagnerian rhythms with kettledrum beats and silver fanfares, he shuffled into the map room, followed by his generals, adjutants and staff officers, their spurs tinkling, their voices chorusing behind him:

"Yea, lovely and light, lovely and light!"

The tall folding doors closed behind them.

"Permit me. . . ." Relaxing his pose, Colonel Egath conducted the veiled girl, still followed by Prince Ferdinand, upstairs.

Major-Domo Schellbaum motioned to a serving man to open the door beside the enormous stone fireplace. Muffled steps were heard approaching. Four S.S. soldiers appeared and took up their positions, rifles planted at their sides, flanking the doorway, and grinned at each other under their clumsy steel helmets. Almost a minute passed before the sound of rustling heavy taffeta was heard through the passageway. A man of imposing presence, dressed in a cardinal's robes, entered the hall, his purple cassock hanging in rich folds. Behind him walked two Jesuits in coal-black.

"Does Herr Faulhaber desire an audience at once?" the Major-Domo asked.

"His Eminence," one of the secretaries whispered, rubbing his hands, "was informed three weeks ago by the Nuncio of the Holy See, that precisely this hour had been fixed for his audience."

The door of the map room opened. Hitler came slowly out, staring straight ahead, muttering:

"Fine, fine! When the wind begins to blow around the gallows in Poland—I say that will be fine!"

Colonel Engel, a magnificently built man in the forties, stepped forward and, with a gesture of ironical amazement, quietly called his Führer's attention to the Cardinal, where he stood waiting between the four armed soldiers. Hitler looked at him—and giggled. Suddenly he beckoned with his index finger. The Cardinal looked at his secretaries questioningly. At length he came submissively forward in two long strides, and stood, in all the quiet dignity of his high calling, before the Supreme Reichsführer.

"Well, come on! Come on, little one! . . . You don't suppose I'm going to have a telephone strung up between us, do you? Come on over here!"

The Cardinal shrugged his shoulders and moved forward a few more steps.

"Bitt schön! You're here as an emissary of your Holy Father's? I happen to know the Pope quite well. Cuts a fine figure! Quite intelligent—ha-ha! I once sat next to him at the Reichspräsident's table, at a dinner given by the Prussian Ministry. He was wearing a violet robe, lined with red. And a fur collar like the one my Aunt Resi wears in winter. . . . He was very fond of Hindenburg . . . he respected him—and why not? Well, what's new in Christendom? What's blowing up? My Colonel Engel tells me you want to lodge a complaint because I've locked up a couple of debauched monks and whores who have been cheating the State out of money. Sir! the first Christians were far less comfortable living in their catacombs, than my guests are in Dachau today. Everyone knows that.—Well, what does the Vatican want me to do?" As Faulhaber remained silent, he went on:

"Have I yet, like Nero, thrown your people to the lions? Have I used them for torches to light my gardens? . . . . Now, look, Your Eminence, I am not a monster! My parents were Christians. And when in Matthew 19:26 and Luke 1:37 it says that God plants faith in children while they are yet in the womb . . . Bitt schön, Herr Cardinal, at all events, God forgot to plant it in me!"

"Herr Führer. . . ." The Cardinal's hand, graced with an amethyst an inch in diameter set in his pastoral ring, toyed with the long gold chain about his neck. "Here is a list of 627 innocent Christians and Jews who have been shot. . . . Here is a report on the intolerable

29

conditions in the prison caves at Theresienstadt . . . Here is—"

"Bitt schön—Aunt Resi was always saying that in Jeremiah I, Chapter 5, and Galatians I, Chapter 15, it was written that there were cases in which God had predestined a child in the womb to holy tasks. But unfortunately I'm not one of them, Your Eminence!" He grinned at the Cardinal. "Otherwise, I'd already have been made Pope—ha-ha!"

"Pastor Niemöller protests against it. . . ."

"Bitt schön—who next? You, a Catholic! Be so good as not to trouble me with your lists of atrocities! . . . Besides, your Christ expressly said: 'He who would follow me—let him take up his cross!' " He exchanged a broad grin with Colonel Engel. "But I very much doubt whether he meant such a magnificent golden cross, set with precious stones as you, Your Eminence, are wearing on your red cassock. . . ."

"My Führer—" Prince Ferdinand had come down the hall and was reporting sotto voce—"Olenka Olschewska is waiting in your workroom. . . ."

"Who?"

"The dancer from Warsaw—who recently enjoyed the extreme honor—of displaying her art before you in the Palace of the Reich Chancellery."

"Ah-h-h-h!" The muscles in Hitler's face twitched like baby mice. "Your Eminence—learn to suffer . . . without complaining!" With two fingers he lightly tapped the Cardinal's cheek, and ran to the stairway.

But there he stopped and took a medal out of his pocket. "This is the Benedictus medal my Aunt Resi gave me for my first communion —to protect me against the devil! Look, Your Eminence! . . . And now people say that I am the devil myself!" His laugh came so gutturally that one of the two Jesuits put his hands over his ears.

"Here, bitt schön, I bestow this consecrated thing on you! You can wear it like a decoration on a string around your neck." He threw it at the priest; it jingled and rolled across the floor. "Furthermore, I forbid these everlasting complaints . . . or we'll never reach the Urals.

"Well, Prince!" He pinched Prince Ferdinand's buttocks. "Where've you got that girl?"

"Upstairs, my Führer!" He mounted the stairway.

"St. John says," whispered one of the secretaries: 'Whoever even greets him becomes a party to his evil works!' "

Toward Hitler's retreating form—and as if to protect his own breast —Cardinal Faulhaber made the sign of the cross.

30

CHAPTER SIX

Once upstairs, Hitler took an apple from a basket of fruit and bit nervously into it. Suddenly he left the Hohenzollern Prince and disappeared a few doors farther on—into his private projection room. He turned a lever and on the screen his pompous entry into Nürnberg on Party Day appeared in flickering light. After seating himself comfortably and relishing his picture, he cautiously drew a bundle of papers from underneath the upholstery of his chair, and scribbled a pageful. But when the wild cries of the interminable Nazi masses became ear-splitting, he rose and, with outstretched arm, saluted his own picture. Suddenly, through the actual film, there appeared upon the screen—more and more clearly defined—the thin face of a soldier.

"Stop! Who's blundering into my film, damn it! Stop it! Get that head away or you'll all land in Dachau." He hid behind a chair and stared at the screen. "You pale-faced pioneer! Are you back again? I threw a hand grenade into your stupid milk-toast mug, and saw you roll down into the trenches!"

Colonel Egath had silently entered the room unobserved and was therefore an involuntary witness of this scene. When Hitler saw him, he quickly switched off the picture. It was dark. Egath snapped on his flashlight.

"My Führer."

"What do you want, you old spy? Since when has my Colonel of the Gestapo taken up spying?" And then he bit his lips. "You were once a Spartacist?"

"At your orders! Are we to bring the girl here?"

"Egath, before I came over from my Tyrolese mountains, to you Reich Germans, I say there was chaos between the Rhine and the Elbe. The place was crawling with pale Bolsheviks with pointed beards. Yes"—he pulled Egath's ear—"even a pure blue-eyed, old-stock German and Aryan like you fell for them. Tell me what did you dolt-heads expect from Moscow? Didn't you know that the East—lies in the East? And that since the days of the Knights Templar the West can have no kinship with the red wolves of the Caucasus? What!"— he pulled his ear harder— "A Junker like you—you wore the red star of Zion and the hammer and sickle on your left arm? Hmm? Who had to come and tell you German blockheads what you are? Who? Who?"

31

"The dancer asks if she may bring her pianist with her?"

"Colonel, didn't you see that I was working? The opus *Mein Kampf* has now become more popular all over the world than the Bible of the Jews! But the opus *Mein Sieg!* will put everything into the shade! And you saw how hard I was working at it just now? Nothing clearer than that the curiosity of the world public, and the curiosity of my Party friends and enemies—including those closest to me!— would just love to get a look at a page or so—hm?—to learn exactly what the world-renowned Führer of the Greater Aryan Race has to say in his 'Last Will,' about the future—what he thinks about the next ten thousand years! Right? Especially at the Russian Embassy! I hear they've brought in a whole army of spies!

"Egath," he yelled suddenly, "if you ever again dare to enter my room without knocking, I'll shove your idiotic Bolshevik brains down into your Nazi arse! Understand?!"

He shuffled away. Egath looked after him coldly. Suddenly he took a vase from the table and smashed it on the floor.

CHAPTER SEVEN MEANWHILE THREE CHAMBER-MAIDS WERE BUSILY PULLING AND PINNING THE DANCER INTO HER COS-tume. When at last she was sufficiently powdered and combed they conducted her to a turn in the corridor, where they handed her over to a waiting footman. Without a word, he preceded her down the full length of the corridor, over heavy rugs, between flowers, tapestries, carved chests, and shaded lamps, in his turn committing her to the good offices of two giant aides de camp. With smiles and bows they led her through a low-ceilinged library where a sphinxlike cat sat purring between leather-bound books and an open box of paints. Waiting at the head of a short flight of steps, the castle housekeeper curtseyed and sprayed the girl with pine scent. At this instant, an S.S. subaltern popped out from behind a green brocade curtain and with white-gloved hands, proffered a tray with glasses of Madeira. The two young platinum-blond lieutenants handed her one of the Bohemian glasses and drank her health.

"Excited?"

"Olala . . . a little!"

"Did you see what the 'Völkischer Beobachter' wrote about you
ter you danced for the Führer? 'Her dancing gives the lie to that
d Briton, Isaac Newton. When she dances, the law of gravity ceases
exist. The apple no longer falls to the ground. When she dances,
erything around her becomes weightless. It is as if we were per-
itted to behold the soul of our Führer, defying the laws of physics,
aking possible the impossible.' Ha-ha!"

"Shall you still be at the castle tomorrow?"

"Why?"

"Then we could show you around the park. Another glass? No?
hen our mission is accomplished."

The one who wore silver insignia on his collar opened a small door
ush with the wall. "Here is the Supreme Reichsführer's workroom.
. . Heil Hitler!" Both aides de camp extended their arms in salute,
d touched her curls, while she, ducking, crossed the threshold. Then
e door behind her closed.

And now she stood alone in a room of huge dimensions. Cautiously
e ventured forward between the strange pieces of furniture. She
scended three steps, then through a great arch on her left she saw—
hat so many photographs had made familiar—the huge, impossible,
all-sized window, through which the Bavarian mountains under the
tting sun, their white snowfields glittering, gave the effect of a
inted Alpine landscape. As this room too was empty (not an aide
a footman anywhere) she decided to risk going on across the yards
mirror-smooth parquet floor. Suddenly she was standing before
olonel Egath. He was polishing his monocle.

"Ah, Fräulein, stage fright?"

"No, no—but you'll be here?"

"Unfortunately, no!" Egath smiled. "Come, come—you're not
raid? You are not in Dachau here! You're in the Supreme Reichs-
hrer's study. But, Fräulein," he said softly, with a look at the door,
nay I in all humility make a suggestion?"

Still watching the door, he spoke even more softly. "Item one: It is
e Führer's custom to talk for hours on end. Don't interrupt him.
em two: When artists have finished their performances, he invari-
ly asks them what they want him to give them."

"What they want . . . ?"

"So don't permit any intimacy until after that," Egath whispered.

"Intimacy! I'm here to *dance* for him."

"Ask him whether he has . . . remembered you in his will."

"Me? In his will?"

"Well, everybody writes his will—when things go badly, and I ju
saw him working on his. He had it in his hand. . . ."

"He's coming!"

"No"—he listened. "They're only changing the guard downstairs

"But I hear steps."

"Fräulein," he suddenly whispered, "we need his will. We unde
stand each other, don't we? Be careful—if we should not understan
each other, I should report you to the Gestapo as a suspicious cha
acter. I should say that you have come here to steal a document." H
gave her a quick, savage look. "Do we understand each other?" An
he was gone.

The dancer stood stock-still, forlorn and alone in the vast worl
room. Her eyes fell on a carved Gothic Madonna, standing betwee
two chests. The tragic, weeping face of the Mater Dolorosa so frigh
ened her that, sinking to her knees, she pressed her freshly shampooe
curls against the hard oaken knee of the Queen of Heaven.

"Well, let's go, little one—let's see you dance!"

The girl sprang to her feet and looked around. There was Hitle
sitting well forward on the window seat and smiling. "Snap into it!

"But. . . . what. . . . ?" she stammered, trembling.

"What?" Heaving himself to his feet, he stalked as if on stilts acros
the thirty feet of polished flooring and pressed a button in the wal
Immediately the rhythms of Ketelby's "Persian Market" resounde
from a concealed phonograph.

Retreating into the shadow of a huge chest, she slipped out of he
silk gown, wrapped a long black gauze scarf around her, and reap
peared before the Führer, who was leaning against the wall, hands i
his trouser pockets, whistling the melody off key.

"Well, go on!"

"But . . . I hate that piece!" She laughed, embarrassed. "The san
old 'Persian Dance'—woman standing up in the marketplace befo
man . . . a slave. . . ."

"Woman a slave! Bitt schön! Yes! That's another Jewish innovatio
Introduced by Pasha Abraham! Ha-ha! And the Bolsheviks have gor
even further in giving women an undignified place in the social ord
. . . Anyhow, Fräulein, I'm glad you feel that way about it. An
when, at the Brown House recently, my Minister of Propaganda, D
Göbbels, showed me photographs of women in the blessed Sovi
paradise—bitt schön! Nobody knew whether to vomit or curse! I
one picture there were about six hundred women, sitting in rows o
benches, each one with her left breast out. Male attendants were goin

34

from bench to bench, drawing the milk. There was a caption under it: 'Production of Milk for Infants in the Soviet Union.' Ugh! If it weren't for me! If *I* didn't exist! Never mind that now . . . Come on. . . . snap into it!"

The veils fluttered and floated around her whirling body. All at once she came to a stop—she could not see him anywhere. Was he perhaps lying on the divan behind the great table? What could have become of him? She shrugged her shoulders and went on dancing.

"Well—about time for the usual stunts, isn't it?" his voice grated from somewhere. "Go on! Wriggle out of those veils, please. . . . let's see something!"

She let the silver veils slip from her shoulders one by one.

"Did they have a bath ready for you when you arrived? Have you bathed, Fräulein? Come, don't be ashamed in front of me! As a painter I've seen more naked models in the studios than the world press dreams I have! You're not the first one! So come on over here!"

"Olala. . . ."

"Have you got tights on?" He leaned across the breadth of the table. "Better be safe than sorry . . ."

"Safe! That's rich! Well, never mind! We haven't come to the end yet! Ha-ha!"

The slave-market music stopped. As he did not put on another record, Olenka Olschewska rested for a moment in a chair. A pair of ravens flew past the window. When their hungry croaking had become inaudible, she rose. She was just stooping to pick up her veils, when suddenly Hitler called out of the darkness from another corner of the room:

"Don't move! Stay as you are!" He scuffled forward as if he had on house-slippers—slowly, wearily. Carrying a glass bowl full of candy in one hand and stuffing himself with sweets, one after another, he reconnoitered her all round.

"Bravo! Very neat! As Poncet is always saying: 'Une femme!' " He sniffed the air about her. "Yes, I was up there recently, on the mountains, with this Poncet fellow! Took him up in the elevator the other day. Right to the top. Of course, you know who Poncet is? The sentimental admirer of Goethe, Ambassador of the decadent French Republic! . . . Have a chocolate? Help yourself! They're from Magda Göbbels. . . . go ahead! You need strength. Your dancing is first-rate. Go ahead, child, have some more! And there I stood, beside—or rather, Poncet stood there beside me. Across the valley, the Zugspitze was purple as a cyclamen. The snow was just the blue of Alpine violets.

And high in the air, over the valleys already lost in mist, a pair of brown eagles sailed, hardly moving their wings. They spiraled higher and higher. It was as if they would conquer infinite space. I said to Poncet: 'Herr Ambassador—Lebens-r-raum!" (He rolled the "r.") "The eagle must have Lebensr-r-r-aum."

He threw out one arm as if to embrace infinity. Then he began shuffling around the girl again, stroking her spine with moist fingers. "R-r-r-raum!" he screeched, hurling the glass bowl against the wall. Then his eyes filled with tears, and he whimpered: "R-r-r-raum! R-r-r-raum! My many and various Ambassadorial Excellencies! Yes! You're not the only ones—the German eagle needs R-r-r-raum, too! What's more, his wings shall conquer space. Even if that sticks in your democratic cockerel's crowing gullet. Let him rot with his painted hens, down there on the dung heap. Let them all rot—the whole lot of them! But we Germans are going to have R-r-r-raum! . . . R-r-r-raum to breathe in!"

He threw himself down on the couch, sobbing. Olenka appeared to be astounded at this amazing spectacle. He looked at her through narrowed eyes, distrustfully, with a certain disgust.

"Woman! Out with it! What do you want of me? Or do you think I can't see through your game? Your paltry, stinking intrigue! You're supposed to weaken me—eh?—so that I'll no longer have the strength of the brown eagles in the upper air! Why are you standing there like that? What's next on the program? . . . Let's not talk nonsense, as if I were the marrying kind. Of course there's always gossip, like that story of my being engaged to the daughter of my photographer. . . . Woman, I am engaged to the Future! How ridiculous any other marriage is. I deliberately forced that creature, Göring, to marry!" He stuck out his stomach, put on an idiotic smirk, and grunted.

"Right! I forced him into it!" His mustache jiggled as he laughed. "I can still see my faithful Hermann in Berlin, waddling down the cathedral steps beneath the crossed swords of his Air Generals, Emmy on his arm, and squeezing into the car. . . . Ha-ha!

"You're pretty!—I ask you, what comes of such fiddle-faddle? A baby in the cradle, of course! Well and good. . . . I even went to the baptism in Karin Hall, took a look at that wrinkled-faced chimpanzee! A child. . . . I am fifty now. When that child is ten, I'll be sixty. When he's twenty, I'll be seventy. . . . What's the sense of it? . . .

"Go and get your clothes on, woman. I don't want your idiotic breasts simpering at me!

"Do you know that picture over there? My friend Mussolini gave it to me. That little painting represents the Jewess Judith returning home in triumph with the head of the Fascist Holofernes. Out with it, girl—who sent you here? Was it Göring's idea?" He made a sudden leap and caught her: "Listen to me! I'm no Holofernes!" He pushed her back, step by step, forcing her down onto a bench. "Now then, out with it!" he growled. "Who sent you here? What are you up to? What're you supposed to do to me? Answer me!"

She managed to think something up. "I wanted to see your eyes."

"My eyes?"

"Yes, a writer from Budapest told me you had such kind eyes."

"Kind eyes?" He squinted at her. "So then you believe in kindness and goodness? Answer me, girl! . . . As for me, I believe in something quite different! Far too lofty for you to understand. . . . What I believe—there it is!" He pounded on a huge sideboard. "At least that's where Hess thinks I've locked it up. But he's wrong. It is here—right here—" and he glided to the other wall, lifted the corner of a Gobelin tapestry, stared at the wall behind it, and said mysteriously:

"There is my Last Will and Testament. But," he whispered, "no one knows—not even Göbbels. Girl"—she did not come fast enough, so he began to bellow—"have the goodness to run when your Führer calls you!" But then, without any transition, he put his arm around her, his voice became coaxing:

"Would you like to see it? My will? For you can't think I'd be such a fool as to really hide it in the wall here? Ha-ha! Göring was looking for it only a few days ago in my night table. Himmler thinks I have it walled up in my bathroom behind the water-closet! Child, shall I tell you where it is? . . . You tell me what goodness is! Then I'll tell you. See that table?" He pulled out a drawer. "Come here! Those are all building plans. Here" . . . . he unrolled a blue-print—"this is my idea for the capital city of the Aryan world! And that's how the prisons for the non-Aryan world are going to look. Do you like it? But behind all those rolls—if you just reach your little hand in there. . . . Stand back!"

He gave her such a sudden push that she reeled back several yards. He was on her in an instant: "Child, I presume you understand that I can kill you at any moment?" He tickled her about the breasts. "Right—at any moment! And nobody'll ask what became of you. I do as I please. Anything! If I kill you, my little dancer, you're killed—and no questions asked! Somehow, I think. . . . you don't believe me. You don't believe I'd do such a thing?"

"No!" she laughed hysterically. "I can't believe you would do that."

"No? My eyes are too kind, eh?"

He dragged her over to the window, pointing down at the immense terrace with its granite balustrade. "You see all those officers in their white jackets? Do you? Ah, there comes Ribbentrop now! That's he driving like mad around the serpentine up from Lake Fuschel. There! He's getting out of his car now, rubbing the dust out of his eyes. Who's that with him—the Russian Ambassador? What a nuisance Ribbentrop is! Always pestering me day and night, with: 'A superb opportunity! Une occasion superbe!' That's what he calls anything he wants me to do. For twenty years I've fought the Red Star of Bolshevism. But no! My Minister of Foreign Affairs wants an alliance with the Reds. And my Deputy Führer, Hess, wants an alliance with England *against* the Reds! Ha-ha! But my little Göbbels, you notice, doesn't take any part in the officers' pink tea down there. Just look how my Marshal Göring chatters at them! And the joke of it is that, while he talks, I do the work. . . . See how Göbbels keeps his ears cocked toward this window! Listening for his master's voice! So—now, my little dancer, you don't think I could 'liquidate' anyone I want to in that group down there—whenever I like? Just watch! . . ."

Before she could sense his meaning, he had fired. The little knot of officers scattered. Then someone dragged one of the two young platinum-blond aides off the terrace. Wolfhounds, wagging their tails, licked up the blood from the flagging. She felt ice-cold. Suddenly the murderer began to stroke her trembling arm with the utmost tenderness. She jerked convulsively as if with cramp.

"Child, tell me—do you believe in such a thing as life after death? If there isn't any, then why should I be 'kind'?" He let her go, and slipped the empty cartridge out of his revolver.

She wanted to seize the moment, to run out the door. But her knees failed her.

"Girl," he looked at her broodingly. "Do you imagine that the soul of that young Storm Trooper can find its way out of his uniform and materialize now, and then go wandering about this place? That would be something!

"Are you a Christian? . . . You know, my astrologer is sitting upstairs in his observatory in the attic, calculating from old horoscopes just when that pale bewhiskered Jesus Christ of yours will return to the earth! Ha-ha! Child, according to a prophecy of the Jew Nostradamus, your Messiah is supposed to return to earth—this year!"

He pressed his nose against the windowpane. "Hollah! Isn't that somebody up there stamping around in the snow? Perhaps that's your

HE. . . . just landed in a parachute from the Kingdom of Heaven! Look. . . . over there! Isn't that He up there on the glacier?" His laugh made Olenka's hair stand on end.

"I left my fur cloak in the other room. May I go and get it?"

"Stay where you are!" And he ran to get it, hung the feather-light cape around her, offered her his arm, led her to the couch, and spread a swastika-embroidered coverlet carefully over her legs. Then he took her hand—and was silent.

It was growing dark. He turned his face to the great window almost apprehensively, as if he saw something out there. But in the gathering twilight it disappeared. The girl covered her eyes with her scarf, gave a sigh, and said softly, "It all seems so unbelievable. . . ." Suddenly the mountain peaks turned red, like iron held in a forge. He nodded:

"Right, little dancer! That's the alpenglow! Beautiful, isn't it? Yes . . . Nature! And whenever I go for a stroll through these woods of mine, I feel myself at one with that infinity out there. Then I can talk! Yes, I can talk as I run uphill, down dale, through the fir trees. And the firs understand me and run after me. And the grasses murmur and rustle. . . . I understand them, too, because I am one with them. The blue jay falls silent. The animals all know me—" Olenka Olschewska looked at him, wide-eyed. Suddenly she asked:

"Why did you do it? That young lieutenant . . ." She covered her face with her hands. Hitler was lost in the spell of the twilight:

"Why? Because— Beautiful dancer, have you ever watched a linden blossom drift earthward, slowly spinning as it falls? Did you ever feel a thrill up and down your spine when your foot stirred the first dry leaf—and you knew that autumn had come? . . . Look! How ghostly the mountains are now! . . . Ashes! Only a moment ago they were fire. . . . Now—ashes—nothing but ashes!" He laughed aloud— "Ashes!"

He walked across the room, slowly, head bowed, hands clasped behind him, as if following a bier. Key in hand, he fiddled with the molding on the farther wall. A section of the paneling, about four yards square, slid back, revealing a row of urns, standing like books on a shelf. It looked like a cabinet in an old-fashioned apothecary's shop.

The girl did not move. Even when he beckoned impatiently, she remained seated. He returned as slowly as he had gone, his voice rumbling: "And yet, they want me to marry. Only Hess, the old sly-puss, the old Egyptian Mephistopheles, with his black eyebrows, advises me against it. He's always telling me I must do something for the new Germanic Era . . . . build a pyramid a hundred times as big as the ones on the Nile . . . . and a Sphinx that smiles. . . . Hess doesn't like my mustache. Yet I keep telling him that the Sphinx of the Twentieth Century has a mustache. But this Sphinx is not going to marry! Not even if they all want me to! . . . Out of the question!

"You have pretty legs. Nice slender, smooth legs. Incontestably pretty legs. It would be unfair to deny it! But I can't understand why you're wearing tights! Is there anything wrong with your skin? With your permission—"

She sprang to her feet with a stifled cry. But he caught her by the hair and pulled her back. "It won't hurt—" Using the point of his dagger, he slit the tricot from the neck down. As if paralyzed, she made no resistance—not even when his hand reached out and tore it off her. "H-m-m-m! Fräulein! Not at all bad! A sculptor like myself has an eye for these things. I remember Mussolini's showing me a statue in Rome. To be sure, the left breast was missing. You've still got a left breast, firm and sound. . . . Nice smooth skin, too. . . . Astounding! Ha-ha!

"Stand up, Fräulein. Just walk a few steps. The whole insane jest lies hidden in those legs of yours. I could slap them! . . . But there's no point in that. The eyes continually try to penetrate their secret. I could tear the flesh off the bones with my nails. But that's not it. . . . Darling, there's one thing I like about you. You don't talk and you do as I tell you! . . . Tell me, could you do the split the way they do it on the stage, so that your buttocks touch the floor? Of course, it isn't exactly your buttocks. More precisely—it's something else. Never mind! The truth is, it always gives me goose-flesh when I see a dancer —quite shamelessly, in front of a lot of men—simply let herself drop from a standing position, legs wide apart, and come down hard on the floor. Amazing! The way you can spread your legs out from that narrow pelvis in a straight line like the arms of a compass. Great! Let's see you do it right now."

She blushed. But she rose to her feet, with a short, embarrassed laugh. "Doesn't mean a thing. Just one of the regular exercises we have to learn at the ballet school. . . . It's actually the first." Without further ado, she illustrated the position.

"Farther down!" He pressed his hand on her head, rocking her back and forth until she touched the floor. "There!" he said. "Contact! Contact with the earth. And far better"—he trembled all over with excitement—"far better than contact with a man! All these people want me to make that kind of contact. It's called 'The Mount of Venus,' isn't it? Very pretty! No man who is a man would underestimate it! Yes,

whenever I hear *Tannhäuser* in Bayreuth: 'Oh, Du mein holder Abendstern. . . .' " He strode to the window, pointing to the silver gleaming
of the stars and bawling ecstatically,—" 'Wie seh' ich Deinen Glanz so
gern!' "

While his attention was thus distracted, she rose and crept back into
the shadow behind the table. At the sound, he whirled around.

"Where are you, my little Venus, eh? Ha-ha! . . . Just look at the
salmon! When the salmon has to spat, the slightest stimulation is
enough to make him loose his sperm. The slightest irritation! All the
females have to do is to swim around in the same water, and rake in the
profits! . . . An irritation, a mere tickling! Girl, have you ever really
thought what that tickling means? . . . You have beautiful legs. Well
and good! None the less, when you did the split for me—you'll forgive
me, but I felt absolutely nothing. Not a thing. My male instinct does
not react to such crude contortions of the female form. I am an archi-
tect!" He unrolled some of the plans and rolled them up again. Picking
up the biggest roll, he went to the window, held it to his eye like a
telescope and said, in a matter-of-fact tone: "I think it's Orion! However, it may be Cassiopeia. When the center star in the handle of the
Big Dipper rises between the Zugspitze and that glacier there—or so
my stupid astrologer says—things look good for me . . ."

He waited. After several minutes during which Olenka continued to
hope that something would happen which would free her—he came
back from the window. He still carried the roll—but now it was as
Göring used to carry his marshal's baton. He was grinning:

"Things look good for me.—But, to get back to the subject. Do you
know what kind of tickling interests me? Don't move! I'll tell you.
When I ask you if you believe in a life after death—that tickles me.
What it would mean to hear from a girl—an ordinary, two-legged
dancing-girl!—if she knows any other solution but the usual one—
something different from Pastor Niemöller. . . . or Cardinal Faulhaber . . . or Spellman in New York or Innitzer in Vienna. . . .
Ha-ha! Hess, for instance, is an atheist. Göbbels believes in me, Göring
in monarchy. And I? What do I believe? But first I want to know if
you believe there's a life after death . . ."

"Mon Dieu! Let me go . . ."

"Are you afraid? Is it getting too dark in here? Shall I turn on the
light? Tell me—did you ever get up in the middle of the night because
the wind was rustling so funnily outside the window? Hm? Hm?. . . .
Child, when I was a boy in Braunau, I used to walk down the street in
October, with the icy wind blowing in from the fields, people in their

black Sunday frock coats throwing pitiful nonsense at each other above
the gray stone walls, and I'd think: If Death would only come now,
from way down the far end of the street, his scythe so shining with
cold that people freeze at the sight of it, and he'd mow them all down
like hay, in rhythmic sweeps—people, walls, houses—that would be
fun! Why are you shivering? Ha-ha! Because either there's an after-
life, or there isn't! Everything depends on that. Are you afraid of
death? . . . When my friend Röhm toppled over, that was a fine
military scene! There he stood against the wall on the parade ground,
the spotlights all turned on him. A roll of drums, a salvo of guns—bang!
—and—'Finis Polonia!' ' "

He stroked her hand: "You're Polish? Colonel Egath was telling me.
What do I care for those imbecile satraps in Poland—the Patotskys,
Podbielskys, Radziwils, and all the rest of them! Every Polish peasant
will sigh with relief when I've liberated him from that plague of
aristocrats. . . . Bitt schön, darling, what if I say to you now: in three
minutes you must die? Tell me, sweetheart, would you be afraid? Or
do you believe in Heaven?" He took her between his knees. "I'd really
like to see that face of yours if I should actually decide to kill you."

"Un fou! un fou! . . ." she muttered to herself, and tried to think of
any possible way to escape. But he watched every move she made.

"Sweetheart, if you really believe in a life after death, it must be
quite agreeable—to die? Mustn't it?

"Then when you're a beautiful, pale ghost you can float around, cold
as death, and just about midnight when I'm dropping off to sleep, you
and all the other ghosts can come to my bedside and sing! And dance!
. . . . just when I really want to rest from my superhuman exertions
for the Greater German Reich. . . . My little angel"—he pinched her
buttocks—"you can dance around my bed with the Röhms and the
Heines and all the other ghosts. Ha-ha! You think that would bother
me!" His face was so close to her that she smelled his sour breath.

"Olala! Someone knocked!"

"What?"

He moved stealthily to the center of the room. Then, tonelessly:
"Did someone knock? It must be my astrologer. It's about time for his
daily report on his transcendental calculations. . . ."

His eyes fixed themselves on the window. "Say! What's that? Up
on the peaks? Look, girl! Isn't that someone glaring out of the glacier!"
His legs teetered. With one movement, he pulled the huge curtain, like
a sail, over the whole width of the window, blotting out the ghostly
Alpine landscape.

42

"Shall I light the fire? Do you like to hear it crackling?" He touched a match to shavings, chips, and leaves under the massive oak logs piled in the fireplace.

Gigantic shadows played hide and seek across the walls and ceilings. With a quick, apprehensive glance at those racing shadows, he darted back and forth across the room, switching on lights. Under the blinding glare, he let out a jubilant shout: "There, Fräulein! Do you see anything black here now? They're gone—all the black things—gone! Haha! Including the Jews and the rats!" He let out a yodel and hopped around like a peasant at a country fair. "Dance, girl, dance! See here, I can dance better than you! By God in Heaven, you shall dance! Haha!" He took her by the hips.

There was an energetic knocking at the door. The chimney smoke billowed into the room. Coughing and clearing his throat, he cursed:

"Who the devil is it? Who's there?"

"It's I!" replied a thick, beery voice.

"Who is I?"

"Meissner, my Führer!"

"Meissner?" Hitler cackled like a parrot. "What do you want, fathead? Why am I always being disturbed by the Chief Clerk of my Reich Chancellery?" He whispered to the girl: "It's only Meissner—the scholarship boy from Heidelberg—the son of a beadle! I've nothing against that! I'm a son of the people too. But this Meissner creature! Girl! He's a, a miserable worm. Why don't I step on him? Why, indeed!" All at once he stormed aloud: "Get away from there!" His voice dropped as he winked at the dancer: "Or, shall I let him in? You want to see something funny? Shall I present him to you? In the costume I've designed for the sponge-belly, he looks exactly like a stuffed frog disguised as a cinema doorman. At least, it's something for my S.S. and S.A. boys to laugh at." He went to the door.

It opened. Heels clicked. The Chief Clerk of the Reich Chancellery raised his arm.

"Na, Meissnerkin, you realize that any moment I can have you shot?"

"That would be inadvisable, my Führer!"

"Inadvisable?" The Führer raised his fist, but immediately patted him in a fatherly fashion on the shoulder. "Switched from Ebert to Hindenburg, and from Hindenburg to me? And all without the slightest pang of conscience! Without the slightest shame or remorse in the night? Without sweating off a single pound of fat? One minute in white tie and tails at every ball given by the Jewish press—and the next in white lapels with the National Socialist dagger in your belt! You half-witted chameleon, you! . . . I wonder what he takes me for."

"For my Führer!"

"Meissner, you want to know what I take you for? To me, your Excellency, you're the democratic abscess that I fortunately cut open! Never mind! Tell me, what's new in Prussian Berlin? Did you come by rail or plane? Meissner, this young lady with me is a dancer. This immaculate virgin, Herr Chief of the Reich Chancellery, is my future wife! What? He's not even astonished? Stands there stiff as a stick. I'll have her do the split for you! . . . Doesn't even budge when I tell him this is my future wife! . . . . Sclerotic, eh? The Chief of my Reich Chancellery turns out to be a paralytic! . . ." He kicked his shin—"Where is Hindenburg's will, eh? In America? In a democratic safe deposit? You monarchist simpleton! Bitt' schön, will the time ever come when you'll cry out, from the bottom of your heart: 'Heil Hitler'?"

Meissner brushed off his trousers, straightened up, snapped his heels together, and purred: "My Führer!"

"My Führer? My Führer? You fool, you!" He grabbed him by the collar and shook him: "Listen, Meissner! I was in the crematory watching when they burned the body of Party Member Röhm. . . . Do you follow me? His feet, legs, knees, and thighs were still intact, but his thick rebel's head made a splendid torch. . . . Herr Chief of the Reich Chancellery. . . . !" He led him by the ear to the wall where the urns were arranged, pointing: "Urn No. 1, Röhm's ashes! Urn No. 2, Heines' ashes! Three-four-five-six-seven—there! See that urn? That one's for you! One day all your superfluous flesh will trickle in there. There'll be a nice label: 'Meissner's Ashes'."

He took down one of the urns, removed the lid, and poured out the ashes on the rug. One after the other, he emptied them until there was a little mound of white ashes. He beckoned to the dancer. "Now, my little dancer, my Salome, go ahead and dance! I wish my friend Richard Strauss were here. This would be an inspiration for him! Not even his Salome was ever given real dead men's ashes to dance in! Röhm's ashes—Heines' ashes—Dance!"

"In their ashes?"

"Instanter."

"No!" she suddenly pulled herself together.

"What! you don't want to dance?"

"You can't force me to dance in the ashes of the dead!"

"I can't, eh? Dance, you bitch!" he yelled, "or else. . . ." He

44

reached for something to hit her with. She began to dance. The ashes whirled about her feet. Then she collapsed.

"Dust! Dust! All is dust!" The Führer raised both arms to Heaven. "O Divine Providence! Dust! Nothing but dust!"

For a moment there was silence, then he pinched Meissner.

"You damned villain! Where's my Will? I'll wager you've drawn up an official dossier about it. Where is it? It was in my night table, and it's gone. . . . Where is it? You know, and I know you know! Open that trap of yours. You've had a copy of it made in secret? You've sent it across the ocean to be sold to the 'Arsenal of Democracy'? You've sold me—for dollars, you? Where is my Will? Open your mouth, swine, or I'll open it for you! Have you had it translated into Anglo-Saxon? My translator just told me that God himself couldn't translate it! So speak up, please, or I'll have them beat that blubber off your back, inch by inch, in Dachau! I'll have them smoke your carcass on the spit. Get out of here! Out!"

"My Führer, the Duce is waiting on the telephone."

"Get out! Did you hear me? Out! Out!" He drove Meissner out of the door, slamming it behind him.

In the pause that followed, he wiped his face, grinning furtively at the dancer. . . . Then softly, tiptoeing over to the window, he fished out a manuscript from behind the radiator.

"Here it is!" He waved the sheaf of papers back and forth like a fan. "But nobody knows it! Quiet!" He listened at the door. "You see, Meissner and Himmler are working together. Now, where shall I put it? In the chest of drawers over there? Or, better still, behind that Rembrandt. Or shall I stick it inside the piano? Look, there's a little trap door in the floor here. When I open it, there's a pane of glass, you see, and I can look down and watch what my Party Comrades are up to, when they think they are alone. Ha-ha! Shall I hide it here? No. . . . Hess knows about the trap door. Won't do! But perhaps here? Will you look at that! A microphone? . . . . . So—my faithful Himmler, eh? Yes, my girl! Ears . . . . Ears . . . . Everywhere ears—" Suddenly he broke off, recoiling from the girl as if in terror. "Girl, this is terrible! Until now, we've been having such an amusing time and all that. But now—things are different! My wonderful dancer! Now I'm in dead earnest! You must die! Too bad, but there's nothing to be done about it. You've seen my Will."

His glance wavered uncertainly. In her unspeakable terror, the girl stammered: "Olala! It must be getting late! I've got to catch the next plane!"

45

"Where to?"

She managed to find an answer. "To Paris!"

"What do you want in that effeminate place? Fräulein, let me tell you something. Anyone who has once danced for me—"

"Let me go!"

"Late, is it? Is that so! Too bad! Well, then, perhaps it is late. . . . A woman changes every month with the moon. You'd never know how to keep my secret. So—it will have to be. Let's get it over with. Would you like another chocolate?" His nose was touching hers. All at once he threw her on the divan, crawling over her, the muzzle of his revolver at her ear, his mouth running with saliva.

"Come! Come!" he coaxed. "I'll whisper the language of love in that sweet little ear of yours! . . . . Love is hate and death! Come! Come! and then—off you go, an eddy amidst the storm of the worlds! Come, now! It'll sound like Götterdämmerung! Like the kettledrum when my Furtwängler conducts! That's how it will crash! What an exquisite little ear! . . . Does it rustle and roar inside there like the cosmic waves? . . . Ha-ha-ha!" He raised his head. "God in Heaven! Why are any of you still alive? . . . . Look out! I'm going to do it just as the Manual of Arms prescribes. The base of my first finger's pressing on the trigger. It's coming! Right away! It's coming! You dear little bitch, with your enticing legs! Yes!" He yelled like a drowning man. "It's coming! Here it comes!—Now!"

At that instant, the revolver dropped out of his limp fingers with a clatter, and, like a lifeless mass, he rolled off the divan onto the floor.

Outside the door there was the sound of running feet. The dancer cleared the body in a single leap. Impatient knuckles rapped demanding admission!

"Meissner again, my Führer!"

The dancer ducked down behind the divan.

"My Führer!"

The Chief of the Reich Chancellery burst into the room. Brought up short at the sight of his Lord and Master lying, apparently exhausted, beside the divan, he stopped, and, helping him to his feet, rattled off his report:

"His Excellency, Premier Mussolini, urgently demands to speak to you on the telephone. He says the President of the International World War Veterans' Association has sent him a telegram in the name of its four thousand members now holding their annual convention in Paris—"

"Bitt schön—Dr. Sauerbruch recently warned me that I was working too hard. I'm terribly tired, Meissner. Even though I'm a superman, I'm still a man. And that scene with Faulhaber. . . ."

"And in the telegram he begs the Duce—just as he did last September—in view of the present crisis threatening world peace, to intervene with you in the name of those four thousand World War Veterans. . . ."

"Four thousand World War Veterans? . . . Bitt' schön. . . . four thousand World War Veterans. . . ." And supported by Meissner's thick arm, the Führer shuffled out of the room, chewing on the phrase. The door was left wide open.

The dancer, turning her head nervously, saw the bundle of papers on the table. Snatching it up, she hurriedly wrapped her veils around it, then slipped on her dress and dashed for the door. Startled at the obsequious clicking of heels by the guard, she ran back across the room, and up the short flight of steps the way she had come. Turning the corner, she looked vainly for the low door in the wall by which she had been admitted. At that moment, a large painting moved aside, seemingly of itself. Colonel Egath stood before her and whispered: "Quick! Quick!" Then he pushed her through the opening. Slowly the painting slid back into position.

CHAPTER EIGHT H ITLER'S TELEPHONE CONVERSATION WITH MUSSOLINI LASTED TWENTY MINUTES. THERE WAS SILENCE IN the Führer's workroom. The logs in the fireplace burned out. All of a sudden there was a clash like the smashing of a windowpane. Then the clatter of boots. Hitler appeared. He took both steps in one jump and stopped, thunderstruck, at the door.

"Where did that girl go?" He rushed to the table and made a wild hunt over and around it.

Meissner came on the run. Hitler grabbed him by his arms, then stretched his fingers like claws, and questioned him in a rasping whisper:

"Where is my Will?"

"What—what's that, my Führer?"

"Egath," Hitler roared. "Where is Colonel Egath?"

Instead of Egath, the head of the Gestapo came in with his eyeglasses askew.

Hitler spoke sharply: "Himmler, who's in command of the Fifth Column in Paris?"

"I don't know offhand."

"You don't?" Hitler kicked him in the shins. "Get out of my way." The next instant he was screaming down the outside staircase into the park.

Alarm bells rang.

Himmler squinted at Meissner. In came Hess, Prince Ferdinand, Prince August Wilhelm, Milch, and other Nazi leaders, all with flushed faces, visibly excited. They had evidently heard the news.

"His Will has disappeared?" Hess asked.

"Forward!" Himmler bellowed at the princes. "Alert the entire fifth column in Paris!" Then he began searching through drawers and closets with Hess, until Colonel Engel hurried in and reported:

"Your Excellency, any private plane approaching the French frontier will be blasted out of the skies!"

CHAPTER NINE "MONSIEUR UHLE! MONSIEUR UHLE! . . ." THE PORTER PADDED DOWN THE NARROW HALL OF THE Hotel Balzac toward the guest who, his full six feet and muscular build ill-concealed beneath a long, black raincape, stood waiting, his hand on the door knob, about to enter No. 3.

"Monsieur Uhle—you haven't filled out the foreign visitor's blank."

"Have you a pencil?" Holding the form flat against the wall under the glazed electric bulb, Uhle read: "Last stopping-place." He wrote, "Verdun." And answering the porter's astonished look he added:

"Mais oui, I've just come from the battlefields." Drawn and haggard, his broad features twitched.

"Permanent residence?" the porter prompted.

"Same as ever, Monsieur Pierre—Pylar-sur-Mer."

"Near the oyster fisheries, eh? . . . Ah!" The porter smacked his lips. "And how long does Monsieur expect to stay with us this time?"

"Two or three days." Uhle's ash-blond hair shone silvery in the half-light as he handed back the pencil.

"Excusez, Monsieur . . . Your passport—?"

"As you know, I've nothing but my carte d'identité. A former

German officer, deprived of citizenship—"

"And the other gentleman?" The man nodded at the door before which they were standing.

"From the battlefields, too."

"His name . . . excusez. . . ."

"I'll write it down for you."

"Monsieur—" The porter attemped to decipher Uhle's handwriting. "Mais . . . Ça va! Ça va!"

"This gentleman will be leaving when I do."

"Would Monsieur Uhle care to have some fruit sent up, as usual?"

"Bon! . . . bon . . . What room have you given me this time?"

"Number 11. I've already brought up your bags." Tipping his gold-embroidered cap, he turned to go. "Pardon! Encore une chose: A lady phoned a little while ago . . ."

"A lady?"

"Mais oui! Wouldn't say who she was and wouldn't leave her number. But she'll phone again later."

"Merci."

Crossing the threshold, Uhle entered No. 3 and found it in semi-darkness. In the early autumn twilight a man sat there at the table, motionless—a soldier. Without shoulder straps or other insignia. From his shoulders hung a long cloak, whose original color it would have been difficult to determine. An indefinable, dirty red-brown, which seemed here and there to glow into a poisonous green, like cloth that had been discolored by years of mud and mist and poison gas in No Man's Land. The haggard, immobile face, framed by a dark beard, showed an almost masklike profile against the wallpaper. Only the eyes were alive—they had a strangely distant luster. On his knees lay a battered trench helmet.

Uhle bent over his motionless guest with concern. "Tired? Do you want to lie down?" Picking up the helmet, Uhle led the soldier to the wide bed, making him comfortable, arranging the pillows and finally covering him with the cloak. "Do you want something to eat? No? Feel like sleeping? Good! Have a good rest. I'll look in again a little later."

Quietly leaving him, he walked down the corridor a few doors to his own room, No. 11.

CHAPTER TEN ENTERING THE MODEST MANSARD ROOM, WITH ITS SLANTING WALL, HE OPENED THE WINDOW AND STOOD IN front of it, looking out over the countless roofs of Paris glistening under the rain. The roar of the streets rose inarticulately.

"Paris . . ." he murmured. "Over there—Montparnasse. Over there —the Eiffel Tower." He took off his black raincape, pulled a chair to the table, took out a sheet of letter paper, and prepared to write. But he laid down the pen. "What? a woman telephoned?" And then he laughed at himself. "Oh, we men! Will our lust for adventure never leave us in peace? The man wasn't so wrong who once said: 'Every normal man, even the most sensible, loses his composure the minute a beautiful woman enters the room.' "

He looked around the room. Yes, the effect was certainly Bohemian. He lit a candle, and picked up the pen again. But his thoughts strayed to the comfortable double bed in the alcove. He leaned back in his chair. The white spread and the two pillows looked so inviting in the candlelight. The shadows of the pillows played on the flowered wallpaper. Across the room the muslin window curtains swayed in the evening breeze like a dancer's skirt.

"Irene," he began writing, "in just such a little room as this, Rouget de Lisle composed the 'Marseillaise.' And I—what am I doing here? I have just come back from a battlefield where millions of soldiers fought for the 'sacred love of country.' " He hummed a few notes of the battle song of freedom: "Amour sacrée de la patrie . . ." For a moment he covered his face with his hands. Then with a sigh he went on writing: "And in all those shattered woods round Verdun, in the fields, on the hills and in the valleys, as far as the eye can see, what has this sacred love of country produced? Graves—nothing but graves! To be sure, it is written: 'Greater love hath no man than this, that he lay down his life for his brother.' But is it not a greater love, to *live* your life for your brother? In your last letter, you wrote: 'It was a great mystic who said, "My soul is unquiet until it rests in thee, O God." ' And you went on, 'Is not this the secret of true love?' Irene! Do you remember how one spring evening on the Riviera we strolled along the water's edge, where the gardens come down to the sea? A crescent moon was in the sky, hardly bigger than a strand of golden hair. The nightingales were singing in the almond trees.

The air was heavy with the scent of orange blossoms. And you said: 'Uhle, our love for each other, which we believe will be for eternity— if ever we let it die, where could either of us find love . . . or eternity?—' And after you had gone to bed, I walked for a long time by the sea. I felt such joy! Only so, I thought, can we create eternity within ourselves. *Amour sacrée*— 'Consecrated love': that is how we would rewrite our own 'Marseillaise.'

"This became irrevocably clear to me down there among those millions of graves: Only he who feels love—whether for a woman, or for whomever—as eternal in himself, only he who has conquered his own conflicting passions, can build the mighty tower of peace. . . .

"Forgive me! These broken thoughts chase each other across the page, helter-skelter, because I am reluctant—I hesitate to tell you about a most extraordinary thing that has happened . . . But before I go on: please prepare the guest room with the view of the high dunes. I am bringing a guest who will require much care. However, I hope that in that fresh, salt air he will soon be better. I would have started with him this evening and come straight to you on the night train, but I want to take him tomorrow morning to see our friend, Dr. Goldschmidt, and find out exactly what sort of treatment we should give him . . ." At a knock on the door, Uhle started up in his chair, listening.

Since there was no further sound, he continued writing:

"—Day before yesterday, in a dugout underground—Please, follow this closely, Irene . . . You are the first human being to whom I am confiding something absolutely incomprehensible—day before yesterday, at noon, in Haudroumont Quarry, thirty-three steps under the ground, I found a soldier—wounded in 1916—still alive."

He unfastened his collar and sighed, as if he felt that he had freed himself of something.

There was a more insistent knocking at the door. Quickly slipping the letter under the blotting pad, he called:

"Who is it? Mais entrez donc!" The door opened slowly . . .

"Olala . . . May I—?"

"You!" Uhle jumped up as the dancer, heavily veiled, came into the room. "Back so soon?"

She brushed past him, and with a quick thrust shoved her violin case far under the bed.

"What are you hiding?"

"I'll explain everything later . . ." She started toward the door, as if to listen, but collapsed onto a chair. Uhle brought her a glass of water from the washstand. She drank it. Troubled by his inquiring look, she began to set her hair to rights, like a cat rescued from under a shower bath. Gradually, the metallic sheen quickened to life in the drying strands.

"They're right on my heels! Actually! I'm being followed! Will you take care of me?"

"What's in that violin case?" Uhle moved toward the bed.

"Don't touch it!" The mingled scent of lilac and the rain drifted out as she loosened her furs, revealing her delicately modeled throat. Evading his eyes, she moved about, her every step weightless, as if sprung from the heel.

"Mais oui, Monsieur." She came to a halt. "I danced for him! I was there—first with his officers—then alone with him!"

There was a heavy silence. She sensed his suspicion, for all of a sudden she said very softly:

"Uhle, I beg of you—please have confidence in me! Won't you? Olala . . . How can I ever tell you—how my poor, stupid heart faltered . . ."

He saw the tears come to her eyes.

"You're crying—?"

"I?" She shook her head violently. "Oh, no!"

Her expression suddenly changed. "You know, darling, until yesterday nothing in the whole world interested me, except my dancing! But—since I was with him last night . . . Mon Dieu! Mon Dieu!" She leaned forward, her forehead resting on the table, and was seized with such a convulsive trembling that Uhle came to her and gently laid a hand on her shoulder. Shuddering, she pulled herself together. Suddenly she raised her head with a jerk.

"Listen! . . . Isn't there somebody outside the door?"

"I'll see." Uhle opened the door and looked out. "No one."

"Please! Please! . . . Lock the door! His whole pack is after me! I'm terrified! The best thing for me would be not to stir out of this room! Darling"—she groped for his hand—"I can't go back to my pension again! . . . Where on earth shall I go? Please, please help me!"

The room telephone rang.

"Hello?" he answered. "Who? Monsieur Gunther? He's on his way up?"

"Who's that? Mon Dieu! Mon Dieu! Where can I go?"

"A friend of mine . . . if you don't want to see him, hide there." Leading her into the alcove, he drew the chintz curtain across it.

As he turned away, there was a knock at the door.

52

"Come in!"

A man of medium stature, in his fifties, supporting himself on a stout stick, his wooden leg only a slight hindrance, entered the room.

"Diable! Have you read it yet?"

"Read what?" Uhle offered him an armchair. Seating himself, the visitor stretched out his wooden leg, nervously rolled and lit a cigarette, and pulled a newspaper out of his pocket.

"Has there been another murder?" Sitting down on the couch opposite, Uhle coughed to distract his attention—through the curtain, he had seen Olenka reach down and silently pull the violin case from under the bed.

"Diable! Cher Uhle! You haven't seen the evening edition of 'Le Temps'?"

"No." Then Uhle went slowly to the window. The clop-clop of hoofs was heard from the roadway below. Leaning out, he saw a squadron of the Garde Mobile trotting by, black horse tails streaming from golden helmets. After them came a regiment of Moroccan soldiers. More and more troops followed, quickstep, with no blare of bands, marching down the street in the direction of the station.

"You really don't know?" Gunther puffed furiously. "You haven't read Hitler's reply to yesterday's speech by the President of our International World War Veterans? Diable! Believe me, mon ami, nothing has ever made my blood boil like reading the Reich Chancellor's shamelessly cynical answer to our clearly formulated desire to bring about a world-wide reconciliation! . . .

"Eh bien!" With his good leg Gunther stamped out his cigarette. "You wonder why I'm bothering you so late at night? You've already spoken for us so effectively on the radio. Mon cher Uhle, I'd like to have you speak for us again, tomorrow evening at the General Assembly of four thousand Veterans! It would do my heart good to have you, a German, answer this insolent telegram of Hitler's on short-wave! Agreed?"

"I!" Uhle shook his head. "An expatriated World War Veteran? What good would that do?"

"Here! 'Le Temps'; read it and you'll see!"

"You want me to speak? Against bombers? No. Look! In this little room every object casts a clean shadow, this candlestick, that glass, my bag, your wooden leg—but a word when it comes out of our mouths—"

"What?" Gunther said, lighting a new cigarette. "You want a word to throw a shadow?"

53

"Was it not written once, 'In the beginning was the word'? The word created the heavens and the earth. The word separated *light* from *darkness*. In those days a word could cast a shadow! But we—our words—certainly, we *speak* against darkness. But there is no connection between the brain and the heart; therefore there is no creative power, no *light* within us which could make a shadow, no substance, to again separate *light* from *darkness*."

"Eh bien, does that mean you refuse?"

Uhle was silent.

"Bravo!" Gunther laid his hand on Uhle's knee. "Then we shall expect you tomorrow night? Agreed? And before the meeting you're going to drink a bottle of wine with me, wine from the lime-gray Champagne. You will? And then!" Rising to his feet, he stamped his wooden leg. "Diable! Then—!" He walked to the door, Uhle accompanying him.

Closing and locking the door behind him, Uhle cautiously pulled aside the curtain before the alcove.

Olenka was sitting on the bed. The violin case lay open, and the bedspread was strewn with sheets of paper. As he approached, the girl swiftly swept them all together and stuffed them into the case again.

"So! Now you've seen it!"

"Seen what?"

"What I have here. Now, don't faint! This is the authentic, handwritten manuscript of—the Last Will and Testament—of the most fantastic monster—"

Uhle sat down beside her. "What on earth are you talking about?"

"You'll find out!" She nodded. "You understand me perfectly well, Monsieur Uhle!" Her brow flushed with excitement, she spoke in a half-whisper. "For over a hundred million Aryans this sheaf of papers constitutes the final and definite refutation of both the Old and New Testaments. At least that's the way your friend Colonel Egath explained it to me on the way down the mountain to the plane."

"To the plane?"

"Olala—yes! It was full of nothing but diplomats!—Even the German Ambassador!—and Prince August Wilhelm! . . . But not one of them recognized me—not even when we landed in Le Bourget . . . the Customs didn't even examine my baggage! That's how well Egath looked after your little dancer . . ."

Under his steady gaze, she felt unsure of herself.

After long consideration, he suddenly grabbed at the papers. But she snatched them away and crammed them back in her violin case,

54

holding it like a prey.

"Look me straight in the eyes—"

"You don't trust me? . . . You don't believe this really is his Will?"

"And what am I to do with it?"

"I told Colonel Egath—that I knew you. And because he wants the papers out of the Reich—no matter how—he implores you in the name of your old comradeship, to keep them until he comes to Paris . . . they're not safe in my hands . . ."

"No! No! . . . I don't want anything to do with such stuff, and Egath knows it. I don't want any contact with his damned Gestapo—"

Suddenly he took his raincape and walked heavily to the door.

"Where are you going?" She ran after him. "Where—?"

"I'm going to the police! That's the best place to take your Nazi documents."

"But Uhle!" She clung to him. "But Uhle—"

"You're to stay here." He freed himself from her hands. "I'm going to lock you in."

"Lock me in?" Her face was radiant with relief. "Then I can stay here—in your room?"

His eyes seemed to look right through her. In an instant he had put on his raincape and was gone. Outside, he locked the door and paused for a moment. Then he strode down the corridor to No. 3. He listened at the door for several minutes. Hearing nothing, he breathed more freely.

"Thank God—he's asleep . . ."

When Uhle's footsteps had ceased the first time, Olenka had thought him gone. When, after a lapse of several minutes, she heard what she believed to be a strange tread in the corridor, she froze into immobility. She felt ready to collapse. As always, in moments of terror, a scene from her childhood flashed through her mind with cinemalike vividness. As a seven-year-old girl, she had been driven away in an old carriage from her father's manorhouse near Cracow. The house had been set on fire by the Russians. As the terrified black horses galloped jerkily, Olenka, clutching her doll to her breast, and peering through the little window in the back of the carriage, had seen the great house crash to the ground in smoke and flames. She remembered the first dreadful night she had spent in the house of her old aunts— bigoted old women who had thenceforth made her life a misery with their old-maid regulations. She tried to efface these memories. She recalled the moment when she first met Uhle. . . . Pictures moved across the shadow screen of her mind in rapid sequence. As the footsteps receded, she breathed a little more freely.

She walked nervously around the room. She turned over Uhle's knapsack curiously, but thought better of opening it. Suddenly she discovered, on the writing table, the letter which Uhle had pushed half under the blotting pad. She turned chalk-white, and slowly drew it out, as if moved by some irresistible compulsion.

CHAPTER ELEVEN HIS HEAD BURIED IN THE EVENING PAPER, THE HOTEL PORTER WAS LEANING AGAINST THE KEY RACK, UTTERLY absorbed in the day's sensation:

GERMAN MURDERER TO BE EXECUTED.

We have it on the best authority that the ruthless slayer of women, Weidmann, in a confession made today, has shed new and gruesome light on the startling series of murders which have terrorized Paris in recent months. According to the killer's latest revelation, several of these murders, some of them committed under circumstances not yet cleared up, were carried out by Weidmann or his accomplices under orders from the German High Military Command. He alleges that this 'little salad,' as he puts it, was deliberately planned in order to distract French public opinion from the really 'big salad,' i.e., the massing of gigantic German military forces on our borders . . .

Engrossed as he was, the porter glanced up just in time to see Uhle come down the stairs and, without greeting him, step out into the street.

Uhle had no sooner made his exit than a stoutish man—a typical Montmartre bohemian, flowing tie, broad-brimmed velour hat, and all—came forward from his seat in the foyer, carrying an address book.

"Porter!" he asked pointedly. "Was that the manager who just went out?"

"Mais non! A foreigner. A writer."

"Is that so? Is that so?" He tugged thoughtfully at the brim of his monstrous black hat. "A foreigner! And from what part of the world?"

"That, Monsieur—"

A metal badge flashed as the bohemian turned back the lapel of his coat.

"Oh! . . . Pardon! Monsieur is the Commissioner of Police?"

"Yes! Let me see your register . . . Merci." He made some notes.

"By the way, does this gentleman often receive—visits from ladies? What is his room number?"

"Number 11."

While the detective and the house porter were going up in the elevator, Uhle was hurrying in the direction of the Champs Elysées. His plan of informing the police he abandoned almost as soon as he had got outside into the fresh air. Instead, he bought some roses at a flower stand and buried his face in their cool freshness and fragrance. He felt now that he wanted to go back to Olenka. But a milling crowd around a newspaper kiosk held him. The evening papers screamed in gigantic headlines:

PRESIDENT ROOSEVELT FLAYS DICTATORS.

Women and girls brushed past him, silks rustling, hips swaying. Eyes, the long lashes deftly mascaraed, looked at him limpidly. Coins passed, indifferent hands crammed ink-saturated, evil-smelling newssheets into noncommittal pockets, their owners making for the nearest sidewalk café and the evening apéritif. Others linked arms with some young vision in filmy, clinging stuffs palpitant as the wings of a butterfly.

The menu in the window of a restaurant gave him the idea of telephoning to Olenka and asking her to dinner. Through the plate-glass windows, the purple hue of burgundy and liquid amber of sauterne caught and held the light in the facets of cut-glass carafes. There was heaped on display all the abundance of the 'doux pays de France': long loaves of crisp bread, Bordeaux oysters, Moroccan pineapples, Riviera peaches, roast-brown chickens, hams from Provence, crimson lobsters, fish from the Mediterranean. . . .

He began to look for a telephone, and pushed his way into the Café George V between the close-packed rows of apéritif-drinkers on the sidewalk. But as the telephone booths were occupied, he hailed a waiter and ordered a glass of port.

At the next table foreign refugees were discussing how long it took the United States to build a 7000-ton ship.

"What? Three weeks!?" One of the disputants rubbed his eyes under his glasses. "You're crazy! In one day they can build two ships of 7000 tons! That's 98,000 tons a week, or 3,528,000 tons a year. Mais oui! Production! Production! I tell you, America will be the master of the world!"

"Voilà!" The waiter brought Uhle's drink, glanced at the paper, and winked. "Twenty years after, and it's to be la guerre again?"

Uhle sipped his drink, lit a cigarette, slowly exhaling . . . Then, seeing the image of a gendarme reflected in one of the café windows, he stood up and was considering whether to speak to him or not, when someone grasped his arm from behind.

He turned to face Baron Jacques, his former translator.

"Hello! Hello!" The Baron, squiring a lady, was beaming. "Had no idea you were in Paris! Haven't seen you in ages! What a coincidence!"

Plump and rosy, in his forties, with a characteristic gesture he stroked his pasted, shiny black hair, and adjusting his monocle, looked banteringly at Uhle.

"May I introduce Miss Inwood? She's just arrived from Nice, to write up Weidmann's execution tomorrow morning."

Tall, languid, and beautifully built, his companion could have passed anywhere for a typical showgirl. She wore an ostentatious breastpin of diamonds and rubies. A gold chain anklet gleamed through a sheer silk stocking. The breeze, lifting her short coral-red skirt, billowed it about her hips, revealing tan thighs surmounted by a triangle of white silk. Calmly smoothing down her skirt, the girl sat at the table, crossing her legs and allowing one gaudy wedge shoe to dangle.

"Whiskey!" the Baron ordered and, successfully foiling Uhle's repeated attempts to depart, forced him back into his chair. "Écoutez, mon ami! Miss Inwood is to do a series of articles on this antiquated Europe of ours before it becomes an American colony, as she thinks it will. And so it happens that, before the general debacle, I'm supposed to show her some of the sights . . . Do sit still! Voilà!" He slapped Uhle's knee. "Mademoiselle, you can begin right here and now! There's one—sitting in front of you!"

The girl faced Uhle, pencil and notebook in hand. "Have you murdered anybody? Jumped off the Eiffel Tower? Are you a famous explorer—or a surrealist? 'German tourist?' Gestapo—or Cheka?"

"Mais non!" Baron Jacques removed his eyeglass, thrusting out his chin. "He's a refugee. Expatriated—from the Third Reich! His father, a high-ranking General, would certainly turn in his grave—"

"Another refugee! You promised me something new!"

"His brothers are all top drawer in the German Army—"

"Then he isn't a Jew?"

"Au contraire! Why, he even wants to give us a 'new' religion!"

"A new religion? As if we didn't have enough trouble with the old one! Why start something you can't finish?"

"Witness your own 'new Messiah' and his fourteen Points! But we in Europe had our prophets, too. Ha-ha!" He pointed at Uhle. "In 1918, after the Armistice, when everything was topsy-turvy, this ex-officer stood up among the ruins and talked about the 'Dream of the Front-line Soldiers'! . . . Ha-ha! . . . About a new and exalted kind of relations between man and woman! Ha-ha!" The Baron ended in a burst of laughter.

"Miss Inwood!" Uhle looked at her. "If you have really come across the Atlantic to our old continent to interview celebrities, you couldn't do better than to begin with this gentleman—one of the heirs of the French Revolution! Baron Jacques was brought up in the noble tradition of the Rights of Man! When I met him in 1918, he was a fanatical believer in the evolution of the individual toward freedom! . . . In 1939 he appears to be a still more fanatical believer in the annihilation of the rights of the individual by the dictators."

" 'Der Mensch ist nicht geboren—frei zu sein'." The Baron sprang to his feet. " 'Man is not born—to be free!' Your own Goethe said that! Ha-ha! 'Liberty!' . . . 'Democracy!' Ha-ha! The world domination of the Jews? . . . Mais non! No, thank you! C'est la gloire, et seulement la gloire—'Fame is the spur that the (in this case *muddy*) spirit can raise' to immortality—and then only *perhaps*. We're dealing with the offal of humanity."

"Gloire?" Uhle looked straight at him. "Of course! Because your Unknown Soldier under the bronze tablet at the Arc de Triomphe can't answer you any longer—he's dead. And the soldiers under ground at Haudroumont—they're dead too. But one of them is not dead, Jacques! And let every traitor bear that in mind!" He paid and left.

"Que veux-tu?" the Frenchman roared after him, biting his nails. "Il faut frotter le peuple avec gloire! And let every traitor bear that in mind!"

Miss Inwood gave him a Broadway wink. The Baron tossed the roses Uhle had left on the table into her lap:

"Excusez! But my friend Monsieur Abetz is expecting me at the German Embassy. I'm sorry I can't spend the evening with you in Montparnasse. Une autre fois!"

CHAPTER TWELVE "GLOIRE! GLOIRE! FAME!" UHLE

REPEATED. HE WAS STANDING IN THE ÉTOILE, LOOKING ACROSS THE MERRY-go-round of shining automobiles at the Arc de Triomphe. Spotlights played on it from all directions. "Yes, they all marched through you! All those who sought fame. All the *Well-known* Soldiers. First Napoleon. And after *he* was finally defeated, those who had defeated him marched through—the Czar of All the Russias—with Field Marshal Blücher and the Duke of Wellington. The King of Prussia, with His Apostolic Majesty the Emperor of Austria and Hungary. And two generations later, Wilhelm I, with his paladins Bismarck and Moltke. And you too, my father, you too, as a Guards Lieutenant, rode through next to Hindenburg—in front of the music and the floating silk flags—and then down the Champs Elysées and across the Place de la Concorde and on to the Louvre. And again, forty years later, Wilhelm II was going to march through the Arc de Triomphe 'before the leaves fell' and after that, as the General Staff used to put it, 'drown everything with black hair in the Bay of Biscay.' And I myself? Wasn't I so near to Paris with a patrol in 1914 that I could see the Eiffel Tower through my Zeiss glasses? Kaspar Friedrich, what are you doing here? All alone in the capital of France? A German against his people? A brother against his brothers and his kin?!—Oh my unknown soldier, sleep well! But when you have had your fill of sleep, arise and come forth. For, so long as there are still triumphal arches, so long as mankind floods them every night with useless light—so long will there be another and yet another Supreme War Lord or Commander of Legions to march through them. So long will one nation seek to triumph over another."

He stood a long time, staring at the arch. Long after the spotlights had gone out around it, he was still standing there. Out of the vast sky of night the stars glittered. He leaned against the wall of a house. The cold of the stone penetrated his neck. He shuddered.

CHAPTER THIRTEEN LATE AS IT WAS, ON HIS WAY HOME, UHLE SAW A LIGHT IN THE WINDOW OF THE SHOP THAT BELONGED to his friend and fellow veteran, the French antiquarian Laroche. Pipe in mouth, Basque beret awry on his straggling gray hair, Laroche sat behind the counter, carefully polishing a misshapen, carved wooden torso, strangely out of place amid the dusty clutter of his wares. In the scant light from a rusty iron lantern, Uhle could barely make out what it was. Gradually he perceived one outstretched arm of the wooden figure, the palm of the hand pierced through. The right arm was missing. The head, inclined as if in pain, showed traces of crude peasant coloring, the hair and beard smeared with red. The naked torso appeared to be pockmarked with innumerable bullet holes. It was such a figure as he had seen propped up on the battlefield.

Uhle drew closer, unobserved by the old antiquarian. Putting on his spectacles, Laroche went to work with a polishing cloth on the ribs. The gaunt and bearded features, drawn with pain, bore such a striking similarity to the face of his unknown soldier in the Hotel Balzac, that Uhle stared in breathless wonder.

"Eh alors!" The antiquary had seen him, and put out his hand. "How do you like him, mon vieux? I brought him back from the battlefields. The Curé of Notre Dame has already been in and left a deposit. He calls it 'The Christ of the Trenches'. His Eminence intends to install it on the high altar tomorrow evening with appropriate ceremonies . . ."

" 'The Christ of the Trenches'?" Uhle stroked the weather-beaten wooden curls.

"Yes! He paid 1000 francs down on it . . . Look!" He pointed to the holes: "He's all pitted with bullet marks!"

"Yes, I've seen him before. After my first engagement in 1914 . . . I had to ride to Vitry-le-Reims with dispatches . . . The endless chalk roads . . . past the countless corpses . . . Far ahead, the burning towers of Reims Cathedral glowing through the murk . . . clouds of white mist rising from the meadows . . . I lost my way . . . I had to ride more and more slowly—over broken bodies everywhere! . . . Oh, Laroche, if I could only make that murderer up on the Obersalzberg see the whites of those upturned eyes! . . . the waxen faces with haggard features . . . dark-framed by a soldier's beard! . . ." His fingers followed the grooves of the carved beard on the wooden Christ

61

of the Trenches . . .

"Even my mare shuddered . . . saddle and bridle dripping wet . . ." He held the figure up before him, gazing transfixed. "I dismounted, groping about, literally feeling my way until at last I found a pole stuck in the ground! Thinking it was a signpost, I climbed up and, holding on with one arm, lit my lighter. Oh, if I could only make *him* see what I saw—that tiny flame burning steady and clear against this blood-stained brow! . . ."

"Mon vieux! Mean to say you'd climbed a crucifix in the fog?"

"Oh, if only I could paint that 'head so full of blood and wounds,' in the heavens, so that, looking out of his vast windows across the Bavarian Alps, *he* would see what I saw then! . . ."

"Eh bien, mon ami," Laroche raised his bushy eyebrows. "So you like my 'Christ of the Trenches'?"

"Oh! if I could only hammer into *his* eardrums, through all the loud-speakers on earth!—those cries! . . . Out of that deaf and death-white mist the cries, now here, now there, of some dying soldier . . . through the endless night . . . growing weaker—ever weaker! . . . until finally it ceased . . . And I clung to my mare's warm neck . . . seized by terror . . . a terror of myself! . . ."

Suddenly, he hurried out of the shop. He was afraid that, during his absence, the hotel porter might have reported the arrival of his soldier to the police . . .

CHAPTER FOURTEEN HE FLUNG OPEN THE DOOR OF NUMBER 3, AND CALLED:

"Hello? Are you there?" Instantly, the unutterable peace of the room seemed to seal his lips. On the chair before the window, the steel helmet shone milkily in a faint glimmer of moonlight. His eyes searching the dusk, pallid with the silvery light of moon and stars, he perceived his comrade-in-arms lying on the bed just as he had left him earlier in the evening. Not a fold was disturbed of the torn cloak over his legs.

The silence was like that of a death chamber . . . And yet, the soldier was alive. Uhle cautiously held his wrist. The pulse beat was firm . . . To his ear it came resonant as a bell—like the periodic undeviating ticking of Eternity.

His head bent above the sleeping man, Uhle whispered: "Are you awake? . . ." There was no answer.

In the path of a moonbeam, slantwise from cheek to brow on the bloodless, bearded face, one eye, picked out by that cosmic radiance, seemed in itself a lambent planet lifted out of surrounding darkness, atremble in some distant constellation, the other side of space . . . Stepping back from the bed, Uhle gazed—and gazed . . . Such inner quiet was almost unbearable to his racing, hunted thoughts . . . Even so must Christ have lain and slept in a little boat on the stormy Sea of Galilee, while his disciples, trembling in fear of death, fancied that from moment to moment their fragile boat must be overturned by the raging waters and they go down . . .

The night wind blew coolly on Uhle's hot face. Oh! how insignificant —here in the soldier's presence—seemed the hubbub of all the people down in the city's streets. What was it—compared with this penetrating feeling of peace, with this stillness that seemed to come from another center altogether—as if from the heart of the Creator itself!

He left the room on tiptoe, shut the door as quietly as possible, and made his way down the hall, past the pairs of shoes outside their owners' doors, back to his own room. Even before he had reached it he saw to his surprise that the door, which he had carefully double-locked, was wide open. Entering, he was astonished to find Olenka gone. And with her, the violin case. Only the heavy, flowery odor of her perfume still hung in the alcove. He picked up the telephone, but put it down again. Suddenly a terrible thought came to him: Could she be a spy in disguise? The idea made him feel so faint that he had to sit down. What other reason could there be for her not waiting for him to come back? And *who* had opened the door for her?

Assailed by bitter thoughts, he turned on the light, and began to undress. While he was bending over to take off his boots, he saw some crumpled sheets of paper on the floor under the table. Retrieving them, he noticed for the first time that the chair by the bed had been overturned and the cover of the night table was dragging on the floor. "What's all this?" He smoothed out the wrinkled sheets, laid them on the table, moved the light nearer, and then, as if hypnotized, began to read, word by word, sentence by sentence:

"'I believe in Almighty God, the Creator of heaven and earth.'"

In the space immediately below was scrawled:

"Hogwash!"

A penciled line straggled down the paper, to where the text continued.

"When I first had to memorize this hogwash as part of the catechism in Bible class, I refused. And why did I refuse? Because I could not understand such hogwash. And why didn't I understand it? Because there's nothing to understand about it! If it had said:

"'I believe in Moses Almighty, the Creator of the Jewish people . . .' that I might have understood! But, in that event, it would have been incomprehensible why, for instance, an American, a Bulgarian, an Albanian, a Norwegian—and least of all, a German—should have to learn by heart a sentence from the Jewish creed! . . . And because the Jewish world propaganda knows this perfectly well, it substitutes for Moses —an 'Almighty Creator!' And instead of Palestine, it substitutes 'heaven and earth'! Of course, that was their propaganda trick, a stroke of genius, I admit. But I say that, by inventing this international God, the Jewish people wanted to make all the other nations of the world adherents of their own purely nationalistic, Jewish existence! And I say, thanks, but we're not having any of such hogwash! We non-Jews have not the slightest intention of making this imaginary Jewish God responsible for our existence! We non-Jews flatly decline to accept such bilge! We don't for an instant believe that Judah's God (alias Moses) created the German earth and the German heaven! That would be a fine state of affairs! . . . Or perhaps it was this God Almighty of heaven and earth (alias Moses!) who arranged for my Aunt Resi, with the red nose, to stand as godmother beside my cradle? Perhaps it was He who buttoned up my father, in his ridiculous uniform of an Austrian customs official? Was it He, perhaps, Who, on the death of my father, denied the pension claims raised by my ailing, beloved mother in order to give her children the barest education? Was it Judah's God (alias Moses) who picked out for me that wretched hovel in Braunau so that I, too, should one day become a customs official of the corrupt Hapsburg Monarchy? No! No! I won't hear of it! . . . Bitt schön! . . .

"Indeed, that was the most decisive moment of my life when, in place of this pan-Jewish hogwash of lies, I had the courage once and for all to substitute my own name! Yes!

64

That was the hour of my spiritual birth when in the toolshed behind our house, I wrote in chalk on the wall:

" 'I believe only in myself—Adolf Hitler!'

"Certainly I never dreamed at the time that I should one day become the Creator of the Greater German Reich. But, that I was determined to become the Creator of Myself,—that at least I had irrevocably decided. . . ."

The telephone rang and Uhle hastily hid the pages in a bureau drawer, picking up the receiver.

"Hello? . . ."

"Olala!" It was Olenka's voice, hesitant and scarcely audible. "Olala! I don't know how often I've phoned. Why didn't you answer? . . . I could hear quite distinctly each time you took up the receiver: I could even hear your breathing . . . I must talk quickly: by the grace of God I've managed to get out here safely to my aunt's house in Neuilly . . . I only hope you didn't let the detective know anything. Dieu merci, he didn't ask me anything and I was able to get away immediately. For the love of God, don't say anything to anybody! Of course, it's quite impossible for me to get back to you . . . But I'll meet you tomorrow morning at nine in the Bagatelle Park: there's nobody there then. I'll be down by the grotto near the lake . . . Hello! . . . And if for any reason I can't get there, then I'll be in Notre Dame about six—in one of the side chapels . . . and . . ."

"Hello! Hello! . . . We've been cut off!?" He hung up the receiver. "A detective? . . . What is all this? And why in the Bagatelle Park, of all places?" Pulling his Baedeker from his coat pocket, he studied the map of Paris.

". . . Arc de Triomphe . . . Avenue de Neuilly . . . It must be here somewhere . . . Jardin d'Acclimation . . . Porte Maillot . . . Aha! Then you go to the left. Aha! . . . Tomorrow morning at nine?—"

CHAPTER FIFTEEN NEXT MORNING UHLE WAS AT THE BAGATELLE PARK AT THE APPOINTED TIME. FOR AN HOUR HE WAITED IN the grotto beside the lake, where Olenka had said she would meet him. He could see through reeds and drooping willow branches the narrow path along the bank. "Almost ten o'clock?" He grew impatient. "Where is she . . . ?"

Turquoise-blue dragon-flies flashed sparkling over the water. Black swans with crimson bills, rejoicing in their own slender beauty, sailed past. Now—they were hidden by the delicately swaying branches of a weeping willow.

A sound made him turn round . . . But it was only a family of ducks. Chattering, half out of water, wings frantic, they scattered in flight from a water rat. With long, naked, rudderlike tail, the mirror-clear water curling above its whiskered snout, the rat swam across to the opposite bank . . . As it scrambled up the shore, a single petal drifted down, twirling to the dark water from a rosebush on the water's edge . . .

Uhle looked at his watch again. Was it possible that Olenka had lured him here only to hand him over to the Paris agents of the Gestapo? . . . But then he thought of her candid eyes . . . He remembered the anxiety in her voice over the telephone: "If not in the Bagatelle Park—then—about six o'clock in Notre Dame!" He decided to wait ten minutes longer. He leaned against a stone block and yawned. He had not had enough sleep the night before. He had spent almost the entire night sitting beside his soldier. Finally, he had drowsed off. He had had a strange dream. Once again he had seen the battered wooden figure of the Christ. He was standing somewhere in the Russian steppes. All round moved cloudy-gray cubes—closing in on him—now moving to the east, now to the west, obeying some mysterious command. Soldiers—nothing but soldiers everywhere! Suddenly they formed a front. Then came a hollow rumbling, like thunder. Immediately afterward, the Crucified was called from the ranks. He approached slowly . . . the rusty barbed wire whipping around his forehead with every step. A general who looked like Trotsky ordered him to lay his head on a block. Now he inclined his head, with the reddish beard . . . And then the general, in his purple, silver-frogged uniform, cut off his head with a penknife and roared, "Go!" And the other went, headless, into the unending gray mist. Uhle's horse galloped after him with flying stirrups. Suddenly the horse stopped and pawed the earth. Uhle dismounted, and stood before a gigantic crucifix! Instead of the Crucified a soldier hung on it. His rigid palms were pierced, and fixed to the arms of the cross, with bayonets . . . His feet, in crude army boots, were laid one over the other and tied to the cross with suspenders. A dirty steel helmet cast a shadow over one half of his haggard, white, unshaven face.

It began to rain. Uhle turned up the collar of his overcoat and was

66

about to go, but just then he felt a hand on his shoulder. It was a gardener, standing behind him, carrying a saw. "Eh alors? . . ." he said, puffing at his pipe. Then, carefully wiping his saw with some waste, "All right, all right," and went his way.

Uhle stood irresolutely until he heard the metallic whining and rasping of the saw, working back and forth in a tree near-by. Then he sidled along from one tree to another. There was no sign of the girl. He heard footsteps approaching. He plunged into the shrubbery.

It began to rain hard. Wading through the dripping bushes, he was soaked to the knees. The downpour increased. The rain spattered and sprayed from branch to branch. The earth steamed—one after another the showers draped silver veils through the woods about him. . . .

Uhle could not go on . . . He found shelter under a stout beech tree. Wild geranium and trodden grass gave off a mingled scent, bittersweet. The noise of the rain now became a steady hum, echoing around him like an ancient monody.

All of a sudden Uhle hid behind the beech, suppressing an outcry: "But that's Auwi!" He stared out into the open. Yes, there he came . . . the fourth son of the Ex-Kaiser Wilhelm! On his long head, a bowler. Uhle held his breath. Not ten paces from him, August Wilhelm, the prince whom Hitler had made a Nazi General, stopped suspiciously, lighting a cigarette . . .

Uhle had not seen him since 1916 at Verdun. But that horselike profile was unmistakable. It stood out clearly against the background of yellowing foliage. The Prince, in an elegant close-fitting black frock coat, moved forward, stepping gingerly so as not to soil his patent-leather shoes, poking aside the wet grass and twigs with his cane. A rain-drop put out his cigarette, he took a fresh one from a gold case and lit it. He listened, drew a whistle from his pocket, and blew a low, short blast. The same birdlike call was repeated right and left. Reassured, he called out in a guarded tone:

"Wilzschek!"

A moment later, Uhle heard branches being thrust aside and a gentleman, also faultlessly dressed, appeared through the trees, leading a dachshund on a leash. The dog sniffed excitedly among the damp leaves.

"Seen anything of the dancer, Wilzschek?"

"Not even a glimpse of her fanny!"

"Nor I! Nobody's fool enough to be out in this rain but a Prussian Prince and the German Ambassador!" He laughed with a high raucous whinny.

"She must be a long way from here with those papers by now!"

"What makes you think so? Our people heard what she said on the phone, didn't they? No, she must be here in the park somewhere!"

"I still believe she thought it too dangerous to stay, and left at once. In any case, Your Royal Highness, I urgently suggest that we go back. One of our men has seen French police patrolling in the underbrush to the south."

"Very well—let us go. How moldy it smells here." Suddenly he clenched his fist: "But, I'll tell that Austrian postcard-painter: A Hohenzollern like myself. . . ."

"Not so loud, Your Highness! Not so loud!"

"In 1933 he made me a solemn oath that my son should be German Kaiser."

"Then he'll certainly keep his oath!"

"No, by God in Heaven, he has broken it. Come on—back to our search! If I get hold of that ballet girl and it comes out that what Meissner told me about the Will"—his eyes stood out as if he had an overactive thyroid—"is true, then, Wilzschek, if he has really broken his oath to me . . . !"

"For Christ's sake, Your Highness . . . not so loud!" The ambassador clasped his hands, then wheeled three or four times on his heels, peering about in abject terror lest they had been overheard. With an emphatic gesture, he removed his top hat, held it straight out before him, and shouted, his forehead bathed in perspiration:

"Heil Hitler!"

At this, Prince August Wilhelm tore the hat from his grasp, threw it in a wide arc downhill, and unleashing the dachshund, urged: "Fetch it! Fetch it!"

The dog frisked with joy, and dashed away. The Prince slammed his great hand down on the German Ambassador's shoulder and gave him a forward thrust that sent him flying after the hat.

At that moment a shot rang through the trees. They both stood rooted to the spot. Then the Prince yelled:

"There she goes. See her running down there!"

Both started to run in the direction from which the shot had come.

Uhle, in anguish for the dancer, sprang out of the bushes. But the way down was barred by policemen. He ran straight through the trees, and came to a halt, breathless, on one of the terraces of the yellow Bagatelle Château. Another gardener was digging in a flower bed.

"Pardon . . . Did a young lady go by this way?"

As the gardener seemed to be deaf and made no answer, Uhle ran down the terrace steps between the flower beds to the park gate. Cautiously he glanced up and down the path. Yes . . . there in the wet sand, among the tracks of several men's shoes, was the fresh imprint of a woman's heel.

Hearing whistles and the barking of dogs approaching, he ran on, heading toward Longchamps. The sun was coming out. A few birds began to sing in the trees.

Suddenly he felt that he was being followed. A man he had not seen before was coming up behind him. Uhle considered whether to turn off to the right through the fields, or to the left through the woods. But instead, he about-faced and walked straight up to the other:

"Excusez . . ." he said, "what time is it?"

With his cane the other pushed back the dripping hat off his forehead, and warned:

"Hurry! Hurry! The police! Come on!—Uhle! Don't you recognize me?"

Uhle looked at him suspiciously, and started away.

"Stop!" The other took him by the arm and hailed a taxi. "No, no, my dear Uhle! I'm not going to leave you to your fate alone in the middle of the Bois de Boulogne! In with you!" He practically shoved Uhle into the cab, sat down beside him, and whispered a direction to the driver. And they started back to Paris.

They met no one on their way except a few horseback riders.

"Uhle! You really don't know me? Just think a minute!"

"Is it possible that you are a certain gaunt General Staff officer, who always went into battle before Rheims with his helmet uncovered—so that the French would be sure to see his Guards' star and silver trimmings?"

"At your service!" He twirled his mustache. "That's who I am. 1914 to 1918: Moyencourt—Ercheu—Roy—Ham—St.Quentin—18th Army Corps . . . Verdun."

"Captain Bruckner? You're certainly fatter than you were!"

"Possibly, possibly! Since the shameful Treaty of Versailles, I've had to lead the life of a civilian . . . yes, a civilian!" He whipped his cane through the air. "And may I ask what *you* were doing alone in the Bagatelle Park at this early hour? Or weren't you alone in the bushes there?" He tugged at his beard and winked: "Apropos, what do you say to a bite of lunch with me? Come along! 'Pigsfeet with sauerkraut!' —'What barbarians!' as the French would say . . .

"Well, why don't you say something? Do you regard me as a 'dangerous Hun'? I know you're no Nazi. But aren't you a monarchist? What the devil are you then?"

Suddenly he grasped Uhle firmly by the wrist and, looking him in the eye, declaimed Schiller's lines:

"To the dear Fatherland do thou be true!
Hold fast with might and main, with heart and soul!
There in the alien world thou art alone,
A trembling reed, snapped off by every storm . . ."

Stroking the back of Uhle's hand, he rambled on: "Or are you such a strong man that you can stand alone? You know what happens to the Prodigal Son. They kill the fatted calf for him—*when he comes home* . . . Seriously: Haven't you had enough of eating *husks* among these democratic swine? Don't you ever get a hankering for the taste of real German wine? A bottle of Mosel? How about cracking a bottle of Bocksbeutel with me? . . . Let's see: where are we? Ah, the Eiffel Tower, Trocadéro! I understand your silence and respect it! What else could you say but 'Pater, peccavi!' 'Father, I have sinned!' That isn't easy, I know. Huppla!"

Suddenly, at a turning, he threw his whole weight against Uhle and whispered:

"Come on, hand it over. A certain ballet dancer was with you in your hotel yesterday! I know all about it— Hand it over, damn it! Or . . ." He drove his hand into Uhle's inside coat pocket, snatched out the contents, and said in a completely changed voice:

"Sit still. Otherwise it'll be just too bad for you . . ."

The driver, having witnessed the incident in his traffic mirror, drew up to the curb beside one of the gilded eagles on the Pont d'Iéna, and hailed a policeman. Swinging his white truncheon, the gendarme approached.

"Shut up!" whispered Captain Bruckner, "—the police!" Furiously, he leaned over Uhle. "Uhle, keep your mouth shut, or you'll never get out of Paris alive . . . This is the last thing I wanted to happen . . . damn it . . . !" Politely he handed his diplomatic passport as a Military Attaché to the gendarme, who saluted.

"And you?" the gendarme demanded. Getting out of the cab, Uhle handed him his green carte d'identité.

"This card is not in order. It has not been renewed. You must come with me!" He seized his arm.

Uhle tore himself loose, and clung to the side of the taxi. "My pocketbook! Give me my pocketbook!" he stammered.

Captain Bruckner leaned forward, his voice cutting: "You have been deprived of your citizenship. For you there's no such thing as 'my pocketbook!' Your property has, according to law, been confiscated by the State! Driver—Hepp! Hepp!"

As the taxi gathered speed and pulled away, Bruckner leaned out of the window and shouted:

"You're on the wrong side, old man! . . . On the wrong side of the Seine! Ha-ha-ha!"

CHAPTER SIXTEEN   "COME ALONG!" THE GENDARME GRASPED UHLE'S SLEEVE. UHLE FOLLOWED HIM THROUGH THE CURIOUS glances of the passers-by. In an effort to calm himself he began to tell the story of his visit to the battlefields. At first the gendarme listened indifferently. As they went on through street after street, he began to show signs of interest. At the door of the 'Poste de Police' in the rue de Grenelle, the gendarme turned in, beckoning Uhle to follow him.

They climbed a short spiral staircase, and entered a badly lighted room with a wooden barrier framing a small space inside the door. Beyond the railing in half-darkness sat three men in civilian clothes, wearing the typical bureaucrat's linen half-sleeves. The office desks, heaped with official documents, were covered with dust. The fly-specked wall clock ticked a full minute before the rattling of paper ceased, and one of the three, who was bald, hoisted his spectacles onto his forehead, pushed back his chair and looked up. Eyeing Uhle, he motioned to the gendarme. The gendarme spread Uhle's identity card on the narrow wooden barrier and with one hairy finger pointed to a circle in red ink next to the official stamp. Then he began to whisper.

Apparently he was telling the story of his prisoner's strange experience in Haudroumont Quarry. The youngest of the three took copious notes. When he had finished, all three bureaucrats climbed off their leather-covered high stools and craned their necks over their collars. Then the tallest—Sergeant-Major Grumbach—removed a pipe from his mouth, brushed the ashes off his alpaca office jacket, and motioned to Uhle to approach:

"Qu'est-ce que c'est que ça, Monsieur? Your card is not in order, pas du tout!"

"Non?"

"Mais non! Du tout, du tout, du tout!"

"Have you no other papers?" asked the bald-headed man. When Uhle shook his head, the youngest bureaucrat, a man with bushy, black hair, picked up his notes and retired to another room, where for several minutes he could be dimly heard telephoning. On his return, he murmured to his colleagues: "The Chief is on his way." Then he pointed to a chair, and said to Uhle: "Sit down and wait!"

Uhle was baffled, but obeyed. The gendarme produced a blue package of cigarettes, and the air was soon filled with the reek of black tobacco. Through the clouds of smoke, Uhle watched the play of significant glances among the four servants of the Republic. Bending over as if to tie his shoelace, he felt in his inside pocket. Thank God, the manuscript pages were still there! And Captain Bruckner had found nothing in his pocketbook but a hundred francs, a small photograph of Uhle's parents, and a few unimportant addresses.

"Monsieur!" The bald-headed man, having polished his glasses, tapped a bundle of documents as if tingling with expectation: "Tomorrow morning, that monstrous woman-killer Weidmann will be beheaded. He pays for his crimes against society. Apropos, he is a German too, n'est-ce pas? He was born in Frankfurt if I'm not mistaken. And you—you were born on the Rhine? Right?"

All puffed heavily as they awaited Uhle's reply. It grew darker—clouds were drawing across the sky. The youngest official motioned to the gendarme to turn on the lights. Directing the shaded, hanging lamp full upon Uhle's face, the bald man grinned ecstatically:

"Weidmann is blond too! Just a minute—"

Outside they heard the grinding of automobile brakes. The gendarme opened the door just in time to admit a short, stocky man, broad-shouldered, wearing a light-gray suit, with the red band of the Legion of Honor in his buttonhole. Tossing a briefcase stuffed to bursting onto one of the desks, gesturing with his low-crowned straw hat, he waved aside the respectful greetings of his subordinates:

"Ça va! Ça va! Porca Madonna! Where is the fellow?" he bowed slightly to Uhle and introduced himself: "Armoni, Special Commissioner! . . . Your name?"

"Kaspar Friedrich Uhle."

"Most happy! Be seated. Please be seated!" Drawing up a chair, he sat down. "Your carte d'identité?"

The gendarme handed it to Armoni, who looked at it, ripped open his briefcase, compared Uhle's name with some papers in it, and gave him a hard penetrating look from his black eyes.

"Mon ami, you've been in Paris since . . . since when? Why have you not reported before this? Don't you know that all foreigners have to register with the police within twelve hours of their arrival?"

"No. I didn't know it."

"Eh bien, ça va!" He tossed the green card across the barrier onto a table, pulled the chair still closer and questioned: "What is your business in Paris?"

"My business? The Secretary of your Société des Anciens Combattants invited me to speak over the radio at the General Convention of World War Veterans at the Trocadéro tonight."

"Hm! That's very interesting!"

At this, the gendarme broke in: "Chief, he was with the German Military Attaché from Bulgaria in a taxi near the Pont d'Iéna."

"Still more interesting! And how do you happen to know the German Military Attaché from Bulgaria?"

"Through the World War. We were in the same army corps."

"Amazing! And your name is Uhle!" He pointed to a typed document from his briefcase. "You were a Captain in the Uhlans?"

"In the Uhlans?" Sergeant-Major Grumbach lit his pipe. "Which Uhlans?"

"The Sixth Uhlans, stationed in Hanau."

The sergeant spat into the spittoon behind his chair. He was about to ask another question, but a look from Armoni stopped him. Muttering to himself, he turned to a cupboard and, producing a bottle of Burgundy, filled two glasses, which he offered to Uhle and Armoni. Armoni's swift, impetuous gesture betrayed the typical southerner.

He clinked glasses with Uhle—"Salut!"—slapped him on the thigh, and with evident relish continued: "We have your record. You're stopping at the Hotel Balzac? Porca Madonna! Didn't the woman-killer Weidmann spend a night there, too? Ha-ha! But—God be praised—tomorrow morning he'll be shorter by a head—one blond head."

"Pardon!" Uhle set his glass aside. "I don't understand any of this . . ."

"Quoi!" The pupils of Armoni's eyes narrowed to pin-points. "How long are you going to stay in Paris?"

"Mais, Monsieur!" Uhle, not to be restrained, jumped up. "I can't for the life of me understand—"

"Mon ami," Armoni smiled, "if you'll just answer my questions, I shall be much obliged! If you won't, I suppose I shall have to let you go. Only one thing: you must leave your carte d'identité here. You can have it back tomorrow morning."

"Then I can go—?"

"Why not? Certainly you can go." He looked at the others: "You've made a note of his permanent address? But first, let me ask you what you think of these facts: This morning, twenty-four hours before his execution, Weidmann—who is known to have murdered at least seven women—swears that someone higher up forced him to commit his crimes and that there is a German hand in all this. He admits that on a certain day, he had a meeting not far from the French border with a German citizen, about five feet ten in height." He turned to the gendarme: "Let's see that card again!" After carefully reading each item of Uhle's personal description, he continued: "And this mysterious S.A. man whom Weidmann claims he met in a garden-restaurant not a stone's throw from the French border patrol—this same unknown"—his vivacious, black eyes searched Uhle's face—"carried a knapsack like yours!"

"Monsieur le Commissaire!" Uhle's patience was exhausted. "What has all this got to do with me? I really—"

"Calm down! Calm down!" Without further ceremony, the four officials hustled Uhle behind the barrier into the inner sanctum.

"Are you crazy!? Let me out! As if I were the only person in the world with a knapsack!"

"Crazy? You be careful, you're dealing with officials of the French Republic! Capito?" There was no mistaking the hostility in their attitude.

Wedged in between chairs and surrounded on all sides, Uhle watched Armoni pour himself another glass. The farcical absurdity of his position drew from him another protest, this time delivered with perfect composure:

"Messieurs, will you kindly permit me to leave? Will you please telephone the Secretary of the Société des Anciens Combattants?" As no one moved, he continued with rising anger: "I am a German exile, deprived of citizenship, supposed to be enjoying the freedom and hospitality of your republic. And so you permit the Nazi German Military Attaché from Bulgaria to steal my pocketbook, while you tell me stories about the murderer Weidmann."

At this moment the door opened. Entered the slouch-hatted detective who, the preceding evening, at his hotel, had displayed such an interest in Uhle's movements.

CHAPTER SEVENTEEN OBVIOUSLY HE WAS A PERSON OF CONSEQUENCE, FOR ALL THE POLICE SCRAMBLED TO THEIR FEET. WITH A broad, theatrical gesture, the newcomer produced from under his black velvet cape a knapsack, depositing it dramatically on the table beside the wine bottle.

"Is that your knapsack?" he demanded.

"What consummate gall!" Uhle jumped to his feet. "So it was *you* who broke into my room?"

"Is that your knapsack? Porca Madonna!"

"Yes. What business is it of yours?"

"Take it easy!"

Uhle again constrained to his seat, Armoni unbuckled the knapsack and withdrew from it a packet wrapped in tissue paper. The contents of this he let trickle out in a small heap on the back of his hand, like sand running out of an hour-glass.

"And now, mon ami, what's this?"

"That, Messieurs, is a handful of earth from Verdun!"

"Earth from Verdun! And this?" Armoni extricated from the knapsack something in soiled linen, which he unrolled. In the midst of breathless excitement, he laid the bones of a human hand on the table. "So! So! Not cherries—and not earth from Verdun—now what can it be!" Armoni's tones were acid.

"No! Messieurs . . . . I found that hand in a meadow outside Beaumont. Perhaps it is the hand of a fallen brother of yours, Sergeant—or of mine! Or perhaps it was your father's hand, Monsieur!" He turned to the youngest of those present. "You must still have been going to school in 1916!"

"Ça va!" Armoni rolled the ghastly relic in its wrapping and stuffed it back into the knapsack.

A captive blue-bottle fly buzzed in the heat and settled on the perspiring, alcoholic nose of the detective. Sergeant-Major Grumbach opened the window, fanning his face. "It's hot!" A heavy draft, foretelling rain, began to flutter the papers so that he closed the window immediately. Then, looking Uhle straight in the eye, he said: "I fought at Verdun, too!"

Armoni gazed reproachfully at his subordinate, distressed to note signs of a beginning camaraderie with Uhle. Grumbach turned to the telephone.

"About time we phoned the Société des Anciens Combattants. If what he says is true, Dr. Gunther can identify him at once."

Clapping his hand over the receiver, Armoni snapped: "Who's conducting this examination—you or I?"

"So, you admit this is an examination! Let me use that telephone!" Uhle took a step toward Armoni.

"Grab him!" yelled Armoni. Uhle was seized and held despite his struggles and slapped vigorously fore and aft. Before he knew it, Armoni's practiced fingers had wrested from Uhle's hip pocket an object which, until then, he had completely forgotten.

Armoni clicked his tongue: "And now perhaps you'll explain this."

"That . . . ?" Uhle encountered the interchange of significant glances. "That—is a revolver—" and he felt his jaw drop.

"And just how do you happen to possess this neat little toy?" The fat detective took off his slouch hat. "Have you, perhaps, a license to carry this lethal weapon? Just talk yourself out of that if you can!"

"How I happen to have this revolver—?" Uhle drew a deep breath. "But what's the use?—you won't believe me!"

"Just go ahead and talk!" The weapon was passed from hand to hand, Armoni finally depositing the star exhibit triumphantly in the center of the table beside the bottle of red wine. "Mon ami, tell your story!"

"But you certainly won't believe me!"

"Get on with it!"

As Uhle still remained obstinately silent, Armoni signed to the detective to read the stenographic record of the gendarme's report on what Uhle had told him while they were walking to the police station. The detective read it through to the end. Armoni leaned back in his swivel chair, shook his head, looked ironically at Uhle, and said:

"What a cock-and-bull story! How long do we have to listen to this kind of drivel?"

Brushing down his short, amber-yellow mustache with the mouthpiece of his pipe, Grumbach spoke with deliberation:

"Monsieur le Commissaire, whoever fought with us at Verdun knows there are all sorts of improbable things down under the ground there.—So please go on with your story, Monsieur le Capitaine!" There was an unwonted tone of respect in his voice.

Furious, Armoni glared at him, poured out a glass of wine and gulped it down; the wind increased, the windowpanes began to rattle. All of a sudden the detective stood up, scratched his head and began ponderously pacing back and forth in the narrow room. He cleared his throat, shot his forefinger at Uhle, and said:

"It was you—who were in the Bagatelle Park early this morning?"

Startled by the sudden question, Uhle felt all the blood leave his face.

"Come on now! Were you in the Bagatelle Park, or weren't you?"

When Uhle still did not answer, the detective flung the door open, shouting: "Monsieur Pierre!"

At the far end of the dark corridor a door opened, heavy steps sounded. Wearing a green woolen shawl over his leather jacket, a man in wooden shoes clumped into the room. Uhle immediately recognized the gardener whom he had encountered in the Bagatelle Park.

At that moment, picking up the revolver, the detective emptied its chambers on the table in front of Armoni and said:

"There's one cartridge missing!"

"Porca Madonna! Will you kindly tell us how that one cartridge happens to be missing!"

Uhle pulled himself together. But before he could utter a word, the detective continued, suddenly in an icy tone of voice: "You had better tell us too why you fired a shot at that girl. . . ."

"I?" Uhle's voice broke. "Did someone shoot at a girl?" He looked anxiously from one to the other.

"Monsieur Pierre here saw you hiding behind a tree in the Bagatelle Park. When he heard the shot, he immediately told the police that it must have been you who fired!"

"But gentlemen! . . ." Frantically afraid for Olenka, Uhle felt the sweat break out on his forehead. "Will you listen to reason?"

CHAPTER EIGHTEEN BEFORE UHLE COULD SAY ANY-
THING MORE, THE GENDARME HAD SNAPPED HANDCUFFS ON HIS WRISTS.

He pulled so hard that the steel cut into his flesh. Throwing his whole weight against him, Uhle knocked him off the stool and trampled his way to the telephone. But the others forced him back against the wall.

"Porca Madonna!" Armoni tore the black cover from a typewriter and ordered Sergeant-Major Grumbach to take down Uhle's story.

"Now—a straight story and no more trimmings! This time it's going to be a proper statement. And the whole truth!"

"As long as I'm handcuffed, you won't get a word out of me . . ."

The gendarme pulled off his belt, and was on the point of striking Uhle. But the detective stepped between them. Then, dismissing the gardener, he stationed himself behind Grumbach, who was ready at the typewriter, and said firmly:

"Monsieur Uhle, we are giving you an opportunity to improve your situation . . . by making a full confession. Now tell us! How did you come to fire that shot? . . . . Did you have a quarrel with the lady in your hotel last night? . . . Was it jealousy? Or was our attention to be distracted from the 'big salad,' as the murderer Weidmann calls it?"

A brief pause. The man in the slouch hat blew cigarette smoke into Uhle's face. "In spite of the fact that your hotel porter must have informed you," he said slowly, "that the Governor of Paris has ordered all soldiers to remain in their barracks, you took a particularly suspicious character in uniform up to your hotel room, didn't you? Mais oui. The hotel reported it. The two of you were together all night."

"Is that to go down in the dossier, damn it?"

"Coquin!" The detective tapped Uhle's cheek with a ruler. "You're both fifth columnists, aren't you?"

"Messieurs! Why don't you let me telephone Gunther?"

"Young man!" The fat man came close to him. "I'm going to confront you with your accomplices—right here. So out with it! You Boches think you have the jump on us—but we'll show you! Talk!"

"I repeat: you will not believe what I have to tell you."

"Chief!" Grumbach put a new sheet into his typewriter. "Do you really want all this in the dossier?"

"Go on and type! Par exemple!" Then the detective took a large flask of brandy out of his pocket, unscrewed it, held it to Uhle's lips, and made him drink a few swallows. "That'll buck you up. And now get busy and find yourself a decent alibi! You can't expect us to swallow the fairy story you've—"

"Fairy story?" Uhle looked at him astonished. "Mais non, Messieurs!"

"Quoi? You mean you really did see an underground depot full of corpse-gas bombs!"

"Gentlemen!" Uhle's voice was suddenly dead serious. "Whether you believe it or not, thirty-three steps underground Captain Hermann said to me: 'Boy, when you're in command of dead men—like me—can you imagine the problems? What do all the bonzes in Berlin know about my heavy duties? Those nitwits in their red-striped trousers! Keitel, for instance—or Göring! We've got their number, we old-time cadets. We know what it's all about! Well, mum's the word. But on the other hand, if one of those muck-a-mucks upstairs strikes a pose and commands "Fire!" and everything topples over, now I ask you, my boy, is that anything special?' "

" 'Anything special'? Did he say that? Damnation!" And then Grumbach nervously resumed his typing.

" 'Fire! Why, any donkey can say that,' he said. I give you my word, Messieurs, for a full minute Captain Hermann stared through the fissures of the lusterless mercury of his rococo mirror. Suddenly he gave a shout, took the chalice, filled it—I don't know how many times—raised it, his hands shaking, to the level of his mouth, and drained it in one gulp. 'To the dregs, my boy!' He turned the chalice upside down—"

"Go on! Porca Madonna! What are you stopping for?"

"What's he stopping for! Par exemple! He's stopping because he's run out of lies. That's what he's stopping for! Right?—You booby! Or maybe the story about the pioneer 'from the seven planets' is true too?" He laughed at Uhle mockingly.

CHAPTER NINETEEN "STOP!" SERGEANT-MAJOR GRUMBACH SHOUTED ACROSS THEIR LAUGHTER, HIS CHEEKS FLECKED WITH RED blotches. "Chef!" He turned to Armoni. "Monsieur le Capitaine is not lying! I know it now." And then he gave the examination an unexpected turn by maintaining that just such a pioneer "from the seven planets" had turned up in his own section of the lines in 1916. "And because of that God-damned face I didn't get the Iron Cross!"

In spite of Armoni's admonishing glance at the photograph of the President of the Republic above the desk, Grumbach, the Alsatian, snorted:

"I should fool myself! Even if I were to get the Légion d'Honneur six times, that wouldn't compensate me for not getting the Iron Cross! After all, I was a German Sergeant-Major!"

"You were what? You're French!"

"I am an Alsatian, born in Strassburg, where we still remember

Kaiser and Reich! I was a Uhlan too! What of it? You can't cut those things out of a man's heart with a knife . . . I tell you, if it hadn't been for that pioneer, I would have had the Iron Cross. Imagine that soldier popping up in our trenches, helmet and all, and underneath it, a perfectly honest-to-God face! And what eyes! Well, for some unknown reason, from the time that face appeared in our dugout, all our gay and sparkling fighting spirit died a natural death! If anyone asked him where he came from, he just stared at you like a ghost, and said:

" 'I come from the seven planets' . . .

"But the damnedest thing was that the toughest fighters in our company pricked up their ears, stared at each other, and began studying the casualty lists with him! Instead of keeping their rifles pointed at the enemy over the trench parapet, they began to feed mice! It was as if we'd been jinxed. Finally it boiled down into a regular argument: was war necessary and legitimate and in the nature of things—or not? What do you think of that, Chef? One day I found the pioneer standing on the firing ledge. He had just put a sandbag on the parapet.

" 'Boy,' I said, 'since you come from the seven planets, you must certainly know what your people up there think about war, and where war gets started.'

"He just looked at me, pushed his helmet back on his forehead, pointed out a loophole, as though he were sighting a rifle barrel— into No Man's Land, where the dead were hanging on the wire. He looked at me out of his pale mug and said: 'Ask him! Not me!'

"I thought to myself: *whom* am I to ask?

"Then I took a squint through the loophole and I saw—by God, Chef, it makes my flesh creep!—I saw a French captain of Spahis lying in front of our barbed wire. A freak shot had caught him in the lower belly and burned away his uniform, so that his organ stuck up at least three times life size—stiff and swollen and black, against a sky that threatened snow. His red Moroccan cavalry cloak lay beside him like a pool of blood."

Grumbach stopped, and took a few puffs from his pipe. No one said anything, so he went on:

"—Suddenly the pioneer nodded . . . And then he began to put out some more of his blue planetary nonsense—"

"What was it, Sergeant? Par exemple! What did he say?"

"He said, 'Comrade, the phallus darkens the sun of peace for us mortals'—"

80

"Porca Madonna, did he say that, did he say that?"

"Right you are, Chef—and I was just going to slam him, but he'd already hoisted that mug of his out of the trench. He slipped out under our wire to the Spahi Captain, picked the red cloak up out of the snow and was just going to throw it over that unholy mess when suddenly they got him. With his arms out he staggered through the fire, zigzagging around in front of our barbed wire. Finally he tumbled back—and there he was, lying in our trench.

"That night, our men knocked together a sort of cross out of planks and strapped the planet-boy's body to it with suspenders and belts. The next morning, in the first rays of the winter sun coming up behind Fort Vaux—I swear it, Messieurs—I suddenly saw that bloody X-Y soldier raised above our trenches like the Crucified. And everybody in the trenches all around there saw it, too. It was a horrible sight—rising against the snow."

"What? What?" several of the police officers asked together.

"What?—why, the Cross of Vaux—for so it was now called all along the Front. But all the artillery staffs must have seen it too, through their field glasses, because before I could order it taken down, it had been laid low by a rain of shell fire from all directions.

" 'He's alive! He's alive!' my men began to shout, and ran. And actually, when they laid him in the bottom of the trench, he was still breathing. We yelled, 'Stretcher-bearers! Stretcher-bearers!'

"But the next minute our trenches were attacked and I never saw that mug again! But that wasn't the end of the silly business." He clenched his fist. "Colonel von Türkheim sent for me afterwards. I went to his dugout. And that was the end of the Iron Cross for me."

In the long pause that followed, Grumbach relit his pipe and chewed the stem. His eyes, under the heavy brows, kept glancing expectantly at his old comrade in the Uhlans—Uhle.

"Sergeant," said Uhle quietly, "I thank you." Then he looked across at the detective. "You see, Monsieur, what I said about my pioneer is the truth. For it was that same thin X-Y soldier, that same shadowy, bearded face the Sergeant has been telling you about, that I saw again yesterday behind that rococo mirror—"

"What!" Grumbach said haltingly. "Captain Uhle! You don't really mean to say that you saw *my* pioneer!"

"Yes, I do. It is the truth. Just as I was telling your gendarme on the way here. The bullet that the General of the Mirror meant to drive me out with . . . missed its aim. For a long time the report raised ghostly echoes down there among the dead—"

"Astounding," Grumbach panted through his mustache. "And what then?"

"Then I jumped at the mad officer, knocked the revolver out of his hand—"

"This revolver here?"

"Yes, gentlemen. And that is the only explanation I can give you for the missing cartridge. I am telling the truth."

CHAPTER TWENTY "PAR EXEMPLE!" THE DETECTIVE PUT ON HIS HAT. ARMONI SHOVED THE REVOLVER, TOGETHER WITH THE remaining cartridges, into a drawer.

Outside, the rain rattled against the windows. Suddenly Grumbach got up from the typewriter, went to the barrier, poured a glass of wine, looked at the others uncertainly—and forced a laugh!

"What do you think of that, Chef! And now may I suggest that Captain Uhle finish his "fairy story" for us? He might tell us—how his encounter with his General ended—"

"Bravo! Porca Madonna! Yes, Herr Uhle, you may as well lie yourself dry!"

"D'accord!" The detective threw his cigarette away and pounded the table. "Par exemple!"

"You want to know how the encounter ended? Very well, gentlemen! I finally succeeded—it took all my strength—in freeing myself from the iron grip of his hands, stepped across him, and on to the mirror. But at that, he went down on his knees to me, grabbed me with both arms, and pulled and tugged until finally his weight drew me down beside him. So there we knelt, face to face. He was sobbing and whimpering like a child:

" 'My boy! Are you going to betray me? And I thought you had come down here to stand by me in my onerous duties! Isn't it true? It can't be you're a traitor! Don't tell me that! My boy, have you any idea what a tremendous responsibility rests on my shoulders?'

"His face, chalk-white to the end of his nose, twitched with indescribable fear.

" 'Boy, listen: every night about midnight, when it's dead quiet in the Cadaver Utilization Factory—you don't know how still it is, boy, in the middle of the night—and then it begins to strike twelve in Verdun from the cathedral tower—so crystal-clear—one!—two!—three!—boy, can you imagine what happens then? . . .

" 'Suddenly—something begins to shimmer through that mirror! It fluoresces like azure evidence. You've heard about radium—how they say it shines by its own power? Well, there you are! It's exactly like that. As soon as the twelfth stroke has sounded, that evidence shines in the rococo mirror . . .

" 'Think, boy! . . . Here I stand . . . nothing but my sense of duty keeps me here. And I say to myself: "To Hell with that azure evidence! A brave heart has its own center of gravity," I say to myself.

" 'But then, all of a sudden, everything here comes alive, in all the caves and graves . . . there are so many shadows, boy! Do you understand? And there I stand, revolver in hand, finger on trigger, and then . . . and then they arrive . . . Out from every plowed field where blood has spurted, they arrive . . . out from the dark Flanders highway, out from the Argonne, from the hero-devouring plain of Vœuvre, from L'Homme Mort . . . They glide along . . . still in their blood-soaked uniforms . . . thronging together . . . O-o-oh! and every one of them wants to get at the mirror! . . . wants to open it. Wants to let *him* out—the Little Jew Jesus! . . . .

" 'But it's just that, boy, that I'm here to prevent! . . . Under any circumstances! Those are my orders from the Supreme Cabinet! But *they're all dead*, boy. And how they whirl! O-o-oh! . . . They flutter out of the dark like moths, flutter up toward that azure evidence behind the mirror!

" 'I knock them off the frame like gnats—*but they're all dead*, boy! I yell at them: "What do you want with the Little Jew Jesus? Get away from that mirror!"

" 'Then they pull at my beard! And they pull at my coat! They pull me here and pull me there. "Life! . . . We want to live!" moans the damned rabble from the grave. Life! Can you beat that, boy?

" 'Then I stand there! Just like this! Like iron, I tell you! Under my steel helmet! . . . like an Archangel! And, boy, nothing but respect for the Prussian General's shoulder straps I wear, no-o-o-thing but their drilled-in terror at the sight of these topnotch Prussian decorations around my neck—only that has held the dogs in check so far! . . . But for how long, boy, how long! You'll never know how ice-cold it is with all of them whispering and muttering around my ears! . . . Then I just jam my helmet on tighter, I glare at them like an eagle, and I shout:

" 'What do you want with the Little Jew Jesus? He can't help you! Or did he help you when you were drowned in shell fire? When you called on him then? Answer me that! Did he help you then? . . . So just get away from that mirror and stay away! Supposing you did let out the Little Jew Jesus, what good would it do? Do you suppose he could bring you to life again? Not a chance, you nit-wits!

" 'For that was really the disastrous mistake he made: the promise of the Kingdom of Heaven! . . . Are you going to get away from that mirror?! . . . I say: Supposing he did come out among you now, you miserable oxen, what would he do? I'll tell you what he'd do! He'd certainly retract everything he ever preached two thousand years ago! I swear to you by my sacred honor! By the three silver stars of a Prussian Full General I swear to you that he would no longer be "international"! He would be a nationalist! He'd stick the Star of David in his buttonhole. It might not be a diamond one like Baroness Rothschild's, but it would be all-metal! You morons! Nationalism—that would be his new blessing! So if you don't get away from that mirror—

" 'Think a minute: if He had been right, if there really were a moral world order—then the World War would have had to be followed by a World Order! But since there is no such thing . . . since the premise is false— What are you saying? "Turn the other cheek?" No!—that presupposes that man is good! But man is not only good: he is good *and* bad, both! So stop rattling your jawbones at me!

" 'Ten-shun! Chest out! Let your hearts beat high!—or whatever it is you've got behind those ribs! You dogs! Don't show me your wounds! Suffer! Suffer willingly! You can suffer cheerfully—now that Germany has an army again! Get it? Atoms that you are, you have had the honor to serve a world purpose! Even if your flabby brains haven't grasped the fact!

" 'Pack of fools!! Fall in! Formations—as you were! Dress your lines! God damn it! Now then back you go and behave yourselves, straight to your own mass graves in your own sectors of the Front. You there in the third rank, what are you muttering about? Got anything to grouse about? Can any of you say that your General hasn't always treated you right?'

"His voice became sentimental. 'Not a day passes that I don't stick nice, new little crosses, row after row, straight-ranked on your graves! Not an Easter or Whitsunday but some big shot, hand at his helmet, or with silk hat over his heart, pays grateful tribute to you—and women and children gladly put a rose or any inexpensive greenery the florist wants to get rid of—on your graves!

" 'So— Heads up, and spirits high! Wasn't it sweet and honorable to die for the Fatherland? You tramps! What are you back here whimpering about the Little Jew Jesus for? . . . The great achievement of the War was: always to ask first whether a thing is necessary or not. But was the Little Jew Jesus necessary in order for you to get shot in the guts? Do you need to have his New Testament in your knapsack in order to batter out your enemy's brains with a rifle-butt? No! . . .

" 'Is Goethe's Faust a necessity when you want to stick a bayonet through your opponent's chest? Not at all! Cattle! . . . But—b-u-u-t —for you to give up your individual lives, you see, boys, *that* was necessary! And by doing so you served a world law—the Law of Might! And might not only smashes right, it also breaks bones!

" 'No help for it! So stop drooling about "Life"! All you Grenadiers, Dragoons, Fusiliers, Hussars, Pioneers, Cuirrassiers, airmen—when you came back to barracks from the dance-halls, your heads dulled by the beer breaths of a girl in silk and satin, I think you knew then . . . to the dregs . . . what this whorehouse and floosie Life is worth. I think we all know how the joy-bells sound— Ding-dong . . . Ding-dong . . .

" 'But, if there's anybody here who thinks otherwise, just let him step forward and I'll break his dome so wide open there'll be nothing left of him but a stupid smile. Ha, ha, ha!

" 'What the hell! You consider yourselves sons of sergeants and drum-majors? Grandsons and great-grandsons of three generations of atheists who went to the garrison church every Sunday and sat on the back benches and snored through the sermon! Get away from that mirror, you filth! Oh, the childish idiocy of the common man! The Little Jew Jesus is pure fiction! Soldiers! Is the shark, instead of filling his belly on the milliards of herrings, to go hungry—out of pure altruism? Or out of respect to the ideology of a League of Nations?

" 'Company—march! Back to your graves! The Little Jew Jesus was only born of a woman, too—né d'une femme! "Consider the lilies of the field"—from now on the tank divisions roll over them! The whole Good Friday spell has been definitely gassed!

" 'Dogs!' He turned so pale that you could see it under his mustache. 'Back! This is insubordination! This is mutiny! This is what is called unlawful assembly of the dead . . .'

"His words burst out like dull explosions from the depths of his fear. I felt he was only trying to keep on talking, because, all the while he talked, something was glimmering, becoming more and more distinctly outlined behind the mirror . . . More and more clearly a face began to emerge . . . a visage with eyes—

"And then a voice—a voice without a mouth— As if out of the farthest depths of space . . . came words . . . in waves . . . like pure music! Words—that cast shadows—"

"Words?"

"Yes. Four terrible words."

"What words?"

"I—COME—TO—JUDGE."

CHAPTER TWENTY-ONE UHLE HAD BARELY UTTERED THESE FOUR WORDS BEFORE HE DROPPED LIKE A STONE. AT THE NOISE, THE police blinked at each other as if startled out of a hypnotic sleep. Armoni was the first to find his tongue:

"Porca Madonna!" He thrust his little finger into his ear, and worked it around as if something were tickling his eardrum. "Hi!" He gave Uhle a push. "Get up from there!" But Uhle lay where he had fallen between the stools, unconscious. The Commissioner raged:

"Either this man is crazy—in which case we'll send him to La Salpétrière! Or he's trying to pull the wool over our eyes with his ghost stories, porca Madonna! But he can't fool me." He picked up the telephone:

"Hello! Commissioner Armoni speaking. Quoi? Mais oui. Get me the District Police Superintendent of Verdun. Right away! Mais vite!"

"Bravo!" the detective joined in now. "And he can connect us with the Battlefield Police."

"Porca Madonna! And then we shall know once and for all if there is any such underground dugout in Haudroumont Quarry. We shall find out," he laughed, "whether there actually is a crazy General living thirty-three steps underground, or not!"

"And that soldier of his behind the rococo mirror," the gendarme added to the joke, adjusting his new yellow leather belt around his hips.

This sally evoked roars of laughter from everybody except Sergeant-Major Grumbach.

"Just take a look at our colleague Grumbach!" The bald man wiped his neck. "He looks as if he were seeing things."

Ignoring their jibes Grumbach took the typed document out of his machine and read it over. The telephone rang. Armoni went to it.

"No answer!" He gave a number. "Mais oui! Send over a police car at once! The bastard ought to be before an examining magistrate this minute!"

Outside, it was growing darker and darker. Huge black clouds lowered over the roofs. Then the storm which had been threatening burst in full fury. The wind blew so violently that the French windows flew open and all the official papers that were not under weights or put away scattered and flurried about the room. Then the lights went out everywhere.

"Lights!" Armoni shouted. "Porca Madonna!"

"Short circuit, Chef!"

While the gendarme was vainly clicking switches around the room, a sudden vivid flash of lightning revealed a white face. For seconds the police stared at it.

But before they could make up their minds whether they had been the victims of a hallucination produced by the lightning or whether someone had really come into the room from the landing, there was a second even more vivid flash.

"That struck!" whispered the junior bureaucrat, cowering under the table. And now it was totally dark in the room. Only the thunder— sounding like exploding bombs—rolled through the rue de Grenelle, shaking the stone buildings to their foundations.

The detective finally succeeded in lighting a candle. They saw Armoni standing with both arms in the air. "Porca Madonna!" The words came almost voicelessly. "Where is Monsieur Uhle?" And they all stared at the empty floor. "Where the hell is he?" Armoni raced through the open door and down the dark stairs. But he returned immediately, and screamed in a flustered voice: "The bastard has got away!"

They looked at each other shamefacedly. Sergeant-Major Grumbach put his whole weight against the window and succeeded in closing it. Then he stared out at the quivering lightning flashes that riddled the sky.

"For God's sake!" He leaned against the window frame. "What do you suppose that mug was?"

"Quoi?" Armoni straightened his tie and pushed the gendarme to the telephone. "Get going! Notify every police station." And then he suddenly clapped his limp hand to his forehead as though he had had a revelation. He had remembered that there was an express train for Germany due to leave about this time. Stumblingly he worked his way through the darkness, down the stairs, and into the street. Then, like a bloodhound on the trail, he ran on past the houses—doing his best to keep the ever-increasing rain off his head with his jacket.

A solitary taxi turned into the street ahead of him. He signaled to it, jumped in as it drew up, and through the thunder and lightning shouted to the driver:

"Gare de l'Est! Mais vite, vite, vite!"

BOOK TWO

CHAPTER ONE T HE LONG WAGON-LITS TRAIN FROM MUNICH AND STRASSBURG ROLLED SLOWLY INTO THE GARE DE L'EST. AS THE streamlined locomotive, steaming and puffing from every exhaust, valve, and piston, came to rest with a long-drawn hiss, gendarmes posted themselves at every door. No one was allowed to alight. The railway police, advised by Armoni, had arranged to let no passengers on or off trains to or from Germany.

The passengers crowded the windows and asked—first curiously, then excitedly—what was the matter. Meanwhile the rain sluiced down, dinning on the station's huge glass roof. Irritation mounted, tempers grew high, and curses flew, until the Commissioner had the guards pass the word along that a distinguished foreign personage was arriving in a special train on the track alongside. They must just have patience. And then the rumor spread from compartment to compartment: "The German Foreign Minister, von Ribbentrop, is arriving."

"Who is arriving?" A head appeared, craning out of the window of a first-class sleeping compartment, and cursing in practically all the languages of Europe.

"Plague and Lenin! I can't get off this train because of Ribbentröpfchen! I'm somebody myself!"

The fierce draft in the station caught his gray-green Caucasian cap and whirled it like a plate along the platform and down between the rails. The skin tight drawn over his oval skull, which resembled Lenin's, was yellow. The three heavy creases in his forehead glistened like neon tubes, reflecting the changing signal lights of the station. His coal-black eyes sparkled, darting here and there. Retrieving his cap, a gendarme politely handed it back to him.

"Plague and Satan! Let me off this train! I have things to do! Or are you afraid of the World Revolution?"

Commissioner Armoni—short and broad-shouldered in his light-gray suit with the red Légion d'Honneur ribbon in his buttonhole—

stepped up to the window, demanding his papers.

"Papers! Plague and Death! What papers! Do you want my baggage check? Smirnow!" He beckoned to his companion in the sleeping compartment. "These Paris Kulaks still put their faith in papers, like Shylock! Death and Democracy! A paper culture! Papers, papers! Hasn't the eastern sun risen yet on you western galley-slaves? Is that why you're still asking for papers? I am a general of cavalry—And what's more, I am going to sing Don Quixote tonight in your opera house. So open the door. I'm catching a chill in this drafty station! Monsieur, have you ever heard of Chaliapin, the famous singer? I see you have. Well, he's dead! But I'm alive, and I'm more famous than he ever was! Plague and Paris! Is this your reception committee? Let me out of here this minute! Smirnow! The bags! Get the bags! At once!"

He opened the door and maneuvered his huge carcass onto the platform.

Through all this flood of words, the Commissioner's quick, small, expressionless eyes had observed him with greater and greater interest. Now he stepped forward.

"Monsieur Schleich, your passport, please!"

"Plague and thunder! How do you know my name? Smirnow, show him our passports! Now you open your eyes, eh! A diplomatic passport! Let me tell you something: the next time a Revolutionary comes to Paris, no one will ask him for his passport. Plague and Danton!"

The Russian colossus made off toward the exit, his secretary trailing him, loaded down with expensive bags and briefcases. Armoni blinked after him. Then he ran to the nearest telephone booth:

"Hello! Commissioner Armoni speaking from the Gare de l'Est. One of the twelve men who murdered the Czar is on his way out of this station. He's traveling under the name of Christlieb Schleich. He is president of the OWRA. Coming from where? From Munich. Quoi? You don't know what OWRA means? It's the cover-up name for the Communist Sabotage Centrum. Schleich is responsible for all the murders and acts of sabotage committed in the past few weeks. The kidnaping of Colonel Popov—the attempt to blow up the Citadel in Warsaw—the bombings in the Balkans, Washington, and Persia. Quoi? Mais non! He's going to the Ritz. But I saw an attaché of the German Embassy waiting outside the station. Quoi? Shall I have someone trail him? No? Porca Madonna! Have it your own way . . ."

Meanwhile Schleich had reached the street. An aristocratic-looking man about thirty-five years of age, wearing a camel's-hair overcoat, hastened to meet him, quietly introduced himself as Prince Ferdinand,

and handed him a telegram. Schleich tore it open, read it, stuck it in his pocket and growled: "All right!" Nodding to another man—less elegantly attired—who was trying to get a word with him, he said: "No time now! Speak to my secretary.

"Plague and Lenin!" He took Prince Ferdinand's arm. "Are you going to take me to the Soviet Embassy?"

"No, your Excellency, I must return to the German Embassy at once."

"What's all this going on in Paris?"

"I don't understand, your Excellency!"

"Whom are they keeping the station cleared for?"

"There are all kinds of rumors."

"Rumors?" Schleich glanced through the telegram again.

"Yes. For example, that preparations for a revolt have been brought to light in Poland."

"That's favorable—very favorable. Plague and the Vistula! Don't you think it's very favorable, Prince?"

"Your Excellency, all Poles are swine."

CHAPTER TWO Smirnow watched schleich get into a motorcar, then turned to the hatless communist, prince Ferdinand's unequal partner in waiting.

"Comrade, let's get something to eat. I haven't had breakfast yet. Comrade Schleich is going to pig it at the Embassy, so why shouldn't we have a bite?" They entered the station restaurant.

"I'm Leo Münzer," said the other, seating himself with Smirnow at a table near the buffet. "Just arrived this morning from Constantinople."

"So? Is that so? Inspecting the Asiatic oil centers? Do you belong to the OWRA news service or the oil-field saboteurs? . . . Never mind! I have another policy: Delenda est Anglia! Down with England! That's the main thing . . . Garçon! Coffee, rolls, butter, fried eggs! . . . Well! Just arrived from Turkey, eh? How goes it in the land of Abdul Hamid of blessed memory? And does the Golden Horn prefer 'the sweet water of Europe' to 'the sweet waters of Asia'? Any signs of the Asiatic wind in Stambul? No more harems, I hear. Instead, the

Father of all the Turks commends 'adopted daughters' for diversion! I hope, for instance, you—"

"Herr von Papen," Münzer interrupted, "has left for Bagdad."

"He has? Well, even the tales of the thousand and one nights finally all get told. Bagdad, eh?" Smirnow yawned elaborately, snatching the dishes, cups, and saucers from the waiter's tray. "I feel like the morning after! Didn't get any sleep at all!" He wolfed the food and wiped up the last of the egg with a piece of bread.

"A-ah! That's better!" He lit a cigarette. "Comrade, haven't we met before somewhere? Wasn't it at the Soviet Embassy in Berlin, Unter den Linden? In the White Salon? At the reception for the German General Staff? Do you remember Lenin's portrait just above the aspidistras and rubber plants? Somebody at the Embassy, I think it was Kreszinsky, demonstrated the latest invention for coaxing music out of the ether . . . Weren't you living at the time under the alias of Axelrot?

"Now I remember: we gorged on caviar dished up on the former Imperial service. And Lunacharsky's beautiful film-star wife coquetted with the Prussians. And all the time General von Stülpnagel angled with golden bait for anyone who gave the least hint of being anti-Stalinist . . . Yes, that was in 1929. Kreszinsky was shot long since. So were Bugoslawsky and Bukharin and—"

"All the real communists . . ." Münzer raged.

"Shot! All shot! Who knows, Comrade, when . . ."

"That damned Stalin!" Leo Münzer clenched his fists. "The spawn of Tiflis! Trying to turn our beautiful communism into Ghengis-Khanism! That block of basalt—with nerves like the veins in a stone! The Little Father all over again! The devil! Why can't someone be found to finish him off in his dacha or somewhere? . . . You're silent, Smirnow. Or are you thinking of our comrade Schleich?"

"Just before we left Moscow, he was walking with Stalin down a dark corridor in the Kremlin. Both had their heads down. Suddenly Stalin threw open the door of a small garret room. They stepped in together. But although their voices were loud and hoarse, I couldn't understand anything they were saying, because they were talking in Georgian and in the dialect of the Tiflis street urchins. I caught only a few words of Stalin's. He said:

" 'The Party line is no longer communism!' "

"And what the hell does he say it is?" Münzer asked.

" 'Asia, awake!' "

"Is that a fact? Did Stalin really say that? The fiend! You know, for us old Bolsheviks, there is only one hope of saving Leninism, and that is Schleich. I envy you, the secretary to Schleich, the 'Red Singer' whom Field Marshal Trotsky embraced at the front in 1917. On the other hand—"

"On the other hand—?"

"We-e-ell! There are rumors in the Dardanelles . . ."

"What sort of rumors?"

"Tell me, Comrade Smirnow, man to man, is it true he's suffering from progressive paralysis?"

"Unfortunately, it is true. And the latest injection of malarial serum was entirely without effect."

"Comrade, another question: is Schleich a Jew?"

"Not he! What makes you think that? The Jews would be pleased! Why, he spits on all Israel! He hates Moses for giving the world the Ten Commandments. No, Schleich is no Jew. He comes from the same Caucasian village of Gori as Stalin. They went to school together and like our 'Soso' Stalin, Schleich was originally a pickpocket, practical joker, cynic, Bohemian, street-fighter, and pimp. That was before they entered the same dark divinity school together. They sat together before the blessed silver cross of the Madonna of Gelati. But they didn't learn to be priests—they learned to hate God. Later they went different ways. Schleich bummed around the capitals of Europe until someone discovered his voice in Vienna—"

"Tell me, does he really sing as well as he thinks he does?"

"Yes! That's one thing he can do. Yes, he belongs in opera—but not on the stage of politics! Of course he thinks that he can simply climb up his scales to the highest rung of a party congress. But, my dear Münzer, communism is a serious matter. Isn't it? Or does a zany like Schleich—just because he can sing a few notes—think that that makes him fit to—How I go on! But believe me: Schleich is neither a Bolshevist nor a Communist—"

"He was walking with a tailor's dummy back there—"

"From the German Embassy? Yes, I saw it too."

"What does that mean?"

"Whenever I try to make him talk about his actual connection with the Nazis he always gives the same answer: 'What is the name of the only tower in the Kremlin? Tainik! . . . And tainik means secret!' . . . And then he laughs like a bear . . ."

"You don't suspect that he . . . with the Nazis?—"

"Why, no! A vain Caruso! that's what he is! Believe me, when women shout 'encore,' he simply loses his head. He thinks the program of the proletariat is nothing but a sheet of music and all he needs to do is to open his mouth and everything will come out just the way everyone wants it. The whole house shouts 'Schleich! Schleich!' Then he steps in front of the curtain, bows, and he thinks: 'Well, here am I! and what are Stalin or Lenin? Garbage!' . . . But how I go on! My dear Münzer, really I don't want to work with him any longer . . .'

"Don't want to work with him? Go on! Tell me the rest of it!"

"Listen! Last night in the sleeper he called me. Only the little blue night light was burning. In his dark-red silk pyjamas, with great chunks of him bulging out here and there, he sat on the narrow mattress and croaked. His bare, swollen, purple feet padded the air.

"'Smirnow!' he yammered, drawing me down beside him. 'I can't sleep! Plague and Lenin! I haven't slept a wink!' With that, he grabbed me by the shoulder, glaring at me in the weirdest fashion, and said:

"'Comrade, do you believe in His second coming?'

"Whose second coming?

"'His of course,' he whispered. 'It is written: "After two thousand years, He will return."' Perfectly stupefied, I just looked at him. Anything to get out of there—so I said: 'Do you want me to get you a sleeping powder?' I wish you could have seen him! He turned pale, clutched me here by the throat, and screamed:

"'A sleeping powder! You mean, a pill from the Tibetan monk of the Urals? From the medicine man of the Cheka? So, Smirnow, you're supposed to poison me? You were picked for the job. Brother Stalin! He set you on!' And he shook me till I thought I'd fly apart. The only way I could get him quiet was by threatening to pull the emergency cord.

"His face was a sickly green, he leaned back in his berth, groaning. Suddenly he began:

"'Comrade, the dead Czar is on board this train. Plague and Satan! When we stopped at Munich I saw him get on. He came into the dining car. After we left Strassburg there he was again staggering along the corridor . . . While we were crossing the Marne Bridge, he put his pale royal hand in at the door of my compartment and asked me if I had washed yet. I ran to the toilet and locked myself in. Just before Paris—while we were running through the suburbs—he knocked on the door and asked: "Schleich, have you reset your watch yet?'"

"I can't believe it! 'Reset your watch yet'?"

"Yes, what can I answer to things like that? Schleich is a very sick man, and I've lost all desire to be secretary to a paralytic. You say you envy me, Comrade Münzer. The Communist Olympus is open! Help yourself! Perhaps you'll get the Lenin badge too. Help yourself!"

Smirnow rose and paid the bill. Münzer sank his head in his hands. Then he ran after him. To their amazement they saw their comrade Schleich, still sitting in his taxi, wedged in between troops, so that he could neither get forward nor back.

CHAPTER THREE   BLUE DRAGOONS, SQUADRON AFTER SQUADRON, CAME TROTTING OUT OF THE RUE LA FAYETTE, HEADED TOWARD the rue St. Martin, their little standard fluttering in front. No sooner had the tail of the last horse disappeared around the corner than small-sized tanks began rattling past. From each tank tower, a cramped poilu stared, holding a pennant.

Schleich berated his chauffeur.

"What's all this—the revolution? Is the proletariat descending on Paris from the suburbs? What's the meaning of this? Can't you get started? Hey, chauffeur, isn't there any other way to the Russian Embassy? Plague and the Volga! Holy Traviata! Here comes the infantry, too! What are they—hysterical in Paris? Do you all lose your heads every time you see a soldier? What are you mobilizing for? Against the workers? Now here comes the whole colonial Empire! All Algiers and Tunis! Come on—I haven't got time to sit here, chauffeur. Are you going to wait for all these Africans in khaki to go by? Take the rue du Temple, turn off at La Madeleine, and cross the Place de la Concorde. Then we'll be there!"

"Ça va!" The chauffeur tucked his "Paris Soir" in behind the instrument board, released the brake, and shot past the tanks, turning left along the rue St. Martin . . . down the rue Magenta, debouching into the Place de la République at such speed that Schleich shouted:

"Hey, chauffeur! You're going the wrong way! Stop! Not the rue Funiculaire! Where the devil are you going? Have you lost your senses? Stop!" Stepping on the gas, the chauffeur turned off into the rue du Combat. "Do you hear me? Stop! Where is the idiot taking me? Into the working quarter? Stop! Halt! . . ."

The downpour struck him full in the face. The taxi was going faster and faster. He tried to read the names on the street signs.

95

"Plague and the Devil! Where is he driving me? Rue de Belleville! Avenue Jean Jaurès! Rue Moreau! Rue du Général Bolivar! Rue St. Jean Baptiste . . . He's out of his mind! . . . Stop! . . . Trees? Here we are in the country! Arrêtez! Arrêtez! Canaille!"

He jabbed the chauffeur between the shoulders as the cab turned off from the rue Fessard and swung through a gate into the Parc des Buttes Chaumont. At sixty miles an hour they tore along the deserted, tree-lined avenue.

"Damn you, are you deaf! I said 'Stop!'" Whereupon the chauffeur stopped so suddenly that Schleich flew off the seat onto the floor.

"Imbecile! Driving me out here! What impertinence!" He pulled out a notebook, licked the point of his pencil, and demanded: "What's your name? . . . Drives me out here! In a thunderstorm! Instead of to the rue de Grenelle! Such impertinence! What's your name?"

"My name?" The chauffeur turned round. Under the pushed-back cap, under the cropped hair, two wide eyes stared at Schleich out of a once-beautiful woman's face.

"Aha! A woman! I might have known it! Plague and Satan! A woman! Doesn't even know the map of Paris yet! Drives me out to a park! Your name!"

For answer, she drew a revolver and said quietly: "Hands up, Monsieur!"

"Vous plaisantez, Madame!" The pencil fell out of his hands.

"Hands up, I said!" She barely opened her thin lips. The words came huskily: "Higher! Or don't you recognize me? I recognized you at once at the Gare de l'Est . . . in that mirror there. You are Schleich, the Red Singer! Keep your hands up! Now do you recognize me? I am Tatyana Trouhanova, the wife of Colonel Popov, who was president of the former Imperial Guard Officers' clubs in Paris and Belgrade! So keep those hands up!

"You lured my husband into a trap, brought him from Amsterdam on the *Rykowa* back to Russia and turned him over to the Cheka? . . . Keep your hands up! I'm the little girl who had to stand and watch you chase my fourteen-year-old brother round and round our summer-house until he dropped. In Charkow, on our estate. My mother stood at an upstairs window and watched too while you started again and chased Fedya round the dahlia bed till he fell to his knees. Hands up! . . . You stamped on his belly with your boots. And then you made him get up and run again, until you shot him down before our eyes! My mother went mad the next day.

"Don't you recognize me? Perhaps not. In those days I had long

96

silky hair, like a fairy story. It's gone, turned gray. But Schleich is the picture of health—fat and not a wrinkle. The Singer—the Red Singer! At first he never sang anything but the song of the revolution. But when the White Russians advanced under General Kornilov, and Colonel Popov took him prisoner, Schleich tore down the placards that read 'Tonight the Red Singer will sing for the soldiers and workers'— tore them down off the houses—Keep your hands up!—and then in spite of your revolutionary conscience you sang Czarist songs, and sang them well. But when the White Army was defeated, Schleich was the Singer of the Revolution again! Ha-ha! And he sang his way up over corpses and burning tears, up from the Volga to the heights of the Winter Palace and from there to the Red Olympus in the Kremlin—"

"Vous plaisantez, Madame!" Schleich looked about him. "Vous plaisantez—Or have you made a bargain with Stalin?"

"Don't you take your hands down!"

"Help! Help!" Schleich roared like a bear. "Au secours!"

"Shout as much as you like! Nobody can hear you here except that robin there, and the rain on the roof—and the leaves. Not a soul can hear you! Keep your damned hands up. The Metropolitan of Kiev told me in church that I was predestined—Hands up—yes I, little worthless Trouhanova—God has delivered you into my weak hands. You the murderer of the Czar! Murderer of the lovely Princesses! Butcher of the Czarevitch! Murderer—Anti-Christ! Hands up!"

She aimed. In terror of his life, Schleich burst out, making that sombre 'cello tone of his more beautiful than ever, singing the aria from Mozart's *Don Giovanni* into the revolver barrel: "La ci darem la mano." The voice poured straight into her blood. Her arm relaxed. Quick as lightning, Schleich drew a dagger and stabbed her in the neck. She was dead.

He got out of the cab, wiped the dagger in the wet grass and clover until the blade showed no blood, replaced it in its leather sheath, and washed his hands in the streaming rain, as calmly as if he were in a washroom. And all the while he went on singing—so loud that the birds began to twitter an accompaniment: "La ci darem la mano, la mi dirai di si."

Plunging into the wet bushes, he reappeared about a hundred yards away on a wooded knoll. There he turned off to the right through the undergrowth, but came back again and obliterated his footprints in the grass. Suddenly he started running as fast as his legs would carry his heavy body, straight through the woods, until he came to a waterfall. On the far side of a small lake, outside an unpretentious restaurant, he

97

saw an open, yellow sport car standing untended. Ducking from tree to tree he worked his way around until he was close to the car. Then, dashing from his shelter, he jumped in, stepped on the gas, and roared through the park at sixty miles an hour, until he got back to the rue Bolivar.

Regardless of traffic, he raced on to the rue du Temple, turned into it and roared on to the Place de la République. There he jumped out, abandoning the car, and hailed a taxi. He was going to say "Rue de Grenelle." But, realizing that someone might have heard him give that address at the Gare de l'Est, he ordered: "Place de la Concorde." But at Les Halles he got out again, and took the subway.

Arrived at the Soviet Embassy at last, he walked slowly and undecidedly into the big entrance gate. The porter accompanied him across the courtyard.

"Anybody ask for me, Fedor? I'm late! It was the accursed traffic held me up—troops all around the Gare de l'Est. My taxi couldn't get through." He nervously lit a cigarette but it dropped out of his mouth . . . "Is the Ambassador here?"

"No, the Comrade is at the Quai d'Orsay. But your new secretary has phoned several times. What was his name again? Eberlein or something. He is waiting for you at the Ritz."

"Is that so? Then call him up at once! Tell him to go and get the papers . . . Plague and Budapest! He knows what I mean. By the way, is Comrade Stalin's Hutuktu at the Embassy too?"

"Do you mean that Mongolian from the political police?"

"Tainik!" He tickled the porter under the chin, grinning, then abruptly turned round. "I want to go to the barber's first." And out he went into the street. He thought for a moment, then strode off. He entered a branch postoffice, made certain that nobody was watching him, took the telegram from his coat pocket and a little secret code book from his vest and decoded the Gestapo wire: "WATCH THE TRAVEL BUREAU STOP PREVENT THE WILL GETTING ABROAD STOP THE DANCER HAS RELATIVES IN NEUILLY STOP OBSERVE ACTIONS OF MAJOR BUCH AND HESS."

Schleich smiled. He tore a blank from the rack and wrote the following message: "Himmler, München, Braunes Haus. Am on the trail stop suspect Hess bloody fingers stop await full powers."

Just as he was about to translate the words into code, a gray-haired gendarme stepped up to the desk beside him, took a blank from the rack, and, as Schleich made room for him, said:

"To my son! Yes! in 1870 my father was fighting the boches! In 1914 it was my turn—four years at the front. Now they've sent my eldest

98

son into the Maginot Line. Oh, Monsieur! I wish I could eat every German alive—every boche!"

Schleich slowly put his message into his inside coat pocket, brought his strong fist down on the man's shoulders and winked:

"D'accord, Monsieur! I agree with you!"

But on the street again he saw that the gendarme was following him. He slipped down onto the quais along the Seine. From there he turned off into the maze of small streets and alleys of the University quarter, then followed the rue de la Bibliothèque, past all the small antique shops, one after another. All of a sudden he stopped in front of Laroche's shop. There stood the Christ of the Trenches, conspicuously displayed in front of a piece of old damask. Schleich's eyes almost popped out of his head. Suddenly the gendarme appeared around the corner. The Russian vanished into the shop, and watched the gendarme stalk by in the direction of the library and finally take up his stand in front of a small café.

Since Hitler's rise to power the café—which was run in Viennese style by a Viennese—had become a meeting place for crowds of refugees from various Nazi hells. Here you would find ex-ministers, Spanish revolutionaries, exiled Czechs, Italian anti-Fascists and so on. But since, above all, the place was filled night and day with the mournful, eternal lament of the dispossessed Jews, the students in the quarter called it the "Wailing Wall Café."

As the policeman thought that Schleich might be in there, he now peered carefully into the room with his best detective eye.

CHAPTER FOUR   Because of the thunderstorm the lights were out. The waiters had distributed candle stubs among the many small round marble-topped tables, but they gave only a feeble light. Through the thick, smoky, steaming atmosphere the customers entering and leaving by the revolving door looked—in their dripping raincoats and galoshes—like fantastic kobolds in a driving fog.

"Oi-oi!" groaned a man of letters transplanted to Paris from the Romanisches Café in Berlin. "If only—" he stared at the rain pouring down the windowpanes—"if only it were the Deluge! God! If only it were the Deluge!" Then he took a "Paris Soir" from a newsboy and read the headline:

"WEIDMANN TO BE EXECUTED."

"Oi-oi!" He turned to a melancholy, meditative group. "Did you read that—?" He put in his monocle. "A girl fished out of the Bagatelle lake this morning? Oi-oi! Although Mr. Weidmann is sitting in his cell waiting for the guillotine? The murders go right on? The eighth woman murdered since summer? It's terrific, my God! Terrific . . ."

"Silence!" the chess-players at the next table hissed.

"What!" The man of letters threw back his head. The skin of his face and neck looked like scuffed leather. "Our generation was born into a world of ice and fire! Eight women murdered one after the other!— oi-oi—that sets a record for belligerent skepticism! That's what I call murder as the basis of a new consciousness. That shatters not only our bourgois concepts, but the American Four Freedoms. Oi-oi! Gentlemen of Hitler's Jewry, there's nothing left for us intellectuals but to go under, or else take up murder as a profession."

"Since when did you turn anarchist, Herr Krah?" Mr. Thompson laid aside his "Times" and smiled at Krah.

"Since when? Mr. Editor, anarchism is the touchstone of the inde-structible! Yes! And the desire for destruction is no less of a desire than the others. Waiter!" He took out his monocle and polished it. "Another beer!" He slipped off his jacket and appeared in a red silk shirt, a dis-quieting figure among the other dark-suited customers.

"My dear gentlemen of Hitler's Jewry! I have at last arrived at the point where nothingness itself seems better than democracy—including my own personal polarity. So"—he breathed familiarly into the editor's face—"I am no longer a demo-cretin! Oi-oi! Krah will no longer con-sent to be the die-punching machine for your bankrupt liberal phrase-ology . . ."

The challenge was not taken up by any of his threadbare colleagues. Their care-lined, tortured faces, stamped with all the sorrows of the homeless, showed that their thoughts were elsewhere.

"Oi-oi—" Krah turned to a white-haired professor of the Sorbonne, who was playing chess with Dr. Lamm. "Once upon a time these people were known all over Europe! Hirschlein! Friedrich Wilhelm Loewi! Oi-oi, my dear gentlemen of Hitler's Jewry, don't you react any more? The test of genius is its ability to react! Shall I stick a pin in you? My God, what a bunch of jelly-fish! Paper! pen and ink! . . . Eight murders! It's worth a ballad."

He began to write, then:

"Dr. Wolff!—He's not asleep, is he?"

"What's wrong?" Rabbi Wolff came to with a start. "Yes, I sleep, but only for two hours out of the twenty-four!

> I think of Germany in the night
> And from my sleep I start upright!"

"Yes, yes!" One of the others nodded. "Like Job the afflicted, Dr. Wolff was born May the sixth."

There was a pause while Krah scribbled. Then he threw his pen down and groaned. "God, am I empty! Look! I began up there in the top lefthand corner, writing as small as possible. This Schickelgruber is a vampire. Oi-oi! He sucks the very brain out of your head! God, am I empty! And yet I'd like to see myself in print again—and not on my visiting card!" He stared around the café.

Christlieb Schleich entered the café through the revolving door on the opposite side, coming from the rue de la Bibliothèque. Behind him came Eberlein, carrying a wooden figure wrapped in blue paper—the Christ of the Trenches. One wooden hand projected from the wrapping. The Russian pushed his way through the crowded tables, settled his huge bulk on one of the leather-covered wall seats, took the package from his secretary, and laid it beside him. "Plague and pawnshops! What was that antiquarian swindler's name?"

"Laroche, tee-hee!" And then Eberlein whispered so that those at the next table could not hear: "He went for the police!"

"For the police? Why, because of this scarecrow here! I paid the fellow 1000 francs for it! Plague and Christ! And it is not worth even ten francs! Worm-eaten wood, that's what it is! And he asked 3000 francs!"

Schleich took a blue lapis-lazuli fountain pen from his pocket and, as the waiter bent down with his napkin, ordered, "One Pernod!"

"Tee-hee, Comrade." The secretary covertly slipped him a bit of paper. "This number called you. I think it's the German Embassy! Tee-hee! I'm told that the Nazi High Priests have arranged to hear your irresistible voice at a banquet tonight. Right?"

"What? What?" Schleich interrupted him and stared at the secret number.

"Yes, yes, Eberlein! my irresistible voice! Ha-ha! Plague and Braunau! My creed is: An iron bed for everyone, as little work as possible for everyone, but, above all, as much erotic satisfaction as possible —for everyone! And you can call it just what you like, Eberlein—Bolshevism, or Nazism, or the Reason of the Future—it makes not an atom of difference to an ex-baritone of all the first-rate opera companies in the world—like myself. Only one thing matters: to have a voice in your throat. Plague and orchestras. Eberlein, I always say, the world is a woman. And only the man with a song on his lips—eh?" And now he was humming into Eberlein's ear: "La ci darem la mano . . . Ha-ha!"

He stuffed a thick cigar into the corner of his mouth and stared at the wooden figure of the Christ of the Trenches. Sweat dripped from him at every pore, then suddenly he fell asleep.

Eberlein permitted himself a giggle and looked straight at his celebrated employer. Then, embarrassed, he murmured toward the next table, whose occupants were making remarks about Schleich:

"A Napoleon . . . can sleep when he, likes!"

Through the revolving door came a young man in a windbreaker. He took off his blue eyeglasses, and shaking the rain out of his blond thatch, looked the place over. Then he went up to a man in a camel's-hair coat, partly hidden from the rest of the café by a heavily loaded coat rack beside the door. He sat down at the table and whispered:

"Heil Hitler!"

The other answered in an undertone: "Who are you?"

"Look . . ." The blond man showed him a small eagle sewn into the lining of his sleeve. "Number 6, Reichs Foreign Service, Frankfurt Division."

"Buch's Murder Division? You should have relieved Hänsel half an hour ago."

"Right. But there were too many police around. And I had to meet my mother at the Gare de l'Est and see her to my pension . . ."

"Your mother! Why did she have to arrive today—just when we're ready to shoot the works?"

"The Old Girl is Leader of the Heidelberg Cultural Division. She's on a special mission, bringing instructions to German women abroad. Ha-ha!"

"Aha!" Feeling Krah's eyes upon him, the other man pulled his cap down on his forehead.

"What's new?"

"Plenty . . . plenty!"

"For example?" The blond lit a cigarette.

"One of our informers in the French police has just reported to Major Buch. That fellow in the Bagatelle Park—and we have reason to suspect that he was a Party man—jumped over the wall with the papers, and got clean away, although he was fired at and three motorcycle gendarmes followed him as far as Neuilly."

"Really?"

"Major Buch has alerted all our available fifth column here. He is having the whole Quarter as far as Notre Dame combed by the Gestapo. Count Wilzschek told me the Führer is in a towering rage. And if his Will isn't forthcoming by this evening, then every man of the S.S. Guard that allowed the dancer to get out of Obersalzberg will be reduced to the ranks or worse—every one of them."

"Damn!" the blond youth puffed hard on his cigarette.

"Our Embassy is terrified, for fear that the Party Comrade—whose identity is still unknown to us—will try to sell Hitler's Last Will and Testament abroad."

"Abroad! Why in the name of—"

"Why? It's worth money! Lots of money! Why, only last week an autograph dealer in Chicago bid $8000 for a few lines in the Führer's hand!"

"Eight thousand dollars! You're joking!" The blond stood up, felt in his breast pocket under the wind-breaker, turned red, and sat down again.

"It's true." The other looked at him through the cigarette smoke. "It's a record. Why, only the other day a letter of Frederick the Great's brought only fifteen dollars at auction!"

"Really? Well, old Frederick has been dead a long time. But $8000! For an autograph of the Führer's—that's impossible!" He touched his breast pocket furtively again.

"Apropos"—the other lit an elegant pipe—"have you heard the rumor that in this new Will the Führer has decreed that all members of royal families are to be banished to Siberia?"

"Not being a Prince, I can't say I'm interested."

"Of course!" The other rose. "You'll be relieved in an hour. Keep your eyes on everybody in civilian clothes. On the slightest suspicion, call this number immediately." He wrote a number on the beer coaster and left. The blond grinned at the retreating back an instant, then he hurriedly unbuttoned his wind-breaker. But, seeing Krah approach his table, he quickly buttoned it up again and began whistling.

"Oi-oi! Wasn't that Prince Ferdinand, the son of the German ex-Crown Prince?"

"Who? Where?" The blond looked at him searchingly.

"The man who just went out the revolving door?"

"Why do you ask, little man?" The blond blew cigarette smoke in his face.

"Oi-oi, I used to know him! Traveled on the same train with him to Sicily in 1929. He was in third class—I was in second. In those days he was still an ardent democrat. Ha-ha!"

"Waiter!" The blond pushed Krah unceremoniously out of the way, and shouted, "Champus!"

"A champagne cup, Monsieur?"

"What a question! A cup! Certainly not! A bottle!"

"Oi-oi!" Krah licked his lips, grinning. "The garçon doesn't seem to think you're the man for a bottle."

"Wha-a-at! Perhaps the idiot supposes I can't pay for it? Or perhaps he thinks I should take yoghurt, like the young lady at the next table! What a charming French face! And that raven-black hair. Fascinating, under that white turban! And that little Peke beside her, ha-ha! . . . Excuse me, Miss Yoghurt, is that your dog? He's a darling . . . Look how indignantly she turns away . . . What do you think? Shall I ask her to drink a glass of champagne with me? I hope, Monsieur, that you will do me the honor . . . ?"

"Oi-oi! Merci beaucoup. Thank you. It's ages since I've drunk champagne."

"Indeed! And why not?"

"Oi-oi, I'm no Rockefeller."

"What's the price of a bottle of champagne? Money buys it. And money is nothing but paper. Ha-ha! Yes, a heap of paper is a heap of money. Where is that idiot with my champagne? I hope he has sense enough to bring a cooler. But Miss Yoghurt here ought to toast us a piece of cheese first. A bit of toasted cheese before you drink champagne—that's perfection. Miss Yoghurt! Will you toast me a piece of cheese?"

"Oi-oi! She's getting up. God, isn't she sweet! Now she's gone and moved to another table. She looks sweeter than ever!"

"Heil! Here he comes at last!"

"Oi-oi! Can I help you? Opening a bottle of champagne comes as close to being a sacrament as anything." They attacked the wine together. The blond let the cork go with a bang. At the report Dr. Lamm leaped from his chair.

"What was that?"

"Champagne. Calm yourself! Oi-oi! Just champagne!" Krah filled two foaming glasses. "Dr. Lamm is used to another kind of popping in the concentration—"

The blond put his arm around Dr. Lamm's shoulder. "Let's load all the guns in the world with champagne instead of shells—shall we? Fine! What a sweet salute to this dunghill of a world! Down with it! It's time everybody got drunk. And when I say everybody I mean

Jewish swine *and* Christian swine. Allow me!" He filled a row of glasses, smashed the empty bottle, and ordered, "Waiter, another bottle! At once!"

"Oi-oi!" Krah grinned at the company. "This is a fine goy!"

"Your health, gentlemen—whatever dungheap of a country you hail from! Prosit!"

"Oi-oi! Let's drink a better toast than that!"

"A better toast? To money, then, you old Pharisee! Let's drink to money! Listen, you from the four corners of the earth—to him who has money, existence is sunny! Money rules the world!" He emptied his glass, smashed it against the wall, and called, "Garçon, another bottle!"

"No, no, please don't order another! I implore you! Not another! I have a wonderful head—but too much champagne! Coffee stimulates the brain. But champagne puts it to sleep. God, how tired I am!" He yawned with such a leonine roar that Schleich woke up . . .

"Plague and poverty!—What is the blond fellow up to?"

"Tee-hee! Your Excellency! The drinks are all on him! Tee-hee!"

"The drinks are on him?" Schleich turned his bald head around to look at the blond, and winked, as Krah put both hands over his glass.

"Non, non . . . assez! Too much champagne equals too many thoughts. Oi-oi, Monsieur—I forgot to ask—what is your name?"

"My name?" The blond banged the bottle down on the marble table top. "Aren't you getting a little familiar? Comes right up and pokes me in the belly—the black Jew! Yes, you Zionist. But I haven't herded any pigs with you yet! God almighty!" He put the champagne bottle to his mouth and drank. Suddenly he pulled himself together, straightened his wind-breaker angrily, glared at Krah, began to speak, but then rose instead and made unsteadily for the washroom.

"Very pretty, very pretty, indeed! Oi-oi! And I thought the boy Viking was going to drink me under the table. And he won't tell us his name? What a goy! Now what do you think of that?" Krah's voice, ravaged by beer, chocolate, and champagne, came out like a crow, and he swayed after the blond. But just as he arrived at the heavy green baize curtain in front of the washroom, Schleich intercepted him, shoved a cigar into his gaping mouth, winked, and went into the washroom alone.

The dispenser of champagne, his wind-breaker wide open, stood in front of the mirror. He had laid a bundle of manuscript precariously on the edge of the wash basin and was feverishly counting the pages, wetting his forefinger from time to time.

"Plague and Himmler!" Schleich recoiled. "Why, that's . . . ! Why, he's got . . . ! Hi!" He tapped the German on the shoulder. "Have you by any chance taken a lease on this wash basin?"

"Quoi!" The blond started up, awkwardly cramming the manuscript under his wind-breaker. "No! If your hands are dirty, go ahead and wash!" He moved aside. "There you are. The soap stinks, but it's still soap!"

"Well, my fine young friend!" Turning on the faucet, the Russian began scrubbing his hands. "Having fun counting the toilet paper?"

"Precisely!" The blond grinned impudently. "Precisely! Ha-ha! Yes . . . that's exactly it!" And, guffawing loudly, he shut himself in the toilet cubicle and shot the bolt. "Precisely! Yes! That's it exactly!"

Schleich turned off the faucet and heard the rustle and rattle of paper begin again behind the wooden door. Then he tiptoed to a little window beside the coat hooks, his eyes measuring whether a man could get out through it. But it was far too narrow, so he retraced his steps and knocked on the door.

"Hi, Monsieur! Aren't you through yet? There are other people waiting to get in!" He listened. No answer. He dropped his cigar butt, and reflected. "Shall I tell him to meet me at the Ritz? Here, someone may come in any minute. I'll talk to him on the street. . . . It certainly looked . . . very much . . . as if this fellow actually had it!"

After a final rattle on the door he went out into the café and sat down, placing himself so that he could keep his eyes on the green curtain in front of the washroom. The waiter had brought his apéritif during his absence. He swallowed it in three long drafts.

"Horrible stuff! This absinthe-green, anisette-tasting dishwater concocted by the Abbé Pernod!" He drained his glass. "Br-rr-r! Ghastly! But after a while it's warm and comforting—eases the stomach!" He lit a fresh cigar. "Eberlein, who's that woman over there?" He looked at a woman seated by the opposite window, apparently writing a letter.

Her green velvet dress was caught up in folds at the shoulder by a diamond brooch. A red fox neckpiece bobbed with every movement. Luxuriant hair, dyed red, tumbled from under a green velvet toque. An unusually large emerald on one tapering red-nailed finger flashed magic signals of green light across to Schleich.

"Eberlein, I'm sure I know her. Can't seem to recollect . . . Does that happen to you too? One second the name's on the tip of your tongue, and the next it's gone! Nothing the matter with me, though. Reflexes in perfect order! Professor Goldschmidt knocked out my streptococci in Prague! Who can she be? . . . Yes, I feel at top form

—potent as a prize bull! Push the champagne-cooler over here, will you? I'll have to soak my head in ice water! But first I'll dictate the manifesto for this evening to you . . ."

"I'm waiting, your Excellency," Eberlein tittered devoutly.

"You're waiting? Plague and Lenin! Aren't we all waiting for the World Revolution! Or are you a Stalinist? Damn it . . . your remarkably brilliant head is shutting off my view of the men's room." He pushed his secretary aside. "But what was I saying?"

Eberlein snickered. "About the manifesto, your Excellency—"

"That's right!" Schleich dipped his handkerchief in the champagne-cooler and rubbed some red spots off his sleeve.

Without warning, he burst into an immense laugh, his big shoulders heaving like a battlefield. The refugees at the neighboring tables looked at him, amazed.

"Eberlein! The Fascists haven't yet made the bullet that could kill me! Plague and Lenin! Schleich still has a lot to accomplish in this world! Do you believe in my star?"

"I believe in the Red Star, your Excellency. Tee-hee!"

"Go ahead and write: 'Workers and Soldiers of Paris! What is the first part of a fish to stink? The head! Once again the capitalists are ready to lead you to the slaughterhouse! Wall Street and the great god Mammon . . .'"

"Hush," Eberlein warned. "People are listening!" Schleich's voice fell to a rumbling mutter.

The woman in green velvet again tore up the letter she had barely begun. Letting the bits of blue-tinted notepaper fall under the table like violets, she took a fresh sheet.

"Dearest Irene," she began, "my little sister. Your letter from Pylar has reached me. I have it here. After all these years—the first sign of life from you! Good God, how we have been tossed around the world! Yes, Adolf the Great sends us little people packing. One to Shanghai! Another to the Dead Sea! Or to Rio! My friend Lily had to go to Venezuela. And you, my little sister, are on the edge of the Atlantic. And I—your Hyacinthe—I am still in Paris . . . Once upon a time— oh, what a sweet life we all had together in our beloved Porzelangasserl in Vienna. Oh, if only, only, there weren't so many great men in the world. Which reminds me that I recently read in a book: 'In the beginning was woman.'—You're surprised. That must have been a very long time ago. Anyhow, nowadays, in the beginning is—man. And man alone. And nothing else. Oh, I have become a great solitary. But you, my little sister, seem to have remained just what you always

107

were. Eh? Still eternally in love? I look at your handwriting—the way the letters are scrawled on the page. It's still the same long curve of ineradicable emotion, Irene! For example, the way you round off your z's. Just like you used to. And do you still hate the capital A because it reminds you of the waning moon? Your letter gives off something as fresh as a sea breeze. And I see you before me as you were that summer in Venice. Your just-blown body in thin, silver-shot muslin. If I shut my eyes, I see you distinctly—the way you stood in the gondola with your great, blue-gray eyes staring up into the stars. You recited 'The God and the Bayadere' so magnificently that Father lovingly spread the softest of silk carpets under your ten bare toes for you to dance on. Your dark hair fluttered free in the wind as we drifted along the Grand Canal. And Father bowed to you more deeply than a Turk to his houris in paradise. And you—do you ever think of those days now? How we bit into yellow rose buds on the Lido, how the scents of the whole world of wild flowers in our exotic garden touched our cheeks like a heavy dew—thyme, wild pomegranate, rosemary, and the sweet breath of anemones. And then the nightingales would begin to sing all around us in the shrubbery, as clear as springs. Oh, my little sister! There you stood under the silver light of Cassiopeia, and your young breasts were taut under your transparent dress—do you remember?—trains were in fashion. And do you remember how we bribed Father's valet to take us—just once—to that night place outside Venice? Do you remember how breathlessly we listened behind the milky-white wool curtain outside under the street lamp? And then we heard—Irene, Irene, do you remember?—the cries of pleasure?—particularly, that one cry? Oh, that one cry! Excuse me—I've made a blot. But just now they've started calling an extra in the café—another woman has been murdered. And the blond monster Weidmann is to be guillotined at cockcrow tomorrow morning. Anyone can go and watch it—it's perfectly public. And people just ask each other, 'Are you coming along to see it?' Little sister, I confess: the word woman-killer exercises a certain attraction upon us women. Or more precisely: upon unloved women! Oh, in a time of such disorder—when only a man has anything to live for—it really has to be something monstrous: to be murdered . . . for lust! torn to pieces! Isn't it better than to die unloved? Yet you—I read it in your letter—have kept your first love. You and your Uhle. And every time you write the word love you make a red circle around it. Oh, what do you think would happen if I were to stand up on my chair in this smoky café and cry out that word love? What answer would I get? People would certainly throw their dirty beer coasters at me. Love? Yes—but only to beget more soldiers. Anyhow, I have never found that purple happiness! And for me now: 'The hour is passed, and yet I lie alone.' So what have you two to do with poor we who are empty of love? What kind of a beginning are you making with me? Of course, I still have impulses, attractions. But then I go out to the old cemetery, buy some pinks, or whatever the market women have, and lay them on a few neglected graves. Little sister, the hour is past. I am sitting here alone in a café, caught in a storm, waiting—for my husband. The word is out. There it stands, just as it stands on the register in the license bureau. Yes, sister, I have a husband. His name? Otto Goldschmidt . . . short and simple. He was First Assistant to the celebrated Voronov, who had his Rejuvenation Institute in Ventimiglia, down on the French-Italian border. But in your dreamland, nobody knows about such things. So I'll explain: the sexual glands of a chimpanzee are used to give the cells of a man exhausted by sexual excesses—new potency. Capito? Ah, sister—better for you to stay inside your little red circle! You ask me if you should come here. For God's sake, no! Here there is nothing but rumors of war, echoes of all kinds of horrible realities! Listen—the worst thing of all, you don't know yet, darling Irene! But today it won't leave me in peace. And I must tell you. Think back— to the days when we were in our teens—that was when I met him. Of course I'm not talking about Otto. Otto? He's fine. He does everything he can. But I'm not talking about him. Sister!" Her writing became very small. "We were sitting together in our loge at the opera in Vienna—you, Mother, and our governess. And *he* was singing Mephistopheles. Oh, Irene—right afterward—you never noticed—I ran to his dressing room. He was still in his red costume with the long cock's feather in his hat. I said freshly: 'You sang the Devil all wrong!' He looked at me—up and down—with such a look. Darling, my heart stopped. I said, 'You must sing Mephistopheles as the Fallen Angel.' How he looked at me then! What eyes! Eyes like Iago's in 'Otello' when he sings, 'E poi? e poi? Nulla!' Nichevo! Nothing! After the performance we met. Instead of going to Uncle's, I went with him. Secretly, of course. We were at Sacher's. He talked and ate and drank. At dessert, I gathered up my courage and said, 'Why don't you kiss me? Every girl has to have a first kiss!' He bent over me smiling. But then he cursed in Russian, 'That damned hat!' I had on my straw hat, the one with the plaid ribbon, remember?—and that was my first kiss. E poi? you ask. All women were mad about him. But he couldn't see me. He called me his 'Little Shadow,' because I was always running after him. After every performance I ran through the streets with him in my high-heeled slippers . . . I could hardly keep up with him. My heels were soon covered with blisters—and how they hurt! But I didn't say anything—. He was always leaving me for other women. He didn't take me seriously. He only wanted to seduce me, to deprave me. Once he asked me to come to his apartment. There was a woman in the kitchen. With one leg up on a chair, she was letting someone button her underdrawers. And he was standing there grinning. Oh, he forced me to witness every kind of vice with him. And I loved him in spite of it. Oh, I was in love with his heavenly voice. Not a word that he spoke was true. He lied. He didn't have a spark of cleverness. But when he sang, everyone had to listen. Such an organ! Tremendous —as if it came straight from the throat of God! Irene—when Otto was courting me, I said, 'You're marrying the singer too.' And he answered, 'All right. But you need someone to take care of you.' And that was how we lived. I helped him with his experiments on monkeys, helped him with dissections and operations, looked after his instruments, kept them polished—and tried to forget. . . . You wouldn't recognize me. Every time I look in the mirror, I'm horrified all over again. God, how I look—like a horse! Pure yellow! One time I'm taking pills to gain, and another time to reduce. Anything to stay in the realm of reality! Not in the clouds, like you! No! This morning, for example, I counted the washing: 5 tablecloths, 7 shirts, 8 napkins, 5 pairs of stocking, 4 pyjamas, a heap of handkerchiefs. And I made a note to get two rolls of toilet paper—just like an oh! so competent housewife. But oh, Irene, often and often I feel such a heart-burning. And I ask myself: What am I wasting all my intelligence on? And what has become of all our lovely poetry? You have held on to yours, Ireneika! Hold on to it—it is the only real thing on this planet. Because everything else—is ghastly. When Hitler came, we fled from Vienna to Prague. And now we're here, in Paris. But four years ago, one day in Prague, Otto had purposely not told me who it was I was getting the operating room ready for. Darling, the most potent of all our monkeys had to do the honors that time. And then, the door opened. A man was brought in—Sister! Sister!—absolutely crippled and bestialized by vice! Sister!—"

Suddenly she stopped. She had seen the Russian across the room. Schleich was still dictating his manifesto. She paled. Collected all her strength. Stood up. And then, tottering, went zigzagging among the tables and out. On the way, she accidentally brushed against Krah. He turned around bristling, jammed in his monocle, and sent a torrent of angry comment after her. Then he undid his shirt collar, gave Schleich a comradely wave with the cigar the latter had bestowed on him, winked toward the green curtain, and grinned:

"What has become of our goy? Oi-oi! He certainly has too much champagne on board! Is he still busy in the toilet?"

CHAPTER FIVE "EBERLEIN!" SCHLEICH STOPPED DICTATING AND POINTED AT KRAH. "WHO IS THAT ATTRACTIVE PHARISEE? Haven't I met him in Moscow? At the editorial office of the 'Word'? Or at that stupid beer party with Stalin and Dimitrov? Eberlein," he whispered into his secretary's ear, "couldn't we make use of him at our railway workers' demonstration tonight—couldn't he carry my scarecrow there in front of the Red Flag? Of course you'd have to explain to him that the wooden Christ wasn't really Christ, but the First Proletarian. A literary yokel in a red shirt is sure to be an atheist. Tell him that all he'd have to do would be to carry my crippled proletarian victim of capitalism in front of the workers' battalions in our protest demonstration. Do you think the inkpot will—What?"

"Tee-hee, your Excellency, if it weren't for the women! Just yesterday I caught him in the telephone booth talking to a certain Nadia, and at the same time he had his hand under the waitress's skirt."

"Good for him!" Schleich grinned. "I like that! Slip him twenty rubles as an advance. Afterwards I'll have him film our demonstration. Did you know I was planning to make a film? I'm going to call it 'The Rubbish Heap of History.' Plague and Lenin! Later I'll give him the run of the gloomy citadel of the Troubetskoi Fortress, where so many brave fighters for freedom lost their lives. Eberlein"—he screwed his fountain pen shut—"is everything clear? Any questions? The workers are to meet in the Rue Solferino."

"And what if the police try to push us off into the Boulevard Saint-Germain?"

"Then we'll march through the Rue Dante to the Quai de Montebello, and from there to Notre Dame. The priestery is going to put on a big show tonight in the cathedral. We'll see if we can't outwave their holy banners with our red flags!"

"Tee-hee-hee-hee-hee!"

"Ha-ha-ha-ha-ha! Vive la France! Vive la Révolution! Ha-ha-ha! Yes, Eberlein, there'll be a show tonight! Well, what about the rest of these people?" He blew the bluish smoke of his Havana in rings like lassos around the heads of the refugees. "Can we make any use of them? Could they carry flags?"

"These people? Tee-hee! No, Your Excellency. They're all intellectuals."

"Plague and intelligence! The intellectuals! Can't they get it into their heads even yet that the rule of a new class has made their intellect superfluous? Utterly superfluous? Plague and Danton! We need at least thirty more flag carriers. Eberlein—" But he suddenly laid his cigar on the table and muttered, "Say! Where has that woman gone?" He stared into the window corner. "Eberlein! There was a woman sitting there—a woman with a red fox fur around her neck! And now there's a man sitting there—a man in a red cape . . .

"Garçon!" Schleich rubbed his eyes and then called, "Another Pernod! Plague and spooks! There *was* a woman sitting there! And now—Eberlein, I must have my eyes examined again! Come and take a look at my pupils. All right, aren't they? Queer, isn't it—I'm in perfect health. Ha-ha! And then—what can it be?—suddenly there's a sort of fog in front of my eyes . . ."

"Voilà!" The waiter warningly set a fresh glass down in front of Schleich. "It's your third Pernod, Monsieur . . . 90 per cent alcohol."

"Ninety per cent alcohol?" The Russian drained the glass in one swallow. "What business is it of his—the damned plate-licker . . ." Suddenly he was listening. "Eberlein! Listen! There's a very strange sound in the air . . ."

"Where, Comrade?"

"Like the beginning of the Revolution!"

"Tee-hee! It's only the bells of Notre-Dame."

"But it sounds like the bells of the Usepenski Cathedral tolling for the dead. Say! don't you smell something?" He sniffed. "There's such a funny smell all of a sudden."

"It's sulphur, Comrade. Tee-hee! After all the thunderstorms today, there's a smell of sulphur."

"The thunderstorms today? It smells just like it used to in St. Michael's Cathedral on Easter Day, when the miserable monks brewed the chrism in their silver censers. Their 'holy oil'—ha-ha! And then the giant bells in the Ivan Velicki Tower, and the sixteen thousand other bells in the City of the Kremlin, would start banging and booming—like a horrible delirium. Eberlein!" He stared at his secretary,

112

startled. "I distinctly see colors before my eyes. And flames—like polished gold on an altar. I see icons. And the broad waves of light from ten thousand electric bulbs and candles! Eberlein! Don't you see anything?"

"I? No, nothing. Tee-hee!"

"What? But I know I'm perfectly normal!" He puffed more heavily. Then he pointed to the film of tobacco in the air: "There! Against the blue background—the crown. Don't you see it? And the red and white arms of the Chmeleitzky, who handed over the Ukraine and the Cossacks to the Czar. By the holy bones in all the monasteries in Siberia! Eberlein, who on earth is that funny-looking man there? The one sitting where the woman was? He looks almost like . . . the Czar . . . with his pointed beard!" He clutched his secretary's arm.

"Who? Where?" Eberlein squinted across the room. "That soldier there? Looks like a corpse on furlough! Tee-hee!"

"Coffee? Tea?" the waitress was asking the man in the red cavalry cloak by the window. But as he only looked at her without answering, she wiped off the table. Suddenly she said, "Monsieur, you remind me of someone. But he never . . . came back. He always took two lumps of sugar in his tea. Will you have milk or lemon with your tea?" As if bewildered, she set a basket of rolls in front of him, and went back to the buffet.

"Eberlein!" Schleich let himself slide down on the sofa and stared at the soldier. "What does that dead Romanov want here? Look! That thing shining through his red beard—isn't it the blue Order of the Holy Apostle Andrew?"

"But Comrade Schleich! Tee-hee! Czar Nicholas has been dead and moldy for a long time. Tee-hee! You shouldn't drink so much Pernod. Ninety per cent alcohol, the waiter said."

"Or does yonder Romanov think that Russia is going to carry the baldachin for him again—with the Byzantine angels inside, and the four white elephants? Eberlein, do me a favor! Go and tell him to disappear. I don't belong to his hierarchy. Go and tell him that in our Party Congress we had no intention of leading him up the fifteen steps to the throne in the magic lamplight—not ever again. But perhaps he hopes that the imbecile Metropolitan of Moscow will put on his golden protodiaconal cope and slobber out the text of the imperial oath to him up there again—and touch his eyes and brow and nose and mouth with the golden rod dipped in myrrh—"

"But Comrade!" Eberlein was beginning to sweat. "Perhaps I ought to get you a doctor? There's a doctor sitting over there—"

"Stay where you are!" He held Eberlein's arm convulsively. "You can't go now! Stay here!" And suddenly he rattled at the soldier in the dark corner:

"What are you doing here, Nicholas Alexandrovitch, Czar of Kazan, Lord of Astrakhan, Grand Duke of Siberia, Czar of Georgia, Prince of Finland and Lithuania, Duke of Rostov and Podolsk, Lord of Great Russia, Little Russia, and White Russia!" He spat the consonants across the table, and seemed, as he spoke the names, to be savoring what Bolshevism had done in Russia since 1917. "Plague and Lenin! Mr. Romanov, the new day *has* come—long since. Do you follow me? There's not a kulak left to pay forty thousand rubles for the pleasure of gaping at you from a café window on coronation day. So be gone from here! In your Malachite Hall, or your Strelitz Hall, the marble statues are gone, the precious tapestries are gone, with your All-Powerful Czardom. Hah! There is not a single state bed for you. The stamped Spanish leather of your carpets and your chairs of state—look here!—I had these boots made out of it. Ha-ha! So away with you! The great, gold-framed oil-painted hams of your ancestors—we've done them over in red. So what do you hope for? Along the Nevsky Prospect, not your proud Preobrachevsky Regiment marches—but the columns of the Russian people in their long green cloaks, with their sheepskin caps on their heads. We shot down your Life Guard Hussars and your two Cossack bodyguards. So vanish! The marble stairs of your palace are full of bloodstains. Even your lackeys in their blue and red liveries . . . ." His wide mouth tried to laugh, but his eyes became duller and glassier.

Eberlein looked anxiously round at the revolving door. But Schleich leaned forward across him toward the window corner where his vis-à-vis still sat—silent and unchanged, his face half shadowed by the hood of his cavalry cloak, one hand crumbling a roll.

"We, the class-conscious workers, stood them all up against the wall—all the ghosts of Tsarskoe Selo—and your silver-white Horse Guards—and your Knights of St. George and St. Michael. All the butchers of the proletariat, with the pretty beasts in their coats-of-arms—ha-ha—the lions and griffins and two-headed eagles. So take yourself off! The people of Moscow will never again hold your stirrup while you mount your dapple-gray horse, to show your small, aristocratic features among all the slit-eyed Khirgis and Georgians and Tatars and Poles and Samoyeds. Vanish, vanish! We the people want no Porphyrogenitus, no 'man born to the purple.' So away with you! Get out! And don't come back! Or don't you recognize me? I am the man! It was I who shot you down. In Ekaterinenburg on the edge of the primeval forest of Siberia—in the cellar of the merchant Ipatiev's house. Three months before your fiftieth birthday. So get out! I remember seeing the blood trickling out of your high boots. Vanish! Or do you think some boyar is still going to wipe the stains off you with his long beard?"

Eberlein, who had listened in terror to this weird monologue of his chief's, suddenly squeezed himself carefully out between the bench and the table, took the package containing the wooden figure, and whispering, "A doctor, Comrade. I'm going to get a doctor," slipped quietly away.

CHAPTER SIX

Dr. LAMM, WHO FOR SOME TIME HAD BEEN DIVIDING HIS ATTENTION BETWEEN THE SOLDIER IN THE WINDOW corner and his chess game with the white-haired professor, suddenly got up too, swept the chessmen off the board, and put on his raincoat. "What!" His partner held him back. "Going so soon?"

"Oi-oi!" Krah looked at the clock. "Has the Angelus already rung from the Sorbonne? Then just about now our Lammkin is due to tell us—for the hundred and first time—the terrible tale of how the dear Gestapo paid a visit to his house in Schöneberg to do a little studying in his priceless library—twenty thousand volumes—and then how the black S.S. troopers peppered all his de luxe editions out the windows onto the heads of the passers-by—oi-oi! wasn't that it, Lammkin? Including the manuscript of Schiller's *Don Carlos*. 'Sire, grant us liberty of thought!'—ha-ha! And, last but not least, how finally Count Helldorf addressed his venerable mother as 'You dirty Jewish sow'!"

"What is the use?" Dr. Lamm had turned pale. He put on his hat. "Didn't a certain Hesiod arraign mankind centuries ago? 'They are a sinful folk. But one day God will weed them out. And then babes shall be born with gray hair. And then shall not Right be named, but the Sword. And city shall ravage city—' "

"Oi-oi! Stop it, Lammkin. Don't be such a pessimist."

"Pessimist?" Dr. Lamm still stood by his table. "Herr Krah, I tell you: Until this day only one man has stood sinless in the world which mankind has corrupted. And that one man, we Jews handed over to the Roman Fascists."

"Oi-oi! Who is he talking about?" Krah shouted over his beer glass. "The fool of Nazareth?" He rose and faced Lamm. "Do you want to make *us* responsible for what happened in Jerusalem two thousand years ago?"

"A thousand years are but as the day that is passed." And then Dr. Lamm met the others' puzzled faces with a look of painful earnestness. Suddenly he cried out: "Messieurs! Mesdames. Say what you will—one thing I know: If ever again they ask, 'Will you have Christ freed, or the thief Barabbas,' I shall shout, 'Free Christ, free Christ'!" And, as if aghast at himself, he slunk around the coat racks and hurried out into the street and the rain.

Krah, startled and embarrassed, screwed his monocle into his eye. "Oi! Oi! Our Lammkin! God, how he ran! Oi-oi! Do you think I should go after him? and bring him back?" He put on his coat. But as he was taking his hat off the hook, he saw the soldier. "Oi-oi!" He exchanged his monocle for his spectacles, and smiled, delighted to be able to sidestep the painful incident of Dr. Lamm. "Who's that sitting there among us democrats? Another wearer of the purple? Possibly a future Catholic King of Austria? God, how red his cloak is! Just so red was Caesar's toga after he was murdered—ha-ha! Monsieur le militaire," he buzzed on, and in order to see better, picked up a candle stub from the table, "may I? What regiment does he belong to? Oi-oi! Do you really march off to war in that theatrical costume?"

"War?" The rabbi turned round as if at a cue, and laughed. "A pity our Dr. Lamm isn't here! For with Christ and the ethics of the Sermon on the Mount, our democracy can hardly stand up successfully against the Führer and Chancellor of the Third Reich! Am I right, soldier?" Dr. Wolff rose and approached. "Or when—and the sooner the better, I say—you are standing behind a machine gun, and the hordes of the Third Reich swarm out against you—I ask you, when some Nazi 'smites your right cheek' with the butt of his rifle, are you going to turn him the left? Are you going to say mildly, 'Come, frère allemand, help yourself!'? Or are you going to shoot? If I'm not mistaken, soldier, you're going to shoot. Bang-bang-bang—shoot, shoot!"

The soldier's forehead had been in shadow. As Krah raised his candle stub, a brightness fell on it, as of frost—and so white, that the refugees at the near-by tables blinked. But an exiled Russian at once set himself to explain the unnatural coloring.

116

"Our Czarina Marie—" he poured himself a vodka—"she used to look as pale as that. She had had porcelain injected under her skin, so that she would never get old-looking. But afterward she could neither laugh nor cry."

"Neither laugh nor cry?" Krah grew more and more nervous as he watched the calm of the soldier, whose eyes constantly brightened and darkened, as if he were one of those planetary beings of whom it is said that they talk to each other only with their eyes, despising speech as too gross.

As a whisper ran from table to table, Schleich blinked:

"Yes! Plague and Lenin! Just look at him! A face like that, and the counterrevolution will begin all over again! Friends! Was it for this that we smelled the smoke of battle in the October massacre and bayoneted all the lieutenants in the belly? Plague and Moscow!" He jumped up and flung himself toward the soldier at the table. "You," he snarled at him, "was it for this that I ripped off all my old decorations at the Proletarian Victory Festival in the Glinka Opera House, and publicly stamped on them in front of the prompter's box? You red-cloaked mummy, out with it! Who are you?"

All present looked expectantly at the soldier. As if mechanically, he opened his mouth.

"Plague and revolution! Who are you? We want to know!"

"One of many . . ."

"Oi-oi—did you hear that?"

"You!" Schleich showed him a hairy fist. "What's behind you?"

"Nothing . . ."

"Did you hear that? Listen, you!" Schleich was foaming at the mouth. "Was it for this that we blew up St. Saviour's Church in the dead of winter? Answer me! What kind of a swindle are you starting now? Answer me! Let me tell you—I'm the man who has thrashed more conductors than Chaliapin! I even threw a chair at the Czar's head once at a rehearsal! You—you—" suddenly he ripped an iron stool into the air. But the others jumped between them. Schleich turned on them: "What do you mean, you kulaks! You kulaks!" And then, like a man on the deck of a ship in a high sea, he lurched left and right clinging to the tables, made the revolving door, and vanished.

CHAPTER SEVEN "N<small>U</small>!" THE RABBI STROKED HIS BEARD. "IT'S A GOOD THING HE'S GONE. THE MAD RED GUARDSMAN—CALLING us kulaks!"

"Messieurs"—the waiter whisked his napkin—"what do you expect? He gulped three glasses of Pernod. Ninety per cent alcohol. Et alors?"

"Pernod? Oi-oi, a good idea. Waiter, bring two—Monsieur le militaire, you'll—" Krah said, turning to the window corner. But the words stopped. For the bench behind the coat racks was empty. "Waiter! Oi-oi! What has become of our soldier?"

"Isn't he there?" The others turned around. "Has he gone?"

"Oi-oi!" Krah struck his forehead, and then squeaked, "I have a shrewd suspicion—God, what a revelation I shall make! Yes, yes, gentlemen of Hitler's Jewry—the man who was sitting there, in the red cloak—" he became mysterious—"no, he wasn't the Grand Candle Lighter to the Negus of Abyssinia—no, God! am I on a hot scent! Do you know who he was?"

"He?" The waitress, not seeing the soldier, sadly set a tea tray at his empty place. "What else should he be but what he was, Herr Krah—a Spahi! From the new regiment that's been forming in Strassburg. But only a man with a high mark in his examination can apply, Herr Krah—only a man who's tops can get to be a Spahi—"

"A Spahi!" He jumped up as if shot from a spring. "Oi-oi! God! am I a Sherlock Holmes! He was—Do you know what I suspected?" But he stopped suddenly. From behind the washroom curtain the blond head of the young man who had bought him champagne appeared, and mocked:

"Go on—what do you suspect?"

"Oi-oi! Did you vomit? You look green enough!"

"Of course. Finger down my throat like a Roman. Then I can start over again. Ha-ha! Waiter! Bring a fourth bottle! That is"—he swaggered over to Krah—"first you must tell me what you suspect . . ."

"Oi-oi—that blond murderer—"

"What, darling? I'm blond too, you know . . ."

"Yes, and every blond carries a dagger. And then afterwards the daughters of Zion are found murdered in front of the Madeleine—or the Louvre. Or they're fished out of the Bagatelle Pond, like the drowned girl this morning—"

118

"Precious!" He gave Krah a resounding kiss. "You're absolutely priceless!"

"Priceless? Oi-oi! but not a pervert!—And why don't the police find the murderer? Because they're not on the right track."

"What right track?"

"Oi-oi! The one that leads to the German Embassy, of course."

"To the German Embassy? You haven't any idea how priceless it is there. Or does blond simply mean 'murderer' to you?" He burst out laughing. "But where's my fourth bottle? Waiter! This is a wretched dump! Champagne! God be praised, there comes the monkey with the bottle. My dear friends from the four corners of the earth, if a scrap of paper is worth eight thousand dollars, how much are sixty-seven scraps worth? Eh? How much does that come to, according to the latest discoveries in higher mathematics?"

"What was that?" Krah pricked up his ears. "Has the goy been playing the lottery?"

"So now we're off! Glasses!"

"Oi-oi!" The red shirt held out his beer glass and rumbled out, "And Pharaoh, oh Pharaoh, he drowned in the Red Sea."

"Glasses! Hold them out!"

"No, I don't drink," the Rabbi refused, lifted his long beard to the level of his chin on the palm of one hand, and puffed through it.

"Oi-oi! Dr. Wolff, isn't this piece of blond humanity one of God's mysteries too?"

"Not to me, Herr Krah. And I'd rather drink Seine water alone, than champagne with such as he."

"The Seine is an enchanting river. Priceless! And covered with broad barges. Yesterday, on the quais, I watched cargoes being unloaded. Wheat! Melons! Artichokes and oats! Peas, bananas, and those heavy, juicy, purple eggplants! Endless celery and tomatoes! But only people with money can buy. Money, money!" He beat his breast. "Money! That's the stuff. Anything for money! On the Bourse I read the inscription: *Numisma est mensura omnium rer—*"

"I deny that," the Rabbi flashed. "No! Money is not the measure of all things. The measure of all things—"

"Is what?"

"The Ten Commandments delivered on Mount Sinai—"

"What? I can't understand that. And I'm twenty-nine years old. Or how old am I? Besides—I always say: If anyone wants to be a Hussite, let him go and get himself burned in Bohemia. As for me, I want to eat tonight—fish and roast, or dumplings—and I'll eat with anyone who'll eat with me. So hold out your glasses, my copains from the four corners of the earth. Monsieur, I know all there is to know about the Embassy. But as for what went on in Mt. Sinai—I'm not interested. And I'd much rather sample different wines with you all than go skating in Dr. Darkbeard's brain. Hold out your glasses, you anti-Fascists and anti-Nazis. After all, I'm not responsible for what the German people is forced to do! All I know is that the earth is going to shake and quake." He pounded the table. Suddenly he grabbed Krah and shouted, "Kneel down, I tell you, and lick my arse. You creaking crow! You black master of ceremonies from Mt. Sinai!"

"He's drunk!" The others tried to free Krah. "Let him go! We're not in Dachau here! Or in the S.A. Headquarters in Motzstrasse—"

"The nerve of you, God damn it!" And then he shoved unconcernedly through the tumult he had aroused around him in the café and went for Krah again. "Out of my way, you damned cormorants, you democratic town-councillors—"

"Cormorants!" the Rabbi roared. "You brown gangster!"

"Brown gangster?" He kicked his shins. "Don't you know who I am?"

"Well, who are you?"

"I am a German!"

At that, Krah reared up and spat straight into his face. For a moment the blond did not react. Then he dipped his handkerchief in the champagne bucket and wiped off his cheek. Then he twirled the bottle around in the ice. Then he ripped it out and smashed it down on Krah's skull.

CHAPTER EIGHT WHILE SOME RAN GESTICULATING AFTER THE YOUTH IN THE WIND-BREAKER, OTHERS LAID HIS VICTIM ON the cushioned wall seat and washed and dressed his wound.

"Into the can with 'em, the whole brown gang from Armin to Göring." A smartly dressed Communist, his shoulders heavily padded and a Swiss passport in his pocket, came forward. "Think they can stamp down the whole world with their brown boots! Into the can with the whole brown gang! And pull the chain!"

"Oi! Oi!" Krah sat up, groaning, and looked about him. "Am I dead?"

"Not quite, mon cher! You're not dead yet! You and I and all of us will live to see someone else dead—someone quite different from you! And then into the ashcan with the devil's brood of them! And shut the lid!"

"S-s-s-sh! S-s-s-sh! All passports, please!" The paunchy, fat-faced proprietor came forward making his way from table to table. "No disturbance, please!" He played with the heavy gold chain across his vest. "It never rains but it pours! Everything happens in threes! The light goes out! The money goes—out! Herr Krah goes—out. A fresh murder every hour! Naturally the police are on edge. So have your passports ready. Don't get excited. Go right on drinking. The gendarmes are beginning back there. A routine check-up! I know the police, I know my guests. Herr Krah—I know you left your passport at the San Salvador Consulate! I'll fix it. How do you feel? He's lying there just like our blessed Dollfuss. The blood is still running. Put a plate there to catch it!" He motioned to the waitress. "Have you enough cotton?"

"It's just a scratch, Herr Anzengruber." The waitress wiped the stains off the cushioned seat. "He ought to have a brandy."

"A brandy! Yes, give him a brandy! And you, too, Baron?"

"No thank you." The Rabbi shook his head, and looked at Krah with concentrated fury. "Give it to the invalid. By Moses and the prophets, Herr Krah! That's what you get for your pains! You and your kind, sitting around in cafés all over the world, drinking with goys—instead of behaving like Jews! You blame the brown gangster, but I tell you that blow came from above, from God on Sinai! To wake you up out of your damned internationalist democratic dream of a happier humanity. To reawaken you to your own national virtues!" Cramming on his big hat, Dr. Wolff departed in scorn.

"Oi-oi!" Krah grinned after him. "The gaze of a cobra is not more dangerous than the eyes of an angry priest! God, was he wild!"

Without warning, he had sat up. He tore off his bandage and dashed to the window. Outside, a girl who looked like a dancer was springing light as a deer over the rainwater puddles, hurrying in the direction of Notre-Dame.

"What's got into him? . . . Krah! What's up?"

"Oi-oi! Did you see that girl outside? God, what a woman! She's got black rubbers on!" Forgetting his pains, Krah squeaked and wriggled with delight. "The lady hasn't got her gray fur quite closed. Only a gentlewoman knows how to hold her fur together like that! Oi-oi! It's ages since I had such a sweet young thing in bed with me! Oh, gentlemen of Hitler's Jewry! When will life be normal again? When shall we be able to whisper into honey eyes, 'Well, sweetie, was it fine?' "

"One must really fall in love!" The writer from Budapest raised his round priestly face and puffed on his long cigarette. "Crazy, head over heels in love! Everything else is sh—"

"Yes! Into the can with everything else—and pull the chain! God! What a shameless wind! God! How I'd like to be that wind! Just look how it nuzzles her cute little knees! Oi-oi! Did you see that? She hasn't any garters on! Has elastic tops to her stockings! Oi-oi!" Snatching his hat he was going to run after her, but as he set the revolving door spinning like a merry-go-round, Sergeant-Major Grumbach grasped his jacket.

"Blast you! Where are you going? Didn't you hear? Nobody leaves! Those were the orders! Your papers!"

CHAPTER NINE ON ESCAPING FROM THE POLICE STATION, UHLE BECAUSE OF HIS HANDCUFFED HANDS, HAD FIRST SLUNK from doorway to doorway. Now he had reached the great open plaza that lies between the Ministère de la Guerre and the Seine. His next thought was a telephone booth, from which he could immediately get in touch with the Secretary of the Société des Anciens Combattants. But just then the storm broke again.

Spiral eddies of dust, whipped by faster and faster falling rain, reared up and charged to and fro like frightened horses. Scraps of paper whirled high over trees and houses, hovered a moment in the air, then, taken by the new, exploding downpour, dropped back, to end in the gutter.

Lightning was blazing all around the horizon—behind the Eiffel Tower, behind the Sacré-Cœur, over the Tuileries Gardens—jagged axes hurled by giants. For an instant the whitish green of wind-blown tree crowns foamed out of the steel-blue air. And now through the sprawling city roared the thunder, as Nero's lions roared when the Christians were whipped out to them from the catacombs.

Each instant the vast sky changed color. Now raspberry-red, now livid-white. Pedestrians who had not found shelter were struggling with umbrellas blown inside out. Hats ran races, while the storm stared smoky-eyed at its wild image in the wet.

122

Cowering from the storm, his back pressed against the broad trunk of a plane, Uhle waited for a chance to go on. Scraps of newspaper, cigarette butts, cabbage leaves streamed past him in dizzying vortices. Each raindrop splashed and splattered on the sidewalk like a separate small fountain. But now the wind drove him on too, along with the leaves in the gutter. Again he took momentary refuge in a doorway, to rest and catch breath.

From the opposite curb the black-haired girl who had been in the "Wailing-Wall" café was steering straight for the house. The wind had blown her dress up girdle-high; delicate fingers tried bashfully to hide naked thighs—But her little feet were forced to take yard-long jumps over puddles and lakes of rain. Her curly dog pulled her through the downpour so hard that his leash looked like a thin black iron rod. Uhle stepped back. She took off her raincape and yanked at the dog, which was trying to sniff him. "Come here, or I'll break your neck," she said in English. On her small head she wore a white woolen shawl, wound twice around like a turban, the fringed ends hanging down on one shoulder. All the life in her delicately modeled, powdered face shone from the black jewels of her eyes. The line of her eyebrows dominated a flawless domed forehead. About half an inch of her hair showed below her turban. Her lips, which she kept closed, were as thin as eyebrows. She made no acknowledgment of Uhle's presence, except to give him one look, at the same time shrugging open the voluminous silver-fox neckpiece that her raincape could hardly confine. Then she made her way up the wooden flight of stairs, dragging the dog after her and not looking back.

Uhle's eyes had now become accustomed to the darkness of the entry. He saw that there was a glass door behind the projecting staircase. Over it a sign, on which was the name "Mathias Westermann." He approached cautiously. There was an odor of glue and fresh varnish. Through the glass he saw a workroom. Inside, suspended on racks, hung violins—one after the other. And halves of violins. The red polished wood gleamed like something precious. Glue pots stood on carpenters' benches. Saws, wood-wool, and shavings. On the wall, under a small dim oil lamp, a picture of the Virgin Mary. The rear of the workshop was lost in darkness. Uhle listened. There seemed to be no one inside. On one of the tables, among a number of augers and knives, shone the roughened surface of a wide file. He clicked open the unlocked door, softly asked: "Is anyone here?" As no one answered, he went on into the room. The only light came from a murky rear court. Something like a holiday stillness lay over it. Just as he was going to set the file to his handcuffs, the house door creaked.

A man without a hat, his curly gray hair dripping around the tanned face of an artist, entered the workroom in three heavy steps.

"Et alors?" he looked at Uhle quickly, obviously mistaking him for someone else. "Ah oui, Monsieur—I know—the Polish young lady has sent you about that violin there! Ja, mein Herr"—he began to mix German with his French—"Is Mademoiselle Olenka back in Paris? It will take a few more days. It's a good violin—no Stradivarius, of course. But the tone is not too bad. Please ask her to be patient a few more days. After all, a violin is a living thing. Right? Or do you insist on taking the instrument with you? But please"—he offered him a chair, but not before dusting it off with his sleeve—"please sit down. Mademoiselle Olenka was telling me—you both live in the same pension? A refugee too? Naturally—our much-beloved Adolf . . . I am from Colmar. Violin-maker Mathias Westermann is my name. My brother was the village priest in Moosheim. I wonder where he is now. In what concentration camp have they put him to meditate on Our Lord! Well—"

His clear gaze found the image of the Virgin on the wall, and he slowly made the sign of the Cross.

"God will be with him. Right? God is everywhere! Oh, how we used to laugh when he would tell about trying to explain the omnipresence of God to the children in catechism class. And then suddenly little Hans in the seventh row raised his hand: 'Father, Father.' And my worthy brother said, 'What is it, Hans?' 'Father, if God is present everywhere, is He in my father's wine cellar, too?' 'Yes, of course, Hans. I have just been telling you: God is everywhere. God sees everything. God hears everything. There is nowhere where God is not present. Ergo, He is in your father's wine cellar, too.' And then the little scamp snapped his fingers and said, 'Caught you that time, Father. My father hasn't any wine cellar!'" And now the violin-maker was laughing so hard that it echoed through the workroom. "But now it is time we kindled the light of reason." He turned on a light—"There!" —took off his much spotted overcoat, hung it up, and laid a piece of wood, which he had brought in with him, carefully on the table. "I've just come from the Bois. Yes, whenever there is a storm, Mathias Westermann goes to the woods. I always did it in Colmar . . . and I do it in Paris—and shall do it however much farther that Antichrist may send me. For a violin-maker, Monsieur—in case you don't know it—is not a man who saws pieces of wood and glues them together and stains them and polishes them. Oh no! A violin-maker—at least if he under-

stands his work—is a sort of Merlin. You've heard of Merlin, I suppose—king of the woods and magician? So—whenever my wounds
from the last war begin to tickle, I know that the clouds are going to
be scene-shifted. And then I leave saw and plane, put on my coat—
right? And I don't stop until I'm out of the city and all alone in the
middle of the woods somewhere. It grows darker and darker. There's
already thunder on the horizon. The glass trembles. There is a sound
in the tree trunks. From root to crown they fill with electricity. Phew!
And then the first wind comes, gusting through the tree tops. It roars
—ha-ha! Yes, and then Mathias Westermann stands there among all
the tree trunks, as if he were standing among organ pipes. And he listens. For, like Merlin, I want to understand what the wind says. And I
understand it. Ha-ha! And then, my friend, the first lightning flickers
white-hot through the twigs, and flames flash over the bark and the
birds in the leaves are sprinkled white with sparks . . . ha-ha! And
then it is so cool, so fresh—as though God were breathing through
the woods. Ah, my friend—and then all the tree trunks sway up out
of the moss like masts, and bend, and creak, and strike one another, and
their excitement never stops growing. Suddenly, they are all still again,
as if they were listening for the sound of the first heavy raindrops on
their leaves. And then they creak again, creak and creak until the wind
lays hold of more and more twigs, as if it were his harp in the storm.
And then Mathias Westermann stands leaning against a tree, and listens. He takes his tuning fork out of his pocket. And he waits. And
when at last the storm deepens and strengthens—right?—when the
thunder rolls through the woods like a drum roll in a Beethoven sym-
phony . . . and the branches whip and groan . . . and it grows as
dark as it did on the day of the Flood, before old Noah went running
into the Ark—I say: then, when the sluices of almighty heaven are
opened and the mass of waters pours down on the trees, so that you
think—right?—that the Last Day has come and the Fiery Spirit will
show itself any minute from behind a tree—I say, then Mathias Westermann stands there with his tuning fork and listens and watches and
waits. And suddenly he is sure: it is that tree—or that other one over
there. That is the tree that gives the best tone, the tree that has understood what the Fiery Spirit said to it. And then Mathias Westermann
makes a sign in the bark of that tree, as once the Jews in Egypt did
when they smeared their doors so that the angel of the Lord should
know where the children of God lived. For that particular trunk, sir,
no longer creaks like the others. It sings high now, it sings in eternity,
like the unending song. In that wood now there is spirit. I am a Catholic

—right? And out of the piece of that tree which I sawed in the woods and brought home from the woods, Mathias Westermann is going to make a violin—right?—a red, slender violin—do you understand me? And it will be the life work of my little life—do you understand?—to bring out the voice of the Fiery Spirit, to make it sound in that wood. Yes! And one day the violin will be finished—right?—and then an artist will come—a man's hand or a girl's hand—a human hand. And that hand will draw the bow over the strings of my violin—right? And then the voices that I heard in the woods will sound—right? A song of freedom sung by tongues of fire—right?—right? And if Adolf Hitler's eardrums are not made of stone—then the tone that Mathias Westermann captured in the woods, in the midst of the storm—when God asked me, 'Is all well on this my earth?' And I cried to him through the tearing hurricane, 'No, my Lord and my Master! No!'—then the Creator's question and the answer of his tortured creature will blast that accursed, music-deaf, inhuman, butchering brain to atoms, like dynamite!" He collapsed over his saws and planes, his body shaken by sobs from his inmost being.

Through the open door the noise of the rain mingled with that human sobbing. It sounded like rivers of tears . . . like the welling and the dropping of the tears of tortured humanity.

Uhle dragged himself to the foot of the stairway. Outside in the street, the houses opposite were reflected in wet wavy lines on the asphalt . . . the narrow street looked like a little canal in Venice. Uhle wanted to start out. But he hesitated. Were his thoughts, perhaps, moving in the black gondola of fate, traveling out of reality into that magical Venice made of rosy pearl—the city that refugees, despairing of reaching the mainland, had built centuries since in the lagoons? Was the manacled Uhlan moving in fancy in a gondola on the Grand Canal, toward a better future? Beyond the Ponte dei Sospiri—beyond the Bridge of Sighs and the prisons—oh!—thither, where the bells of Santa Maria del Salute sound, and a fresh wind urges the painted boats of simple fisherfolk peacefully into the night?

CHAPTER TEN "S<small>H-H-H! SH-H-H!</small>"

<small>STARTLED, UHLE FACED ABOUT. THERE STOOD THE GIRL IN THE WHITE</small>
turban, laughing and pointing at the downpour. "Darling, are you
going to stand here till the weather clears? Come along!" She beckoned
him.

From the fifth floor her dog barked insistently. She started up the
stairs, and Uhle followed.

On the second floor there were glass doors bearing the signs of firms
dealing in coal and coke. Apparently nobody lived on the third floor.
The fourth floor rang with the hard tapping of many typewriters.
After that, it became so dark that Uhle could no longer distinguish her
form—only by the soft creaking of her fine leather sandals could he tell
that she was still ahead of him.

"Here we are." She stood aside and motioned to him to enter, gave
the yelping dog a kick, and shut the door. A colored lantern illuminated a small anteroom, the walls of which were lined with books. The
scent of flowers rose from a bowl before a deep armchair.

"Signor, siete sorpreso? Ma, s'accomodi!" And then she began to
mix Italian with French, English, and German. With a mischievous
look, she opened a closet door. "Ecco! My bar," she explained proudly.
"Used to be a clothes closet! Ma prego, caro amico, approchez!"

The miniature bar was all done in red lacquer. A mirror covering
the whole rear wall gave a feeling of spaciousness. A narrow board,
covered with blue leather, separated the mixer from the guests. Rows
of glasses, together with choice liqueurs in swollen-bellied, four-square,
or slender, fluted bottles, shimmered on the shelves.

"Chéri, an egg and cognac? Mamma mia! Doesn't he think I'm real?
You're not allowed to look at me like that! Or do you prefer a Cordial
Medoc? Mais oui!—whenever I can't sleep at night, or if I've had horrible dreams, I sit here alone, and drink. Makes me sleepy, finally. Monsieur!" She filled two glasses. "Here's how! Sit on that stool! But the
board stays between us! I'm so thankful you can keep me company!
This is the time of day my flesh crawls. A friend of mine says: 'Six
o'clock in the evening is the hour when Christ vanished from the
tomb, to descend into hell!' I have to kill time until He comes back.
Ha-ha! Salut!" She raised her glass, then turned on her stool to confront the mirror. . . . "Oh, my! Do I look terrible! Deep rings under

my eyes! Because I don't get any sleep any more. Well, Monsieur! what sort of person do you think I am? But why don't you take off your raincoat? Drop it on the floor. Much too hot in here! . . . Foffo, tais-toi!" she called, and the little dog became quiet.

"You came to see the old violin-maker? I think Himmler knocked out his front teeth. Darling, I hope you're not a Nazi? Hm? Tell me, what sort of a man are you? . . . With a head of hair like that? An artist? You're certainly not French? You look Scandinavian. . . . Yesterday the young Duke d'Aguillon was here. . . . Charles hates the Republic. He sat right where you are and made long monarchist speeches. He's completely in love with himself. Calls the Count of Paris his 'illustrious cousin'! Drank up a whole bottle of egg and cognac and then prophesied: 'In 1955 France will once again be a powerful monarchy!' Then he drank up another bottle of egg and cognac to drown his grief over the fact that Henry IV is dead. Ha-ha! He invited me to the country. He keeps wonderful women there. How he hates democracy! The Pope recently gave him a private audience. Oh hell!" She added cognac to her cordial, winking at Uhle. "You know, I could die laughing at you! Don't you ever say anything? I suppose you're thinking! Hm? Well, what do you think of me? Une grande courtisane? . . . Wrong guess! I'm an actress—at present without an engagement. Why I've no engagement? Because I loathe the theater. Even when I *do* play Judith! The Holofernes is nothing but a wretched actor. And after I've finished him off—when I've finally beheaded the butcher of Jews in his bed—then the curtain comes down, and there we are side by side, taking our bows! But everybody who sees me in the part is simply bowled over! Anything that amuses me, I can do. Unfortunately, nothing amuses me any more. Mornings, when I get up, I'd just as lief go right to sleep again! Who knows what that means . . . ?"

Her complexion had a faint golden tint. The big turquoises in her ears made her look like some slim, silken-clad Princess of Tibet.

Leaning back against the mirror, she hummed:

> Jesus Christ, the Saviour
> Ate his fish and bread;
> The Abbess of Port Royal
> Crammed eggs until she's dead! . . .

Suddenly she bent forward, stared searchingly into Uhle's eyes, and whispered: "My name's Nadia. Red Stalin's little wife was named Nadia, too. 'Nadia Alleluia,' to be precise. What's your name? But it doesn't matter! You don't have to tell me." She laid her head on the bar, smiling. "Monsieur, am I talking too much? What are you brooding about? Why don't you drink? What's the use of so much thinking? Doesn't lead to anything! The brain is a labyrinth. And we run round and round inside—just like Mickey Mouse. Where's the way out?"

She stared into space. "You know, I'm half Jewish. I tell every gentleman that beforehand. I want them to know it." Since Uhle made no reply, she wrinkled her nose. "So, if you don't want to clink glasses with me any more"—she raised the cognac bottle to her mouth—"I'll drink all by myself until I'm . . . dead!"

Uhle, who had hitherto carefully kept his hands hidden under his cape, now tried to take the bottle away from her. She saw his handcuffs . . . and let the bottle go. Her eyes dilated. Abruptly, she clapped back the bar, and brushing past him, she let the dog out of the kitchen, shouting, "Too hot in here! Why do you stink so?" And then, with forced composure, she walked slowly along the book shelves to a small winding staircase. Step by step, as if heavily burdened, she pulled herself up the stairs.

Uhle listened and wondered if she were phoning the police. But there was not a sound in the apartment—it was so still that his ears began to hum. He went quietly to the door, but hearing voices on the stairs, he cautiously closed it again. Tiptoeing back to the bar, he seated himself and waited, undecided what to do. Several minutes passed. His thoughts chased each other. Now it was the dancer, and then the police. If only he could lay his hands on a telephone! Gunther would certainly help him. . . . Or should he go find the little actress and frankly tell her the plight he was in? And if she didn't believe him?

From somewhere upstairs came the thin chime of a clock. He started, knocked down a glass; it fell with a tinkling clatter. The dog scratched at a door. Again silence.

As Uhle stooped to pick up the fragments of the glass, the sheets of paper in his breast pocket rustled. He realized then that he had forgotten all about the Will. Despite his handcuffed hands, he managed to withdraw the pages and spread them out on the bar. He put the candle beside them and began to read the irregular script:

"The journalists of the world have felt themselves obliged to snuffle through all the rooms and houses that ever enjoyed the honor of sheltering me; and not only have they snuffled through the cupboards, commodes, beds, hangings, washstands, and waterclosets to see if they could find some pornographic or erotic scandal that would make me, the Supreme Reichsführer impossible in the eyes of their democratic

129

world, but these snufflers have also shied at no expense and no distant journey no matter how fantastically far, simply to turn up in my Austrian homeland some postman—or washwoman—or baggage porter—or any other obscure person they could find who might eventually dish up some gossip and tittle-tattle about my love-life. Well, gentlemen of the press, I have always had lots of fun watching you! The fact is, your snuffling always was and is hopeless! For this reason: Adolf Hitler has no love-life! And today, after so many years, even the rabble of writers for the press will flatly have to admit that they have been incapable of tying even the slightest scandal onto me. The fact is, Adolf Hitler is neither a Bluebeard nor a Don Juan or Casanova! The Boccaccios will therefore never find in my biography any material for their pig-sty effusions! And herewith, German Folk Comrades, I come to one of the major secrets of my gigantic successes. Hitherto, I have confided it to no one, not even to my bosom friend, Hess. But to you, my Last Will and Testament—come what may, I must whisper it truthfully into your so-called ears. . . . Yes! The Future shall know it. But will there ever be a generation of men which will comprehend the secret of their Supreme Führer? That which he now, with a shudder of pride, for the first time entrusts to a plain and simple sheet of paper? Indeed, I ask myself: will the Pan-German youth understand me when I, the Triumpher over Europe, speak to them? I, Adolf Hitler, the Supreme Reichsführer and Chancellor of the Pan-German Reich—I have never in my whole life wasted or squirted away a single drop of my own substance. And if I have said 'Hitler is no Don Juan!' that does not mean to say—as many of my effeminate enemies absolutely at a loss to account for the phenomenon of my life, would like to imagine—that I was an onanist! . . . 'Ni l'un ni l'autre! Messieurs, Mesdames!' as the frogs say. So now—you Hitler Scout of the Pan-German Future—prick up your ears and listen: I am just as normal as you are! Of course I have also felt certain stirrings. For instance, when I saw little Seppl Gruber standing naked in the brook, or when Liesl Hofgärtner at the hay-making, behind the shed, couldn't get her shirt to button over her breast—Puh! ! BUT! And this is the great difference! For instance, when our teacher once drew for us on the blackboard a diagram showing the difference between the male and the female elderblossoms, Seppl Gruber and I examined ourselves. Heavens! The mere word 'female' or 'male' used to twitch through me as if my legs were frogs' legs that you hold to an electric wire. Later on, after supper, we were in the village street. The elders were in bloom and the girls were singing outside the houses. We walked on and on and then turned left to the haystacks. All at once Seppl Gruber put his arm around me. A wonderful feeling! I remember we danced together. And only when a nightingale began to sing in the black-thorns did we stop. Seppl, of course, wanted to sit down in the hay and listen . . . I had picked up a stone and was prowling about the bush: I wanted to hit that nightingale. But Seppl caught hold of me, and began rough-housing. Suddenly I was lying in the grass, the night-ingale was singing and sobbing, and some shooting stars fell! 'God!' said I. All of a sudden Seppl Gruber got nasty. He took hold of me in such a way that I was dumbfounded. But I sprang up and—strangled him. A few seconds later he flopped over backward, like a lifeless some-thing, into the brook. . . . There I stood. The moon rose red over the woods. A couple of rabbits chased each other. The water gurgled and murmured past . . . But let me say right away: I felt absolutely noth-ing; a definite proof that I had done the right thing. The nightingale stopped singing, probably frightened by Seppl's plunking into the water. As I went to the bush to cut myself a switch, it flew away. . . . You German Hitler Scouts! Your Supreme Reichsführer does not ex-aggerate when he maintains that he stood there like Siegfried after overcoming the dragon. Yes! An unbelievable feeling suddenly stormed through my blood! Something so heroic yanked my head straight up out of my collar, so heroic that I could only compare it to the magical glitter of the stars in the blue of the night above me. I lashed my switch through the air and strode along in the furrow as if I had wings. At home everybody had gone to sleep. I threw myself down on the straw in the tool shed. Outside, the light flickered in the lantern. Oh, you National Socialist Youth! I repeat once again: I do not exag-gerate when I say that, with folded hands, I prayed aloud to myself!

"On the following day, the yammering and yelling about the mur-dered Seppl Gruber, found in the brook by a trout fisherman, did not in the least upset my composure. And inasmuch as nobody among my stupid relatives and friends would ever have thought of me in connec-tion with any such great deed, I kept silent. Even when they accused the old dealer in chinaware of having drowned Seppl because the week before he had deliberately smashed some of the best china in his shop —I only laughed proudly inside myself. And when the police came to take him away, I picked up a stone from the street and threw it after him. That afternoon, at the burial, I stood beside Seppl Gruber's grave and scattered on his coffin his favorite flowers—dandelions (we used to call them 'butter-flowers' too). . . . Yes, you Scouts! that's the way it was. And the second creature that dared to try and inveigle my substance into a so-called love affair was a pretty girl. Naturally, that was many years later. It was my creative genius she admired. For hours on end she could fly into ecstasies of enthusiasm over my drawings and architectural designs. Once in Munich, we had just had some tea and lots of cookies . . . I sat on the red plush sofa and as usual gave expression to my splendid fantasies, grandiose reveries, and the tremendous, creative intuitions of my sublime genius. The young thing was just about to clear away the tea-cups when my genius caught fire in her. She stared at me entranced and asked if I would please permit her to sit down on the sofa beside me. Of course I permitted her: why should I have denied the young lady such a thing? But then came the tragedy! Misinterpreting my sublime, creative processes of thought— for she was, of course, a woman—she suddenly attempted to degrade my essence by dragging me down into the enervating nonsense of love. But thou, O Scout of my Pan-German future!—spare me the description of the repulsive scene which followed—and which naturally could not possibly terminate except by . . . her death! . . ."

CHAPTER ELEVEN

NADIA HAD COME DOWN SO SILENTLY THAT UHLE HAD NOT HEARD HER. SHE STOOD BEHIND HIM IN A white silk down-lined negligee. She had rouged her cheeks. Her black ringlets spiraled down over her shoulders, as if Eros had curled them.

"Hold still!" she whispered, and before Uhle could hide the sheets, she had brought out a pair of pliers and squeezed and twisted at one of the links until it snapped. "There you are! Free!" She gave him a theatrical look, threw the pliers down, and gave a half-humorous imitation of an actor's bow at the end of a well-played scene.

Uhle flexed and shook his hands.

"Monsieur, do you know why I did that?" She lit a cigarette. "No? Can't you guess?" She blew smoke in his face. "Well, I know—and that's what counts. Ever since I was fourteen and ran away from home, I made up my mind to do whatever Papa forbade me to do. As, to pry the handcuffs off a strange man! Ha-ha!" She made a face. "Mais chéri, why so silent? How do you feel? Are you all right now? Your skin is chafed—do you want some powder? Or cold cream? No doubt I disturbed you now in the midst of 'important' reading? But I don't want to know. I'm not curious. Unfortunately, you can't spend the night. The Duke d'Aguillon is coming to dinner. But you must meet him. When he sees those handcuffs, he'll make you a member of his Monarchist Club at once! . . . Darling!"—she stroked his wrist. "Do say something! . . . Hm? . . . You'll stay? We'll just have a dinner à trois. Oh! I'm a wonderful cook!" Suddenly she was listening. "Pssst! . . . Did you hear steps on the stairs? Please don't leave me alone now! Last night I had already gone to bed when all of a sudden I heard 'tap-tap-tap' on the stairs . . . and the dog whining . . . I jumped out of bed and came down. Nobody! But as soon as I was back in bed upstairs, I heard 'tap-tap-tap' . . . !"

"Fear . . ." Uhle murmured. "Fear . . . Our metaphysical fear!"

"Quoi? Mais non. I am very brave! But of course I am an awful coward too. Sometimes I feel as if there was no way out. Then the tips of my fingers hurt so horribly. I always know what's the matter—those Nazi dogs are tearing the nails off some poor creature! . . . I hide in bed and make myself very small and pull the covers over my head. But I see them still, their backs all flayed and their faces broken from kicks . . ."

She covered her eyes with her hands. "Hélas! Is there no God at all? And if there is a God, why does he permit such things? Or perhaps there isn't any God at all—only the Devil!"

Uhle's mouth twitched. She said quickly, "Chéri, tell me—do you believe in God?" Neither spoke for a moment. Then she smiled and said:

"Come, I want to show you my bedroom." She climbed the stairs humming, and turned round transformed, a high-spirited child, her outstretched arms barring the doorway. "Arrêtez! You're not to laugh! Promise? I'm so ashamed. My bedroom is so absolutely feminine. It's all in white silk—everything white!" She looked at him wide-eyed, like a schoolgirl. "After all, I'm not a man! So please . . . please don't laugh!"

And with this preamble she led him into a room of almost geometric symmetry, cleanliness, and order. Only gradually did Uhle perceive the perfumed atmosphere of a boudoir: Chanel and Quelques Fleurs wafted their cool breath through the spacious room. Heavy, quilted hangings of white silk hung before the two windows. On the night table, yellow wax candles burned, with unstirring flames, beside an enormous bed. Against the opposite wall stood a tall baroque clothes chest of inlaid wood, the warm color of an old bass-viol. An ornamental gilt key, from which hung a red damask tassel, stood in the lock.

133

Behind the bed, and along the wall as far as the door, was a multi-paneled mirror. Her dressing table, too, was all of mirror glass. Crystal flasks, filled with heavy gold essences of distilled spring flowers, refracted the candlelight like polished gems.

"Do you like it?" she asked anxiously. "You know, I believe I really do have talent—not only for the stage. Whatever I try, I can do. Only one thing puzzles me. Can you give me your advice? Hm? Does that Maria Theresia clothes chest go well in here—or doesn't it? Downstairs I have a Jesuit chest; its lines are much more severe. This morning I had two workmen here and they did nothing but carry first one down, then the other up. But I still couldn't make up my mind which is best in a bedroom. Mon Dieu! It's like my uncle, who has such a long beard that he never knows whether to sleep with it under the covers or on top of the covers!" She laughed so heartily that her toy dog came bounding into the room, jumping around her and licking her hands. Abruptly he stopped and crawled under the bed.

"Someone's calling!" Uhle listened.

"Where? Oh, only the violin-maker downstairs. Sometimes he calls out like that in the middle of the night! Doesn't it sound as if he were tearing all the strings off his violins? Awful! Thank God you're here! Otherwise I'd begin peering under the bed again. I'd open all the closets and look in every corner. I begin to have that feeling of fear. Well, anyway, tomorrow that Nazi Weidmann's to be beheaded. The Duke wants to take me to see it. It's public." She yawned nervously. "Once I saw a chicken get its head chopped off. Its body ran away, but in the still head, the little eye moved, suddenly it got milky white, then slowly the beak opened. Hélas, mon ami! What horrors are waiting for all of us? Chéri!" She clutched Uhle. "Do you really think that this 'race' madness is going to spread to every last corner of the earth?"

"Pardon?" He started, as if he had been lost in thought. "At least, if we don't get together against the beast—I mean—" He sank his head in his hands and wept.

"Go on!" Nadia huddled closer to him, beseeching. "Please go on talking! I can't sleep any more for the fear! I've no appetite! Never hungry—just chuck the food down. And when I try to read, the letters dance before my eyes. You know—sometimes I think: perhaps this is all over and done for? . . . all this white, white silk . . . my precious perfumes! . . . my pleasant face creams . . . And this enormous, clean bed . . . where you can feel so wonderful . . . where you can make love! . . . Oh, lo-o-ove!"

She jumped off the bed—"Excusez!"—and ran into the bathroom.

There was a noise of running water. Back again, she moved her hands over her slender body.

"I still function perfectly. That's how I keep my figure. Oh!" She took a rose from the vase on her dressing table and held it up to Uhle's face. "What a beautiful flower! And in full perfection! Hélas, Monsieur, perhaps there is nothing more beautiful than a rose . . . Oh! that we can still have a rose in the agony of a world—is a miracle!"

"It is!" Uhle looked at the rose. "For, after all, this flower found the way out of the agony . . . the rose believed in the light! . . ."

Nadia turned toward him, puzzled, then she lit a cigarette; the blue smoke veiled her face. She paced back and forth on the Angora rug by the bed; then suddenly stood stock still. She laid her hot hand on Uhle's fingers. "Tell me—don't you like women? Or are you a homo? Hah!" She squealed with delight. "You know, nowadays most men are homos! Or are you only attracted by blondes? Is that why you're so cold?" She ran her fingers through her curls. "Of course, you don't have to tell me anything. I'm certainly not a Madonna to listen to confessions. Mais non! I'm no Madonna! Ha-ha! Sometimes I ask myself whether I'm not just a charming little whore? Ha-ha! Darling, you wouldn't believe it, but it's not so long ago that I didn't even know the real difference between a man and a woman. Still mooning? Got a date with someone else? How many sweethearts have you, boy? What a gorgeous neck you've got!" Abruptly she tore the rose out of his hand, threw it into a bowl, and looked at him invitingly. Her negligee opened a little. As Uhle saw that she was naked under it, she touched his knee with her toes and sighed.

"Chéri! Are you attracted to me?"

"Yes!" Uhle looked at her small foot. "I am."

"Merci, Monsieur!" She came closer. "Then you might be a little bit nicer to me!"

"Nicer?"

"Mais oui. Ha-ha! Do you know what the Duke always says? 'Breasts like yours are usually found only in the Mediterranean type—so high and firm!'" She touched them, unashamed.

"Do you know—" Uhle watched her, embarrassed—"every pore in your skin has a separate fascination. And—like it or not—I mean—do you know what you arouse in a man?"

"What?"

"The beast!"

"The be-e-e-east?" She lay back on the bed relaxed and laughing. But suddenly she sat up again and bit him in the hand with her little teeth, so hard that he cried "Ouch!"

"Quoi? I arouse the beast in you? Which beast, out of all the beasts in the zoo, chéri? Tell me which! Is it the lion with his golden mane? Hm? Do you want to eat me up? Eat me then!"

He freed himself from her, finger by finger, and then, while she relapsed into laughter, dropped into the soft, blue, silk-upholstered chair by the clothes chest. And, unable to take his mind from the pages of Hitler's Will in his pocket, he began to mutter to himself:

"How was that? . . . in order to realize his devil's dreams, he hoarded up his substance?! Spent not a drop of it? Is that where his strength lies? his uncanny power over all the others? And we! Uhle, Uhle! To realize our dream of mankind, what did we do with our substance?"

"Hi!" she called to him over the end of the bed. "What is my lion growling about?"

"Oh, I was just getting a better look at you and your fascinating charms! Yes, you! on your paradisal featherbed supported on snow-white lacquer! And it reminded me of a verse in the Bible."

"A verse in the Bible," she laughed, still in the same playful mood. Then she beckoned him to come closer. He went back to her, and said:

"The General Epistle of James, chapter 4: 'From whence come wars and fightings among you? come they not hence, even of your lusts that war in your members?' "

"What's that?" she giggled. "You funny lion . . ."

"You know"—he put his finger under her chin—"that little face . . . with all that black mass of hair around it . . . it looks like a waterlily in a night-dark pool."

"Like a waterlily?" She sat up, flattered, turned to the mirror, and ran her fingers through her curls. Then she sighed, "Mais non! It's horrible! I hate my hair!"

"But why? It's extremely lovely."

"Extremely lovely?" she hissed at him like a viper. "You don't mean that. . . . Hello! what are you looking at in the mirror? Nice, isn't it, the way it reflects all this?"

She looked into the quicksilver as if into a clear pool.

"There are the curtains—so white! And you too! And me right beside you!"

"Yes . . . And from behind the rococo mirror someone else is watching us."

"Someone else? Who? Besides, my mirror isn't rococo at all."

"Darling," he rubbed his face against her hair. "I wanted to know whether—in such a sweet moment—my Unknown Soldier would still be thinking of his innumerable fallen comrades."

"Who? Darling"—she pinched his ear—"tell me! Or are you an ascetic? Mais non—with lips like yours, you couldn't be an ascetic, Dieu merci! You're a warm-blooded, sensual creature!" She took his face in her hands and kissed him as if her lips would never let go. He drew her to him so violently that her white silk negligee flew wide open.

"Darling!" he whispered hoarsely against her body. Then, "But I! what am I to do? When the beast rises in me and demands pleasure! Pleasure! What am I to do?"

"Eat me up," she gasped into his ear, "won't you? Eat me up!"

"And when it's all over? I mean: après. Then I go downstairs. Take a taxi, and ride to the Trocadéro. And then, I stand at the microphone in front of four thousand World War veterans. And open my trap in praise of freedom! Eh?" He dug his chin into her neck. "In praise—of freedom! Hm? Sounding the call of freedom for all peoples! Hm? And all the time I know inside me that a few minutes ago I was in bed with a girl—no better than a slave myself—a slave to her tyrannical desires. Unable to free myself from that hot, thought-drugging pleasure!"

"Freedom?" She looked at him, puzzled.

"Yes! But how is that divine word to fire the millions—when there is no truth behind me? No truth! How, how? Or do I really want anything but what all the other slaves of lust want? Eh? Do I want freedom? No! I will fulfill myself here in your white arms! Darling, darling!" He forced her down on the mattress. "We shall feel pleasure! Yes! What if God and the angels weep over it? Nuts! What matter what oaths or what corpses we tread down? Eh? What do we care? If only the beast in us gets his fill of our luscious flesh! Eh?"

"Are you crazy? Oh God, what is life without pleasure! Come, lion! As for me, I want pleasure. Come! The chain mustn't break! Come! Nothing else has any meaning—Why don't you come to me?"

"Mademoiselle"—he sat up with a jerk—"do you know that twenty minutes ago we were total strangers?" He freed himself from her arms.

"And now the beasts in us are sniffing and licking at each other like dogs in the gutter!"

"Pardon!" He straightened his collar. "But why can't we sit beside each other like two reasonable beings and talk? God knows there are enough important subjects to talk about in this day and age!"

"Love! Love—is there anything more important than that? Come! Listen—I tell you, if you don't tear me to pieces—I'll tear you to

137

pieces!"

"Uhle, are you obliged to go crazy because a girl has dimples in her cheeks? And those red-painted claws? And a good make-up? Let's get out of this witches' kitchen of pleasure!—Nadia," he cried, so loud that she jumped up and stared at him thunderstruck. "Nadia," he said then, softly and with deep shame. And then again, stammeringly, "Nadia!"

He went to the window and threw it open. The cool, ozone-filled air, cleansed by the storm, poured in. And with it, across the roofs, came a deep humming sound.

"What's that?" He smoothed down his hair. "Is it six already? Is that the bell of Notre-Dame?"

"I'm freezing! Do shut the window! What on earth are you trying to see?"

"If he is coming. I want to see if he is coming. The edges of the clouds are catching fire everywhere, as if to receive him."

"Who do you think is coming? You mad apache!"

"Who?" He turned to her. "Who else but HE? He who is calling us to get up out of bed at last! And rub the sleep out of our eyes!"

Under the bed, her dog moved all four feet, running in a dream.

"Little one!" He came back to her slowly while the bell boomed on, sat down on the bed, and took her moist hand. "We two could form a first cell here—I mean, here in our will and our blood! A beginning, a new movement! Do you understand? Listen: A countermovement—against the Brown House croaker of Munich. For what he could accomplish for evil, we two could accomplish for good. Eh?"

"You idiot! And it was so wonderful just now! Why don't you kiss me? Why do you suppose I opened your handcuffs?" And with all her strength she tried to draw him down beside her. But he pushed her off. Her head struck hard against the back of the bed.

"Oh! Hurt yourself?" He bent over her, shocked. As she did not answer he found a bottle of cologne on her dressing table and doused her temples.

She wound a strand of her hair around her finger and tugged at it. "Mais oui! Yours is blond. Mine is black. Et voilà! that's the only difference. But that's no reason for you to want to make me cold!"

Suddenly she sat up, stared at him out of her pale face, and hissed, "Get out! I hate you!" She stamped at him. But immediately she pulled him back again. "Darling, darling! Écoutez: A blond like you came into my aunt's room in Duisburg once. And do you know what Aunt Rosi did? She smashed the chamberpot over his murderous skull. Hélas!" She looked around the room, exhausted. "Unfortunately, I

138

haven't anything here but extremely precious vases.—Get out! Get out!" And she flew at him with her fists.

The telephone rang. She lay back, her mouth wide open, and sobbed. Finally she reluctantly took up the receiver and said tonelessly, "Hello? Quoi? Mais non!" She sat up. "Trouhanova? Une Russe? Quoi—assassinée? Mais c'est terrible! In which park? Mais c'est effrayant!" The receiver dropped from her hand.

Uhle meanwhile had gone to the door.

"Excusez!" She stared at him . . . and hesitated. "It was the Duke."

Uhle left the room without answering. Quickly she called into the mouthpiece, "Hello, Duke? Still there? Come here this instant! Why? Don't ask. But hurry! Hurry!" And then she hung up. She slipped cautiously to the open door and peered out. Uhle was just opening the apartment door downstairs. He heard her.

"Nadia." He waved to her. And then, in a completely different tone. "We're not afraid any more, are we? Quiet, are you? I'm leaving you alone now. Yes—I'm going. But I know this: ·

> One day shall evil pass away
> And good shall triumph on that day.

So we're not afraid any more! Quiet, aren't you?"

She listened breathlessly until his steps had stopped sounding on the house stairs. Then she glided downstairs, put on the heavy door-chain, and remained for a long time leaning against the bookshelves, breathing slowly and heavily. After a while she made her way to the kitchen, and dropped onto a stool. Her legs were trembling. Lost in thought, she opened a can of sardines, forked one out of the oil, and ate it.

Suddenly she dashed back to the apartment door, took off the chain, and shouted down the stairs—

"Hello! . . . Hello! . . . Hello!"

But Uhle was long since gone.

CHAPTER TWELVE "PLAGUE AND ARYANS! WHAT HAVE I DONE TO OFFEND YOU?" THE RUSSIAN WHO HAD BEEN TRYING TO waylay the young blond ever since their encounter in the washroom, had now caught up with him a couple of street-lamps from the Wailing-Wall café. "Stop, young fellow!" He caught hold of his wind-breaker. "What are you running away for? Calm down! Just because I took the liberty of asking you the whereabouts of certain secret Obersalzberg papers—you feel offended? Boy," the Russian muttered, "you must know something! Or else why did you lock yourself in the toilet a while back? Heh? You can't pull the wool over my eyes!"

"Stop your gassing!" The other gave him a dig in the ribs, at the same time winking broadly. Schleich looked around.

"Is someone following us? Plague and the police! What does that gendarme want to tail us all over the place for? Stand still, young fellow! Let him be on his way! . . . Well . . . well! The way he looked at you!"

"What do you mean, looked at me? Nix! He was looking at *you!* Damn it! he's stopping again!"

"Then we'll stay right where we are!" Out of the corner of his eye Schleich watched the gendarme sauntering down the street, his truncheon swinging, until, coming to a halt, he lowered the rubber hood from his visored cap, for meanwhile it had stopped storming. Here and there the sky was brightening through broken clouds.

"Stay here!" The Red Singer tugged at the hatless man's sleeve. "I've nothing to do with the police! Why are you so suspicious? I've already shown you my American passport! Isn't that enough?"

"Mister, you're simply priceless!" The blond continued on his way until, stopping before one of several antique shops, he turned and winked gaily at Schleich. "Well! so you're from Chicago! A Yankee, eh? Yes, once upon a time I even thought myself of joining the Indians! Well, who knows? Who can tell how things will turn out?" He was glowering at the window display, in which a confused pile of decorations, medals, and orders of all countries, their shining metal disks attached to gaily colored silk ribbons, was exposed for sale. "Look at those decorations! Ha-ha! Yes, Mister—whoever's got money can buy what he likes! Ha-ha! See that! A hat of the great Napoleon's! Says 'authentic' under it! Gorgeous! Ha-ha! You have to admit it's a good-sized hat. But in spite of all that, the Emperor of the French didn't finally succeed in cramming all the nations under his lid! Ha-ha! . . . Yes! You—Yankee!" He poked the Russian in the belly. "There's only one man in all the world who can get away with that!"

"Young fellow," Schleich scolded, "do you really mean to say you believe the world should all be clapped under one single man's lid?"

"Oh, I forgot—you're from the Land of the Free. A Brutus—eh? With the plaster-of-Paris Statue of Liberty in New York Harbor?

Ha-ha!"

"There's one thing you can be sure of: if such a Caesar should arise, I'd batter his ugly mug in!"

"You don't mean it?" The young Scout laughed aloud and then fell to brooding. "But God damn it, mister—what happens when you've done away with Caesar? What's left then? Of course, for the noble Brutus there still remained such a thing as 'Freedom'! Ha-ha! . . . But what would be left for somebody like me if the Führer were knocked off? 'Liberalism'? 'Humanity'? Or 'Democracy'? Ha-ha! No, mister! Nihil! Nichts! Absolutely nothing!"

"Nothing? Nothing? Ha! . . . Plague and the bankers! There's always one thing left—and that is money! The dollar, boy! Listen!" The Russian chewed on his cigar. "I'm ready to do you a good turn! Plague and luck! It's your good luck that you ran into me!"

"Well, well, well!"

"I mean it. You're at the parting of the ways! Won't be so long now and there'll be only cats and rats slinking through the streets of Europe! So it's high time you made up your mind! . . . I tell you confidentially that, after 1945, anybody like you that calls himself a blond, Nordic German, won't be allowed on the streets off the leash or without a muzzle! You take it from me! I know what I'm talking about! Washington is simply going to deprive all you blondlings of any human rights whatsoever!"

" 'Human rights'? 'The rights of man'! Ha-ha! You certainly are an inveterate Yankee!"

"Plague and the White House! I know what I'm talking about. There is, of course, one way out, and that is: take your suitcase and skedaddle to the New World! That is, provided you've got what it takes in your pocket! . . . Big Boy!"—he breathed into his neck—"you can't have too many dollars in your pocket when the deluge comes! And the Supreme Court is not going to fool around with you! So, hop to it! Tell me once and for all: where is your Caesar's stolen will? What I'm driving at is this." He winked. "I'm a great autograph collector. And if you put a good thing in my way, of course it goes without saying I'll pay you the usual ten per cent. Hm? So where is it?"

He opened his alligator-leather billfold and ruffled the thick wad of notes. "Here's your chance! Go to it! Grab hold of Fortune while you can! You see I'm not joking. I can pay! And afterwards, like the Jew Columbus, you can sail west to the Land of the Dollar! . . . It's not going to be very cozy for you Scouts around here in the Old World!

Ha-ha! You cute Gestapo boys have been living on the fat of the land for the last ten years! You've been having the time of your lives! It's been one long glorious orgy of human blood! You gluttons!" He gave the blond a light tap on the cheek. "And of course for *that* pleasure you must naturally pay the penalty! And soon! On the other hand—if you manage to get away to America first—well, then, you are beyond reach! . . . So now, where are the documents? As I said, for an authentic manuscript in the handwriting of Adolphus Magnus I am ready to pay on the nail! Ha-ha! . . . And with your commission you can build yourself a bungalow out there on the sunny hills of Los Angeles, like all the others, with a panorama of the whole Pacific Ocean! You can settle down and write your memoirs. 'The Facts about'—you know what! Ha-ha! The Book of the Month Club is waiting for you! Dollars, dollars, boy! Ha-ha! You'll have Negro boys in white patent-leather gloves to serve you Madeira before dinner, and Chinese boys to bring you coffee after dinner. While, over here in Europe, they'll be serving your blond Party Comrades something quite different! Sudden death! A few thousand hangings! That will be the mildest you'll get! Yes, I heard a Jew say that they're planning to sterilize the whole German nation."

"Mister!" The blond fixed the Russian with expressionless eyes. "How much would you be willing—if the occasion arises—to pay per page . . . cold cash?"

"What's that? Well, of course we'd have to discuss that! Business is business . . . But not here in the middle of the street! Let's get going. Come along with me. There's a quiet corner in the Ritz Bar where we can talk undisturbed."

"Not so fast! Not so fast! Don't rush me like that! Damn it, what's the idea, Big Shot? You've got the cart before the horse! Understand? You certainly are a Yankee—the way you do things! But you're all wrong if you think a seasoned Storm Trooper like me is going to stand here and listen to a capitalist like you!" He walked on. But at the next corner he turned round again. "One thing more, mister! you've got another guess coming if you think that in 1945 we blonds'll be the ones to wear muzzles! No, mister! It's not we blonds who're going to build canals and dams and fortress walls criss-cross around the globe! No, mister! It'll be somebody else altogether! And it'll be a sad day for the mother's son of you that says: 'I can't go on'! No! No dog muzzles for *us!* . . . And you can put this in your pipe and smoke it, Mr. Yankee: Before that happens to us, the whole damn world will have been blown to pieces. Ha-ha!"

142

With a broad laugh, he left Schleich and crossed the street. Non-plused, Schleich watched him go. The next instant he dashed after him. But the pitiful yelping of a small dog that had been run over stopped him. Out of nowhere a crowd gathered. In the thick of it, the Red Singer lost sight of his blond. Gendarmes appeared and began to disperse the crowd.

"Mais circulez! . . . Circulez donc!"

As the crowd broke up, a soldier was seen stooping over the terrier, from whose mouth a thin trickle of blood was dripping.

"Mais circulez!" a policeman urged at Schleich's elbow. But the Russian stood staring at the soldier's red cape, and began to talk to the policeman.

"Plague and the army! Who is that Good Samaritan? He stands there among the others like a soldier on leave with an indecipherable ticket. Look at him—taking the dog in his arms! and wandering off toward the Seine! Is that what he's doing? Sergeant! Plague and the Kremlin! What district does that bearded saint come from? Go on—why don't you arrest that anemic Czar?" The shock of this second meeting with the soldier whom he had seen earlier in the Wailing-Wall café, seemed to bewilder Schleich's thoughts completely, for he babbled on:

"I'll have the exorcized Pope in Mantua wash my feet in his full regalia. I'll make him braid together the pigtails of all the kulaks, magicians, and astrologers at midnight in the middle of the Caspian Sea, before I'll let that imbecile Nicholas, shot dead by our brave revolutionaries, go wandering around this way, through the streets of the Jacobins!"

He took a fresh Havana from his vest pocket and tried to bite off the tip. But his teeth were chattering so uncontrollably that he found it impossible. Instead, he fished inside his coat, and produced a dagger, with which he cut his cigar.

"Tiens! Tiens!" One of the gendarmes raised his eyebrows. "A dagger? Vous permettez?" He took the blade from the Russian and tried the edge.

"Plague and the Cheka!" Schleich nodded. "General! I warn you . . . look out for that dead man. . . ."

"Et alors, Monsieur? Here on the blade . . . there is blood!"

"And how! And good red blood it is! It's human blood, that's why! I just bit my tongue again! B-b-b-lo-ood!" He stumbled over the syllable. His face turned purple, his upper lip twisted out of shape. The gendarme wrapped Schleich's dagger in a piece of paper. Then, having looked the Russian over from head to foot, he said:

"Vos papiers!"

"Plague and my tongue! . . . The Russian kept wiping off his lips and staring at the blood on his handkerchief. "After all, I can't discuss the higher metaphysics of the proletariat with a notorious corpse! . . . These chilly ignoramuses still think that the seat of the brain is the head! Yes, Sergeant, the white pack of them still doesn't know that the hurricane is going to descend from the Caucasus!"

"Nom de Dieu!" An elderly lady dodged aside as Schleich clutched at her. "The poor wretch must be out of his mind!"

"Pardon, where was I?" Schleich goggled, unconscious of the general laughter. "Only a bunch of kulaks like you would ever contend that . . . the End of the World had been postponed . . ."

At this juncture a car drew up alongside. Her fox fur wrapped about her, Hyacinthe, whose flaming red hair had attracted attention at the Wailing-Wall café, sat at the wheel. Catching sight of her the Red Singer opened his eyes wide. Then he dashed forward:

"Well! How do you do? Delighted to see you—delighted! Yes, it's always the same thing: blood—blood—blood! I've gone and bitten my tongue again! Had too many shocks recently, sweet. Too dreadful shocks! And the whole time I eat nothing but lemons and mirabel plums! . . ." He got into the car.

"Excusez, Madame!" the gendarme insisted. "This gentleman must first come along with me to the police station."

"Forward!" Slamming the door of the car, Schleich yelled: "What's got into you, Governor? Keep your hands off me! Let go! Power is the symbol of existence! Capito? . . . And, furthermore, I know the dungeons of Moscow! . . . Drive on, Madame!" Offering the gendarme a cigar, he winked at Hyacinthe. "Don't make so much fuss, General! The fact is, I have to accompany this pale, red-headed Messalina out to the cemetery. Vous comprenez?"

"Arrêtez! Stop!" Gesticulating, the gendarme tried to force him out of the car, but at that instant Hyacinthe let out the clutch and drove off.

Having covered some distance in silence, Hyacinthe was arrested by Schleich's outcry:

"Wait! Stop!" She brought the car to a standstill. Staring over her shoulder, Schleich murmured: "Pardon! I simply can't make out—what has suddenly become of the whole earth!—including the 7th Tank Division! Chauffeur, mean to say Madame, don't you notice how it's dripping from the sun? Eberlein, is that the newly discovered red star—one hundred times as big as the well-known sun! . . . Allez!

What are you stopping here for? Haven't got a moment to lose!"

Suddenly, without her being aware of it, he gave himself a hypodermic. The effect was instantaneous. He sat up straight, his features assuming their normal cast. "There!" He handed Hyacinthe an address. "Drive to 123, Quai de Seine."

She wrapped the fur more closely around her, and drove on, finally bringing the car to a stop before a corner house near one of the smaller Seine bridges.

"Is this 123? Bon! Here we are! Plague and Gutenberg! This is the office of the refugees' paper, 'Postwar.' Ha-ha! These intellectual Jews are all convinced that the whole world is going to be Americanized— including Asia! Plague and Stalin! Here's where I've got to hand out some more money!" He got out. "We'll need at least two or three more wars, before all the kulaks are killed off." He dashed into the building and on to the elevator. As she entered and stood alongside him, he removed his beret.

"What floor, young lady?" She pushed back a lock of hair from her forehead, looked straight at him, and, drawing a deep breath, asked, "Don't you recognize me?"

"Pardon! Of course, of course! Didn't you manicure me at the hotel the other day? Or where did we meet? Tell me, angel, would you have a little time for me this afternoon again? But, first, I have to go up to the fourth floor—"

"You don't remember me any more? Your 'petite amie' in the straw hat with the plaid ribbon?" The little elevator carried them up; she laid her hand gently on his arm. "And Vienna? Don't you remember Vienna?"

The elevator came to a halt. Schleich ran down the corridor to the publisher's office. Through the glass doors, several dusty and grimy rooms, filled with editors, were visible.

"Your Excellency!" Eberlein came timidly to greet him. "Tee-hee! Are you here already?"

"Plague and the workers! Is everything humming?"

"Tee-hee! . . . Everything's just fine!"

"How many proletarians have struck?"

"So far, about three thousand railroad workers have started on the march!"

"Is that all?" He shouldered Eberlein aside and barged on into the next room, apparently taking for granted Hyacinthe's following at his heels. He even gallantly offered her a swivel chair. Then he threw open a window between the rooms and shouted:

145

"Hello! Eberlein! Have you found a standard-bearer? Anybody to carry my scarecrow? Who's going to carry the wooden crucifix along when we start?"

"A butcher's boy. He's volunteered, Comrade Schleich!"

At the sound of a cannon shot in the distance, he slammed down the window, cowering. Eberlein stuck his head through the door.

"That's the artillery, already, Your Excellency! Tee-hee! . . . They're shouting extras in the streets!"

"Extras?" The Russian rose. "Plague and Paris! Mean to say they're at it already?"

"War is the father of all things, Your Excellency!"

"Right, Eberlein. But the Revolution, Eberlein, is the mother of all things!" He grinned at Hyacinthe. "And I always tell my proletarians in every barracks and cadet corps: 'Study your chemistry! But only just enough to know how to make powder and saltpeter for the final rounds with all these bloody kulaks!' Hop to it, Eberlein! What are you giggling around here about? . . . Go on! Get yourself up to the assembly point in Montparnasse! Hey, got some coffee for me? I need coffee! Go on, Eberlein! I'm coming right along!"

Relighting his cigar, which had gone out, he smirked comfortably.

"Yes indeed, young woman, Vienna is a delicious spot! Women like alabaster! Though I never have understood why your Waltz King should have christened the Danube 'Blue'! Or was he always drunk? Ha-ha!"

A stenographer brought in a cup of steaming coffee. Schleich took it greedily, gulped it down, and smacked his lips. As soon as the door had closed, he went on:

"Dearie"—he turned to Hyacinthe—"you've certainly become more beautiful! You smell like a Siberian mare. Of course, I recognized you at once. It goes without saying! Bu-u-ut, obviously—" He stroked her glove. "Listen! You could do me a tremendous favor! Hm? We'll leave everything personal until later! Are you free? Can you have dinner with me this evening? Hm? Ha-ha!"

Without further warning, Hyacinthe sprang to her feet, trembling in every limb, snatched a lamp from the desk and began hammering Schleich with it as if she had lost her senses.

"You monster! You've messed up my entire life!"

The Red Singer took refuge in the next room, Hyacinthe pursuing him. Wedged curiously in the doorway, the office force heard now Schleich's yells, now Hyacinthe's screams. Eberlein, who was just leaving, came back, blushing crimson. He had just rushed to the tele-

146

phone, believing his Chief had suffered an attack of insanity, when Schleich re-entered. Seating himself at the desk, he stuck out his tongue at the terrified office force, and then, with a tired gesture, motioned to them to leave the room.

As soon as he was alone, Hyacinthe appeared again too, sat down in the swivel chair and began rocking back and forth. Her laughter broke the silence.

"Go ahead and sleep with the whole damn world! That doesn't cancel out the fact that you belong to me!—I have never stopped adoring you. Never, you monster, never! I adore you beyond anything! Because—no matter what—your voice is a direct gift from God!"

Schleich leaned against the blue-baize covered door and wiped his brow with the back of his hand.

"As I was saying, I lost him in the crowd! The damned Hitlerite mongrel! But he's sure to be waiting in the Ritz—he sees money in it. But I've got to go along now and steer this demonstration in the right direction—so you would be doing me a very special favor if you'd just run along, as you are, to the Ritz Bar in my place. Will you? He has flax-blond hair. Wait for me there and keep your eyes peeled. Just make up to him a bit. Coax him into having a few cocktails—and keep him there until I arrive. The fool has got wind of a certain secret document—the significance of which I'm sorry I cannot reveal to such a beautiful angel as yourself! I can only tell you this: I've got to have that document! Listen!" He became confidential. "I've simply got to find out if this occidental junta of kulaks in Wall Street and the Bank of England have already concluded ninety-nine-year treaties against the East with this ABC-dolf in Berchtesgaden—or whether the East has got to open an account in Wall Street!" He pinched Hyacinthe and ran through the editorial rooms to the elevator.

"Hello! Comrade Schleich!" Münzer came out of the office with Smirnow and dragged him back again. "You had no time for me at the Gare de l'Est."

"Plague and impertinence! . . . I have no time for you now either!"

"Then steal the time! Comrade Schleich . . . Sit down . . . I am just back from Turkey.

"The Shah of Persia has good wool to be shorn, but not I! So let me out. Plague and the proletariat!"

"Comrade Schleich! We anti-Stalinists trust you."

"Très honoré, coquin! Très honoré!"

"You have made Eberlein head of today's workers' demonstration?"

"Comrade—are you Lenin that I must answer you? Clear the road! Or there'll be an August Revolution around here! Out of my way, Comrade! Even if you have just come back from Turkey, that's no reason for you to play grand vizier! Right?"

"You want to assemble the steelworkers of Paris for an anti-war demonstration. You want to prevent the proletariat from revolting against Hitler and Fascism, Comrade Schleich. I repeat, we trust you. And if Comrade Stalin drinks whiskey with Herr von Ribbentrop in the Kremlin, or if Comrade Molotov has tea with the Führer—well then, Communism stinks."

"You stink—you stupid! Let the leaders of this world meet wherever they want to—in Iraq, or for a tête-à-tête with the Sphinx! . . . What business is that of yours, you German ox?" He was red with anger.

"Comrade Schleich, I drudged for the great Lenin."

"You're a Trotzkyite!" Schleich yelled. "Out of my way, trouble-maker! Your brain doesn't reach any further than from Nuremberg to Fürth. Let go of my sleeve!"

"Comrade Schleich, in the name of all decent communists, I beg you to give up this anti-war demonstration, which can only further the ends of the betrayer of the workers, Schickelgruber."

"Give it up!" Schleich threw his hat between the typewriters. "Herr Münzer!" He chewed on his cigar. "I know you're an idealist and that you have no idea what reality is like, so don't try to hold back the flood, or there'll be trouble! Your native village might have been painted by Dürer or Breughel. You may know how to slaughter a sow in the fall and drink its blood hot. But that doesn't teach you anything. Plague and Moscow! You German communists all lack the will to power; you did not crave power. Otherwise you wouldn't be refugees, sitting around here doing nothing. You didn't have the guts, the guts, the guts—" he whipped the word into Münzer's face. "You're not democrats. And you're not Bolsheviks. You're . . . yes-men. All you can do is obey. You can't move until you hear a word of command. You lack the Red drive. The sow has more red blood under her fat than you have, Comrade Münzer! And now I give you a word of command. Get out of my way—I'm taking the elevator!"

Münzer grew purple in the face and taking a broad posture, he said threateningly, although at first shaking: "Comrade, you have just insulted the German communists. Allow me to reply to that."

"Do you want to fight a duel with me, you old bourgeois?"

"The German oxen—as you call them, Comrade Schleich—were in

1527—that is, 250 years before the French Revolution and 400 years before the Russian—the first proletarians! Workers! Soldiers and Peasants! who fought against their oppressors and for their rights, with scythes, clubs, and pitchforks. Comrade Schleich, those German oxen from the Odenwald, the Harz, Allgäu, the Tyrol hunted the knights and junkers out of their castles on August 18, 1525. Those German oxen hunted down Count Helfenstein with their pikes. Those German yes-men didn't wait for any word of command when they drove the high and mighty daughter of the Emperor Maximilian to Heilbronn in a dung cart—and set 292 noblemen on fire for torches to light the procession—"

"Shut up!" Schleich threw a paperweight at him. "Or are you going to start preaching theocratic communism all over again?"

"Comrade Schleich! Without any word of command, those German oxen started the greatest of mass movements, the most dangerous of revolutions, for the proletarians of all future time. And paid for Protestant freedom and the equality of all men in the eyes of God— not with the blood of a slaughtered sow, Comrade Schleich! No! With their German proletarian blood they—"

"Out of my way! Get out of my way!"

"Or who was it, four hundred years before your 'points' and 'programs', on whose German peasant banner was written, 'No discrimination between rich and poor'? Who was it who threw the words 'Common Ownership of Goods' into the powder keg like a torch? Who else, but the German revolutionary peasantry! Comrade Schleich! 'Freedom of the woods! Freedom of lakes and streams! Freedom to fish!'—Who brought that about? Who abolished the flax monopoly? And did away with tithes on cattle? Who, who, who?— Comrade Schleich, these German oxen here are going to stop your demonstration *for* Fascism!" Coughing with excitement, he ran to the elevator and went down.

"Damned kulak!" Schleich spat after him. "Damned Trotskyite, damned German ox"—and then he let Hyacinthe, who had come out when she heard them quarreling and had stood all through it protectingly behind him, lead him back to the small office. He sat down and, glaring ahead of him, drank the cold coffee she offered him. Then he lit a cigar and puffed like a locomotive.

Hyacinthe slowly took off her left glove, hooked the fastener of her fur collar and, looking steadily at Schleich, whispered:

"Man . . . And what about your singing? In God's name, what do you care about all this insane game of politics and rivalry of nations?

You—to whom God has given such a voice! Oh, Schleich! Tell me who ever seduced you into this Hell's kitchen? What woman was it? What infamous woman?!"

"Do be on your way, dearie." He interrupted her and stood up. "It's getting late! Get yourself downstairs as quick as you can, and drive to the Ritz Bar. The fellow is wearing a wind-breaker. Off with you!"

"And—what about your favorite role? What has happened to our opera 'King Agarthi'? That was the title role. You said you wanted to sing that role—where King Agarthi—where the King of all souls ascends from the underground kingdom where he was imprisoned so long—and then, at last—at last, the Reign of Goodness begins . . . !" Tears ran down her cheeks. "Oh, I simply can't bear it any more! We're starving—all of us—for Goodness! Darling, tell me—why don't you sing it with that divine voice of yours? . . ." She let him go and, to hide her emotion, went to the window.

Down on the quai along the Seine, still stood—the soldier. Before him on the broad stone parapet lay the little terrier, to which life seemed to be returning under his hands. For a moment the breeze soughed in the tall plane trees along the river bank and then again silence fell on the Seine. Behind the blue silhouette of Notre Dame, the dull disk of the autumn sun sank steadily, its rays shimmering on the soldier's red cape and on the swirling, muddy waters of the yellow stream.

When Hyacinthe turned round again she saw—instead of Schleich —two gendarmes in the room.

BOOK THREE

CHAPTER ONE   **U**HLE, ACCOMPANIED BY MATHIAS
WESTERMANN, ENTERED THE LEFTHAND PORTAL OF NOTRE DAME. AS HE
had passed the violinmaker's door on the way down from Nadia's
apartment, Westermann, on the pretext that he must go to inspect the
organ in Notre Dame, had joined him. The leather-quilt door swung to
behind them, and they stood still. The darkness inside the cathedral
came on them so suddenly that they had to grope their way for the
first few steps. At the font, the violin-maker dipped his whole hand
into the water, touching his forehead and making the sign of the Cross.

Two nuns, who had been kneeling on the folds of their heavy
habits, rose ceremoniously, each holding out an alms bag toward them.
Westermann dropped in a coin and smiled at the nun's soft word of
thanks. A beadle in felt slippers had seen him give the alms; he
twirled a brush in the holy water, sprinkled the violin-maker—and
held out his hand until Westermann gave him a few sous too. The
church was almost empty. A service seemed to be going on at the
rear, to the right of the high altar. Now and then, they could hear
the echoing mutter of a priest's voice. There was a smell of mold
in the air.

"Well—" Standing beside Uhle, Westermann looked into the arched
dome above their heads, well over a hundred feet high—"we seem to
have got back into a forest again! Right? Not a forest of trees, but
a forest of stone! Right? How still it is! From here back to the apse
it is 410 feet. I've paced it myself. And the cathedral is 150 feet wide.
There are seventy-five pillars, see how they stand, round and slender!
They remind me of old beech trees." From somewhere out of the
dusk of the side chapels, a boy's voice soared and became distinct:

"Eterna madre:
madre mia
madre cara
madre dolcissima . . ."

" 'Madre dolcissima . . .' " Westermann repeated in a deep bass, "that sounds better than 'Heil Hitler'! Right? 'Eterna madre . . .' " He looked up at the windows through which the late afternoon light threw all the colors of the rainbow. "Would you like to come up to the organ with me? Or do you want to pray? Those were the good old days when men still prayed before they went to work! Right? If you'd grown up in Strassburg as I did, Gothic would mean something to you! . . . Right? My minster! 'Madre Mia'. Out of the plains of Europe, the spires of minsters and cathedrals, sheer and perfect, flamed up to the Creator! In Ulm . . . in Laon . . . in Cologne . . . in Dijon, Freiburg, and Milan! . . . The world forgotten in infinity! Right? Those were the days of the burghers! They were strong men then—right? Lübeck. Danzig. Nuremberg. Burghers! Bourgeois!—It was no insult then, but a proud title. And today those brown termites want to make it an insult! Dürer . . . Bach . . . Cranach . . . Holbein . . . Van der Goes! And the Master of Bamberg! Right? That was a supernational Christian art! Right? And they managed without any League of Nations or Hague Court! As various as a forest—and yet all aspiring to one common goal: Eternal Madre! Amor deae immensis! Yes, mon cher! And what is the goal today?"

Uhle expelled a deep breath. The violin-maker pressed his arm. "Well, my friend! I must get up to my organ now. What shall I play? The Requiem? Or would you rather hear Schubert? Or the Appassionata? Yes, the German genius! 'Be embraced, ye millions! This kiss to the whole world! . . .' Not the same thing as: 'You can be strangled and butchered by the millions and be damned.' Right? When I sit up there before those keys, I say to myself: 'Mathias Westermann, play well! Eternity is spinning its circle above you' " . . . With rapid tread he disappeared behind the columns.

Uhle stood there, forlorn. Not until he heard the grating of stools and benches in the organ loft and several long-drawn-out tones from the pipes, did he look about him. He crossed over to the other side. But as he did not see the dancer anywhere, he sat down to wait. "Eternity is spinning its circle above you!" He remembered Westermann's words and bowed his head. The violin-maker was trying out the organ, picking tones at random, running from a thundering crash to an abrupt squeak, as if a brake were too swiftly applied. Then silence again.

Uhle hitched his collar up to his ears and slid along the bench, because he seemed to feel a draft from a door suddenly opened. Then he became aware of something: a red cloak billowed in many folds against the gray background of the church wall. He sat erect, hiding his eyes in his arm. A chill ran over him. Slowly he went nearer, dazed and surprised, whispering: "Is it you? You? My Little Jew Jesus? . . . You . . ." Suddenly he slid to his knees. He clutched the folds—which were growing a deeper and deeper red, and wrapped them—"You! You!"—around him. A naked soul . . . freezing.

Such loneliness!

He crouched on the cold flagstones, his whole being immersed in the burning evening light. Before his eyes there swam a purple radiance, as if the crystalline All had become a single warmth!—green, azure-blue, and orange seas! A heavenly-sweet fire, where all thinking ceased, all happiness began!

At length, almost blinded by the brightness, he turned his head away. For the first time he saw that his hands were only clutching the curtain of a confessional. The dying sun, shining through the red armor of the Archangel in the stained-glass window of the Virgin, had turned the dark-green material into a glowing mass of red fire. And now that light was gone.

He stood up, pushed the curtain aside. The confessional was empty. Exhausted, he sank down in it. Staring into the darkness, he murmured:

"What could it have been? A vision? How could I have seen your pale, wonderful face? They say that the cortex of the brain is the instrument of the spirit. Oh, inscrutable substance contained in the skull! Under the microscope a slice of the brain is like a tremendous forest! Each nerve a great tree with a taproot! And every time a thought stirs in the brain there is agitation, like a wind blowing through all the twigs and branches that are its nerves. . . . Like Mathias Westermann in his forest I stray among the tree trunks and branches of the brain! Am I, too, listening with my tuning fork for the right tone? Trying to find the place where I can hear the highest vibration of my own substance?" He clasped his hands.

"You Unknown Soldier of Verdun! Were you trying to establish communication with me? Have you come from the deep realm of those to whom—crumpled over a bombed flower pot—or a sewing machine—you came—in the Dead Sea of their lives—and showed them the way out of their misery—and under Your hand, the torn wings of their souls were healed, and spread again? Have you come from all those unknown men who, under the high, still moon of No Man's Land—or wherever they lay—propped themselves up once more on their cartridge cases and—out of that pitiless infinity—their eyes already glazed—cried out their faith in you—over the battle-field—and up, up to your all-embracing memory of every smallest, unknown, unseen 'good deed'—before they fell back—faithful unto death—a bundle of torn bloody rags, like all the others?

"Was it you who came to me just now? Can it really be that you have seen some cell in my brain worthy to vibrate in response to you?

"Oh, then blow everything else, corrupt with decay, out of my being! And if my brain does not give out your light, then toss my head like a rattling burnt-out bulb onto the refuse-heap. Or push it aside if, in the morning when I shave, instead of the Azure Evidence of your eyes, a diseased vanity is reflected back from the quicksilver surface of my mirror.

"Oh! Erich my beloved brother! And you, Werner, my comrade! And you, Vopelius! All of you there under the grass: I say to you: Rather slay me, if you can no longer evoke in me the sound of eternity—lest your eternal silence give that false Unknown Soldier, that flayer of mankind Adolf Hitler, still longer leave to doubt that *you are alive!* That it is not you who are the phantoms, you Unknown Soldiers!—but he!"

Uhle heard the heavy tread of feet on the flagstones. Two men were coming from the sacristy, stopping now and then in conversation. One spoke in a whisper, the other in ordinary tones. Uhle recognized the antiquarian, Laroche—his coarse face was wrinkled with anxiety. The grinning man beside him was the red-bearded Swiss. He pushed back his bicorne, trimmed with black ostrich feathers, tucked the stick with its alms bag under his left arm, and swinging his halberd in the other hand like a walking stick, clattered on over the flags in his buckled shoes.

They stopped in front of the confessional. As Uhle remained hidden in the shadow of a double column, the beadle apparently suspected the presence of no one in the yawning emptiness of the church. He propped his halberd up against a life-size bronze statue of a poilu, squeezed into a pew, and fished out of the skirt pocket of his laced livery a small plate onto which he poured the contents of the alms bag.

He began to count eagerly: "Un sou—deux sous— You know what I told you before you went to ask His Reverence for His expert counsel? What consolation did he give you in regard to the plunder-ing of your shop—and the loss of the Christ of the Trenches?"

"Rien.—Et alors?"

"Did His Reverence give you any money?"

154

"Rien."

"Rien? Was that all the consolation you got? You're a faithful Catholic, my son. His Reverence must certainly have given you some hope."

"Rien! Rien! Rien!"

"Aha! My son! You mean to say that His Reverence did not at least hold out to you the prospect of God's meting out every possible punishment at the Last Judgment to the bolshevik thieves who stole your Christ of the Trenches?"

"Mais oui. Évidemment!"

"Surely, His Reverence promised you that you would get back your Christ of the Trenches! He is a benevolent, kind-hearted man!" He went on counting. "My son, we've known each other for many years now. You know I've done what I could: I've managed to smuggle out to you from our trash here, Gothic velvets, worm-eaten candlesticks. And even a patten from the time of Pepin the Less. Yes. But what was I telling you only last week? 'My son,' I said, 'don't go on hoping for too much from relics dating from the Night of the Long Knives! . . . We no longer live in those glorious days when an honest Swiss would sometimes find a gold sou in the alms bag! When a Swiss could manage a bottle of wine out of Peter's Pence!' I said to you, 'Don't go on being a junk dealer! You must become a dealer only in new and worth-while things! Instead of that worm-eaten Christ, display the headgear of Adolf the Great in your shop window! Then you'll see something! Instead of Gothic velvets, display a pair of Adolf the Great's brown breeches in your show window!—then you'll see something!' "

"Tais-toi! Are you a Frenchman—or a swine?"

"I? My son, I am Xaver Grün—since 1920 the Swiss of Notre Dame. Do you think that priests or bishops or exalted spiritual rulers would entrust a halberd like this to a 'swine'? Such a plumed hat? Such silver buttons, with the illustrious coat-of-arms of the Cardinal of Paris, sewed on my coat? 'Quot Deus bene vostat', as His Reverence loves to say . . . Chin up, my son! Why be blind? Why do we say 'God'? Because we think God will help us. Isn't that so? Because we believe God is God! But what if God should turn out to be, not God —but just a topic for discussion—nothing but a subject for a sermon? . . ." He suddenly raised his voice—"Ave Maria!"—and made the sign of the Cross for the benefit of a passing nun.

He raised his head as the rustle of her robes died away. "Suppose, for instance, that Christ there above the pulpit should say to one of the members of His Party: 'What is the greatest, most wonderful, most glorious thing you can do—something never done before—for the Party of Christianity?' What happens then? . . . sixteen sous in the alms bag! Didn't I tell you the alms bag is the barometer of faith? . . . . But now, for instance, our Adolf—! You will soon see! I tell you, everything else is a swindle—nothing but bluff! Like the old story that the earth is round! Now, I always say, 'How could it be?' That's only a trick of your theologians to make fools of us. Just the same as when they say: 'The dead shall rise again!' They just want to make fools of us! They just do it to keep us down! . . . Do you see the tablet to Charles the Bold over there? Well, under that, a staircase leads down to the catacombs. I've often had to take Cook's-Tour people down there to visit the dead. And what do you see when you get down there? Corpses! Nothing but corpses! It's a safe guess, there are several hundred thousand, male and female! And all of them the most Christian-Christian corpses from the various centuries of this most Christian-Christian City of Paris! And what are they there for? Why, they were all victims of the plague—or of wars!

"Now, son, when I guide a party down there, and the first thing I have to do is drive away the bats with my flashlight because the damned beasts are hanging and clinging to the bones like leeches, and when I have to beat a path through the piled-up kings and bishops before I can get to a really interesting corpse, and there is no other resurrection of the dead except the mice that scatter and scamper up the walls into the topmost tower gallery . . . now I ask you, my son, what kind of resurrection of the dead do you call that? Ah—I see you begin to meditate! Yes, my son, scratch your brains and think a long time: Is there a God? Or isn't there a God? For one thing is indispensable: a Party Member in our day and generation can't get around that question! If there is a God—then Adolf the Great is a robber! A thief! A murderer! . . . But if there isn't any God—then Adolf is the greatest man in the history of our Church! . . . . Twenty sous . . . That's the take for today . . ."

He stuffed the small coins into his pocket. "Not even a bottle of white wine can I get with that! Twenty sous!!! And you expect me to believe in the resurrection of the dead? . . . My son, have you still got that pail of goose-fat behind the Henry IV cabinet in your shop?—In that case, I might as well have dinner with you this evening. Hm? I've a sort of feeling I ought to stay with you in your hour of misfortune . . . Yes! because despite the Disciple from Emmaus—Wall Street rules the world. The bloodsuckers!"

"La pauvre France! . . . to plunder my shop! . . . et alors? Is that civilization?" Laroche moaned. "Those dogs of the Front Populaire have stolen my Christ of the Trenches!"

"Courage, my son, courage!" Suddenly he was whispering. "A while ago I saw a detachment of police with a sergeant-major in command, ride up the rue de Lille to the German Embassy!" Xaver Grün pulled a memorandum out of his sleeve. "They say: *He* is in Paris!"

"Quoi? Who? Who?"

"Shhh!" The beadle peered about in all directions. "Nobody knows it! Only we Party Members! My son!" He slapped Laroche on the back. "I ask you: Would you like to see *him?* . . . He is your enemy—that's what His Reverence says every day as he puts on his stole. Entendu! But after all, isn't it Christianity that teaches us to love our enemies?" With grim humor, he picked up the alms bag and stood up . . . "Allez!" Pushing the antiquarian out of the pew, he retrieved his halberd and brought it down with a smart rap repeating: "Allez! Jews, Democrats, and Christians—the time will come when they'll all rot in the latrine!" Jamming on his bicorne, he grabbed Laroche under the arm and broke into: "Deux étions et n'avions qu'un cœur!", the tapping of his halberd gradually dying away in the distance.

The Uhlan rose to his feet, every muscle in his broad features firm and determined—shoulder to shoulder with the poilu cast in bronze—beside the granite pillar on which were cut the names of the dead in the First World War, and before which the poilu stood his timeless, endless watch.

CHAPTER TWO   "OLALA!"   WHISPERED THE DANCER'S VOICE AT HIS EAR—ITS INTONATION SOFT AND SUBTLE, IN ITS Slav way, expressive of every emotional nuance.

Uhle turned around.

She looked steadily at him out of her brown eyes—shaking the corkscrew curls that framed her face.

For a moment or two, he could not say a word. Seeing his discomfiture, she carried the candle that a nun had just sold her over to the Altar of the Madonna—to the marble statue venerated for centuries as 'Notre Dame de Paris'. On a table below the statue, the tiny flames of many votive lamps, rippled by imperceptible air currents, moved back and forth with a watery, wavelike motion. Olenka stuck her slender, burning taper in among a score of others standing on an iron plate. In the surrounding vases, there were bunches of dark autumn flowers. The yellowed, marble image of the Virgin, polished by the touch of countless pious hands, shone like alabaster. Above the statue hung a sky-blue baldachin studded with gold-embroidered stars, its heavy folds inlaid with dust.

Uhle had followed the girl and, when she knelt at the altar rail, he did likewise. For a long time they said no word, kneeling side by side. Her gloves and handbag lay on the straw-bottomed chair beside her. As if frozen in the gesture of wringing her hands, she held them before her lips, murmuring her prayers, her red-gold hair gleaming in the candlelight. Now and then, she looked up into the vaulting, and the irises of her eyes glistened like drops of dew in the cup of a lily.

"You're pale!" Uhle said.

"My dear! When I couldn't find you anywhere, I had such a strange feeling that one day I should be all alone in this cathedral. I would make a beautiful corpse . . . wouldn't I?" She looked anxiously into his eyes. The heavy waves of incense came and went. The candle wicks crackled faintly. Behind the chair, a woman's voice rose: "Madre di ogni grazie . . ." Olenka began to tell her rosary. Up in the gallery, Westermann commenced a fugue—the mighty organ tones rumbling through the twilight of the vaulting. Suddenly he stopped. The girl raised her head: "My knees hurt." She sat down and Uhle pulled a chair beside her. She was crumpling her gloves, nervously.

"Look!" She pointed to an inscription on the wall: 'Love is repaid by love.' . . . How beautiful! . . . But is it true?" She pressed Uhle's hand. "I've been looking for you everywhere. Olala! I was so afraid, so worried about you! Where have you been?"

"I—I was in the Bagatelle Park! But where were you?"

"Oh! Uhle—"

"What is it?—You look well—"

"Because you're looking at me. When you're not, I'm wretched—"

"What made you blush just now?"

"Because you stare at me so hard. The blood just rushes up . . . stop looking at me! No!" She pressed his arm—"Look at me. Tell me—were you really in the Bagatelle Park?"

158

"Yes, really. But where were you?"

"I? Olala! I went out so early this morning. The birds were still asleep. The wind was roaring in the branches. I found a grasshopper in the grass! I had no idea that grasshoppers grow so big! I couldn't stand it any longer in my little bedroom at my aunt's. Oh! You have no idea how much room just a little heart asks for! Fame? No! No! I have a horror of it now! And you, darling? Have you thought it over yet—" she laid both hands on his thigh—"tell me: do you love me? Then please say 'Tak, tak!' That means 'yes' in Polish."

A priest in vestments, carrying a monstrance, came out of one of the side chapels, preceded by an acolyte bearing the cross. As they vanished into the sacristy, Olenka was still looking questioningly at Uhle.

"Why won't you talk to me, darling? What are you thinking about? Hm? Oh, I want to know every thought you think! Every one of your thoughts—from the day you were born, on!"

Uhle started—as if the Angel of the Last Judgment had spoken to him.

"Every one of my thoughts," he repeated, "from the day I was born!" He stared at her. After a long pause he looked away from her brown eyes. And then asked, matter-of-factly:

"Where is your violin case?"

"Oh!" She leaned her head on his shoulder. "I don't want to know anything any more! Nothing but you! Only you!" Her eyes were lost in the candlelight before the Madonna.

Uhle took her hand. "I simply can't understand where you were this morning. I looked all around the lake for you. Did you go up the winding stairs into the grotto?"

"Dearest!" Her eyelids trembled. "When I went out into the meadow, to see if you were coming at last—there was a man standing there with a cap on and a black mask over half his face, and he shouted: 'Hands up!' I was terrified and ran and ran down the hill . . . he fired a shot at me. So I just threw the violin case into the high grass and ran and ran.—Olala! Uhle! Don't make me think about it any more—please! All I want to think about is you. Nothing but you!" And then she whispered imploringly, "Let's not talk about it any more. Promise me—will you?"

Uhle was going to answer—but the Swiss tapped his shoulder.

"Monsieur! Is your name Uhle?"

"Why?"

"Psssst!" He winked. "Somebody over there behind the pillar, son, wants to speak to you—" But the rest of the beadle's message was lost in the sudden, inharmonious counterpoint between a litany that had begun behind the high altar, and its echo in the vaults. Then a single voice broke through the alternating petitions of the choir:

"God, have mercy on us!"

"Christ, have mercy on us!"

"Christ, hear us!"

"Christ, Dispenser of Grace, hear us!"

"Holy Mary, hear us! . . . ."

"Pssst! Monsieur Uhle." The Swiss plucked his cape. "The gentleman is waiting for you in front of the Altar of Saint Anthony."

"The police?" Uhle rose.

"Come on!" Xaver Grün winked his reddish eyelashes. "He's here!"

"Who?"

"The Rescuer, my son!" Grinning, he quietly pushed aside a priedieu with his halberd. "Come on—you'll see!" He crossed himself and, in unison with the litany, launched forth mechanically:

> "Saint Anthony of Padua!
> Pillar of the Church!
> Teacher of truth!
> Vanquisher of heretics!
> Terror of sinners!
> Consolation of the afflicted!
> Helper in our need!
> Liberator of captives!—
> Saint Adolf of Braunau!
> Help us poor Christians!
> Amen!"

Suddenly his foot slipped—the halberd clattered metallically on the stones. His bicorne flew in a wide arc into a nun's lap. Several worshipers hurried to help the beadle to his feet.

"Olala!" Startled by the noise, Olenka became aware that the chair next to her was empty. She discovered Uhle three columns away, watching a group of men in the shadow of a side chapel. One of them looked to him like Prince August Wilhelm—but, if it was, he had changed from the black frock coat he had worn in the Bagatelle Park that morning to a military raincoat, with shoulder straps and a belt.

Olenka ran to Uhle, hung on his arm, and said:

"Let's go!"

"Yes, we're going!" They edged their way through the pews across

160

he aisle. Just as they were about to go out into the street, however,
he dancer recoiled.

"There's Egath!—at the door!"

"Egath?"

"Quick! Quick! Quick!" Olenka dragged Uhle back into the cathedral. Seeing a ticket window and a sign showing the prices for the
scent of the tower, she quickly bought two tickets. Then she ran
o the narrow winding stairs of the north tower, and beckoned Uhle
o follow. But before he realized the situation, Colonel Egath had
caught up with him.

"Where is the Will? Quick! Rudolf Hess and his men are outside."
He pushed him behind the enormous stone font where they argued
with such heat that the Swiss cautioned them with his halberd. They
disappeared behind a pillar whispering. Suddenly Uhle came out alone
and started for the tower. But again, Egath overtook him.

"My dear Uhle—"

"Pardon," Uhle blazed at him, "you said that Prince August Wilhelm
ent you to me?"

"He offers you the chance of going down in history . . ." and he
drew Uhle back into the shadow of the pillar. After he had murmured
omething persuasively to him, Uhle laughed aloud.

"What am I supposed to do? Shoot your All-highest War Lord?
Pardon me—but I mean—why don't you do it?" He looked with
contempt at his former war comrade.

"Egath! Tell me—how was it possible for a man like you to become
a Nazi? You—who on November 28, 1917, read to me with great
enthusiasm Lenin's manifesto, 'Long Live the World Revolution.' "

Egath polished his monocle: "What do you expect? The situation
demanded it. When *he* came to power in 1933, was there any class-
conscious proletariat left? Or was I to fight him single-handed in the
Bülowplatz?"

" 'The situation demanded it,' " Uhle repeated bitterly . . . "You
mean opportunism was written on your banner: small positions, bigger
ones . . . advancement. Man! You knew better! At least you did,
when the shells burst around us at Verdun like flaming trees! You
said to me then: 'Uhle, if I were to be asked now, why all this beastly
work?—for my country? for honor? for greater Germany?—my only
answer would have been to curse!'—And now—with the Gestapo!"

"I hate the ex-corporal almost as much as you do."

"How can I believe that? Oh, no! You will have to give me stronger
proofs. Or do you feel your game is up, and are you merely looking

for a safe hiding-place before Judgment Day? . . . When I warned you—against him—you told me that I was an idealist, that the individual must make way for the masses, that only the masses counted! And now you try to persuade the scorned idealist to perform a deed—for which you realists are no doubt too cowardly."

He turned and left him. Colonel Egath was so dazed that he did not see Uhle disappear into the tower.

CHAPTER THREE OLENKA IN THE MEANTIME HAD CLIMBED SO FAST, TAKING TWO STEPS AT A TIME, THAT HE HAD DIFFICULTY in catching up with her. Not until he had reached the second landing did they meet. There he listened—to hear whether Egath was following him. But no one came.

"How you can climb!"

"Olala! And my skirt is much too tight! Did Egath see us?"

"Be still . . . footsteps!" He pressed her against the wall.

Just then two poilus on the gallery above called down: "Courage, Madame!" One of them laughed, "256 steps! You'll soon be there." Then they clattered on down the stone steps in their nailed boots.

"Courage—that's it!" And she let Uhle, who had gone ahead, pull her along. "Enfin—arrivés!" She felt his heart. "How fast it beats! You climbed too quickly."

He stepped out on the roof and breathed deeply. His dispute with Egath ran like poison through his veins. Should he tell her about it?

The sun had just gone down, but the autumn afterglow still shone on the broad and winding surface of the Seine, broken by many bridges. The storm had withdrawn to the horizon. Mountain peaks of clouds were towering behind the Sacré-Cœur, whose high cupolas and towers glowed like a Fata Morgana out of the raspberry-red Paris haze.

Uhle looked cautiously over the balustrade of the tower gallery and down into the little square in front of the cathedral. Olenka gazed about, fascinated by the stone gargoyles, uncannily alive and real, squatting gray-black on the balustrade against the turquoise evening sky. For centuries the rain had poured through them and then out of the narrow lead pipes between their paws, spurting down on the ant-like human beings below.

162

The play of lights and illuminated signs began in the mist below
hem. Between colorless masses of buildings lay the Jardins des Tuileries, a black oblong.

"Olala! How the earth pulls!"

"Come here!" Uhle dragged her back from the balustrade.

"Why? Afraid—I might jump? Mais non, Monsieur! Only if you
don't want me. Only then!"

"Stay back! They can see us from down there!"

"Who do you mean?" She leaned over. Suddenly she cried, "Listen!
There goes a bell. Someone's ringing."

"Perhaps they're closing the tower."

"But I don't want to go down yet!"

"There it goes again!"

"Do you suppose it's for us! He's ringing like mad."

"I wonder when the tower does close?"

"About seven, I think."

"But it's still light—"

"Now they've stopped! Uhle! Perhaps they've locked us in!"

"Yes . . . perhaps the Swiss didn't know we came up—"

"Olala! Then shall we spend the night up here together? Darling!
We can cover ourselves with my fur coat. It's warm enough . . . Or
are you too fascinated by these stone demons? Is that why you look
so stern? Look! There's the first star! Here's a place that's dry: shall
I make our bed here? Oh? a pigeon? it was asleep already! Do you
really think we're locked up here?"

"The bell's stopped ringing."

"Then come and sit down here beside me—close to me! When do
you think they'll open up again? At seven in the morning? Or later?
Oh, Uhle!" She threw herself happily on his shoulder and seemed to
have forgotten everything besides. "Dear one! To think of spending
the whole night with you alone!"

Suddenly she jumped up and called, "Catch me!" Then ran away,
her long legs flying. But she came back directly, disappointed, for he
had not followed her, and asked, "What are you brooding about?"
Suddenly she noticed a long dark hair on his coat collar. "Whose is
that?" And then, after a silence, she asked, "Is your wife in Paris?"
But as Uhle did not answer she took the hair off his shoulder and let
it drop over the balustrade.

"No, I'm not jealous. I'd like to bring you all the most beautiful
peasant girls in Poland. Real madonnas! You ought to have a child by
every one of them! I shouldn't mind if you had a whole brigade!

Just so long as those eyes of yours were reproduced every time!"

"By the way," Uhle interrupted her, "why didn't you tell me anything about the detective who let you out of my room?"

"What?" and then she muttered something in Polish. And then
coaxingly, "Darling, I told you all about it on the telephone—"

"And another thing"—Uhle gave her a side glance—"how did
Colonel Egath happen to know that I would be at Notre-Dame? Did
you mention it? Hm?—You must have told him that we had an
appointment here."

The dancer gave him a desperate look. Suddenly she took his hand.
"If only I could just take you to Poland with me!"

Uhle was silent. The more he looked at the dancer, the more he felt
a deep melancholy.

"Darling!" she undid his black raincape and snuggled against him
and went on playfully: "After our wedding, you see, we'll go right to
the country. Far up in the mountains, to a lost village! There's an
inn just across from the railway station. And then—for the first time
—we'll be alone together in a little white-washed room. As Monsieur
and Madame! Only a chair between the beds! And I hang my wedding
dress on an old iron peg so that it won't get wrinkled! And there I
am—in bed—all in pink! And outside we can hear an old locomotive
switching back and forth—Uhle! Uhle! Say something! Or would
you rather be in town with me—in my house in Cracow! It was left
to me by a great aunt. Not at all comfortable, but it's on the most
beautiful square in the city. So old that it's under the protection of
the Fine Arts authorities! Just opposite the Town Hall. It has only
two windows on the front, but it is built long and deep and narrow,
with thick stone walls. Of course, there's no running water! You
won't mind? But the rooms are enormous, dear! And in the bedroom,
there's a bed that is wide and comfortable. And in front of one of
those old-fashioned leather armchairs, there's a stand holding an enormous Bible, bound in heavy silver—another heirloom."

"A Bible?" Uhle repeated slowly, while his thoughts wandered back
to Egath.

"Yes! There's a book for you to study in! And in the morning,
old Joseph knocks at the door: 'Madame, I've brought you hot water
to wash with.' Olala! I want to see his face when he has to say
'Madame' to me! Ha-ha! Later he'll ask if we'd rather have tea or
coffee. When we ring he'll set the wobbly Baroque table with our old
chipped and cracked juniper-wood service and old tarnished silver!
They don't have any like it nowadays. Dear!" She squeezed his fingers.

164

"Then we start eating breakfast. And the sun shines in all the windows! And such a marvelous view! The golden towers and clocks of the Church of the Virgin! And down below, the market, with all the women selling fruits and vegetables under enormous, colored umbrellas—like flowers in a dream. Or darling, would you rather go to my father's estate? There everything's always in disorder downstairs: Mother's knitting and everything higgledy-piggledy, all mixed up with baskets of corn, melons, tomatoes—Father always solemnly invites me upstairs to have tea with him. But first he picks the most beautiful flowers he can find in the garden. He doesn't care for any except wild flowers. You should see how gracefully he picks them and hands them to me, Uhle! Uhle! He's always saying he's never made anything out of his life, and therefore *I* must become somebody! He's always dreaming that I shall become the most famous Polish violinist! He hates my dancing—he's always wanting me to practice the violin. Ten hours—" Suddenly she stopped and looked up. "Darling! Unfortunately my bedroom at home is cold and damp, and my sister sleeps in the room next to mine. Olala! how she talks in her sleep! And outside my window there's the poplar walk. Sometimes at night the wind rustles so funnily in the tree tops. I get up in my nightgown —so old-fashioned—"

"The flowered one?"

"Yes, that one! Ha-ha! And there I stand, barefoot, up so high— lots of strange black-winged birds flying across the moon! Make me shiver!"

A number of brilliant searchlights began to play from Montmartre. "What are they searching the sky for? Are they looking for God? Hm? Whom do you suppose . . . ?" She hid behind his back. He stroked her hair. So they sat for some minutes without a word. But then he said: "If I only knew how Egath found out that I would be in Notre-Dame?"

"Darling, I wish I were going down the poplar walk with you now —out into the fields. There are loads of haystacks! There's always a little brown falcon sitting on one of them—and then he flies away. In the distance, nothing but plowed fields and hills, deep blue all the way to the horizon. Olala! But the most beautiful thing of all—transparent as crystal—is the Tatra! And then we throw ourselves into the hay together! Beetles crawling all around us. And the smell! Olala! Look, there's the falcon back again! He's looking at us! What a sharp beak! Off again? Where is he? There! How he floats! without ever moving his wings! Oh, Uhle, Uhle! How you would love my Poland!" She threw her arms around his neck. But all at once her eyes looked terrified.

"No—away from Europe altogether! Darling, I don't want to stay in Europe any longer!" She covered her face with both hands and her shoulders trembled. Uhle took her hands.

"Have you an affidavit?"

"No! And you?"

"Neither have I!"

"It doesn't matter!—I know a steamship line that would take us anyway—banana ships from Marseilles, with only one or two passengers. And if we haven't any money—that's all right too. The Captain will give us some bananas . . . Uhle, I have plenty of clothes, too—enough for at least two years. A suit—très chic! And a tulle evening dress—blue-black! Makes me look like the fabled phoenix. Oui! Like a fairy princess . . . And then"—she rubbed her cheek against his shoulder —"and then, away we sail, out over the sea, to our Magic Island! I found it in the atlas! It lies west of South America . . . in the blue, blue ocean!"

"Our Magic Island?" Uhle smiled.

As the wind grew colder, they huddled closer together.

"You know"—she covered his knees with the fur coat—"I have a permanent room here in Paris. Whenever I come from Warsaw to dance here—I stay there. I can't bear to go there any longer, though. Too many refugees! I can't stay at my aunt's now. They'd find me . . . the beasts! No, no! They'd put me in a concentration camp. Uhle! on my floor, there's the nephew of a Rabbi: he's an editor from Mainz —tall and pale—he has such burning eyes! He escaped from a concentration camp. He says they made him drink a whole bottle of castor-oil, and then, with the cramps in his stomach, he had to climb a ladder in the middle of the courtyard and impersonate King Solomon . . ."

"King Solomon?" Uhle bit his lips together.

"Yes! Tell me, do you think such a thing is possible?"

"Possible? In a world that crucified Christ what is *not* possible?" After a gloomy silence—

"On a ladder, you said? It was on a ladder of seven metals that Jacob once saw angels climbing up and down—" He stood up. Strange! Since he had found his unknown soldier on the Field of Verdun, something had awakened in him. Uhle felt that—like Jacob once—he too was fated to wrestle for salvation with the messenger of eternity.

"Where are you going? Please stay! Olala! Do you hear something?

166

It's only the wind . . . the wind . . . He's rattling the tiles on the roof. Don't go, Uhle! Where are you going? Downstairs? But the tower is closed!" He walked along the gallery and started around the tower.

"Uhle! are you going to leave me up here alone?" She ran after him.

CHAPTER FOUR

THEY COULD HEAR FOOTSTEPS MOUNTING THE WINDING STAIRS. OSCILLATING SHADOWS FELL ON THE opposite wall, rising higher and higher. It was the Swiss, Xaver Grün, and a soldier for whom Grün lifted his small iron lantern so that he could see the last few steps.

"En avant, son!" Xaver Grün rattled his big bunch of keys. "Tu sais—maybe this Monsieur Westermann is a good violin-maker. But he doesn't understand our organ. So, son, I'll show you the air intake that connects with the organ bellows behind the tower there— It may be stopped with dirt. If you want to help fix it, I'll get you an extra absolution from our Curé. As I told you, we need the organ tonight for the 'Hallelujah' during procession. Just a minute; first let me put out my lantern!" He blew it out.

"Yes, son, I wouldn't dare go out on the tower gallery with a light —the good people of Paris would think there were ghosts up here! Come along, my beloved in Christ—" he stroked his beard, grinning. "Yes, I have charge of the tower. Viens! Viens! You must realize, son—" He led the soldier in the red Spahi cape along the railing to a gargoyle.

"In 1793 and 1794, this so-called cathedral was known as the Temple of Reason!" He laughed. "And the smart sans-culottes, reeking of 'reason,' went to the trouble of smashing the noses on all the finest stone carvings we have. Yes! Yes! and that's not all! Didn't the reds behead some two hundred thousand aristocrats? Ha-ha-ha!" As his companion looked out over Paris without answering, the Swiss beck- oned to him:

"Viens! From here, son, you have the finest view of Paris. Tiens! There go the bells! You're lucky! Ding-dong! Listen! I know them all apart. That's the tenor bell of St. Jacques. Over there to the right— that low one—is from the Hôtel de Ville. Our murderous Marat often

167

used to ring it in honor of Madame Guillotine. Listen! That deep, bronze tone comes from St. Germain. Yes, son!" He put his hand on the silent soldier's back. "That bell was the signal for the Massacre of St. Bartholomew . . . You know—when the Catholics killed all the Huguenots. I hope you are a Christian—a soldier ought to be a Christian; otherwise there would be no blessing on his rifle. Apropos, son, there's half a bottle of brandy there behind the stove. How about a drink to the soldier's honor? Are you a sergeant? Did you go through the war? Hello—what's up? Is the storm coming back? What a wind —it's drawing the clouds over the roofs, looks exactly like galloping blue squadrons, doesn't it? Are you a cavalryman?—By the way, did you come in by the Sainte Anne door or the main door? I ask because I thought I'd locked them both. There goes the big bell in the south tower; boom-bam, boom-bam! Cast in 1686, weighs 13,000 kilograms.

"Maybe afterwards you'd like to see Napoleon's coronation robes? It's on account of the key, I ask . . . Look, that cannon ball in the wall behind you dates from the Franco-Prussian war. Plenty of history these walls have seen. Apropos—that relief in the wall there represents the so-called 'Christ Triumphant!'" He struck a match and lighted the figure for a moment—an unshaven man with outstretched arms. As the soldier approached, the match went out.

"Yes, son, people keep asking me: 'What's He triumphant about?' Ah, comrade, how can I answer that? I always say: Who is there that still hopes? Who is there that still loves? Who is there that still believes? Am I right, son? Or maybe you believe in Immortality Triumphant? Ha-ha! As for me, hélas! I have a wife . . . also a little daughter!" Laughing aloud he led the soldier away with him over the roof.

CHAPTER FIVE OLENKA'S ACCOUNT OF THE JEW-
ISH EDITOR'S TORTURE ON THE LADDER IN THE CONCENTRATION CAMP HAD moved Uhle profoundly. The more he imagined the horrible scene, the more he believed that he saw the finger of God in Prince August Wilhelm's proposal that he shoot Hitler.

On his way back to the tower stairs, however, he was gripped and again brought to a halt by a strange apparition. On a raised platform between the two towers stood a colossal marble angel, in form like a slim youth. He held a shepherd's horn in his left hand; his face was up-turned, with the long index finger of his right hand he pointed toward the stars. Around him—much larger than the gargoyles on the roof—there crouched monstrous granite beasts with pointed pigs' snouts, and wide browless skulls. Monkeys, birds with women's breasts, and grinning sphinxes, black with soot.

In the gathering twilight, Uhle stood motionless, gazing at the Gothic master's fantasy sculptured in stone. He moved nearer. "There indeed they sit—all the beasts who dominate us human beings! That baboon, for instance, does he not symbolize our ghoulish vanity? Or the heavy feline head of that lion, our thirst for power? And the bat at the left—the spreading of false rumors! And there the disgusting dirt-sniffing dog—and just beside him the half-man, half-beast—who with his gigantic arms tries to free himself from the animal world! But he cannot do it! For eons he has tried, but cannot! Even though the Angel in the midst of the beasts has been calling him for untold eons—calling, calling, to help us get out of the animal world—

"How lightly poised you are!" Uhle touched the stone figure—"seemingly without any weight, as if at any moment you would fly up from the cathedral roof . . . high . . . higher . . . where?"

Then he smiled bitterly and murmured, "Stone, nothing but cold stone."

Unnoticed, Olenka had come up. She stepped behind Uhle, and whispered, "You smell wonderful . . . like earth . . ., like . . ."

Uhle came out of his meditation. Then he put her lightly aside. "Olenka . . ."

"Olenka? Say it again! Darling—" Her head nestled on his shoulder. "You smell like verbena. And your hair smells of camomile!"

"Olala! I just washed it for you. Is that your stomach rumbling? You haven't eaten anything! Shall I buy some radishes? And slice them small on bread? Uhle! Do you hear me? What are you looking at, up there on the tower?"

The tops of the two truncated towers were lost in darkness. The square-hewn stone masses cast shadows as geometrically precise as their outlines.

Olenka looked around her, feeling as if she had no room to breathe. In the silent vastness of all those hard, granite blocks, laboriously hewn and set one on the other, she suddenly felt lost. Uhle, too, felt a chill run over him. She noticed it. Uneasily she watched the stone beasts —growing out of their own shadows . . . growing larger . . . ever larger.

From somewhere in the cathedral a clock hammered out its metallic strokes . . . Olenka pressed as close to Uhle as she could get. Through the soft folds of her fur coat, he could feel her body.

"Phew! It's too hot!" She unhooked her coat. Warmth rose from her dress in waves. Suddenly she pressed her thighs softly against his.

The great bell in the south tower began to reverberate in deep bronze-bass. The stone vibrated lightly. And then Olenka kissed him. The sweet music of his senses, aroused by the tip of her tongue, called to his blood. It was as if from the mysterious stirring of life, when it first appeared on our cooling planet, something had called to him.

And through the touch of her young womanhood came over him, without his willing it, an overwhelming force—just as eons before, when there was as yet no law to divide woman from man . . . no good and evil . . . but only, in the midst of cosmic darkness, in the utter cold of space, the sharp unbounded desire to create, to people the yet unquickened body of the world with life, as a means of salvation, as a protest against death.

Her longing grew as Uhle's desire mounted. She half closed her eyes. Suddenly, she sank down at his feet, as if pulled by a force from the earth's very center. One of her curls lay on the stone foot of the giant frog gargoyle. "Come," she stammered hoarsely, "come—I want you so much."

As she lay on the granite pavement, her slim body seemed to sink into the stone, as if it yielded to the weight of her desire. Uhle stood tense. Desire drove through him, from his brain to the marrow of his bones . . . and further . . . until it flared in all his veins.

All at once above the crying of the wind, over the roof and round the sharp-edged towers, strange sounds came flying—just such sounds as had come to him while he wandered at night, when will-o'-the-wisps in zig-zag flight lure travelers into swamps—sounds like smacking, sucking water. He felt as if the soles of his feet were being pulled down.

"Come . . . come . . ." The imploring tone rose up to him.

Shrill voices seemed to come out of the wind. As he listened, his eyes fell on the girl's slender white thighs. Under the fur and the dress, they called him to the gate of the flesh as into primal forgetfulness.

"Why struggle so?" groaned his senses, "why not give yourself up to the sweet flood of ecstasy?"

"Come to me . . ." she moved, heavy with longing. White silk showed in the pale light of the night. Uhle bent over her.

"How smooth your skin is—"

Just as his hands touched her knees, something happened. One of the searchlights on Montparnasse had focused on the stone figure of the angel, so that it stood in a blinding brightness. The two wings seemed to reach up to the polestar. Out of the marble face, which in that strange light looked like the mask of his unknown soldier, eyes seemed to flame awake. Suddenly there came a voice: "Thou shalt not commit whoredom."

Uhle was terrified to the marrow. He looked around. There was no one in sight. Then suddenly there was a whisper in his other ear:

"Why bother about that angel? It's just a stone figure, covered with pigeon-droppings . . ."

The sweat broke out on Uhle's forehead. Were there people standing there, in the shadow of the tower, watching him?

"Go to it, son," came another whisper. "What are you waiting for? Take the girl. Don't be a booby. Help yourself to the dainty dish. Then, 'after taking,' our cold friend there—immortality's office boy —will have the damned duty—as soon as you've repented properly— of whisking you up to heaven pickaback between his wings. One, two, three—hop! And away you go, caught up into the forgiveness of sins. Ha-ha!"

"Thou shalt not commit adultery." Again the voice in his other ear. Uhle tried to pull himself together. He listened with strained attention.

"So what!" came the voice in his left ear. "Take your fun. All men do it."

"Don't be concerned with what others do!"

As he listened and listened he suddenly heard distinctly the voices in his own breast.

"*You* must begin!" came the clear command.

"What's he got to begin with?" the other laughed. "He wants his fun. He's normal, isn't he? He'd like to grab all the pleasure he can in this short life!"

"Uhle!" The whisper in his heart was more imperious. "Think of No Man's Land. Think of the dead Spahi in the snow at Verdun. Remember how swollen, how black against the shell-torn earth—Uhle! Uhle! the phallus, for us men, darkens the sun. Can you not tame it? Must it always run wild? Don't you know yet that *there* is where all wretchedness begins? In your own passions that fight within you! Uhle, Uhle, beware: Here, in your own self-seeking, the Nazi in you begins."

Gusts of wind cried round the cornices, like the whimpering of maltreated creatures, like the cries for help from the camp-straw be-

hind bars and barbed wire. Suddenly he saw faces above him in the air
—pale, tortured faces . . . and then . . . one face, a delicate oval.

"What do you want? . . . Who are you?"

"Don't you recognize that face?" The voice within him was still
clearer. "Or do you want to have done with your feeling for Irene
here and now? Did you not once think it was to be forever? . . . eternal?"

"Forever? . . . eternal?" It was the mocking voice. "How can a
feeling in a fly like you . . . be eternal? Ha-ha!"

"If once you let a love that you have felt in your soul to be eternal
—if once you let it die in you, let it grow cold, then for you there is
no love and no eternity. Understand that! Begin! Even if other men
change their feelings as a waiter changes plates! *You* begin! The Yes
is in *you*. The No is in *you!* As *you* decide, so shall it be! Stand up!
In *you* is the will to the beast. In *you* is the will to God. *You* begin!"

And then he heard it—as if from every part of himself—from the
soles of his feet, through the veins of his legs, in every blood corpuscle,
in the very dance of their atoms—somber, heavy, and dull against his
ribs, like the thumping of his heart: "*You* begin, *you* begin, *you*
begin!"

The contours of the tower blurred before his eyes. Slowly he rose
from her embrace. He drew a deep breath. And then forced the rebellious lust of his loins back into his will. Into his heart and brain. And
further still. He raised his eyes, beyond the beasts and the angel, and
once more gave direction and purpose to his flesh. In the mysterious
cells of his masculine essence he transmuted the excitement of a fleeting sensuality into the silver sap of a higher end.

There he stood, between the towers of Notre-Dame, firmly braced
on his two feet. Above him was infinite space. Suddenly, in all the
glitter of the night sky, one star shone out, unwontedly bright. It
looked like an eye full of clear light, like the eye of his soldier.

Uhle looked up at it, until he had brought that azure evidence from
the far-off, unspoiled realms of innocence into line again with his own
pupils and the four heart chambers in his breast. And then one ray
after another reached him and worked magically in him. He trembled
—like a mother when a new life first stirs within her. For that light
was urging him, driving him to the birth of a new love.

The night wind blew cool over his damp forehead.

CHAPTER SIX "HELP ME!" THE DANCER SAT UP.
"I WANT TO GET UP . . . IT'S GETTING COLD." SHE RUMPLED HER HAIR.
"Heh, Monsieur, they seem to have forgotten we're up here. What
time is it?" She looked at her wrist watch. "Olala, it's not late at all.
It's only seven. I'd have guessed midnight, at least. Uhle, what are you
thinking about? . . . something a thousand miles away?" She yawned.
"Olala . . . très fatiguée . . . Hélas!" She stood up and sauntered
over to the parapet. She put her hand on the hump of the gargoyle
whose two-pronged horns tickled the night sky. "Eh, bien, Monsieur
Stone-Devil, you blink as if you were quite content with the ocean of
houses down there . . . apparently you're satisfied with Paris.

"Uuuu-hle," she turned around and prolonged the sound of his name
caressingly. "Isn't Paris exciting? It excites me! But don't worry on
that account. I'm not going to force you. Oh no! I don't force anything. Everything must develop harmoniously. Yes—I believe in that.
And besides, over us there is destiny—Kismet."

She ran toward him suddenly, and shook him. But then she left him.
She slipped off her coat and began to undress—as if she were going to
do a dance for him. Tossing her stockings at his head, with swift movements she pulled her dress up over her head, kicked off her shoes in
different directions—"That's Polish housekeeping!"—and finally lay
down flat on her fur coat. She stretched her legs straight up and began
swinging them from her narrow hips—three times to the right, three
times to the left. Then she jumped to her feet, wriggled out of her
thin silk combination and stood there before him with a touchingly
serious face.

"Voilà! . . . Here you have me just as God made me. Now, if you
want me, just say so. If not—that's too bad! I can't offer you anything
else but myself . . . This is the way I am; front and back view! Oh!"
She spread her arms wide. "What a breeze! It's heavenly! Deliciously
cool! Even better than bathing naked in the sea at night . . ."

Tiptoeing to a rain puddle, she sprinkled herself with glistening
drops, then let herself dry in the wind. An uncertain light glowed
faintly in all the fine down of her body, even to the small triangle between her legs . . . As Uhle did not stir, she tripped away in her
nakedness, and began to run in a circle. Suddenly she stopped short and
sat down astride one of the rain pipes, as if in a saddle.

173

"Look! Here in this crack, there's a real dandelion growing!" She picked the round, frail, white thing and held it up. "It's gone to seed. In Poland we say that every seed is a soul . . ." She blew the delicately feathered seeds from the stalk. One of them stuck to her fingertip.

"Tell me whose soul are you?" she asked. "Are you a Pole? Or are you an U-u-u-uhle?" She blew with all her might. Watching it float away, she rose a little. The light of the lantern shone on her back. But abruptly she hid her face in her curls, and hummed:

> Though drear the nights and dull the days,
> Waits the Dark Rider, his charger neighs . . .
> And whenever I will, He will clasp me beside,
> And together we'll ride . . ride far and wide!

Suddenly she lunged toward the balustrade, clambered quickly up it, and balanced herself between two rain-spouts. Then she played with her slim toes as if she were running her fingers over a piano keyboard. Suddenly she slipped, and wavered uncertainly on the treacherous stone. "Olenka," Uhle cried out, and rushed to catch her by the knees. He tried to force her down from the parapet. But as if to spite him, she balanced herself like a tightrope dancer, and spread her arms far out in the air over the yawning abyss.

"My bridegroom, when I was making myself beautiful for you this afternoon, I thought that perhaps by this time I'd be your bride."

Rhythmic shudders ran through her body. With her long hair fluttering around her, she tried to let herself fall into space. But Uhle's hands held her in an iron grip.

"Oh, all ye stars!" she sighed up into the sky. "Oh, love. Blissful reunion."

Then she shut her eyes and let Uhle pull her back between the two rainspouts. After he had covered her trembling body with his raincape, she peered at him out of the corners of her eyes.

"Then you were just a little concerned about me? . . ." she leaned her head back and whispered. "Tell me!"

"Do you trust me?"

"Only you!"

Rather clumsily he helped her to dress. He put her fur coat around her and led her over to a bench. Then he waited until they were both relaxed. "Do you know"—he stroked her forehead—"day before yesterday at Verdun, in that kingdom of the dead, while I was wandering around alone among the countless graves of all those unknown children of men who had died in the slaughter, I asked myself this question: How is it thinkable that in the twentieth century we can still butcher each other—how, year after year can we drive each other—as if in an orgy of destruction—into such morasses of blood? There must be a fearful cause for it, somewhere . . . somewhere . . . there's no effect without a cause. That is the basis of all magic. Do you understand? And then I thought: There is something wrong in us . . ."

"Wrong in us?" The girl looked at him questioningly. "Go on, tell me—"

"That is hard to do," he whispered, "hard—because perhaps the cause of all evil is . . . here!" He pointed first to himself, then to her. "I mean, here, between man and woman. Particularly in—sexual desire."

"Desire?" She stared at him in amazement. "Olala! But Uhle, I love you!"

"Love?" he murmured after a long silence. "Yes . . . but tomorrow, we'll say the same thing to somebody else . . . that word . . . And yesterday? . . . and day after tomorrow?"

"And yesterday? . . . and day after tomorrow?" she repeated, feeling a fear that she could not comprehend.

He looked at her with his heart full. He wanted not to hurt her with any more words. Suddenly she covered her face with her hands. Then she peered out at him through her long slender fingers, like a bird from its cage, and asked tenderly, "But you love me a little, just a little?"

"Surely there is . . . there must be . . . mankind must find some new . . . some fixed point of reference—"

"Point of reference? What's that?"

"I mean a love no longer bound up with the 'you' and the 'I'."

"But what else is there?"—She shivered and drew his raincape around her shoulders. "For me, Uhle, from now on, there's only one fixed point."

"And that is?"

"You!"

"Me?" He smiled and shook his head. They looked out into the blue night sky, which was as transparent as a glass dome behind which there looked out on them from countless eyes only good spirits.

"Listen . . ." she took hold of his hand and laid it carefully over her left breast. "Do you feel how it beats? That is my very self, all alone in the universe."

"All alone?" he repeated. "Feel my heart, too. Do you feel how it beats?—That is my very self—all alone in the universe."

"And the woman," Olenka was trembling, "to whom you started to write last night in your hotel room . . . is Irene too alone in the universe?"

Several seconds passed. Then Uhle asked softly: "Or will it never be possible for us lovers to shape the first bridal feeling in ourselves, to build it up—I mean, through snow and rain, through heat and lightning, into such beautiful fulfillment as this Gothic cathedral? . . . Hm? Darling, does it not stand here as if it fitted into the cosmic order? While we . . . ?"

Once more there was a long pause. A weak moonlight brought into clearer outline some of the stone animals in the shadow of the tower.

"Yes—" he looked around—"what is all political or economic tyranny compared with the age-old dictatorship of the beast within us?"

"Shhh!" Olenka laid her fingers on his lips. She rose from the bench and with luminous face looked out toward the flickering star worlds. "How light it is! Yes, you are right! And everything seems to fall into place in the cosmic order. Oh, Uhle. . . ."

"What?"

"But that giant stone frog there? and the pig? and the marble monkey behind him?—and Hitler in Berchtesgaden? Oh, Uhle, Uhle!" She turned away so quickly that her tears sprayed into the wind.

"Olenka"—he turned her face toward him—"can't we form the first cell—begin a new movement against the beast in us?"

"See how bright it has become all around us . . . almost as bright as a concert hall. Yes"—she craned out into the night—"a first cell! Darling! A new movement!" Her slim figure grew slimmer. "Darling! And then I would no longer be alone in the universe?"

"No. For one soul can become many. And many, a hundred. And even more . . . Oh, countless souls who will have understood the symbol of that stone trumpet in the angel's hand there—who will finally have heard in themselves the sound of eternity, through which the spirit summons our souls out of animal chaos into its spheral music."

"Oh, Uhle—" her hair blew across his face. Far below them where the Seine flowed they could hear the steady, even roar of the great city. Suddenly Olenka was blinded by the glare of a flashlight in her face.

"Mademoiselle," the Swiss Xaver Grün grinned, "are you Olenka Olschewska? There's a gentleman here to see you . . ." He pointed to Colonel Egath, who was approaching with a covered violin case in his hand.

"Is this yours, Fräulein?" Egath lifted his hat. "This empty violin case was found in the Bagatelle Park . . ."

"Quoi?" Stammering, the dancer tried to regain her self-control.

"Your name and address are inside the lid. That's not very fore-sighted. Please come with me to the tower guard's cabin over there. I have a few questions to ask you—"

But before Egath saw what was happening, Uhle had caught Olenka's hand. Then they both ran as fast as they could along the gallery and around the corner of the tower.

Xaver Grün blinked his flashlight at the astounded Colonel. Then he showed him back to the tower stairs by the shortest way. As they went, he growled out an old army song:

> And the cow does more
> Than the nightingale!
> And the cow does more
> Than the nightingale.
> But most of all, beneath his tail
> The bull does most—and he has no pail!

CHAPTER SEVEN THROUGH A LABYRINTH OF PITCH-DARK STAIRS AND NARROW PASSAGEWAYS, STRIKING ONE MATCH AFTER another, Uhle had meanwhile taken the dancer out of reach of the Ge-stapo. Now neither of them knew where in Notre-Dame they were. And while they held their breath, listening to hear whether Egath was following them, they heard organ notes. They felt their way toward the sounds, and saw ahead of them the dark violet shimmer of a church window illuminated from within. Just beside it was a small wooden door, which opened. From the top of the narrow stone staircase they could see down into the choir. The huge organ pipes shone dull-silver in the light of a single electric bulb.

Uhle bounded back. His unknown soldier was seated at the keys. Westermann was pumping the bellows and explaining why he thought the mechanism didn't work. The other listened attentively and then began to strike a fifth or an octave here and there. The violin-maker listened happily, because the invalided war veteran whom the Swiss had introduced to him as an organ expert was handling the fragile century-old mechanism almost like a wise doctor treating a living organism.

The rest of the cathedral was shadowy and empty, except for a few women who were busy cleaning the bishop's throne for the evening procession.

But now Xaver Grün appeared from the sacristy. He distributed worn Gothic velvet cushions, meanwhile impatiently raising his red eyelashes toward the squeaking organ. One of the old women who was dipping her cleaning brush in the water pail, secretly took a drink from Grün's bottle of brandy, which was standing on the altar steps.

Under the soldier's hands, the organ notes grew slowly clearer and finally lost their previous wheeziness entirely. Uhle looked down at him as if spellbound. Suddenly, as though following an inner impulse, he hurried down the little stairway. Olenka started to follow him. But she was so shocked at the sight of her own gigantic shadow on the wall, that her knees gave way under her. And then, as in the ballet of "Death and the Maiden," which she had so often danced, it seemed to her that the shadow suddenly beckoned strangely, like the skeleton in the black cloak. She had to sit down, she felt so faint. But the violin-maker had already climbed up the stairs to her.

Surprised that the bellows had stopped, the soldier turned his head. He saw Uhle, and took his fingers off the keys. Uhle waited until Westermann had led the dancer safely away from the stairs. Then he went to the soldier and sat down beside him on the organ bench. As the noise of scrubbing in the apse stopped for a moment, Uhle whispered wonderingly:

"You here? This morning, when I looked in on you at the hotel, you were sleeping so quietly. And now—here in Notre-Dame?—But don't let me interrupt you. Play! Play!"

The other improvised softly again. Uhle listened. Then he wrote something down and slid closer.

"Here! That's the address of the Secretary of the Société des Anciens Combattants, Monsieur Gunther. He's expecting me later at a banquet for four thousand veterans in the Trocadéro. Please go in my place. Really I—do you understand?—I have an appointment."

The other was silent.

"Strange," Uhle thought, "his mask shines with the same gas-green, trench-complexion color as the wooden face of the Christ of the Trenches! And his Moroccan cloak is as dark as dried blood. Like the blood from the nail wounds." But in the eyes of the man at the organ there was an enigmatic light—such as we see in the eyes of soldiers who have come back to their homes out of the hell of mechanized warfare, and can find no connection between the butchery enforced on them out there and the unforced, swarming life in the streets at home. There was something touchingly helpless in his look. But something inexpressibly desperate too! Horrors were reflected in his pupils—corpses, shot-torn faces. And the longer those eyes that had seen the Front looked at Uhle, the surer he felt that only such eyes, eyes which had returned from the slaughter still whole, could give direction and a goal in the midst of the world's chaos.

But suddenly behind the soldier's head Uhle saw, crowning a pointed arch, a Gothic stone face, like the stupid pale face of a parishioner—or did it perhaps represent the Devil? As he looked more clearly, it visibly took on a resemblance to Hitler's grimacing countenance. But then it occurred to him that it was a quite ordinary face—where had he seen it first? In the shop on the corner? And in the streetcar. And at the postoffice window. And in the railway station. Everywhere! Even one of the gendarmes had had that face. The longer he looked, the more gigantic that everyday face on the wall became. Yes, that calcified, narrow-minded, mass-production face changed before his eyes into the likeness of that devil—he whose ossified stupidity will never tolerate new paths, whose bespectacled eyes never see a new direction, and who is therefore the eternal enemy of eyes like the soldier's, which see the way out.

He stood up, and staring at the granite mask, moaned, "By the living God, I'll shoot you down! You, you!"

Outside in the tower a clock began to strike, softly as velvet. After it had stopped, Uhle nodded.

"Yes! Tonight I shall shoot you down. In you, I shall blast the brain of Nazism into its constituent atoms."

The soldier looked at him. But not until Uhle laid his hand on his arm did he stop playing and asked, "Who gave you that idea?"

"Who? Well—I suppose—obviously everybody who wants to see the end of that face. I mean—everybody! But to make it possible to put the idea into execution—you see, Comrade—Prince August Wilhelm is going to arrange an audience for me at the banquet for the generals at the German Embassy tonight."

"Who? Prince August Wilhelm? That astonishes me. One of the founders of the Nazi Party!"

"The European princes want to get rid of their Hitler again."

"The European princes?" The other played a few notes while he spoke. "Didn't the Marshal of the German nobility—in the name of all the dynasts—solemnly present him with a replica of Charlemagne's sword as a symbol of their 'unchanging fidelity and fealty'? That was at the Party Day in Nuremberg in 1934."

"How do you know that?"

"In the twenty years of my solitude underground behind the rococo mirror, I have listened to all your radio speeches. Including everything with which you up here have hourly prostituted the miracle of the ether waves. Yes, I heard the twaddle about a lasting peace—in Haudroumont Quarry. But I heard your presidents and ministers and generals too, when they shouted into the microphone, 'Only military power counts in our world of realities! Only power! The power of artillery and bombs and motorized armies! If you want peace, prepare for war.—Si vis pacem, para bellum.' But I didn't hear anyone shout over the ether waves, against that age-old dictum of Caesar's, the new dictum—the dictum of the unknown soldiers: 'Si vis pacem, para pacem!' "

Suddenly his eyes burned angrily out of his mask.

"Oh, I know, ever since we swore our oath for peace, there on the battlefield, over the graves of the 'unknown soldiers'—I know what lies and promises have come from the 'well-known soldiers.' And now you think that by shooting one man you can blow out the brains of Nazism? Don't you know that to do that you would have to shoot brain after brain? He could never have swollen up into such a world-wide black plague all by himself!"

Uhle looked down. The maimed soldier pulled out one of the stops, until a very delicate tone vibrated. "In any event, don't you know that his movement has spread over the whole world? An organization of evil, in which everyone is involved."

"Movement?" Uhle's attention was caught, for he was reminded of what he had said twice that day—first to Nadia and then to Olenka.

But before the soldier could answer, he wrapped himself in his red cape, as if he were cold, and rose. Then he looked up at the stone face: "Yes! Everyone is involved! You parents, who let your children play at war in the streets, like savages, with toy revolvers in their belts! *You* have made him great! You have made him great! And you girls, too, who float around the city streets picking up soldiers on leave, crazy about a uniform—or take sailors upstairs out of bars for an hour! You have made him great! Everyone who has talked to his fellow citizens about freedom or democracy in front of a plaster-of-Paris statue of liberty—but who in his own home, in apartments, drawing rooms, private dining rooms, or in secret sessions with vice, has not

180

defended freedom against the slavish swarm of his own sensual desires
—he has made him great! Every actor who has sung war songs or hate
songs or victory songs or revenge songs to an audience—has made him
great! A democratic state that gives citizenship to a refugee from a
dictatorship the minute he puts on its uniform and shoulders a gun, but
classes him as an 'enemy alien' if he 'only' defends freedom and peace
with his brains—that state has made him great! Every man who drowns
his mind in alcohol and lets his desire for freedom be talked to sleep by
the proponents of the doctrine that 'there's always been war and
always will be'—he has made him great! Everyone who says 'God' and
'hallelujah' and sings hymns in church on Sunday and goes back to the
office on Monday and serves Satan—has made him great!"

Uhle was profoundly frightened by the tone in which these words
were spoken. Timidly he went to him and asked,

"Comrade, could not we undo his greatness?"

As the soldier remained silent, Uhle whispered over his shoulder,
"Comrade! Could not we two together form a first cell of good men
against evil? I mean—an organization of good men, a counter movement against the beast, in which everyone can take part."

The soldier turned. For seconds they looked into each other's eyes.
Then the war cripple went back to the organ. After a long silence, he
took a notebook from his pocket and handed it to Uhle.

"I found this once in a fallen lieutenant's coat."

Uhle turned over the pages. Then, on a page stained with blood and
rain, he read the following sentences:

"'Strange fact: Belligerents exchange characteristics. And so we
shall presumably find the goosestep and the drum majors of the German army (if it is defeated) turning up again in Russia in the Red
Army. Or the Prussian military state will be destroyed, only to live
again in Washington.'"

The Uhlan handed back the notebook without a word.

"Brother," the maimed man from Verdun said, "do you not know
that God said, 'Revenge is *mine*'? Or has He made *you* the judge—that
you undertake to shoot His Accursed at tonight's banquet? Have you
so little faith in the justice of God? Do you not know that every blow
you give to another finally, in some mysterious, often roundabout way,
comes back to yourself?"

"What do you want of me?" Uhle threw his head back defiantly.
"Or perhaps you think that the flood will come and swallow everything?"

"Who can hold back the flood when its waters rise higher and higher out of the depths of sin? Do you think *you* can—by shooting down the man who controls the factories that turn out the raw material of sin? By shortening by seconds the terrible span of torment irrevocably decreed for him by the unalterable laws of universal justice? Do you want to fire your one bullet to free him from the ineluctable logic of evil?"

Uhle stared up at the organ pipes.

"Brother, think! Whatever evil a man does, he does to himself. But whatever good a man does, he does to himself too. That is as much an irrevocable law as gravitation is in physics."

"You ask the impossible!" Uhle put his hands to his temples. "No! Men will sooner believe in the devil than in such things! What you maintain is utterly horrible. What! The whole responsibility for the Nazi catastrophe, you lay not on him but on us! Upon every single one of us! During your twenty years of solitude did you never hear that there were people who fought against him day and night? Don't you know that there are innumerable men who warned against him—in schools, in congresses, in committees, from the stage, at mass meetings?"

"Brother!" The unknown soldier touched Uhle's shoulder with his fingers. "Do you not know that hypocrisy is even worse than the warmonger himself?"

"What?" Uhle started. Then he stood up straight, set his jaw, and started away.

But the other looked at him inexorably, like a new conscience. More than a minute passed. Then he asked gently:

"Where are you going? Listen! In my dugout behind the mirror I learned that to put an end to darkness light needs no other weapons than the power of its own ever brighter rays. And with them alone, the uttermost darkness will at last be bright!"

But as Uhle continued to stand there defiantly, the other drew him back to the organ bench.

"Brother!" He put his face close to Uhle's. "No one knows where the wrong began. But the first man who cuts clean through the endless tangle of the curse, who dares to speak out and say: *I!*—that man has thrown open the lion gate of peace."

Uhle wanted to answer. But he had to catch hold of the organ bench. His head sank down onto the keys. His whole body shook. Then the soldier from Verdun laid one hand on his head. With the other he softly played a melody, not learned in this world.

CHAPTER EIGHT "GO ON—IN HERE!" THE UHLAN WAS ORDERED BY A YOUNG MAN, WHO GOT OUT OF THE CAR CLOSE BEHIND him and who, nudging him with the barrels of the revolvers concealed in his coat pockets, forced him to enter a palatial residence near the Tuileries. "Keep going!" he called, poking him up a wide circular staircase, at whose curved iron railings Uhle occasionally caught.

When they arrived on the top floor, the man in the camel's-hair coat rang the bell over a small brass plate with the name "Dr. Schids." His coat opened, revealing a glimpse of silver braid on a black S.S. uniform. A pair of eyes looked through a peephole. Then there was the sound of a door chain being removed. A footman opened the door. They entered a dimly lighted anteroom, luxuriously furnished. There Uhle's companion, taking his cap off, bared his young and well-groomed head and revealed himself to be Prince Ferdinand. Just as the footman was about to take the Uhlan's cape, a gentleman in evening clothes appeared —his baby face looked devastated and bloated . . .

"Hello there, Mackensen!" The Prince pointed triumphantly at Uhle. "Here he is!"

"Excellent!" The almost sixty-year-old son of Marshal Mackensen inserted his monocle and listened smirkingly to the Prince's report— delivered in an undertone:

"It was Rudolf Hess—and my humble self—who caught him in front of Notre-Dame, coming out of the cathedral with a very chic lady . . . Unfortunately the beauty got away in the darkness under the trees along the quai." At these words, Uhle drew a deep breath. The Prince twinkled on to Mackensen:

"But Party Comrade Hess and Colonel Egath, are tracing her. I was supposed to deliver Uhle at once to Major Buch to be crossexamined at the German Travel Bureau in the rue de l'Opéra. But, according to my arrangement with you gentlemen, I have brought the noble demo-crat here first."

"Excellent!" Mackensen clicked his heels. "I shall immediately in-form your uncle August Wilhelm. He is at dinner with the others." Mackensen, who had been ordered to Paris for a few days from his post in the Embassy at Rome, beckoned to the footman. After the latter had left the room with the Uhlan, Mackensen whispered quickly into Ferdinand's ear:

"Your Imperial Highness, will you take my car and drive at once to a place well-known to your palate—Prunier's! Ask for the yellow private dining room. All the representatives of the crown-wearers of the future who are in Paris at the moment are assembled there—strictly incognito—for a monarchist dinner. Report to the chairman—the Duke d'Aguillon—what has taken place. He will then take matters in hand . . . !"

"What wouldn't any of us do—to foster the common great cause!" Ferdinand smilingly lit a cigarette, puffed clouds of smoke into the gray hair of the Hussar Marshal's son, buttoned up his coat again over his Gestapo jacket, and disappeared down the corridor.

Mackensen looked uneasily after him through the peephole. Then he carefully fastened the door chain again.

"Mr. Ambassador . . . I have taken the man into the big salon . . ."

"Excellent." Mackensen went past the footman and on into the olive-green-paneled rococo room. The logs in the fireplace crackled. Lamps were lit in various corners, their voluptuously shaded lights, reflected in the mirrors, shone on almost endlessly.

"Asseyez-vous!"

Bowing slightly, Mackensen offered the Uhlan a chair, and put cigarettes on a small marble table in front of him. Then tiptoeing noiselessly over the carpets he went back through several rooms, into the dining room.

For a moment the noise of a merry dinner party could be heard. Then the door was closed, and everything was still again. Uhle sat there, motionless. He did not once look at all the costly furniture and oil paintings. His dirty boots contrasted with the delicate colors of the silky Persian carpets. The footman had previously told him that Prince August Wilhelm was dining here . . . Uhle, who, it will be remembered, had already met his former schoolmate in the Bagatelle Park that morning, was determined, in spite of his conversation with the soldier in the organ loft, to accept his proposal. Yet he dreamed too of meeting the Austrian mass murderer alone and unarmed, trusting only in God's word and his own good cause.—Still his princely schoolfellow did not appear. "Olenka!" he whispered happily to himself. "At least they didn't catch you."

The door opened behind him. With hasty steps the fourth son of the Kaiser entered. He was wearing a dinner jacket. Behind him came Mackensen and Major Bruckner.

"Hello!" Prince August Wilhelm waved at the Uhlan—and then the three took chairs opposite him. Uhle sat there, like a soldier newly taken prisoner and brought before the enemy's general staff. In his eyes there still burned the reflection of his experiences at Notre-Dame—experiences whose importance these officers, who looked so sure of themselves in the protection of their caste, were incapable of suspecting.

The Hohenzollern now made a sign to Major Bruckner . . . Whereupon the latter rose and handed Uhle the pocketbook of which he had robbed him in the taxi by the Seine bridge that noon.

The Prince took from his vest a cigarette case with a crowned monogram and offered cigarettes to his companions. All three began to smoke. Through the clouds of tobacco Uhle watched the Hohenzollern's face. He thought of where, when, and how he had last seen him! It was in 1915, at Saint-Quentin. Filthy—just as they had been pulled out of the mud-holes along the Somme—his gun slung around his neck, wearing his steel helmet—he and many other soldiers, carrying heavy packs, hardly resembling human beings, had floundered past the Prince's shining yellow special train, to be crammed into cattle cars and be carried off to the offensive at Verdun . . . Mackensen, at that time aide-de-camp to the Prince, had called Uhle into the special train. August Wilhelm was spread over a voluptuous chaise longue upholstered in blue silk. His uniform was unbuttoned. "Makki" had to draw the curtains—so that the crowd of "Front swine," streaming past the car, could not see him. . . . And then the Prince had said:

"Congratulations, Uhle, on the privilege of fighting in the coming winter campaign. I am going to Potsdam—to my wife and child—over Christmas . . . Looking forward to getting back to the woods and feeding the hungry fallow-deer . . . in the glittering snow. . . . Or on December 24th in the afternoon—to accompanying my father from the New Palace through the snowy avenues of the park . . . to Sanssouci!" Yes! Now the Uhlan again heard the starting signal . . . Oh! In what a cursed hurry he had had to leave that magnificent special train—to be loaded with the rest of the unexpended human materiel!

In the meantime the Prince, too, had looked at his former schoolfellow closely. In the high, nasal tone of an erstwhile officer of the Guards, he suddenly said:

"Well, Uhle old man, since when have you been a Catholic? Ferdinand tells me you have taken to praying to the Madonna?" He grinned at his companions. Suddenly he exchanged glances with Mackensen, who drew Major Bruckner into a corner. There, among the bookshelves, they remained, quietly whispering. The footman, too, did not move.

"Tell me!" Prince August Wilhelm drew his chair closer to Uhle. "What exactly are you doing in this city of the crazy Gauls? Were you just sight-seeing with that charming lady in Notre-Dame out of pure love of the arts? Heh-heh! A cigarette? A glass of whiskey?" . . . He poured some into iced glasses and drank to Uhle.

"Yes, old man!" He twirled his small beard. "About the year 1000, France really played a leading role in the arts—at least so they told me at the University. Heh-heh!" He drank his glass empty and immediately refilled it. "Yes, sir! The good old history of art—heh-heh! Well, about the year 1000, too, for the first time, people began to worry about the end of the world. And now we're right back where we were —don't you think?—frightened of the end of the world. Hm? Good old Uhle! You must admit that I foresaw the whole thing." He looked at the others—then went to the fireplace and stared into the flames.

"When on November 11th, 1918, I telegraphed you from Baden-Baden and, in Germany's darkest hour, begged you to come to me, you did not come!" He looked darkly at the Uhlan. "A Prussian officer and the friend of the Kaiser's sons, you Uhle, went over to Judocracy!" He crushed out his cigarette against the fireplace. Then he went on, almost as if he were talking to himself: "My royal father and the Crown Prince had fled over the Dutch border. There I stood, all alone, in the mist and rain of that deserted watering-place, and I said to myself: 'Everything that is happening to us now is so insane that we can only be saved by something still more insane!' Yes!" He turned his head to Uhle. "I even went so far as to imagine that we two—I, the art-loving Prince, and you, the celebrated author—I thought that we two would be able to restore the might and dignity of the down-trodden Monarchy . . ."

"Monarchy . . . ?" Uhle moved impatiently. For a moment the two former classmates, who had not talked together for twenty years, stared at each other in a manner so estranged that the Prince suddenly rose to his feet, crossed the carpet, and opened the door onto the balcony. The autumn wind blew leaves into the room.

The Prince picked one of them up, shut the door, and came back and held the withered leaf against the lamp. "An oak leaf. Looks done for. Yet there must be strength in it still. Otherwise, how could it decay?" He laid it on the table. "The Greeks—everyone knows they fought for Helen. The Middle Ages fought for the Holy Sepulcher. But what this age is fighting for—good old Uhle, haven't you found that out yet?"

"Yes. I know it more clearly than ever."

"Bravo!" The Prince hunched his chair closer. "Because in those days

186

you didn't know. You didn't come. And I had to go to Potsdam alone that night to be with my mother in the New Palace. The Kaiserin was all alone, guarded by a 'Soldiers' Council.' I tried to get them to let her telephone to Holland. It was cold as the devil and they refused to give us wood to burn. My poor mother waited by the telephone till long past midnight. But the Kaiser never called. Of course, we had no idea that meanwhile Princess Hermine—it was vile—simply vile! . . . When I wanted to get into my villa, there stood a band of drunken sailors with the red rag round their arms, barring the way. It never entered their heads to present arms!" Cold rage twisted the corner of his mouth. "In my living room, my wife's blue velvet armchair was empty—she had cleared out. I never took the trouble to inquire who she eloped with. Later she achieved the sorry fame of being the first Royal Prussian Princess who, along with the hoi polloi, became an American citizen. Disgraceful! Makki!" he called back: "What did my great-great-grandfather, 'Old Fritz', use to say? 'The State is like a pyramid!'—wasn't that what he said?"

"Right! 'And the people are its base—' " The ambassador stepped forward. "But the crown is the apex! Without a base no apex!"

"And without an apex, no base! Heh-heh! Did you hear that, Uhle? You see, we have nothing at all against the base! In that, even I am a democrat! Goes without saying: there has to be a base—the people. But the apex—that's something else again! Do you follow me? It's the God-ordained pinnacle—It's the apex—that's all." He studied Uhle out of the corner of his eye. "What more is there to say? So now I ask you: Who is the apex today?"

In the tense pause that followed, Uhle replied quietly: "Who? Why do you ask me? The Austrian, of course! The man whom, for the past fifteen years, you have called 'my master'!"

The Prussian Prince turned lobster-red. Shielding his eyes from the lamp, he cleared his throat: "Do you suppose for a minute I would have discarded the uniform of the First Guards Regiment and buttoned on 'his' brown shirt, if I had not felt: Here is the man the civilized world needs against the Bolsheviki?! I ask you, who else was there? When the Spartacist mob tore the tapestries out of my mother's bedroom in the Berlin Palace—who was there? When that loathsome Jewish spider Rosa Luxemburg ripped the gilt Prussian Crown from the balcony in my ancestors' palace and threw it down into the street for the rabble to play football with—who was there?" He drummed on the table with his fingers. "Who was there when the stinking stream of your 'new humanity' poured in from the fields and threatened to inundate the palaces of Emperors and Kings? When the stupid cattle bleated and bellowed: 'Hurrah for Ebert!' 'Down with Ebert!' 'Hurrah for Scheidemann!' 'Down with Scheidemann!' 'Hurrah for Lieb-knecht!' 'Down with Liebknecht!' Anything! Anybody!

"Where were *you* when the hordes with their red banners, bawling the 'International,' streamed along the Tiergarten, and the Communist litterati and deputies stood up at their loaded tables in Hiller's triple-sec restaurant and raised their champagne glasses and piped: 'Long live the Revolution!' . . . Who was there *except* Adolf Hitler?"

He poured out a glass of water and gulped it down. "On my sacred honor, that's the only reason why I put this unknown Austrian on his feet! At least the fellow knew the ordinary language of the people—not the sort of thing our kind learns in the cradle! And it was not until *I* pinned the Silver Star of the Order of the Black Eagle on my Nazi shirt that people, one after another, began to say: 'If our Prince August Wilhelm can manage to get along with that man, so can we!' In Hell's name! Yes!—It was I! Long before Herr Göbbels! I, the Prussian Prince who, clad in the velvet of highest rank, used to stand with all the princes of the blood, beside the throne!—It was I who called the rabble-rouser 'My master'! Gladly and willingly! It was I who brought the German nobility into the camp of the Austrian plebeian! Yes!—I persuaded them all: The Archdukes of Hesse-Nassau and bei Rhein! The Landgraves of Hesse! The Princes of Lippe-Biesterfeld auf Det-mold! The Duke of Coburg! Duchess Hilda of Baden! The Mecklem-burgs! The Oldenburgs! The Princess of Thurn and Taxis! The Prince Solms and Isenburg! By God in heaven! Except for Ruprecht of Bavaria, I managed to drum all the crowned heads of Germany into the train of the bully-boy of Braunau! I was even able, after hours of argu-ment with my most Gracious Kaiser and Father in Doorn, to get him to part with astronomical sums, paid over to him as compensation and damages by the Weimar Republic!" August Wilhelm laughed with grim humor.

"Yes, my dear Uhle, it was *I* who, on a beautiful spring day in 1933, when everything was in bloom, drove this patriotic nonentity through the Mark Brandenburg to the old Monastery of Chorin. There, in the library, I read to him a prophecy dating from the eleventh century, ac-cording to which that man should become ruler of all Europe who would exterminate the black pestilence of the Jews! What could the wretched house-painter have done if I had not demonstrated to him the historic justification of his purely instinctive loathing for the Jews! Does that astound you?

"Afterward, we rowed out on the lake. There sat the former lance-corporal, dreamily watching the water drip from the oars while he listened, all ears, to what I had to say: 'Providence has chosen you, Adolf Hitler, to annihilate the corrupt processes of thought which, first from the French Revolution and then from the Bolshevist Revolution, have crept into German thinking. Liberty! Equality! Fraternity! Man is not free, I told him. Not equal! Not fraternal! . . . Only the decadent Jewish intellect, out of revenge for its own impotence, could have invented such a basic error! We must grind the viper under our heels! —All of a sudden, across the lake we heard some excursionists singing:

A Crown there lies in the Rhine so green,
Of magic gold and diamonds sheen. . . .
Who brings it up to the sun's bright ray
Shall be crowned in Aachen the self-same day!

"I shall never forget how he turned and listened, a sparkling light in his eyes! For fifteen minutes we did not speak. The boat floated far out from shore. His arms plunged to the elbow in water, he suddenly began to howl: 'Of magic gold and diamonds sheen . . . Who brings it up to the sun's bright rays . . .' Startled by a pair of herons rising, he sat up straight, shaking the water from his fingers. Watching the gnats dance in the air, he raised his right arm and shouted: 'I would rather be a gnat in my own country than Emperor in a foreign land!' And then he screamed: 'Deutschland! Deutschland über alles!'

"Late that evening, when we were driving back to dinner at Magda Göbbels', just as we passed the Berlin Palace, he suddenly grabbed my knee and said: 'Party Comrade August Wilhelm, you have fought the good fight with me! You have not only brought the so-called people over to me, but the cream of society too. At a time when only a few believed in me, you stuck to me through thick and thin! So, when I manage to fish the German Imperial Crown out of the mud and filth of democracy—then—' "

"Then?" Uhle smiled. "I suppose your 'master' will set it on your head?"

Red blotches appeared in August Wilhelm's face. Inserting a finger in his high collar, he stretched the starched linen back and forth over his Adam's apple with such force that it squeaked. He pushed his Hohenzollern seal-ring up and down on his finger. He avoided Uhle's eyes. "Naturally, I declined the Führer's noble offer for myself. But— I accepted it for my son." Finding his cigarette case empty, he snapped it shut.

"Eh bien! A short time later, His Excellency Herr Meissner, Chief of the Reich Chancellery, came to see me in Potsdam. He told me confidentially that in his Will, which he had just finished writing, the Supreme Führer had arranged that after his death my son was to be Emperor of the Greater German Reich. Meissner and I celebrated the occasion well into the morning hours.—Didn't we, Makki?"

The ambassador rose and clicked his heels. Prince August Wilhelm rose too, pacing back and forth among the furniture as if he were in a cage. Abruptly, he stopped, stared at Uhle, seized the table beside the armchair, raised it, and brought it down with such force that it groaned. If Uhle had not caught the lamp, it would have crashed to the floor.

"And this swine who owes everything to me—this filthy, wallowing swine—has crossed out the paragraph! This Austrian abortion! That is the Habsburgs' revenge against us Hohenzollerns!"

"Oh, perfidious Maria-Theresia revenge!" retorted Mackensen, clenching his fists—"The Viennese revenge against our Fridericus Rex in Sanssouci! And his seven-year-long fight and victory against Austria!"

"This disgusting product of Viennese Ballplatz intrigue dares to call himself Supreme War Lord of the Prussian army!"

"War Lord!" Mackensen gnashed his teeth. "That lackey! That waiter, that clown from the Wurstelprater!"

"Makki!" The Prince stood with clenched fists. "Herr Uhle doesn't seem to believe us. Here!" He brought down his fist on a Russian leather brief case.

"Here are all the documents. At the risk of his life, Herr Meissner rendered me an inestimable service and wrote down page 27 of the Will from memory."

In the anteroom the bronze mechanism of a clock started to whirr. With long pauses between the strokes it struck eight.

The Prince looked at the door. There had been a ring, and the footman went out.

"So now, Uhle, it is time to enlighten you about the reason for your presence here.—Or did our friend Colonel Egath tell you? No? I am acting in the name of the International Monarchists' Club." The house door opened and closed again. There was a murmur of voices. "Uhle, old man, we are giving you the chance of your lifetime! More than that, Uhle! We count on you to accomplish a great deed! And if you succeed—"

Prince Ferdinand entered, and announced with a grin:

"Uncle, the Duke d'Aguillon!"

"Is he here? Well Uhle, of course you know the Prefect of Police is temporarily ignoring the strong probability that you have committed a murder, and has turned over the handling of your case to his friend the Duke d'Aguillon. That young French nobleman, who is waiting outside, represents the Count of Paris, the future King of France. Since the anti-monarchists spy on us everywhere, I have asked the Duke to come up here. But"—he pointed to the door which the footman had thrown open—"there he is now!"

A young dandy in an opera hat, his black satin evening cape draped picturesquely over his left shoulder, entered. He was followed by a short, thickset man in dinner clothes, with a scarf around his neck.

"Excusez, mon cher cousin!" The French Duke gave the Prussian Prince his hand. "So sorry to be late! This person"—tapping the shoulder of his companion with the wine-reddened face—"is the treasurer of our club. A thorough scoundrel, but I can't get along without him! Eh, chéri?" They both laughed. "Eh bien, Messieurs!" He lit a cigarette and inhaled deeply. "Now—where is the young man—the one who is to . . . ?"

Prince August Wilhelm held the lampshade so that the light fell full on Uhle's face. The Duke inserted his monocle and stroked his diminutive, soot-black beard.

"Charmant! Très charmant!"

"Votre Altesse Royale!" The Treasurer bowed to the Hohenzollern, and his pockmarked face grinned. "You will allow me to speak to your protégé?"

"Naturally."

"Merci, mon Prince!" He drew Uhle into the window corner. "Mon vieux," he said hoarsely, "you managed to escape from the police station in the rue de Grenelle? Écoutez: I have read your dossier. Eh bien! You know, of course, that Weidmann still sticks to his story that he knows you? Tiens, tiens! There's a button missing from your sleeve? . . . Here it is—I've brought it along! This matches your other buttons, doesn't it? Eh bien! We have photographed your footprints in the Bagatelle Park. So my best advice to you is: if you want to avoid the criminal police—agree to the proposition of these gentlemen . . ."

"Un moment!" the Duke d'Aguillon interrupted him. The doorbell had rung several times. Then he smiled at the Prussian Prince: "My dear Hohenzollern, our illustrious club members have arrived. Shall we go to welcome them?"

"What for?" August Wilhelm licked his finger and nervously ran it

191

over his eyebrows.

Again the high folding doors opened and a group of men in evening clothes and dinner clothes came in. Patent-leather pumps glistened. An Austrian Imperial Order peeped out through the folds of a scarf. The Star of the Spanish Crown glistened from a black coat. The wide satin ribbons of the highest European Household Orders shimmered in the changing light. After the greetings were over, the Duke stationed himself in front of Uhle and said solemnly, "Mes augustes princes, le voilà!"

There was a play of curious glances. Without further ceremony, Prince August Wilhelm took some penciled sheets from the Russian leather brief case:

"Most illustrious Rulers and Princes of Europe!" he began in a voice that shook with excitement. "I, Prince August Wilhelm of Prussia, have the honor to bring to the attention of your Imperial and Royal Highnesses this accurate copy of pages 27, 28, and 29 from the Will of the German Reich Chancellor. These pages deal with the monarchist principle. Confidentially, of course, damn it! Shut that door back there!"

The footman shut the door. Prince Ferdinand placed himself in front of it and the assembled grands seigneurs moved breathlessly nearer to the Prince. The latter approached the lamp and then read the brilliantly formulated sentences he had been given by Meissner—as if they were the original text of Hitler's Will.

" 'German Folk Comrades! Before I, Adolf Hitler, enter upon my fiftieth year, it is befitting that I, blood of your blood, should bequeath to you an unequivocal word, which shall, if in the course of human events anything should happen to me, regulate the succession to my office of Führer, conferred upon me by your majority vote . . . Malicious tongues have often attempted to make you believe that your Supreme Chancellor of the Greater German Reich would be guilty of the same wretched nonsense as the erstwhile Napoleon Bonaparte, and in order to certify himself in your eyes, would dig some crown or other out of the moth-eaten treasury of the decadent dynasties and set it upon his own head. German Folk Comrades! . . . I have no need of any other crown than your confidence in me! We have already experienced to the full the worthlessness and futility of the entire rabble of European crowned heads. My friend Mussolini despises these dregs of humanity just as much as I despise them. Providence, on the other hand, has placed the Duce, inspired genius though he is, within the frame of circumstances governed by royal etiquette, inconsequential though it is. Every time I have had the honor to stand beside the Duce, I have been seized with an unspeakable emotion of proud satisfaction that I did not have to function as the Prime Minister of any ridiculous 'Royal Majesty,' but that on the contrary, I have been called solely and exclusively to represent the Majesty of the National Socialist State.

" 'The last strands of the mythical bond between throne and people were torn to shreds in the trenches of the War of 1914-18. Has any of you, for instance, ever seen a single one of these Sovereigns, anointed by 'God's Grace,' in the midst of the fire of battle? Myself, a simple lance-corporal, on all my errands of duty, I never ran into one of their illustrious gang . . .' "

Prince August Wilhelm ceased reading for a moment and asked: "Do your Imperial and Royal Highnesses desire that I continue?" There was an oppressive silence. Not a breath was heard, not a word uttered. "Eh bien, then I shall continue the reading of these amusing testamentary dispositions. Herr Hitler declares:

" 'And if the President of the United States wants to collect all this most illustrious rag-tag and bob-tail we have hunted off the thrones and out of the principalities of Europe, and hand them over to the Indians for a curio cabinet—let him do so! We have no further use for them. Do you suppose that one of these nit-wits—as for instance, the Coburg idiot—imagines I cannot see through his illustrious chicanery and that I don't know why he has put on the brown shirt of my National Socialist Party? Does the half-witted Prince of Hesse imagine for a single instant that I do not know the true color of his opinions through my Gestapo? Does Prince August Wilhelm think his visits to Holland in the uniform of the First Guards Regiment are unknown to me? When he is with me, he wears the brown shirt, but when he is with his monarchist, nose-in-the-air relatives, then of course our plain brown shirt isn't fine enough for him.

" 'German Folk Comrades!

" 'You don't need any such illustrious blockheads in Europe any longer! It's been long enough that these beribboned, un-German, most gracious landlords have been selling you and haggling over you as if you were cattle, solely and exclusively for the benefit of their own princely interests. . . . Oh, German People, read and read again your German history! And then ask yourselves what these Orléans and Hapsburgs, these Hesses and Bourbons have ever done for your "Strength through Joy"! Wasn't it a Hapsburg, for instance, who betrayed that German of Germans, heart and soul a German man, Andreas Hofer, in Mantua, straight into the rifle mouths of your enemies? No!—I would rather end my life as a simple German private than, at the pinnacle of all my triumphs, set upon my head any one of those crowns drenched in your blood, O People!

" 'I, therefore, your Führer, herewith declare and determine that: Whoever—after me—shall in your name, O German People, have the conduct of the affairs of this world—shall forever be, unto the farthest millennium, only my representative, deputy, and appointee! Even after my death, I shall be always present with you! Whether you sow or whether you reap, whether you fire a rifle against Bolshevism or whether you give the boot to the last remaining Jew in Europe!—Yes, even in the moment of cohabitation, when you are procreating our invincible divisions of German soldiers for the defense of the National Socialist People's Community!—always and ever, the immortal image of your Führer shall hover over your beds! Heil Hitler!' "

A nasal voice inquired: "Is that all?"

"Not yet, Your Imperial Highness. Here is a postscript:

" 'If ever'—it says here—'a Hohenzollern or a Wittelsbach, a Nassau or an Orléans, or anyone else from the mausoleum of moldy potentates, dares to approach you as a pretender, O you my Greater German People! on that day and in that hour—and this is my last Will—pick up a hammer or a pitchfork or a dagger or whatever you may have at hand, and smash and cram and jam anybody who has managed to set himself on a throne and taken your power unto himself! Beat him, slay him, slash him, and smash him until every Gauleiter or S.S. Storm Troop Leader or Reich Deputy Governor shall once again through the mist and smoke of battle, behold the beloved countenance of his Führer! Heil Hitler!' "

Some of those present had put their hands over their ears. The same nasal voice as before demanded: "Is that the end of it?"

"Yes." Prince August Wilhelm put the sheets back into the Russian leather brief case.

There was a murmur of indignation and gradually single words shrilled out:

"Swine!" "Monster!" "Bolshevik!" "Wring his neck!" "What impertinence!" The angry eyes of all the dynasts focused beseechingly on Uhle. He brushed his hand back over his head and sat weighing their lust for revenge, looking straight ahead of him at the table. Then suddenly he stood up:

"Most Exalted and Illustrious Rulers!" he began ironically. "Imperial and Royal Highnesses! Eminent Eminences! Illustrious Princes, Counts, Barons and other Wearers of the Purple! . . . You who do all in your power to serve the insignificant, common man to his last breath—!"

"What! What!" The Treasurer gave him a push. But Uhle did not budge:

"Gentlemen, in September 1914, I myself was present when the German heavy artillery in the neighborhood of Nesle bombarded the village of Champien to atoms, and your Imperial Father"—for the first time he looked directly at August Wilhelm—"made known his intention of seeing with his own eyes the effect of the firing on the 'common man'—"

The Treasurer undid the scarf around his neck, tugged at his black tie, and said ominously: "Et alors?"

"That is to say—the All-Highest edict of the All-Highest Authority was issued: The village must be instantly cleared of every last corpse of a 'common man,' because his Imperial Majesty in the greatness of his most exalted heart, could under no circumstances bear the sight of the scraps and cadavers of the 'common man'—that is, should the All-Highest condescend immediately to appear at the scene of the battle . . ."

". . . Condescend immediately to appear?" . . . There was a scraping of feet, but Uhle continued remorselessly:

"Whereupon the remains of the wretchedly maimed and shattered common man were hastily wheel-barrowed out of the still smoking ruins and devastated vegetable gardens along the village street to the square in front of the burning church. There, the Major in command of the Imperial Military Police had ordered the digging of a mass grave, 32 feet long, 26 feet wide, and over 15 feet deep. The first victims of the All-Highest bombardment were quickly and unceremoniously dumped into the ditch. Unfortunately, one young woman, with both legs smashed to ribbons, had to be fished out again because the M.P.'s had forgotten to take the rings off her fingers. Inasmuch however, as a wild and tangled disorder of the common man had resulted down in the grave, the Major gave the order to straighten out the torn bodies, rearrange them, orderly fashion, in rows, and pile them up on top of one another in layers. The command was carried out: Blue coats, field-gray uniforms, red trousers, women's dresses, peasant jackets, Indian turbans, khaki overcoats containing British soldiers, Negroes, and many examples of the German common man, were expertly built up the way bricks are laid. And if, Illustrious Rulers, these common men have up to the present hour not been able to express to you their most subservient thanks, it is because the

M.P.'s probably let the earth trickle too quickly into their open mouths, rigid in death. And besides, there was really not enough room for such a demonstration of submissiveness . . . And the top layer was already sticking out above the earth which the M.P.'s had shoveled on in the last haste of excitement. And inasmuch as there were still piles and stacks of other common men lying about among the pear trees behind the cemetery wall, and your Imperial Father was approaching at a brisk pace along the Route Nationale—the fanfare from 'Lohengrin,' blown on a trumpet by the silver-liveried chasseur seated beside the chauffeur, could already be heard in the air! —the Major was yanking the hairs of his moustache like mad. Suddenly he gave a command. 'Chuck the rest of that muck on top and tramp the whole piggery down! Go on! Stamp it down! Harder! Be quick about it!'

"And now the nine M.P.'s formed a chain and, with their brand-new, oiled, brown boots stamped in all the corpses that refused to make themselves comfortable under the earth—step by step, like grass seed!"

"Stop!" one or two of the perfumed grands seigneurs gesticulated. But Uhle slowly turned the lamp in such fashion that all their faces were in the light.

"The last corpse they dragged up was that of a common soldier— a splendid physical specimen in the prime of his youth. In his gaunt and waxen face, with its growth of untrimmed beard, the whites of the eyes rolled back mournfully, as if to say: 'What a pity! The wind is blowing so lightly among the dangling, ripe pears . . . The swallows are flitting so joyously back and forth. . . . The grasses are bowing and dancing . . . The butterflies are sucking honey from asters and dahlias . . . What a pity!' But he, like the rest, was thrown on the heap. Unhappily, his left arm stuck up so stiff and straight that the earth would not cover it. The motor horn of the Supreme War Lord was already heard at the beginning of the village—Ta-ti-ta-taaa —resounding with operatic magniloquence on the air of that still, golden September afternoon. The Major snatched a shovel out of the hand of an M.P., heaped chunks of earth on top of the obstinate arm of that common man, sticking up out of the earth. Every time he threw a spadeful, the obstreperous arm simply teetered and waved back and forth. His brow sweating, the Major passed the shovel on. 'Go on! Get that damn thing covered up!' And now the M.P.'s heaved such masses of earth on the obtrusive, flagging arm, that they made a regular hillock. Notwithstanding, the hand of the corpse still wobbled and waved out of the top of the pile! This was too much for the Major! he took a run and jumped on top of it, his saber rattling. The bone snapped . . .

" 'Taaa-ti . . . ta-taaa!' . . . The Kaiser's yellow standard breezed onto the village square at fifty miles an hour. The Major snapped to attention like a railway signal arm. Up there, on top of the mass grave, the M.P.'s snapped their heels together. Your Father, the All-Highest, drove forward, slowing down. In the gold-braided uniform of a Prussian Field Marshal General, he saluted graciously with his swagger-stick:

" 'Oh, grandiose!' he rejoiced. 'Our artillery certainly did a beautiful job!' . . ."

Uhle looked out onto the balcony. Without another word, he walked past the assembled dynasts—who stood there confused, as if the hatred they felt were too much to cope with—and out into the adjoining room.

CHAPTER NINE   AUGUST WILHELM'S FACE WAS GRAY. THE ZIG-ZAG VEINS ON HIS PRINCELY TEMPLES WERE SWOLLEN BLUE. Lips barely parted, he muttered nasally:

"Mon cher Aguillon! My illustrious cousins and princes—what shall we do with this swine?"

"Your Royal Highness!"

"Count Schimmelsporn?"

"May I be permitted humbly to suggest that the Club adopt a resolution that our tried-and-true Treasurer go after the swine and see to it that—one way or another—he takes the decision with which we are at this moment solely and irremediably concerned?"

"Messieurs—" Prince August Wilhelm took off his cap—"are all present in agreement with this proposal?" There was no response.

"Eh bien!" D'Aguillon gave his pockmarked companion a shove. "Allez! And make a good job of it!"

Knotting the scarf about his neck, the Treasurer disappeared.

"Mais calmez-vous, mon cher Hohenzollern! . . ." One of the group offered him a cigarette. "Mon Dieu! We Orléans are well acquainted with the chronique scandaleuse of ingratitude! Yet the silver Loire still winds its ancient way."

Gradually the indignation of the frozen assembly began to thaw.

"As I was coming through the rue St. Jacques just now on my way here"—Aguillon was sucking on a bonbon—"I happened to think of that saying of Pascal's: 'The "I" is detestable!'—'Le moi est haïssable . . .'"

"Certainly not *our* 'I'." One of the Princes wiped his face with his handkerchief.

"Swine!" August Wilhelm sat back, exhausted, on the bench. "Here we go, making these swine capable of appreciating the niceties of court life—and what happens? For centuries, we have to listen to their servile whimperings on the parquet of our palaces. And then these 'most obedient servants and servitors' suddenly go and discover in their hearts—what? 'The rights of man!' Ha-ha! They go wild because a miserable limb of a corpse won't stay put. On the slightest pretext, this rabble of subjects goes and gets excited!"

"Calmez-vous! Prince August!" The young D'Aguillon handed him the water bottle. "'The world is a dung heap!' as Voltaire said. And only our Crowns—only the Crowns of the dynasts—can gild such manure so that you'd really believe there was something to it!"

"You give such gentry"—August Wilhelm's voice trembled—"swords of honor, cravats, autographed photos—and all of a sudden some boor like that takes it into his head to be impertinent!"

"Mais calmez-vous, mon cousin! The people in this world will continue to crawl around on all fours until we are seated on our proper thrones again—and then we'll show them—how to stand up on their hind legs!—So-o-o!—Paws up!"

"Yes, yes!" They all laughed, and began to imitate begging dogs. "There's a good doggy! That's the best you can get out of such human scum! Take the whip to them! Nice doggy! Sit up! Lie down! Roll over—dead dog!"

"My Illustrious Cousins"—August Wilhelm was gradually regaining his self-possession—"perhaps it's just as well we've heard this with our own ears. And if the Monarchist Principle does not pretty quickly stamp out the spawn of such anarchy—it won't be long before people like us, of rank and station, will simply have ceased to exist!"

"Always look for the silver lining, mon prince!"—the Duke d'Aguillon combed back his oily, black hair—"Always keep your head up, and never look down at the dirt! We alone, Messieurs—we are what we are by the Grace of God!" This pronouncement completely restored to them all their seignorial complacency.

The Treasurer stepped through the doorway, bare-headed and grinning with satisfaction.

"Et alors?" There was a general movement in his direction.

"Gloria! Gloria!"

"You mean he agrees?"

"He raved! Let him rave! The main thing is—he agrees!"

"Just a moment!" One spoke up: "Just how has the list covering the restoration of the European crowns and thrones among us—*after* the event—been worked out?"

"The list of what? What kind of a list? France to Orléans! As to the German thrones, you thirty princes must come to an agreement among yourselves!"

"We are agreed—and united!" August Wilhelm half rose from his seat. "My Father, the Emperor, and his heir, my dear son, have already been advised to prepare for the event."

"Prince Obelinski?"

"Here! We Poles—"

"You are representing the Romanovs?"

"No! My cousin, the Grand Duke Cyril, is here to represent the sacred rights of the Sole Ruler of all the Russians!"

"Bon!—And who are you?" asked the Duke d'Aguillon of a tall dynast.

"I represent the claim to the Throne of the Most Illustrious Princely House of Reuss, of the Twenty-ninth Line!"

"And who is here for Austria?"

"The Archduke!"

"Good!—And you?"

"I represent the claim to the Throne of His Serene Highness Prince zu Lippe-Detmold."

"And the Mecklemburg Archdukes?—"

"Are at their palace of Schwerin, awaiting word by telephone of a successful attack on the Führer."

"And Hilda von Baden?"

"Awaits the news at the residence of her tennis-playing cousin, the King of Sweden, in Nice."

"Good!" The Duke tapped with his seal ring on the table top. "The exalted representatives of the princely houses of Europe are virtually all present. But, before the deed is accomplished, we must agree on our program. My dear Hohenzollern, early this morning Count Schimmelsporn demanded, in the name of His Royal and Imperial Apostolic Majesty the Archduke of Austria, in the event of a successful restoration, the return of both the two Silesian provinces, stolen from the most Illustrious House of Hapsburg by your Illustrious ancestor Frederick the Great, during his predatory Seven Years' War—"

"Duke!" Prince August Wilhelm brought his fist down on the table. "The German Imperial Crown rules over the territory of the German Reich, including Silesia, Poland, Moravia, the Tyrol, Alsace-Lorraine—"

"Pardon? pardon! pardon! Alsace-Lorraine? A great-great-grandson of the Roi-Soleil will never set his signature to that!"

"Pardon!" August Wilhelm's tone was cutting. "Nonetheless and notwithstanding, it was expressly so agreed at Doorn, in May of this year, in the presence of my Imperial Father, His Majesty Wilhelm II, and in the presence of the Illustrious Ruling Families of the Netherlands, Spain, Serbia, Rumania, and Norway.—What! And now we're supposed to give Silesia back to Austria?" August Wilhelm shook his fist in the air. "The Devil you say! We'll go to war first! Strike me dead if I wouldn't rather let the Bolsheviki have it! Have you Austrians gone mad? If Maria Theresia were still alive! But an exiled Archduke who hasn't even done military service! Silesia?! You Orléans might just as well demand the return of the whole Rhine Province!"

"Mon cher Cousin! On that question we still have to come to an agreement—"

"On the Rhine Province?" August Wilhelm's voice broke with rage. "Perhaps you'd like to retain the status quo of Versailles?"

"Not precisely the status quo, Cousin—but still, some sort of status—"

"Impossible! The German Army will never consent to any such chicanery! If that's the case, the plan is out." He jumped to his feet.

"Ça va! Ça va! Let's not forget, my dear Cousin, that we're in Paris! We're not in Potsdam! The regiments down there along the Seine are still as far as I know the regiments of the French Republic! But when the shot has been fired in the German Embassy—then, my dear Hohenzollern—then all the bayonets from the Place de la Concorde to the Arc de Triomphe, from the Tuileries to Provence, will again be the regiments of His Most Christian Majesty, the King of France . . ."

"My dear Duke!" August Wilhelm burst out into uproarious laughter. "Don't make me laugh! Can it be possible you don't know that the initiative in this matter lay not with the Orléans but with the Hohenzollerns, supported by the German Reichswehr? Your Paris is a wonderful city—I grant you! But you seem to forget that, since they chopped off the head of your illustrious ancestor, Louis XVI, certain cavities have developed beneath your edifice—"

"Quoi? What kind of cavities?"

"Calmez-vous!" someone intervened. "Are we going to darken the sunrise of monarchy in Europe with such squabbles? Dear Prince August, on behalf of His Holiness the Pope, I am instructed to ask the House of Hohenzollern whether a re-enthroned German Kaiser intends to recognize the supreme authority of the Catholic Church—or not? Does that question disturb you, my dear Prince August? Of course, we know you are a Protestant—"

"You know nothing about it! I *was* a Protestant!"

"Oh!" D'Aguillon bowed. "Charmant! Charmant! Bravo! So you've become a Catholic since?"

"Ni l'un, ni l'autre!" August Wilhelm flashed. "We German representatives of monarchy have drawn our own deductions and conclusions from the course of recent events!"

"Deductions? Conclusions? Heh-heh! These Hohenzollerns talk in riddles! What sort of conclusions? At all events, the rest of us crowned heads have long since concluded an agreement with the White House in Washington and His Most Sacred Holiness the Pope, to the effect that in close collaboration with democracy and the Vatican, we intend to make the Pan-Catholic Principle the basis of our mutual international and dynastic relations. Heh-heh-heh! Excuse me! And your mocking smile, Prince August, does not in the slightest degree affect a Frenchman like myself. I am not a bigot, everybody knows! But we rulers of the West are convinced that, since this latest exhibition of mob rule by the godless scum of humanity—from now on, externally at least, we must do everything possible to build an aura of supernatural splendor around the heads of our Monarchies for the benefit of the mob."

"Of supernatural splendor? Heh-heh! The German Reichswehr, at any rate—" August Wilhelm snapped.

"German Reichswehr! German Reichswehr!" The other Princes menaced the Hohenzollern. "What! More religious wars? Do these Prussians want to—"

There was silence as Uhle, upon whose decision all their future dynastic hopes depended, was brought back into the room.

CHAPTER TEN

He WALKED IN BETWEEN THE POCKMARKED TREASURER AND COUNT SCHIMMELSPORN, HIS SHOULDERS set. Picking up a candle from the smoking table, Prince August Wilhelm threw the light directly in Uhle's face. So strange did his former school comrade appear to him that the Kaiser's son set down the candle bewildered.

"Et alors?" asked the Duke, annoyed at the interruption. But behind Uhle's back the Treasurer nodded his head in affirmation for the benefit of the exalted gathering.

All breathed more freely. Nazi General August Wilhelm wiped the sweat from the back of his neck with his handkerchief. Then the tense mouth under the long nose gave the Uhlan a friendly smile. Uhle took the magnificently upholstered chair he offered him. His knees wide apart, his hands resting on them, he waited.

"Good old Uhle!" the Hohenzollern stuttered. "If I interpret our Treasurer's gesture aright, you have decided to fire the shot! Bravo! Magnificent! But we haven't got much time, so let's get down to business: The members of the Monarchists' Club here present have magnanimously declared their willingness to award you, post mortem, the Distinguished Service Cross, Third Class, of their several Household Orders. The implements, weapons, and clothing for your mission will be supplied to you by my nephew, Prince Ferdinand."

"At your service!" The young Prince came to attention at the door. "He will be equipped in the conservatory of the German Embassy."

"Bien, bien!" August Wilhelm nodded, and then turned back to the Uhlan. "Have you any questions? Shall we notify your relatives? Do you need a priest? Any last wishes we are benevolently disposed to grant . . . So!" He wiped his forehead. "Then that's settled! And now, Prince Ferdinand will accompany you. A car is waiting to take you to the scene of operations . . . And—whatever differences have been between us"—he brushed them aside—"are better forgotten! The deed you are about to do wipes your coat-of-arms clean of every democratic maculation! Geh mit Gott!"

All stood silent, eyes greeting Uhle, like a band of conspirators in mingled fear and admiration of a terrorist to whom the lot has fallen to carry out an assassination. Uhle got up from his chair and started for the door. His eyes glittered as if he had been drinking wine.

Abruptly he stopped in front of an unusually tall gentleman wearing dark glasses—below whose bow tie the Order of the Golden Fleece, set with emeralds, gleamed.

"Archduke? I'm not mistaken? Last February, through the mediation of the Spanish Loyalist Münzer, I paid my respects to you here in Paris . . ."

"Yes, indeed!" The tone was kind. "What is it?"

"In the Petit Palais Royal, wasn't it—next door to the Comédie Française? It was snowing—heavy white flakes—"

"Kindly respect the Most Exalted Incognito!" Count Schimmelsporn thrust himself between them.

"No, please—let him talk."

"I waited in the lobby by the artificial palms. Your aide-de-camp finally sent for me. I found the Count sitting by his bed, typing a letter. When he had finished, he opened the door to the next room and said: 'The Emperor is expecting you!' I found you, Archduke, in a small hotel room, your hat and coat on the sofa, a writing case on the marble mantel . . . The curtains were drawn."

"Your Majesty!" Schimmelsporn put down his cigar, painfully moved. "You probably no longer deign to remember this Prussian!"

"Oh, yes I do! Remember quite well! I talked about the traitor Dollfuss and Schuschnigg . . . And then this gentleman talked to me about some kind of a 'better future for humanity.' Ha-ha!"

"That was it! And over your green-shaded desk lamp I gave you an account of a meeting I had with a 'common soldier' in the trenches at Verdun in 1916."

"Correct!" The other smiled at the dynasts through his dark glasses: "In the course of the audience he told me about a pioneer who had called his attention to a grass blade in the middle of a battle."

"To a grass blade?" The princes pricked up their ears and grinned.

"Yes!" Uhle nodded. "It was waving beside our machine guns against the evening sky, like the quintessence of beauty. And that common man looked at me with his Christlike eyes and said, 'Look, comrade. That grass blade lay in the ground as a tiny seed. And the earth weighed on it so hopelessly heavily. What, then, gave it the courage to strive up through the lightless, worm-riddled ground until at last it broke through? Until at last its green tip for the first time knew the infinite light of day!'"

"Christlike eyes?" Count Schimmelsporn raised his eyes to heaven, shook his head, and then looked at his master. "As if there could be anything more beautiful, your Majesty, than that which our All-

203

Highest Redeemer proclaimed more than two thousand years ago!"

"For instance," Uhle's gaze strayed over the Most Christian Potentates, " 'Peace on earth, good will towards men.' "

"Of course!" The Grand Seigneur tugged furiously at his Hollywood beard. "But, if you Prussians make a point of never following the wise precepts of the All-Highest Lord Christ . . ."

"Prussians! Prussians?" August Wilhelm pulled impatiently at his chin as if it were a hard-mouthed horse and turned round to Mackensen.

"That's right!" sneered a Bavarian Prince. "If it weren't for you, the rest of us would have been spared this world-wide cochonnerie . . ."

"Pardon," Uhle interrupted their Catholic Highnesses. "What particular wise precept of the Christ's is under discussion? Is it 'He who draws the sword shall perish by the sword?' "

There was a spontaneous outburst of mocking laughter. Uhle seemed so alone among the dynasts that the Imperial Aide-de-camp felt sorry for him and touched his shoulder almost sympathetically:

"Have the goodness not to forget that our Sacrificial Lamb, with the crown of thorns on His head that day in Jerusalem, laid a command on all Christians: 'Render unto Caesar that which is Caesar's!' Correct, Your Majesty?"

"Correct," all the dynasts nodded. Uhle met their triumphant glances. Then he said coldly:

"And precisely for that reason this beautiful world of ours has been delivered over to Caesars and criminals for the last two thousand years!"

"What was that?! Such impertinence!" There was an angry muttering.

Uhle waited for the tumult to subside . . . then he said still more decisively: "Christ also said, 'Render unto God that which is God's.' "

After an embarrassing pause, a commoner whom Uhle had not noticed before came to the rescue of the high-born gentlemen—a refugee writer from Buda named Zuckerl. The chubby author of prize-winning legends of the saints, who had been offered the post of Minister of Culture when the Hapsburg monarchy should be restored, smirked broadly at the Uhlan:

"Bravo, old man!" He puffed on his long Virginia. "By all means, 'Render unto God that which is God's.' "

"Pardon!" Uhle wrinkled his forehead. "How is it possible to render unto God and at the same time to render unto Caesar? We front-line soldiers could never manage that trick during the slaughter."

"Well, old man"—the other rubbed his hands together like a clergy-man—"you certainly aren't setting out to *change* this world—are you? Give to Authority that which you owe to Authority. The more it demands of you, the better." He bowed to the Archduke, then went on puffing at Uhle: "Old man! Pay your tribute to earthly power! Hand it over all your wordly goods—all of them! That's what God up in Heaven cannot use from you anyway . . . Give until you stand naked without a shirt on your back! Old man!" He sucked comfort-ably at his juicy and stinking Virginia. "Give all your filthy material possessions. Give your body. Give everything but the immaterial part of you!"

"The immaterial part of me?" Uhle looked bitterly at the happily smoking biographer of the saints. "The immaterial part of me? Well, we had to deliver it piece by piece to Authority in our barracks: our dignity, our liberty, our feeling for justice, even our love and our heart-beat—and our very breath . . ."

"La! La! La!" the Judo-Christian, who had turned from Communism to the Church, burst out and fingered the brand-new gold cross on his watch chain. "*Your* heart-beat? Come, come, old man? What do you mean—*your* breath?"

"This Prussian here"—Count Schimmelsporn grinned at the Princes —"behaves as if *he* had created himself! Ha-ha-ha!"

"Pardon!" Uhle cuttingly interrupted their laughter. "Didn't the grass blade we were talking about create itself from its own root, too? Joint by joint! Pushing up through the dark earth, until at last it reached light!—But, of course, if you laugh at our will to light, trample it down before it has a chance to grow . . . or mow it down with your imperial edicts—before the human grass blade can ripen its primal pollen . . . I mean—its innate drive toward light!"

"Its own innate drive?" Zuckerl's face darkened. "Uhle, old man! Don't you know that *nothing* is your own? Nothing! Not your heart-beat—nothing! Not even your breath belongs to you!"

"Nothing?" The corners of Uhle's mouth twitched. "And—may I ask you of what use to your Caesar-God is such a 'nothing'?"

"What?!" The other's eyes almost popped out behind his thick glasses. "You ask me, what use to God is such a 'nothing'? Well," he winked at the princes. "Your Highnesses will agree, I'm sure, that only in God's inconceivable and inexhaustible grace can we sinners find the answer to that question." He was going to drivel on, but Prince Ferdinand pulled the door open.

"Uncle August Wilhelm, 8:20 already. The car is waiting."

"Eh bien!" The pockmarked Treasurer grabbed the Uhlan. "Allez! Allez!"

"Pardon! Before I go I have one word more for you, my erstwhile, respectable brethren of the escutcheon. If God is pleased to permit me to accomplish my purpose on this gigantic imitator of your age-old dreams of power, it will not be so that *you* can start growing your dynastic mushrooms again on what one of Your Highnesses has called 'the dunghill of the people.' No! It is not *you* that I shall represent at my audience with him, but another. Prince August Wilhelm, I go in the name of him to whom at L'Homme Mort before Verdun in 1916, we took a solemn oath to work for peace—while around us the corpses of 'common men' were heaped higher and higher. For him, I take it upon me that the Sacred Law of War which you have been preaching for centuries shall be changed in us into the new Sacred Law of Life!"

"Sire," Count Schimmelsporn shouted above him, "is he going to begin jabbering about the common soldier again?"

"About him with the crown of barbed wire! Who said, 'There shall be wars and rumors of wars, but the end is not yet!' "

While they looked at one another, shocked by the sudden metallic quality of his voice, Uhle walked past them. But on the threshold he turned back to them as if they were ghosts and whispered,

"Danse macabre of rotten imaginations . . ."

Then he was out of the door. Prince Ferdinand and the aide-de-camp hurried after him.

CHAPTER ELEVEN SERGEANT-MAJOR GRUMBACH SAT IN THE NARROW KITCHEN OF THE PENSION ALSACE, WAITING FOR HIS cousin to come downstairs and tell him more of how things were going beyond the Rhine. He had met her at the station that afternoon on her arrival from Germany. The fifty-four-year-old widow of a German officer reported missing in the holocaust of Verdun, she insisted upon being addressed, even by her relatives, as "Frau Captain."

Not very hungry—what he had heard at Uhle's hearing had decidedly upset him—he was nibbling at a ham sandwich which his sister Therese had just made for him. This shriveled, gray-haired old maid in black clothes had followed him to Paris from Alsace in 1918.

Somehow or other she managed to make both ends meet out of her modest earnings from her boarders, most of whom were German refugees. Nevertheless, the many religious pictures on her walls, one of which hung above the kitchen stove, revealed that she had invested her main capital in the Kingdom of Heaven, from which she hoped one day to derive a heavy return.

Wiping his mustache, Grumbach started to make a list of Therese's foreign guests. From time to time he eyed the door in the hope that Frau Captain, who had gone to her room to dress for the evening, would finally come down.

"What can be going on at the German Embassy tonight that she has to make such an elaborate toilet?"

"After all she is the Women's Cultural Leader of Heidelberg!" Therese finished shelling her peas, swept the empty pods off the oilcloth-covered table, went to the kitchen door and listened for a moment for sounds from upstairs. Then she sat down and began laboriously checking her accounts.

"Frau Captain is getting to look more and more like our late-lamented Empress Auguste Viktoria."

"Klärchen has certainly become plump. Who lives in Number 13?"

"Her son, Baldur—"

"Ask him to come down a moment—"

"He doesn't get home until late." She put on her lead-rimmed spectacles. "But the young woman in Number 7 wanted all the noon papers brought to her room yesterday when she got back from her trip."

"Number 7?" He looked down the list. "That's Mademoiselle Olenka Olschewska . . ." Abruptly he rose from his chair. "Here comes Cousin Klärchen! Her silks rustling . . . !"

A pompous female, hair just curled, nails manicured, sailed into the room in a lilac taffeta dress.

Grumbach stroked his amber-colored mustache with his pipe. Wiping off a chair, Therese pushed it forward.

"Or, Frau Captain, perhaps you would prefer to sit down in our living room? You might soil your gown here in the kitchen."

"Don't trouble, Reschen. It's quite nice here. Your living room is gray with cigarette ashes. Everything you touch—ashes! Haven't you anything but Jews here?"

"They are people like ourselves!"

"What! Ressssschen!" She hissed the "s." "If I were not your guest—! Otherwise—!" She heaved her generous bosom, emitting a long-drawn-out whistle through her nostrils. Then suddenly she slapped the corner of the kitchen table with her long gloves, laughing acidly: "Your Rabbi is in there now sticking little flags along the Jordan on the map of Palestine. He's probably figuring out how he can save his battalions by the Dead Sea from our on-rolling tank squadrons! Have you a pin, Cousin? Frau Reich Minister Dr. Magda Göbbels always wears her decolleté an inch lower. Her Excellency Frau Field Marshal Emmy Göring, on the contrary, does not approve. And this evening she will be there! . . . Well . . . This is the last chance to do any shopping in Paris . . . !"

"Frau Captain! Do you mean because of war?"

"War? Who's talking about war! Thank you"—she took the pin, arranging a wisp of black lace discreetly to veil the deep cleft in her bosom. Thereupon, with considerable effort, she pulled the thin kid glove onto her fleshy left hand, finger by finger.

"Well, my dear Sergeant-Major, I suppose you're waiting to hear a word or two from me about your dossier and that queer-looking soldier you were telling me about. Let me state once for all, Cousin, that your processes of thought are utterly foreign to me. You two have been living for such a long time in the Jewish-Christian world of lies . . ."

"Can't we talk about something else?" With a pious upward glance at a religious picture from Lourdes above the steaming pots on the stove, Therese said: "Faith, Frau Captain, is, after all, just what it is —faith!"

"Fine! Reschen, that's the first time we agree. That's just what it is: Faith is faith! On the contrary, superstition is superstition!" She fanned herself vigorously.

Grumbach tamped down his pipe, applied the match, and puffed. "The question is, which is faith and which is superstition?"

"My good man—" She coughed slightly, pushed back her chair violently, waving the clouds of smoke away from her imposing coiffure. "That question was long ago definitely answered by my beloved Führer for the next thousand years. And if you, Cousin, can still believe in such nonsense as that spook of yours behind the rococo mirror you were babbling about a while ago, then I can only say that a National Socialist like myself is more than overblest in the knowledge that your world is falling to ruin! But tell me, in what regiment was the Captain who fed you this pap about the Little Jew Jesus—?"

"In the Uhlans, as I was—"

208

"Acti-i-ive?" she prolonged the vowel.

"No longer active—"

"No longer active!" her shrill laughter cackled. "As soon as I had crossed the Rhine Bridge at Kehl, and the German border was behind me and I stood on French soil, I immediately had the impression that the entire outside world was 'no longer active'!" Her bosom strained with laughter, the taffeta crackling. Her expression again became severe.

"Here!" She undid the string on a small package—"I have brought you the latest issues of 'The Holy Source of German Strength.' You must read them through. You'll find some articles by the second wife of His Excellency Ludendorff, 'the greatest commander-in-chief of all times,' as she calls him, in which she sets forth certain incontrovertible truths—"

Grumbach turned the pages with interest. Now and then he shook his head.

"My dear Cousin, the stuff your inactive Captain of Uhlans was telling you about the coming of the Little Jew Jesus, you will find irrefutably dealt with and settled in the chapter, 'Belief in Ghosts and Spirits.' In that chapter Mathilde Ludendorff, the 'greatest woman philosopher of all times,' as her husband, the Commander-in-Chief, called her, has rebuked and refuted, once and for all, the superstition of a continued existence of the Bolshevik Jew Jesus, crucified two thousand years ago—a superstition diligently created and cultivated by the Freemasons, Quakers, and Jews to stupefy mankind."

Therese, her religious feeling wounded, was carefully basting a roasting chicken with fat, and she now slammed the oven door. "But Mary Magdalen spoke to Our Lord on Easter morning in the garden, after His resurrection! Everyone knows that!"

"Correct! Absolutely correct!" Looking at the kitchen clock, she set her wrist watch. "A completely hysterical Jewess named Mary Magdalen certainly testified that she had met her lover, the Communist Jesus, dressed in white, in the garden that morning. Perfectly correct, Reschen! She was, of course, in love! And a woman in love—is capable of anything! But that was long since incontrovertibly cleared up on a purely scientific basis by Dr. Mathilde Ludendorff. On page 67, you'll find it irrefutably established that: 'The resurrection of the Jew Jesus was a purely erotic fantasy on the part of the Jewess Mary Magdalen.'"

Frau Captain sniffed with appreciation. "Your coffee is so fragrant! How much is it a pound? So—so! Well, our coffee in Heidelberg is not so bad. Of course it hasn't such an aroma." She laughed shrilly. "So the Little Jew Jesus has climbed up out of the dugout at Haudroumont! Wonderful! Marvelous! No, no! Whoever is once dead—is dead!"

Therese was assiduously turning the handle of the coffee-mill. "Frau Captain doesn't even believe in the life after death?"

"I should hope not! Only a lunatic can still believe in such rubbish! Only somebody who still listens to Freemasons, Quakers, and Jews!"

"Cousin, how can you!"

"But it all started in the ninth century, when Charles the Saxon-Slayer, whom you call 'Charlemagne', butchered our German people like cattle at Verden an der Aller, in order to force his beloved Christianity on us Germans. What nauseating poison—this horrible plague of lies from Bethlehem!"

Therese Grumbach poured the freshly ground coffee into the pot. Turning to an altar picture adorned with faded corn flowers, she produced a rosary from under her apron and murmured:

"Holy Mary of Mount Carmel, I promise Thee as soon as I have time—this very night at midnight Mass—to go to confession and satisfy the Divine Righteousness of my sincere repentance for having listened to this pagan!"

"O Mathilde Ludendorff! O profound philosopher!" Klärchen shook her head. "It's simply incomprehensible to me! Only to think that I, too, used to mutter such rubbish! Wearing a gold cross around my neck I, too, used to hurry to church!—Early morning Mass! Noonday Mass! And tonight you're going to midnight Mass! Where?"

"At Notre Dame—"

"Cousin!" She laughed loudly. "Your Lord Jesus isn't going to help you! Thank God, not more than three per cent of the Greater German people today believes in these childish dreams of a ghost-seer!"

"Sweet Jesus!" Therese fell on her knees before another holy picture by the ice box: "I implore Thee, embrace my Cousin in the flames of Thy Love." Then, rising to her feet, she took off her apron, and went to Frau Captain and gave her a kiss.

"Yes, yes!" Painfully moved, Klärchen applied fresh powder to the spot. "You 'poor in spirit'—yours is the kingdom of Heaven! So said your Israelitish itinerant preacher . . . Cousin, you deserve it! Your life has certainly been sour enough. But let's talk about something else! Wasn't that the front door? Somebody's in the corridor! It's probably my boy!" She reconnoitered down the hallway, returning immediately. "It was Baldur! Been on duty until now. He's washing up. Have I shown you what I brought my Baldur from Heidelberg? Where did you put that box, Reschen?"

"In the hall next to the umbrella-stand."

"Let me get it!" Sergeant-Major Grumbach left the room and brought back a box wrapped in blue paper. Setting it on the kitchen table, he helped Frau Captain to unpack it.

"How my Baldur has developed! After the Treaty of Versailles I had no idea how I was going to pull him through, the splendid boy! How was I to keep his spirit uncontaminated in the morass of the Weimar Jew-Republic! At first he ran absolutely wild, the rascal! I almost had to send him to America. I thought he was lost. At the eleventh hour Hitler gathered about him the imperiled youth of Germany! He took them off the streets! He showed them, instead of the fabulous, red swamp blossoms of Marxism, a clear goal shining once again! You poor things! Are you really going to live and die without having known what it means in our time *to be a German!?* You poor unfortunates! What kind of life is this in Paris? Everything so mean!— so dingy!—so huggermugger!—without a bright goal or a clear future! You can't imagine how happy I am! When I think of the last time I marched through Heidelberg, on 'The Day of Work,' with the whole German people! Alongside, His Excellency, Reich Propaganda Minister Dr. Göbbels! Next to him a former master chimney sweep! On my right, the representative of the German Academy of Poets! Behind me, our postman, and next to him our sturdy washwoman! (She still remembers you.) And behind them again, the Reichswehr officers, arm in arm with the butcher who lives opposite, and the lanky orchestra conductor—the one who got all those enticing dollars out of America—and all of them together in stride and step with the awakening people behind our beloved Führer, marching forward to the conquest of the world! . . ."

With eyes shining ecstatically, she stared for a long time at the ceiling. Grumbach and Therese did not dare to breathe. At last, Frau Captain emitted a deep gasp of bliss and babbled on: "And with it all —my proud consciousness of being the widow of one hero and the mother of another!"

Lifting the lid of the box, she exclaimed: "Look! This is Baldur's new uniform—all that's real silver, the embroidery! You didn't have anything like that under the Kaiser! In those days your galloons were only wool! Doesn't it make your mouth water?" Carefully she closed the lid. "Only yesterday at the station, my brother-in-law said to me, just before I got on the train: 'Do a good job, Klärchen! And when we've conquered the East, then we'll buy ourselves another pig! And when we've got the West, as far as Panama and Rio, we'll start a new manure pit!' Yes!" She clapped her hand over her mouth, stifling a coloratura yawn. "Plans! We have our plans—lots of them. We no longer save up the sky-blue taffeta dress in the cedar chest, just to put it on for the last sacraments and then, from our death-beds, drive off in a golden coach with eight horses along the Milky Way direct to the 'Golden House' of the Heavenly Führer—!" Laughing uproariously, she tapped her cousin on the shoulder. "No! We enjo-o-oy everything there is to enjoy in the realm of incontrovertibly justifiable Pan-German Rights! We—" But at that moment she broke off and backed against the wall as if she had seen a rat.

Rabbi Wolff, returning from the Wailing Wall Café, entered the kitchen with his niece, Nadia.

"Bon soir, messieurs dames!" Politely lifting his black slouch hat, he handed the proprietress a slip of paper: "Madame Grumbach, you forgot to put down two beers on my bill."

"Did I forget?" She held the bill up to her face and added the missing item.

"Hurry, Uncle!" Her eyes on the Sergeant-Major, the perfumed little actress tugged the rabbi by the arm. "We're going to the prison. At nine o'clock, they're going to put up the guillotine. And seven hours from now Weidmann is to lose his blond head. But what good will it do? Two more women murdered since this morning! Your police, Monsieur le Commissaire, seem to be helpless—"

"Damnation! Don't say that!"

"Yes, they are! I was just speaking to the Duke d'Aguillon on the phone. He'd just come from the Prefecture, and they're absolutely groping in the dark."

"You can bet it was a Nazi." The Rabbi joined in. "Oh! Until they finally make up their minds to guillotine all those blond beasts, you can be sure that murder isn't going to stop in this world."

"In the name of all Reich Germans, I forbid such insolence in my presence!"

The Rabbi and Nadia turned in the direction of the sharp voice. "Madame!" Dr. Wolff attacked his beard pugnaciously. "Whom do I have the honor—?"

"Ho-o-nor?" Klärchen's mouth was distorted in a grimace. She made one step forward.

"Pardon!" For the first time the Rabbi noticed the Party button on her bosom. "Madame Grumbach, since when do you permit Nazis to stay at your pension? Come on!" Grabbing his niece by her silver-fox collar, he stamped to the door.

"Well, thank God!"

"Thank God?" The Rabbi about-faced, his eyelids narrowed, his nostrils vibrating. "What do *you* know—about God?" The Rabbi slowly nodded his head. His eyes began to burn. "If you knew anything about God—you would know that He has long since pronounced judgment on you Nazis!"

"Judgment?" The voice of the Cultural Leader from Heidelberg shrilled through the kitchen.

"A judgment which will one day bring weeping and wailing and gnashing of teeth to those beyond the Rhine!"

"How terrible! So that's what the 'Chosen People' are dreaming about in exile, is it? That would suit you down to the ground! But let me tell you something—Your Jewish terrors of hell-fire and damnation and the Last Judgment don't frighten us any more! You can't bait National Socialists with that drivel! The greatest historical deed of my Führer was that he purified the German soul of this Jewish, nauseating, cowardly fear of a 'Last Judgment!'"

"Woman!" The Rabbi's burning eyes were fixed upon her. "Is there no shred of moral law left in you Germans?"

"Moral law? You don't suppose I would discuss that question with a Jew? I flatly decline! For the Pan-German people, since the assumption of power, there can be only one moral law!"

"And that is—?"

"Murder!" Nadia screeched between them. "Murder!"

"Jewish sow! Shut your mouth!"

"Jewish sow?" The actress sprang at her, ripping the golden Party button off her dress.

"Shameless pack!" The Nazi screamed. "Sergeant-Major—why don't you help me? The filthy toad! Give me my button! This is an insult to the whole Pan-German Reich!"

"This filth—this symbol of murder!" Nadia shouted over her.

"Mademoiselle," said Grumbach, "hand it over at once! That is a national emblem. Everybody has the right to wear his national emblem and be proud of it!"

"Proud of it!" The Rabbi's voice rose to thunder. "The swastika! The emblem of all the lowest and most infamous instincts."

"Are you going to give that thing back to Frau Captain?"

Therese Grumbach grasped the Rabbi's arm imploringly. "Doctor, you're wearing the same kind of a thing in your buttonhole!"

"The Star of David?"

"And the American in Number 5 keeps saying, 'I am an American!' and wears a little flag! And the Englishman in Number 12, didn't he say last night at dinner: 'My country—right or wrong!'?"

Snatching a saucepan from among the kitchen utensils, Frau Captain, purple with rage, swung it menacingly and roared: "Give me that Party button or I'll—"

"Bitch!" Dashing to the stove the Rabbi's niece lifted up one of the glowing stove lids and threw the National Socialist emblem into the red-flaming coals. "There you are!" she cried triumphantly. "Come and get it! Murderess!"

Then something happened which none of those present expected. With a look ominous with wrath, Frau Captain strode pompously to the stove. Putting her naked right hand into the hole, she groped in the burning coals until she found her Party pin. Her hand and forearm blistered, she calmly pinned the button back on her bosom. Going to the kitchen cupboard, she scooped up a handful of butter and—"You don't mind, Therese?"—smeared it thick over her injured hand. "Ye-ss! There's still butter in Paris!" she said grinning, and then, gritting her teeth, she pulled on the white kid glove as far as it would go. Marching up to the Rabbi, she stood stiffly and mumbled: "You may be sure there will be a sequel to this!" Abruptly, she stretched out her arm horizontally and shouted so loudly that doors in the hallway were opened: "Heil Hitler!"

Before the others could catch their breath, she was gone, slamming the front door behind her.

CHAPTER TWELVE

THERESE GRUMBACH FOLDED HER HANDS PIOUSLY OVER HER BREAST.

"Come!" The Rabbi pushed his niece before him. "By God the Just! A sequel? Here in Paris. I'll soon fix these Fifth Columnists!"

"Where are you going, Doctor?"

"To the police!" And out he stamped with Nadia.

Still gasping with astonishment, Grumbach leaned against the ice box, mopping his brow, and stowed his pipe away.

"Damn! These Jews!"

"Jesus, Brother!"

"What next? A private revolution of their own?"

"Won't you stay for dinner? We're having chicken!"

"Not hungry—"

"There goes the bell!" She clasped her head. "My God, can it be Frau Captain coming back?"

"There it goes again! Damnation! Are you afraid—with a brother in the police? All right, I'll go!" He opened the back door. The Polish dancer dashed past him into the kitchen.

"Madame Grumbach—has anyone telephoned?"

The Sergeant-Major returning, looked questioningly at his sister. But Therese was putting on her apron. She removed the roast chicken from the oven and, with a dangerous-looking knife, cut the appetizingly browned bird in two. The truffled stuffing gushed out onto the platter. Fetching three plates from the cupboard, she set the table. The last touch was a colorful Alsatian vase full of nodding sunflowers. While her brother brought a wooden bowl of salad from the ice box, she heaped a mound of steaming white rice in a dish. Fascinated, she stared into the glowing coals in the stove, replaced the stove lid, pushed the chairs up to the table and sat down, mumbling: "Sweet Jesus, Sweet Jesus!"

Without a word, her brother took the place across from her and allowed himself to be served a juicy drumstick. Then he held out his glass. She filled it with foaming beer, which he swallowed at a single draft.

"Mademoiselle Olschewska," Therese said, "won't you eat with us? Our cousin brought this chicken all the way from Heidelberg. Do you think I should have basted it more?"

"Non! Non!" Her brother was gobbling busily. "Delicious! Tender as a baby's behind! Melts in the mouth! Well, Mademoiselle"—he looked up from his plate—"you're not hungry?"

"Jesus! My angel, I forgot to congratulate you!"

"What is it? Damnation! A birthday?"

"Mais non!" Therese giggled slyly. "But only a little while ago I saw this young lady and her 'fiancé' in Notre Dame, standing in front of the Madonna for Ave-Maria."

Olenka ran her fingers slowly through her hair. Then she sat down at the table, began to stuff salad leaves into her mouth, and chewed on them with a noise like grating pebbles.

"Engaged!"—Grumbach gouged into his mouth with a toothpick, squinting at the girl over his denuded chicken bones. "Engaged? Are

215

you the young lady in Number 7?" Pulling out his notebook, he checked his list of foreign guests.

"Engaged!" Therese wiped her plate with a piece of bread. "That used to be my dream! But in a world like this!" She solemnly wagged her head. "No, not in this world!"

"What is your fiancé's name?—I drink to his health!"

"Jesus! Let her eat in peace! Another little piece, Mademoiselle? Here's the liver—I saved it for you. Or do you prefer the heart?"

Olenka stood up suddenly, but Therese took her hand.

"Mais restez donc, my poor child! She's been through a lot, Brother. Her father's estate was destroyed by the Russians! At four years of age she saw her home burned down and only saved one doll!"

Olenka put down her knife and fork. "Madame Grumbach, if anyone calls, I'll be in my room!" And she hurried down the corridor.

"What's the matter with her? Jesus! There goes the phone!"

While Grumbach went to the telephone, Therese found her gloves, a black lace veil, a small prayer-book and her rosary. "Who was it?" she asked her brother, who came hurrying back.

"In line of duty!" He wrapped up another piece of chicken, gave her a brotherly smacking kiss in the air, and shoved off.

CHAPTER THIRTEEN "OH, GRACIOUS VIRGIN!" OLENKA THREW HERSELF ON HER KNEES BESIDE THE BED. "THOU WHO HAST NEVER refused Thy help to any! To Thee I come! Oh, Virgin of Virgins! Mary! I kneel before Thee in my heart's anguish! Holy Mary, reject not my plea! Hear me in Thy grace—and answer me: Where is he? Where? Where? Uhle—suddenly you disappeared!" She muffled her face in the counterpane.

The window was wide open. Outside under the street lamps the wind was sighing through the trees in a small park, wedged in between the houses. Suddenly she got up and snapped out the light. She remembered having seen a policeman standing outside.

A cool breeze stirred the curtains. A shimmering blue evening gown of tulle hung from a hanger—forlorn. On the bed table there were photographs of Paderewski and Madame Curie. And with them, a honey-yellow piece of rosin—another memento of her home in Cra-

216

cow.

Had the front door opened? She listened in the corridor. No one!
Out of the clothes closet she fetched a pink stuffed Easter rabbit and
pressed it to her face. "Uhle! Uhle! Uhle! You gave him to me on
Maundy Thursday—and now the leaves are falling. Oh, Uhle!" She
threw herself on the bed. "Where are you?" She cuddled and kissed
the soiled rabbit. And as she kissed it, holding it against her heart, she
gradually became quieter.

Outside, the wind rustled in the tree tops. Someone knocked.

"Come in! Olala!" She half rose and turned on the bed lamp again.
"Is that you, Madame Grumbach?"

"Am I disturbing you?"

"I think—I must have been dreaming. Somebody was shouting 'Out
of the way! Get away! The house is falling down!' I ran as fast as I
could, but everything was tipping over—the stones were rattling . . .

"Why—you're all dressed up? Are you going to church?"

"Yes! To Procession at Notre Dame . . . I thought you might like
to come with me?"

Olenka shook her head. "Olala! I can't."

"Sweet Jesus! What's happened?"

"Please pray for me. . . ."

After a long pause, she looked up at the owner of the pension. Suddenly she made the sign of the Cross. "Go, Madame Grumbach. Go
and pray for me. . . ."

"Jesus! Mademoiselle Olenka, there is no relying on men . . . Only
on God! Jesus! Jesus!"

When Madame Grumbach had gone, Olenka rubbed her eyes. Then
she slowly took off her fur coat and restlessly paced up and down the
room. Then she stood still again, picked up a little glass box and held
it to the electric light, looking at the laurel leaf that lay in it like a
jewel. It was a souvenir she had pilfered from the wreath under the
'Manifesto' of her country's great poet Mickiewicz in the Polish National Museum. Oh! . . . she knew it by heart: "Without heart," it
began, "without soul!—the people of this world are only shadows!"
The leaf was her talisman, so far from her native land.

Setting it in front of a vase of roses, the petals of which trembled
and fell at a touch, she resumed her pacing up and down. Finally she
stopped in front of the mirror, picked up her powder puff and dabbed
at the red spot that excitement had brought back to her throat. Then
she put on her hat and coat; she would follow Therese to Notre Dame.

Along the dimly lit hall she groped her way between pieces of baggage, shoes, and laundry bags. In front of Number 11, she paused. Wasn't this that young Mr. Hermann's room? Whenever she had danced in Paris, he had brought her candy and had shown himself attentive. She had not wanted to speak to Madame Grumbach about her terrible fear for Uhle . . . But it choked her. She had to talk about it to someone. Hesitantly she knocked. There was no sound.

"Olala! Isn't he in?"

CHAPTER FOURTEEN $\qquad$ C AUTIOUSLY, SHE TURNED THE KNOB. A STRANGE SPECTACLE MET HER EYES. BALDUR HERMANN, HIS FACE flushed from alcohol, sat in front of the full-length mirror of his wardrobe. To the right and left of him, heavy wax candles, thick as a man's fist, stuck in glass tumblers, burned, shedding their light upon a heap of close-written manuscript pages, the object of his feverish scrutiny.

Of all the S.S. agents set upon the trail of the dancer, Baldur alone disguised as a Paris rowdy, had succeeded in getting the violin case with its precious contents away from the girl in the Bagatelle Park. But instead of following his orders to turn it over to those "higher up" in the Gestapo, he had followed a vague impulse and—as we have seen—had lost himself in the human stream of the metropolis, eluding all pursuit.

Later, in the Wailing Wall café, learning from Prince Ferdinand the sensational value of the lost document, he had felt the urge of an unbounded greed for money, which, after his talk with the Russian, had sent him to numerous rendezvous in dark streets. From these— his courage bolstered by much drinking—he had returned to the pension with the definite decision (despite pressing orders to appear at the German Embassy that evening) to turn the Last Will and Testament of his Führer into money and promptly fade out of the picture, westward, via Bordeaux.

So now the Nazi—drunk with joy over his find—was taking a 'last, long leave' of the new uniform which, symbolizing his promotion to the rank of Standard-bearer in the Bodyguard, his mother had just brought him. Olenka stood hesitating on the threshold, torn between the impulse to withdraw, the fascination of his weird behavior, and the resemblance of the sheets over which he was poring to those of Hitler's Will.

The blond rose, his underpinnings rather insecure, elaborately depositing the pages on the seat he had just vacated, and began decking out his brown shirt with a quantity of medals. Brushing his disheveled hair flat till it shone like a metal helmet, he slung over his shoulders the dazzling, silver-worked new tunic and stood there, his ice-blue eyes goggling dazedly at his own reflected image.

Suddenly he caught sight of the dancer in the mirror. He hastily piled some cushions on the papers in the chair and—"Damn it! Wasn't the door locked?"—extinguished the two candles with the flat of his hand. One candle remained burning smokily on his bedside table. Bowing unsteadily, he pointed with a clumsy gesture to the giddy array of decorations on his shirt, grinned, and detached them one by one, dropping them into a cardboard box.

"Olala!" She pointed at his open bags and half-packed trunk. "Am I disturbing you, Herr Baldur? Are you going away?"

"Right you are! But to what do I owe the honor of your charming visit? When did you get to Paris?"

He looked into her face. His eyes narrowed mistrustfully. Had Olenka recognized him that morning in the Bagatelle Park, in spite of his mask? But after a long, practical scrutiny, he was convinced that she suspected nothing. So he said gaily,

"What bad luck! You don't drop in until I'm packing to leave!"

"Olala! Yes, it *is* bad luck. Oh, Herr Baldur, I did so much want to ask your advice!"

"My advice?" He pricked up his ears. "Good advice is expensive! Ha-ha! But please be seated!" Her beauty had so confused him that he offered her the chair in which the papers were hidden. The valuable sheets fluttered all over the room. As Olenka stooped to them, his face changed, and he pushed her away so violently that she stumbled against the wall.

"Hands off!" His head under the table, in the act of picking up the pages, he barked: "Stand back, I tell you! Or I'll knock the enamel off your nails!"

After he had angled the last page out from under the bed, he sat down on the mattress, licked his forefinger, and without a further glance at the girl, began counting and recounting, back and forth. Then he took off his garters and wound them around the bundle of sheets.

"Olala!" She looked at him flabbergasted. "Were you afraid I would read it?—Is it your diary?" she asked.

"You wouldn't think I had so much to say! But—one sees, one hears —and keeps notes!"

"There's so much material today! For a writer—you only have to fill your pen—"

"But the main thing is—never write in ink."

He looked at her brazenly. "I'll make you a proposition: you help me finish packing and then—we'll spend the evening together. Agreed? Can't talk here . . . But outside, somewhere—for instance, Neuilly. I've rented a little house there—a villa."

"You—have a villa?"

"That is tops! Let's go! Take the Metro to the end of the line. Then —off we go, across the meadows, through the woods and—there we are! Here's the key to the garden gate! What do you say? Is it a deal? Nice little dinner, tête-à-tête! Vegetarian—cook it all myself! After dinner"—from his night table he produced two bottles of Benedictine which he cradled, one in each arm—"we'll crack a bottle or two! In August, Neuilly's sometimes as foggy as in November. We'll light the fire in the open fireplace! What do you say? And when the flames leap high—somebody breathes on the back of your neck, 'Turn back! turn back! you lovely girl! You're in a murderer's house.' "

"Olala!" Olenka sidled over to the bundle of papers. "It sounds like a detective story."

"Hands off!—No, so far I haven't seen hide nor hair of a detective out there. Except for the postman and the baker's boy who leaves bread on my windowsill, we'll be absolutely entre nous."

"Entre nous? Herr Baldur—"

"That's right—so let's get along—." Hiccoughing, he linked his arm in hers. "You said you wanted my advice? Can't give it to you here. Walls have ears! Besides—the Old Girl, my mother, has arrived— sticks her nose into everything!" Putting the bottles down he began packing his socks. "Come and help me! Soon finished and then . . . ! Take it from me . . . I know what little girls like! No news to me! What I always say: 'The love of woman corresponds to the basic tone!' " He came close to her, impudently. "Yes! The song of songs rises from the ovaries!"

He slammed the lid of his trunk and pulled off his brown shirt. Then he went to the washstand, splashing water over his head and chest, gargled, and dried himself. Uncorking one of the bottles, he filled two drinking glasses with Benedictine and offered her one.

"Hail Bacchus!" He poured the sticky syrup down his throat so

quickly that his neck jerked back with a crackling sound. "Ouch! . . .
Oh! The skull sits up there on the topmost vertebra! Ha—after all—
we're all bones . . . nothing but bones! And our hair grows like prai-
rie-grass round the think-tank! . . . Drink! Why don't you drink?
Takes some time to get there by Metro. . . ."

Feeling more and more uneasy, Olenka edged away from him,
watching her chance to get out of the room without trouble.

"If you're not going to drink it, I will." Putting on a white shirt, he
snapped his suspenders over his shoulders. "Everything ready? Then,
let's go!"

"Oh, no! I'm expecting a telephone call . . . "

"Quoi!" and before she realized what was coming, he had his knee
between her legs.

"Let me go! Olala! Mais vous êtes drôle—"

"Drôle?" He stuffed his shirt into his trousers and followed her
around the table. "Aha! A skeleton in the closet! You're expecting a
telephone call? Look at her get red as a tomato! If that doesn't tie
everything. Anyhow, you won't get any call! Girlie, you might as
well know now: I belong to the Police secrète allemande—"

"Olala!" She stared at him, uncomprehendingly—"You belong to
the—"

"At your service! Where are you going?" Before she could reach
the door, he shot the bolt and gripped her arm, wheezing alcoholically
in her face: "What's the sense of your waiting? No sense! He won't
telephone you—he can't."

"He can't?" She was shocked. "What do you mean?"

"Don't lose your girdle! Chin up! Girlie, I thought you came into
my modest retreat to ask my advice? Sweetheart, if you want my
advice, it's this—"

"Herr Baldur!" She tried to break loose.

"Now, if he only had money! Or is his portemonnaie as empty as
Notre-Dame on Monday? And a poule like you ought to be the
smartest and best dressed woman in the four world-empires! But to
be chic takes money! And that's what I've got!" He looked avari-
ciously at the manuscript on the table. "Nothing I can't buy now!
Even you!"

With a desperate effort she freed herself from his grasp.

"What!" He barred her way to the door. "So—milady turns out
to be angry, even though I offer free advice! So she's angry, is she?
Well—go ahead and drink! There!" He filled her glass. "Drink until
you forget! Drink, I tell you! And then—off we go—to the four

corners of the earth! Mind you, I'm not so bad—just as I am! But with money! What do you think? Money! Money! Drink, damn you!"

Olenka sipped at her glass. Was he just talking—or did he really know what was delaying Uhle? In the midst of her heart's deep anxiety, she had a sudden thought. Looking innocently around the room, she forced a laugh.

"Your health, Herr Baldur! Don't you think it's rather nice of me to have come to see you? You remember the first time we met on the stairs, you said you wanted to show me your treasures—"

"Treasures?" Flattered, he set his glass down, slapped the pages of the Will and boasted: "This is the only treasure that means anything to me now! This afternoon some of the leading collectors of the world offered me astronomical sums—for *this!*" He waved the bundle. "I don't know how many glasses one of them poured into me so that I'd sell him this particular treasure! Astrono-o-mical sums, I tell you!"

"But"—she pricked up her ears—"what about your pictures? You said you wanted to show me—"

"Pictures!" He glanced at the wall, adorned with photographs of all sizes and shapes. "By the Almighty, I'd almost forgotten to pack my beauties!" He climbed unsteadily on a chair and, with his knife, began prying the thumb-tacks out of the wallpaper. "There! Aren't those beauties! The most prominent men of our male world-era! Every one of them is an earth-shaker. For instance, this head—you recognize that bald-headed Caesar?"

"Mussolini, of course!"

"Right! That's just who he is. Yes! This is the Roman who, in 1936, coined the pregnant phrase: 'The entire League of Nations in Geneva is nothing but a bunch of democratic cattle, consisting of lisping English aunts at their knitting and Salvation Army lassies!' And here's Adolf. In 1933 the Prince of German poets called him 'the greatest German since Luther.'

"Looks like I'm forgetting my old man!" He detached a framed picture from the wall. "Papa, did you think I'd forgotten you?—May I introduce you to Captain Hermann, reported missing in the holocaust of Verdun, 1916." He stared at the portrait. "When my good mother received the official postcard, she lost, not her mind, but her faith in God!"

"Olala! How awful!"

"Awful? Why? Are you a Catholic—hm? Still a believer? I hate the whole damned show! But—if I may ask—what is it you believe in? Do you believe in him?" He fished around in his trunk and brought out a

222

color reproduction of the famous "Crucifixion" by Matthias Grüne-wald.

"In him? That hung above the bridal bed of my beloved parents . . . Ha! But then, later on, Mother threw it on the rubbish-heap. I dug it out again to add it to my curios. There He is!" He shied the picture onto the floor. "You Saviour of humanity! Ecce homo. 'Good Friday Magic,' as Mother used to say . . . Yes! Under that execution scene, dear little Baldur was procreated."

"Don't blaspheme. . . ."

"Blaspheme? The sight of your World Saviour on Golgotha was too much of a dose even for his Heavenly Father! And in His sublime wisdom He answered the wails of His only-begotten Son with total darkness! You call that blaspheming? How so? When the Gestapo of the Syrian Gauleiter took this tortured Communist of a Jesus and finally began to polish him off with spears and lances, did God the Father in Heaven move His little finger to save Him?"

"Stop! Stop!"

"Why? Mother says: 'Baldur, we Germans can only believe in a God who can muster the National-Socialist courage to look on, with total indifference, when His little Son, no matter for what reasons, comes to a miserable end on a dump heap. Only such a God is the stuff for a Gestapo-man.' "

"Olala!" Olenka hid her face, as if in religious terror. "Your mother says that? Oh! Aren't you afraid?—"

"Afraid? I believe in neither God, man, nor Devil! For me there is nothing but courage . . . and cowardice!"

There was a hail of pebbles against the windowpane. He turned white.

CHAPTER FIFTEEN "SHHHH!" HE PULLED OFF HIS SHOES. "NOT A PEEP OUT OF YOU!" FROM UNDER THE MATTRESS HE PULLED a rifle, cocked it, and tiptoed to the window.

"Baldur!" a man's voice called.

"Shhhh!" Baldur motioned to the girl. After several more appeals, the voice ceased and they heard departing steps. Baldur pulled the curtains together and hid his weapon under the mattress again. He looked quickly round:

"Where are you going?"

"Olala!" She was at the door again. "Please! Let me out!"

"Let you out? What for? Nothing doing!"

He dropped down on the sofa, stretched out his legs, and fell to brooding aloud: "Hell! If somebody would only clear up one point for me: how many do you have to bump off before you're a hero? For instance, Freiherr von Richthofen in 1917 shot sixty-five Englishmen out of the clouds! When that pinnacle of achievement was announced in Berlin, the entire German Reichstag stood up in reverence. Bölke later liquidated a mere thirty-two! And Reich Marshal Göring, as far as I know, made cold corpses of only nineteen mothers' sons . . . Sit down and tell me: how many do I have to have chalked up before I can be called a hero?"

He stood up and put on his wind-breaker. "For instance—when I was in the concentration camp . . ."

"You were in a concentration camp? Olala!"

"Yes, as a guard in Cassel. On June 3rd I received orders to take a Jew named Max Hirsch out of his cell on June 4th at 3:50 a.m., turn him loose, and shoot him down when he started to run." He knotted a bright silk scarf around his throat. "Orders are orders! So I stayed up on night duty. The guard room was full of S.A. men, singing and drinking beer. The list of prisoners was on the camp commander's table. I lay down on a bench and dozed off a couple of hours. But I woke up again—I heard such a funny hissing sound. I blinked and there was some kind of a fly flirting with the candle flame. All of a sudden it flopped on the blotter. I picked up the commander's big magnifying glass and studied the creature. It was spotted red and yellow like a salamander, with a long stinger in its head. Lifting it on my knife, I held it up to the flame. It almost doubled up. When I held it away from the flame, it cleaned its singed stinger with its front legs like a soldier cleaning his gun. I held it up to the flame again—something made me. It went 'ksss' again."

He paced up and down and then sat down in the corner of the sofa, kneading both hands deep in his coat pockets, staring straight before him. "Yes, girlie. And then I inspected it some more through the lens: its eyes—simply eno-o-ormous! Held it up to the flame—'k-s-s-s' it went! But this time it stuck to the wick—charred black."

Olenka quietly sat down beside him. "The little fly—?"

"Hm?" He came to with a jerk, and then suddenly dropped his head on her hands. Olenka felt them become moist. She stroked his hair, and repeated,

"The little fly?"

"Pardon!" He leaned back. "Yes! The rest had long since turned in or the night. I was alone in the guard room. The clock struck four—I jumped up, put on my cap, tightened my belt, and beat it into the courtyard. The morning sky was crystal-clear, the stars fading. I ran along the barbed wire—the stars ran with me! I stood still—and they stood still! I made a fresh start and ran all the way to his cell. Dr. Hirsch was sound asleep on his straw. I bent down, shook him awake, and yelled: 'Get up! lousy Jew!' He stood up. Through the little barred window, damn it, Aurora's doggone light fell on his pasty-white face. He asked: 'What is it now?'

"I told him, 'Change camps!' and he looked at me—his eyes simply enormous. 'Stinking Jew!' I yelled. 'Get the hell out of here!' And I helped him make a get-away."

The blinds rattled in the wind. Baldur went to the door and opened it.

"Olala! You want me to go?"

He stared at the flickering candle on the night table.

"And afterward, I went to the camp commander. It was 7 A.M. by that time. Several S.S. officers were smoking and drinking their coffee in the barracks. Prince August Wilhelm was there, too. I said, 'Heil Hi!' They all stretched their arms and yawned, 'Heil Hi!' Then I reported to Major Buch: 'Orders not carried out!'

" 'So the kike is still alive?'

" 'Major!' I said: 'I've kicked a lot of people in the teeth and walked on their faces—but—killing!' And Prince August Wilhelm screeched: 'Heels together! What! You can't bring yourself to bump off a dirty, kinky-headed Jew from behind?'

"I shouted: 'Your Royal Highness, I cannot kill!'

"At that Major Buch takes an army pistol from behind the typewriter, looks me straight in the eye, and says:

" 'This pistol belonged to your heroic father, Captain Hermann, reported missing at Verdun. Either you now carry out another special assignment—or you take this pistol, go to the latrine, and pay the penalty for your cowardice!'

"I thought it over—and decided on the special assignment. Major Buch nodded, and Prince August Wilhelm went out the door, motioned to me, and I followed. We stopped in a field some distance outside the camp.

" 'Baldur,' he said: 'One day in the Cadet Corps my brother Oskar and I and some others were ordered to finish off a cat in the stables, after our riding lesson. Our tutor, Colonel von Gontard, insisted on that kind of bayonet drill. So when we left the riding ring, we brough[t] along our rifles and bayonets. We found a gray-striped tiger to[m] backed into the whitewashed corner of the stable yard, spitting. Gon[-] tard gave the command: "Go!" And then we had to practice bayone[t] thrusting, according to the rules, with the cat for target. Myself firs[t,] then Oskar, then the others. Time after time, we jabbed that three[-] edged bayonet into the terrified, scratching, howling beast. Bloo[d] spurted everywhere. Every thrust went home. The creature's how[l] became so awful that the grooms came running. And every time w[e] thought, "No, let's hope it's dead now"—it was still alive! Such a toug[h] animal! Gontard was rubbing his hands: "Go to it! Drive it hom[e,] boys!" And then such a blood-lust took hold of us fifteen-year-o[ld] boys that we stabbed at that cat absolutely unconsciously.

" 'Yes, Baldur, my boy, murder is the bell that wakes a man to lif[e!] Romeo was a murderer! Orestes was a murderer! And Queen Elizabet[h] of England! And Hamlet, Prince of Denmark! And St. Joan of Ar[c!] Alexander the Great and Brutus were murderers! From Dr. Faust t[o] my Master in his "Eagle's Nest," history is nothing but one lon[g] bloody murder! . . . Yes, murder is the bell that wakes a man to life[!]' He picked a few buttercups, handed them to me, and turned his hors[e's] face to the dawn. 'Now go, Baldur! Carry out your special assignmen[t] so that your hero-father can be proud of you! Heil Hi!'

"To prepare for my special assignment I went to the slaughte[r] houses every day. I watched, learned how they hold the knife, and ho[w] they stick it in. Finally I got used to looking at carcasses. I would stan[d] and look into the butcher shops and watch the cooks and housewive[s] inspect the slaughtered animals. I watched women pinch the breasts o[f] chickens and weigh them in their hands—watched how they'd pic[k] out a calf's head, its muzzle drained dead white and grinning aroun[d] the teeth!—Once I saw a woman put her spectacles on its nose an[d] stick an aster behind its ear for a joke, while the blood dribbled dow[n] into her market basket. A cook like that—she had it over me! The wa[y] they smacked their lips and petted the animals, living or dead! Yes— that's an art! you have to learn it. But finally, I could do it too!"

"What could you do?"

"What?" Suddenly he looked at her fixedly, breathlessly, like [a] hunter at his prey, stalked to the bed, pulled out his rifle again, an[d] aimed at her: "That's what I could do! Ha-ha! Bullet in the back of th[e] neck—"

As Olenka hid herself with a cry of horror, he grounded the rifl[e] and grinned mockingly: "So—you take to cover like a soldier in battl[e!]

226

. . eh? Come on out from behind that sofa! Come on!"

"Vous êtes fou!" Trembling in every limb, she stood up and stared at
the rifle's mouth.

Somewhere in the pension a door banged shut. He laid the rifle on
the bed.

"Wonder if that's the Old Girl? Mother was going to come for me."
Quickly he wrapped up the Will in a plaid scarf. "Let's get out of
here! Got to beat her to it!" But as no one came he undid the bundle,
tightened the garters around the roll, and put on his hat. "Quick!
Before she comes . . . If there's one thing under heaven Mother
wants, it's for me to be a hero! But I'm going on strike! Not enough
for her to have a hero for a husband, her coffee doesn't taste good without a hero for a son. This afternoon she was telling me: 'In the Eternal
War that's coming, your S.S. Corps will be transformed into a Black
Elite Division, and then, there will be global opportunities for "good-
for-nothings like you"! If you don't die in France,' she said, 'there's still
plenty of chance in Poland! In Serbia! In the Orient! At the equator!
Wherever the jungle beasts are looking for an extra tidbit!' She can't
wait for the Medal for Bravery to be handed to her, in my name—after
I'm dead!"

He picked up the package and poised it in his hand as though weighing it.

"Kill? All right with me! But to be killed? No! There's a whopping
difference! And all the brave boys who talk so big about heroes—in
their Palazzo Chigis or somewhere else under safe cover—they have
that difference before their eyes as clear as crystal— Not one of them
contemplates being dumped into a mass grave. No-o-o! Not a single
one! Girlie, either man is just a fly—it went 'k-s-s-s!'—or—man is *not*
a fly! And he who wrote these pages here had no intention of being
a fly. Of course, he never betrayed that fact to anybody—not even
Göring! Not to speak of Hess! Not to anybody in the Party! And I
wouldn't know it if he hadn't written it down here in his own hand!"

The dancer wanted to dash for the papers, but she could not move
her legs.

"Come, come, angel. There—take your hands down from your face!
You're not ashamed because you were a coward just now? You needn't
be. Nobody need be! Better five minutes of being a coward than dead
your whole life! And this chap here"—he kissed the manuscript—"he
was a coward, too! Wrote it down himself! At first he didn't want to
—but then he had to. It was like a command—that's what he writes.
His handwriting sticks to the paper as if fear had sweated it on there—

227

Want to see it? Did you ever see such crazy writing? But I've made
out! He was going to tear it up afterward, he writes. But now *I've g*
it!" He gave the pages another resounding kiss. "Yes! Now *I've* got i
Listen to what he says:

"September 14th at the crossing of the Meuse—in the gorge—righ
and left, trenches full of smashed-up horses—their hind legs straddlin
their hind quarters yellow (he writes). His major, bullet in his back,
the first-aid station. Everywhere stinking putrescence! The blue sk
of autumn echoing to exploding shrapnel . . . There he stands on
little hillside, in 'Death Corner' (he writes). Up on top, his comrad
falling like flies. 'Forward!' his sergeant-major yelled, ordering him u
to the top of the hill to take the place of dead gunner Maier. But h
ducked down behind an alder—his face lead white—his trousers dow
—crap—And then here (he writes), all of a sudden, a pioneer looks
him through the underbrush—just looks at him! So he takes a pot
the pioneer. Out! So then—there was nobody had seen he was
coward . . . Yes, girlie, that's what he writes! Get it?

"But later, at Verdun—suddenly (he writes) there was that sam
damn pioneer again—just looking at him! So what does he do? H
kicks him down into an empty dugout—and every time that blood
pioneer tries to climb out, he kicks him in the face with his heavy boo
—until he's out (he writes). Yes! isn't that something? 'Until he wa
out'! So then nobody knew—and nobody knows! Except one perso
—and that's me! Yes! And now let 'em talk to me about—

"Come on, girlie, let's go! We're going places. I've got what
takes!"—He clutched the Will—"Money! And on the Mississippi we'
buy a farm—with money!—bungalow! terraces! palms! wild pigeor
cooing on the roof! Hop! Take your violin with you! After dinner—
music! dancing! Solos—duets—quartets—trios—anything you like!
'Little Night Music!' The primeval forest is listening to you! Th
moon! The Pacific! And me smoking my pipe! And then, 10 P.M
sharp, the news over the air—how the flies are exterminating eac
other in all four world empires! *But*—our hero Baldur is not havin
any! Ha-ha! Then, if Mother dares to say her Baldur was a coward!
they bother me—if they get in my way, you know what I'll do? I'
shoot my mouth off!—I'll tell the press of the whole world somethin
they'd like to know about their 'beloved Führer!'—

"Let's go!" Taking his rifle apart, he packed it among his suit
slapped the lid of the trunk down and locked it. But suddenly, dis
turbed by a sound at the blind, he swung on his heels, and stared at th
window as if he were seeing a ghost through the curtains.

> " 'Come tell me true and tell me true,
>   'Who's there outside the window?' ' "

He pressed his hand to his ribs. His knees gave way. He sat down on his trunk and shut his eyes. "Sometimes I have—such a sharp pain here —and all around my heart! Then I ask myself: 'What's the use of the whole rotten mess?' This afternoon in Montparnasse, I stood watching the people go by. God! How they all rushed. Their faces green, like slimy shellfish! And in their eyes—greed! Nothing but greed! Yes— everybody wants to live! Even the old man, hobbling along on his stick! Even flies! Flies? Ha-ha! Even *he*—the top of them all—even he behind the alder back there, chose to live! Ergo, life certainly must be something colossal! But what the hell *is it*, after all? For instance: I aim at a girl like you—a bullet in the back of her neck—and she falls on the carpet—and in her death throes her knees make silly jerks—and her nose gets so pointed and her lips turn black—I can always tell exactly: *This* is—death! Why the hell can't I tell exactly: *This* is life?"

He stood up, threw his hat on the bed, kicked the trunk out of the way, and stared at Olenka:

"Do you know exactly? Is it in the act? Or before? Or after? Or only in that moment—in the ictus? Hm? If you know, tell me! Hess says it's lust! Hitler says it's the Aryan Race! Mother says it's the Führer! Your Jesus says it's 'Love thy neighbor'! Prince August Wilhelm says murder is life! . . . What the hell is it? Or is this entire dump of a world nothing but a nut house—where nobody knows anything!—Girlie, I've heard you playing Chopin through these paste-board walls, I've said to myself: 'Bravo! Bravo! But what *is* it? Is *that* life?' Last Friday at a concert, I simply couldn't stand it any longer— sitting in a numbered seat among all those season-ticket-proud philis-tines. It suddenly came to me that all this artistic blah is a total waste of time."

He chewed on his cold cigar. Suddenly he whispered to her: "Tell me—do you love him? Do you love Uhle? I've got to know!"

He came at her with strangely short strides. And before she saw what he was about, he had slammed her down on the sofa so hard that the springs squeaked. She tried to get up, but he had her by the calf. His breath whistled. He moved his hand higher.

"Do you love him? Out with it!"

"Ouch! I'll scream!"

"That's what they all say! Answer me!"

"Let me go!"

229

"Always the same old line? Never anything new? Just another show-window dummy, with plenty of powder and paint? But this heat between your legs—that's real—I hope!"

"Let me go! Madame Grumbach!"

"Don't yell!" He held her fast by the thigh. "Don't yell or I'll—" He pulled a revolver from under the sofa cushions behind her. "You can yell when I give it to you—but not before!" With brutal force he turned her over on her back, one hand holding her mouth shut, and threw himself on top of her. The other hand squeezed her throat harder, harder.

Outside a bell rang. He let go of her. Somebody opened the front door. And then, along the corridor, footsteps—like a cuirassier in full field equipment. A bump, and the door was thrust open violently. On the threshold stood Frau Captain.

CHAPTER SIXTEEN THE FACE OF THE CULTURAL LEADER FROM HEIDELBERG GREW STONY. HER HAT FEATHER TREMBLED. Was it difficult for her eyes to accept the reality of the scene before her? Abruptly she commanded:

"Get up!"

"As you wish, Mother." Baldur heaved himself up clumsily from the disarray of the girl's clothes.

"Throw that slut out!"

"Won't you please shut the door?"

"Throw that creature out, I tell you!"

"Won't you have a chair, Mama?"

Without answering, she stamped over to the sofa, pulled the stunned girl to her feet, dragged her to the door, and ejected her so violently that she crumpled against the opposite wall. Thereupon Frau Captain flung out her arm and, with her burned and gloved hand, landed a tremendous box on her son's ear.

"Swine! Such behavior from a newly appointed Standard-bearer in the Bodyguard of my beloved Führer! Put your clothes on! Swine! Pack your things! Not another instant will I permit my son to stay under the same roof with filthy Jews in this filthy pension! Go on! Put your new uniform on, I tell you! The very kind Second Secretary of the Embassy has sent his car for us! We're driving to the Embassy at once! Hurry! Comb your hair! . . . Lousy Jews! . . . But Dr. Schulz told me they'll get what's coming to them! No time to talk to you now! You swine! Are you sure the girl was clean, at least? An Aryan? Hurry! Get dressed and be quick about it!"

"Mother dear! Easy does it. I'm still rather dizzy."

"What's this?" Raising her lorgnette she approached the table as if hypnotized. "I certainly know that handwriting—"

"Mother! For God's sake! Don't touch that!"

"My son—what do I see? Is it possible that Providence?—Baldur!" She pushed him aside. "I certainly know this beloved handwriting." Overwhelmed, she sat down, picked up the pages of the Will and let them glide slowly from her hands into the silken reservoir of her capacious lap. Ecstatically she threw both arms out wide. "Baldur! Come to the trembling heart of your proud and rejoicing mother! My Baldur! Can it be really true that you have found it?"

"At your service!"

"What? You, my own beloved son, my little Baldur!—chosen by the dear, good, kind, German God to bring to nought this despicable theft —about which, thank God, only a few trustworthy people know! You —you darling good-for-nothing—you to foil this robbery, organized and perpetrated by the vile Freemasons! You little imp! You chump! You to have recovered the most sacred Last Will and Testament of the Ruler of our Aryan Reich!" She groaned for joy. Then she tapped his cheek with her glove. Baldur's face was frozen. Picking up the manuscript by the garters, she dangled it back and forth, sighing aloud: "Heil! Oh, Heil! Thou, my beloved Führer!"

And so, a statuesque Walküre, her trembling bosom throbbing like two kettle-drums, she marched with stately strides toward the door.

"Stop!" Baldur sprang after her. "Where are you taking it?" With a powerful lunge, he pushed the heavy sofa in front of the door.

Outside in the hall, Olenka had pulled herself to her feet. Still dizzy, she groped her way along the dark corridor—whispering over and over again, "Un fou! un fou!"—past the empty kitchen, and out through the open door, into the street.

In Baldur's room a scuffle back and forth began. Chairs overturned. The uproar grew. Feet ran. Finally, there was a long-drawn-out strangling gurgle—and then the thud of a heavy body striking the floor.

CHAPTER SEVENTEEN **O**UTSIDE THE MÉTRO STATION ON
THE PLACE DE L'OPÉRA, DR. WOLFF BOUGHT A "PARIS SOIR," SCANNED THE
headlines absently, and with Nadia at his side sauntered through the
evening crowds over to the ornate lamps outside the Opéra.

"Well, what are they giving tonight?" They climbed the broad
flight of steps and read the announcement. "*Lohengrin?*" No, I'd
rather see the Swan as a roast on my table . . . Who's conducting, I
wonder? Let's see, now." He read: "In the presence of the President
of the French Republic and the Diplomatic Corps, for the benefit of
the International Red Cross, the famous director of the Bayreuth
Festivals and friend of Adolf Hitler, Privy Councilor Professor Doctor
Wilhelm Furtwängler, has graciously consented to conduct tonight's
performance of *Lohengrin!*"

Shaking his head, the Rabbi looked out over the bustling crowd
under the sparkling lights on the Place de l'Opéra and murmured:
"Paris? . . . J'accuse!" Reiterating Zola's memorable threat, Dr. Wolff
descended the steps again, his fists clenched.

"If you still want to wait for your Duke d'Aguillon, you may. By
God the Just, as far as I'm concerned, this whole evening has been
spoiled!"

"Don't you want to go out to see the guillotine with me?"

"No, I really don't know why I should look on at preparations
for executing the people of Israel . . ."

"Uncle! Weidmann's a Nazi!"

"Don't talk to me about the murderer! His head will soon be
chopped off . . . But we still have to go round with our chopped-
off heads propped up in stiff collars!"

"All right, then, Uncle—till tomorrow! There's the Duke's car
now." She made for the curb. The Rabbi lit a cigar and walked
straight across the Place de l'Opéra to a telephone booth. Having
dialed the number, he turned his back to the street. Only by the convulsive jerking of his left arm did he betray the fact that the
subject of his conversation was no indifferent matter. Leaving the
booth he put his cigar to his lips—wrong end to. He spat it out, and
cleaned his mouth and beard. He began wandering aimlessly here and
there—purple spots darkened under his eyes. Finally he brought up
against the iron railing around the Métro entrance, and held on to it,

swaying slightly.

"Uncle!" Nadia pushed through the crowd to him. "The Duke isn't free this evening, after all. He was with several of his 'noble cousins', in a ridiculous hurry . . . drove off to his club! . . . Thank God, I found you again!—But what's the matter with you?"

"Oh, nothing. Come!" He leaned with his full weight on her arm.

"Where to?"

"Doesn't matter—"

"You can eat at my apartment. I'm scared to be alone in the place. Shall we go?"

"All right! . . . All right! . . ."

"Hadn't we better take a taxi?"

"No—no! I'd rather get some air," and so they turned slowly into the Avenue de l'Opéra. In front of almost every shop the Rabbi stopped—breathing with difficulty—staring at the luxurious displays. "Nadia!" He looked about him uneasily. "Nadia, listen to me—Madame Grumbach just told me over the phone that Nazi woman is dead— She was found murdered in Number 11! Obviously, I can't go back to the pension. Let me stay with you tonight. I won't put you to any trouble. I'll sleep on the couch . . ."

"Murdered? I can't believe it!"

"Can't believe it! The police are already there . . ."

"Oh God!" Nadia turned white. "Shall I phone Madame Grumbach?"

"No! By God the Just! Better keep our hands out of it! . . . Come, let's go . . . Look there! That's the Sebaldus Church in Nuremberg." He stopped before a garishly lighted window display. "And there's a poster of the Frauenkirche in Munich, the 'City of the Movement.' What is this place?" He looked at the large sign in brass letters over the door: "German Travel Bureau."

"All we need to do is just walk right in and buy a ticket back home!" He laughed grimly. "We Wolffs have lived in Munich ever since 1567." Through the glass he read a small sign in tiny electric light bulbs, flanked by fresh flowers: "Germany!—The Most Beautiful Land for Travel."

"That's no lie." He looked at his niece. "Perfectly true! I couldn't imagine a more beautiful country to travel in, in autumn . . . Our Isar! The Starembergersee!"

"Do let's go on, Uncle!"

He took a step or two and then halted.

"That woman was a mocker. But God lets not His Own be mocked.

And now she lies there dead on the floor. And Madame Grumbach whining over the telephone, 'Such a fine, healthy woman!' Yes, now she's dead—the Nazi! By God the Just! Whoever harms a Jew is accursed! I can see them all, like her, all of them—all dead on the floor. For God is the Lord God of Sabaoth!"

"You know what, Uncle?" His niece, half-terrified, tried to get him to come on. "I'll open a can of asparagus and we'll have a bottle of Burgundy—"

"Niece," he lowered, "I have always dealt uprightly. I gave the goy addresses when he had a toothache—"

"Better if you hadn't—Come on!—then his teeth would have fallen out! Now he's knocking out ours—"

"I found him an inexpensive doctor—"

"Does the Bible command Jews to do that?"

"God the Just knows, whenever there was a collection box standing among the beer glasses, I always gave something."

"And there's your thanks! Here you stand in a thin overcoat, and autumn is coming! Let's go on."

"With my Protestant and Catholic colleagues, I always faithfully upheld the national idea."

"You're all mad!"

"I've blessed German soldiers going to battle quite as often as my Protestant and Catholic colleagues. And when they came back covered with blood like sacrificed beasts, whether they belonged to the Jewish, Protestant, or Catholic faith, I've tended them with my own two hands! Many a Christian I've bandaged, and I remember an Aryan paymaster sergeant who was dying at the front—I gave him the last drink from my field canteen."

"Is that so? Then you can hope that when *you* die, an Aryan will steal your last drink from under your beard!"

"But ever since the days of Queen Esther, it has always been our very persecutors who have consolidated us Jews and awakened among the best of us the affirmation of Judaism and the passionate struggle for a better future! . . . Well—let us go now."

Just as they were passing the door of the Travel Bureau, it was flung open and several hands seized the Rabbi and his niece and whisked them inside. Simultaneously the steel blinds rattled down. It all happened so quickly that passers-by noticed nothing. Nadia did not even have time to scream before a gag was stuffed in her mouth. The Rabbi started to make a gesture demanding an explanation, but he received such a blow behind the ear that his glasses flew onto the

234

floor. A secretary rose from a typewriter and ground the lenses to splinters under his heel.

"You hoary prophet! March! Through that door!" They were thrust into the next room. "Wait here!" They were left alone, in a bare room, lit by only one bulb.

A curled and perfumed man in his fifties entered. He was elegantly dressed in a brand-new striped suit, with a white tie, and a dark red carnation in his buttonhole. He shook his head, removed the gag from Nadia's mouth, threw it in the corner as if revolted, and brought two chairs from the outer office.

"Je suis désolé! Asseyez-vous!" And then he introduced himself amiably: "Doctor Stein . . . Director of the German Travel Bureau . . . Some of my subordinates are a little hard to control!—But you must understand our unpleasant situation: First, a Secretary of the Legation is shot by a coreligionist of yours in broad daylight at the German Embassy. And now, the Leader of our Heidelberg Cultural Division!—a highly distinguished and meritorious woman! You will therefore find it understandable that we should ask people who lived in the same pension—and in the same corridor—as Frau Captain Hermann to help us with their doubtless valuable testimony, which may shed some light on the darkness of this latest crime . . . You're looking for something?"

"Yes, my glasses . . ."

"Dr. Stein, I wish to phone my lawyer—"

"Of course, Mademoiselle, of course! May I get you the number?" He brought over a telephone extension. "I forgot—the French have already discontinued our phone. We're on the eve of being closed down. Today or tomorrow, the present democratic government of France is closing all German consulates and travel bureaus."

"Dr. Stein is your name?" The Rabbi produced and adjusted a pair of spectacles. "By God the Just! Of course! We know each other, Doctor! I've a good memory for faces—" The Director squirmed on his chair. "Nu! I have it! I can even remember place, day, and hour. 1912 in the Theatinerstrasse! You remember? Prince Regent Luitpold had just died—"

"Of course I remember! And Wilhelm II came to Munich for the first time—"

"Now perhaps, you'll remember the number of the corner house, from the third floor window of which you and two pretty actresses watched the funeral procession—"

"I recall it! It was over the Lion Apothecary Shop! But how do you know that?"

"How? It was my apartment! Am I right?"

"Holy St. Sebaldus!" The other gave him his hand. "Of course, of course!" He smiled pleasantly at Nadia. "And there stood the champagne all for nothing—the funeral took so long."

"How the gendarmes galloped past the Bräuhauskeller! Then the troops lining the streets presented arms. You could hear the Chopin Funeral March in the distance. And then slowly—heads bobbing, ostrich feathers swaying—along came eight shining black horses. The coffin was hidden under wreaths and flowers . . . Anyhow, nobody paid any attention to that! All eyes were looking for only one person—"

"How he remembers—"

"Why shouldn't I remember? It was my Kaiser! And then he came —all alone behind the hearse. A long black streamer of crepe fluttered from his golden cuirassier's helmet—"

"Your uncle! The way he remembers everything!"

"I can see it now! Above the broad brown beaver collar of the imperial mantle, his face, pale as marble, with that gaze of his, as if he were looking through the snow toward Valhalla!"

"Just how it was! Holy St. Sebaldus! Just so! And to right and left of his nose, the waxed points of his imperial mustache, sticking up straight as iron rods!"

"And his long field-marshal's baton! And his mantle swinging open at every step! And his snow-white cuirassier's breeches! And his feet in his high shining black boots! Yes, Niece, that was the way he walked! How would you describe it? Like a dancer—eh, my friend?" He slapped the Director on the thigh. "Like a dancer! Toes always pointing down."

"Yes, Mademoiselle! Slowly, slowly he set his feet down in the snow—like a slow-motion picture—ten paces in front of the whole crowd of German Princes!"

The rabbi laughed aloud. "Do you remember how August, King of Saxony, hobbled along?"

"And the Grand Duke of Oldenburg? Scandalous!"

"And Ernst Ludwig of Darmstadt?"

"Like a corkscrew! Just as if he hadn't any spurs to his boots. Scandalous!—And the Belgian! That lanky Albert! Rolling from one leg to the other as if he were mountain-climbing! Scandalous! And all the other Princes! Ha-ha! Scandalous! The Briton! The Dane! The Swede in his theatrical uniform! A scandal—by St. Sebaldus!"

236

"But our Kaiser, Niece! Whoever missed that—! How he marched along! By the Lord God of Sabaoth! Like a Maccabaeus!"

One of the doors opened with a bang. "Making any progress?" The secretary who had trodden on Rabbi Wolff's glasses stood in the doorway insolently. Nadia jumped up.

"Herr Kuhnert!" Doctor Stein began rummaging through a heap of travel folders. "Let's hear what the other one has to say, first."

"Nonsense! All at the same time!"

With sudden foreboding Nadia clutched the Director's arm.

"Come, come, my little lady! . . . Nothing to be afraid of! But you'll have to excuse me! You see the way things look here—and tomorrow morning we have to shut up shop. Endless things to do—"

Nadia tried to follow him out. But together with the rabbi, she was hustled into another room.

There one of the close-cropped men pushed and pummeled them over to a partition. Behind it sat Colonel Egath in a gray sport suit, smoking a cigarette and poring over some documents. Only the upper forehead was white in the square, tanned face.

"Heil!" One of the Travel Bureau secretaries came in. "Major Buch wants to know when you'll be finished with the Jews."

Egath, pretending not to have noticed his impertinence, growled, "In a few minutes." The S.S. man left. Egath—who was still so agitated by his encounter with Uhle and the dancer that he kept throwing his cigarettes away half-smoked—lit a fresh one and looked at the young Jewess behind the Rabbi. Then he beckoned them both to come closer.

"Your name?"

"Dr. Wolff—"

"Come here." He threw his cigarette away and immediately lit another. "You are a refugee from Munich?"

"Colonel, in 1914 I was about to become an officer in the field artillery—"

"Answer my question!—Things are not going to be easy for you, I'm afraid." He offered Nadia a chair. "What was I saying? Has either of you anything to do with this murder in your pension? Do you know anything about the missing documents? Out with it! I have a couple of passports here"—he glanced at Nadia—"and in memory of my sainted father who was a pastor in Cassel and rigorously condemned any kind of religious persecution, I'll let you slide out of this . . ."

"Colonel, I wish everybody's conscience were as clean—"

"Is this young lady your niece?"

237

Egath looked straight in front of him, a strained expression on his face. At that instant the secretary returned. "Major Buch wants to know if you've finished with them?"

Egath struck a match and blew it out.

"Yes, damn it!" As he spoke, the Rabbi and his niece were pushed through another door, and down a staircase that led to a large cellar.

CHAPTER EIGHTEEN

FROM THE VAULTED CEILING HUNG A KEROSENE LAMP WHICH SHED LITTLE LIGHT. AMONG THE PACKING CASES, several men in civilian clothes were exhaling smoke at each other's smooth-shaven Nazi heads. None of them turned round to look at Nadia and the rabbi, because their chief, who looked remarkably like the murdered Röhm, was just examining the visiting card of a gentleman with a high standing collar and blue spectacles.

"Count Willzscheck? . . . Good!" The fat man made his cigar glow.

"And who are you?"

"Me? Major Buch, Chief of the popular Murder Division."

"Excellent! My dear Major—you have the dancer? Fine! . . . Where is she?"

"That's her, lying back there. The doctor's looking after her. Our boys were right behind her, and then the silly fool jumped into the Seine! What luck!—there wasn't a policeman on the quai! So we were able to fish her out ourselves . . ."

"Fish her out? Ha-ha! Congratulations! And apart from that? Everything perfectly clear?"

"Clear as crystal! We do what we can. Anything else?"

"No—that's all."

"Want me to show you the way, Your Excellency?"

"Merci! I'll manage to find way out by myself." Count Willzscheck's footsteps died away behind the packing cases.

"Count of No-account! Idiot!" Major Buch spat. "These diplomats! Hänsel!" He motioned to a golden-blond young man with an exceptionally broad posterior. "Go get Colonel Egath and bring him down here." As Hänsel ran off, the Chief of the Murder Division whistled and sang:

> "We were betrothed—
> You know by whom.
> By the bulfinch . . ."

The last line of this comic-opera song he bellowed, mouth wide open, on a tremendous shattering yawn: "We we-e-re betrothed!" Jamming his cigar between his teeth, he sat down in front of a barrel, stolidly watching Colonel Egath approach.

"You wanted me?"

"My dear Colonel, I only wanted to tell you—Our Ambassador was just here, ants in his pants, chirping: 'If we haven't found a clew to the lost document by this evening, we can all be buried in soup-and-fish tomorrow morning early . . .'"

"Chirping, eh?"

"Yes!" Half-turning his head, Major Buch yelled back over his shoulder: "You there, Doctor! How's it coming? Hasn't that damn ballet dancer opened her trap yet?"

"Not yet, Major." At this, Buch stood up and walked over to a body which was covered with old sacks.

"Now—snap to it! Have you pumped the water out of her according to directions?"

"Been pumping her arms right along until now, Major—"

"Yes! You're sweating all right! That's all you first-aid people are good for! Gangway!" He came nearer, raising one corner of the sacking to reveal the dancer, and felt her pulse. "My dear Schmidt, did you give her camphor?" With comical puffed-out lips, he munched his cigar, rolling it over his tongue. "Well, my good Doctor, what are we going to do?"

"I'm going to try something else."

"Excellent! Don't forget, she mustn't kick the bucket! We've got to have her confession! So hop to it, old saw-bones! Show us what the Red Cross can do! Doctor Schmidt," he threatened, "let me tell you that if you can't put life into this corpse, then you can have yourself embalmed with her tomorrow." Roaring the last words like a man demented, he turned around and marched back to the barrel. "Hänsel! Hell! Where did Colonel Egath go?"

"Colonel Egath! . . . Colonel Egath! . . ."

"The Colonel seems to have left—"

"Seems to have left? . . . That's fine! Ha-ha!" Suddenly he picked up an ash tray and hurled it over the packing case at the Rabbi, shouting: "The God-damned swine! Bring that lousy Isaac over here!"

239

The Rabbi was unbound and brought before him. Leaning back against a packing case, Major Buch puffed heavily on his cigar, exhaling clouds of smoke to fumigate the Jew. Then he rose to the trot astride the packing case.

"At it again, you Isaacs, eh? Stirring up another world conspiracy against us poor Aryans! That corpse back there—she's on your conscience too! You Elder of Zion, let me tell you—your dirty Jewish mug is just as nauseating to me as it would be to the author of 'Mein Kampf!' I know you'll say you can't help that! But that's precisely the great tragedy of it all! In God's name keep your snout shut and don't annoy me, or there'll be Sodom and Gomorrah around here! I'll bet, you bloody Talmudist, you know what that means! . . . Do you hear me!" He sprang forward. "If you keep up this provocative silence, you'll soon find yourself turned into a pillar of salt!" With his gloved hand, he clawed and yanked at the Rabbi's beard. "I hope you've understood me, Isaac! One fine day the children of Israel will have a good deal to answer for! So—you're the 'Chosen People'. Your megalomania is already costing the world enough trouble! Hey, Hänsel! How about a little singe for the hair in the prophet's nose! Disgusting! The old swine never seems to go to the barber's." His assistant Hänsel in the close-fitting blue suit struck a match.

"Wait! Not so fast!" The fat Major blew it out. "Otherwise, this Isaac of ours will think we're barbarians! Listen, old Moses, I've got the best reference work for the treatment of defeated enemies." He took a pocket Bible from his coat and laid it on the barrel. "There you are! The Gestapo doesn't have to beat its brains to find out how to tickle you. Every rule you can think of for handling prisoners is here. And our fat Luther translated it into German for those of us who can't speak Hebrew. Tells here what your Jehovah recommends, for instance, in the Book of Kings: 'You shall stamp out my enemies in the wine-press of my anger until your thighs are sprinkled red with their blood!' Also it says here, Jehovah commands: 'You shall lift up the skirts of the captive women so that their nakedness may be seen!' Or—" But he clapped the Bible shut. "Yes, you broken-down Isaac, I have become quite a student of the Bible! But, tell me now—whatever put it into your heads to throttle the Cultural Leader of Heidelberg?"

"By God the Just, we had nothing to do—!"

"Shut up! The Jew's getting insolent! Come, Isaac, what do you say: isn't this latest Jewish murder in direct contradiction to your Moses's commandment: Thou shalt not kill? For God's sake, keep your dirty trap shut! Hey! Hänsel, the swine is looking so surly, it's

about time for a little cooking . . . There!" He lit a candle stump.
"And now the smoke of sacrifice can ascend unto your nostrils!"

"By God the Just! No! No! No!"

"Hold it, Hänsel! He seems to want to make a statement. Well?
Just have confidence, Isaac, and get it off your chest! How does this
murder hang together with the theft of the document?"

"I know absolutely nothing—"

"Hänsel, go to it! Isaac, nature is cruel! But you Jews have been
torturing us Germans for the last two thousand years. Hänsel, turn
on the heat! . . . The first murderer was the well-known Cain—at
least, it says so in the Bible! Cain—he was a tough one like you, and
he only hated Abel because he was blond! Had nothing to do with the
fruits of the field! Hänsel, get on with it! Look here, you moldy
Isaac, I'm here to carry out the orders of those higher up! Exactly like
your Abraham! And when his God on Sinai demanded that monstrous
thing of him—that he should butcher his own whelp—then Abraham
didn't get sentimental—he simply said, 'Hinemi!' which in our language
means, 'Here am I', or, as we soldiers say, 'At your orders.' So when
my own God up on the Obersalzberg commands me not to stand on
ceremony with the dearest thing I possess—a little Jew like you, Isaac,
old boy—you could hardly expect me to find better words than your
forefather did! Hinemi! That is: 'Heil Hitler!' " He held the burning
candle closer to the Rabbi's nostrils. "Are you going to talk, Isaakel?
Go ahead and talk! Help me! Where did you hide that Will?"

With his last remaining strength, Dr. Wolff groaned:

> . . . If I said: Let the darkness cover me,
> Night would become day!
> For with Thee there is no night!
> For the darkness and the light
> Are both alike to Thee . . . !

The words became unintelligible. Giving him a kick in the belly,
Major Buch blew out the candle. The rabbi lay motionless between the
packing cases.

"Excellent! And now while we're waiting for our good Isaac to
feel the flame of reason rising through his nostrils into his brain and
to condescend to give us a satisfactory statement—just bring that little
Jewish witch over here!"

CHAPTER NINETEEN

W HEN NADIA SAW HER UNCLE WHIMPERING ON THE STONE FLOOR, SHE THREW HERSELF ON HIM AND covered his face with kisses. Suddenly she recoiled and sprang up like a cobra. "Gangsters! Murderers! Gangsters! Beasts! Fiends!" And again she fell back prostrate over the Rabbi.

"You all heard what she said?" The fat Major turned, grinning, to his henchmen who had come running to the barrel from all directions to witness this little scene. "We all know the words of the 'Song of Songs of Charity': 'Though I speak with the tongues of men and angels, and have not charity'—" His audience grinned appreciatively. "So! Now then just pry our little Jewish witch loose from that touching family scene—and she can sing some more out of the Psalter of Charity . . ."

They seized Nadia right and left under her silver-fox collar. She was jerked to her feet by both arms, her face red, her eyes wide open.

"Beasts! You may as well know I can't stand pain! I'll scream horribly! But I won't answer questions! If you want to get anything out of me, you'll have to take me before Hitler himself! I won't tell you anything! Beasts! Beasts! Beasts!"

" 'Behold, thou art fair, my love,' " puffed the fat Major, who meanwhile had opened the Bible. With the unction of a clergyman and to the delight of the others, he read on:

" 'Behold, thou art fair: Thou hast doves' eyes within thy locks: thy hair is as a flock of goats, that appear from Mount Gilead. Thy teeth are like a flock of sheep that are even shorn, which came up from the washing; whereof every one beareth twins and none is barren among them.'

"Excellent!" Major Buch puffed heavily. "Only, seems a bit exaggerated . . ."

"Beasts! No! No! You'll break all my teeth!"

"Hänsel, open that muzzle of hers! Maybe she has something to say—"

"Beasts! Beasts!"

"Several teeth missing!" Hans reported, wiping the lipstick from his fingers.

"Yes," Buch continued reading, " 'Thy lips are like a thread of scarlet . . . Thy temples are like a piece of a pomegranate within thy locks . . . Thy two breasts"—he held the Bible nearer the light—"are like two young roes that are twins, which feed among the lilies'—"

He took off his spectacles and studied her. "To make sure of that . . . we'd have to see something. Hänsel!" Crude hands were already tearing off her fur. Underneath it she wore a snug-fitting white silk dress, closed at the neck and with long sleeves down to the palms of her hand.

"Excellent! What a lot of buttons! Take your clothes off."

Nadia, whose face gleamed wet with fear as if drenched in water, shut her eyes.

"Make it snappy, little witch! You heard me! Unbutton that dress!"

"Major!"—the onlookers laughed—"perhaps she only understands Hebrew!"

Buch winked solemnly. "Go to it, German Party Comrades! Let's just make sure if the Bible is right! Are her two breasts like twin roes?" On that cue, Hänsel came round the barrel and, in less time than it takes to tell it, had stripped off her dress and underclothes. Like a finely modeled Tanagra figure, her body stood there among the Nazi serfs.

"Excellent!" The fat Major laid the Bible reverently on the barrel.

"Yes, 'thou art all fair, my love; there is no spot in thee' . . . Except one thing: that you tore the sacred party button off the dress of the Women's Cultural Leader of Heidelberg and threw it into the stove. So the glowing coals seemed to you the most suitable place for it? Not altogether surprising in a daughter of Israel. As I remember, the 'fiery furnace' with the three singing men plays a not unimportant role in the Bible. It wouldn't even surprise me if *you* began to sing if we brought you up to the same temperature."

The eyes of the others lit up with a horrible eagerness; their hands moved uneasily in their trouser pockets. Major Buch blinked to the left where a pot of glue was cooking on a small iron stove.

"So, my little witch, you stick to it? And you won't say anything? . . . Take her over there to the fire . . . Hold it!" His eyes suddenly hardened. "What kind of a stone is it that the witch has on her finger? Let's see it!"

But Nadia was already screaming and wrenching herself away.

"You'll tear the nails off my fingers! Beasts! Beasts! Beasts!"

"Shut your trap!" Buch clapped his glove over her mouth and yanked her across the barrel. "Oh! That seems to be a valuable stone? Karl!! Let Karl take a look at it. He's an expert! Something of a connoisseur in jewels. Take a look! What is that?"

"That?" Karl's nose bent over Nadia's hand. "If it isn't a garnet—it could be a ruby. But I'm not a real expert. Party Member Lettré is the authority on precious stones . . ."

"A ruby? Excellent! You little Jewish witch, how did you get your claws on a ruby like that? It's a historical fact that the whole pack of you once wandered out of the swamps of Poland into the West, arriving poor as church mice! So how did you come to lay hands on such treasures? Dirty work afoot somewhere! Hm? Hänsel! Take that ring off her finger!"

"Ouch! Beasts! Beasts!"

"Go ahead and yelp!" The fat Major laid the ring on the cover of the Bible and studied it, gloating. "Excellent! Just like the Nibelungen treasure! What fires there are in that stone! From what German folk comrades did you swipe that little ring? Oh hell, Hänsel! Clear as the nose on your face. That's a valuable stone! Little witch, my first idea was to throw the ring in the stove there and then invite you to fish it out of the glowing coals again. But since it's a really valuable stone, as Party Comrade Karl tells us—well, we can't do that. Besides, we're not barbarians! Hänsel, you keep the stone for now, and tonight"—he whispered—"Air Marshal Göring is arriving. A nice little gift on our part if we tuck this ruby into his napkin for his little daughter, Edda . . . You know how he loves precious stones . . ."

While all eyes were admiring the ruby, Nadia, picking up her dress and fur, sneaked cat-footed to the stairs. But just then someone came stumbling down them so fast—that she just had time to hide behind a packing case.

CHAPTER TWENTY "**M**AJOR BUCH!"

"WHO WANTS ME?" ALL EYES TURNED AND, AS SUDDENLY, ALL HEELS clicked together, all arms were outstretched in salute.

Rudolf Hess walked up to the barrel. Around his throat he wore an apache scarf. A coal-black strand of hair hung from under his cap, which was pulled down over his eyes. He looked exhausted. An odor of toilet-bowls hung around him. Pale, with agitation, he asked,

"Where is Baldur?"

"The newly appointed bodyguard standard-bearer? Hasn't shown up here—"

"Not shown up? Run, Hänsel! Wait! Call up Sieburg of the 'Frankfurter Zeitung'—Pantheon— You know the number. He's got all the secret addresses—"

The blond secretary dashed off, tripping over Nadia's legs. She was again dragged back. When one of them slugged the girl, Hess's face did not change. Apparently the Deputy Führer was used to such incidents. His glance blazing hate, he looked at her lingerie with disgust.

"Cover the sow up!" They draped her clothes around her.

"She won't say anything, Rudolf Hess!" Major Buch flicked the ash from his cigar. "She'll only discuss the matter with Adolf Hitler personally! Ha-ha! She won't do it for less! Ha!"

"Who? That whore?" Hess cocked an eyebrow. "How very nice of her!"

"Yes! That's her kind of insolence! She won't talk to us beasts! Just calls us beasts and murderers!"

"Unheard of! Such noble characters! Is that nice? Where is Waldmüller?"

"Present!" A piano-mover of a man thrust himself forward.

"Perhaps you'll take care of the lady?"

"At your service!" The other grinned. "Maybe our crazy Felix will make her talk—"

"What crazy Felix?"

"The lusty chimpanzee that the Sultan of Morocco brought from Marakesh as a gift to Count Willzscheck. Rudolf Hess, how about sticking the little witch in the cage with the ape?"

"Excellent!" Major Buch grunted and, quite forgetting party etiquette, slapped the Deputy Führer on his behind. Overlooking this informality, Hess gnawed his nails with pleasure. In the meantime Nadia, entrusted to Waldmüller's tender mercies, was hurried off, her whimpering cries of 'Beasts! Beasts!' dying away in the distance.

"Well—and that thing?" Hess poked the prostrate rabbi with his toe. "One begins to understand why the old Egyptians refused to have these Jewish termites in their country. In Alexandria, for instance, I and a few of my friends in the German colony had a standing agreement with a Bedouin sheik outside the city. And every Schabbes, we used to nab some old piece of carrion from among the Chosen People in the bazaar. We'd take him to Sheik Muhammed's tent. First he'd serve us wonderful Turkish coffee and then we'd smoke nargilehs, sitting there on his beautiful rugs. But later when Luna would rise above the desert like an opal in the fiery green sky—and the jackals signified by appropriate howling that they had not yet scared up their Sunday roast in the stone quarries

—we used to tie our piece of carrion to our stirrups, leap into the saddle, and gallop away with him over the shimmering golden desert . . . Then later, after our mission was accomplished and we were galloping back under the stars—which, I assure you, my Party Comrades, in Africa shine down from the zenith at least six times more brightly than here—and still later, when we were back again in Muhammed's tent, squatting on his beautiful carpets, and drinking endless cups of coffee until dawn . . . I can only tell you that, every time, we shared the same proud feeling that we had 'remembered the Sabbath day to keep it holy' —German-style! . . ." He grinned with relish.

"Is there no balm in Gilead? Nadia! Niece! Is there no doctor here?" The Rabbi groaned and then let his head fall again. "Oh that my head were filled with water and my eyes springs of tears! Oh! Oh! Oh! . . . Day and night would I bewail the destruction of my people!"

Pushing back his cap from his brow, Hess let out at the Rabbi. "If you don't keep your mouth shut, you rotten carrion, we'll soon make a Sunday roast out of you too!" Turning away, he pulled a paper bag of bon-bons from his trouser pocket, stuck a pink fondant in his mouth, and walked up and down, chewing with relish. Abruptly, he stood still. "Prince Ferdinand!—where's he gone?"

Major Buch looked about him.

"Yes, God dammit! Didn't he report to you with that Uhle fellow?"

"To me? No!"

"God in Heaven! I gave him his orders just a while back—" He was going on, but just then Hänsel reappeared with the addresses.

"Here's the number of a bar where Baldur sometimes has an absinthe. The other addresses are in Montparnasse. And here's the secret number of the fifth-column villa in Neuilly—"

"Villa in Neuilly?" Hess gagged on his bon-bon, turning pale and then red. Taking off his cap, he held up a pocket mirror and combed his hair. "What can he be doing there so secretly?" He put the addresses in his pocket. Suddenly, the Doctor called from behind:

"Major! Major! She's breathing—"

"Rudolf Hess!" Buch tried to detain him. "She's breathing—" But the Deputy Führer hurried away, calling back over his shoulder:

"I'll be at the German Embassy at nine. You can report to me then—"

"What's got into him? . . . Running off like that!"

"Major, I never saw him run like that except once in Hamburg when a ship full of handsome sailors came in—"

"Is Baldur a pervert?" Buch made a wry face and spat out: "Well, I'll be damned."

246

CHAPTER TWENTY-ONE "SHE'S COMING TO!" THE DOCTOR PUT DOWN HIS HYPODERMIC AND RUBBED HIS HANDS. AND INDEED THE dancer had opened her eyes a little and was whispering, "Where am I?"

The Chief of the Murder Division bent over her, blowing a cloud of cigar smoke against her trembling lashes.

"Where are you, girlie? You're right here with the Gestapo!"

"With the Gestapo?—" Her voice died away.

"We-e-e-ell, Doctor? Isn't this carrion strong enough to talk yet?"

"Certainly, Major, she only swallowed a bit too much water . . ."

"Can't understand it! Every time I look into somebody's eyes like that, all I see is fear! Fear of good, kind Major Buch and his gentle Gestapo! Well, girlie, we can only die once! So pull yourself together! A little extra courage! Our industrious male-nurse has pulled you round again. Now suppose you tell us something. Having enjoyed the unusual honor of being received as a guest by the Master of Berchtesgaden, you reward him with base ingratitude! Not only with ingratitude—damn it! but with treachery! For meanwhile we've found out there's a Rabbi mixed up in this. We've found out that you have peculiar friends in Paris. For instance, the one with whom you were in the Bagatelle Park . . . Well, Doctor, she doesn't seem to be very lively yet . . . I have the impression that this young woman is still not able to take in my remarks."

"In my opinion, Major, she's quite capable—"

"You mean—just mulishness? So—so—so! Girlie, your passport says you're a Catholic? Well, your blessed Catholic Church's most holy Inquisition tortured many, many more women than the dear, kind Gestapo has ever thought of doing . . . Such a Grand Inquisitor as the Jew Torquemada, for instance—I've just been reading his memoirs—had about three hundred thousand witches burned and, according to his devoted editor, he nevertheless 'after a long and fruitful life, peacefully died in bed in his eighty-second year, comforted in his faith in the Lord'—ha-ha-ha! . . . I hope you can hear me? For I'm asking you one simple, clear, and unequivocal question—comprehensible even to the nit-wit brain of a ballet dancer: Where is the Will? No monkey-business now! Is your dress too tight? Difficult for you to breathe? Wait a second!" He squeezed her left breast out of the brassiere.

247

"There! That ought to be better!" The delicately rosy convex whiteness lifted into the smoke-laden air. The glitter in Buch's eye portended no good.

"Just a moment, Major!"

"What's the matter now? Is she fading out again?"

"One moment!" The doctor poured something down her throat.

"How's that for a pick-me-up? I particularly wouldn't like to lose my patience with you! I'm such a good-natured fellow! Everybody who knows me always says: 'That fat Major Buch is such an amiable fellow!' Like our Julius Streicher, I'm a bird fan too. I've even got a genuine Harz roller—he sings the Horst Wessel Song! And when I come home at night, and he's sitting on his perch, I take off my shoes and walk past his cage in my stocking-feet so as not to disturb the little, golden dear in his sleep. My chief, Heinrich Himmler, always says that even Richard Lionheart declared: 'Only an Aryan is capable of true depth of feeling.' I tell you this just so you'll know you are not in the hands of Huns—as the lying Jewish press is always calling us. No!" He ran his hands through her curls. "Just have confidence, girlie! Just tell us now: Where is that Will! . . . I'll count up to three! If on the count of three, I still don't know, then this burning cigar is going to persuade that innocent breast of yours to speed up your thinking."

He puffed until the tip of his cigar glowed red-hot, then held it close to her nipple. "One! I've counted 'one', girlie! Where is that Will? Two! I've counted 'two'! Where is that Will? When I count three, remember, I'm going to apply the cigar! Now then, where is it? Where have you hidden it? Here goes for 'three'! Will you talk? Three!" He crushed the burning cigar into her breast. The girl's body arched in pain. All the men in the cellar crowded around.

"Girlie!" The fat Major pressed the dancer down flat again. "When the regicide Ravaillac had assassinated Henri IV, and was cross-examined as to his motives by the Paris police of those days, it was a good deal worse than this! So lay off!" With his brutal thumb he stroked her teasingly under the chin. "Little girl, you know what they did to Ravaillac?—They broke every bone in his body, one by one. And then they made him do penance, holding a candle, in front of Notre Dame. And when they brought him to the place of execution and lifted him out of the cart, he screamed so loud you could hear it on Montparnasse. And all that Bolshevik did was to try to kill the king! And what is a king compared with your Benefactor of Obersalzberg? Girlie, have you any idea of the contemptible trick you played? Say you're sorry, and tell nice kind Major Buch where that Will is? You know he might get wild! And if I should have an attack of St. Vitus' dance, then I won't vouch for any more formalities. Where is that Will? Just tell me—and I'll even give you a visa. The dear, kind Gestapo has no objection if you should want to gladden the New World with your presence! We'll even let you write a book—all about your experiences with the dear, kind Gestapo. America's sensations are not our sensations!—So you might as well talk. Spill it, child! Are you going to tell me the truth? Then we'll be good friends. I'm not such a bad fellow! —What do you think, Party Comrades?" He blinked at the others, whose hands were dancing in their pockets. "I believe I know the answer to that! Yes! How can we help it if this chaste virgin under the sheets here won't tell us the truth?" Cigar in mouth, he leaned over again, his head close to her breast. But now suddenly Olenka sat up erect with the unbelievable strength that is given only to the dying at the moment of death. She raised her eyes until they shone all white and then recited the words which her beloved poet, Mickiewicz, had cried out to the youth of Poland almost a century before:

" 'O Youth!' "—her voice rang through the cellar like an S O S call —" 'Poland has fought against Russia nine times! Youth! you must fight against the egoists of this world!' Uhle! Uhle!" Then, in her agony, she transformed the words into an answer to what the Uhlan had whispered into her ear on the roof of Notre Dame. " 'Yes! We will form a first cell! The very first movement against the beast in us! Yes, Uhle, bring down to this lost earth a new world from the sphere of our ideals. Oh, Youth! Youth! Stand we together against the powers of brute force! Yes . . . a first cell, so that our hearts may know warmth at last—warmth in the sun of freedom! Youth! Stand we together! . . . So that we are not so alone—in the universe . . . Not so alone any longer . . ."

She had pulled herself erect, and stared with her dying eyes at the dirty ceiling of the cellar. Suddenly, her breath already failing, she cried: "Uhle, Uhle! Listen! I hear the sound of eternity!"

Major Buch was speechless. All at once he growled:

"I say, if this pig-headed bitch won't shut up, what are we going to do?"

"What?" As if answering a command, the others took their cigarettes from their mouths and hoarsed:

"This!" And then they all pressed their burning cigarettes against the girl's naked flesh. She sagged back without a cry.

When Major Buch snatched up her left arm and let it go, it dropped like stone.

From the distant office the Director came crashing down the stairs, shouting, "Police! The police!"

"Who?" Buch threw down his cigar and snatched the sheet back over the girl's body. "Lights out! Boxes in front there! Shut the doors! All the lights out—God damn it!—black it out!"

CHAPTER TWENTY-TWO

IN A LONG, NARROW OFFICE DOWNSTAIRS IN THE PREFECTURE OF POLICE, SERGEANT-MAJOR GRUMBACH, HIS mustache bristling with excitement, was taking down a memorandum on the typewriter. Opposite him sat Siegfried Krah, the litterateur, arrested at the Wailing Wall Café. All his protests that he had had nothing to do with the murder in the Pension Alsace had been fruitless. In impotent wrath over the crime perpetrated on his Cousin Klärchen, Grumbach had simply dragged him straight here from his café table.

Before continuing the examination, however, Grumbach clumsily pinned a black mourning band, just brought in to him by a policeman, on his left sleeve. Krah, meanwhile, dreamed out the broad, high window, across the Seine to the Quai Saint Michel, thinking sadly of his brandy glass left standing three-quarters full. Still swollen by the heavy rains, the river flowed darkly, glossed only by the light of a few street lamps, rustling between the quais on either bank. Motorcycle patrols of the Garde Mobile, in their heavy black leather jackets, roared up and disappeared into the court of the Prefecture. Others—in an equal hurry—dashed out, their headlights lancing the night. A coming and going like that before history-laden days.

"Damnation!" Grumbach squared himself back at the machine. "I've already typed the story of your life, Monsieur Krah. But before we go any further, tell me: Don't you feel any remorse? I keep wondering how you can sit there so nonchalantly. In fact, my friend, my astonishment is so great that I could even be driven to drastic physical measures if I were not quite so clear in my head as to the limits of my duty. Damnation! You monster! And I'm deliberately overlooking the fact that the murdered woman was a close relative of mine and, what's more, an Aryan! You say you are an Israelite?"

"Oi-oi—if you poke any more holes in my belly, I'll have to go before a justice and register myself as having suffered a change of sex!"

"Taisez-vous! Damnation! I'll have you handcuffed if you go on this way. Just because you've lost your Palestine, that's no reason why the rest of humanity should pay the piper! Damnation! Are all the white people to be murdered and the nations driven into war just so you can get back to the Jordan? There are philosophers who have incontrovertibly established—dammit—that your Dead Sea has increased its salt content ever since you've been tormenting humanity . . . She was my cousin! And when I say 'she was', that means that I haven't the slightest illusion that Klärchen is now arriving up there in a golden coach, dressed in sky-blue taffeta, to stay as a paying guest with the Dear God! No!" He practically howled the word. "I'm not so dumb! I know Klärchen is just exactly as dead as that fly there on the fly-paper! And precisely for that reason I'd like to wallop this fist between your eye-glasses! For, if there is no more mercy and no more Kingdom of Heaven, then I'd just as soon kick the whole business to Hell! Damnation! Go on, now! But please talk a language that a policeman with common sense can understand! Because there is one thing I'd like to tell you before we go any further: You're not dealing with a stupid bureaucrat, as you might suppose—in your omniscience! No question of that at all! So—that's just by the way! You maintain that you never left the café after noon today? How does it happen then that Sergeant Michel saw you this afternoon with a blonde . . . in the rue de l'Université? Here's his report, you monster—! I'm not one to let you tell me fairy tales! If the Holy Ghost himself were to come up the thirty-three steps from the bombproof shelter at Haudroumont, I'd say to Him: 'The House of Ludendorff has incontrovertibly demonstrated the fact that there's no such thing as a Holy Ghost.' "

"Bravo! Oi-oi! Monsieur le Sergeant!" Krah held out his hand to him across the typewriter . . .

"Wh-a-a-a-at? You monster! You don't believe in the Holy Ghost? Damn it!" He picked up a bell and rang it. "Michel!" The policeman entered. "Come here at once! I have the proof now! This is the murderer! Shut up, you damned atheist!" Rising half out of his seat, he leaned over his typewriter threateningly. "If anyone belongs under the guillotine, it's you—not Weidmann! Damn it, Michel, handcuff this atheist! Here is absolute proof that he murdered Frau Captain!"

"Oi-oi!" Krah regarded his fettered hands with interest. "How am I ever going to write now?"

"Write? You're not going to do any scribbling here! The only writing you'll do is your signature right under this memorandum. And after that you can catch fleas with your fingers in a numbered cell! Do

251

you understand?"

"Oi-oi! Why didn't I leave Paris! I have a visa and three affidavits! I could have been in Hollywood long ago!"

"Dammit! My hands are shaking so!" Grumbach motioned to the gendarme. "You sit down at the machine. I can't do any more! I simply can't do any more!" He held both hands before his eyes. "After all, I'm only human! That magnificent taffeta dress of my cousin's! Mon dieu, Michel, she was a lady! In the truest sense of the word—a lady! Therese always used to say: 'Like the Empress!' You just had to love Germany when you saw that woman! Such stateliness—such an imposing figure! Absolutely different from what you see here . . . Absolutely nothing of the tart about her, like the women here! I tell you, every word she spoke—you'd stand there gaping! Incontrovertibly! She had invited Therese and me to the Trocadéro tomorrow noon—and now the poor thing is lying dead on a bier in the conservatory at the German Embassy! . . ." He stood up and suddenly ran at Krah, with smashing blows right and left to his face. "You fiend!"

Krah grinned all over, his face a mass of wrinkles, offering his cheeks. "Go to it! Oi-oi! Hit me again! If a man strikes you on the right cheek —turn him the left!"

"What? A Jew says that? You scoundrel! That's the commandment for a Christian!"

"Oi-oi! Then why don't you obey it?"

"Damn it!" Grumbach yelled, "I'm no Christian . . ."

"I'm certainly no Jew!"

"Then what the hell are you?"

"What am I? Oi-oi! A poor devil like yourself!"

"What? Now the monster wants to get chummy with me! Equality —what? Fraternity—what? And I suppose Liberty, too! And if possible, you'd like to escape out of here—what?" He gave Krah such a shove that he and his chair fell over together. "If there's ever another revolution here on the Seine—you ogre!—it'll be against you! Understand?" Again he flew at Krah. "You hell-hound, to strangle my Klärchen! You Herod!"

Rushing out from behind the typewriter, Michel dragged the Sergeant-Major back, led him to a water-cooler at the rear, filled a cup for him, and said: "Buvez, mon chef!" Grumbach drank.

"I'm only human, after all! And if there's no longer such a thing as mercy and no Kingdom of Heaven, damnation—I say, if that is incontrovertibly established, then kick the whole business to hell!" Again he sprang at Krah. At that instant, however, the door burst open, and

Armoni and two gendarmes ran in. Glancing at Krah and Grumbach, the Commissioner gestured:

"Porca Madonna! Get out! Get out! Cross-examine him somewhere else! Room Number 3 is free! I have to telephone the Minister."

"Get going!" Grumback pushed Krah into the hallway. "Damnation!"

Armoni shut the door, picked up the receiver, and put through his number, impatiently thumping the table with a paperweight. To his assistants, he shrugged an eloquent shoulder.

"No answer! Mamma mia! Hello! Hello? . . . . Hurry . . . . Hurry . . ." He rattled the hook. "Now . . . Yes . . . Vendôme! Ministry of Justice! Yes! Right! Now! Monsieur le Ministre himself? Monsieur Marchandeaux? Commissioner Armoni speaking! Your Excellency—something sensational! What? But I couldn't reach the Minister of the Interior anywhere! Excellency! Excellency! Monsieur Schickelgruber is arriving in Paris incognito within the hour! What?" Covering the mouthpiece with his hand, Armoni whispered furiously to his colleagues: "He says I'm an idiot! He keeps saying, 'Bluff!' 'Blackmail!'"

"But Monsieur le Ministre!" He screamed into the phone: "We've just raided the German Travel Bureau! . . . What! . . . What! ('Blackmail'—he keeps saying 'blackmail.') . . . Excellency! It is positively established: Monsieur Schleich, the Russian, is a German agent! Being paid by Berlin to start riots here . . . What? . . . Yes, indeed! There are hundreds of German agents scattered among the workers! What? Yes! German officers in civilian clothes, too! Where's Schleich now?—Making a propaganda speech outside the Ministry of War . . . The square is black with people! Seething! He's agitating against the Republic! Against our democracy! One insult after the other! And against the Bishop of Notre-Dame because His Eminence made a radio address in support of war against the Nazis! What's the crowd doing? Excellency—they're acclaiming him. What? What's the weather like? (Asks me what the weather's like!)" Armoni raised his eyes to heaven. "Still stormy and rainy . . . Mais, Monsieur le Ministre—what shall I do? I've received reports that the workers meant to march through the rue Solférino, but the police sidetracked them down the Boulevard Saint Germain. At this moment, Monsieur Schleich is leading his ever-growing mob of protesting workers through the rue Dante to the Quai de Montebello. Looks as if he was taking them to Notre Dame."

Putting down the receiver, Armoni ordered: "Allez! Go get Police Chief Clemenceau! The Minister wants to speak to him. Quick!

Quick!" A sergeant came running in from the corridor and whispered to Armoni, who called into the phone: "Monsieur Clemenceau drove off half an hour ago in full uniform . . . Latest report just in: Reich Foreign Minister von Ribbentrop has arrived at the Hotel Ritz . . . What? Yes, Your Excellency! And four Generals of the Reichswehr with him . . . What? (He says he knows that! Monsieur Abetz has been to see him at the Ministry!)

"Your Excellency!" Armoni's voice edged over into falsetto. "I await your instructions! (Quick! Quick!)" He beckoned for a pencil and pad. "One moment, Excellency! I'm writing down your orders. All ready here. I repeat: 'Monsieur le Ministre instructs me to let the German Embassy and Monsieur Schleich alone!!!' Et alors!? Is that all?! But—your Excellency!" He screamed with rage into the telephone: "But—is that all!?" He slammed the receiver down and glared at his colleagues: "That's all, gentlemen . . . Porca Madonna!" He folded his arms, Napoleon-fashion. "The whole business, from A to Z, is a plot against democracy!" Slapping his straw hat on his head, he straightened his broad shoulders. And then, his eyes sparkling as if he had reached a decision, he raised his arm and shouted, "Vive la liberté!"

He stamped to the door. As he opened it, Siegfried Krah ran past, his face streaming blood, and flew up the stairs to the floor above. "Oi! oi! oi!"

"If there's no more mercy and no more Kingdom of Heaven, I'll kick the whole business to hell!" Sergeant-Major Grumbach ran after him. Armoni clenched his fists. The next instant he was gone. The gendarmes followed him. Downstairs at the entrance to the Prefecture, they watched him running along the quai in the direction of Notre Dame.

"Et alors?" The policemen pushed back their caps—and then they brandished their white rubber truncheons as if they were trying to fight the air.

CHAPTER TWENTY-THREE ARMONI ARRIVED AT THE SQUARE BEFORE NOTRE DAME JUST AS THE IMMENSE PROLETARIAN CROWD BEGAN to stream across from the Quai de Montebello under the brilliant street-lamps of the Pont au Double. The sailors on the barges gliding under the bridge, looked up. Drivers stopped their cars on the quai. Curious spectators stuck their heads out of windows on all floors.

His coat billowing wide, Schleich strode at the head of the workers, talking incessantly. At his side, his feet dragging with fatigue, walked the butcher's boy whom Eberlein had hired, balancing the Christ of the Trenches on his left shoulder. The "International" echoed from the house fronts. The rain-soaked caps and coats of the marching workers looked like a slow flood of withered leaves driven along the gutter. But now and then their care-worn faces gnarled as roots were visible when they bellowed at a gendarme or a soldier:

"À bas la guerre! À bas la guerre!"

"Halt!" Armoni, with six armed bicycle police, opposed the mob. Schleich whistled and immediately a great pushing and shoving began. The workers at the back crammed forward, those in front held their ground. Armoni pointed to weapons at the ready.

"Arrêtez ici!"

"Et pourquoi?"

"Monsieur, I give you fair warning—they are issuing cartridges in the barracks. You had better stop here! The square is closed—"

"Cartridges?" Schleich shook a raindrop out of his ear. "So—you're issuing cartridges? Out of the way! Who the devil are you anyhow?"

"Voilà!" Armoni showed his badge.

"Cartridges?! Monsieur le Commissaire!" Schleich flung the word back at the crowd like a tocsin. "Plague and Justice! Is the bourgeoisie mobilizing its executioners?"

The news that ammunition was being issued to the soldiers in the barracks spread like wildfire through the crowd. A number of square-chinned gentlemen who did not look at all like proletarians at once opened their pocket knives, saluted with them, and then roared out the weighty stanzas of the proletarian hymn in a foreign accent. At the same time bayonets glittered through the greenery of bushes around the square . . . "Aha!" Schleich took them in. "These kulaks are lusting after workers' blood! En avant!"

But just then a long procession of children wound into the square, coming from the Hôtel de Ville through the rue d'Arcole, and the Russian stopped and stood watching them curiously.

Above the shellacked straw hats of hundreds of convent-school boys and girls, silken church banners waved in the forward rhythm of a slow-pacing multitude. Nuns with wide-eared, white-starched head-dresses kept the marchers in order. The nearer they came to the Cathedral, the more distinct became their clear-voiced singing:

"Mary, Holy Mother of God!
Mary, Wondrous Queen!
Immaculate Virgin! Help us!"

"Oh, Mary!" a woman's voice rose above all the others. "Help us to fight against the Devil!" The voice broke off as if terrified.

Therese turned her head to a red-haired lady: "How you can sing!" But Hyacinthe quickly hid, abashed, behind a church banner.

"Plague and Hallelujah!" Schleich broke into wild laughter and snapped his fingers as he watched the little girls in their blue dresses trip modestly by hand in hand.

But as the workers began to murmur in protest at the delay, he shouted: "Comrades! Up with your red banners! And then we shall see if—" His harangue remained unfinished, for at that moment two automobiles crammed with police officers, followed by trucks from which rifle muzzles threatened, zoomed into the square and drew up before the cathedral. A silver-laced major of the Garde municipale alighted.

Behind him the antiquary Laroche, unshaven, Basque beret on his head.

"Je suis ancien combattant! Mon Commandant! Everybody knows me here in this neighborhood. Yes! There he is!" He pointed out Schleich. "Mais oui! Voleur! Voilà . . . Mon Christ des Tranchées! et alors! La France le potoir pour tous les bandites?! Mais non!"

Armoni went up to the major and talked to him, gesturing broadly. Nodding his head, the major lit a cigarette and walked across the square to Schleich:

"Monsieur! I warn you! Pas de bêtises! Lead your followers out of the center of the city at once—and quietly!"

"Plague and liberty!" Schleich stood firm, his legs wide apart. "Are you the ambassador of the bourgeoisie? According to what edict do you dare close the way to the workers of the Republic when they want to march into the more flowery quarters of the city? This is not a stage chorus. These men are iron workers! Every one the father of a family." And now his voice took on the tone of a commanding general: "Comrades!"—he pointed to the wooden figure—"that proletarian there—has yet another cosmic function to fulfill. He is not an individual—but a type! With all the seminal substance of future centuries! En avant, comrades! Be proletarians! That means—the archetype of races! En avant!" He gave the butcher's boy a shove in the back. "We, the international proletariat!—we protest in the name

256

of this mutilated proletarian! You see him here on our flag-bearer's shoulder. We protest against the chicanery of those who are trying to drive the working people once more into the massacre of war! En avant!"

Many hard hands grasped the Christ figure, holding it high in the air, and bawling:

"À bas la guerre!" Thousands of voices responded thunderously, the clamor racing through the streets to the rue Dante—and farther:

"À bas la guerre!"

Then, under the church banners, out of the mouths of the countless children and nuns, frantically intoned, came the reply:

"Vive la guerre!"

The Russian hesitated—but he gave his workers a sign and, with rapid steps, walked alone across the sanded square to where the children were massed. As Armoni and the major stepped out to confront him, he yelled: "Out of my way! Sticking your noses into world history! There's no room for you there! Gangway!" And he had plunged in among the schoolgirls.

"Plague and Maria! You appetizing little daughters of the *non*-working people! Can't you perform your sexual egg-dances somewhere else? We need the whole stage. Out of the way! They've issued cartridges already, and I'd be sorry to see such a delicious little bride—" He pinched one of the prettiest girls on the behind. At her squeals several nuns came sailing up, hissing like angry swans. The eldest of them —hands folded over her domed stomach, stiff convent robe seesawing —marched over to the major and demanded Schleich's arrest . . . Suddenly, inside the cathedral, the organ began to sound with such unaccustomed strength of tone that they all looked at each other.

"Sweet Jesus!" Therese made her way through the crowd of children to the left portal. "Has the procession begun already?" She beckoned to Hyacinthe.

As they were about to enter, Mathias Westermann came out. "Right, Madame, right? How our organ is working now! What a tone! Listen! Just as if Johann Sebastian himself had come straight from Heaven with a cantata he learned from the angels—to give us a first performance right here in Notre Dame—"

"Sweet Jesus—who is it playing?"

"Come inside!" Westermann beckoned, and let the two women slip into the church.

CHAPTER TWENTY-FOUR

Disturbed by the ever mightier organ crescendo, Schleich irritably made water against the cornerstone of the main portal. The nearest convent girls leaped away from the splatter, horrified. Nuns wrung their hands.

"Cochon!" Armoni tore up from behind and gave the Russian a push. "Et alors! Pisser à notre cathédrale?! Cochon!" The air was blue with curses of righteous indignation. "Porca Madonna! On this venerable edifice!"

"On this world-famous, incomparable monument of Gothic Art!" . . .

"Plague and kidneys!" Schleich adjusted his clothes. "What am I supposed to do—burst a bladder?"

Armoni signaled with his straw hat and, at that magic wand, a cordon of police appeared from behind the statue of Charlemagne.

"Messieurs les gendarmes!" Schleich tried to sway them. "Even if your weapons are of polished blue steel, you are nonetheless all of you sons of the people! Not ghostly automata of the bourgeoisie! Stand back!—You don't suppose we're afraid of your bayonets? There's no man living can close the way to the workers! Make room! Everybody move! Gangway!"

There would undoubtedly have been a collision if, at that moment, there had not happened something which occurred only on high holidays. The great central doors of Notre Dame opened and a procession, lighted by many flickering candles, came out, headed by a group of choir boys, of whom the first carried a long staff surmounted by a golden cross. Behind him the singing boys and a body of priests. And last, resplendent in flowered ceremonial vestments, the Curé of Notre Dame. Halting, he made the sign of the Cross to right and left. At a signal from him two priests left the litany-reciting group and went over to the butcher's boy who, still shouldering the Christ of the Trenches, stood flanked by waving red banners. The honey-yellow light of their candles shone on the war-stained wooden face. The butcher's boy was plainly uncomfortable. And when the tonsured, lace-clad priests took his burden, he not only did not resist, but sank to his knees and made the sign of the Cross.

"By Saint Marx and the angels!" Schleich held them fast by their brocade collars. "Where are you going with that? That scarecrow belongs to me!"

"Scarecrow?" Laroche clasped his head . . . "Oh, mes pauvres amis!"

"What! Steal my scarecrow and get away with it! Hey, you police-man, have the goodness to protect me!"

Sensing the increasingly ugly mood of the workers, the Curé sent one of his choir boys for Armoni. Hat doffed, the little commissioner whispered to the priest. Then he hurried across to Schleich.

"Porca Madonna! His Reverence would like to end this difference as quickly as possible in Christian brotherly love. Come! Just name the sum for which you will turn over this relic to the Cathedral Chapter!"

"The sum? Plague and Shylock! I'll not haggle! I'm the leader of an army of workers! And this piece of wood"—he turned the priest hold-ing the figure around—"is soaked with the cries of dying soldiers. You want me to name a sum? Do you think I'm the Pope?"

Encouraged by laughter among his workers, Schleich folded his arms and said:

"Besides—I bought my proletarian for the Kremlin."

"The Christ of the Trenches—for the Kremlin!" Laroche choked with indignation. Then he shouted at Schleich: "Bolshevik! You Bol-shevik—"

"Christ was a proletarian," the Russian outshouted him. "And so I bought him for Moscow. But, under one condition, I would be pre-pared—"

"Vite, vite," Armoni urged.

"If his Reverence, just as he stands there under the dazzle of lights in the doorway—and all his ecclesiastics in the full mumbo-jumbo of their official regalia—including all the lilac and purple-shirted priests who are holding their hands up to protect their candleflames from the wind —I say—if this entire, incense-stinking company puts itself at the head of my proletarians and, preceding our red banners, carries this wooden cripple to the Quai d'Orsay in a solemn march of protest, and, arrived there, in the name of all working men, women, and children, demon-strates against any and all preparations for war—and then—"

"C'est tout?" Fanning his brow with his straw hat, Armoni scurried back to the Curé. At length he returned and, standing at some distance from Schleich, ordered him to withdraw with his forces behind the police cordon—"sans discussion."

"Plague and the Pope! Is that your answer? So you want to see pro-letarian blood flow before the curtain falls? Eh bien!" He seized one of the red flags and was about to give the command to march forward, when he saw his scarecrow being quietly carried into the cathedral.

"Gangsters! Stop!" Forcing his way between two steel helmets of the cordon, he plunged after it, but stopped short on the threshold.

CHAPTER TWENTY-FIVE

JUST AS THE BULLET-RIDDLED FIG-URE OF THE SAVIOUR BECAME VISIBLE BETWEEN THE PILLARS OF THE NAVE, the powerful organ tones which had been filling the vaults broke off. The organist in the loft rose to his feet and looked for his cape among the music stands. But Hyacinthe forestalled him and hung the old Moroccan cloak tenderly around his shoulders.

Then he came forward until he stood just behind the balustrade of the organ loft. From there, with knowing eyes, he gazed down into the church.

Supported on the shoulder of the strongest of the lace-clad officiants, the Christ of the Trenches swayed forward ahead of the choir-boys. Followed by the priests, he teetered, candle-lit, between the pews along the long aisle to the high altar. As He passed, the children curtseyed and crossed themselves. Therese Grumbach, her face covered with a black veil, fell on her knees, not daring to look up. Many curious passers-by followed the procession in from the street. The pews were soon so full of worshipers that there was not a vacant place left. The Curé struck up, and all sang:

> The Son of God goes forth to war,
> A kingly crown to gain;
> His blood-red banner streams afar:
> Who follows in His train? . . .

Meanwhile, the figure was carried up the many steps to the high altar. As the officiating priests arranged themselves on either side, the Curé of Notre Dame raised the wooden sculpture, and set it ceremoni-ously on the altar, between vases full of autumn leaves, in front of the tabernacle.

The children crowded up against the wrought-iron choir screen separating priesthood from laity. Their banners, with their saints and their silver tassels, rocked back and forth above their young heads. The second stanza of the hymn had not yet come to an end when an acolyte

260

rang his silver bell. Then all together sank shuddering to their knees under the vaulting arches, among the pillars and the stone walls. In this pause, shot through with whispered prayers, the Curé took a carved thurible, bowed three times before the Christ of the Trenches, and censed it from all directions with clouds of bluish smoke, fragrant with ambergris.

The soldier in the loft saw the weather-beaten wooden face of the martyred Saviour come alive in the warm sheen of the many altar candles. As if safe and sheltered, and once more arrived in the House of His Father, he was embedded among the autumn leaves. Then the other raised his pale haggard face and looked up into the vaulting. And under that look it was as if the gray, pointed arches and age-old Gothic walls opened wide. And now he filled his lungs anew—with the breath of Love.

The longer Hyacinthe watched the strange soldier, the more her heart seemed too narrow to contain the sudden joy of her soul. For as only genius can, the organist by his playing had stilled the torment of the day in her every cell. In exuberance of emotion, she grasped the hand of Mathias Westermann, who pressed it so hard that it hurt.

Now, as the soldier left the balustrade, they both followed him almost reverently, then went slowly down the stairs behind him. As the sound of his tread came nearer, Schleich withdrew. Into the square in front of Notre Dame trotted a squadron of dragoons, and halted. Bridle by bridle, muzzle by muzzle. Chewing of bits, rattling of chin-straps, scraping of hoofs. Armoni made a gesture of relief toward the blue-steel-helmeted, lance-bearing riders. Then, together with the Major, he hurried into the cathedral, caught Schleich by the coat, and dragged him out.

"Porca Madonna! If you and your mob don't make tracks instantly, we shall open fire!"

"You'll open fire?" Schleich's eyes blazed. Suddenly he marched out into the square and waved his cap.

CHAPTER TWENTY-SIX "EN AVANT!" SCHLEICH URGED THE FLAG-BEARERS ON. "TO THE MINISTRY OF WAR! À BAS LA GUERRE! OR do you want to satisfy your hunger from the bourgeois rubbish pail as in 1914? En avant! Or these kulaks will force you once more into their immense arsenal of destruction to beat your hammers and sickles into bayonets for capitalism."

"À bas la guerre!" came the answer. And the swelling army of workers surged forward.

"Vive la guerre!" A voice suddenly rang above the shouting. A square-built man worked his way through the line of march until he stood before Schleich:

"Comrade Schleich! is that you making such a crazy speech? I protest! You are preventing the French proletarians from going to war against the Nazis!" His gray hair stood like bristles around his ashen face, which was lighted by his threatening eyes. He looked like a people's leader at the time of the Peasant Wars.

"Münzer! Münzer!" He was now recognized by many workers as one of the surviving secretaries of Lenin.

"Plague and Hell," cried the Red Singer even louder. "En avant!"

"Halt!" Münzer stood alone against the forward-marching masses. "Comrades! Now it is either life or death for communism! À bas le Fascisme! À bas les Nazis! Vive la guerre!"

"En avant!" Schleich kicked the butcher's boy in the back. "En avant! I am willing to talk with you about the life and death of communism, but not with such kulaks!" He hit Münzer over the head with a red flag and thundered, "En avant! À bas la guerre!

"Or"—he pointed to the cathedral where the priests had taken the mutilated wooden torso of the Christ—"proletarians! you will soon look like him! Like him, without arms and legs.—That's how the capitalists would like to send you home after the war—so that they wouldn't have to be afraid of you when you demanded higher wages! En avant!"

"Comrade Schleich," Münzer grabbed Schleich's collar. "Can you intend, here and now, to smash the resistance against that Obersalzberg betrayer of the workers?" And now with all his strength he bellowed out to the workers: "À bas Hitler!"

As at a cue, a wild pell-mell of roaring began. "Vive Hitler!" "Vive Stalin!" "Vive la guerre!" "À bas la guerre!" "À bas Stalin!" "Vive la guerre!"

Into the increasing howling of the masses, Münzer shouted hoarsely, "Comrades! We have opened the drafts under the boiler of the revolution for you! Do you want to turn the steam back into the dead machinery of reaction?"

"You ox!" Schleich spat, "what do you know about the secret of the

Kremlin? En avant!" And he led his proletarians on.

Already the advance guard had reached the central portal. The captain of the dragoons saw it. But he hesitated. He even ordered his men to withdraw a little. Their retreat was greeted with howls of triumph. Suddenly a shot was fired. No one knew from where. Schleich threw himself flat on his belly. His workers came to a halt. When the Russian had risen to his feet, the police noted that the bullet had gone through one of the red banners. There was a second of wavering. Then, without further warning, the proletarians began raining stones and other objects on the soldiers. At this point, between the dragoons' horses, infantrymen advanced with fixed bayonets. An infantry lieutenant raised his sword and commanded:

"Ready! Aim!"

Rifles were pointed at the workers. In the pause, like an eternity, before the command 'Fire', the scolding voice of the Swiss Xavier Grün was heard:

"What, son? Play the organ—and then stop playing the organ? Out with you! Go and mount your horse! Allez! En avant! Go and shoot at those Bolsheviki! Get out—I said. Your comrades are already aiming their rifles! Get out!" And he pushed at our unknown soldier with his halberd. Then he closed the giant doors of the central portal of Notre Dame behind him.

The soldier now stood outside . . . Behind him were Mathias Westermann and Hyacinthe. The infantry lieutenant, disturbed by the incident, had neglected to give the command to fire. Schleich, too, instead of leading his workers forward, began, as soon as he saw the red cape, to mutter insanely.

The soldier abruptly strode into the open space between the workers and the armed military. He looked at the aimed rifles, then at the proletarians. Then he freed his arms from the Spahi cloak and spread them wide.

"Out of the way!" the captain of dragoons sprang at him. "We're going to shoot!"

"Shoot!" Hyacinthe screamed, and ran to drag the soldier back. But at that moment, a gendarme on top of a truck turned on a powerful searchlight. The glaring white disk fell full on the head of the organist. His mask was clearly visible. The commanding officer stared at it. Then he spurred his mare back. Here and there an aimed rifle trembled against a soldier's cheek.

"Get out of the line of fire!" yelled the lieutenant with the sword.

"To what regiment does that man belong?" The captain spurred his bay forward again. "Hey! You! What are you doing out of the barracks? Don't you know you're all supposed to be in barracks standing ready for an alarm?"

Suddenly raising both hands to his ears, the soldier slowly lifted off the mask which all had hitherto taken to be his face . . . !

A cry of horror swept across the square. Above the soldier's throat appeared a cluster of bluish-black shadows, without form . . . no nose . . . no mouth . . . nothing but flesh painfully stitched together. The dignity of what had been a human face had found refuge in the eyes, which still remained unharmed.

Green as the eyes of some night-prowling woodland creature blinded by the headlights of an automobile, his eyes fluoresced into the artificial acetylene glare as if out of their own evidence.

"Damnation!" Sergeant-Major Grumbach threw up his arms. "Isn't that my pioneer's mug?" And then he tumbled grotesquely down into the truck.

There was an ominous silence—whose significance the major understood only too well. He seized the horribly mutilated soldier, intending to hustle him out of the spotlight of the general attention into an army car. But then from the sea of workers there rose a shouting that would not be downed: "À bas la guerre!" Like a stream that could no longer be held back, it surged against the police and the soldiers.

Abruptly, from somewhere in the crowd a voice, hard as metal, gave the command in German: "Feuer!"

The French lieutenant of infantry recoiled—then at once he, too, shouted, "Feu!"

A salvo crackled . . . Wounded in the shoulder, the soldier crumpled. Over his prostrate body surged a fighting, fleeing mob. Pandemonium—in front of Notre Dame.

BOOK FOUR

CHAPTER ONE

UNDER THE LONG BLOOD-RED SWASTIKA BANNERS OF THE GERMAN EMBASSY IN THE RUE DE LILLE, THE broad, high, wooden courtyard door closed behind Schleich, who leaned for a moment exhausted against the wall. His shirt stuck to him, drenched with perspiration. He was shaking as with ague. Nevertheless he dragged himself across the small high-walled courtyard past the Honor Guard of S.S. men just dressing ranks, rifles grounded. His eyes still wild, he shambled up the broad flight of steps and was received by footmen in silver-laced livery. Gasping, he looked around the foyer, which rippled with Japanese chrysanthemums. In knee-breeches and buckled shoes, Major-Domo Schellbaum hastened forward and, with smiles and winks, helped the Russian out of his dripping overcoat.

"Plague and Notre Dame!" Schleich winked at the Major-Domo. "Is His Excellency Herr Himmler in the house?"

"Not yet—but the Reich Foreign Minister has asked for Your Excellency several times . . ."

He conducted Schleich upstairs to a guest room where lackeys pulled off his sweat-saturated clothes. An infantry bullet had grazed his left arm, singeing his linen and scratching his skin. Schellbaum cut off the shirt sleeve and put salve on the wound. Since Schleich continued to shake as though with a chill, the Major-Domo suggested a hot bath. The Russian declined, demanding his baggage. A leather suitcase was brought in.

"Plague and the Volga! My dress clothes are in there!"

Opening it, Major-Domo Schellbaum handed the guest of the German Embassy a red-velvet military tunic with gold galloons. "Shall I have it pressed, Your Excellency?"

"No! Stop gabbling at me. Hand me the breeches."

"Here!" Schellbaum handed him a pair of sky-blue breeches and the accompanying red Russian leather boots.

No sooner had the servants left the room than Schleich dashed to

265

the telephone, shielded the receiver with his hand, and in a low voice asked for the Hotel Ritz.

"Hello? Is that the Ritz Bar? François! Is that you? . . . Is the red-haired lady still there? What? You haven't seen any lady with red hair? Plague and cocktails! Listen! . . . was there a fellow in a wind-breaker? I asked him to be there. What? Nobody like that to be seen? . . . What? Listen! . . ." Hearing steps at the door, he had just time to drop the receiver before von Ribbentrop came strolling in without knocking and cordially shook hands.

"Monsieur"—he looked with open admiration at the Russian—"in that costume you could pass for Ivan the Terrible! Ha-ha! We'll build you an ice palace in the Urals—when the time comes! And by the way"—he clicked his heels lightly together—"my Führer deigns to award you, in recognition of your outstanding services against Chris-tianity, the Grand Cross of the Order of the German Eagle! Excuse me —but we're expecting a most distinguished arrival at any moment. A thousand things to be attended to . . . But if you'll drink a glass of champagne?" He clapped his hands . . . "Oh!" He clawed at Schleich's chest. "There's no tape here to pin the Order on." To the valet who entered, he barked: "Quick! Have a tape sewn on His Excellency's tunic at once. . . . My very dear Comrade Schleich! . . ." Bowing, he ran out, his patent-leather pumps twinkling along the corridor.

A chambermaid entered, curtsying, followed by an S.A. man with a bottle of champagne and glasses. Filling a glass for Schleich, he clicked heels and made off. The maid, her straw-yellow hair freshly waved, be-gan deftly sewing with lilac thread on the left side of Schleich's tunic. With an upward flash of moist blue eyes, she asked permission to open the lower three buttons. Pouring the second glass of champagne down his throat like a man dying of thirst, Schleich made no objection. Reaching her soft white hand under the tunic, she adroitly held the tape in place and tacked it down with neat stitches. The scent of her fluffy hair tickled his nostrils. He emptied the third glass. Suddenly he seized the maid by both breasts. With a frightened "Oh!" she nevertheless found his grasp peculiarly agreeable. Without further ceremony, the Russian tumbled her on the floor. She spent the next few minutes moaning under his bearlike weight.

CHAPTER TWO

MEANWHILE, DOWNSTAIRS IN THE
DINING ROOM, A HUGE OVAL TABLE WAS BEING SET WITH CRYSTAL AND
heavy gold service for twenty persons. Opposite the glass doors that
opened on the garden, the waiters set an ornate chair of state.

"Well!" Freshly bathed and powdered, Rudolf Hess came into the
room with a casual air. "Where is Party Comrade Hänsel? Isn't he here
yet?"

Major-Domo Schellbaum paused in the act of lighting the candelabra.

"Why are you looking at me, Peter?" In his role as "lady of the
house" for that evening, Hess skipped about the candle-lighted room
. . . arranging roses in a Sèvres center-piece between the plates . . .
placing them stem by stem in the mirror-basin of water . . . Then he
lit Japanese incense-sticks and, running from corner to corner, dis-
pensed their artificial fragrance through the room. Suddenly, he stood
still:

"Peter, do you hear anything?"

"Where, Your Excellency?"

The major-domo stepped to the sill of the wide-open garden door,
listening. Brushing from his brown gala-livery the rain drops that every
gust of wind sent down from the soaking crowns of the trees, he asked:
"Is it really true, Your Excellency, we're expecting—a visit? I still can't
believe it!"

"Peter! Have you prepared the spinach?"

"À la Mussoliniana . . . 'Spinacci!' . . . The last time he dined
with the Duce in Roma Eterna, the greens tasted especially good to
him."

"And the mushrooms?"

"Riced with carrots. I ordered the eggs from Munich by plane.
French eggs are not for him! The Devil only knows what kind of cooks
they've got here!"

"Clear up this mess here! And don't turn on the fountain till I give
the signal . . ."

"Are you really going to have candles stuck on the turtles out there
on the lawn, Your Excellency?"

"Well, why not, Peter? Good idea—don't you think?"

"And when shall we light the lanterns in the trees?"

"When he has been seated, Peter, and begins on his celery soup.

What are those bottles? . . . Heavy wines and liqueurs? . . . Who are those for?"

"General Jünger ordered them! And Colonel von Einem just asked if we had a good old brandy."

"Where are the generals?"

"Gossiping. Your Excellency. There's a rumor . . ."

"Beware of rumors, Peter!" Hess tidied the tablecloth, removing the débris of flowers.

"And General Rommel has arrived too? When Rommel is on the scene—the adjutants were just saying—something's due to happen! He's always for taking a short-cut with his tanks!"

"Peter" . . . Hess brooded. But with a quick change of mood he asked: "Have you given my little Douglo his chopped veal and milk?" Suddenly he nudged the major-domo. "Who's that out there—beyond the fountain—just passing those trees?"

"Where do you mean?" Schellbaum awkwardly adjusted his spectacles. "I don't see anybody . . ."

"Must be General von Blaskowitz. And behind him—old man Mackensen! What the devil is he doing here? Who ever invited that moldy death's-head to Paris?" Tossing the incense sticks on the table, he ran out.

Schellbaum picked up the incense sticks, deposited them on the silver tray that a footman had just brought in, and sent him out of the room. Peering about, he suddenly hurried into the park as far as the first large tree trunk. Ostentatiously he cleared his throat. Around the bed of begonias came Prince Ferdinand.

"Your Royal Highness," Schellbaum whispered, "Hess has just left—"

"Already off to the airport? Fine—fine!"

"Everything remains as planned?"

"Nothing changed. Where's my uncle?"

"Prince August Wilhelm? He slipped down to the furnace room a little while ago. His Majesty has probably arrived from Holland . . ."

"His Majesty!" The young prince in his smart black S.S. jacket gave him a hard look. "That senile old bird from Doorn? Schellbaum!" He pulled the major-domo into the darker shadow behind the tree. "You remember, when I was made a lieutenant at ten years of age, my first parade with the bodyguard—in Potsdam?"

"Yes, Prince! I had a string tied to my side-arms for you—"

"And I held on to it so that I could keep step with you six-foot grenadiers when Their Majesties reviewed the company . . ."

"Your Royal Highness! . . . I would die for you!"

"Dear old faithful!" He embraced him. "You're a grand fellow! But anybody who thinks that I'm sticking around tonight to pull the chestnuts out of the coals for other people—has got another guess coming! Uncle's little sonny-boy is not going to get the Imperial Crown! Get me? As to my grandfather—let him go bury himself! As for being Kaiser, he doesn't know how. He made a wretched mess of it in 1918 . . ."

"Ps-s-s-st!"

"I count on you! Keep your tail up! Be sure everything clicks! It's now or never!"—and he disappeared in the darkness.

Tugging at his necktie, the major-domo breathed deeply with excitement.

CHAPTER THREE "HELLO, PETER! . . . YOU'LL CATCH YOUR DEATH!" RIBBENTROP STOOD IN THE OPEN DOOR OF THE DINING room.

"Your Excellency!" Schellbaum, his voice shaking, trotted back along the gravel path.

"Well, Peter! We'd better close these doors! It's frightfully damp tonight! And you know our Lord and Master has to be careful when it's so humid." Schellbaum slowly closed the two tall glass doors.

"Merci, Peter! Now be so kind as to see if Herr Abetz has already returned from his session with Monsieur Marchandeau at the Ministry of Justice."

"Right away, Your Excellency."

"Wait a minute, Peter, old fellow!" Ribbentrop laid his hand on Schellbaum's shoulder. "What did the Deputy Führer want with you?"

"He asked me if I had fed his dog."

"Oh!—God, I'd like to poison that dog!"

"Why?"

"Because he was bred in England. And the English have got to be wiped off the earth! The Lord Northcliffes, the—"

But he broke off, and looked into the library. "Any idea who that blond adjutant is in the library? What a lovely wave he has."

"That is Party Comrade Hänsel. As far as I know, he's from the German Travel Bureau, must be the Deputy Führer's new secretary."

269

Ribbentrop watched the young S.S. officer tear up some papers, throw them into the fireplace, and sneak away like a thief.

"Well, Peter—go and bring Herr Abetz here!"

As soon as he was alone, the Foreign Minister streaked into the library, picked up the tongs, and poked around in the fire. But the papers were already charred beyond recognition. Puffing his cigar thoughtfully, he sauntered through the dining room and out into the garden. His blood tingled in expectation of his Bräuhaus God. "The devil! Where are all those nice, new young pretties of the bodyguard? Don't see them anywhere!" He strode on.

"Who goes there?"

"I! . . . At ease!"

"Pardon . . ." Prince Ferdinand recognized the Reich Foreign Minister.

"Oh!" Ribbentrop stepped back, embarrassed. "So it's you, Party Comrade!"

"At your service. I'm in charge of the security guard on duty to-night. Himmler has made me responsible. So you'll excuse my challenge, Your Excellency. The wall at the back of the garden is right on the unlighted quais of the Seine."

"Indeed? Well, please don't let me disturb you! I only wanted to see if Colonel Latour's car had arrived. By the way, how many men have you posted in the garden?"

"Two sections—"

"Well, Prince—as ever: The bodyguards answer with their lives for the safety of the Führer!"

"Heil Hi!" Prince Ferdinand extended his arm, his silver galloons glittering.

In high feather, Ribbentrop re-entered the dining room. Looking through the music room, he saw Rudolf Hess bending over, his eye to the keyhole of the conference room. Tiptoeing over the Smyrna rug, he tapped him on his posterior.

"Bonsoir!"

"Bonsoir!" Hess jumped erect and, to cover his embarrassment, re-adjusted his leather belt.

"Is Hess smelling out a conspiracy against his beloved Britons?" Smiling gleefully, the Foreign Minister drew him away and, arm in arm they strolled back the way he had come. "Hm? Arabian perfumes? Everything going smoothly? Congratulations! Can you be perfectly sure of Count Willzscheck's cook? . . . Who's tasting the vegetables?"

270

"I am—as always—"

"Yes, mon cher!" Ribbentrop sighed. "You've been his friend the longest of any of us—the friend of the 'Bad Man', as that clown Churchill calls him . . ."

"Yes—yes—I am his oldest friend . . ."

"And how is your amiable wife, my dear Hess?"

"Oh, thank you—thank you— And yours?"

"Oh, thank you—thank you—. By the way, where on earth did you get that new young adjutant?"

"Pretty as a picture! . . ." Flattered, Hess sniffed at his perfumed handkerchief.

"Personally, I find his torso somewhat too long. But, everyone to his own taste." He sucked appreciatively on his cigar. "Well, Schellbaum"—the major-domo had reappeared—"has Herr Abetz returned?"

"Yes sir, he's upstairs, taking a lukewarm bath . . ."

"Anything else?"

"Yes sir, a telegram from Moscow."

"Hand it over!" The longer Ribbentrop read, the brighter his face became. He rubbed his hands.

Pocketing the telegram, he blew a kiss. "The sea will run red! Smash England dead— And not only England! Hey!" He blustered over to the piano, fingering the accompaniment to the "Meistersinger" motif:

> Winterstürme wichen dem Wonnemond,
> In mildem Lichte leuchtet der Lenz.
> Auf linden Lüften, leicht und lieblich,
> Wunderwebend er sich wiegt. . . .

and humming, "Yea, lovely and light, lovely and light!"

Hess ran into the library. "Hello!" he called into the phone. "Meissner! What? Already at the airport? When? All right!" He banged the receiver down. Spreading his arms wide, he inspected himself nervously in the mirror above the fireplace. "Adolf, you're arriving! And I look a sight!—losing my hair . . ." He spat into the fireplace and muttered angrily in the direction of Ribbentrop's playing: "Damn it! War with England! Perfectly insane!" There was a noise behind him. "Who's that?"

"It's I!—Hänsel!—" The new secretary wagged his broad posterior.

"Well, well! Report!" Hess was livid with excitement.

"Baldur was not in the villa."

"Not there? Did you search it thoroughly for the papers?"

"Thoroughly! I found an envelope in the fireplace."

"With papers?" Hess's exclamation was so loud that he clapped his hand over his mouth in fright. Fishing behind some old folios on the library shelves, Hänsel pulled out a bulky envelope. Hess snatched it from him.

"The Will? . . ." Hess ripped open the buttons of his brown jacket, stuffed the papers under his shirt, and, as quickly, buttoned the jacket again. Embracing the blond secretary, he crowed for joy:

"Hänsel! Hänsel!—after midnight—in my room! Just a minute! There's one thing more, Hänsel. You know I'm expecting Lord Douglo from London. Meet him at the airport. But don't let the Reich Foreign Minister get wind of it. Wait! Try to find some perfectly safe place. Prepare Lord Douglo for the fulfilment of his dreams. I'm going to present him to the Führer. But don't let him drink too much whiskey beforehand." He tore out into the corridor. Snatching his raincoat and hat, he waved to the Ambassador who, standing before a handsome Renaissance tapestry, was discussing the murder of the Cultural Leader from Heidelberg with a group of princes and aides. "Willzscheck!" he beckoned as he ran past. "Quick! Quick! To the airport!"

CHAPTER FOUR IN THE CONFERENCE ROOM, THE AGED FIELD MARSHAL VON MACKENSEN LAID HIS HAND ON THE EDGE OF THE mantelpiece as if seeking support and, after looking cautiously around, murmured to another gray-haired general: "My dear List! Apparently, you don't quite understand what Meissner has just divulged to us—"

"Perfectly! Perfectly, Field Marshal! . . ." Looking round at the door, General von List led Meissner and General von Blaskowitz over to the window out of earshot. Pulling up an armchair for the nearly ninety-year-old Marshal of Hussars, he adjusted his monocle, once again inspected walls, windows, and doors with the eyes of a General Staff officer, and then, bending over Mackensen, said softly:

"Certainly—I understand! . . . Meissner came out flat with it: There's to be a shot fired—and, if I surmise correctly—it will be in the course of this evening . . . ?"

"That's it!" The Field Marshal craned his head forward: "There's to be a shot fired! Quite certainly!" He stroked his snow-white mustache. Then both muttered together. List's hand flew to his ear, pulling at the lobe.

"But, Field Marshal—such an enterprise demands long and careful preparation! This comes too quickly!"

"The quicker the better!" Mackensen spat like a tomcat, thrusting his chin forward.

"Furthermore"—the lean, lanky Blaskowitz stretched to his full height—"in 1918 the Crown disappeared into Holland. Why should we restore it now?"

"What?" Mackensen grasped the hilt of his saber. "A Prussian General talking like that? Unbelievable!" And he spat into the room.

"Field Marshal," Meissner whispered from the other side, "have the assembled generals heard about the circular letter the Brown House is sending out tomorrow to all leaders of the Reichswehr?" The generals pricked up their ears. "The text runs: 'To all Generals and Staff Officers of the Reichswehr!—The Christian faith is the mortal enemy of National Socialism; whoever has not severed all connection with the Christian religion by September first will suffer the penalty for his refusal.' "

In the ensuing pause, General von List looked at General von Blaskowitz in amazement. Suddenly he asked: "Field Marshal, where is the Ex-Monarch now?" Meissner bent down, unfastening the lowest button of his waistcoat, wiping his throat with a handkerchief, and was about to answer when von Ribbentrop entered the room.

"Excusez! Do I intrude? . . ."

"A Reich Foreign Minister"—Mackensen laughed shortly—"always intrudes when generals are together!" All laughed.

"The Foreign Minister"—Meissner held his middle fingers to the stripes on his trousers—"seems to be standing on hot coals?"

"Our fat Meissner's ears are too big for him, ha-ha!" He blew cigar smoke into his face and sang: " 'Yea, lovely and light.' Gentlemen, I have a telegram in my pocket that is positively itching!"

"A telegram? We're all on tenterhooks!"

"Soon we'll be up on the box, driving the world like a coach-and-four as Bismarck said. Yes!—'Yea, lovely and light!' "

He hopped along the wall like a kangaroo and then stood still. "What Homeric laughter is that from the map room?" He opened the door.

A wild hullabaloo greeted him. A rabble of staff officers appeared, all sorts of hats jammed on the backs of their heads, swinging their sticks. In front, General Jünger carrying the Christ of the Trenches like a punch bowl. He set it up on the long polished table. Behind him—and standing on their heads in the mirror of the table surface—were

273

General Milch, Chief of the Luftwaffe, General Rommel, Chief of the Tank Division, General Krebs, Head of Microbe Warfare, Colonel von Einem of the Cuirassiers, Lieutenant Colonel Tot and General von Stülpnagel of the Supreme General Staff.

As soon as they saw the venerable Field Marshal, their racketing ceased, heels clicked together, and arms stretched out—"Heil Hitler!"

Old Mackensen spat on the parquet, pulling his chair around so energetically to face them that the old gilded worm-eaten wood creaked.

"Damn it, you puppies! Where've you been? Trooping in here like drunken Indians! The celebration hasn't even begun, and you're already drunk."

"Field Marshal!" General Jünger shoved the Christ of the Trenches nearer to him. "I report with all deference: the Battle of Notre Dame this evening ended with a total victory over the moth-eaten 'Rights of Man'!" There was loud laughter. "There were even some casualties."

"Yea, lovely and light!" Ribbentrop slapped his thigh with pleasure. "And what did the French Government do?"

"Nothing! Ha-ha-ha!" General Jünger smoothed his hair. "Thank God, the Minister of Justice no longer goes by the name of Danton, as in 1792!"

"No, today he goes by the name of Marchandeau!" Ribbentrop whinnied. "The patron and benefactor of our Abetzel!"

"But did that Russian, Schleich, get here safely?" asked General Krebs.

"The damn Boleshevik disappeared all of a sudden! Field Marshal, 'we simple French workingmen' have conquered the French dragoons with nothing but our sticks!"

"And this trophy"—General Jünger's voice broke into falsetto laughter—"we nabbed from the high altar of Notre Dame—"

The veteran Mackensen put on his glasses and goggled. "Damn it! What kind of a totem-pole is that?"

"Bravo!" Ribbentrop rubbed his hands. "The Field Marshal is already such a thorough-going National-Socialist that he doesn't even recognize the Nazarene!"

"I don't know anything about antiques."

"Field Marshal!" General Jünger turned the wooden figure slowly around. "This is the only begotten Son of God! Ha-ha! But before Verdun our artillery shot Him down off his party symbol, the Cross!"

"Damn it!" Mackensen removed his glasses. "He certainly shows a lot of direct hits!"

"A lot? What do you mean? In the Argonne I was hit seven times myself!"

"Damn it, what a comparison!"

"Well, why not?" General Jünger's voice edged sharply. "I think we front-line soldiers all went through our own Golgothas! And World War Number II, Field Marshal, will call the Fourth Estate solidly into the arena of history!"

"You puppy!" The Field Marshal squinted at Jünger. "What has the Fourth Estate got to do with front-line soldiers?"

"What has it to do? Well, in any case our Führer succeeded in doing what Wilhelm II was never able—"

"And that was—?" The old general joggled his chair with rage. "And that was—?"

"To mobilize the tremendous energy of the entire Fourth Estate behind a purely military government!"

"What? That's going a bit too far for a Prussian Field Marshal! You fool!" With one powerful thrust, Mackensen turned his back on him.

"How about it, gentlemen"—Ribbentrop wiped tears of laughter out of his eyes—"could we settle this argument with a glass of champagne? It's getting chilly standing here so long in pious contemplation of our 'Saviour'—" He looked ominously at Colonel Egath who had just joined them, and who, white-faced, was staring at the wooden torso. Suddenly Egath murmured: "I must confess—that thing strikes home."

"Glad to hear you say that, Colonel!" The Marshal pulled on his gloves. "Yes, you puppies! In 1864, against the Danes—in 1866, against the Austrians—in 1870, at Mars-la-Tour and Gravelotte—and even through all the last war—your old Mackensen always had his hymn book in his saddlebag. Yes, you puppies! As long as 'Glory' was the watchword in the Prussian Army—a good soldier was always a good Christian!"

"What a pity, what a pity, Field Marshal!" Ribbentrop rocked irritably back and forth on his heels. "But this time—when it's double or nothing, our marching goal is no longer going to be the Crucifix!"

"Indeed? And instead—?"

Major-domo Schellbaum appeared with bottles of champagne and glasses. Ribbentrop poured. "Field Marshal"—he offered him a glass—"it happens that I had the rare privilege of sitting in his luxurious private library face to face with the terrestrial representative of the Nazarene . . ." He drank to the company and then refilled the glasses.

"Yes, my dear Party Comrades! In 1938, I, Joachim von Ribbentrop, sat as close as this to the Living Ghost of the Christian rigmarole, in his pompous gold and red brocade armchair! And I can well believe that, since the written history of German Emperors and Roman Popes, there has never been a German who looked the Turnkey of a problematic Kingdom of Heaven in the eye with such feelings of triumph as I! You shake your head, my good Colonel von Einem? I can assure you that all my nerves and muscles were so filled to bursting with the reality of National Socialism that Pius XII, well known to me as the former Papal Nuncio in Berlin, stared at me like a gaffer who could only poorly conceal behind his spectacles his envy of me—because, for once in his career, he had to deal with a man who contained within himself the whole ardent life of a new millennium!"

"Colonel Egath!" The Field Marshal lifted his champagne glass. "Your health!"

"Field Marshal!" Egath drew himself up rigid, emptied his glass . . .

"I swear to you"—Ribbentrop licked his lips—"the discrepancy between two visions of the world, as represented by the Foreign Minister of the Third Reich and the Turnkey of Saint Peter, became so electrical that Pius XII quaked. His white taffeta robe, buttoned down in front from the collar to the buckles on his shoes, swished as his knees shook. Suddenly he bent toward me, staring at me through those thick magnifying glasses of his, as much as to say: 'Amico mio! Can we not work together?'" He laughed, and gurgled out champagne. "I kept silent, of course, and let him flounder. Finally, he couldn't stand it any longer. He muttered—"

"What did he mutter, Your Excellency?" General Jünger refilled his own glass.

"He muttered: 'Eccelenza, pensa bene. Anche il Duce, l'amico del vostro cancelliere del Reich. . . .'"

"In German, please! In German!" There was a general chorus.

"All right. Here's what he said: 'I should like you to consider the fact that even the Duce, the friend of your Reich Chancellor, has, in spite of the spirit of Fascism, found a modus vivendi with the Vatican. You see,' the Pope said, 'in this very library, His Excellency the Premier of Italy and Duce of the Fascist Party knelt before my Blessed Predecessor, His Holiness Pope Pius XI. I myself, at that time Papal Secretary of State, was an eye-witness when His Holiness raised Mussolini from this very carpet, decorated with the chain of the Order of the Annunciation, and kissed him.'"

"Damn it!" General Jünger exploded. "You mean to tell me the

276

Duce knelt before the Pope?"

" 'In this very room,' the Pope spoke more and more softly, 'at this very desk, where the same ebony and ivory crucifix is standing, the Lateran Treaty was signed between the Holy See and the Fascist Government.' Quite apart from the spiritual benefits that accrued, both contracting parties were fully satisfied. The yearly payment of two billion lire by the Fascist State to the Vatican was an altogether shrewd gesture on the part of worldly power toward spiritual power. Ecco! Guarda, cara Eccellenza! How shrewdly and foresightedly the Duce handled this matter was demonstrated in 1936, that critical year for Italy, when the League of Nations, on the motion of Anthony Eden, was absolutely determined to prevent Il Duce from declaring war on the Negus of Ethiopia. In that decisive crisis for Fascism—affecting the balance of power between might and right—the Holy See put its entire weight in the scale for might. Even the justifiable pleas of his African Eminence, the Bishop of Ethiopia, as well as the entreaties of the priests at the Ethiopian Seminary in the Vatican—even the fact that the Ethiopians are one of the oldest Catholic communities in the world—all these could not prevail upon the Holy See to withhold Our Apostolic blessing from a war which the national interests of Italy made excusable. On the contrary: in spite of all the League's protests, our entire priesthood obeyed the Vatican's orders and placed itself wholeheartedly at the service of the *national* cause. Although many million Catholic Ethiopians were gassed by Count Ciano's and young Mussolini's bombing squadrons, the wounded were, of course, at the behest of the Holy See and with the meritorious assistance of the Red Cross, given whatever treatment was possible—especially the severest cases of burnt-out lungs, etc.

" 'However'—here the Pope sat up straight in his chair—'I shall not now discuss with you any sort of alignment of Catholic and National Socialist interests. I would simply like to bring home to you, and ask you to consider, the power which the Church represents! Caro amico, I really do not believe that your Third Reich has, in the long run, any chance of successfully defying it . . . Here, lining these walls, you see unnumbered manifestations of the spiritual resources of theology: works by inspired thinkers such as St. Augustine and St. Thomas Aquinas! What these saints have accomplished for the spiritual development of the human race is beyond dispute.' "

"Says he! The Pope?!" General Jünger broke in. "There's one thing certain. We 'front swine' in the trenches got a very concrete idea of what they have accomplished!"

277

"Come, come!" The venerable Marshal of Hussars picked up his busby from the floor beside his chair.

"I am sorry, Field Marshal—but the world-rejecting theory of salvation set going by that Hebrew there"—General Jünger looked contemptuously at the Christ figure—"was the one great error in our Manual of Arms!"

Mackensen was helped out of his chair by General Blaskowitz. He stood, leaning on his cavalry saber, his eyes blazing at General Jünger. Unable to find words for his indignation, he finally said:

"My dear Meissner, where can I wash my hands?"

"This way, Field Marshal!" He opened a door and the old Hussar left the conference room, rapping the parquet with his saber at every step.

CHAPTER FIVE "OUF!" RIBBENTROP OPENED THE WINDOW. "I SMELL MUMMY . . . FRESH AIR!" HE FANNED HIMSELF. "Oh, what an ambrosial night! A cigar, General Jünger!"

"Thank you very much!" He accepted a light from Ribbentrop's lighter. "Yes, Field Marshal! A National Socialist must even have the courage to do away with the very last prop of blind faith—to reach the point where even nothingness seems more desirable than such dubious nonsense about a Saviour!"

"Dubious nonsense about a Saviour?" Egath growled, saluted, and left the room.

"Damn it, I think somebody like me, who was a storm-troop leader for four long years, has a right to attack any system of thought, even one invented by St. Augustine himself!"

"Bravissimo!" Ribbentrop slapped Jünger on the shoulder. "I say: We not only have the right, it's our duty to fight all this priestly nonsense. Gentlemen, sitting opposite Pius XII, I got such a horrible whiff of the corpse of a two-thousand-year-old crime against the life of our German people, that I literally felt nauseated. And the fact that, for so many centuries, Germans have let themselves be talked out of following their predestined path by such specters!—that in itself suddenly struck me as such a deception of the poor, benighted German citizen, that I had to get up and get out as quickly as possible—out of that stuffy Papal library with its walls plastered with pictures of saints —out into the fresh air . . . And then—it became perfectly clear to me"—he blew symmetrical smoke rings at the ceiling—"that for a National Socialist, the Pope is no longer a fact."

"Your Excellency! . . . Prosit!" General Jünger's eyes sparkled. "On this globe—there is one single global fact that cannot be contested—"

"And that is, my dear General?"

"And that is"—General Jünger looked at his comrades with the objective eyes of a technician discussing his subject—"and that is the evidence of a bomber and of a machine-gun!"

"Tak-tak-tak-tak!" The younger generals imitated the rattle of machine-gun fire and drank enthusiastic prosits to Ribbentrop. Suddenly, with a snarl of "Perish Judah!" General Milch gave the Christ of the Trenches such a push that He slid to the edge of the polished table.

"Field Marshal von Keitel"—Ribbentrop jumped in the air for joy —"would now say: 'Why don't they send up the 'A Hack' rocket?'"

The elder generals, Blaskowitz and List, who during the conversation of their juniors had been silently studying a map, now looked up, and one of them asked:

"Where is Field Marshal von Keitel?"

"He's part of the escort."

"The escort? Devil take it!"

General Jünger puffed so powerfully on his cigar that it sent out sparks. "I can't tell you how I long for the boom-boom of the heavy artillery! Damn it all! And the colored gasses of explosives! I love that milky vapor, my dear Milch, that creeps away so lazily over the heaps of rubble after a direct hit, licking everything with its sulphurous yellow tongue! I'm dying to sniff the prickling, brown fumes of powder again, when finally the black explosion bursts in the middle of a swinish bunch of Tommies like an enormous sack full of soot."

"Caro amico!" Ribbentrop tenderly laid his hand on his golden epaulette. "I promise you, General, you shall taste those pleasures to the full! To the full!"

"Remember"—Jünger saluted Ribbentrop with his cigar as if it were a sword—"Your Excellency has made me a solemn promise! Oh, when the 'A Hack' rocket goes up and bursts green and red and white, with long shimmering tails and—"

"Hello!" Meissner yelled into the room. "Gentlemen, take your places!"

"He's here?" Ribbentrop sprang to the door.

"No, Your Excellency! But he has just landed at the airport!"

The young generals stormed out into the courtyard.

CHAPTER SIX

A MAN OF SOME EIGHTY YEARS, DRESSED LIKE A PROTESTANT CLERGYMAN, WAS PACING UP AND DOWN UNder the laurel shrubs in front of the conservatory. His well-cut black frock coat was buttoned up to the throat like a Quaker's. As he memorized the text of his address he kept running his fingers through his silky-white hair. On a small garden table stood a bottle of champagne in a cooler and a single glass and each time he passed it he stopped and took a sip. A lantern in a tree shone down upon the stretch of gravel path between the bushes. Again he stopped for a drink and then declaimed aloud:

"Here speaks a Nobel Prize Winner, talking from Paris. . . . I have the honor to stand beside the sarcophagus of a murdered woman folk comrade, in order to broadcast these few simple words of commemoration to all parts of the world . . ." Taking a slip of paper from his pocket, he held it to the light, read it through, and maundered on:

"My highly honored friends of this Gala Assembly, in the presence of the Supreme Führer of the German Reich, I address you, I, Dr. Gerhardus! And I am justified in hoping that my sincere expressions will also be heard three thousand miles away, across the Atlantic Ocean, where German-Americans in Yorkville still sympathize in joy and sorrow with their one-time folk comrades . . . In this coffin lies Old Heidelberg! What?" He looked at the piece of paper again. "Oh no! In this coffin lies a murdered woman folk-comrade! Under many flowers she reposes—as I said—in this coffin! A horrible murder carried her off at the height of her powers." He went to the table, drank down a glassful, and resumed his pose. "Yes, in this coffin sleeps a mother—and what is more: a German mother! And what is still more: a National Socialist Mother. J'accuse!"

"Honored Master—!"

"Hello!" Dr. Gerhardus tottered and wheeled round. Out of the shadows, into the lantern light, stepped Colonel Egath.

"Colonel!" Dr. Gerhardus bowed to the Gestapo chief. "To what do I owe the honor? For I am—how shall I put it? A small dress rehearsal . . . I was called to Paris at the command of Herr Propaganda Minister Dr. Göbbels as the sole representative of our Pan-German intellectual life— Excuse me, but my address is not yet firmly imprinted in my memory. So, any other time. But may I offer you a glass of champagne?"

"Thank you very much. I don't drink."

"You don't drink? . . . Well—in that case, I raise my glass to Victory, Colonel—to Victory!" His little, crafty parrot eyes opened wide; his forehead rippled into countless folds. "We had the pleasure, Colonel, as I remember, of conversing frankly once before, at the Hotel Adlon, in Berlin. As far as I understood you at that time, you harbored the idea of handing in your resignation? In spite of the black police uniform, your spirit—I might say your mind—had to a certain extent—a leaning toward 'Liberty!' " . . . He looked about cautiously. "But please be seated! If you'll allow me, Colonel, I'll go on quickly memorizing my little gala speech to the end!"

"Oh, please, please!"

"My German folk comrades! In contemplation of this National-Socialist corpse—"

"Dear Master, may I most obediently ask you for a bit of purely personal advice?"

"You may, indeed! Indeed! But let us not have such a harassed expression!" He licked his swollen lips. "What a dainty little maid that is, scampering by! Hello!" He called to the chambermaid. "I hope you're not going to carry off my champagne! Just look at her! How she skips over the lawn! Probably going into the conservatory to sew a few more ribbons onto the wreaths on the coffin . . ." The object of his speculation reappeared, curtseying.

"Have you gentlemen by any chance seen a young actress here in the garden?"

"No! My, look how she runs!" He watched her. "Ravishing! . . . A young actress! That would be ravishing!"

"Master, many years ago you wrote a revolutionary play about the workers, dealing with the exploitation of the poor Silesian weavers by the factory-owners—"

"That's a long time ago—"

"But for me, Master, it's still freshly engraved in my heart. Those downtrodden creatures—the world proletariat—" Egath put his finger in his collar—"When you championed the cause of the downtrodden in your play, your heart must have felt an unutterable compassion for misused humanity—"

"Obviously, obviously! By the way, Herr von Ribbentrop's champagne is at least as good as his foreign policy: it makes the gas come up and gives the kidneys plenty to do! You'll excuse me!" He stood up. "I'm an octogenarian—!"

He disappeared behind a bed of sun flowers. Over the high stems only a bit of forehead with its aureole of white hair could be seen. There was a copious splashing. "Colonel, is that the Big Dipper or the Little Dipper over our heads? Well, at all events they're stars. And I'd really like to know if our Relativity fiend, Professor Einstein, in his Princeton bungalow, sometimes ponders how infinitely distant one human being is from another! . . . There!" He reappeared. "Naturally, there's always something very enticing about a trip to America! Nevertheless, my esteemed Colonel, in your fatherland you are a well-groomed staff officer, with a monthly salary and silver galloons! You are, if I may permit myself to say so, a person of consequence! Yes, indeed! Yes, indeed! On the contrary, however, when you arrive on the other side and walk down the gangplank as a refugee, suitcase in hand, in civilian clothes, alone, among all those skyscrapers in New York—what are you then? An enemy alien! I ask you: who over there knows anything about your meritorious services? Not a soul! Nobody at all!"

"Nevertheless, Dr. Gerhardus, there is such a thing as conflict of conscience!"

"What?" Blinking at him, the Nobel Prize Winner refilled his glass. "What conflict of conscience could be great enough to make you leave your fatherland? Colonel!?"—he became pressing—"do you want to stand on the George Washington Bridge one day—a broken man—and jump into the Hudson out of pure homesickness?"

Egath looked at him in astonishment, adjusted his revolver holster, and got to his feet. An uneasy pause fell between them, like an unanswerable question.

"Ah!" Dr. Gerhardus wagged his head sagely. "After all, who can give anyone else advice? I got over doing that long ago. As the saying is, 'Each man forges his own destiny!' So, why shouldn't you go to America? We mustn't forget that it was an aide-de-camp of Frederick the Great, General von Steuben, who traveled over there and rendered outstanding services to George Washington. So I can quite well imagine that you might be eminently serviceable in training the American Armies for the coming conflict between the peoples of the West and the East—say in Fort Dix, or Indianapolis, or Chicago! Prussian Generals have drilled the Japanese, the Argentines, the Bolivians. On the whole, wherever on this planet they're standing at attention or swinging their legs on parade, there you may be certain the military spirit of Potsdam has stood godfather. So—why not?"

"Dr. Gerhardus, if I ever take off this uniform, it will certainly not be to put on another."

"Dear Colonel, the uniform today is a Bastille that it won't be so easy to capture. And a man with shoulder straps would best leave the downtrodden to God to look after. Refugees are plentiful as fleas. But a colonel is—a colonel!"

"And that is your advice, Dr. Gerhardus?"

"That is not my advice, but the philosophy culled from three generations of experience . . ."

"Will you be joining us later at the Führer's table?"

"I hope so! The cook told me a secret: There's going to be trout!" He clicked his tongue, and was about to say something else, when someone shyly plucked his coat from behind. Wonderingly he raised his eyebrows, turned around, and then clapped his hands together, enchanted.

CHAPTER SEVEN BAREFOOT, HER HAIR DAMP, NADIA STOOD ON THE GRASS IN A MOSS-GREEN BATHING CAPE, LIKE A FOREST FAIRY just emerged from the bushes. Her freshly bathed body gave off the fragrance of all flowers. Her dark eyes stared at the old man with indescribable idolatry. She seemed to see nothing else.

"How perfectly ravishing!" He smiled with vanity. "You are doubtless the young actress the chambermaid was looking for a while ago. Been having a quick before-dinner dip in the fountain among the roses?"

"Dr. Gerhardus!" She breathed—and turned away her eyes.

"I am he, my dear! And never have I so gladly been just who I am, as at this instant!"

"This instant! To be really standing face to face with you! Something I've dreamed of my whole life long!"

"A very short dream, Fräulein! I shouldn't think you were twenty yet.—She's ravishing—absolutely ravishing!"

"Not twenty? I've already acted in almost all your plays!"

"That does honor to my plays. And in my next one—I'm building up a scene with a minuet for elves, moths, and crickets around a lantern under an old elm tree at midnight—you shall play the moth!"

"Oh, Dr. Gerhardus!" Her knees gave way. Like a drowning man, she seized both his hands, and hid her face in them.

"How perfectly ravishing!" Smirking, he looked around at Egath. "Colonel, I wouldn't exchange this moment for all your epaulettes! Give me a glass of champagne! The exquisite lines of such girlish curls!" He stooped down to her.

"My dear, you'll catch cold! I've an inkling you've nothing much under that bathing cape except your marble-smooth, wonderful skin. May I offer you a glass of champagne?" He lifted the bottle out of the cooler. "There's still enough for two glasses. How perfectly ravishing! . . . Colonel, this dainty sylph has acted in all my plays. At least, so she says. In that case, she must have made her first appearance in diapers!"

Catching sight of the Gestapo officer, the Rabbi's niece closed her eyes. Egath did not move. He wondered if the girl remembered seeing him at the Travel Bureau—he had had on civilian clothes there, now he was in uniform. Suddenly the actress embraced the dramatist's knees.

"Protect me!"

"How perfectly ravishing! Did you hear that, Colonel? I—a man who will soon be a centenarian!—am asked to protect this sweet child." He laughed. "Of course, Fräulein! Is the great god Pan after you?" He put his arm around her. "Of course! I'll protect you from anybody you like! . . . Bare toes in the dew? You'll permit me?" He lifted her from the lawn to the garden table, spread out his handkerchief under her feet on the chair—and then, with a grand air, kissed the fingertips of both her hands. Pouring out the champagne, he handed her the crystal glass. She took it and then stared, huddled together in fright, over the foaming champagne.

"Dr. Gerhardus," she whispered, "I'm suddenly so tired!" And she leaned her black curls against his frock coat and sank into a swoon.

"How perfectly enchanting! Colonel"—his voice dropped—"I think —the child is sleeping . . . If only the waters of the Grand Canal in Venice were gurgling beyond that iron garden gate! . . . If only a black gondola would appear around the corner, from behind that plane tree—I'd lay this ravishing child on the black leather cushions . . . Then away we'd float through the lagoons, past the palaces of the

284

Doges, past the clear marble dome of Santa Maria della Salute to the Piazza San Marco . . . Nonsense, let's leave that whole candy-stick Venezia behind us! The gondolier shall row us far out—out to the sea . . . Climb aboard, Colonel! You can come too! And out there, where the horizon is round and free again at last, I shall toss my pearl tie-pin—something I've always wished for, but never possessed!—in a wide arc into the emerald-green, crystalline flood . . . and the drops of water, translucent with moonlight, will sparkle and glitter about us like Murano glass! And though I shall not be married to the sea like a Doge—nevertheless, this little one here shall not be deprived of her rights! . . . Gondola! Gondola!" He began a kind of singsong, and all the while his eyes followed the hurrying little pearls that kept bursting on the surface of his champagne. "And then, chaste Luna, in thy chariot of golden light we shall journey on and on—until at last we have left this world behind!" He drank and trickled the last few drops onto the crown of Nadia's head. "How perfectly ravishing! But this table is much too hard for such a trim little girl's behind. Come, Colonel! Behind those trees, there's a pavilion built in 1714 . . . Come! Help me—I saw a Hollywood swing in there . . . Come!"

Colonel Egath lifted the actress by the shoulders, Dr. Gerhardus carefully taking her feet, and so they carried her between the flower beds to the pavilion and laid her on the luxurious flowered cushions in the swing. From somewhere a ray of light fell through the heavy black branches onto her graceful figure. Enraptured, the poet turned to the Gestapo man.

"Colonel," he murmured, "let someone else give the funeral oration! . . . She's perfectly ravishing! Girl, what is your name?" Opening her long-lashed eyes, she nestled her head back in her curls, and whispered:

"Nadia— My name's Nadia."

"How perfectly enchanting! Nadia? You wake up in the morning and you call, 'Nadia'! If that isn't bewitching! 'Nadia!' And then— there she comes! Nadia! Now, alas, I understand why I've never really successfully achieved Dionysian verse! Nadia!—Nadia! Who told you that I was in the garden? Colonel, this would be the very moment for one of Schubert's songs played on the violin—and then out of an overflowing heart one could only say to the dear God: 'Bravo'!" With two fingers he pushed a curl back from her forehead, his face closer and closer to hers. She smiled timidly and shrank away, out of the yellow lantern light. Then, cowering like a child, she whispered:

"Master!"

"What is it, Mignonne?"

"I am—a Jewess!"

"How perfectly ravishing!" Suddenly, he drew himself pompously to his full height, ran his hands through his hair, and then looked around at the Gestapo chief to see if he had heard her. But Egath, his features inscrutable, stood stiffly in front of his long black shadow against the cream-and-gilt rococo door.

"You are—a Jewess?" He caressed her fingers, then was silent for several seconds. Abruptly, he lifted his head challengingly. "Is the Jewish Problem to be the tragedy of my old age? No! Either you go crazy or—you don't go crazy! But to anyone in his senses—! Besides, my little odalisque, the line of your throat—bewitching! Exactly like Princess Nefertiti's!

"Colonel, if I now say, 'You're all idiots—all of you!,' I naturally mean, always excepting yourself, this sweet child, and myself . . . Good heavens! You mean to say the Egyptians threw out anything as exquisite as that?"

"Dr. Gerhardus," she begged, "at what hotel are you staying?"

"The Hotel Ritz, Place Vendôme—and you, child?"

"I have an apartment in the rue de Grenelle. Please take me home! Please! I'll open a can of asparagus for you. Master, you're fond of good wine? The Duke d'Aguillon sent me six bottles of very old Sauterne only yesterday"

"Sauterne? How perfectly ravishing! My dear Colonel, what do you say? Couldn't you tell them in the Embassy—the old man was taken ill suddenly? Isn't there a garden gate at the back where we can get out without being seen? Colonel, surely you have the keys! The corpse in the conservatory will certainly never come to life again! But here"— he raised the actress gently from the cushions and kissed her—"here is life, sprightly and blithe as a leaping trout! Gerhardus!" He slapped his imposing brow. "This is not a dream! You're really in Paris, alone with little Nadia!—What thighs! I can sympathize with that old glutton Herod! Nadia—"

"Please take me away from here."

"Stand up, my child!" He picked her up in his arms, stood with her in front of Egath, and winked: "Come, my dear Egath! Fish your keys out of your pocket and extricate us from this complication! And then, as far as I'm concerned, off we go—anywhere—where a free wind may once more play about my bare head!" And he carried his light and lovely burden out of the pavilion and under the trees across the lawn. Colonel Egath followed.

Suddenly the bright glare of an electric torch drenched the three in its white light. Nadia cried out, but Colonel Egath, holding his big hand before her face, asked tersely, sotto voce:

"Who's there?"

"It's me—Waldmüller, Colonel!" The piano-mover from the German Travel Bureau came a step nearer. Instead of blue overalls, he now wore impeccable evening-clothes, his piqué tie shone above a dazzling white shirt front, which crackled every time he moved. Some distance behind him stood Hänsel—Hess's new adjutant—and the chambermaid.

"Colonel"—Waldmüller pulled a rope out of his pocket—"for the past half hour we've been looking for this sow!" Going slowly up to him, Egath muttered:

"Waldmüller—"

"Sir?"

"You haven't seen anything! Be on your way!"

The piano-mover slammed his heels together, about-faced, and walked off.

"Pardon!" Raising his right arm, Hänsel came forward firmly, making an energetic signal for Waldmüller to remain. "Sir!" He saluted the Colonel. "We have orders from the Deputy Führer to scrub and clothe this bitch and then hold her in reserve for a little joke after dinner."

"What kind of a joke?" Egath knocked Hänsel's flashlight down so that it made only a small disk of light in the grass, darkness enveloping them all above the knees. "Hänsel!" Egath's voice became confidential. "You know me—"

"At your service, Colonel!"

"Hänsel, did you ever have any cause for complaint against me?"

"Never, Colonel."

"Who brought you to Paris as a foreign correspondent?"

"You, Colonel!"

"Who introduced you to the Deputy Führer?"

"You, Colonel!"

"Yes, it was I! Hänsel, what kind of joke have they planned for this little Jewess?"

"I don't know."

"Hänsel—"

"Yes?"

"Disappear! You have seen nothing!"

"I can't do that, Colonel."

"Hänsel, be off!"

287

"Official orders from Rudolf Hess—"

"Don't be a fool. Be off!" Giving Dr. Gerhardus a push, he whispered: "Go ahead!"

Dr. Gerhardus, who had overheard this exchange between Egath and the brand-new adjutant with growing astonishment, went falteringly on. But Hänsel's flashlight and his loud "Halt!" stopped him in his tracks.

"Colonel, I must know this man's name."

"Hänsel, do you mean to say you don't recognize the prince of German poets?"

"I have my orders. If this gentleman wants to take the Jewess with him, I must have his name and address! We're on the trail of a certain affair—can't make any exceptions whatsoever!"

"What's all this balderdash?" Returning to the attack, Waldmüller stuck out his chin. Colonel Egath seized him roughly:

"Shut up!"

"What?" Waldmüller wagged his neck loutishly in his wing collar. "On account of that Jew bitch? Hand her over!"

"No!" Nadia threw her arms around Gerhardus' neck. "Don't let them—! This brute wants to lock me in a cage with an ape! He's tried to make me drunk! The beast!—He's already stuck a hypodermic in my arm, so that I have a burning fever! Beasts! Oh, Master! Only a few yards—and we'll be outside! Out there by the Seine—and I'll be free!"

The dramatist squinted, bedazzled by the flashlight. Then he tried unsuccessfully to free his neck from Nadia's arms, looking desperately at the Gestapo men:

"In God's name, what's all this about? As far as I can see—and—since I had absolutely no knowledge of any such orders from the Deputy Führer! . . . But my dear girl—for Heaven's sake, let go of me! Please let go! And if His Excellency Rudolf Hess wants this young lady—I was totally unaware of the fact! Damn it! Now—will you please let go of me?" He twisted her fingers until they finally let go and she sank at his feet in the grass, shuddering.

"My highly honorable Herr Adjutant!" Dr. Gerhardus bowed deferentially to Hänsel. "To tell the truth, I am very much distressed. This lady simply threw herself at me! The Colonel here is my witness. I swear—I was taken absolutely unaware! And I have absolutely no intention of acting contrary to orders given by any Reich Minister! Oh heavens!" His hand flew to his head. "My little funeral oration— I still haven't got the text fixed in my mind! And so, my most honor-

288

able gentlemen, you will be good enough to excuse me—"

"Dr. Gerhardus!" Nadia screamed and held his boots so that he could not stir. "Master! You won't give me over to that beast? You—the poet of the human heart—?"

"Let go!"

"What crime have I committed—?"

"Let go of my feet—!"

"Master! You—with your great heart—!"

"My great heart?" The dramatist did his best to shake off the girl's hands. "I admit: I have a great heart! Unfortunately, it was far too great! Unfortunately! Besides—as I was recently telling the Hitler Youth—according to the latest researches, the heart is the most inferior organ in the body—ha-ha—a mere pump, my dear lady—that's all! That's absolutely all! So now, for the last time, will you kindly let go?"

"Don't let them! Oh please don't let them—! You *must* save me!"

"And"—Waldmüller swung his rope like a lasso—"why should this particular gentleman save you?"

"That's it—that's just it! Bravo! I don't even know you! God in Heaven! Will you let go! I'm certainly not going to land in the Devil's kitchen on your account! Let go of me!"

"Dr. Gerhardus!"—Colonel Egath moved to his side—"perhaps if you, with your wonderful powers of persuasion, were to say a few words on her behalf—?"

"What do you mean?" He warded off Egath's whisper. "As long ago as 1933, asked whether or not I was willing to serve the Third Reich, I gave a clear and definite answer! Every time there was an election—and the last time, when I was in Italy, I telegraphed my irrevocable 'Yes' across the Alps to Berlin. I'm certainly not going to divorce myself from my fatherland simply because there may happen to be a fire raging there!"

"A fire raging? Beasts! Beasts!"

"Keep your mouth shut, Fräulein!" The poet had lost his temper. "To call honorable men beasts simply because they keep faith with their own people—? No, little girl, Gerhardus won't countenance that! God in Heaven! You needn't go imagining you're just a lot of beautiful angels—out there in the cold! You'd have loved to stay if you hadn't been shown the door! I know all about it—the tragedy of fear and suspense, of cringing and servility—until, in spite of everything, you are finally driven away! People have envied me for my house! My books! My blood! And my fatherland!"

"Help me! Help me! Help me!"

"Let go! Anybody who has to wear the yellow patch on his clothes —he obviously can't expect to wear the Swastika armband!"

"I rather like him," Waldmüller grinned broadly.

"But anyone who is an Aryan, like myself— Is this little nuisance never going to let go of my feet?"

"Dr. Gerhardus—honored master . . ." Colonel Egath whispered.

"What on earth am I expected to do? I am no Savonarola! I've no intention of being roasted in a bonfire on account of this person! Let go! You don't suppose one of you Jews would do such a thing for a goy? You Jews fix and contrive everything your own way! Not one of you accuses his own people! All you talk about is *one* people! One destiny! One dream of a military state on the Jordan! Do you suppose there's anybody in the whole world—a Chinaman, an American, an Englishman, a Canadian—who would desert his country on your account? . . . Let go of my feet! I'm not going to end up in Dachau because of you! She won't let go of my feet! My highly respected gentlemen of the Gestapo—this Jewess is out of her mind!"

"But your humanity!" Nadia clamped her arms around his ankles still more firmly. "Your humanity!"

"Will you please let me alone! What's my humanity got to do with you? I certainly don't belong to the species of world-reformers. What on earth"—he wiped saliva from his chin—"would happen if a poet began making of what he wrote the rule of his life! That would be utter insanity! And I'm not speaking only for myself! I'm speaking as the representative of our entire intellectual and spiritual life! Let go!"

And he managed to give her such a push with his old legs that she rolled over to the piano-mover's feet. There she lay, whimpering. Waldmüller was just about to tie her hands with his rope when there was an outbreak of shouts in the Embassy:

"The Führer! The Führer!"

The whole house was transformed into a humming beehive. Colonel Egath snatched Nadia up and vanished with her into the shadows, Waldmüller on his heels.

As soon as the octogenarian dramatist had smoothed his hair and put his frock coat to rights, he strode pompously down the garden path back to the Embassy. Outside the illuminated dining room, he stopped, bowed till he could bow no lower, then straightened up again with great dignity and, stretching his arm tense to the tips of his alcohol-swollen fingers, he said with deep emotion:

"Heil Hitler! . . . ."

290

CHAPTER EIGHT

Reich Foreign Minister von Ribbentrop galloped upstairs to the first floor of the embassy and along the corridor, shouting:

"Abetzel! Abetzel!" Opening the door of a guest room Ribbentrop was greeted by the indignant "Shh! Shh!" of a blonde chambermaid ironing a shirt. His voice fell. On the huge double bed, he saw Schleich, flat on his stomach, sprawled across the red silk bedspread, snoring like a Caucasian bear. Closing the door, he continued his search.

"Abetzel! Abetzel!" From behind the third door farther on, a sleepy voice answered flatly:

"Hm?"

"It's I, Abetzel!" The door was unlocked and Ribbentrop flung himself on a chintz-covered chair, stretching his legs, his eyes bulging. A well-built young man, blond, just out of his bath, dressed in sky-blue and red-striped pyjamas, shut the door and eyed the Foreign Minister with astonishment.

"But Jochen! What's the matter?"

"Get dressed! Get dressed!"

"Calm down!"

"*He's* already here!"

"*He?* Are you crazy? What time is it? The devil! I just had a bath—" Abetz peeled off his pyjamas, darting about the room and snatching up various portions of his uniform.

"Yes, he's here! The elite of the German colony drawn up along the courtyard and up the steps—and he walked past as if worlds away, without looking at a soul, and so—into the house!"

"Did he notice my absence?"

"Nonsense! Your absence? Didn't even notice me!"

"The devil! Has anything happened? Who was with him?"

"Göring, Hess, and Keitel—"

"Jochen, was he—any different to you than usual?"

"Never mind that! Only one thing now:—we must control our nerves."

"Where is he now?"

"Downstairs in the library—"

"Are you keeping something from me? You can't expect me to *smell* what's happening—even if I do like your new perfume! Chanel No. 5?

Heavenly! And thanks for the bewitching silk handkerchief. Did you buy it across from the Tuileries? I hope you're not hurt because I wasn't down for the reception. But I've been running around all day long, like hare-and-hounds! First the Quai d'Orsay! And finally, till eight o'clock, with Marchandeau at the Ministry of Justice. This city of females is full of perpetual intrigues! I had to wait in the anteroom. Had to wait forever! But finally a hundred francs to the porter did the trick! I was admitted. My friend Marchandeau had just thrown out a certain Police Commissioner Armoni who was boring him with an account of a shooting affray in front of Notre Dame. That intuitive angel of a policeman had put the bee in his bonnet that Adolf Hitler is here! So the upright Republican demanded nothing more and nothing less than that my friend Marchandeau close the rue de Lille and the Quai d'Orsay with a military guard."

Slipping on his tunic, Abetz tied the ribbon of the Order of the Italian Crown, First Class, round his neck. "You can just imagine, Jochen, how I had to gabble on until the worthy Minister of Justice was convinced that our Führer was not in Paris and nothing of any importance was going on here at the Embassy tonight. Luckily, afterwards, I ran into my friend Baron Jacques on the Place Vendôme. Arranged everything else with him . . . And—if their senile Marshal Pétain agrees—his First Adjutant, Colonel Latour, will come here secretly this evening to discuss our world coup d'état with the Führer personally. . . . There!" He brushed his hair once more. "I'm ready! But Jochen, what's wrong with you? I've never seen you so totally pickled before! Shall we go?" He ran his hand through Ribbentrop's hair.

"What?" Ribbentrop came out of his daze. "Where to?"

"Downstairs—to *him!*"

"He's locked himself in!"

"Locked himself in? What does that mean?"

"Abetzel!" Ribbentrop got up and sat down on the bed, sniffing the discarded pajamas. "We two have got to keep our heads now! You and I! The greatest stake in the history of the world is on the table! And I do not intend to let anyone mess it up for me! Not even if, at the prospect of such a gigantic throw, our Adolf loses his head at the last minute! We're not going to lose ours! Your hand on that, Abetzel!"

"Right! But why all the melodrama? Come to the point!" He slapped Ribbentrop on the knee.

"All right . . . *He* threw his cap on a chest. His Hess helped him

292

take off his raincoat—. He had on his brown uniform—"

"And then—?"

"Adolf tidied his hair, and sat down behind that gaudy Louis XVI writing table—"

"Well—why not?"

"He made a gesture, and old Franz, stooping a little in his gala livery, drew back the heavy brocade curtains, opened the wooden blinds, and threw the tall double windows wide open. Adolf inhaled deeply. Out there in the garden you could see the gray-blue steel of the Bodyguard men—their helmets and rifles shimmering in the candlelight. All of a sudden he looked at us—standing between the library and the dining room, breathlessly waiting for a word from him—as if he had never seen us before. No one spoke. You could hear the fire crackling. I swear, not even I opened my mouth. Suddenly he shouts: 'Himmler!' He clicks his heels. And then, with that dead-pan policeman's face of his clamped onto his monocle, he steps forward. Biting his lips, the Führer snaps:

" 'Well, where is she? Where've you got her?' "

"She? Who, Jochen?"

"Who? Why, the dancer that escaped from Berchtesgaden of course!"

"What? Is there any proof at all that she stole his sacred Will? . . . Jochen! Jochen! You're the one I suspect! Cross your heart—where is it?"

"Then he slid his left hand, pale as an octopus, from the inkwell to the flower vase and said, 'Go get her.' "

"Dear me! Is that ballet-rat here at the Embassy? What did the Ambassador say to that?"

"Willzscheck? Oh, Adolf didn't even let him in! He stamped around the room: 'All the way here by air!—and nothing is ready! Taking my time like this!' In the paneling a door opened and two S.A. men carried in a stretcher. Privy Councilor Sauerbruch, who had arrived from Berlin an hour before, followed, with several consulting physicians. She lay under a thin, silk spread . . ."

"She lay? The spy?"

"They set the stretcher down. Adolf starts over—stops—makes a face . . . asks: 'Can't the lady get up?' No answer. 'What did she say under examination?' Silence . . . Suddenly he runs to the stretcher—"

"And what happened?"

Ribbentrop stood up, took a handful of chocolates from a box on the night table, and began following the square pattern around the rug.

Sitting on his pillow, Abetz nervously rolled a cigarette and lit it.

"And what happened then?"

Ribbentrop stopped and bent down to the silver-framed mirror on the dressing table, chewed, withdrew a single tooth from his denture, polished it on his sleeve, and reinserted it. Still without answering, he resumed his tour of the rug.

"Jochen! What! While two worlds are mobilizing for their last tennis match—and the tramp of Caesar's legions thunders to the clouds —I say at this millennial instant of life-and-death decision for the victory of the Male World—from Socrates and Plato down to Oscar Wilde and Stefan George—what!—on the stroke of the hour when at last we begin to see that chaos 'Woman' behind us, and the bright sun of young manhood rising—when we begin to salute Apollo—Jochen! Jochen!—when millions of the most beautiful boys in silver braid, with weapons ready, only await the signal—finally and forever to stamp out of existence that 'Black Flower' Woman! . . . In this crisis for the race of man, the Supreme Führer of our movement leaves the capital and flies after a little dancing bitch!" He jumped to his feet, threw his cigarette on the carpet, and stamped on it as if it were a bedbug.

"Where are you going?" Ribbentrop rushed after him and caught him at the door.

"Since you're all messing your pants—"

"You're not going to the Führer?"

"Where else?" At this Ribbentrop hurled him back so powerfully that he fell among the silk pillows.

"Idiot! Dolt! There's more at stake than l'amour. And now, Mr. Know-it-all, I'm going to give you, word for word, exactly what was just said downstairs in the library! Just keep your face shut till I'm finished. And then you can go get your black-haired friend, Jacques."

"Forgive me, Jochen!" Thoroughly subdued, Abetz rubbed the back of his head. "Forgive me!"

"So—standing beside the stretcher, Hitler murmured: 'Yes, beautiful dancer! This is not exactly how you hoped we'd meet again!' He beckoned Himmler: 'Who arrested her?' "

" 'I, my Führer!' Major Buch came forward, sweating.

" 'Where?'

" 'When she saw we had her surrounded—she jumped into the Seine and tried to escape by swimming—'

" 'I see. She's asleep?' Himmler looked at Buch, who said nothing. Adolf motioned to Privy Councilor Sauerbruch—Suddenly, however, as if embarrassed, he stared at his tanned Reichswehr generals, smiling:

" 'Gentlemen—she was a first-class dancer!' Backing up slowly to the table, he ran forward again, halting a step from the stretcher and bawling:

" 'Get up! At once!' Privy Councilor Sauerbruch looked at me questioningly and—effaced himself. The Führer squinted after him. Then he turned to me:

" 'Why does the Chief Surgeon of my Berlin hospitals walk out? . . . But perhaps one of you stupids will finally condescend to help my beautiful guest to her feet. Come on,' he yelled at us, 'help her up!' At that, one of the staff physicians summoned up his courage and stuttered:

" 'Mein Führer, the girl is dead!' "

"And then?" Abetz slid forward on the bed.

"After a long silence, Adolf suddenly started walking up and down the length of the library. Stopped in front of the fireplace. Stared at the stretcher and ground his teeth:

" 'Yes, dead! For me—she is dead! From me, the sincere admirer of her high-kicking, she stole a unique document, of definitive and colossal importance for the coming epoch! Take that cover off her!'

"Thereupon the red-haired assistant physician pulled the silk covering off the dancer's body. Abetzel! And now the Lord of Obersalzberg put his hand over his eyes. We all thought—any minute he'll go raving mad . . . Far from it! He was perfectly quiet . . .

" 'Come, get going!' he whispered. 'Help the lady! Prop her up with pillows.' So Major Buch took her under the arms and held her up. And that dead face, framed in gold, looked vacantly into the room.

" 'Major!' Hitler came at him threateningly. 'Kindly take your paws off the lady!' Buch let go: she fell back. Adolf nodded and nodded his head. At length he came deliberately over to us, with a peculiar gesture toward the dead girl, clicked his heels together, and smiled:

" 'German Folk Comrades! It was my intention to make that leg-splitter my wife! And now look at her! What a figure the woman makes now! She just keels over!' "

"Make her his wife?" Abetz crammed liqueur bon-bons into his mouth. "I can't believe it!"

"In one long stride he was beside the stretcher again. Fingered her hair. Pulled one of her curls till our flesh crept.

" 'You ungrateful dancer! Come on and tell your admirer—where have you hidden my Will?' Suddenly he broke off and bent slowly down over her:

" 'What kind of a spot is that? There on her breast? Major Buch, speak up! You conducted the examination!'

" 'My Führer!' stammered Buch.

" 'You old murderer!' Hitler took hold of the third button on Buch's tunic. 'At my order, you shot my bosom friend Röhm, in the Grosslichterfeld courtyard! Heines, too! The other traitors, likewise! You killed—' He shook him back and forth, whispering: 'Tell me: Was she actually dead?—when you fished her out of the water?'

" 'No, she still showed signs of life . . .'

" 'Ah! And when did she die?'

" 'During the examination, my Führer.'

" 'And who made this spot?' . . . Abetzel, you should have seen the end of Buch's nose turn dead-white! He said voicelessly:

" 'I.'

" 'You, Major? And—on my wife's skin? With what?'

"The Major stuttered.

" 'With what?' Adolf asked him. 'With what?'

"And the Chief of his Murder Division muttered: 'With my cigar.'

" 'With your cigar? Indeed!' Then he walked straight across the room, stumbled, and sat down in the big armchair. 'With your cigar!' he repeated. 'Indeed! I hate tobacco. The smell of it makes me sick! So!—with your stinking stogie!'—He beckoned him to come nearer— 'Just one question, Major! Could you by any chance put a burning cigar in your right eye?' "

"What?" Abetz held on to the bed with both hands.

"That's exactly the way Major Buch reacted. He lurched to the wall and asked almost inaudibly: 'What!'

"Hitler twiddled his mustache . . . 'Go to it, my dear Buch—try it!'

"A hoarse noise came out of Buch's face: 'No, my Führer! No, no!'

"Hitler's command was icy! 'Come on, Major! Light up!' "

"I can't believe it! And you?—what did you do?"

"We clenched our fists . . ."

"And then what?"

"A footman came up with a box of cigars. Buch took one. I swear to you, Abetzel, I was just going to step up and say something to the Führer—but General Jünger elbowed me aside. Picked up a silver candelabra full of lighted candles from a table, and presented it to Major Buch. He was enjoying it horribly. Buch goggled at the Führer —and waited . . . But Hitler didn't move."

"And you?—And you?—"

"I didn't have the nerve, Abetzel! . . . As Hitler remained motionless, Buch at last held the cigar to the flame of one of the candles.

" 'Doesn't it draw?' "

"Who said that?"

"Who? . . . Why *he*, of course! And then he roared: 'Is it burning?'

" 'At your service'—Buch tottered. 'My Führer—'

"But the Führer cut in: 'Commander of my Murder Division, your Supreme Reich Führer has always closed his eyes to your insolent omissions and commissions. In Vienna, on the Belvedere Terrace, when certain rumors of torture came to my ears, I said to you: "Well! Live and let live!" To which you jokingly answered: "Murder and let murder!" You remember? I see you do, old murderer! So, now stick that cigar in your inane, blue, native German eye! Don't glare at me so! Make a good job of it! Just as you did on the snow-white breast of my wife! Burn it in!—' "

"On the snow-white breast of his wife!" Abetz was thunderstruck.

"Buch goggled at us," Ribbentrop continued. "Suddenly he raised the cigar to his eye—"

"Stop!" Abetz pressed the silk quilt over his eyes.

"The doctors sprang forward. Hitler stared. 'Lieutenant Colonel Buch—General Buch! Polyphemus too had only one eye! At least that's what the legend tells us. Yes! And it takes me to make the most legendary legend come true!' And while the doctors supported the Major out of the room, Adolf burst out laughing:

" 'Yes, killing—you Gestapo gentlemen can do that to perfection! But—to make the dead live again!—who can do that?' And then he grabbed Meissner by the waistcoat. 'Do you believe it possible for your Führer to bring this dead dancer back to life?—Do you believe it?' Suddenly he shouted: 'Or is there anyone here among you who doubts that I, your Supreme War Lord!—that I, Adolf Hitler, possess the power to make that dead woman on the stretcher come back to life, and so alive that she can do the split in front of you all, right here in this miserable French salon? If there is, let him raise his hand!'

"Twisting his neck, Field Marshal Keitel looked us over. Then he raised his marshal's baton and growled:

" 'My Führer! As far as I can ascertain—there's no one here who doubts it!'

"Hitler stuck his hands in his pockets:

" 'I thank you. Although I must say I am not in the slightest degree astonished, gentlemen. For after all, what was your Germany when I—a completely unknown Austrian—came over the border to you? I

—an unknown lance-corporal out of the World War—I alone—called up the already stinking corpse of the German People, out of the vault of the Weimar Republic, out of the shroud of democracy! My word alone awakened eighty million people out of their rigor mortis! Therefore!'—his mustache twitching, he looked contemptuously at the stretcher—'after all, what is a single corpse compared with four hundred million people who, at my word, arise, take up their beds—and run! So, why shouldn't I succeed in setting this dancer up on her slender hind legs again?' "

"Jochen! Jochen!"

"Abetzel—feel my hands! . . . You know the major-domo hasn't called us yet. So, for the past half hour Hitler has been alone with that corpse. And I ask myself, if a man of his energy gets an idea like that in his head—and it doesn't succeed—"

"How could it succeed?"

"I say, and it doesn't succeed! Abetzel!—what happens then?"

"Somebody's knocking . . ."

"Must be Schellbaum. Open up!" Abetz opened the door and the major-domo stood bowing on the threshold.

"Your Excellency, Field Marshal Keitel and His Excellency Herr Meissner have just ventured into the library. Privy Councilor Sauerbruch has sent me to ask Your Excellency if you will please join them."

"Certainly!"

CHAPTER NINE

AS FIELD MARSHAL KEITEL AND MEISSNER ENTERED THE LIBRARY, THEY SAW HITLER SQUATTING ON HIS heels, making a sketch of the corpse. Every now and then he would scramble to the stretcher and, with his pencil, measure the exact length of a toe or the curve of the breast, and then crawl back and draw it, smiling with self-satisfaction. Keitel looked at Meissner out of the corner of his eye. The Chief of the Reich Chancellery, trembling even to his eyelashes, tried to withdraw as quietly as he had entered. Keitel, however, held him fast, and thus they remained, as if chained to each other by their common fear, standing near the door and neither daring to breathe. Not noticing them, their Führer crept forward again on his knees, over the polished parquet, raised the linen sheet from the middle of the body, and stood his pencil upright in the navel, studying it as if it were a tower. Apparently he was watching to see if it would vibrate. Then, licking his pencil point, he lay down flat on the floor. Without moving their heads, Keitel and Meissner exchanged glances.

With a slow roll of his body from the head, he again attained a sitting position, wrapped one hand around a leg of the stretcher, and shook it. As the shadow of the corpse oscillated on the carpet, he clutched at his throat. Suddenly he ran once around the stretcher on all fours, like a dog. He brought his face close to the feet, and bit the corpse in the toes. Meissner would indubitably have fallen over in a dead faint if at the last moment the powerful hand of the Field Marshal had not caught him by the waistband. Startled by the noise, Hitler looked up.

"Who are you?"

"It's us, my Führer—"

"You shouldn't be too sure of that—"

"It's I: Field Marshal Keitel . . ."

"And"—Meissner hid behind the broad back of the Chief of the Reichswehr—"I, my Führer—"

"I"— Hitler gazed blankly into space. "Yes, I! Naturally! Who else! Goes without saying—I!" And he turned his back on them. Abruptly he stood up, put his left foot on the stretcher, and went on as if to himself: "If Japan is on one side of the Himalayas—and I on the other side—then we shall see what becomes of all the fakirs! Let no one imagine,"—his voice became louder and louder—"that the Caucasus runs from left to right solely to present an obstacle to National Socialism . . . I am precisely the man, who—even if it doesn't suit certain people—certain people in Washington!—will certainly not use the Panama Canal to cultivate straw hats. If you, therefore, behind me, are of the opinion that I stand before you, so that you can make jokes behind my back!—then,"—he spun round like lightning, shrieking so that the windows rattled—"you can both of you take a running jump in the shit-hole! Back to the muck! In the old days, when I was a mason, I used to feel a stitch in my heart every time the workers called each other 'muck', which was about every three seconds . . . But Field Marshal, since I have the honor to have harnessed the destiny of this dubious world, the word 'muck' has become my only authentic term for such scum as you!" He dashed at them. "Who gave you permission to sneak in here, into the workshop of your Supreme Reich

299

Führer? You'd like to steal my ideas! Just as you've already stolen my document!"

"But, my Führer—" Keitel stuttered.

"Shut up! You old mustache-brush! Shut up! Snap your heels together! You've robbed me! Eavesdropping and listening behind every wall! In the vain hope that you might at last snatch the sparks of my genius! Just what you haven't got! But I still have my spark in this head of mine, Field Marshal! And I don't intend to give it to you for a pocket flashlight! Get out, you damned pack of thieves!"

Keitel and Meissner were about to retire. Meissner had his hand on the knob, but just as he succeeded in opening the door, Hitler gave it such a kick with his boot that it banged shut. Thereupon he bellowed at the Chief of the Reich Chancellery: "Quiet, damn you! Imbecile frog! On your tiptoes! Why do those patent-leather pumps I bought for you squeak so? Herr Chief of my Reich Chancellery, there's a dead woman in this room! Quiet!" His tone became matter-of-fact: "My good Keitel, please shut the window. The girl will catch cold. Pull the curtains, too. Thank you . . . This Meissner creature was actually present when my deceased wife danced, at top form, in the ashes of Heines and Röhm—"

"May I be permitted to withdraw?" Meissner asked.

"Keep your voice down as you would in church! Halt! Cover up the corpse!"

Meissner looked at Keitel, then he obeyed. Shaking as if he had the ague, he drew the sheet over the stretcher.

"Naturally"—Hitler folded his arms—"the Field Marshal has already sat down at the spinet. Our good Keitel needs music! He used to play the drum. But since he's with me, he even calls his wolfhound 'Walküre.' He's taught him to play the piano with one paw. 'Hoi-hoto —hohui!' " At the last syllable of the Valkyrie's cry, Meissner doubled up as if with cramps. Laughing, in the best of humor, Hitler strutted across the room and sat down at the writing table.

"Meissner, Meissner, how can I ever thank Providence for sending me you, along with all the furniture of the Second Reich, plump in the middle of the Third Reich! Oh, Keitel, I never have to go to the circus! *One* look at our superknave, Meissner—and I really have my fill of laughing! If you don't go down in German history as the shabbiest intriguer that ever betrayed his temporal lord between the Rhine and the Elbe—then Adolf Hitler knows nothing about history. Well, don't goggle so stupidly, but go and look on those shelves and see if among all those senseless books you can find the most senseless book of all."

300

"Which book is that, my Führer?"

"You don't know which is the most senseless book of all?"

"My Führer, I only read documents . . ."

"I know, you scamp! That's how you know so much about my Will!
. . . Now, get that carcass of yours over there and dig out the Bible!"

Coat-tails flying, Meissner hurried to open the glass doors of the book shelves. He put on his spectacles and quickly scanned the richly tooled leather bindings. At length, dragging out a yard-long, thick, parchment-bound Luther Bible, he reported:

"Of the seventeenth century, my Führer. Belongs to Count Willz-scheck." Hitler pulled his chair up to the writing table.

"Just go on playing, Field Marshal. I rather like the tone of a spinet. Reminds me of my Vienna . . . Ha! You Heidelberg cask!" Jabbing Meissner in the stomach, he turned the pages of the Bible. "Göbbels once read to me in the Brown House, just for the fun of it, some of the bilge in this Jewish history book. Meissner, do you know the chapter about the Roman centurion of Capernaum?"

"Of course, my Führer."

"Dig in then! Find it!" Meissner's pudgy old student's head, slashed like a beefsteak, bent over the yellowed pages.

"My dear Field Marshal, you presumably know of the incident? A Roman captain is on his way home from drill. A non-com gallops out the highway on a donkey and reports to the worthy captain that, while he's been drilling recruits out on the parade-ground, his child had meanwhile suddenly died of the measles. The poor father is frantic. Dismissing his soldiers from the highway into the fields, he sat down in the ditch and sobbed. When suddenly—at least so they claim—the Jew Jesus happened by on one of his propaganda tours. He was quite tired and covered with dust, trudging along from milestone to milestone. The Roman centurion had heard some of the flub-dub about the wonder-working activities of the Israelite fakir. And so, dear Keitel, what does he do? He stands up, straightens his helmet, climbs out of the ditch onto the highway, salutes the bearded Jew, and asks if he may speak to him a moment about a purely personal matter. The white-robed pacifist naturally feels his fur smoothed the right way when a centurion of the Roman army of occupation even condescends to speak to him. Scratching his beard, he asks the Roman what's on his mind. Our worthy centurion turns over the company to the sergeant-major and goes strolling along past the olive trees with the sandal-flapping fakir of Nazareth, his toes kicking up the dust. Coming to a stand-still in the shadow of an olive tree he removes his helmet to cool his

301

head, and on a sudden impulse he addresses the Jew as 'Master' and tells him the sad story of how his little boy died that very morning. The weary Bolshevik asks the centurion what he can do for him in the matter. The Roman looks at him with wondering, big eyes for, of course, he thought the miracle-working medium, notorious throughout Palestine, would already have guessed his need. But since the other pretends to be thick-witted, he finally says: 'Master, come with me into the city and raise my little son from the dead!' The Jew makes an evasive, dubious sort of face, trying to get out of it. But, true soldier-fashion, our centurion is adamant. He grabs the Hebrew by his toga and pronounces certain words, which, my dear Field Marshal, always providing they're true, certainly have their significance for us National Socialists today."

"What did he say?"

" 'When I say to one of my soldiers, Go, he goeth; and to another, Come, he cometh. When, therefore thou, Master, shalt say to my son, Arise, he shall rise up from his bed and live.' At that, the Jew Jesus looks at him, thunderstruck. He simply can't get through his Jewish head the fatuity of the worthy centurion. At the same time, however, he senses the possibility of a gigantic propaganda trick and wiping the dust out of his ears, he speaks to him familiarly: 'Well, trot along home now! That kid of yours will live. Your faith has helped you!' "

Hitler leaned back in his chair and smiled to himself. "My good Keitel! What do you think? Is such a thing possible?"

"I've studied strategy—but not the Bible. Still, if that's the way Luther translated it—"

"Well, and you, old suet-pudding?" He slapped Meissner's posterior. "Did I get the story straight?"

"I simply can't find it, my Führer!"

"What!" Standing up, Hitler slammed the Bible shut under Meissner's nose. Then he went to the fireplace and looked a while at the corpse. Suddenly he said:

"Come here, Meissner! Sit down here on that salmon-pink, silk chair. Ha-ha! Yes, the rococo certainly never provided for such an emergency as your behind! Are you seated?"

"About half, my Führer!" the other bleated from his uncomfortable position.

"Then, just keep still as a church mouse . . . and you, Keitel—what kind of a tune is that?"

"I'm trying to mix Beethoven with Wagner . . ."

"Ha-ha! He was always a good card-player . . . Meissner, did **you** ever happen to think that our Field Marshal over there at the spinet went through the whole four long years of the War without even receiving a decoration?"

"My Führer, I don't give a hoot for decorations—"

"Go on playing your drum! Until 1938, Keitel was totally unknown . . . Field Marshal, you were just another one of those desk-work officers on the General Staff. Who had to come along and discover you? I!"

"That's right!"

"Right! So it's to be hoped you won't consider me insane for digging the truth out of the documentary dust of wholesale Jewish lies. Meissner, don't gape at me like a dumb ox!" Hitler took a piece of wood from the fireplace and extinguished the two candelabras in front of the mirror, candle by candle. Quietly moving about, he put out all the other candles except one, leaving the spacious library in a golden-brown dusk. From the fireplace, the firelight flickered about the stretcher; shadows began to play on the walls. Field Marshal Keitel softly struck up the 'Rhine Maidens' motif. To the accompaniment of his rippling pianissimo, Hitler took off his brown tunic and untied his necktie. Standing in front of Meissner, he stuck out first his right leg, then his left, for the other to pull off his soft leather boots. Then, in his socks, he danced around the room, gathering here a Chinese vase, there a jade ash-tray. From the mantel a porcelain goldfinch. From the table beside it, a couple of chessmen. And then he stood there, like a Santa Claus, his arms full of rarities.

"Just go on playing, Keitel!" Waltzing with an invisible partner, he circled toward the dancer, and set the various vases, porcelain birds, and chessmen round about the stretcher like a sly child. Then, his face like an Indian out of "Robinson Crusoe," he went back to the writing table, crept up on the vase, ambushing and decimating the flowers, leaving only a solitary lilac-tinted aster. Carrying that, he went back to the corpse and, with a look that made Meissner turn his head away, inserted eight petals in the spaces between the toes. Then he stood up and scratched himself jubilantly.

Meissner tried to catch Keitel's attention, but the Field Marshal sat and improvised, head tilted back, his shock of gray hair against the wall, his big, cruel eyes gazing sadly at the ceiling. He was liberating his bureaucratic spirit from its narrow Prussian sphere of duties, through the soaring and flowing fantasy of Wagner's melodies, up into the enticing, shimmering barracks of the German gods of Valhalla. Meanwhile, his Supreme Führer squatted at the head of the stretcher,

303

giggling. Meissner, wishing he were far away, stealthily unbuttoned the waistcoat under his heavy official coat.

Suddenly the sliding doors to the dining room were cautiously pushed open. Little by little, Ribbentrop's head appeared through the aperture. With one eye on the Supreme Reich Führer, the Chief of the Reich Chancellery whispered: 'Sauerbruch . . . Sauerbruch!' The Foreign Minister's brow broke into a sweat, and he quietly closed the door again.

Hitler was still giggling. The elderly Heidelberg student on his rococo chair was changing color like a chameleon. He gestured to the Field Marshal, but the latter went on playing and rumbling in a groaning bass:

> Das Vöglein, das heut morgen sang,
> dem war der Schnabel hold gewachsen . . .
> Macht er den Meistern bang—
> gefiel er doch Hans Sachsen . . .

and then lost himself still deeper in Wagnerian intoxication.

Hitler suddenly dashed across the carpet to Meissner, muttering: "Don't take things so easy! . . . Listen to me: I'm going to make a little experiment. If it doesn't succeed—then I want to know to whom we'll have to send my marriage announcements with a black border?"

"My Führer!" Meissner solemnly cleared his throat. "We have plenty of good addresses in South America . . ."

"Tell me—Josef Stalin—at fifty he married a fourteen-year-old girl —didn't he?"

"I don't know, my Führer . . ."

"Oh yes he did! And begot children! Ribbentrop was telling me: Every evening when he comes from the Kremlin to his dacha, the Russian shoemaker's son sits in the kitchen, drinking a bottle of Georgian wine . . . Now and then he blows the smoke from his pipe into the little monkey face of his cry-baby son in the cradle . . . And when the baby won't stop bawling, he sticks his stinking pipe in its trap—and is tickled pink! He—the great Stalin! The Red Pope! . . . Meissner!"—he pinched the calf of his leg—"just you watch me!"

He crawled back to the stretcher. The fire sparkled and crackled in the fireplace.

The little door in the paneling opened and Privy Councilor Sauerbruch entered.

Rising to his feet, Hitler looked at him suspiciously. "Yes, Doctor, we've got that far already—she's dead!"

The surgeon made a gesture of regret.

"Yes, you're a world-famous doctor. Under your knife, many a patient has seen the doors of heaven . . . But I didn't send for you! What do you want?"

"My Führer, I only wanted to assure myself—"

"—that she's dead? Yes, the girl no longer lives. But now that you're here, answer a question . . ."

"Anything you wish . . ."

"You're a specialist?" Privy Councilor Sauerbruch shrugged his shoulders. "So far—so good!" Leading the doctor to the fireplace, he offered him a chair and sat down facing him. "This lady here interests me . . ."

"What can I do for you?"

"I'm interested in her brain. As an expert, you can surely tell me whether or not it's thinkable that certain images, ideas, or thoughts can possibly have remained engraved in her brain-substance—like speeches recorded on wax records, which can be reproduced by means of the phonograph? In other words: is there a possibility that, if you crack open her skull, you have any clever device by which you can reproduce the last thoughts recorded in her brain-substance before her death? That would be enormously important to me! Well, you look pretty skeptical! My dear doctor, what's the difference? A man like myself is not unused to skepticism. It's you specialists and carcass-carvers who unhappily always stop just at the point where you should carry on. If I had stopped every time the so-called laws of possibility and probability set up their limitations, I certainly would not be today the great man that I am . . . Now then, Doctor! Do you feel capable of undertaking such an experiment in my presence?"

For the space of thirty seconds, Sauerbruch looked at him without answering. Then, entering into the spirit of the thing, he said:

"If the Reich Führer would come with me to my laboratory, there is no reason why I shouldn't undertake such an experiment."

"What laboratory?"

"There I have all the latest devices . . ."

"But, practically speaking? Do you think it practicable? Have you a laboratory in Paris?"

"I have an old friend in the Institut Pasteur here in Paris who would place such a laboratory at my disposal at any time."

"Fine!"

"If you'll allow me, my Führer, I can take you there at once."

"Wait! First tell me something: from a purely technical point of view, how does a thought actually get into the brain-substance?"

"That's something I don't know."

"Oh! He doesn't know that! The great Sauerbruch!"

"No—that is one of the secrets of nature . . ."

"What? Field Marshal Keitel! Meissner! And I always thought a doctor like you could muster the National-Socialist courage to dig out the last secrets of nature with his knife!"

"That's what I've been doing all my life."

"Bravo! Well—then you're just the man!" He threw a log on the fire. "Now, will you please explain to me: how could the Jew Jesus actually get the little son of the centurion of Capernaum to live again?"

"Perhaps he only seemed to be dead."

"Bravo! Keitel! Did you hear that? Yes, if he only seemed to be dead —then, there was certainly no particular art in that! But it states explicitly that he *was* dead! Correct, Meissner?"

"Yes, my Führer!"

"Then how could the Jew Jesus make a dead body come to life again? Or do you believe that Nazarene had supernatural powers?"

"In order for me to answer that question, the Lord Jesus would have to come to see me during office hours."

"Sauerbruch! With what sort of powers do you credit me?"

The doctor removed his spectacles. "The same as those with which you credit yourself."

"Hear! Hear! I credit myself with some considerable powers, Privy Councilor!"

"Do you need to tell me that?"

"I even credit myself with the power to raise that dead girl there on the stretcher and bring her back to life . . ."

"In that event you will suffer your first defeat!"

"What was that?" Hitler's ears were red. "Doctor-r-r, you can thank Providence you've already had your appendix removed! Talks quite cheerfully about 'my first defeat'! My good Doctor!" He rapped his knuckles on Sauerbruch's forehead. "Do you know *who* smuggled such a shameless suggestion into that dome of yours?"

"Yes indeed, my Führer!"

"All right, then—who?"

"Common sense!"

"No! You belly-slitter—the Jews! It's Judah who haunts your brain! 'My first defeat'! That is Judah's dream! For no real Pan-German would ever dare let the word 'defeat' slip out before Adolf Hitler! That's Jewish machination! In the pupils of your black eyes, I can see

306

the Jew shrieking his hate at me! 'My first defeat'!" Slowly he raised both hands as if he wanted to throttle the doctor. Quietly smiling, unmoved and confident of his own ability, Dr. Sauerbruch pressed the Führer's arms down.

"Herr Reich Chancellor, your opinion that thoughts are introduced to the brain from *outside* is undoubtedly sound."

"From outside? What? Ha-ha! According to that, you believe that there's something else outside of us? Hm? Hm? Hm? But that bogs us right down in the middle of the Pan-Jewish hogwash again. Doesn't it? Let's get this straight: Adolf Hitler sharply rejects any such Jewish process of thought! I am—what I am—through myself alone! In this world-famous head"—he stroked his cheeks—"not even a dust mote has ever been introduced from 'outside'! Every thought I ever had was generated in me alone! And I absolutely forbid any idea that any sort of thought transference from 'outside' is possible, as far as I'm concerned!"

"Your pardon, my Führer, if I cite yourself as an example to the contrary! For you have actually transferred your thoughts into millions of other heads—"

"What?" The Führer looked flattered. "Well, if that's the case, you will certainly credit me, just as much as the Jew Jesus, with the power of raising the dead! You will certainly admit that I—who have accomplished rather more than that Jordan Bolshevik—I say: you'll agree that I—that is, if I want to—hitherto I haven't even wanted to!—if I will to do so!!—I can raise this little doll here from her mattress?"

Dr. Sauerbruch produced his cigar case, lit a Havana, and bowed slightly.

"My Führer—if you are a Christ—then nobody will be happier than Privy Councilor Sauerbruch!"

He walked quietly out of the library. As Meissner attempted to sidle out after him, Hitler roared:

"Stay here!"

CHAPTER TEN

IN HIS PANIC, MEISSNER STUMBLED OVER THE ONE REMAINING CANDLE ON THE FLOOR. THERE WAS TOTAL DARKness, until Hitler heaved three logs onto the fire, when the changing play of reddish light from the flames flickered over the room. Leaning against the bookcase Hitler wiped his nose with a handkerchief. In the pause which followed the conversation with Sauerbruch, Keitel's uninterrupted soft murmuring chords at the spinet relieved the ominous silence—which the presence of the corpse would otherwise have rendered unbearable—by introducing an element of the fantastic.

"Yes!" The voice of the madman came tonelessly, almost in a sigh. "But whoever did credit me with anything at all? It began as far back as Aunt Resi . . ." He groaned, and the pupils of his eyes sidled lecherously in the direction of the stretcher, peering through the shadow-thronged firelight. "I remember one Sunday, Field Marshal, when we children were invited to Uncle's to pick blackberries. It simply drove me wild—not a soul paid the slightest attention to little Adolf! So I stole away, sneaked round behind the barn, up to the old witch tower, and set it on fire! I swear, that tower burned like a flaming torch! Yelling! Tumult in the village! Suddenly, the old tower, wrapped in *my* flames, became the focus of that long, boring Sunday afternoon! Such a feeling came over me, Field Marshal! For *I* had set that tower on fire! I! . . . I! . . . I! . . ." He ran around in a circle.

"Whatever I have accomplished—I have always accomplished by myself. Your confidence in me has always limped along behind my success! You dung hound!" He spat. "You scheming moron! . . . And notwithstanding, I am now about to do you both the highest honor! For you two shall be witnesses of the most world-shaking event! . . . Field Marshal Keitel! In spite of this notorious medical skepticism—or rather precisely because of it—while you've been unconcernedly tinkling out your trills—I have decided upon an enterprise which certainly no other mortal besides myself has even thought of attempting. With every last atom of National-Socialist courage, I am now going to undertake an event—an event of which, naturally, not a horned ox of you all on this terrestrial globe even believes me capable!

"Get your chair out of the way, Meissner! So! And now I'm going to say to that lovely girl there on the stretcher: 'Stand up!' . . . And then we shall see if Adolf Hitler who, for so many years, has never had to record a defeat! . . . will now—Halt! Where are you going, you beer-barrel? Why are you fluttering around like a wounded sparrow?"

"My Führer—may I please? The fact is—I've drunk a good deal of beer today . . ."

"Even if you were so tanked up the Rhine Maidens could swim around in you"—seizing him by the waistcoat, he plumped him down on a sofa—"you stay here!"

Feeling his way along the paneled wall, the Führer crept up behind Keitel and, craning his neck over the spinet, whispered:

"Field Marshal, can Adolf Hitler raise the dead? Keitel! You and I! In other words the supreme power in the Greater German Realm! We're going to find out, once and for all: Can a man like me—who up to now could do everything—also raise the dead?! . . . I know—an extremely delicate question! And much more difficult to answer definitely than whether we shall dictate the terms of peace in Washington in the summer of '44 or in the spring of '45. Look here, Keitel—that centurion of Capernaum—he really had a hunch! He really believed! And don't the clergy say: 'Faith can remove mountains'? Keitel!" He gnashed his teeth. "Keitel-boy! Can you scare up as much belief as that Roman centurion? Think well! Titanic things depend on your answer! Not merely on account of my Will—for then this thief will have to tell me whom she slipped it to! It's not just that, Field Marshal! But if we really want to wipe out two thousand years of Christianity and replace them by endless millennia of our National Socialism—then we've still got to clear up this point! Understand me? It's unthinkable that I!—the all-highest Führer of our Movement—can play second fiddle to a Jew in this business of resurrecting the dead! . . ."

The Field Marshal breathed heavily. His gray cadet's face nervously evaded the challenging gaze of his superior. He could feel only too clearly that with his answer the foundations of his military dreams would stand firm or fall. Unhooking his gold-embroidered collar, he struck a few keys. But then he could no longer withstand the magic spell of his master's obsession.

"Why, damn it!" he growled. "Herr Hitler, our Reichswehr is, after all, not a plaything! Do you seriously believe, Herr Reich Chancellor, that an Alexander the Great, a Caesar, a Frederick the Great, or a Napoleon!—damn it, do you really think any of those 'Greatest of the Great' would ever have asked his commander-in-chief such a foolish question?"

"Foolish question?" Hitler's hand corkscrewed out at him. "Foolish question!"

"Damn it!" Keitel hoarsed on. "Damn it, what's this question got to do with us?—whether we can raise the dead? Can you possibly imagine, my dear Herr Hitler—Old Man Hindenburg at Tannenberg suddenly asking himself if he could make the three hundred thousand Russians drowned in the Masurian swamps come back to life? Even if the Hero of Tannenberg had been able to do it—I say: 'Even if'—why, it certainly would not have been desirable in the interests of feeding the

German people!"

"You bureaucratic straw-man!" His fingers closed tighter aroun[d] the Field Marshal's throat. "We're not talking about three hundre[d] thousand drowned Russians—but about victory—or defeat! Th[e] twenty-eight-year-old girl"—he let go of Keitel—"that would be [a] laugh!"

Tugging at his forelock, he pressed himself flat against the wall an[d] stared at the corpse in the shadowy corner, fifteen feet away. Th[e] warm firelight shone on one curl. Even the dead pallor of her smoot[h] and lovely face was rosy in that light.

"Keitel,"—his voice was toneless—"listen to me! My flesh is craw[l]ing, right down to the fingertips! My blood tingles as if there were an[ts] in my veins! What?" He drummed one heel against the wall. "Wouldn['t] that be a laugh if such superhuman energy as Adolf Hitler's—co[n]fronted with the cellular structure of such a slender girl's corpse—" H[e] crashed his fist on the keys of the spinet so that the strings twanged a[s] if snapped. "Oh, of course, perhaps it will cost a lot of sweat! But I'[m] accustomed to pouring out my sweat for Greater Germany! Fiel[d] Marshal! As your immediate superior and Supreme War Lord, [I] solemnly ask you: 'Do you believe that I can get that dead dancer u[p] off that stretcher?'"

In the long pause that followed, the only sound was an asthmati[c] rustling whistle from the choked, fatty lungs of Meissner. The Chief [of] the Reichswehr straightened up, his bobbing Adam's apple seeking su[p]port on the rim of his collar. His eyes glazed, he lifted his well-man[i]cured hands high above the keys and came down with all ten finge[rs] like hammers on the strings:

"Damm—dada—daaa!" He banged out the first bars of the "Meiste[r]singer" Overture: "Da—da—da—daaa—daaa!"

Stepping away from the wallpaper at the first "damm," Hitl[er] marched one pace forward. During the next beats he marked time. An[d] with each following fanfare, he took another step forward in perfe[ct] rhythm. And so, clattering his heels across the bare parquet, he arrive[d] beside the corpse. Squeezing the cheeks of his posterior together, he[el] to heel, his feet forming an angle of ninety degrees, his throat muscl[es] strained and swollen, he stretched out his right arm, every inch of [it] knotted muscle, above the dancer:

"I, Adolf Hitler, Supreme Reich Führer and Head of all Forwar[d] Movements, hereby give you my official order: 'Get up!'" The shado[w] of his hand moved, black and gigantic, across the ceiling. No sound. N[o] movement on the stretcher. The Führer stood as if petrified. The Fie[ld]

310

arshal stopped playing, got up and, no less forcefully, marched, spurs
ttling, to his Führer's side, came to attention, and whispered:
"Repeat the command! Go on! The command again!"
Hitler remained silent. The clock on the mantel ticked. Abruptly the
eld Marshal seized the pale girl by the hair, yanked up her head,
cked up her body, dragged it over to the writing table, and threw it
to the armchair like a dummy.
Meissner made his escape out the door.
Hitler stood, his arm still outstretched, like a statue. The Field
arshal lit a candle, took it from the chess table, and set it on the desk
front of the corpse:
"Girl! You surely don't want that fat Meissner—that notorious
atter-box—to go around now telling everybody in the Embassy,
he Führer has suffered his first defeat'? You surely don't want that
happen? Child! You don't want a whispering to begin behind tapes-
ies and mirrors!? Is it to go so far that the two double-posted guards
front of the Villa Wahnfried, when Adolf goes to the Obersalzberg
estival, will wink at each other behind their rifles, presenting arms,
d say: 'He didn't make the dancer come to life again!' Little girl!"
e tidied the disarrayed curls around her pale head and let them fall
er her shoulders. "Oh, joy of joys, oh, enchantress! Do you really
tend to disobey the official order of the Führer of nearly a half billion
man beings? That would be blasphemy against National Socialism!"
Shyly, with distended, glassy eyes, he turned his head toward Hitler.
hen suddenly he tickled the dead girl under the breast— "Ee-eek!" At
e same time, two heavy tears rolled down his leathery cheeks.
Out of the nadir of disappointment came Hitler's voice: "Here we
conquering countries—besieging cities!—setting up Gauleiters—
stalling governors!—chasing parliaments away!—packing kings off
their travels! . . . transporting whole nationalities! . . ."
Whimpering, Field Marshal Keitel went to the spinet and got his
arshal's baton, returning to face his Führer. Standing swiftly at at-
ntion, he saluted him with a broad, sweeping gesture. Like a somnam-
list awakening, Hitler let his outstretched arm fall and squinted at
e Marshal. Then suddenly he seized him with both hands, as if seeking
pport, and tottered against his display of medals. Abruptly, he tore
f Keitel's right epaulette, then the left, and threw them into the
adows . . . Then he snatched his marshal's baton and began beating
m with it like a berserker, clinging to his coat, while the Marshal re-
eated step by step, shielding his head with his arms:
"Swine! You didn't believe in me! You dried-up bureaucrat! You

don't want me to have any more victories! Envious swine! Couldn
have any more faith than that in your Führer! The faith that mov
mountains! Swine! Swine!"

Abruptly he let go. His face swollen, spongelike, eyelids puffed, h
pointed nose like something made of rubber, his expression was li
that of a man drunk. Not with alcohol, but with megalomania r
longer sure of its footing. He staggered away from the Field Marsh
to the fireplace. There he listened—like a surrounded criminal on
moonlit night, who first hears the police dogs barking around th
house.

What he heard was the wind in the chimney high above his hea
howling in ever renewed gusts—the first harbingers of autumn. A
though it was still August, their cheeks were already swollen with
November gale. Hitler, his three folds of chin pressed down on h
collar with dread, shuddered. At every fresh moan and bellow of th
ethereal element, borne out of dusk and storm clouds, he flinched.

At that moment a particularly vehement blast of wind came dow
the chimney, so that even the dying embers were caught up in a sing
sheer flame, with satellites of swirling sparks. Blinded and terrified b
the blazing embers showering onto the carpet, Hitler sprang away fro
the grate. A groan was wrung from his throat, still slavering curses,
if an invisible hand were gripping his windpipe. In the blue-red gla
of the pyramidal flame that licked up to the ceiling, the dead girl reste
in the armchair, not at all like a corpse— It was as if, under her sk
and through all her cells, there coursed something from another atmo
phere. Sparks rolled over the carpet to her feet, and the shroud arour
her legs fluttered. Even her curls moved. As if no longer corporeal, h
face and her throat, against the shadows, were white as fire.

Hitler swayed back. Then he pointed at the refulgence and cried o
in a stifled voice:

"Keitel! Field Marshal Keitel!"

And doubtless, his madness would have cried: "She lives!"—B
there his tongue and vocal cords failed him. For the light from outsic
and beyond, that effervesced ever more weirdly from the fireplac
falling now on the beauty that he had abused even in death—touchir
now her closed eyelids—drew from them a smile from other realm
from other dreams. A smile of bliss! In that dreary rococo librar
crammed with nooses, revolvers, seniority stripes, and musty wi
bureaucratic fug, her delicate, girlish face smiled with such a brightne
of touching grace at the brown shirt of the Supreme Führer and Char
cellor of the Third Reich that it seemed to set the material slow

312

on fire. Buttonhole by buttonhole, pleat by pleat. Like a Nessus shirt, it seared into the emotionless, empty breast of the banal brawler, son of a narrow-minded customs-official of Braunau—for minutes on end.

But suddenly the charred embers rustled through the bottom of the grate. The room was plunged into darkness except for the one remaining candle. As if dropped from the zenith, the Führer collapsed across the stretcher and from there bumped to the floor.

The door in the paneling opened and Dr. Sauerbruch hurried in, Meissner at his heels. Taking in the situation at a glance, the doctor bent and picked up the Führer. While the corpse was being placed back on the stretcher and carried out, he laid Hitler on a sofa and listened to his heart. Taking a hypodermic from his pocket, he was about to locate a suitable vein, when the Führer hit him with his fist between the eyes.

"You old knife-grinder! At my order, through a simple trick on the operating table, you sent that saddle-maker Ebert, first president of the Weimar-Republic, to his grave! At my order, you gave the necessary assistance to that old fogey, Hindenburg, so that he could pole-vault out of his tax evasion scandal and up into Valhalla! Get the hell out of here—you and your damn needle! I don't need your assistance —not yet, Doctor!"

The physicians effaced themselves. Hitler got up from the sofa, hic-cuped, found his boots, and pulled them on. Neatly looping and knot-ting his tie in front of the mirror, with a small pocket brush he care-fully rearranged his disordered hair until it shone.

"Field Marshal! Lights! Now! Hurry up there!" he yapped, tramp-ing about. "Lights—! You heard me!"

Groping his hand along the wall, Keitel found the switch and turned it. The huge chandelier of delicate Murano crystal coruscated in the light of countless electric candles.

"Well—well!" Once more he was seated at the Louis XVI writing table, his voice again matter-of-fact. Retrieving and fastening on his epaulettes, the Field Marshal stood ready, the thick veins in his temples throbbing. Hitler let him stand as if summoned to hear a reprimand in the Reich Chancellery Palace. Playing with a paper knife, the Führer snarled:

"Dear Field Marshal! Thanks be to Providence! This has been a great victory! At last I've given you conclusive proof! For it must have penetrated even a dim-wit General-Staff brain like yours, Field Marshal, that, if Adolf Hitler can't get a dead body up off a mattress, then the Jew Jesus was just as incapable of doing the thing two thou-sand years ago! And the brazen lie of the Bible is thus exposed through

313

me. Have a bonbon, Your Excellency." Proffering him a small paper
bag, he stuffed his own mouth full. "Oh, Hell! I feel refreshed and
strengthened—just like after a good hot bath! Field Marshal!" Leaning
across the writing table he patted Keitel's cheek. "Now at last, I feel
there is nothing on earth that I can't do. For the next thousand years
the watchword will be—"

"—Heil Hitler!" The Field Marshal's face shone. Raising his head
he went back to the spinet, clapped open the lid, and once more
hammered out: "Damm—dada—daaa! Da—damm—da—daaa!"

His left hand akimbo on his leather belt, Hitler picked up his cap
from the chair and put it on. Accompanied by the racket of the "Meistersinger" Overture, which threatened to burst the spinet, he arrived,
arm outstretched, at the door. It opened. Through the mist of tobacco
and candle smoke, the red faces of his generals and S.S. officers grinned
at him. Only the death's-head face of his overworked Chief of Staff
appeared washed out and ghostly among the others. Field Marshals
von Brauchitsch, von Rundstedt, and von Bock-und-Pollach swung
their marshal's batons—whereupon the younger generals welcomed
their Führer with a thundering:

"Heil!"

He laughed like a magpie, then turned to Keitel:

"Field Marshal! Forward! Here's where we guzzle!" Arm in arm
with him he marched, between the honor guard of shaven-headed cold-
eyed war craftsmen of the Supreme General Staff, into the dining
room, seething with black and brown uniforms, where glittering gold-
liveried footmen stood waiting to serve dinner.

CHAPTER ELEVEN WHILE THE LIVERIED SLAVES,
AMID A SURGING ROAR OF JOCULARITY, PUSHED CHAIRS UNDER THE OFFI-
cers' behinds, Meissner shoved the chair of state under the brown
breeches of his Führer. Then with a rapid gesture, he joggled the
major-domo, who was just about to pour some fruit juice into Hitler's
glass. The red liquid spilt all over his own waistcoat and he wormed his
way out between the soup-bearing waiters and into the music room.
There he looked around, and ran past the grand piano into the conference room, where he waited to see if Schellbaum had understood his

ignal. When the latter put in his appearance, they reconnoitered to-
ether into the map room.

"Your Excellency"—slinking behind him, Schellbaum tried to wipe
ff Meissner's stiff shirt with a napkin—"you look as if you'd come
rom the battlefield—simply dripping!"

"Peter!" Meissner whispered, and once again looked cautiously
ound the room, "I did that purposely, so that I could come out here
nd tell you—what's next on the program. Listen: first—"

"Shhhh!"

"Somebody's tapping at the window."

"That's Prince Ferdinand. Four taps!—Our signal!" Schellbaum
pened the window onto the garden a little way. Prince Ferdinand
eered in.

"P-s-s-s-t! Friend Meissner, I was watching through our peephole—
aw you leave the dining room. Meissner, why is everything so de-
ayed?"

"Ah! Prince! Prince!"

"This Uhle chap hasn't even got his costume yet! He's getting im-
atient. Haven't you a glass of old brandy for our assassin?"

"Peter!" Meissner nudged Schellbaum. "In the cupboard, back by
he mirror, there are bottles! . . . Ah, Your Royal Highness—without
God, we're beasts!" He handed a dust-filmed bottle out the window.

"Prince! Is it an absolutely sure thing?"

"Absolutely, Meissner! Absolutely. We're only waiting for Colonel
Latour. The cloth and the chloroform are all ready—we'll put him out
n a flash. And then we dress our noble democrat Uhle in the Colonel's
magnificent Spahi uniform . . ."

"And then he'll shoot?"

"And hit his mark!"

"And hit his mark!" Raising his eyes, Meissner folded his hands.
"But I can't find Uncle August Wilhelm anywhere . . ."

"Prince August Wilhelm has just gone downstairs to speak to His
Majesty in the furnace room."

"In the furnace room? I didn't find him on stairway C. Perhaps he
used the other one—near the conservatory?"

"Shhh!" warned Schellbaum. "There's a sentry!" They listened to
he strong, quiet tread on the gravel, approaching and then receding.

"Meissner, when will the banquet be over?"

"The fish is just being served, Your Royal Highness."

"Peter!" The Prince pushed the window a little farther open with
his dagger. "And when the liqueurs are being handed round . . ."

"Then I'll let the musicians into the dining room. The first note o
the violin is the signal."

"Good!"

"Oh, Prince"—Schellbaum's hand reached for Ferdinand's—"if onl
the dear, kind God stands by us now! . . . When I brought his la:
glass of Vichy to Field Marshal von Hindenburg on his deathbed, h
looked at me and said: "Peter! you'll live to see it: The Kaiser wi
come back.""

"O God! O God!" Meissner, too, clutched the Prince's hand. "You
Royal Highness! . . . We need a ruler once more who bends his knee
before God! Not someone who looks at you with the eyes of Sata
himself! My hand in yours, Prince Ferdinand:—I vow eternal loyalt
to His Majesty, with blood, with goods, with heart and hand! Utterl
and irrevocably—until my last breath! If only the Lord in Heaven wi
stand by us this one time! If only He will deliver us from this were
wolf."

"Shhh! Shhh!" Prince Ferdinand closed the window. "See yo
later!"

"Here's another cushion, Prince—for His Majesty, so that he won'
be too uncomfortable in the cellar."

"Per aspera ad astra!" Ferdinand's eyes glittered, lynxlike witl
cupidity, and he disappeared into the garden.

His heart overflowing with hope, Meissner hugged Major-Dom
Schellbaum, and growled:

> A mighty fortress is our God,
> A bulwark never failing,
> Our helper He amid the flood
> Of mortal ills prevailing.
> Yet still our ancient foe
> Doth seek to work us woe—
> His craft and power are great,
> And armed with cruel hate—

"Ah, Peter, Peter, Peter!"

"Shhh! Your Excellency!"

A servant shuffled in: "The Führer has asked for you twice!"

CHAPTER TWELVE

BEHIND THE CONSERVATORY, PRINCE FERDINAND STOOD FOR A MOMENT UNDER THE SINGLE ELECTRIC-LIGHT BULB in a wall socket on the winding stone stairs designated 'V', which led down to the furnace room. His face twitched with grim spite as he chewed the cud of Meissner's name.

"Meissner! . . . Idiot! Power! Policy! God! Idiot! Your head is as fat as your belly!" Stifling an involuntary laugh, he took a piece of paper out of his breast pocket, but immediately replaced it at the sound of footsteps coming up from the cellar. Quickly remounting a few steps, he stood still, listening.

There were sounds of labored breathing as Prince August Wilhelm ascended. On his brown uniform he wore the Star of the Order of the Black Eagle. At sight of his nephew crouching so strangely against the wall, he recoiled.

"Lord, Ferdi! No hitch in the program, I hope?"

"What kind of hitch, Uncle?"

"Have they sat down to dinner at last?"

"They have! And Peter Schellbaum was just telling me they're finding it excellent."

"Funny thing! About ten minutes ago Himmler passed me in the garden without a sign that he knew me—and with such a queer expression!"

"What do we care about Himmler? All sentries tonight are under my command!"

"Are your fellows all perfectly dependable?"

"Damn it, Your Royal Highness, you don't suppose I'd put any S.S. man I didn't know on this job?"

"Good, good!" August Wilhelm exhaled with relief, his hand on his nephew's arm. "Your imperial grandfather is wearing his uniform of the Hussar Bodyguard. In cellar No. 5! So far he's quite fresh, seems to be bearing up all right in the close confinement. If only it doesn't last too long!" His tense features the color of chalk, he looked at Ferdinand.

"Uncle August Wilhelm, don't get nervous! Uhle's just having a brandy. Must keep your nerves in hand! I've fixed everything with Peter Schellbaum! Like clockwork! It's bound to click! It must!"

"Hope this Uhle hits the bull's eye!"

317

"Why shouldn't he, Uncle? It's no great stunt—firing a revolver."

Removing his own weapon from the holster, he put its muzzle to his uncle's forehead.

"Are you crazy, Ferdi?"

"Just a matter of form, Uncle. Before that shot is fired there's some business to be settled between you and me!"

"Oh—please!" August Wilhelm's eyes were furtive.

"Up on the next landing! We can talk there!" Waving his uncle ahead with the revolver, he followed close behind. "Stop! Don't move! Nice romantic session of the Monarchists' Club you had up there. As I'm not entitled to be considered a legitimate successor to the throne, you didn't invite me, of course! Nevertheless, you're going to hear what I have to say! And my words, too, will have their weight in the scale of destiny. The legitimate successor to the throne—mon frère ainé —ha-ha!—he hangs around with the democratic utopists in London— waiting to see which way the wind blows! Well, I'm not having any part of it! Keep your mouth shut! Don't move! I'll do the talking! Since the collapse of the monarchy, you and I have had many a lively dispute about the eventual succession to the throne should the Hohenzollern dynasty be restored. Uncle—"

"Lord! That's no reason why you should come after me with a revolver like a gangster!"

"Shh! Don't raise your voice! Since 1918 I've had decided differences with my illustrious family! Fact is, I was the only prince with the guts to gain the confidence of the leaders among this democratic set-up and so convince myself of the factual value of the boss-ocratic ideal. I was the only one of the lot who, in greasy overalls, punched the clock day after day and took my stand at the machines in Ford's Fort Lee factories on the Hudson. I'm therefore the only one of you who knows not only how a motor is built, but also how it runs! And how to drive it! Fact is, I'm the unique example among all your illustrious High-and-mightinesses who knows how the motor of democracy is put together!"

"Please don't rub my nose with that damn revolver!"

"Little thing like that bother you? Doesn't bother me! To put it briefly: if I may be so bold, on the basis of all my experience in the western world, I'm the only one among you, as I stand here, a National Socialist air-fighter—"

"Why harp on the 'National Socialist,' Ferdi?" August Wilhelm growled. "Only a few yards from where we stand—down there in the cellar, my father is waiting—His Majesty, Kaiser Wilhelm—to ascend the throne of our ancestors—and you stand here insisting you're a—"

"—National Socialist! Yes, your Royal Highness!"

"I must say, I doubt—" August Wilhelm made a short turn and would have gone.

"Halt! Or I shoot!"

"Ferdinand!" His uncle came to an abrupt stop and leaned against the wall, trembling and staring at his nephew.

"So! Now let's get down to brass tacks! What your imperial father is up to down there among the coal bins—leaves me absolutely cold! Furthermore, I care even less what his sons—and among them you, my illustrious Uncle—are up to along with him! Thanks to your pitiful ineptitude in 1918, the Prussian monarchy was handed over on a gold platter to the hordes of the Revolution. Shut up! I'm talking now! You've no right to wear the Star of the Black Eagle, my dear Uncle. All you did in the World War was to loaf around out of harm's way! So now you can just keep your mouth shut! And instead of urging your imperial father in that critical moment of 1918, between victory and defeat, to mount his dapple-gray and, together with his sons and his general staff, to gallop at the head of the Imperial Bodyguard through the breach of Amiens against the American tanks, and so at least, in one grandiose, symbolic act of heroic behavior preserve the myth of the crown and of 'the Grace of God'—instead of that, the whole pack of you scattered like scared rabbits over the border in all directions! What you did do was to leave our glorious army—at whose head a worthier stands today—you left it to its fate!"

"You rat!" August Wilhelm whipped a revolver out of his trouser pocket. But his nephew was quicker. With a swift kick, he knocked the small Browning out of his uncle's hand.

"Hands at your sides!" He pressed his own weapon against his uncle's throat. "You don't suppose my generation will ever let such a pack of cowards return to the throne! Let Wilhelm II keep on growing roses in Holland! My own father can go on fooling around. . . . But your little boy in Potsdam, Uncle—he's not going to have the imperial German crown to play with!"

His lips blue, August Wilhelm mumbled incoherently.

"I'll have you know"—Ferdinand's voice was hoarse as he traced the contour of his uncle's skull with his revolver muzzle—"I idolize Adolf Hitler! And there's only one reason why I have agreed to let him be finished off—and that is because I intend to seize power myself! Because power fascinates and intoxicates me! Do you get me? Because there's one thing I learned among the Ford workers, and that is that a man without power, if he doesn't have the guts to seize it and be somebody, even if it's only a gangster—is the most miserable creature on earth—my illustrious Uncle! I am mad for power! Mad! Mad!"

August Wilhelm, his fifty years suddenly wilted, let his arms dangle limply. His nephew produced a sheet of paper from his pocket, held it out to him with a fountain pen, and commanded: "Sign!"

"Sign what, Ferdi?"

"Sign!" The gun menaced him. "The contents are O.K. You needn't bother to read it!"

"I can't do that! I won't sign anything I haven't read!"

"Si-i-i-ign! Or else—I'll go up these stairs, and report to Adolf Hitler that he can bag the whole cowardly crew of Kaiser and Princes down among the furnaces—like mice! The whole litter isn't even fit to wipe the mud off his boots! . . . So go ahead and sign! Your Monarchists' Club will have to content itself with the fact that one dynastic representative will be sitting on top!"

Prince August Wilhelm, his jaw wobbling, signed.

"Many thanks, Uncle! Now you can go downstairs nicely and just wait for things to take their course. I promise you to dig up some tenantless crown somewhere in Europe and have it hammered egg-shape to fit your horse's skull! And you must graciously forgive my informality! So sorry that I could not stick strictly to court etiquette! And when you get down—keep your mouth shut! One false step— even the slightest attempt to doublecross me—and the whole mess of you will be jacked up against the wall in Grosslichterfelde to-morrow morning!"

Replacing the document with his uncle's signature in his pocket, Ferdinand picked up the Browning, handing it back to its owner with elaborate courtesy, and trotted smartly upstairs.

Prince August Wilhelm eased his shirt a little away from his dripping chest. Suddenly he slid weakly down the wall. And there he sat, on the white-washed stone stairs—like a wax figure.

CHAPTER THIRTEEN Since ten o'clock that evening, EX-KAISER WILHELM II AND HIS HIGH, HIGHER, AND ALL-HIGHEST ASSO-ciates, had sat, still as mice, jammed and crammed together, deep down under the Embassy garden, inside the dungeon walls of cellar No. 5.

His fourth son, August Wilhelm, despatched a quarter of an hour ago, was expected to return at any moment with the longed-for message of liberation.

The all-highest War Lord of the First World War sat between the many oil-dripping pipes which conducted steam into rust-red boilers, on a coal bin, provisionally draped with velvet. He was smoking over-size cigarettes—a gift from the erstwhile Sultan Abdul Hamid. At his side stood a well-dressed and well-nourished civilian, the President of the Austrian Olympics. A guest of the Kaiser in Doorn, charming raconteur and court fool, Dr. Schids had been included in the retinue so that he might distract and entertain the All-highest. At this precise moment he was handing His Majesty with most submissive devotion a slender crystal goblet of the champagne Meissner had managed to smuggle down. The sparkling liquid foamed over onto the cinnabar-red tunic of the lavishly gold-embroidered hussar's uniform which the ex-Kaiser had donned for the solemn moment of his restoration. Some-what bowed under the metal burden of his many medals, orders, epaulettes, and galloons, the octogenarian ex-ruler vainly sought for something to lean against behind the Watteau Gobelin faintly swaying in the cellar air. Thanks to Meissner's efforts, a setting to some extent befitting His Majesty had in all secrecy and haste been staged among the coal shovels, cobwebs, and other cellar fixtures.

"Your Majesty!" Dr. Schids took the liberty of raising his glass, and murmured: "The resurrection is just about due!"

"Damn it! I'm no corpse!"

"Sire, for your first drive through the streets as Kaiser, I have taken the liberty of placing my Olympic sedan at Your Majesty's disposition."

"I can't understand how Meissner could have been so mistaken about the time! I was promised the event would take place at ten—damn it! —What's become of my sons?"

"Their Royal Highnesses"—Dr. Schids bowed—"are awaiting the promised telephone call at the Netherlands Embassy. But here comes Countess Egmont, Lady-in-waiting to her Royal Highness, the Crown Princess of the Netherlands."

"Why hasn't her Prince Consort, Bernhard zur Lippe, put in his appearance?"

Dr. Schids guided the Countess between the oil-smeared boilers to the Kaiser.

Wilhelm rose slightly from the coal bin and sat down again immediately. "Any word from the House of Nassau-Orange?"

"Their Royal Highnesses"—the Countess curtseyed—"sincerely wished to shake hands with Your Majesty quietly before the event—but, in view of the delicate situation here in Paris—"

"Well—I certainly shan't forget that, coming from the House of Nassau-Orange!"

His aides grinned. Suddenly the Kaiser turned his head, seeming to recognize the footsteps that were approaching. His second consort, a voluminous female in a huge feather hat, her bosom bedecked with medals, made a rustling entrance from Corridor A.

"Herminchen!" Wilhelm called to her expectantly, his yellow face reanimated under the high forehead upon which the waved white hair formed a sort of top-knot.

"Dear Kaiser!" She sat down quickly on a box pushed forward by Dr. Schids. "Our good Peter Schellbaum has just sent word by Ferdinand that we should stay quietly where we are. The person in question is still sitting at table. But the event can't be far off."

"Kaiserin Hermine!" Wilhelm blinked at her, and excitedly clutched his golden galloons. His watery-blue eyes took on that fanatic glare known for over forty years, in Germany and outside it, as "the Hohenzollern gaze." But immediately he became nervous.

"Cotton! I can't bear the sound of firing! Cotton for my ears! Ever since 1918— Damn it—where's the cotton?"

"But, dearest Kaiser!" Princess Hermine reassured him. "Down here, God be praised!—we won't hear anything. The shot will be fired in the library."

Stirred by the contagious excitement, the others rose from their ramshackle seats and, with carefully muted voices, cried out:

"His Majesty, our most gracious Kaiser and King!—Hurrah!" In acknowledgment of the subterranean hurrah, the octogenarian rose to his full height, supported by the strong arm of his second wife. Setting his field marshal's baton against his hip, the slack skin taut across his cheekbones, he said as if in thanks:

"Gott mit uns!"

Again footsteps were heard approaching through Corridor A. Field Marshal Mackensen, his saber and busby on his left arm, edged along, supporting himself against the cellar wall. Standing before the Kaiser, bow-legged, he poised the curved saber with its point against the toe of his left boot. Twisting the points of his white mustache until they stood rigid, he made such a profound obeisance as only a courtier's back, accustomed to many years of bending, could achieve.

"See there! My Marshal of the Danzig Death's-head Hussars stands before me—a trifle shaky, to be sure!"

"My most gracious Lord!" The aged hussar reverently kissed his hand. "There are a lot of damned swine in the world!"

"Whom are you telling that, my old friend!"

"Your Majesty—first of all, before I forget it again: Meissner has sent word that the iron door behind that last boiler back there opens into a subterranean passage which comes out two blocks away in the cellar of a German watchmaker. Outside his shop there are three powerful Mercedes cars waiting."

"Mercedes cars? What for?"

"Sire, in the event that the attack should fail, this is the way of retreat which must be taken without an instant's delay."

"Fail? What does that mean, damn it? I was certainly told that—there was not the slightest risk."

"Your Majesty, I was only able to excuse myself under the pretext of obeying a need of nature. I must therefore return immediately. They are just serving the capons."

"Mercedes cars? 'In the event that the attack should fail'? I don't understand it."

"Your Majesty, behind that water gage there's a bell. If it rings once, the All-Highest Person of your Majesty will have the goodness to mount as quickly as possible the stairs that lead from Corridor B up to the conservatory."

"Like a flash, eh?"

"Your Majesty's sons, the Princes and other representatives of the throne, will then be conducted in person by Prince Ferdinand through Secret Door C into the extraterritorial grounds of the German Embassy, where the presence of these princely personages will lend legal force before the whole world to the restoration of the monarchy."

"Damn it, that was a long sentence! Certainly cost the old man a lot of breath! My aides—has everything been noted down for me?"

"Yes, Your Majesty!"

"Sire!" Mackensen raised three fingers of his gloved hand. "If, on the other hand, the bell rings *three times!* . . . then we most humbly implore Your Majesty and the ladies and gentlemen here present to leave these premises as swiftly as possible, by Door 13, thus reaching the three Mercedes cars and making every effort to cross the Dutch border with lightning rapidity . . ."

"What a grand old man he is!" Wilhelm laughed. "Damn it—I remember well how, at maneuvers, I used to love to ride to the attack with him! How we'd dash along! Across plowed fields! The whole

323

thundering cavalry corps! And there he was, at full gallop, always reining his horse just a head short of mine! The earth rumbling with the hoofs of the cuirassiers, dragoons, hussars, and the rest, every man-jack of them firm in the saddle, damn it! And even later on, in Rumania, in 1917, we could still show them our hoofs! . . . But today, I see, the old bird's a bit shy! Ha-ha! 'Mercedes cars! Door No. 13!' And 'every effort to cross the Dutch border!' Well, well! Go along, old boy! The capons are calling."

"Sire!" The Marshal of Hussars again bowed low from the waist. "I remain as ever Your Majesty's most subservient vassal and liege . . ." With sword scraping and spurs jingling, he brushed his way along the cellar corridor, returning to the dining room.

"Damn it—'Be faithful unto death, and I shall give thee the crown of life!' Well, I have been faithful! So I don't see any reason at all to be so anxious. Almighty God is in honor bound—in fact, it's His plain damn duty—to give me back the crown. But, damn it, right now I'd rather have one of those caviar canapés!"

"Here, dear Kaiser!" Princess Hermine handed him some sandwiches divested of their greasy wax-paper wrappings. "They are the last you'll ever have to eat in exile."

"Damn it!" Wilhelm looked hard at Countess Egmont. "The word 'exile' has been pronounced. And I feel impelled out of my overflowing imperial heart to request you, Countess, to convey the expression of my profound thanks to her Royal Highness. Princess Juliane and her Royal Mother have accorded me the warm succor of kinship during my exile in Doorn. They not only did *not* surrender the illustrious head of the German Kaiser to the hyenas of democracy, as stipulated by the Treaty of Versailles . . . No! . . . On the contrary, with constantly renewed and magnanimous demonstrations of their all-highest compassion, they comforted and rejoiced the spirit of the sorely tried German Kaiser . . .

"Isn't it so, Hermine? Damn it, only recently, on the occasion of the marriage of my little nephew Ferdinand to that charming Slavic daughter of the heir to the Russian Imperial Crown— Ah! that was a rare feast for the soul! There was I, King and Kaiser, surrounded by representatives of all the proudest princely houses of Europe, each one bedecked with the most ancient and honorable orders. The Princess, with the ribbon of the Order of the House of Nassau across her breast, sat there before me between Prince Ferdinand in his black S.S. uniform and my charming daughter the Crown Princess Cäcelie. That was in 1937 . . . or even later. Looking round on that wedding day,

I knew that democracy's days were numbered.—Hey! Hey! What's up now?" he called to the hastening aide who approached. "Is it a fait accompli?"

"Your Majesty," General von Friedeburg reported breathlessly, "two field marshals of the Reichswehr are coming down . . ."

"Damn it, do you mean to say we didn't hear the bell? Has the attack succeeded?" He stared dreamily into space. "When I make my entry into Berlin through my Brandenburger Tor, I have in mind a sumptuous display of splendor! I remember, more than forty years ago, when I was visiting His Holiness, the doddering Pope Leo XIII, in the Vatican, I said to my Chief Chamberlain, Count Eulenberg: 'Damn it! I! An Imperator and Rex! I, a wearer of the purple! I feel positively embarrassed in the presence of the imperial magnificence of the Vicar of Christ on earth!' And during these bitter years of exile, I vowed, if God the Highest should ever deign to guide my footsteps back to the throne of my glorious ancestors, I would from then on take as my model, in respect to the display of glory and power, only the Vicar and Turnkey of the Lord Jesus!" He sank into his memories of Papal power and magnificence.

"Your Majesty, the two field marshals . . ."

"Be quick about it!"

The aides-de-camp skipped off, calling out into Corridor B: "His Majesty has most graciously deigned to grant your most humble request for an audience."

Their spurs rattling, the two gray-haired generals, von List and von Blaskowitz, came proudly forward. With a slight bow to their former Supreme War Lord, they straightened up, in their narrow-waisted, close-fitting uniforms.

The Kaiser glared at them: "Is the person in question dead yet?"

"Your Majesty—" Blaskowitz began, his left hand resting on a glittering sword hilt.

"My good Blaskowitz! Your Kaiser has always cultivated a manly spirit in the German people. Therefore, I know a good deal more than most people on this earth! My dear List, what's the matter with you that you don't click your heels? I was once company chief! I was squadron chief, battery chief, and regimental commander before I was king! The drill-book for true Christians prescribes that you bring your heels together in the presence of your All-highest Emperor and King! In good times and in bad times my heart has always been close to the soldier . . . And now, aren't you ashamed to stand there in such a posture before your All-highest Lord? Damn it, my achievements on behalf of the army laid the foundation for everything you're doing up there! It was I who developed the machine gun from its modest beginnings to become the backbone of the whole fighting power of modern infantry! For every innovation in the field of combat the armies of the world have to thank me! Even the introduction of the traveling field-kitchen is due to the efforts of the German Kaiser! . . . Legs together! . . . When as a ten-year-old prince, I proudly stood at attention before my grandfather Wilhelm I on the second of May, 1869, I certainly never dreamed the day would come when two Prussian generals wouldn't know enough to bring their heels together before me! . . . Get out of here!"

The two Reichswehr generals saluted and took their departure.

Princess Hermine shook her head. Schids edged forward. "Sire, shall I not bring the marshals back again?"

"Swine!" The Kaiser fulminated, waving his marshal's baton. "Such swine! Swine, every one of them! I am almost too tired to reign again over so many swine!" Wearily, he sat down on the coal bin. "A Prussian field marshal who no longer snaps his heels together before his Supreme War Lord! Hermine, I begin to comprehend the torments of Jesus in the Garden of Gethsemane! . . . Just doesn't click his heels together before his Kaiser, damn it! Well, Thy will, O God, is inscrutable! Notwithstanding, I say: 'Thy will be done! Amen!' "

Disconsolate, he fell into a daze in the candlelight, but all at once became animated again. "God has revealed Himself to us through sages, priests, saints, Christians, Jews, and Kaisers. Damn it, He spoke through Hammurabi! Moses! Abraham! Homer! Charlemagne! Luther! Gœthe! and Kant! But, damn it, God also spoke through your Kaiser. If the world had only listened to me! Didn't the German Kaiser as long ago as 1900 warn the world against the Asiatics! 'People of Europe, preserve your most sacred possessions!' " . . .

"S-s-sh! Dear Kaiser! Here comes Doctor Schids again, alone!"

"Sire!" The president of the Austrian Olympics rubbed his hands with embarrassment. "With most humble regret, I most unhappily report to Your Imperial Majesty the impotence of my heartfelt good will. The two handsome Reichswehr marshals—"

Wilhelm nodded. "Learn to suffer without complaint." He accepted one of Abdul Hamid's long cigarettes and a light at the hands of Prince Fürstenberg. His gaze lost in the blue clouds of sweet-smelling cigarette smoke, he did not observe the reappearance of Prince August Wilhelm. Glancing all about him, the prince played his flashlight into the dark corners. With a knifelike smile of suppressed rage, he stood

326

before his father.

"Damn it! You—August Wilhelm?" The Kaiser fanned the smoke away from his eyes with his glove. "Well? . . . Well?"

"Don't be nervous, Papa!" Prince August Wilhelm elbowed Doctor Schids to one side, behind the steam pipes. "The fellow who's doing the job is having a glass of brandy."

"And can the fellow really shoot?"

"He was a captain of Uhlans—why shouldn't he be able to shoot?"

"But the Kaiser means: Is his aim good?"

"Why shouldn't it be, Madame? It's not difficult!" Pulling his pistol out of his pocket, he aimed at his father. There were cries of alarm. Princess Hermine stepped protectingly in front of the Kaiser. Several members of the retinue jumped out from behind the furnace toward Prince August Wilhelm. The aides picked the Kaiser up. Cringing, the terrified sycophants eyed the prince.

"Understand me, ladies and gentlemen! The slightest attempt on your part to doublecross me—" the poison generated by those words of Ferdinand's spurted out of him with the same envenomed vanity— "and I'll have the Gestapo clean out the whole cellar!" In the stunned silence that followed, he continued: "Well, Papa! Now you and I are going to talk straight."

Supported by Princess Hermine and Lieutenant General Friedeburg, the Kaiser looked at his son:

"Your Royal Highness! I have talked straight all my life. Damn it— comb your hair!"

"My dear Sir—"

"Dear Sir—?" Wilhelm's voice shook. "Bring your heels together! You're standing before your Kaiser!"

"Papa dear," the bleating voice resumed, "in 1918, if you had mounted your dapple-gray and, at the head of the Imperial Bodyguard —had galloped through the breach of Amiens against the American tanks—" Ferdinand's words poured involuntarily from his lips.

"August Wilhelm!" The Kaiser raised his fist. "By the myth of the crown! . . ."

"The myth of the crown? . . . my dear Sir, you yourself annihilated that myth when, like a miserable coward, you ran away across the Dutch border—"

"August Wilhelm—" A moan issued from his father's white mustache.

"Prince August Wilhelm!" Princess Hermine clutched her breast. "You talk like a dyed-in-the-wool Nazi! And just at the moment when

327

your Imperial Father, His Majesty, stands here in all humility, to receive the crown once again by the grace of God and set it upon his venerable royal head—"

"Madame! In the name of Her erstwhile Majesty, the Kaiserin Auguste Viktoria, my mother!—I forbid you to shoot off your mouth in this loose fashion!"

"Eau de Cologne! . . . Friedeburg! Eau de Cologne! . . ."

"By the grace of God?" The Prince turned to the Kaiser again, who was mournfully fingering his galloons. "No!" and then in his boiling hate, he could think of nothing else but what Uhle had said in Dr. Schid's apartment before the assembled grands seigneurs—"No!" He whipped a piece of paper out of his pocket and scribbled something on it. "Either you sign this formula with your own hand—or—!" With lips compressed, the Kaiser looked about at the members of his suite.

"My son has gone crazy—"

"Here!" August Wilhelm held out the paper. "Sign! Even if I were crazy—anything would be better! Nothing to do but put a stop to such power-lusting fools! . . . Sign!"

"You read it, Hermine! I haven't my glasses."

"Dear Kaiser, it says here: 'We, Wilhelm!—by the grace of the Unknown Soldier!—give our solemn assurance that when we ascend the throne—"

"Here—give me that!" Wilhelm snatched the paper out of her hand. "What is it this swine wants of me?"

"Sign! You needn't bother to read it! It's the correct formula all right!" With his revolver muzzle the prince pointed at the text, a fanatic gleam in his eyes.

Using a pair of spectacles lent by an aide, the ex-potentate read the formula. "By the grace of what Unknown Soldier? What's he talking about? Can't he understand that when one has reigned as I have for forty years by the grace of God, one's head is in the right place—that is, where God the All-highest has put it? An Unknown Soldier? Friedeburg—what do you make of this? Where is my court physician?—Am I supposed to reign by the grace of buck private Joe—whose business it is to see that he brings his heels together before his Emperor and King? Your Excellencies"—his eyes flashed at his suite—"if you don't want your Kaiser to lose his senses entirely, then drive this whelp out of my sight! He is no longer my son!"

"Get back! I'll shoot!" Prince August Wilhelm stood braced against the wall.

"I believe . . . from 1914 to 1918 . . . about twelve million buck privates must have fallen!" The Kaiser trembled so that his medals and orders gave off a faint tinkling. "The next thing you know," he shouted, his cheeks blue, "this—this—in God's name, what shall I call this renegade Hohenzollern?—the next thing you know he'll demand my signature—he'll ask for a receipt stating that I'm a mass-murderer! What?—I'm supposed to wear the crown in the name of the Unknown Soldier? That would be democracy—not monarchy!" With imperial scorn he threw the scrap of paper at his son's feet. The prince picked it up and left the cellar.

"But—Prince August Wilhelm!" Princess Hermine ran after him over the coal and threw her whole weight on his shoulder. "We can still talk it over! It's all so sudden! You must give us time to think! Grant us another minute! . . . And dear, dear Kaiser!" she called back to him: "Only think what would happen if your son really did go up to the person in question! . . . Dear Kaiser! All on account of such a stupid formality? . . . Willi!" she moaned, "sweetheart! My Mutzi!" She whispered: "Just give in to these Nazis and Democrats—anything they ask, darling! Say 'Yes' to everything! Until we get on top again! Mutzi! We want to be Kaiser! With you I have shared sorrow and joy from your sixtieth to your eightieth year! I have dedicated my young life solely and singly to this dream: that we shall yet sit on the throne in the white salon in Berlin! Willi! So please sign!"

"I shan't wait any longer!" August Wilhelm made as if to go.

"Wait! He'll sign! Won't you?" From among the many fountain pens offered him, the Kaiser picked out a white one and thereupon signed his name to the paper with broad loops and imperial flourishes. Immediately below it, he set his 'I.R.'—that is: Imperator Rex.

Tearing it out of his hand, his pupils distended more and more, August Wilhelm pranced among the boilers and partitions to the stairs, neighed wildly, and disappeared.

"Damn it!" The Kaiser brushed a tear from his eyes. "My heart is constricted with pain and sorrow! But one thing I swear: If I come out of here tonight, by God's help, with the imperial German crown on my scorned and slandered head—then the first thing I shall do will be to erect a fitting tomb for my grandparents. The old mausoleum in Charlottenburg won't do any longer. It's too cramped . . . Damn it, how cramped it is down here! So cramped—cramped—cramped—" From the edge of his improvised chair of state, he sank down onto the coals. There he sat, mute and stiff as his own figure in a waxworks show.

329

CHAPTER FOURTEEN

AT THE REAR OF THE EMBASSY GARDEN, AGAINST THE WALL THAT SEPARATED IT FROM THE QUAI, UHLE stood under an old moss-covered elm. It was so dark that almost nothing was distinguishable. There was no sound except, at a short distance, the metallic clatter of a patrolling sentry stationed by Prince Ferdinand to watch Uhle. Only now and then was there a faint sighing among the leaves of the tall and many-branched elm.

Around the ancient trunk the flutter of moths was like a faint, soft melody. Each time the breeze stirred the foliage and a branch moved, from a lantern somewhere a dull yellow glow fell upon Uhle. Prince Ferdinand had shut him up in a small enclosure, the Embassy's private menagerie, to spend the last minutes before the attempt. On a garden chair beside him stood a bottle of brandy and a plate of cakes. A few yards away, in front of a small green shed, a fawn slept on some straw. In the darkness the white spots on its brown coat shone like flowers.

Tired with his long wait, Uhle sat down, stretched his legs, sipping the brandy and listening. Nothing but the steady tread of the sentry. A gnawing sound at the food-trough startled him . . . Probably a rat, after scraps.

On the other side of the wall, an automobile drew up and stopped. There were voices. Uhle listened.

"Probably Colonel Latour has arrived."

Then the car drove off again. And again there was quiet. The elm was so quiet . . . That quietude of the tree in the night strangely affected the Uhlan . . . His feet had carried him now here, now there . . . And all that time the trunk of the elm had grown—round and firm—from its great, spreading roots—always in the same place . . . And yet in its leaves and twigs it had taken to itself all colors from the sun. High up in its crown, it was moving its most delicate leaves, like a chime of tiny bells. Now and then, from high in the firmament, a star twinkled through its branches and caressed its rough bark with silver rays . . . so cool . . . so good . . . as with hands of peace. Indeed, the tree was like some man of prayer, ripened into perfection. It reminded him, in its repose, of his soldier from Verdun.

Uhle clutched at his laboring chest.

"Has God chosen you to be his judge?" the soldier had asked him

330

at the organ. "Have you the right to judge?—Or do you not know that hypocrisy is worse than the Devil?"

Suddenly Uhle, seized by a great anxiety, took from his pocket a small New Testament, given to him by his mother when he went to war in 1914. It had been his great-grandfather's, and his grandfather's, and his father's.

Under the lantern he opened it and read by the dim light from the Revelation of St. John the Divine: "His eyes were as a flame of fire." And then: "Fear not: I am the First and the Last." And then: "I am he that liveth, and was dead; and behold, I am alive for evermore."

Through the park the drunken voices of the Nazi chiefs and the Reichswehr generals resounded louder and louder. Uhle closed his eyes and imagined that he saw that wonderful figure of the Saviour. Thoughtfully he put the little book back in his pocket. Suddenly he remembered that at this hour he should be with his friend Gunther, Secretary of the Anciens Combattants—they were to have drunk a bottle of wine together. And yet: Was it not better that he should confront this "false unknown soldier," here at the Embassy—than that he should stand in front of a microphone in the Trocadéro? And then Uhle dreamed that perhaps he might be given the power so to depict the fact of the *true* Unknown Soldier that the lance-corporal would remember what all the unknown soldiers had promised one another in the hell of the trenches.

He pressed his hands together. "Yes—why should it not be possible at last to lead the poor, peace-loving, common people of this world out of—"

"Hi! Uhle!" Prince Ferdinand whispered through the wire fence. "I'll have your clothes immediately! . . . How many cartridges have you? Three? Or how many? You'll have everything in just a minute. I'll come back for you."

He made off in the darkness. Frightened by the noise, the fawn ran on slender legs, with swift jumps, from one end of the enclosure to the other. Its ears flicked back and forth—and it sniffed. The lantern light played on its small, moist black muzzle. All at once it snuggled in the straw again. Uhle went to it and stroked the supple, softly breathing body. The red-brown pelt felt like Olenka's hair.

"Darling! I saw my first deer as a child in a meadow in the Black Forest. Out of the dark firs, it came shyly into the clearing. It looked at me. Then it streaked through the slanting sunrays to the other side of the meadow and disappeared again, into the night of the forest.

Quaking-grass and bluebells swayed to and fro behind it. Through the crane's-bill and the sorrel Saint Ottilie's Spring rippled over the white pebbles fresh and clear . . . Oh, homeland! homeland!" He suddenly sighed, and listened to the growing racket of the Embassy banquet.

All the music and poetry of the German genius! . . . In that bitter moment he could hear it only in the dark murmuring of the elm leaves above him. For the blast and uproar of the Nazi orgy—bursting into the sacred silence of the night—was a blast of barbarism.

Suddenly, not far from him, behind some bushes, a small iron gate in the garden wall was surreptitiously opened. Then two shadowy figures, unrecognizable in the darkness, carried out a stretcher. He experienced a momentary shock, for it seemed to him that under the coverings he distinguished the body of a woman. As the wall was too high to look over, he climbed up on a pile of old boards. From this he was able to raise himself high enough to look out, over the wide, faintly lighted Quai de Solférino.

Where could they be going with the stretcher? Uhle leaned far over the tree-shadowed wall. The men went to the Seine. There they glanced cautiously around. Uhle wanted to follow them. But one of the S.S. sentries came along below him and halted beside the deer, scratching its ears. In a moment, however, he resumed his beat, whistling.

As soon as the sentry was out of sight, Uhle climbed over the wall, let himself down on the quai, and ran after the men. When they saw him, they thought it was the police and abandoned the stretcher.

Uhle approached. . . . Suddenly he gave a cry. . . . The others took flight.

"Olenka!" Uhle threw himself wildly at the dead body and caressed it. Then he drew back, afraid, before the power of her immortal presence. The moon shone on her smooth face. Just as in the library, when Field Marshal Keitel had put the dead girl in the chair before the fireplace and the wind-roused flames had lighted her so magically—so now the same smile of beauty rested on her face.

"How quietly you lie there! As if the sound of eternity had kissed your lips. Olenka"—he mourned over her—"have you left us alone in the universe? Alone in this dance of death?" He moved his fingers hesitatingly through her curls, wet from his tears. "You! You! . . . What mysterious happiness smiles at me behind your closed eyelids? What is it that you see? A land where there is true freedom? Where we are released from this tension? Where over again we may rejoice in a grass blade or in a little swallow on a telegraph wire? Do you still remember it—that house in the meadow? You asked me under the stars: 'What is to become of this dark world?' I said: 'Be silent and be pure!' No! Now I say: 'Act and be pure!' Olenka! You wanted to know all my thoughts? From my birth on? Hm? Did you feel too that your question startled me awake, like the voice of an angel on the Day of Judgment? You! Be now my guardian spirit! Do you hear me?—Where are you now? Somewhere on your Magic Island? In the blue, blue sea?—And your wedding dress? Ah!"—he leaned his head on her—"do you believe that we shall ever see each other again—in the universe?"

Down below, the waters of the Seine, still swollen by the thunderstorm, gurgled along the embankment of the quai, sinister and black.

Meanwhile, the sentries had noticed Uhle's absence and, throwing on civilian overcoats, they came cautiously out of the Embassy garden with Prince Ferdinand. They looked around, then ran across the quai. Suddenly they saw Uhle.

"Are you crazy—" The S.S. Prince tore him away from the body and pushed him back into the Embassy garden. Only there—when Uhle heard the splash of water, as if a heavy object had been thrown into the Seine—did he become conscious again. He stared at the Prince and shouted:

"Murderer!"

"Not so much noise!" The Prince threw a cloth over his head, and he was pummeled back into the little deerhouse. One of the sentries picked up the brandy bottle, which had fallen over during the struggle with Uhle, and asked:

"Shall we get him another?"

"No," grinned the Hohenzollern, "*he* won't need any more brandy. Not he! He has pure rage in his veins now!"

CHAPTER FIFTEEN   MEANWHILE, THE ROARING OF THE MILITARISTS SEEMED TO HAVE REACHED THE STAGE OF DESSERT, FOR champagne corks were popping.

Meissner came breathlessly galloping through a bed of salvias. When he saw Field Marshal Mackensen, who was walking under the shadow of the trees with Generals von Blaskowitz and List on their way back from their visit to the Kaiser in the furnace room, he stopped and waved excitedly:

"Field Marshal! The coffee's being served! The coffee's being served!"

"Come, come!" The old hussar slapped the Nazi official on the shoulder. "A little civilian courage!"

"Oh! I can't help feeling suspicious! . . . The way the person in question has been sitting there in his chair of state, ever since the banquet began—just watching us all! Quite unlike his usual self—he hasn't said a word! He hasn't eaten anything. Just keeps fiddling with that dead ballet girl's little sandal. And I had to lay out her flowered dress on the empty chair beside him! Oh, Your Excellency! do you suppose he knows what we are up to? And is going to have Himmler arrest us all?"

"Come, come, man! But who's that playing the violin so beautifully?"

"That unbelievable Bolshevik Schleich assembled an unbelievable gang of gypsies from Montmartre, and now the whole unbelievable rag-tag and bobtail are dancing around like mad in red shirts. And General Jünger is chasing moths away from the candles with one of the gypsy-girls' striped shawls—"

"Indeed? Well, then let's get back inside to his 'Fourth Estate!' Ha-ha!" He marched bow-leggedly to the Embassy and reconnoitered into the dining room through the rhododendron bushes. "Meissner, who's that sitting next to Keitel? Is that the Crown Prince?"

"Who? No, it's Prince August Wilhelm."

"The devil!" Mackensen twirled his white hussar's mustache. "To the attack, fellow monarchists!" He made water into a rose bush.

CHAPTER SIXTEEN AMID THE GENERAL HUBBUB OF DRINKING, THE RETURN OF THE FIELD MARSHAL AND HIS TWO GENERALS was unnoticed. All eyes were centered on Schleich. Temporarily restored, by a sound sleep, from the trying experiences of the workers' demonstration in front of Notre Dame, and egged on by von Ribbentrop, he was now performing an ancient Georgian sword-dance which he had learned in his youth with Stalin in their native Tiflis. A knife between his teeth, his knees bent, he flung out first one leg, then the other, keeping time to the frenzied clapping of the gypsies. The dancer Tchechova, in high spirits because that very afternoon the Gestapo had done away with a dangerous competitor for the favor of her 'beloved Führer', was screeching Russian songs in accompaniment. And so loudly that the Red Singer, in spite of his orchestra-conquering baritone, was no match for her. Every time he roared out 'For the Cossack chieftain, well he knew!' she raised her champagne glass to Hitler and whinnied like a mare in heat:

> Into the saddle, Beloved! Mount and away!
> The land of the Finns is too misty and white—

But her "Adi" was not even listening. Was it perhaps his discontent because that explosive force of his, with which he had often magnetized millions, had failed him before the dead dancer? For even now, when the Asiatic Silenus reached the climax of his dance, hurling his limbs about with such fury that Frau Göring rose from her chair and, wrapping her pompous, milk-white ermine cloak around her, ambled off like a pregnant polar bear—even now, the Supreme Reich Führer did not budge. Nor did he join in the uproarious laughter of the whole table when the Russian, catching the toe of one boot in the film star's cascades of tulle, tumbled over backwards, and collided with the footmen who were carrying in trays of liqueurs.

As they helped him to his feet, pudgy Air Marshal Göring noticed that on one of his hairy paws the Russian was wearing a ruby of such exceptional bigness that it coruscated in his eyes as something at least four times as valuable as the red stone from Nadia's ring which the Chief of the Murder Division had tucked into the napkin of his consort Emmy. The fat flyer, with his hydrocephalic, carnivorous face, growled ungraciously at his neighbor, Major Buch, who was wearing a bandage over his head and a brand-new general's uniform. Then he rose and with his marshal's baton tickled the Russian, who was being painfully helped to his feet by the major-domo: "Come, Schleichowsky, where did you ever manage to bag that colossal ruby? Is it the fashion for Communists to wear such sunbursts on their Marxist paws? I have never seen such a whopper of a ruby in the rue de la Paix!"

"You do me too much honor!" Obviously embarrassed, Schleich grinned, hiding his hand in his pocket.

"Damn it! Russopofsky! What a magnificent red carbuncle! He surely didn't fish that out of the pale blue Neva? Schleichowsky!"

A belch from the depths of that spongy paunch hissed through his teeth. "Looks to me like the seal-ring of your murdered Czar?"

"Plague and bombers!" Irritated by the pointed irony, Schleich mopped his fungoid bald head.

"Come on! Hop to it!" Göring tickled him harder. "Let's see it! It's certain our Führer has never seen such a ring even among Maria Theresa's crown jewels in Vienna. Not even the All-holiest Pope has such a juggernaut in his fisherman's ring! Looks as if the blood of your three-and-a-half million massacred bourgeois, petrified by the Terror, were concentrated in that stone! Hop to it!" He tickled his ribs again. "Let's see it!"

"The idea! Plague and Moscow! . . . I'm one of the guests of honor here!" Smoothing out the wrinkles in his red velvet jacket, he made a deep bow to the Führer, murmuring:

"Vnisokoprevoskhoditelstov . . ."

As Hitler shrugged with annoyance, the stout interpreter, Dr. Schmidt, explained:

"That's Russian. It means: 'Your exalted Excellency!' "

Ribbentrop waved his fork at the silent Führer:

"That's Schleich! The Russian I was telling you about—"

"Herr Schleich," Dr. Schmidt whispered hurriedly, "is descended from the famous rebel, Stenkya Razin, whose torch set fire to many a nobleman's impregnable retreat along the banks of the Volga."

"Bitt' schön, please keep your seat." The Führer eyed Schleich strangely. Abruptly he brought his fist down on the table between the glasses. "There's one thing I want to tell you! Not one of you has plumbed the depths of pain and suffering! There are explosions ahead . . . And I am going to make the sedentary bottoms of humanity galvanize to the goosestep! The whole thing's perfectly insane! Absolutely senseless! But now let us speak for a moment about our neighbor Russia"—he bowed to Schleich. "I've heard that Your Excellency took an active part in the shooting of the Czar of all the Russias?"

"Plague and Siberia . . ." Schleich coughed violently, raised his glass of brandy, and sniffed at it.

"Bitt' schön . . ." The Führer drummed nervously with his finger-nails on the Iron Cross under his breast pocket. "You're an Asiatic! And yet you speak German so fluently? . . . My interpreter was telling me upstairs that you and your Communist Stalin both took an active part in it together? That is a very important matter to me! The fact is, in spite of my fondness for the worthy Russian people, I have not the slightest intention of immortalizing your Communist Stalin! . . .

336

And since—as Himmler was just telling me—you personally shot down the All-highest Czar, I am in hopes that, by way of the grand tour over some most distinguished corpses, we can, in a new German-Russian future, become friends. Prost! . . . Bitt' schön—now then, first —according to Himmler at least—you led your Czar down into the cellar—?"

"No! Plague and the Volga! First—the four daughters—"

"Of course they screamed with fear? Bitt' schön? . . ."

"Not at all. They went down the stairs, pale and silent—"

"And then you fired?" The query assailed him from all sides.

"I think so . . ."

"Bitt' schön—and then came the Czar?"

"No. First the Czarina . . . When she saw the Princesses Olga and Tatyana lying there dead—she screamed—"

"She screamed, did she? Bitt' schön—Ribbentrop, did you hear that?"

"Yes!" Schleich sipped his brandy. "And then she clasped the Czarevitch's feet. But—"

"But—?"

"Ah!" With a deep groan the Russian held out his glass for the major-domo to refill.

"Come—was it as bad as that? Bitt' schön—?"

"Herr Reich Führer . . . those blood-stained dresses! . . . Plague and murder! Their beautiful breasts! . . . Tatyana had such full breasts!"

"Breasts?" Hess was apparently revolted.

"Well—and when did you finally get around to the Almightiest Czar?"

"When?" Setting his glass down on the silver tray, Schleich stared through the clouds of tobacco smoke into the candleflames. "The world will never find that out—"

"Never?" Hitler's laugh was short and shrill. "Not even when I arrive in Moscow?"

"It was gruesome, Herr Reich Führer! Plague and nightmares! Gruesome . . ."

"You think there's anything gruesome I don't know about? . . . Himmler-r-r!"

"My Führer!" The Chief of the Gestapo leaped to his feet and took off his glasses.

"Heinrich, what is the most gruesome thing you ever experienced?"

"My Führer"—he polished his glasses on his sleeve and put them on again—"I've never experienced anything particularly gruesome . . ."

"Is that so?" Hitler grinned at the dumbfounded generals. "Hear, hear! So says my Supreme Chief of Police! . . . Heinrich!" He drank to him in lemonade. "Just sit down again, and go right on peeling your orange . . . It appears, however, that His Excellency here *has* experienced something gruesome . . . But Comrade Schleich, you were going to tell us some more about the blood-stained dresses—"

"Plague and dresses! Well—finally all eleven of them were dead . . ."

"Why only eleven?" Himmler asked, and pushed a fragrant orange section into his mouth.

"Why, gentlemen!" Schleich counted on his fingers: "First, the four princesses—"

"Come, come!" Göring drained the champagne from his golden goblet. "You've told us that already."

"Plague and Romanov! . . . Princess Maria was the fourth . . . As I was saying, the four beautiful girls were pale and silent as they came down into the cellar and—"

"He keeps saying the same thing!" Göring whispered across a bowl of bonbons to Hitler, and then, behind his hand: "You know, the swine has syphilis . . ."

"First—they got everything all wet—and then they were dead!"

"Just one question!" Hitler rose slightly out of his silken chair of state. "How did you go about shooting them?"

"We used our army revolvers, Herr Reich Führer. How else should we? The Almightiest Czar wanted to kneel. But one of my colleagues yanked him up off the stone floor, yelling: 'Hands at your side! Chest out! 'Ten-shun!' And then Comrade Beloborodov slugged him in the face with his fist. And then he lay there—"

"And then he lay there? Who? Czar Nicholas? Ha-ha-ha!" Hitler leaned back in his chair and laughed till his ears turned red. "What? First he had to stand at attention! . . . Himmler! Did you hear that?"

"Quite clearly, my Führer!" The Gestapo Chief bit into a banana. "First he had to stand at attention, hands at his sides."

"Well—bitt' schön! . . . And then Beloborodov slugged him in the kisser! . . . Well, isn't that gruesome?"

"What's gruesome about it, my Führer?"

Abruptly Hitler stood up, thrust both hands in his trouser pockets, and began snickering:

". . . First—'ten-shun! Then—one in the kisser! . . . Czar Nicky! ha-ha-ha! . . . First—'ten-shun! Then—one in the kisser! . . ." He

338

threw himself back into his chair. "First—'ten-shun! Then—one in the kisser!"

"Plague and Satan!" yelled Schleich. "Will you please stop laughing!"

But his protest only incited the whole table to still greater salvos of laughter.

"Adolf!" Göring had unbuttoned the lower buttons of his tunic, "And now this Bolsheviko is obsessed with the idea that Czar Nicholas is always after him—trying to get his ring back . . ."

"What?" Hitler grinned at the Russian. "Well—if you believe the dead can come back again, why do you go killing the living off so grandiosely in the first place? Ha-ha! If afterwards you begin to think they can come back!"

Suddenly his face darkened. He rapped on his glass. The laughter ceased instantly. Some of the generals, laying their cigars down, sat up straight, expecting a speech. Instead, their Supreme War Lord pointed to the door.

"What is it?" Picking up his marshal's baton from the table, Göring was all ears. The others too twisted their necks.

Slowly a tapestried door, flush with the wall, opened. Hitler's astrologer, his white robe embroidered all over with the signs of the zodiac, appeared. Meissner got up in a flurry, and, politely bowing to one lady after another, indicated that the assembled beauties should now leave the gentlemen to themselves.

The wives of the Nazi chieftains rose, clicked their evening slippers together, stretched out their bare arms, and obeyed without a murmur. In a glitter of precious stones they took their departure, leaving a cloud of Parisian perfumes to be devoured by tobacco smoke. Then the gypsies were sent out too.

CHAPTER SEVENTEEN A S SOON AS SCHELLBAUM HAD CLOSED THE DOORS, THE STAR-GAZER APPROACHED THE REICH FÜHRER weaving circles around him with a white wand. Bending to Hitler's ear he muttered for half a minute—apparently saying something so astounding that the Chancellor, at first incredulous, finally put his hands over his eyes with a shudder, as if before something unimaginable.

Meissner, hidden by the center-piece, had turned pale. He exchanged alarmed glances with Field Marshal Mackensen. Generals von List and Blaskowitz also looked at each other covertly. Could it be that the monarchist conspiracy had been uncovered? There ensued a general, surreptitious observation of each other among all the members of the abruptly silenced officers' clique. For every one of them was up to something. . . .

After the face-powdered astrologer had at last straightened up, he answered the anxiously questioning glances of those present with such portentous winking and shaking of his head, that none of them dared to ask him anything. Only Hitler beckoned him back to his ear.

"You idiotic disciple of the Jew Nostradamus—bitt' schön, *Who* is here?"

"Shhh!" . . . the other murmured, and moved the huge silver candelabra so that they both were hidden from the company. "He! . . . from the Crossing of the Meuse—1914 . . . Pioneer X, from your company."

"And where has he turned up?"

"In Paris . . ."

"Are you insane? He's dead. Dead. And if you ever come to me with any such astrological nonsense again, all the animals of your zodiac should devour you . . ."

Noiselessly, as he had come, the star-reader disappeared.

The faithful Keitel squinted at his master. Still feeling under his marshal's tunic the smart of the blows he had received in the library, he wanted at all costs to avoid a renewed outburst of rage on the part of his unpredictable Supreme Commander. Sensing the dangerous thoughts that were hatching in the long silence, he broke it by loudly clearing his throat, and then asked:

"Damn it, what's happened to the conversation? A propos, whose turn was it to tell us about the finest moment in his life?"

"Göring!" Ribbentrop blew the ash from the tip of his cigar. "What's become of him?"

"He went out with Herr Schleich," Schellbaum reported.

"The devil!" The Marshal of Hussars winked at Meissner. "If the Air Marshal has gone, why, let the Reich Foreign Minister perform! We are all ears!"

"All ears? Superb!" Ribbentrop puffed some smoke clouds at the ceiling. Pushing aside another of the candelabras so as to have an unobstructed view of the Reich Führer, who was still sitting as though in a trance, he began with evident pleasure at the opportunity to proclaim is experience: "Eh bien, awhile back we were talking about the actual content of truth in the various religions and Colonel von Einem asked me Pilate's old question, 'What is Truth?' . . . Gentlemen, I forwent my soup, but I ate my pâté de foie gras, and by the time we got to the roast it was perfectly clear: the question no longer presents any problem to a National Socialist. Messieurs, in 1937, at my first audience in Buckingham Palace, when to the great dismay of the English Court I greeted the young King George VI with outstretched arm and 'Heil Hitler'—*that* was the truth. There was neither the shadow of a doubt nor a lie about that gesture. And incontestably the gentlemen on the Thames understood it! Yes, through that gesture, National Socialism probably first became something tangible to those democrats."

"Bravo!" General Jünger held a moth to a candle and, with obvious relish, burnt off its antennae.

"Eh bien!" Ribbentrop continued. "One afternoon, as I was driving back along the highway from Starnberg to Munich in a pouring rain, a man I'd never seen before stepped right out in front of me. Yes!" He cracked a few almonds from the little silver dish before his plate. "And he stood there waving his arms, and finally I put on the brakes and stopped . . . 'Can you give me a lift? Got to make a speech in the Bräuhauskeller. I'm sopping wet!' . . . 'Come along! In you get!' . . . I took him along with me in my little car. For a fact, he talked for hours in the Bräuhauskeller, through the smoke, to hundreds of Munich citizens. I was thinking: 'What kind of stuff is this' . . . But suddenly I clapped a hand to my brow and dashed into the street. I whizzed across Munich, and ended up at my wine-dealer's, an old business acquaintance of mine. As usual, he started to babble on about the blessings of democracy. I stared at his long hooked nose until his black eyes began to blink nervously at me. And then I asked him: 'Eh bien, Herr Wolf! And what about the Treaty of Versailles?' He smirked, and was just going to offer me a glass of wine, as he usually did when we talked business. At that I picked up the very best bottle on the table and I banged that Jew over the head . . ."

"Bravissimo!" Meissner, squirming with anxiety, burst into applause.

"Then I went back to the Bräuhauskeller. My man was still talking. When he finally came to the end, I went up to him and said: 'When you got into my car,' said I, 'who was I then—a wretched little drummer, traveling for the Henkel champagne firm. And who am I now?'" He jumped up from his chair. "My Führer! That meeting with you!—that was the finest moment of my otherwise humdrum existence!"

He picked up his glass. "Colonel von Einem, you wanted to know what truth is? Eh bien! There! At the head of our table—behind those candles—there sits the Truth! And there is no other! Gentlemen—Adolf Hitler!" With the exception of Prince August Wilhelm, the whole company clanked and clashed to their feet and—like a gang of conspirators who once again feel sure of themselves—holding their champagne glasses level with the second-highest button of their tunics, they chorused:

"Sieg Heil! Sieg Heil!"

Not until the third "Sieg Heil!" did Hitler open his eyes again. Then still yawning nervously, he blinked his way back into reality. Suddenly he seized a bottle of champagne from the table and tossed it over the candelabra to his Foreign Minister. Catching it lightly, Ribbentrop arched his back in a reverent bow, with professional hands, uncorked the bottle without letting it pop. Putting it to his lips, he drained it without setting it down. The generals jiggled in their chairs, gloating. General Jünger even got up and enthusiastically supported the Foreign Minister's head. White-faced, Ribbentrop let the empty bottle drop from his hands to the floor and, swaying slightly, supported by footmen, made his exit amid salvos of applause.

"My Führer!" Field Marshal Mackensen purred out of his tomcat face. "As a young lieutenant, I remember once, in the presence of Bismarck, the Queen of England, the Czar, and other luminaries, I drained a hussar's boot, filled with champagne to the brim. And then leaped on my thoroughbred and jumped three card tables, without so much as wobbling in the saddle . . ."

"Do it now!" Hitler had regained all his mobility. "Bring in a horse—someone! First you lose World War No. 1, and then you lie low as if nothing had happened! Here!" Pulling off one of his boots he threw it to a waiter. "Fill it up with champagne! Damn it—since then Saturn and Jupiter have been in conjunction three times in Pisces . . . Exactly as in the year 7—Colonel von Einem—the year 7 before the birth of your Jesus Christ!—bitt' schön!—who, of course, died especially to save you!" He barked with hysterical rage: "Get going! Where's my boot? Fill it up! But, damn it, what are you doing here at this table? Herr Mackensen! Didn't I bury you? Or was that old Hindenburg? I certainly walked along behind your coffin! Put some more champagne in it! I—in my fifties!—I'll survive all of you! Come on now—hand that Death's-head Hussar my boot! Drink it down!"

"My Führer!" The Field Marshal cleared his throat. "I'll soon be as old as Methuselah! So if you want to kill me—and walk behind my coffin . . . I'm at your disposal! Come here with that!" he snarled at

liveried footmen behind him. "Canaille! Have you filled it full? It
ells of the Führer principle!" He sniffed, and the whole table
ghed. "If any of you think a Prussian field marshal hasn't got a bet-
 stomach than a Reich Foreign Minister!—then the Devil take the
ole fatherland! Pour some more in! Canaille! Is it full yet? The
an boot doesn't hold! Look at that! The champagne's running out
 the seams and cracks! Mein Herr!" He handed the boot over the
delabra. "It's not my fault that your Führer's boot has a hole in it!"
'A hole? You moth-eaten hussar! Through that hole I'll—!"
'General Jünger!" Keitel hurried to stave off an outburst. "It's Jün-
's turn now!"
'Bravo!" cried the Hussar. "Yes! Let that young puppy tell his tale.
neral Jünger! Hop to it!"
'No!" Hitler thundered at the Field Marshal and—raging—tore
 dancer's golden sandal to shreds. Then, through the clouds of to-
:co smoke, he studied their Prussian faces one by one. Suddenly, his
·s remained fixed on the sole civilian among all the officers. With
ish of unexpected favor for the man whom Göbbels had once called
e erstwhile favorite of the Jew Republic," he called: "Well, poet,
at was the finest moment in your democratic life?"
'My highly respected Führer!" Dr. Gerhardus rose. "But first I
uld like to ask my highly honorable neighbor at table, General Jodl,
be so kind as to fill my glass! A thousand thanks!—Herr Hitler, I
 a man of the people—"
'And so am I!" The Führer tossed him a flower. "Yes!" He stuck
 his chin at his Reichswehr officers. "A man of the people! Like
·self!"
'Most honorable Führer!" Gerhardus played with the dahlia as if
vere a little girl. One by one he plucked off the petals. "Ravishing
bsolutely ravishing! . . . It so happened that when the pious Mufti
fiz, at eighty years of age, laid by his priestly robes to devote him-
 finally and exclusively to the religion of lovely flowers and girls
. Because their fluttering skirts . . . But their curls too . . . Any-
w! . . . for what is this whole so-called present world to us? Per-
tly ravishing! Eminent Führer! This wonderfully blue flower from
ur supremely noble Reich Führer hand— Yes, this is indeed the
est moment of my life!"
Glasses tinkled against each other, and the smoke-hoarse laughter of
 Reichswehr generals drowned the rest of what he was saying. But
 soon had their attention again.
'My highly respected representatives of the armed forces . . . Par-

343

don, I have never been armed! But, if I may say so, I was neverthele
a force! Although not an armed force!"

"Bravo! Long live our poet!"

"My father was a simple innkeeper! And when I see you, my hono
able Excellencies, carousing here around this oval table— Yes, pardo
Then I can't help asking myself, what will be the state of things whe
everything is all eaten up? How many empty bottles? What were tl
takings? What the expenses? Have the revels been worthwhile? A
we certain that none of the highly respected guests here present w
carry away a case of mushroom poisoning or fish poisoning? Has tl
Almighty Spirit blessed the toasts of the various gala speakers? In
word: Were the Muses—and all the other gods of this so-called worl
whatever their names—satisfied with my menu?"

"Bravo! Splendid! Bravo!"

"Most noble Herr Reich Führer, I am an old man! And I humbl
beg you to grant me the distinguished favor of permitting me to st
outside now and look at the stars!" Amid a general hallooing, he move
with dignity, then with some haste, out of the room.

"General Jünger!" Meissner shifted back and forth on his chair
if he were sitting on hot coals. "Now it is General Jünger's turn."

"Well, why not? I know some anecdotes, just like anybody else . .
But if the Führer doesn't mind, I should just like to take off my Pour
Mérite and unhook my collar. Ever since the cheese, that black-an
white ribbon has been scratching my throat . . . All right! Here v
go! I am certainly no poet!"—he gargled on a mouthful of wine—"I
a soldier! And, as is well known even among the termites, the soldi
constitutes a fantastic exception—ha-ha! Well, I begin: It was in tl
year of grace 1916, in Champagne. Opposite me there was a compar
of daredevil Scottish Highlanders— Yes!" He lit his cigar at a candl
"And the Captain! Yes, gentlemen! He was a model! A beautiful, han
some, healthy, round-limbed, angelically blond boy with violet-bl
eyes. I watched him for weeks through the periscope. There was on
about seven yards between us. The Scotchman was so beautiful, Fie
Marshal, that if he hadn't had a downy little mustache he could ha
been taken for a Ziegfeld girl in a British uniform."

"Do you hear that, Adolf?" Rudolf Hess, who had been sitting siler
edged his chair nearer, smiling sweetly. "Do you hear that?"

"His thighs were like Doric columns. Gentlemen, my attitude t
ward women is neither overintense, nor animal—but rather, probler
atic! For instance, during my many hours of lying wounded in bed
hospitals, I could never bear to have any nurses except nuns, who

344

severe costume concealed the female form. For even if our poet Gœthe maintains: 'The Eternal Feminine draws us upward and on . . .'"

"Stuff!" Rudolf Hess spooned his lemon sherbet. "The Eternal Feminine pulls us downward and under!"

Through the mingled cries of protest and shouts of agreement, Jünger said:

"Although my opinion is not as drastic as that of our Deputy Führer, I must confess that this Scottish Captain of Highlanders had me going." He took a glass of Munich beer from the silver tray presented at his elbow. "Yes, indeed! And in the long monotonous hours in the trenches I gradually became possessed with something like a longing to exchange a good, strong hand-clasp with the slender, blond-haired angel of a Scot . . . Your Excellencies—I finally succeeded!"

"You finally succeeded?" Pushing his glass aside, Hess breathed heavily.

"Yes! By means of all kinds of sign language we finally came to an understanding that we would not shoot at each other. And at a given moment we all climbed out of our trenches: German soldiers joyously clambering across the refuse of corpses in no-man's land to meet the enemy Highlanders. And while my men were swapping uniform buttons, chocolate, and cigarettes with the Tommies—ha-ha!—like a love-sick boy I shyly shook hands with my Captain of Highlanders. His violet-blue eyes looked at me from under his gray trench helmet, no less lovingly than my rather mouse-gray eyes held his. Too bad! The various artillery staffs had spotted this harmless bit of fun, and things began to happen. From all sides the heavy guns let loose at us! It was a speedy parting. Like a weasel I squirmed the few yards back to my trench, jumped down, dashed for the machine gun and, before my blond boy had got back to the English trenches—tak-tak-tak!—I had potted him! He fell over backwards and disappeared behind the barbed wire—"

"The devil!" Mackensen slapped his knee. "The devil you say!"

"And then?" His face reddening, the listening Supreme War Lord gnawed at the dancer's sandal, and squinted up at him: "And then?"

"And then?" General Jünger held his long black cigar between two fingers. "My longing began to be a positive obsession! Come what might—I began to have the fixed idea that I must conquer the section of trench where the fallen Scotchman would be found. I made the most minute preparations! As far as humanly possible, I was determined to succeed. And—gentlemen—I did succeed! With the expected losses, we took the English trenches. Our bayonets made mince-meat of the Tommies that didn't surrender . . . Late that night, after a long search with my flashlight in the dugouts and among the corpses on the floor of the trench, I finally found my fallen boy. There he lay, half-propped up against the wall, his violet-blue eyes wide open, and alongside him two bottles of whiskey . . . In the pockets of his excellent overcoat I found some excellent cigarettes, some biscuits, a jar of jam and another of marmalade—treats we had long been denied. After settling my company in the new trenches, I set up housekeeping, snug in the dugout, along with my dead angel. With the stub of a candle burning on the little trench table, I sat quietly to gorge on biscuits and orange marmalade, etc. I also drank up the two bottles of whiskey. In the silver light of dawn, I began to feel hot! Holding the incredibly beautiful boy's pale paw, I sat watching the stars fade and —gentlemen—I'm bound to say: that death watch with the Captain of Highlanders in the conquered trench was, without the slightest exaggeration, the finest moment of my life!"

The generals looked at one another uncertainly. Hess's eyes were swimming. He clenched his fists. Hitler stared at General Jünger, who put on his "Pour le Mérite" Order again.

"Yes!" With long swallows he emptied his beer glass, wiped the foam from his upper lip, and said: "Prost! Men! . . . Yes!! to live means—to kill!"

The World War lance-corporal had paled; now he slithered along behind the chairs until he reached General Jünger's. Binding the golden leather lace from the torn sandal around the general's forehead, he knotted it in a chaplet of victory; then, holding him fast by both gold epaulettes, gasped as if shaken by spasms of lust. The deep blue shadows pulsing under his eyes, he murmured as if to himself: "Heil Hitler!"

Jünger jumped to his feet, fingering the chaplet as if it were the highest possible honor, and saluted . . . But then someone knocked on the glass of the garden door. The scars on Meissner's cross-hacked student's face turned purple as he motioned to the major-domo. Schellbaum drew back the heavy brocade curtains and opened the door.

CHAPTER EIGHTEEN

"PRINCE FERDINAND? . . ." THE MURMUR OF VOICES ROSE.

"Officer on Duty of the Bodyguard Watch! I respectfully report: A French army automobile has just driven up to the rear garden gate that leads to the Seine."

"A French army automobile?" Hess looked from one to the other and searched Ribbentrop's face.

"A private rang the night bell. In answer to my personal interrogation, the poilu replied that Marshal Pétain's First Adjutant, Colonel Latour, is waiting in the car with a message to you, my Führer, from his chief."

"Latour?" Hitler too sniffed around. "With a message from Pétain?"

"Don't receive him!" Hess whispered. "This is Ribbentrop's doing —and without asking your permission!"

"And at this hour?" Hitler stood up.

But Prince August Wilhelm, who throughout the banquet had not opened his mouth, stood up too and, bending, retrieved the champagne bottle Ribbentrop had let fall. In one graceful stride he reached his nephew—and brought the bottle down on his head. The young Nazi prince dropped like a stone.

"Damn it!" The house-painter from Braunau turned and stared at the two princes of the blood. "What was that?"

"That?" With complete satisfaction, the prince set the bottle on the table and piped deliriously: "That was the finest moment of my life! And that's exactly what"—his shrill, high tenor flung at Hitler—"that's exactly what's going to happen to anyone who breaks his oath to me —Prince August Wilhelm!" Taken aback at first, his "Master" said nothing, then muttered something unintelligible.

Meanwhile, assisted to his feet by Peter Schellbaum, Prince Ferdinand shook his head dazedly once or twice, then, without a quaver, asked:

"My Führer, what are your orders? What answer shall I give Colonel Latour?"

"Party Comrade August Wilhelm! You'll excuse me for venturing to call your attention to the fact that we are not at present in the 'Arsenal of Democracy' where, it is a well-known fact, every prince hungry for a crown still considers himself useful as a figure on the chessboard of global policy! But if your all-highest cranium is afraid that—without the German Imperial Crown to cover it—it will catch the Hohenzollern catarrh—" With a darting glance, he picked up from the buffet an enormous bowl full of caviar and deftly inverted it on August Wilhelm's head.

Field Marshal Mackensen put on his busby—furious. The enormous, silver death's-head against the fur grinned threateningly at the scene— in which a member of the Ruling House which for five hundred years had kept Europe in fear and trembling, now stood before them, his equine head crawling and dripping with stinking fish-spawn—like a battered blackamoor effigy in a shooting gallery.

Meissner exploded in salvos of hysterical laughter: "Oh-oh-oh! Ha-ha-ha! A-o-ouw! Like a witch doctor! Like a negro! . . ."

"You idiotic chameleon!" Hitler gave him a shove and then glowered at the Reichswehr generals. "Either the whole pack of you are drunk! . . . or—you're not drunk! . . . But, between that 'either' and that 'or' "—the veins of his head swelled—"there stands my Heinrich Himmler as Chief of the Gestapo with loaded rifles!" The last word was an animal scream. Then he ran out the door and slammed it shut behind him.

CHAPTER NINETEEN THUNDERHEADS OF LOWERING RE-SENTMENT HUNG OVER THE TABLE AS THE CHIEF OF THE MURDER DIVISION quietly rose to his feet, adjusted the bandage over his eye, and followed Hitler out. The object of his search was not in the music room. Nor in the conference room—where a solitary Staff Officer sat poring over maps under the bright glare of a small lamp; he was plotting out future battle positions in red and blue pencil. The one-eyed general proceeded cautiously, opening door after door . . . searching on. In the last room —the so-called smoking room—he saw Field Marshal Göring. Buch stepped back behind a curtain.

The Air Marshal was trying, with his marshal's baton, to reach Schleich, who had barricaded himself behind a battery of brandy bottles.

"Herr Göring"—the Russian clapped his hand to his head—"if it were *my* ring— Plague and snowstorms! But it's not mine."

"You dragon!" Göring caught him, while bottles tumbled to the floor. "Then where did you get it?" And he continued to jab at him with his baton, while sweat broke out under his armpits and stained his snow-white uniform.

"Don't suppose, Comrade, that I'm going to let you out of here with that ring. No! My wife has wanted a ruby like that for a long, long time. Stand still, you. What fire!—it shines like the Holy Grail. I can't see rhyme nor reason to a Bolshevik like you wearing a ring like that on his finger." And then he tickled Schleich so hard that the Russian vomited, bespattering Göring's piqué waistcoat. "See here"—the Marshal held his nose—"how would you like to have your name in the English Court Circular, the way Stalin's was recently?"

"Plague and bliss! I feel better. In the crowd there I was having chills and fevers. Too many shocks, Marshal. I've been racing all over Russia in my private car—it used to belong to the Czar's special train. Ah, the steppes of the Volga—plague and Cossacks." Suddenly he started singing, to distract Göring's attention from the ring. But Göring only held him faster.

"You sing like a canary. Is that Leporello's aria? I'll hire you for the State Opera. Wonderful! What other songs do you know?"

> "Czar Nicholas without his furs
> Ran out of the Winter Palace,
> Ran out of the Winter Palace . . ."

"Wonderful! Out of the Winter Palace! What a joke! You can really see him running! Holla!" He whirled round—General Buch had been unable to control a sneeze. "Who's there? Damn it! No one? One gets to feel almost like Nero—before the murder—" He went to the door. When he saw the Chief of the Murder Division standing there, he squinted at him and then his eyes grew as big as eggs. He went back and lay down on a chaise longue. Spread his legs, belched, and sighed:

"My dear Schleichovsky, hand me that brandy bottle, will you? Thank you. Well, before we're murdered, the moon will rise and set many a time. So—where did that gigantic ruby come from? I can't keep my eyes off it—it's enormous . . ."

"My dear Marshal," Schleich became confidential, "parole d'honneur—"

"None of your nonsense! I'm a field marshal and you're a Bolshevik. And a Bolshevik can never be a field marshal. If he does, he isn't a Bolshevik any longer. So don't give me any nonsense about your honor. Otherwise, my instinct will begin to wake up—you red dragon. And Emmy always says that then my eyes get like a cat with a robin in its

349

mouth. Speaking of 'red'"—he ran the point of his sword along Schleich's coronal suture—"when I see red, I get very different impressions. For example—at the opera, when I go to 'Aïda' and the fanfares sound for victory and the king comes out in his red mantle, I always have a heroic feeling. But when I see the red of your ruby, you dragon, the mystic in me comes to the surface. Although ordinarily I'm an absolute realist. So give me that ring—or—"

"Marshal"—Schleich lit a cigar—"it so happens that the Kremlin is right here in my head. And with it, the whole secret!"

"So there's a secret in the Kremlin, is there? My friend, you stink so of vodka that I can hear troika bells! Come on, take that ruby off your finger and give it to me!—I can't understand it at all! If you didn't hack it off the martyred Czar's hand, where can it have come from?"

"Marshal, it came from the subterranean vaults under the Kremlin."

"What? I thought you red swine had pawned all that stuff in New York long ago."

"No! In those vaults there are still ten-thousand-carat diamonds. There's one solitaire—twice as big as this ruby. And fire! you have to wear glasses to look at it, it's so bright. There's another stone as green as a fresh-cut lawn. And another—belonged to Czar Paul too—is orange, like sunset over the Black Sea. And there are yellow stones—like the ones the Living Buddha wears. And stones that are pale red, like a girl's tongue—"

"That would be something! Damned if it wouldn't!"

"—In 1812, when Napoleon went down the subterranean passage in the middle of the Kremlin to the treasure vaults, he said: 'For one such stone, the mastery of the world!' . . ."

"Did he say that? Then why didn't he help himself?"

"Why didn't he? Just then his grenadiers stumbled against some chests—"

"What kind of chests?"

"And out of those chests there came such mysterious music that—"

"Music is always mysterious—you dragon!" Suddenly he rushed at the Russian. "The ring! You dragon, give me the ring!"

But suddenly Schleich gave the Air Marshal such a kick in the belly that nothing more was to be heard except a noise like a rolling barrel.

General Buch grinned. However, he did not help the Reich Marshal but went on trying door after door looking for the Führer. At length, when he came to the pantry next to the kitchen, he found him sitting on a wooden stool at a table covered with cleared-away dishes and half-empty glasses.

CHAPTER TWENTY

IN FRONT OF THE ICE-BOX STOOD SEV-ERAL FOOTMEN, SHOOED AWAY FROM THEIR GOURMANDIZING, THEIR POSES suggesting that for them the last trump had sounded. At a sign from Buch, they goose-stepped away and disappeared.

Hitler was nibbling at a drumstick and, at the same time, abstractedly pouring champagne from one glass to another. On the gold and silver dishes, greasy sauces had congealed. A broken joint of roast goose stuck out of its ornate, fringed paper cuff, stippled with swastikas. With his fingers he clawed a few string beans out of a dish, holding them in front of his nose and snapping at them as if they were spaghetti. Loosening his belt a notch or two he belched, and then with a soiled dishtowel began drying some of the rinsed dishes, piling them on top of each other in orderly fashion.

With his one remaining eye, Buch blinked as if he were seeing a vision. Could the morphine injections have made him delirious? But the voice of his Führer waked him:

"Just look at this!" Hitler fell into the Austrian dialect: "Sakrament! Isn't that a scandal? Here's this sow Willzscheck still using porcelain with the monogram of Kaiser Wilhelm on it, and a crown on top of it! Sakra! What a sow!" He smashed the plate against a faucet, delightedly watching the pieces fly. "Here! Buch, get a towel—and help me!" The Chief of the Murder Division unhooked a towel from the wall, drying the wet plates that Hitler handed him.

The kitchen door opened and the chef, his face, under his tall white cap, red with heat from the stove, gave the Hitler salute.

"My Führer! In the name of the entire kitchen personnel I wish to thank you for the great honor you have done us!"

"Have you a couple of sausages for General Buch? The poor invalid's hungry."

"And what may I offer my Führer?"

"What else have you?"

"Did the mushrooms riced with carrots please the palate of our Supreme Führer?"

"Listen!" He pulled the chef down by the ear: "Have you got any more caviar? The kind from the Black Sea? There's none left in the dining room! What do you say to that, Buch— Ha-ha! Though, of course, I'm only a vegetarian! Ha-ha!"

"My Führer!" The chef ventured tremblingly. "There's an old friend of mine here in the kitchen—an Alsatian—the Swiss beadle of Notre Dame! He carries the halberd. It would be the supreme fulfillment of all his earthly dreams if he were permitted to gaze upon the world-commanding, National Socialist Ruler of the National Socialist World Party!"

"Go on—and don't forget the toast! Be sure it's good and hot!" He extended his arm. "Heil Chef!"

"W-w-w-w-what! My Supremely Beloved Führer!" The chef tumbled to his knees and laying his towering white cap at Hitler's feet, implored: "Please step on it!" When his Führer had graciously complied, he pressed the soiled imprint to his lips. Struggling to his feet again, he set the cap on his head reverently, as if it were a tiara, his face shining. "Most submissive thanks! . . . But there's a Frenchman outside too—an Ancien Combattant! He keeps a small antique shop and, like all the rest of us, he spits on 'Humanité'! My Führer, if only Providence would grant him the opportunity for a single instant to rise above the daily filth of the République Française and gaze into the cosmic sun of the new millennium—"

"Go on, Buch! You take a look at them first!"

The newly appointed general followed the chef.

Hitler remained alone. The information given him by his astrologer made him nervous; he began picking his teeth and murmured:

"Pioneer X? What? That milk-toast face of his . . . from my company?" Suddenly he wiped off some silver knives and then, distractedly, began dissecting parts of the skeleton of a capon. Whenever he cracked one of the small bones he would say: "That is impossible, the fellow is dead. I know it"—and his features resembled those of a medieval torturer.

Suddenly there was a noise . . . Looking up, he saw a hand outside the window drawing something on the pane with a piece of soap.

First a thick horizontal. Then, across it, an even thicker vertical. Flinging open the window, he tried to shout! But the gust of night air gripped his throat so that he choked on a cough. Just as he began to be calm again, he heard a well-known voice coming out of the darkness of the garden:

"Kismet! The horoscopes check. As in the year 7 B.C. Three times Jupiter and Saturn! The time is fulfilled! He is here. He is here."

He shut the window again with a rattle, and sat down, staring into the darkness, not moving a muscle. Then he began boring out the dead eyes in the many fish heads that lay goggling on a platter among

352

scraped bones. Suddenly he started flicking them at the windowpane.

Warily, one after another, Keitel, General Halder, Göbbels, and Ernst Jünger stuck their noses round the corner of a dish rack. They risked one puzzled glance into the pantry; then they withdrew. For their Party Chief in his pantry corner gave them a look of such whole-hearted hate as only one of another class can give the "gentry" when they leave their part of the house to flit for a moment through the kitchen and scullery.

Several minutes passed before General Buch returned from the kitchen.

"Bitt' schön"—Hitler started to his feet. "Oh—it's you—you old murderer! Listen, you Bible scholar! Tell me: Do you believe in any such thing as astrology?"

"My Führer!" Buch grinned. "In the Book of Samuel, it says expressly: 'God hates wizards and soothsayers!' "

"It says that? But did you ever pay ten pfennigs on the street to look at the stars through a long telescope?"

"No! But I've just been looking at a list of the names of the plotters in an international monarchist conspiracy against you!"

"Kismet!" Hitler yawned. But abruptly he clenched his fists. "Don't let them try anything funny with me or—" he broke off.

Xaver Grün, wearing an old-fashioned shiny black frock coat entered the pantry. Behind him came Laroche. Both sidled forward warily, as if the Supreme Chieftain of Nazism were a high-tension wire. Pressing the skirts of their coats down smoothly, they stood looking at the floor, their faces turkey-red.

"Well, fellows—which of you is the halberdier?"

In their embarrassment, the two squirmed against each other as if they were going to do a modern dance. In his excitement the Swiss suddenly emitted a well-modulated trumpet tone. At this, Laroche, his cheeks blue with mortification, dropped his chin still lower on his white shirt front. Their knees were shaking. All at once the halberdier gave the Frenchman a jab in the ribs, jostling him back into the kitchen, and cursing: "Cochon!"

Bending over the sink, Hitler turned on the faucet, washed his face with both hands and dried himself on an apron. Then he slowly and thoughtfully ate up the remains of some compote in a bowl. Abruptly, the tiny red veins in his eyes more inflamed than ever, he clutched a fork!

"Buch, people can think I'm great or not great!—a genius or a blank zero!—a god or a devil! What they think leaves me absolutely cold!

Buch—you'll notice my voice is perfectly normal, just as if I were ordering pretzels and radishes. And notwithstanding you must believe me when I say: Arrest my stupid star-gazer immediately! And then let him eat kitchen soap until he tells you all he really knows about a certain Pioneer X. And then communicate at once with the French police."

"It shall be done!" The General winked from under his bandage, and then asked: "May I smoke?"

"Far as I'm concerned—stink as much as you like! One thing about you: You're no princely specter licking your chops for a crown! Ha-ha! Bitt' schön! One fine day we shall make chromium-plate furniture out of your ribs!"

Profoundly affected, the Chief of the Murder Division kissed his Führer's hand. Then, lighting a cigar, he did his best to anesthetize the pain in his empty socket with smoke.

"And you branded the nipple of my dancer with such a disgusting piece of punk? You lout!" Darting the prongs of the fork in all directions, he pricked the general here and there as if he were trying a roast in the oven.

"You look magnificent in that bandage. It's very becoming to you! You just wait and see! They'll spin all kinds of legends about you in the Party! 'Buch—the One-eyed!' Ha-ha! Like Wotan in his slouch hat! Ta-ti"—he began—"ta-taaa! Ta-ta-taaa! Wagner! Doesn't that sound exactly as if you could hear our flame-throwers and hand grenades exploding in the flanks of the Jewish dragon of Democracy? Verily, verily: To live means to kill! And I always feel exactly like that Count Leo Tolstoy, who wrote in his diary of the Crimean War: 'To tell the truth, it's a rare pleasure to watch people killing each other. Morning and evening, I spend hours sitting in my carriage just watching how they kill each other! It's a really magnificent spectacle, especially at night!' . . ."

"Indeed? Count Leo Tolstoy? Well, well! And I always thought that Russian prophet was a pacifist!"

"He was. But only later. Later! And who knows?" He stroked Buch's hairy hands. "Who knows what we'll be like when we lie by the fireside, toothless lions, beginning to feel the sclerosis in our tails? Yes, yes! At ninety—that's when we become saints, when the grub begins to be thinner and thinner in the food trough! Yes!" His yawn was cyclopean. "Yes, indeed! Those were Tolstoy's words. Old killer! But as long as the 'Ta-ti—ta-ta!' still gives off its fanfare in us—"

"What's the matter?" Buch leaned forward because his chief had ceased speaking and was staring at the window. Had he seen something

354

suspicious outside? All the many little fish eyes that had stuck to the windowpane suddenly shone, ogling iridescently, as the pantry door opened and light entered from the hall.

"It's me!" Ribbentrop came in, smiling behind Hitler's back. "Here I am again! Jochen! Vomited the whole business. Feel tip-top again."

"It's all nonsense—pure nonsense!"

The Führer spat at the fish eyes on the window and cursed.

Ribbentrop pointed to the door. "May I request your presence? Colonel Latour is waiting in the library. And it's most desirable—"

"What?" Hitler whirled round. "Well, let's get on with it! Ta-ti—ta-ta-a-a!—" He snaked along behind Ribbentrop, prodding him at every step with his knees, through the laundry and other rooms, Jochen opening the doors for him. At this moment the Foreign Minister's England-hating brain was possessed with but one idea: A swift military alliance with France in order to bring the despised English to their knees and disrupt the entire British Empire.

The Deputy Führer, on the other hand, determined at all costs to prevent a war against their Aryan cousins on the Thames, had meanwhile made arrangements of his own. While the England-hating Foreign Minister was in the toilet soaking his champagne-hot head in cold water, Hess had closeted the supposed Colonel Latour with Prince Ferdinand in the audience room. He had left his most trusted party friends on guard in front of the door, with orders to use their revolvers in case of necessity. And now, to keep his Führer away until Lord Douglo's arrival, he had adopted an idea of Waldmüller's and made of it a magnificent theatrical trick. So, as Ribbentrop triumphantly opened the sliding doors to the music room, Hess stepped out from behind a Japanese screen, leading a young lady, and conducted her quickly past the waiting Generals Keitel, Halder, and Jünger and straight across the room to his bosom friend Adolf.

CHAPTER TWENTY-ONE GRACEFUL—SHYNESS IN THE SLIGHT CANT OF HER SHOULDERS—NADIA STOOD THERE. HER CLOSE-FITTING white velvet dress, fairly well restored and buttoned up to the neck, shone in the candlelight even whiter than the tuberoses in her black hair. It was all too evident, from one look at her vague expression, that

Waldmüller, after preventing Egath from taking her with him on his flight, had been busy with his drugs, preparing the poor girl for this moment.

Hitler started. His eyes turned suspiciously from one party comrade to another. From the dining room could be heard the drunken singing of a few officers still sitting at the table: "A crown there lies in the Rhine so green—"

Abetz nudged Ribbentrop. Whereupon the Foreign Minister begged his Supreme Chief 'most obediently' to have the goodness to continue on his way to the library to interview Colonel Latour. But Hess blocked the way, smiled at Ribbentrop, and taking a candle from the piano, set it on the floor in front of Nadia, and made a sign to Waldmüller. The piano-mover disappeared through the curtains to the sun porch, where the chimpanzee Felix was ready in his cage for what Hess had in mind.

"Adolf!" Hess indicated Nadia. "The Princess had expressed the greatest yearning to be introduced to you . . ."

"Pardon!" Ribbentrop irritably elbowed him aside. "It happens that Colonel Latour is waiting, on a mission from Marshal Pétain which can no longer be postponed."

Hitler, at first undecided, finally started to follow the Reich Foreign Minister. But just as he reached the door, Nadia called out in such a softly penetrating voice, "Hello—" that he turned back again. Pointing to a moth fluttering drunkenly around the electric bulb on the wall near where he stood, she said:

"White with orange-red wings? That's an aurora moth!"

"My Führer!" Ribbentrop raged at the delay. "Mademoiselle seems to know all about lepidoptera—"

"Oh yes!"

But then, as if her memory had failed, her face lost all expression.

Hess quickly handed her a demitasse of black coffee, and grinned: "The Princess comes from the land of coffee."

Leaning against the mantelpiece, Hitler watched Nadia. "Why doesn't somebody offer the Princess a chair?"

At once the various officers hastened forward, pushing chairs.

"Merci!" Sitting down, Nadia watched the aurora moth. "Last week my cousin in Shanghai sent me some butterflies as big as plovers! One was blue, with two thin silver stripes on each wing. But look! There's a male aurora—two!—three! Shut the window! Once I saw 127 male auroras come to a female within a couple of hours!"

The expression in his eyes more and more uncanny, Hitler gaped at her. To please him, Ribbentrop went over to Nadia and, with exaggerated gallantry, placed a damask cushion under her feet.

"Merci! Merci!—For instance, in your garden, the ephemerides are swarming under the elms now! The female sits quite still on a grass blade. But suddenly she begins to soar—higher and higher. The males with their turbanlike eyes catch sight of her from below and—swish!— they're after her, higher and higher, up into the topmost layer of light . . ."

"The topmost layer of light?" Hitler pricked up his ears. "Bitt' schön, where's that to be found?"

Field Marshal Keitel's spurs rattled. He caught General Halder's eye. The Reichswehr Chief of the General Staff approached the Supreme War Lord in precise goose-step.

"My Führer!" he rumbled, adjusting his glasses, a malicious smile on his tired features: "When I was a boy I collected insects too. For instance, the neat little flying louse that lives on the bat. But over there in the map room, we have sketched out the line of march of our armies against the English-speaking world. Now, if it's agreeable to you, we'd like you to worm out of this Colonel Latour—" Just then Nadia stood up, stretching her lithe body in a gesture of profound yearning—so he made a sign to Göbbels, who at once limped over to the actress. But the Reich Führer, like a theater-goer wanting to hear what is said in an important scene, impatiently waved him away. "Sh-h-h-h-h-h!"

Slowly lifting her arms above her head, Nadia turned round and round, dancing in exquisite steps, at first in a narrow orbit, but then swinging out in increasing arcs upon the mirrorlike polished parquet. As if it had been an insult, Hitler snatched away a little rococo stool in her path. To please his master, Ribbentrop tiptoed to the piano, touched the keys a few times, and then fell to playing. To his clumsy rhythms, Nadia improvised such enchantingly buoyant movements that Hitler, completely carried away, suddenly dashed forward and picked her up, revolving with her in a spin that took her feet off the ground. His long wet hands linked under her breasts, he propelled her in ever more frenzied revolutions, like a white cartwheel, until her legs, swinging out horizontally, struck against a table. Her cry of pain recalling him to his senses, he threw her onto the nearest sofa. While she sat moaning and rubbing her ankles, he stood alone in the center of the music room, stupid and sweating.

The pale, drawn, ghostly face of his Chief of the General Staff, assumed an even more mocking expression. Fanning himself with his handkerchief, the Führer walked over to him:

"Come, my good Halder. Surprised? Didn't know your Supreme

War Lord was a great dancer too? Yet—I remember in Braunau, when I was twelve, I couldn't manage to get Elschen Gerstengruber even to turn her head round when I was on the dance floor! Ha-ha!" And he burst into a laugh so vulgar that even such a mercenary as Ernst Jünger set down his beer glass in surprise.

"Yes, my Field Marshals! It's only since this so-called humanity trembles before me that these females come running from all points of the compass!" He made eyes at Nadia, who was still rubbing her ankles. "Yes! All of a sudden these brown and blonde and gray and red and black curly-heads are fluttering around my feet! No, Princess —it's not 127 males that swarm around one female! On the contrary— 127 females swarm around one male!" He puffed out his chest. "Am I right, my dear Keitel? The minute you open a door nowadays, there stands another Miss Issippi and throws herself at you! . . ."

"Hoping, of course"—Göbbels rubbed his hands—"to fill at least three volumes of her memoirs with a single inspired thought of Adolf Hitler's!"

"Yes! You honorable sons of the Prussian Drillbook! Today—at fifty —I—the son of a narrow-minded Austrian customs official—know this: that only the man who breaks into their bedrooms with the blood of victory on his fist—he's the only man that weak, two-legged sex will turn around to look at—" Throwing himself into a chair he let his legs hang over the arm.

CHAPTER TWENTY-TWO **D**URING THIS TIRADE BY THE SU-PREME REICH FÜHRER, GENERAL HALDER HAD BEEN POLISHING HIS GLASSES. He now inclined his head, shaved smooth except for a small patch of gray hair, and beamed at Keitel, as much as to say: "It ought to be much easier in our coming wars to find suitable pastimes at head-quarters for this sexual Austrian cock-of-the-walk, than it was to keep Wilhelm II busy! And all we had to do with him was to let him gorge himself on tasty tidbits and then, after dinner, turn on his imitation war-lord look, seat him between Hindenburg and Ludendorff, and let the press of the world bombard him with their cameras . . ."

The various chieftains of the Reichswehr withdrew giggling. Facing about at the door to the map room, heels clicking, spurs jingling, each made a smart bow to his 'War Lord,' and in turn vanished.

General Jünger was the only one who remained. With ears schooled at the front to the humor of the trenches, he had listened to Hitler's boasts of sexual prowess. Benignly splashing some brandy into a tumbler, Jünger sniffed it like a connoisseur and drank it down. In a sudden access of jollity, he jumped up from his seat and sauntered, cigar plugging his mouth like a bowsprit, over to where Nadia was nursing her shins. And just as in wartime, after shooting up a village, he would flirt with any surviving female, just to kill time between battles, so he sat down now beside Nadia, blowing smoke rings like lassos around her.

Instantly Hitler, 'Protector of the Defenseless,' was on his feet.

"You cigar-slobberer!" He tore the Havana out of his mouth and threw it on the carpet. "You slobberer!" The general's face was one of infantile imbecility. Getting up, he ground out the cigar with his heel and left the room. Ribbentrop took advantage of the moment to snap his notebook loudly shut and mention Latour's name again. But his Chancellor did not react. Instead, he suddenly picked up the candle from the floor, wandered around the room with it, finally bringing up in front of one of the tall French windows. Half-opening one of the blinds, he pressed his nose against the pane. Something flickered out there under the tree. Or was it only from the play of light from his candle? No! There, beyond the flower bed, he saw it again: a peculiar light signal. Quickly shutting the blind, he faced round. Hess was coming across the room, humming in high humor.

"Come, Adolf!" He tried to take his arm, but the Führer pushed him away.

"Send Himmler to me at once!"

"Here!" The commander of the Gestapo popped out from behind a curtain, removing his glasses . . .

"Where's Göring?" Himmler shrugged his shoulders. "General Buch?" But the Murder Chief, feeling the effects of morphine, sat dozing in a chair. "Himmler, do you realize that your Führer is actually in Paris!"

"At your orders!"

"Right in the middle of the Jewish-Democratic-Monarchist world conspiracy! Himmler! . . . A deadly enemy of mine has turned up in Paris."

"I have to report—"

"What's up?" Hitler clutched his forelock.

"Colonel Egath has—deserted."

"Who? What?" He seized his Police Chief by the throat. "Deserted? Where's Göring? Why did the field marshals leave? . . . My Colonel Egath—deserted?" He let go of Himmler.

"My Führer!" Himmler glared uncertainly at Nadia. "With your permission!" He slid across the floor to her as if over ice. "Sow! What are you doing here?"

The actress arched her back defensively in the corner of the sofa like a cat. Her red nails clawed at the damask. She tossed back her hair, and looked from one to the other, her long lashes trembling:

"Please! Please! You must excuse me! It's all because for once I departed from my principle: always to tell every gentleman who falls in love with me, right at the beginning, so that he knows where he stands: 'Monsieur, I'm a Jewess!' "

"A Jewess!" Hitler swallowed, and then stammered: "Who's responsible for this?"

Ribbentrop and Abetz ducked behind their notebooks. Göbbels tried to make himself smaller than he was. For, since that night in Bad Kreuznach in July of '34, before the flight to Munich to murder Röhm, he had not seen the Führer with such a wild look.

While he brooded more and more ominously, Nadia lit a cigarette, blew the little opium clouds up to the chandelier, and held the miniature torch, reddened by her lips, theatrically—as if she were on the stage, waiting for a cue. But as the cue did not come, she began—just to keep the scene going—to talk in the direction of the various Nazis, who were already sweating with terror:

"As a matter of fact, when my Duke d'Aguillon heard that the great poet of the Psalms, King David, was my forefather, he put a ruby on my finger! Alas, that fat man there on the chair stole it from me!" She pointed to Buch and blew a few more rings into the silence, pregnant with evil.

Suddenly she shuddered. "Ah! Do let me go! I'm tired. Upstairs, where you did my hair, there's a bed! Of course, you know, I'm a girl who can't go to sleep without love. Mais oui," she called to Hitler drowsily, "without love, I'm nothing. So let's go! In my apartment I have a bed that's twice as big. Monsieur! Heh! Please be nice! I promise you before we lie down, I'll light one of my yellow wax candles! Suddenly I'll say: 'Sh-h-h-h! Do you hear something? I heard something.' You'll lift your head above the white taffeta spread and growl: 'Shut up! Don't babble! That's the rain at the window!' 'Nonsense!' I'll say, 'That's not the rain!' 'What is it then?' you'll ask. 'Those are tears,' I'll say, 'lots of tears! Listen! They're tapping at the window, and they

360

want to get into your tear-glands! . . . A-a-a-dulf! Don't go to sleep. Look! Your tear glands are already swelling with them! Watch out! Soon you won't be able to see anything or hear anything—your whole face is nothing but a single tear gland! Wait! I'll get a pair of tweezers from the dressing table. Keep still! Now I'm going to puncture it!'

"There you are! See the tears flow out! See how they run! Oh, how they run! At first you think perhaps the water was left running in the bathroom. So I jump into my slippers and take a peek! But no!—the faucet is turned off! What do you say to that? Nevertheless, there's a whole flood around the bed . . . A-a-adulf! Look—the water's rising higher and higher! Soon it'll be over the night table! You just sit there in bed, goggling. Inch by inch, it rises. You cry out: 'Turn off the water! It's already up to my breast!' But it keeps on rising! It's already gurgling round your throat! You try to swim, but the salt from the tears chokes you! You have to cough! And the more you cough, the more tears you swallow! You get so weighted down that you sink! Only the top of your head sticks up out of the flood! You try to cry out—but at that instant a tear drops down from Heaven—so hot that you scream! For it burns! You can't stand the pain any more! All at once there's a sob from above: 'That is your little Braunau mother's tear!' And with that your skull cracks in two! . . ."

With a loud, staccato snore, General Buch came out of his morphine stupor, adjusted his bandage, and smacked his lips.

"My Fü'! . . . What are you deliberating?"

"What?" Hitler started. "Oh! I'm just deliberating—the best way to pull out the ten toes"—suddenly he roared as if haranguing a crowd in the Berlin Sportpalast—"of that ghetto sow there—!" Before he could finish, Nadia had sprung screaming from the sofa across the smoking table and had him by the throat, hanging on with both hands, biting and scratching like a wildcat. Only by twisting her arms and legs was Waldmüller finally able to tear her away.

She fell to the floor. Together with General Buch, the piano-mover dragged her through the curtain onto the sun porch where they stuffed her into the chimpanzee Felix's cage.

His face the color of curds, Ribbentrop bobbed up from behind the piano, found a napkin, and wiped the blood from Hitler's face.

"We've cause to be grateful, dearest Führer, that your jugular was protected by your collar . . ."

"What a stinking sow!" Returning, General Buch brushed the powder off his Führer's brown uniform. Then he pushed the curtains aside so that they could see into the sun porch. Oriental hanging lamps of many colors illuminated it voluptuously. At the top of the cage a chimpanzee bigger than a man hung, startled out of his sleep, panting.

CHAPTER TWENTY-THREE "GHETTO SOW—" HITLER CRANED HIS NECK AND STARED THROUGH THE BARS OF THE CAGE. BUT then his face turned such a sickly green that Buch and Göbbels helped him away and laid him on a garden sofa. Hess, able to breathe again because the anger of his bosom friend had not lighted upon himself, brought iced chocolate and candies. His still bleeding master drank a few swallows, and then stared glassily around, white with rage.

On Göbbel's orders, the exotic plants usually housed in the sun porch —which was a glassed enclosure six yards long by four wide—had been carried over into the conservatory where they now enshrined the coffin of the Cultural Leader from Heidelberg. In consequence the sun porch looked rather bare. At the front of the cage Waldmüller had attached an electric bulb in such a position that the shadow of the iron bars now fell criss-cross on walls, ceiling, and floor. The resulting effect was that of a prison-cell into which Hitler, with his assistants, Rudolf Hess, Göbbels, and General Buch, together with the torturer Waldmüller, had just walked—ready to be regaled once more with the torments of a defenseless human being.

Bowing clumsily, the piano-mover in evening clothes approached. His left eye wide open, he drew his boorish face into an expression of servility:

"My Führer—the ape is named Felix. He's three years old. Count Willzscheck—"

"Willzscheck? Where's that ambassador of mine?"

The Propaganda Minister limped hurriedly off to find him.

"And tomorrow morning, our lusty Felix is going to give what they call a 'testicular transfer.'"

"Just between ourselves," Hess whispered into his Führer's ear, "his fantastic jungle potency is to be applied tomorrow, in line with Voronoff's latest researches, to the sexual apparatus of that Bolshevik swine Schleich, worn out from whoring with females!"

"My Fü—'!" Göbbels came back at top speed. "Party Comrade Willzscheck is just briefing your head pilot for the return trip to Munich. However, he'll be delighted, he says, if, for your entertainment, before his emasculation Felix can have his plai-s-i-i-i-r with a female of his own blood group!"

"Well, then—get on with it!" Hitler impatiently worked his toes in his boots, and looked at Nadia, who, her eyes slowly opening, had heard what was said. Beside her on the sanded floor of the cage was a pile of eggshells, half-chewed carrots, and lumps of sugar.

Rudolf Hess, uncertain whether or not his bosom friend might not yet find out who had been guilty of this contretemps with the Jewess, timidly offered him bonbons, and began deliberately to chatter. He wanted, too, to thwart Ribbentrop's intrigue with Colonel Latour.

"You know, Adolf, the Jewish race owes its origin to just such a 'love-scene!'"

"Romeo and Jew-liet!" Göbbels thrust forward his sausage face lecherously.

Hess nodded to the piano-mover, who shaded the bulb so as to concentrate its light on the cage. With a pair of fire tongs, Waldmüller angled through the iron bars, tweaking the chimpanzee's hide. The ape grunted with satisfaction, twitched the skin of his forehead, snapped the blue lids of his eyes shut, and turned his shaggy behind to the company.

"Tchk! Tchk!" Hitler, his chin smeared with candy, bombarded the monkey with coffee bonbons, excitedly reiterating "Tchk! Tchk! Tchk!" But Felix did not budge.

Von Ribbentrop and Abetz sidled in through the curtains, both trying to entice their Chancellor out of the sun porch by the stressed syllables: "Col-onel La-tour!" Hess, however, well aware that his Adolf would never pass up the opportunity to witness the promised piquancies of the scene in the cage, tossed his head at Ribbentrop with a triumphant smile. Then he sat down, comfortably crossed his legs, and, wagging his long index finger, rambled on:

"What I was just about to say, Adula, is the absolute truth. The Aryan racial scholar, Franz von Vendrin, after years of painstaking research up among the prehistoric mountain caves in Sweden, has indisputably established on the basis of ancient runes and cave drawings, that over forty thousand years ago a pair of such chimpanzees, brought from Africa along with other booty by our Germanic forefathers, were the begetters of the Jewish race . . ."

"What?" Hitler drummed with his fingers. "Rudolf! Rudi—"

"Absolutely. And while we Germans happened to be engaged somewhere in honorable battle, the sensual monsters managed to escape from their cage and attacked and violated two of our blonde women."

"Attacked and violated?" Hitler shuffled with his feet. "Where was that?"

"In Mecklenburg-Strelitz, my Füh'! And the bastards thus engendered—those were the very first of the Jewish species . . ."

"Really?!" Hitler was triumphant. "Bitt' schön—now do you understand, my Party Chiefs, why I'm often so proud of myself?" Suddenly he thundered:

"Damn it! Why doesn't that chimpanzee get busy!"

"Dear God, dear God!" Nadia folded her hands behind the bars and her eyes grew big as a child's—"Thou wilt deliver me? Let me go free? Thou wilt?—O dear, good God? Thou!"

"Sow!" General Buch smashed a flowerpot at the cage. "Shut up!"

"Damn it! Can't you fools get that chimpanzee down from his perch? I can't wait all night to see him go for a ghetto sow!"

The piano-mover tweaked the animal harder. Disturbed in his sleep, Felix snatched at the tongs and shook them with such violence that Waldmüller let go and flew back against the wall. The tongs crashed into Felix's pan of water, bespattering Nadia.

"Tchk! Tchk!" Hitler persisted. "The ape doesn't give a hang about this female!"

"Perhaps," Hess giggled, "perhaps, like his ancestors of forty thousand years ago, he only goes for blonde hair!" Salvos of laughter.

"Beasts!" Nadia rose to her feet ecstatically. "Oh! Could I but hear you—you storms around the mountains of Palestine!"

"Ghetto sow!" Hitler jumped up and, seizing the tongs from Waldmüller's hand, frantically jabbed the actress through the iron bars. Her outcries roused the chimpanzee. His forehead twitching, he climbed down, shaking the cage. The Reich Führer retired. Felix, using his yard-long arms like crutches, swung over to the girl and then squatted down, tentatively scratching about with one black, wrinkled paw among the eggshells.

"Now! Now!" The party chiefs nudged one another. "Watch him! He'll go for her now!"

Clinging to the bars, Nadia stared into the hairy creature's eyes, as though hoping to hypnotize him into submission. Through the salacious laughter of the audience, Rudolf Hess whispered:

"Watch, watch, Adi! You know that beast is hyperpotent! . . . Now! Now!"

"Yes, my Party Comrades—now do you understand why your Germanic Führer felt obliged to wage a final war on these black lechers?"

"Poke him again!" screeched Göbbels. "Waldmüller! Give him a good poke! Po-o-o-oke him!"

"And yet"—Hess rose from his basket chair for a better view—"in the year 45,000 B.C. we Germans, in the famous 'Paradise Battle of Meseritz, drove back the ape-people as far as Libya!"

"Shut up, Rudi! Look! Look! What's he doing now?"

"He's pee-ing on her, my Füh'!" Hess was hoarse with delight. "And just as our forefathers utterly defeated the half-apes at Meseritz, so in our era will you defeat the descendants of those shaggy jungle-hoppers!—these democrats!—"

The chimpanzee encircled Nadia's hips with his enormous arm. Her cries were lost in the hullaballoo of shouts and laughter.

"Adula-a-a-a-!" The saliva ran down Hess's chin. "And exactly as the Pharaohs, by their laws against the Jews—to prevent the adulteration and decadence of the noble Egyptian race—hunted the Hebrews away from the Nile—"

"Exactly so"—Hitler raced back to the cage—"will I disinfect the whole world of your kind!—you repulsive ghetto sow!"

"God! God!" Nadia's hands trembled impotently. "But Thou wilt drown them again? Drown them, dear, dear God? In the Red Sea of Blood, in the Sea of Blood! The murderers!"

"What's the whore jabbering about?" Göbbels too limped to the cage, hurriedly put away his notebook, in which he had been making notes for his paper "Der Angriff" while Hess was talking, and jabbed Nadia in the back with a pair of compasses. "Any two-mark whore in the Friedrichstrasse is better than a Jew sow like that! Waldmüller, tear off some of that dress so that the ape can see her flesh! Flesh!"

The piano-mover sneaked up from behind and, before the girl could move, tore the white satin open across her breast. His curiosity roused, the chimpanzee looked on. Rising to his feet, he came nearer . . .

"No! God! Oh, no!" Her voice half stifled, Nadia stared at the tremendous animal. Suddenly, Felix grasped her left leg, twisting it this way and that as if he were playing with a doll. Then he sniffed at her feet.

"Bite her!" Hitler urged the beast on. "Bite her toes! Bite her! Bite her!"

"No!" cried Nadia, terrified. "Dear God! Help me! help me! Help—"

"Shut up!" Göbbels squeaked. "This is too perfect!"

"What's he doing?" Hitler babbled. "What's he up to?"

"He's just about ready!" The Propaganda Minister excitedly rubbed

365

his shriveled ear. "Jab her, Waldmüller! Push that cheap whore nearer to him!"

But when the piano-mover approached the actress, the chimpanzee showed his teeth. Snorting, he hammered the floor with the flat of his hand, whirled round, and gave such a howl that Nadia nearly fainted. Then, plunging at the bars, he shook them so violently that the spectators fled behind their chairs. Howling, the ape whirled round again like lightning, his brow ruffled in heavy folds. Clutching bar after bar, he edged along the cage. His black fingers grasped Nadia between the legs. But then he hesitated, listening, his head swaying from right to left . . . then suddenly, screaming with terror, he climbed back to his perch. His skull half-hidden in his heavy pelt, he blinked down at them curiously.

CHAPTER TWENTY-FOUR

THERE WAS A SOUND OF RUNNING FEET IN THE GARDEN. SOMEONE OPENED THE DOOR TO THE SUN PORCH, and Himmler appeared. Without looking around the room, he went straight to Hitler:

"My Führer, Colonel Egath is here! Two Elite Guards found him in the rue des Pyramides behind the Tuileries Gardens. They're bringing him along."

Foaming at the interruption, Hitler cursed: "Get the hell out of here! Out of my way! I can't see!—Where is he now?"

"Outside, my Führer."

"Tchk! Tchk! Stick him again; get him down off his perch!"

Colonel Egath was led in bare-headed, out of breath from running, his face pearled with perspiration.

"Egath?" Nadia whimpered, and fell into a dead faint, prostrate among the refuse in the bottom of the cage.

"My Füh'!" Himmler removed his glasses. "Colonel Egath has the floor!"

"Well, Egathchen," Hitler joked at his Gestapo staff officer, "you don't seem to be able to hold my Foreign Minister's champagne! How many bottles did you drink, swine? . . . Out of the way! I'll have a word with you later! Get away from in front of that cage!" Suddenly he yelled: "Göbbels! What's the matter?—Can't you get that monkey down?"

366

Colonel Egath turned around and saw Nadia. He looked from the cage to Hitler and from Hitler to the cage. Then in four thundering strides, he was at the cage door. But as he was about to push back the bolt, Waldmüller's boxer's jaw threatened him. Using an old police trick, he landed his bony fist on Waldmüller's windpipe. The piano-mover rocked on his feet. But before Egath could open the cage, he was again seized and held by his S.S. captors.

"Come, Egathchen!" Hitler walked slowly up to him. "So the Negus of Abyssinia up there on his perch has given you an attack of the tropical fits? Hess, make the Colonel comfortable in this basket chair! Himmlerchen, come, come—take off those handcuffs! What kind of horseplay is this? Where will we get to if you take to handcuffing my Gestapo officers? Ha-ha! Göbbels, bring him a glass of water! General Buch, offer your colleague a cigarette! There we are! And now, my honorable, loyal, zealous, and dutiful Party Comrade Egath, I, your Supreme Chief, am this once prepared to forget the stupidity of which you in your drunkenness have been guilty! Yes—alcohol is the very devil. It makes creatures you'd barely recognize out of good old-time National Socialists! That's why, year in and year out, I drink only fruit juice! The old Germans, however, of whom our friend Hess was talking a while ago, were unfortunately mostly to be found in the condition you're in now, Egathchen!" He tickled Egath under the nose. "Police chiefs who don't know how to behave! S.S. officers who dishonor the uniform!" He stretched his fingers until they cracked. "Such deserters!" In a sudden access of rage he tore the silver epaulettes from Egath's shoulders. "Such—such—" And he spat on the Colonel's boots. "You dirty dog! You tried to let this ghetto sow get away out of the back garden gate? You imbecile! Tell me, who on this continent is the supreme criminal judge? And who is a certain Herr Egath to presume, on his own initiative—?"

Colonel Egath had at first leaned his head back, exhausted. But now he sat up straight, his square-boned, hard-jawed features closer and closer to Hitler's.

"If I'm drunk, Party Comrade—then I'm drunk! And if alcohol is the very devil, then it would be rather advisable for you to keep your distance from me. For it's very likely that a drunken devil might say something that might possibly sound strange to the ears of such a sober Reich Chancellor . . . Therefore, in the name of the Devil, I ask you, mein Herr, to wipe your spittle off my boots!"

"Apparently," Hitler whinnied, "the concept of subordination has curdled in this fellow's brainpan! Party Comrades"—he looked about, his eyes flashing—"if none of you top-men knows what to do or say, then your Supreme Reich Führer *once again* finds it necessary—as he has times without number!—to make his own decisions, solo! Blackguard!" He slapped Egath's face. There was a muttering of voices which was only interrupted because the chimpanzee, his curiosity aroused, shuffled over to the bars.

"Adolf Hitler!" Egath's voice was low. "Are you not ashamed?"

Hitler put his hands in his pockets and sat down on a swing, whistling to himself. Then he called out:

"Back to your seats, gentlemen! Snap out of it, Egathchen—you, too! Take a front seat! And now I want to see what a black, super-Jew from Africa can really do at his ruttish best! Ha-ha!"

Waldmüller turned the electric light so that it dazzled the ape on his perch overhead. Egath jumped up from his chair.

"Sit down!" roared Hitler. "Sit down!"

"With your permission, I—"

"Sit down! Or would you rather be stood up against the wall in Lichterfeld?"

"Gentlemen—"

"Shut your mouth!"

"My esteemed Führer of the National Socialist Party! I stand here before you without epaulettes! When, in 1918, after four years of war, I returned as a dragoon captain to the fatherland, on the corner of Friedrichstrasse, a Bolshevik tore off my epaulettes, with such insults as 'blackguard,' 'son of a bitch,' and—"

"If you don't keep still, you drunken fool, I'll have you arrested!"

"I, a front-line officer—"

"Silence, you Bolshevik you!"

"And so, my epaulettes gone, I tried to hide myself in the darkness of the trees in the Tiergarten. Wiping the Bolshevik's spittle off my ear, I walked on and on through the trees. Without a goal. Simply on and on. Coming to an arc-light, I stood still, burning as if with fever. In front of me was a well-tended bed of blue hydrangeas, in the middle of which stood the white marble base of the statue of Queen Louise. I said: 'O Queen! Has this Bolshevik no shame, so to attack a soldier who, for four long years, did his duty as best he could, under fire for his fatherland, and who today, beaten, defeated, and covered with wounds, returns to his native land? Yes, has this Bolshevik no shame at all?'" Abruptly, he put his hands over his face, and trembled so, that Rudolf Hess lowered his eyes and Göbbels, painfully moved, offered his Führer chocolates.

368

"Well"—Hitler stuffed his mouth full of sweets—"has the swine finished talking? He's simply frightening the ape with his wretched drivel."

"And then I said"—Egath uncovered his face—"O Queen! By the memory of my blessed father, the devout pastor of St. John's Church in Cassel, I vow to you—you who, in 1806, in the deepest misfortune of our fatherland, showed the courage of a man, when you went to the tyrant Napoleon at Tilsit—I vow that from this time forth, I will dedicate my whole strength, however small, to him, whoever he may be, who shall at last liberate us from such noisome riff-raff and once again restore justice and decency even to such poor defeated soldiers as I!' Herr Führer"—his eyes shone as he looked at Hitler—"when at a meeting in 1923 I first heard your promises, I enrolled as a party member in the 'Movement'—

"Yes, comrades," he looked at two generals whose heads had appeared around the curtain near the music room. "And today, twenty years later, here I stand again—without epaulettes!" His voice faltered. Nadia had moved in the cage. Oh, that white face of terror! As if multiplied in a thousand mirrors, it looked at him from everywhere—out of cattlecars, crammed with prisoners . . . out of cellars and dungeons . . . out of the twisted features of the hanged, dangling from a lamp-post . . .

"Herr Reich Chancellor"—he clutched his own throat—"if I tried to count up all those martyred and murdered in my command-district alone up to the time of your entry into Prague—" But he got no further. His Führer had grasped his wrist, and for fully half a minute held him fast without being able to utter a word. Then, peering over his nose right and left, Hitler let go and sat down again.

Hess and Göbbels rushed up:

"Let the swine pay the penalty outside—"

"Fools! I want to know how far the Jewish infection has gone in this party member. Bitt' schön, Colonel—" he motioned to Egath. "And why especially up to the time of my entry into Prague?"

"Why? Because there, for the first time, I experienced how you broke your own solemn promises! Yes, the very oaths you had sworn only just before to a free and peaceful nation! An innocent people—"

"Innocent?" Hitler whistled through his teeth. "Innocent? Bitt' schön! Come, has this swine forgotten what those sw-i-i-ine!—those Czech thugs did to German-speaking people!—what murders—what humiliation—!" His voice became so hideous that the chimpanzee embraced his bare perch with both arms as if for protection. His excre-

369

ment fell and Hitler held his nose.

"Pfui! But, bitt' schön, Egathle, go right on with your speech."

"Your standards were hoisted over the Hradschin Castle. You—Herr Reich Chancellor—sat at the long table in Masaryk's library, with all your governors and gauleiters. And all the time nothing but fresh orders for blood-baths were drawn up and signed! Five thousand people! And another ordered the shooting of a whole corps of students who loved their fatherland . . ."

"Go on! . . . *Go on!*"

"Then at last, you stood up from the table and got as far as the brocade window curtains, where you recoiled. And it was not until I assured you that the Nepomuk Church was closed and all Prague was full of S.S. troops with rifles ready, with motorized infantry, and hundreds of armored cars!—not until then did you dare appear at the window. I stood behind you, watching your face. Your eyes wandered unsteadily . . . After one swift glance down over the river, the houses, roofs, towers, and hills of Prague, over which snow lay heavy as a shroud, you hid behind the blinds, with your Neuraths, Seyss-Inquarts, Bock-und-Pollachs, your Prince Philipp of Hesse— afraid!—afraid a bullet might be fired out of any one of the countless windows down below! And then your face, Herr Chancellor and Führer of the Third Reich, took on such a revolting expression of shabby, ordinary cowardice—"

"Have you all been listening? Do you hear what Egathchen is saying?"

"And then you ordered me: 'Go on! Down into the courtyard! And see to it that no Czech swine get near my car!' So I went ahead of you down the castle steps into the courtyard, conducting you through the tall iron gates to your armored car. You sat down beside the chauffeur and drove off through the long rows of bayonets presented by your Reichswehr troops . . . I watched you go—and ever since that instant—"

"Well—what, you drunken Prussian? Ever since that instant—what? Hm? You Prussian swine!"

"Ever since that instant, in my small sphere of command, I have given every creature that was handed down to me for punishment— I've given him a false passport so that he could escape out of this Third Reich, whose Supreme Führer has never kept one promise to the spirit of the front—"

"That's enough, my boy. Time's up—." He clutched the breast of Egath's tunic, but the Gestapo officer knocked his hand down.

"And—this evening—here at the Embassy—I reached my limit! And that's why I opened the gate and ran as fast as my legs would take me—in the opposite direction—along the quais—across the Place de la Concorde—and down the rue de Rivoli . . . Yes! For freedom beckoned me! Freedom called—and waved! . . . And I ran and ran . . . But my boots were already too full of blood!—too heavy with all the blood I have shed in your service, Herr Führer! And so I could no longer even grasp the hand of Freedom! That fellow there"—he pointed to Hess's brand-new adjutant standing at the door to the garden—"that Hänsel!—that Hänsel, to whom I've never said an angry word from the time he was a first-year scout until he got his shining new galloons—he had faster and younger legs than I! And so he caught me! . . . Herr Reich Chancellor!"—He raised his fingers to his throbbing face in a salute—"I am at your disposal!"

Hitler unbuckled his belt and slashed time after time with it across Colonel Egath's head and face and shoulders, until the blood flowed and the terrified chimpanzee fled to the roof of his cage.

"You drunken Prussian! . . . I'll drive the devil of alcohol out of you! . . . You drunken swi-i-i-ine! . . . There! . . . Now take this sodden drunk out into the garden! . . . Let him throw up! . . . Turn the hose on him! Himmler! . . . And when he's sober again, bring him back here! . . . I'll examine him myself!"

Without having once flinched or cringed from the blows, his shoulders high and straight, swaying slightly, Colonel Egath walked to the glass door between Himmler and Hänsel. Suddenly he about-faced, thrust his way back to the cage, pressed his face against the bars, and rumbled hoarsely: "Fräulein—!"

With a touching rush of hope, Nadia stood up, listening breathlessly as if she hoped to learn the way out from his twitching lips. The corner of Hess's mouth curled.

"Well, our Police Colonel has certainly fallen for this garlic blossom!" Göbbels massaged his crumpled ear.

"How he looks at her! A lyric poem."

But Egath could find no more words. Suddenly he took something from his pocket and quickly pushed it through the bars to the Jewess.

"An apple?" Hess rushed at him. "An apple? Doesn't this gentleman of the Gestapo know that, according to the Nuremberg Laws, it's forbidden to give fruit to such carrion?" He pulled Egath away and out of the sun porch into the darkness. Göbbels slammed the glass doors shut so that the panes rattled. And then they all broke into roars of laughter. General Buch even forgot his burned-out eye and, delighted at Egath's discomfiture, hitched at his bandage, scratching his head.

"What a drunken Prussian!" Hitler buckled on his belt again, threw himself in the hammock and, cheerfully swinging his feet, set it going, at the same time blaring out his "Siegfried" motif:

"Ta-ti—ta-ta-a-a—ta-ta-taaaa!"

"Ta-ti—ta-taaaa." The Chief of the Murder Division and Göbbels blared along with him. Hess handed the chocolates around.

CHAPTER TWENTY-FIVE N̲ADIA HAD KNELT DOWN NEAR THE FOOD TROUGH AS IF IN A DREAM. LIKE A FAIRY PRINCESS, SHE HELD the fruit in her hands . . . Her eyes the blue of anemones, her dress in rags, she held her arm outstretched, with an imploring gesture in the direction in which Egath's steps receded faintly on the gravel . . .

"Waldmüller!" Hess snarled. "Will you kindly chase that Wandering Jew down from the top of the cage! The poor beast is absolutely petrified!"

"My Führer!" Göbbels rolled up his shirt-sleeve, scratching the scabby skin of his underarm. "We've just seen in a nutshell what happens when a good solid goy is infected with this Jewish syphilis! But, to understand Colonel Egath's impertinence you don't want to say 'Cherchez la femme!' but, rather, 'Cherchez la juive!' . . . Find the Jewess! Wherever in the world you find anybody raving on with all the democratic insolence of an American President—there's always a Jewess behind it! Well—now let's see this cheap Levantine whore perform some of her erotic tricks! The tricks that disintegrate the Aryan! These painted ghetto whores are responsible for inventing the erotic art of tickling! You've seen how it can drive an Egath to giggling insanity! Let's see how she does it!"

"Shut your mouth, Joseph! Shhh! Look! He's coming down from his perch again . . . This shaggy Adam takes his time. Bet he's after the apple—"

"Wonderful—simply wonderful!"

"Go to it, Eve!" Hitler spat the pit of a brandied cherry at Nadia. "Go on! Show us how you brought about the fall of man—ha-ha!"

"Female!" Hess too was spitting cherry stones into the cage. "Go ahead and show us some original sin!"

"She's biting it!" Göbbels burst out, astonished. "There she goes, just crunching away as if she were at home in the kitchen!"

"Stop!" Hess bombarded her.

But she chewed and crunched at the juicy apple, tears rolling down her cheeks. Softly she chanted the name "Egath," then ceased and murmured, "I cannot but think of thee—thou great King Solomon! A thousand princes waited upon thee! Every day thou didst eat a fatted calf! Queens washed thy feet! And the most exquisite and gayly colored song-birds in the world sang in concert for thee!"

"What's the whore drooling about?"

"Yet, would I rather wash thy feet and sing before thee—Egath! Egath!"

Outside in the garden there could be heard lashes across a man's back. The ape was startled.

"Waldmüller!" Hess screeched, soaking wet under the armpits. "Show the beast some flesh! Show him her flesh!"

Waldmüller tore off his tail coat and sidled up to the cage. "Shut your eyes, Sarah!" Dragging Nadia against the bars by the hair, he pulled her head so far back that her breast arched. The chimpanzee licked his snout. Holding onto the bars with his right hand, he fumbled about in his pelt with the left. Rising to his full jungle height, he waddled nearer and all at once began to peel the white velvet off Nadia's body like the skin of a banana.

Hitler and his gang rose out of their basket chairs, and—cautiously, so as not to disturb the animal—slunk forward expectantly. But suddenly a loud cry of horror escaped from their throats. For, as the chimpanzee bared Nadia's body, they saw her skin covered with clusters of boils the size of peas. Felix clamped his muzzle shut and crept away.

"Adol!" Hess pushed his beloved back. "The carrion has the plague!" And then they all fled, terrified, into the farthest corner, where they stood, a tottering group. Not until Göbbels, slinking along the wall, escaped into the music room moaning, "Professor Sauerbruch! Doctor Sauerbruch!"—did Hitler come to himself. But immediately afterward, as if he had been bitten by a mad dog, he flew out of the sun porch, Hess at his heels, with choked cries of "Fresh Air! Air! Air!" . . . Waldmüller too, who had pushed Nadia back among the eggshells and carrots, fled.

The chimpanzee clambered up into the farthest corner of the cage and hid his head, as if a poisonous snake were in ambush below. Nadia covered herself with her torn dress and cowered—as if somewhere out of the world.

In the music room there was much running to and fro. Chief Staff Physician Dr. Kohler and his assistants, accompanied by Hitler's Press Chief, entered—all dressed in white smocks, wearing masks. Increasing numbers of footmen, maids, and cooks came running through the garden and pressed their noses against the panes of the sun porch.

As soon as Dr. Kohler had examined Nadia, he pulled off his rubber gloves, smiling.

"The plague? Who ever made such a diagnosis?" He looked sarcastically at his colleagues.

Among the liveried servants in the garden Dr. Gerhardus now pressed his imposing profile against the window. "How perfectly ravishing!" He stared into the sun porch so hard that his forehead wrinkled like corrugated iron. "How perfectly ravishing! . . ."

The little Jewess had risen to her feet. Strangely, wonderfully—she paced across the filth in the cage as if it were a rug in Solomon's palace, and the frightened chimpanzee above her a dark guardian of her beauty!

"Egath! . . ." she breathed, over and over, and putting her fingers in her curls, like delicate orchids, she declaimed:

> "Yet shall the evil pass away,
> And good will triumph on that day—

Egath! Egath! . . . Open the cage!" Nadia implored all the faces outside the window. "I implore you! Let me out!" She shook at the iron bars.

The poet of the misery of the weavers winked covertly at the fat actor. Would he help her? But just then Minister Göbbels—clad in germproof clothes—limped onto the scene. When he saw Nadia standing there, like a wild lily in the passion of her longing, the lines in his grimacing face became as deep as sword cuts with his impotent hate. The orders he gave to Waldmüller were so revolting that even the piano-mover could not react immediately.

The white-headed Nobel-Prize winner Gerhardus turned anxiously and obsequiously to the propaganda inventor. Raising his thick finger with its curved nail like a baton, he demanded:

"My highly respectable audience! What belongs to us today?"

"Germany belongs to us today!"

"And tomorrow?"

"The whole world!" came the chorus of concupiscence.

Meanwhile, the piano-mover had ventured back into the sun porch.

374

All those whom the desire to gloat over misery had brought running —footmen, officers, poets, cooks, actors, princes, and chambermaids—glowed with evil delight.

A rout of maggots and ghosts.

Waldmüller tore the girl's quivering body out of the cage . . .

CHAPTER TWENTY-SIX

IN THE MEANTIME HITLER HAD FLED FAR DOWN THE GARDEN AND INTO THE TEA HOUSE—AN OVAL PAVILION hung with yellow tapestries. In the flickering light of a few candles hastily lit by Hess, he lay on a brocade-covered chaise longue between gilded rococo mirrors—groaning up at the ceiling, which was painted with Japanese landscapes, like a man doomed to death.

Hess, kneeling beside him, felt his pulse. Twigs scratched at the tall, many-paned, open window. The wind sighed in the tree tops. In front of one of the candles, a finger-long praying mantis crawled on its long, thin, grass-green legs. Its pale-ivory insect head eyed the whimpering chief of the Aryan race. Abruptly, spreading its wings, it whirred its frail orange-tinted body, and was gone in the darkness.

"Where is Sauerbruch? The doctors!" The Führer's voice rattled, and at every instant he inspected another portion of his skin.

"Calm yourself, Adol'! Sauerbruch has been sent for—"

"Calm myself? But I can feel it already! It itches! There!" He pointed to his arm. "Isn't that vein turning black? That ghetto sow has infected me!"

The bald-headed little doctor in the white smock, who had just examined Nadia, entered, carrying a medicine kit as big as a suitcase.

"Dr. Kohler, Colonel in the Medical Corps!"

"Charlatan!" shouted Hitler. "Where's Sauerbruch?"

"Flown back to Berlin—"

"What? Without my permission? Just flies off like a fly? He'd better not try that again!" Suddenly he gasped: "Come over here. How long am I supposed to wait on your exalted pleasure? Going to stand there till I'm a blackened cadaver? You miserable intern, you! I've got the plague! Can't you see my veins are getting blacker and blacker? Eh? When are you going to open up that poison kit of yours?"

Dr. Kohler was amazed. Setting his medicine chest on the green malachite table, he took out some medicaments. Addled with excitement, Hess kept asking if it wouldn't perhaps be better to telephone the Institut Pasteur at once. His hypodermic ready, Dr. Kohler, on his oath as an expert, assured both the Supreme Reich Führer and his Deputy that the boils on the actress's body had as little to do with the plague as a sore throat with cancer! They were solely and simply the nervous reaction to nausea.

"Nausea?" Hitler hitched himself up in the cushions. "What can nauseate a ghetto sow?"

But Dr. Kohler did not reveal what Nadia had confided to him in the cage: She had been so revolted because a drop of Hitler's blood had touched her tongue.

"Henry IV," he answered soothingly, "used to have such a rash every time he heard a hen cackling. Catherine of Medici's skin became scabrous if she smelt a rose. Sir Isaac Newton, it is said, suffered a skin eruption every time he saw shellfish. And my own little daughter gets pimples on her hands from looking at a tree louse."

"And the whole human race"—Hitler shouted him down—"as long as this plague of the Jews—"

"May I," the Doctor interrupted, "most respectfully—request you—"

"Why are you rolling up my sleeve?"

"Simply as a precaution, I'd like to give you an injection which will make you absolutely immune."

"Immune?—"

"If you please—" The doctor bent over, but when Hitler saw the long needle, he jumped to his feet.

"What? Sauerbruch gone back to Berlin—just when I need him? Get away with your needle! That's an operation! Get away! Leave me alone!"

"Perhaps the Deputy Führer will try it first?"

"As far as I'm concerned"—Hess rolled his sleeve up to the red band with the swastika—"you can go ahead—though my Douglo always says, 'Pure blood can withstand any bacillus'."

"Is that true?"

"Will you please sit down and rest your arm here . . . That's right! And now clench your fist . . . Thank you!"

"Is that all?"

Eyes narrowed, Hitler had watched closely to see if Hess had experienced any pain. Now he ordered: "Come here! But if it hurts, I'll give you an antiquackery injection in your magnificent staff-physician's brain with the same needle. Ouch! You scoundrel! Why don't you apply a tourniquet first? Ouch!"

"Thank you, my Führer!"

"You devil! It's bleeding! Hess! The fiend jabbed me in the vein! It's bleeding! Are you crazy? It's bleeding!" He turned white. "Rudolf! Rudolf!"

Dr. Kohler placed a small wad of cotton on the almost invisible puncture, folding Hitler's forearm back against his upper arm. "It won't bleed any more now."

"You swine! . . . Yes, I wanted to study medicine once, but the dissecting room always reminded me too unpleasantly of the Treaty of Versailles! The way the attendants used to cart the corpses in, as unconcerned as you please, and, with their ham sandwiches in one hand, passed out arms and legs and other organs to the students with the other! That's precisely the way the Jewish-democratic rabble came to the League of Nations round table with the amputated limbs of the German Reich! Well, get off with you now! As long as you quacks haven't got a hypodermic to make the dead come to life again, so far as I'm concerned you and your medicines can—" He stopped, listened. Then he said shortly to Hess: "Go get Colonel Latour!"

As his friend hesitated, he barked:

"Go on! Jump to it! Stir your stumps!"—and to the doctor: "Where are you going?" He caught him by his white smock before he could follow Hess. "You seem to be in a great hurry! Listen to me. The last few days I've been having a sensation of cold here!"

"In the sinus, my Führer?"

"Yes, as if there were a piece of ice in there. What does that mean? Don't tell me it's just— But what does a urine-smeller like you know —about astral influences? Tell me, according to your staff physician's philosophy, who is closer to life—woman or man?"

"Woman—"

"Prove it!"

"Man is born of woman—"

"But not the superman!—You iodine-painter—take your aspirin mentality out of here!"

Kohler closed his medicine chest.

"And now what?" the Führer asked. "Going off on a binge? What's next on the program?"

"I'm going to the Trocadéro to—"

"Sounds like fun. What's brewing there? A lot of naked women doing the bumps, eh? Paris! Yes, even a gray-haired old dissector like you still yells 'Yes' in Paris. Come, don't look so offended! Tell your racial chieftain—baited by Judah as he is—what's the great attraction in the Trocadéro?"

"They're going to show us doctors a phenomenon—"

"A five-legged steer?"

"No—a soldier—"

"A soldier?" Hitler's tone changed. "French?"

"I don't know exactly. I was only told that it's a gravely wounded soldier who for more than twenty years has managed to exist in a dug-out near Verdun, and we doctors—"

But Dr. Kohler, somehow sensing that what he was saying was disagreeable to his Führer, did not finish his sentence. He quietly made off, the Reich Führer not even noticing his departure.

"What kind of a soldier?" He paled and grew uneasy—like an accused man before a jury, suddenly facing a witness who—he knows—is able to destroy his cleverly planned defense with one look.

"Who's there?" He spun round and his face grew even paler. His mustache looked like the black fur of a mouse that had crawled half-way into his nostrils. "What's that noise?"

He stared out the window. The two bright stars in Libra shone from the night sky—steady and stern, like the eyes of the Cosmic Judge.

"Sakra!" He pulled the curtain to, so quickly that the drawcord snapped . . . Something moved in an alcove behind him. Out of the dark corner came a soft humming—like the wind singing through barbed wire.

"Milarespa?" he asked tonelessly, "is that you? Answer me—boob! Have you brought me more details about the reappearance of the 'promised redeemer'—ha-ha!" He tried to laugh. But there was no sign of his astrologer. There was nothing but that fine, soft humming, like the vibration of a little porcelain ball. He shuddered.

Gradually, among the Chinese lacquer furniture, he discerned a bright-colored figure; at each step he took toward it, its head and hands moved. It was sitting on a table: a cross-legged Buddha of Meissen porcelain, about the size of a baby. Its canary-yellow robe strewn with lilac blossoms was open over its glistening, flesh-colored pot-belly. Each time its fat, wrinkled face nodded forward, a blood-red tongue popped out of its grinning mouth. Heavy chains of coral hung about its neck and down to the gilded navel.

"Heh-heh-heh!" He laughed sheepishly, then louder and louder, flicking the porcelain head so that it nodded more rapidly. "What kind of fakir are you? Have the goodness not to stick your silly tongue

378

out at me so shamelessly! Are you grinning because I wasn't able to raise the little dancer's corpse up on her pirouetting legs again? Heh-heh-heh!"

"You should have lain down on top of her—mouth to mouth!"

"Who's that?" Hitler held his breath. The squeaking voice answered:

"Your astrologer friend told me you should have rattled off Tibetan abracadabras until the corpse stuck out her tongue at you. Then bite quick! Snap! And don't let go! That way, you would have the dancer's soul between your teeth! Snap! Bite and hold fast!"

With a groan of dread, Hitler clutched at his throat:

"Who's there? . . ." And then he saw, sitting in the shadow of the table his Air Marshal. Göring looked at him out of his old cadet's face—like an officer who has surprised his wife's lover, and is ready to duel. His tunic was sluttishly open so that the ribbons and orders about his neck disappeared between eunuchlike breasts. In the corner of his mouth he held a long pipe from which light clouds of sweetish smelling smoke arose.

"Ah, Adolferich? Not disturbing you, I hope? Quite solo? solissimo? in this love-nest by night? Curtains drawn and only a candle on the table? Ho-ho!" Removing the pipe, he admonished: "Don't let me hear any complaints!"

Since his Chief kept silent, eyeing him distrustfully, Göring took a few more puffs:

"What are you looking for? Your Will? I have the honor to report: I strongly suspect that Schleichovsky is an agent of Stalinsky's! I turned him over to Himmler for further investigation. It's true, your Bolsheviko was telling me Stalin's a murderer . . . Well, that wouldn't be so bad! The only trouble is—he reads classic literature! . . . Adolferich! Don't you trust that Russian of yours when he tells you that National Socialism and Bolshevism are two parallel lines that will eventually meet in infinity! Lot of flapdoodle! . . . The truth is: the Cossacks want to be in Potsdam. Watch out, Adolf! You say nothing? Why do you look at me like that? Hope you don't think I stole your Will. Not I! Why should I? I know your Last Will! Didn't you name me your post mortem alter ego before the plenary assembly of all the party nit-wits?" He saluted him ironically with his pipe. "Morituri te salutant!! Adolfus Magnus! But if Schleichovsky spilled even two cents' worth of truth when he was examined, I advise you—" he suddenly whispered—"watch out for Hess! Have your dear friend Rudolf shadowed for a while! Understand? My advice is good! Believe me! . . . What's the matter? Are you peeved at your faithful Hermann?

Are you worried because the emigrant scum in Paris compares me to a sausage stuffed with the blood of all the 'minorities'? Hm? So much dandruff as far as I'm concerned! But unfortunately it isn't dandruff to Emmy! You see? . . . She's more than ever determined that our footmen shall wear brown instead of the fresh and frolicsome hunting green I love! 'In honor of Adolf!' she lisps. Spoils the whole tone for me in my Karin Hall—bison—elks and all!" He hunched his shoulders and drew a few long puffs. Suddenly his eyes blazed green with jealousy.

"Adolferich, where is Emmy? General Milch couldn't find her at the Hotel Ritz. General Tot says Meissner knows where she is—but Meissner doesn't know, he says! Adolf! Emmy is my wife, my matrimonial self! Since she left the table she hasn't been seen anywhere! . . . You put a jeweled garter on her plate! Very nice idea! 'Honi soit qui mal y pense' as my dear old friend Henderson would say . . . Adolf—" He seesawed and wobbled his mountainous body closer. "Emmy has more depth than an artesian well in the Vatican! But I won't even permit the Bishop of the National Socialist liturgy to quench his thirst at my private well! Understand me? Now, where is she? Even if we're no longer Christians—praise God!—we're not among the Eskimos who lend and borrow each others' wives! Understand me? Mark my words, Emmy is no theory of relativity—she's substantial solid flesh and blood! . . . Now, what are you up to here? Is that why you sent your Hess away? Did the doctor give you an injection of hormones to pep things up? Answer me, man!" He waved his pipe in Hitler's face. "Is the child mine or yours? A whole mystery depends upon your answer. You know very well—I don't think much of bombs that only explode in the attic! Come on now—out with it! What are you doing here? I love my child. It always behaves so well when you powder its little fanny. It can already say 'Papa!' Know what I mean? But if it isn't *my* child, I'll have it roasted like a suckling pig and served to the Jews in Dachau for Christmas! Understand me?"

He rattled on, but soon faltered in the face of that countenance, drained of blood, which in its silence was like a fresh-shaved corpse. Like a chief eunuch before his padishah, who perceives from his lord's bloodless lips that he has talked his head into danger, Göring tried to crawl back into the folds of his own fat. Timorously he went on:

"Adolf, please! Only think what it means! After all, it was in your service that, standing between you and Ludendorff in front of the Feldherrnhalle, I received that bullet in the Easter-eggs! Don't forget that! . . . Anyhow that's no reason why you should doubt my

380

ability! It's true, you awarded me the marshal's baton! Bon! But that's only an ersatz honor! Adolfus! . . . I remember seeing, in the grotto in Capri, the so-called 'World-Bull,' with Mithras riding on his back and the serpent eating his testicles! But I bet that didn't hurt him as much as it hurts me if Emmy and you!—and you, I say, with whom I have shared sorrow and joy! . . . I know, you are lord over man and beast! Yours is the jus primae noctis! Yes, Adolfino!" He tried to smile. "But please leave me my quiet place beside the hearth in wintertime! Please leave me one dent in her bosom! . . . Or is it that, to carry out your offensives, you really need something else—something sexual? I've got some nice little girls that would be tickled to death to play eight-handed tiddle-de-winks with you! So if you need some relaxation before your great undertaking—Adolfo caro! You're not angry with me? Don't take offense because I've poured my heart out to you! Good God, say something! Spit at me! Yell at me! Howl at me! Have fits, but don't keep your trap shut so long! I simply can't stand it!" Beads of sweat dripped from his nose.

"God and the Devil! I'm not a creature like Röhm! When you had Ernstel arrested, he called you 'Swine!' I'd never dare do such a thing! Adolfino!" he coaxed, "you don't mean to have me loaded in an armored car and shipped to Grosslichterfelde? At your order, I had all those swine shot down in the court. But I wouldn't mutiny! We two, you and I, are I and you, aren't we? I am you and you are I! And besides, I'm popular, too! It never entered my head to find fault with your creative achievement! You are the incontestable cause of everything! But you can't deny that, with all due modesty, I've done my best to carry out your orders! Adolf!" He held out his fat hand hesitantly. "I've been smoking opium. Just to shake off my misery! Plain, ordinary misery! In the first stage you get a headache. In the second, stomachache and nausea. But after that you begin to see gigantic jewels and shining butterflies over an endless sea! Adolf, please say one word!" He began blubbering: "I tell you, I love Emmy! Yes! As far as my duties permit me—I love Emmy! . . . Your Napoleon said: 'In love, there's only one solution for the man and that is flight!' . . . But I'm not going to take flight! Göring is no cowardly Judocrat! No! Göring is a member of the master race. I wouldn't be worthy of you if I were a coward, Adolfus Magnus! The ancient Germans used to bury cowards alive!"

At these words, Hitler started as if he had received an electric shock. Without warning, he ripped the pipe out of his Air Marshal's teeth with such brutal force that Göring choked. Fearing an outbreak of ungovernable rage the President of the Nazi Reichstag—torn between his consciousness of what was due to his high position and his imminent fear of losing it—discreetly retreated, step by step, out the door.

CHAPTER TWENTY-SEVEN At THE REAR OF THE EMBASSY GARDEN, IN THE SHADOW OF AN ABUTTING WALL, RUDOLF HESS STOOD WAITing impatiently for Hänsel to bring him word of Lord Douglo's arrival. He had begun to think that there was no longer any way for him to keep his Führer out of Ribbentrop's intrigue with Colonel Latour . . . He was almost ready to take Uhle (whom he believed to be the adjutant of Marshal Pétain) out of the audience room again and smuggle him unobtrusively out of the Embassy. Suddenly he saw Marshal Göring sneak out of the tea house, reconnoiter most suspiciously, and then disappear under the trees with Meissner, who had stepped out from behind a bush.

A terrible suspicion flashed through Hess. Had the reactionary patron of dethroned royalty done something to his Führer? As if out of his senses, he tore across the flower beds to the tea house. The door was shut. His heart pounding, he lifted the latch. Then he started back.

Hitler was sitting on a sofa, a long pipe under his dark mustache, puffing away with such fury that the whitish clouds entirely veiled his features.

"God help me!" The Deputy Führer sidled up timidly, not daring to ask his friend why he—who never smoked—had developed this sudden passion for the pipe. He had to clear his throat constantly because of the penetrating, sweetish aroma. For Hitler was blowing the opium smoke out of his pipe bowl as if he were trying to create a cloud that should hide the face that floated in the air before him—the face of the pioneer whose reappearance from the dugout at Verdun his astrologer had announced.

"Adolf!" Hess ventured at last. "I respectfully report: Our English well-wisher Douglo is in Paris."

Hitler only puffed more furiously. Indeed, it seemed uncertain whether he even knew Hess was there, so blankly did he stare through the opium cloud. Now and then he clutched his head and made groaning sounds.

382

"Ado!" The Deputy Führer cautiously sat down beside him and tried unsuccessfully to remove the pipe from his mouth. But as the smoke made him feel more and more nauseated, he got up again and began to speculate whether Göring, with some counter-revolutionary intention, had tempted his bosom friend into opium-smoking. Abruptly he picked up a vase, and—hoping to shock the stupefied smoker out of his lethargy—smashed it on the floor. But Hitler continued calmly puffing.

"Addi!" He made a last desperate attempt to bring the Führer to his senses by calling up 'colossal' memories. "When I was granted the signal honor of composing the Bible of the New Millennium, in the Fortress of Landsberg—"

"Who?—You?" Hitler put down the pipe and, as the air began to clear about his head, reiterated: "You?" His eyelids opened and shut mechanically. Leaning over the arm of the sofa, he appeared to be looking for a basin in which to vomit. So he remained for several seconds. Finally he murmured dully and haltingly:

"Ever-r-r-rybody gets fresh with me! Every single one of you tries to get fresh with me! Although I've yet to see any miracles of color . . . above an endless, deep sea . . . everywhere I look, I see miracles of impertinence." He laid the pipe down behind the Buddha and sat up straight.

"But my stomach can stand anything! My bowels are cast iron! I can even stand Göring! And you! You, too! Everything, ever-r-r-rything! But tell me, how did it happen that *you* composed the Bible of the New Millennium? So—Rudolf Hess is the author of 'Mein Kampf'?" The Führer smiled:

"Where is Colonel Latour? I gave you orders to go and get him."

"Adi!" Hess evaded. "The polestar of your policy must be an alliance with England!"

"Must? Must? But, of course, since Rudolf Hess wrote 'Mein Kampf', he must know! . . ."

"You yourself, in the classic style of which you are a master, formulated as the guiding principle of all your actions, the unity of the Aryan master races!"

"Go see who's knocking . . ."

"Adi!" For the first time in his career, Hess disobeyed the direct command of his Führer, and instead begged: "Adi, please don't receive this adjutant of Marshal Pétain's until you have talked with my Douglo!"

"Douglo? You mean the Duke of—? Where is he?"

"Where?" He looked about mysteriously, and whispered: "He represents the English aristocracy. I have arranged to meet him in a lonely place. Here you're always watched. But there you can speak. Come, Adi. I'll drive you there. I know that a conversation between you and such a super-Englishman will be absolutely decisive for the whole future of the master race!"

"What nonsense are you up to now? What are you doing? Looking through the keyhole? Hanging your cap over it? Is my Ribbentrop standing outside there? Ha-ha! Now, he knows your England better than you do! That green island with its chalk cliffs in the salt North Sea is no longer inhabited by the red-blond knights of King Arthur's round table who would have been worthy of an alliance with Adolf Hitler! No, young man! The waters of the Thames stink with all the noblest swamp blossoms of Judocracy!"

"The true strength of your movement lies in an alliance with England! Adi! Only an Anglo-Saxon can understand the manly German spirit!"

"An Anglo-Saxon? The English are a nation of shopkeepers! Slaves of the Jews! What good are a few exceptions? What have they to say? The country is ruled by democratic swine!"

"Ado . . . Listen: Douglo thinks—!"

"Douglo! Douglo! As if he knew more about it than I do!—Let me also remind you of what Sir Hugh Walpole, the famous British poet, wrote about me after his audience in Berlin: 'I felt his passion for Germany so sincere. It seemed to burn through his boots into the ground, and I liked him.' There you are! And in the Encyclopaedia Britannica it says of me: 'He is sincere!' Ha-ha! But Hess—my Rudolf Hess—believes he must tell me what to do! You!" He began spouting: "The fire of my love for the Greater Germany burns today as yesterday, 'sincerely', through the soles of my boots down into the ground. Ha-ha-ha!"

"Adol!" Hess cuddled his head against his friend's Iron Cross.

"Rudi!" He sniffed. "You're using a different hair tonic? Now then, you anointed Egyptian! Sit up straight and behave!"

"Ado-o-o! In 1916, on the Dixmude highway, the first time you put your arm around me—great God in heaven! Ah! England is just where they understand that best! There are fine-boned, firm-skinned young men waiting for you there! Deliver them from the revolting female rule of the Judocracy! For instance, what has such a handsome young Lieutenant of the Royal Horse Guards to do with these League-of-Nations hyenas?"

"Now, now! you're quite intoxicated by your British Ariels—."

384

"Intoxicated? Oh, dearest, don't ever again do as Wilhelm did in 1914 at Ypres, and send Aryan youths to their graves against Aryan youths. Spare their massed shout of enthusiasm for yourself. All those young men have your picture hanging over their beds! Oh, Ado! Ado! Do you want Judah and the whole raceless rabble of the world to rejoice again over every blond boy killed in battle against England? *No war against England!* Or the red waves of chaos will roll over you as they did over Pharaoh. Adolf! Within a year, the noblest members of our party, the most enthusiastic National Socialists, would all lie in mass graves! And then—what's left for you? Compromisers! Dissidents! Opportunists! Fat-bellied paterfamiliases! Democratic swine, only waiting for your Elite Guard to be killed off so that they can go back to their disgusting marital pastimes with their wives in their stinking beds! . . . Oh, Ado! If only Fortune favors you long enough to—!"

" 'Fortune favors the most industrious!' says Ribbentrop . . ."

"Ribbentrop! Ribbentrop?" screeched Hess. "That changeling slapstick comedian! That ambitious champagne drummer! Simply because they didn't make enough fuss over him in London?"

"Stop yelling at me!"

"Just on account of the sick vanity of a champagne peddler? Adolf! Don't let him drive you into a conflict with our English cousins! Come with me! Come! My Douglo has purposely flown across the Channel to represent the other England, the secret England, the manly England—"

"Rudi!" Hitler rubbed his smoke-reddened eyes, and then looked at him appraisingly, as a lecher looks at a resisting girl. "You're forgetting your setting-up exercises! Getting too fat around the hips! Strange! You used to be so firm and slender . . . And already going bald? What's become of your waist?" He straightened up. "Fräulein Hess!" He pinched his posterior. "You used to have such a delightful behind."

"My Führer!" The Deputy Führer bounded to his feet and ran to the door, clicking his heels together. "May I go—?"

"For all of me." Yawning, Hitler retrieved the pipe from behind the Buddha. "Fact is, the erections of your political organism don't attract me much . . ." He puffed sensually. Hess held out his right arm horizontally, but with the hand turned down at the wrist. Dark looks flashing from under his bushy eyebrows, he growled, "Heil Hitler!" and threw open the door. But then he pulled himself together, and groaned: "Just the same, I used to be—your favorite!"

"The Jew pays nothing for what has been." The Führer puffed so hard that smoke swirled around his face.

"A-a-ah!" Hess exploded, his tone knife-sharp: "So, after all—a Je-e-e-ew—"

Before he could get out another word, Hitler had him by the necktie. The pipe splintered. Squeezing Hess in an iron embrace he tripped him up, threw him down, pulling him by the hair till he lay flat on his back, and then, squatting on his chest, croaked:

"I? A Jew? I?!" Suddenly he felt the packet of papers inside Hess's shirt. "What's that you've got there? Love letters from your Douglo? Hm? What is it? Get up! You're white as a sheet! What are you hiding?" His eyes bored through Hess. "Rudolf!" he said flatly, "I can't believe it! Come on, are you going to get up?" Now his voice was cold. "Answer me!" He pounced on the Deputy Führer, but Hess cursed and ducked round the table. He knew very well that if Hitler found him in possession of the papers Hänsel had brought him—and which, in the confusion of the evening, he had never been alone long enough to read —there would be but one thing ahead for him. The rifles of the Gestapo.

"Stand still!" roared the Führer. Both made false starts—to the right —to the left! And again, and again, around the table—until Hitler stopped out of breath. Taking advantage of that instant, Hess climbed onto the green malachite table top and jumped over the lowered head and shoulders of his Führer to the door. Hitler dashed after him, tackling and holding him by the boots so that he came down in a heap, and then hammered him in the face with both fists until he had a chance to rip the papers out of his shirt. Lurching back to the table, he muttered:

"What is this?"

"Forgive—!" Hess stammered, and raised both hands, like a soldier surrendering.

"Rudi! No. . . . no! Did you—? No!! . . . Did you steal my Will?"

"Forgive me!" Hess fell on his knees.

"What? Rudolf Hess? My old cell comrade?"

Howling, he tore open the brown paper—the package contained the photographs that Baldur had taken down from the wall of his room in the Pension Alsace when he was packing for his departure . . . "What is all this?" Hitler stared at them. "Bitt' schön! What is all this?"

When he saw what the package contained, Hess hitched himself up against the wall and felt his throat, like a condemned man who finds the hangman has undone the noose again. For an instant he stood there, pale as a ghost in front of his own shadow. Then he broke out into insane laughter.

The photographs fell from Hitler's hands. His head bumped down onto the malachite surface of the table. Then he began howling like an Eskimo dog. His Deputy picked up the scattered pictures and kissed them, his eyes raised to heaven in gratitude.

As his friend slowly regained possession of himself, Hess slithered along the edge of the table toward him. Hitler stared at him out of swollen eyes, imploring forgiveness. Slowly and reproachfully, although his heart still pounded against his ribs with fear, Hess nodded.

"Rudi!" Desperately, Hitler caught at him and drew him close, running cold fingers through his thin hair, chattering unintelligibly. Then suddenly he put his mouth to his—teeth against teeth—and kissed him.

Startled by a cough outside, they broke apart.

"Come, Rudi . . ." Hitler looked at his bosom friend with eyes that implored forgiveness, ready to do anything. "Where is he—your English Ariel?"

"Will you really see him?" Hess thought for a moment. Suddenly he whispered . . . "Come. . . ."

And they were able to reach Hess's car without being seen by any of the Gestapo sentries.

BOOK FIVE

CHAPTER ONE   Not far from Neuilly-sur-Seine, in a little wood where detached villas are separated from each other by extensive grounds, Baldur Hermann nervously unlocked the door of the "Villa Michelle" for a tall, well-dressed, good-looking and self-possessed blonde in her mid-twenties. Then he led her cautiously through the vestibule in the hall, from which a wide, carved-wood staircase led to the floor above. The windows and blinds were all closed. The air was damp and sticky. Flashlight in hand, he directed the roving disk of white light over walls and ceiling. Then, his hands shaking, he lit a candle. In the autumn-cold room, the flame seemed strangely small. By its light we now recognize Miss Gloria Inwood, the friend of Abetz's friend Baron Jacques.

Baldur, who had made her acquaintance only an hour earlier in the Ritz Bar, conducted her, now quite unsure of himself, to a luxurious sofa where, with a forced smile, he begged her to make herself comfortable.

Hair coiffed with a band of white roses, Miss Inwood threw herself at full length on the cushions, her red taffeta evening dress, trimmed with fur, opening out fanwise. Kicking off her beaded sandals, she wiggled her toes with adventurous zest. Then, stripping off her black velvet bolero, she arched her breasts, which were concealed only by two narrow bands of gold tulle. Around her soft throat hung a collar of emeralds in an antique gold setting. Her long, dangling earrings were also of emeralds. While Baldur studied her appraisingly, she opened her handbag and put on lipstick. Then suddenly he asked her if he might open the window for a moment. Climbing up on an antique chest, he unfastened the heavy blinds and opened the upper half of the window. The curtain swayed. Night birds cried outside. The wind rustled.

"Oo-ooh, it's cold!" Miss Inwood pulled the hood of her velvet cape over her head. "You'd better shut it again!"

388

Baldur obeyed and then, searching through various closets, found candles, which he lit and stuck on the mantelpiece, the table, and the lower steps of the staircase. Opening a four-panel screen, he arranged it behind the sofa, and smiled:

"Well, Miss! Aren't you afraid?"

"Afraid? Why? My place in California is much more isolated than this."

"You don't say? Sounds marvelous! But now tell me the truth—you mean to say, you noticed me right away in the Ritz Bar? That's queer —I didn't see you."

"Boy—you were much too busy poring over steamship folders!"

"Right! And if you hadn't asked me for a light, I would long ago have been—where? Ha-ha! Always the same joke! A little spark—and the flame squirts out of the lighter! You light the cigarettes of such a beautiful lady! Et voilà!" He offered her some American cigarettes. "So you're from the land of the dollar? That's marvelous! And thanks to my position as bodyguard standard-bearer, I am granted the rare privilege of driving such a de luxe young Park-Avenue Miss all the way from the Place Vendôme through Paris by night to my villa on the Seine? Now, if that isn't marvelous! But, you'll excuse me! I'll just run upstairs and change my things!" Pulling off his wind-breaker, he creaked up the steps.

As soon as he was upstairs, he dashed into the first room to the left, pounced on an old armchair, dug under the cushion, and pulled out a small Browning.

"Hello, up there!" Gloria called impatiently. "Where are you?"

"Be right back!" Cursing, he loaded the weapon. "What the hell am I to do now?" For the umpty-umpth time he had waited in vain in the Ritz Bar in order to conclude the deal with that damn Russian Schleich. —And all the time the police were after him for the murder of his mother.—He must at all costs make his getaway from France. So, in desperation he had hooked this rich American woman. Under false pretenses, naturally. With the help of whiskey, he had succeeded in overcoming her inhibitions by promising to arrange for her to interview Adolf Hitler that very night at the German Embassy . . .

"Say, have you died up there?" She called again, avid with her insatiable hunger for the sensational.

"Oh nuts—" Baldur muttered away a last hesitation, and put the revolver in his pocket. "I've got to get the hell out of here! With pictures of my sainted old girl on every street corner! In all the night editions! Murdered! Another murder! Ha-ha! Tough going, old girl! Yes, but

389

after all I couldn't let you get away with such a big financial invest-ment! This little bundle of papers"—he tapped the roll of manuscript inside his breast pocket—"is just so much cold cash! What?" He took another hurried look through the evening paper. "All the railway sta-tions are being watched? Well, it can't be helped,—I'll have to run through the fields—."

"Hey there!"

"Yes! Coming!" He started, but stopped again. "What the hell! When the time comes to end a thing—you've got to find a way to end it!"

He descended the stairs, holding a half-empty box of chocolates.

"Boy!"—Miss Gloria straightened herself up among the cushions—"not in your uniform yet?"

"Just wanted to offer you something sweet—"

"How late is it?"

"Doesn't matter!"

"Doesn't matter? Must be almost two A.M. What time does his plane leave?"

"Doesn't matter. Perhaps at sunrise. Perhaps not till sunset. Have some chocolates?"

"Crazy about them!"

"Great!" He handed her the box.

"Haven't you got a blanket?"

"Why? Is it so cold?"

"I'm freezing!"

"Does it have to be a blanket?" Throwing back the lid of the old peasant chest under the window, he scooped up two armfuls of femi-nine undergarments and silk pyjamas, tossing them through the air to her like carnival streamers. She began kicking off the entangling lingerie, revealing her legs. Then, made uneasy by his peculiar stare, she slowly pulled her dress down over her knees and lit a fresh ciga-rette!

"You know, before every interview, I always figure out the ques-tions I'm going to ask so that I won't forget anything when I'm con-fronted by some big gazabo. When I finished with Mussolini, he stopped me at the door and asked: 'Do you want to be famous? Then I'll give you a piece of advice. Above all, be sure that you first murder your own heart!'"

"Did the Old Roman say that? Marvelous! . . . Well, let's see if your heart is really dead?" He crawled beside her on the sofa. "Your skin, at any rate—that's alive! And the precious stones on your skin—

390

they're alive, too! Splendid! Are they genuine? Pardon! I only asked because so many ladies nowadays wear imitations and keep the real ones in a safe!"

"Everything about me's genuine . . ." She stretched luxuriously.

"That goes for me, too! Everything—!" He grinned at her.

"Darling!" She blew smoke in his eyes.

"Well—now what? Wait a minute! May I count your emeralds?—One—two—nine! My God!" He fingered each stone. "This junk must be worth a lot of money. What?"

"Darling—"

"Now what's on your mind?" From under the sofa, he pulled out a bottle of Sauterne. "My glasses are all broken! Let's drink out of the bottle!"

Gloria put the bottle to her lips and gulped a few swallows.

"Leave some for me!" Grabbing the bottle, he carefully examined the lipstick on its rim, and then drank. Finally he set it down. "Beautiful, how much time have you?"

"Time? I? What for? Darling! I'm simply waiting for you to change your clothes and take me to the German Embassy! You promised! Or do you think he won't receive me?"

"Of course he will!"

"Of course he will?"

"Well—just recently he received a Dollar Princess like you in the Reich Chancellery. Of course, she happened to know our State Opera singer Milford! Why, it was after three in the morning that she saw him. You know he doesn't sleep well. Of course he'll receive you! The great man would be tickled pink to have such a fairy come and tell him stories between midnight and five A.M.—ha-ha!"

"Is that so? You know, I've read everything there is about your Führer! And everything he's ever written—everything! I know exactly how his bed is made! Know what he has for breakfast! Thoroughly acquainted with all the intrigues around him . . . But that doesn't interest me . . ."

"What does interest you?" He played with the necklace around her throat.

"What does? I have to see things for myself. Facts! Facts! You know"—she drank from the bottle—"when the minister told us from his Sunday pulpit that Christ turned water into wine, and a couple of skeptics snickered, he yelled through the church! 'You must believe it! You must! You must!!' Right then I made up my mind to believe nothing except facts! That's why I became a journalist! Darling!"—

she put the bottle on the table—"enthusiasm and hate don't give us the answer to the secret!"

"What secret?"

"Darling! Darling!" She rubbed her well-manicured hands with excitement. "I have so much curiosity! Boy, boy—so much curiosity!"

"About what?"

"About what?" She laughed. "Well, for instance, I'd very much like to know how this world started . . ."

"How it got going, you mean? Ha-ha! That doesn't interest me one bit. You mean to tell me, you're curious to know what goes on after death too?"

"No . . . no, I'm only interested in this life and how to get the most out of it. In the present. And that's just what I'm doing. It's the best or nothing for me! Oh-boy! I bet none of my friends would ever believe I'd go to the German Embassy in Paris at three in the morning for an interview with your Führer!" She pushed him away. "Hurry up now! There are certain opportunities one can't afford to miss!"

"I'll say there are! Girlie, you know your skin has a fragrance all its own! Marvelous! Is that the way Americans smell? Don't be afraid! That's only my raven back there in the billiard room. Sometimes in its sleep it hops around on its perch—ha-ha!" He caressed her hands. "Quiet isn't it? Not a soul lives around here! It's so quiet . . ."

"Why don't you go and put your clothes on?"

"Right away!" He pulled her chin up. "First show me the tip of your tongue. Why won't you? You've got one? And since you're doing that cigarette the honor—come on—we've still got plenty of time!"

"Darling, you know, sometimes in Los Angeles, I've left a night club at five in the morning, sent my negro chauffeur home, and then I'd go for a walk quite alone—along endless avenues lined with palms . . . The rays of the rising sun would shine on my evening dress . . ."

"The dawn?"

"I'd be walking straight into it—the light getting brighter every minute! Once, darling, a couple of ditch-diggers, warming their stiff hands over a kettle of boiling tar looked at me so—"

"You don't say so! Well, my Fairy Princess, what would you say if I should suddenly pop out from behind a tree and bar your way with a gun?"

"Oh, darling!" She combed his blond mop with her red fingernails. "If it were anyone else, I'd be terrified!" She stared into the blue of his eyes. "But with you, darling!—If I only heard your dark voice, I'd be quite calm . . . Oh! Before I met you in the bar, I would never

392

have dreamed of such a thing! And now, five minutes later, the greatest adventure of my life is going to begin?"

"The greatest adventure?" He put one arm around her shoulders, and whispered: "Miss Gloria, is it *he?* Or is it *me?*" Her eyes widened. Then she smiled:

"I don't know—"

His shot rang out just behind her ear. She sank back, her limbs twitching once or twice. Baldur waited until she lay quite still. Then he unfastened the emerald necklace and spread it carefully out on the table . . . "Marvelous . . . marvelous!" He took off her rings too, and then looked through her bag and found some change and a checkbook. The gold chain on her left ankle wouldn't come off easily, so he left it there. Spreading her evening cloak on the floor, he picked her up from the sofa and rolled her slender form in it as tightly as possible. Then he pulled a ball of string from under the sofa and expertly tied up the body like a mummy. Kicking the carpet aside with his foot, he opened a trap door and dragged the corpse, like a roll of linoleum, down the steps and into a roomy basement whose roof was supported by a single column. Here he dropped his burden and flashed his light about, revealing heaps of dusty boards, garden tools, and hose. Finally, he propped the flashlight so that it concentrated on one corner. A startled mouse fled along the wall into the darkness. This section of the cement flooring showed the rough outlines of several bodies, hastily and clumsily buried, and roughly covered over with plaster and whitewash. Behind the fourth was a narrow depression, sketchily dug out about the length of a grave. Beside it stood a shovel, a pail of plaster, and a pail of water.

Baldur widened this depression about a hand's breadth, rolled the corpse to the edge and tumbled it in. Pouring water into the pail of plaster, he stirred it to a thick paste, and slapped the first few shovels of the resulting mixture down the beaded evening slippers. Not until the body was covered to the hips did he pause for breath. Then, leaning on the shovel, he coolly imitated the voice of a clergyman at a burial:

"Of dust wast thou made! And unto dust thou shalt return!" Then he extended his arm over her and said simply and faithfully:

"Heil Hitler!"

Just as he was about to scoop up more plaster with his trowel to finish his sinister work—he thought he heard footsteps in the hall above. Instantly he threw the water-proof engine cover of his car over Miss Gloria's finger-waved hair—snatched up the flashlight and tore up the steps so fast that he banged his head against the trap door.

393

No mistake about it! There was someone in the vestibule. Soundlessly he crept out and edged over to the screen. "Could it be the police?" He held his breath.

Since there was no further sound, he ventured forward, out through the hall to the vestibule. He pushed aside the beaded hangings that served as a curtain. There stood Schleich. He had an alligator leather brief case under his arm and looked like a man just about to set off on a journey. His breath reeked of vodka.

"Ha-ha-ha! Mr. Yankee?" Baldur laughed uproariously. "Marvelous! In the name of the devil, where have you been keeping yourself?"

"I was just going into the Ritz Bar when I saw you drive off with that stunning girl. I trailed you all the way out here! Plague and speed! I nearly lost you in the darkness! . . . Well, my handsome German Folk Comrade, why didn't you wait for me in the bar? Don't look so distraught. What's the matter? Have I disturbed you at a tête-à-tête?"

"Just one second!" Clicking his heels, Baldur slipped back through the beaded curtain, tiptoed to the trap door, closed it, and noiselessly replaced the rug. He thought for a moment: "Can the Yankee be a detective? Put on my trail by the French police?" Grabbing the murdered girl's jewels and checkbook off the table, he climbed up on the chest, and was just going to jump out the window into the garden when Schleich, entering, called out:

"Now what are you up to?"

"Just going to air the place a bit. It's so stuffy in here. But first let me take your coat."

"No, no!" Schleich's tongue, thick with alcohol, moved with difficulty. "You-are-very-very-kind—German-Folk-Comrade!" He grinned in response to Baldur's saccharine smile. "Oh—what long fingers you have!"

"Long? They're pretty nice, aren't they?"

"Damn! Those are the damned longest hands I've ever seen on a young fellow!"

"Is that so?" The bodyguard standard-bearer stepped tensely behind Schleich, intending to knock him down from behind—a Gestapo trick. But the Red Singer turned around just a second too soon. Seating himself comfortably in a big upholstered chair by the fireplace, he slapped his wallet down on the table in front of him, fingered the banknotes, and asked:

"Well? You handsome rascal—how much?"

Baldur's eyes bulged at the sight of so much money. Nevertheless, he was on his guard. Schleich noticed it, and called toward the door:

"Mr. Tainik! Come in! Come on in!"

The blond drew his revolver, ready to defend himself. But Schleich merely grinned.

"Don't worry, young fellow! It's just a graphologist I brought along —not being an expert myself on Hitler's handwriting. Come in!"

A man whose face was heavily powdered entered and looked at Baldur through narrowed eyes.

"Come in. This young scoundrel is shier than a thoroughbred when the wind blows. Ha-ha! Mr. Tainik is an expert. Recently published an article on Hitler's handwriting, in the New York Times. So, if he's satisfied your document is genuine—I'll buy it."

Unbuttoning his coat, Baldur rather uncertainly took out the pocket containing the sixty pages. The graphologist, squeezing a watchmaker's lupe into his eye, subjected them, one by one, to minute inspection, somewhat after the manner of a dealer in diamonds. Finally, his voice emotionless, he said:

"Mr. Schleich, this manuscript is genuine!"

"Gentlemen"—Baldur's cheeks were feverish with excitement—"can I offer you a glass of wine?"

"No thanks! I've got to be on my way." The Russian pushed a wad of bills across the table to him.

"Money?" Baldur grabbed it greedily and then counted it under the candle—accompanying the counting with indefinable, throaty sounds. Suddenly Schleich pricked up his ears. He felt sure that an automobile was driving up to the gate. Quietly he rose. And, before Baldur could take in what was happening, Schleich and his expert were up and away.

"Hey!"—he leaped up—"Mister Yankee! Hey! Gentlemen!" He dashed after them.

But when he reached the vestibule he heard an automobile brake to a stop on the road. Then he heard voices. The garden gate squeaked.

"A trap? Damnation!" He stumbled up the staircase. He wanted to put out the candles but couldn't muster the nerve to go down into the hall again. On all fours, he crawled into the shadow of the banister on the first floor, crouching there. And then he could not believe his eyes.

"I'll be damned—it's Hess!"

The Deputy Führer pushed back the beaded curtain and, arm in arm with Hitler, came forward, reconnoitering, into the center of the hall.

CHAPTER TWO

W
ELL, WHERE IS THIS ARIEL OF
YOURS?"

"According to Hänsel, Lord Douglo should have been here by this time."

"I certainly saw an automobile following us!"

"Out of the question, Adolf!"

"You're positive no one followed us?"

"Quite certain. Those were the lights of Neuilly. Besides, Douglo would be coming from the other direction—from Longchamps."

"Yes—then where is he? Would his Lordship keep his Aryan god waiting?"

"Douglo!" Hess went to the window, partly opened it, and called, "Hey—Douglo!"

"So! My Deputy Führer already has his own little hide-out on the Seine! Ha-ha! God in heaven, what a smell! There must be mushrooms in the garden . . ."

"Quiet! I heard something."

"Shut the window! Damn it! The mist's coming in . . . This villa of yours reminds me of our house in Champagne. You remember it? Where we had such a wild time during that infantry engagement in 1914."

"I remember."

"That house smelled of mushrooms too."

"The closets had been ransacked, but the stuff was still lying around everywhere."

"Do you remember the corset on the chair, Rudi?"

"In the kitchen, the roast hare was still hot in the oven—that was how fast the French owners had had to flee for their lives from us boches!"

"Hm! Seems to be lots of female underwear lying around here too! Herr Rudolf Hess—since when? Look at him blush! Just what goes on in this hide-out?" He slapped him on the thigh. "Hm? Remember how you put on an enormous female straw hat, trimmed with flowers and dangling velvet ribbons! Ha-ha! But although you had a perfect thirty-six in those days, I still couldn't get that corset tight over your buttocks . . ."

"And Madame's old-fashioned lace panties, Adolf!"

"And how we danced together—we two soldiers! Ha-ha!"

396

"And all the time, behind the house, in the orchard, our machine-guns were going tak-tak-tak!"

Up on the landing Baldur had stuffed a handkerchief in his mouth to muffle his breathing. Between the banister rails, he staired pop-eyed at the scene fifteen feet below. The cramps in the calves of his legs became so unendurable that he was on the point of jumping up and firing his revolver to break the tension. His knees shaking, he hugged the shadows.

"Rudi!" Hitler grasped his friend's hand. "You're such a decent fellow! I swear to you that if your Lord Douglo can give me the slightest evidence that there is a secret movement in England—I shall really put into effect what years ago, in our prison cell in Landsberg, we laid down as the 'leitmotif' of German policy! Damn it!" He laughed with such metallic uproar that it resounded through the hollow silence. Alarmed, Hess ran behind the beaded curtain and double-locked the front door.

"I tell you, I'll swear friendship with 'perfidious Albion'. Yes! And the devil take the rest of the world. But what's become of your Ariel?" He was growing restless. "But I'll throw all the suffragettes and Judocrats into the Thames! Well—where is he?"

"If only Ribbentrop's hand isn't in this!"

"What? I'm thankful to you for tipping me off to the real machinations of my Foreign Minister!"

"Believe me, the only reason he arranged a conversation with Colonel Latour was so that *you* would put his Anglophobia into action!"

"Rudi! You don't think the French General Staff sent that Spahi officer to spy out my plans? Maybe the Quai d'Orsay has made up its mind to ferret out at last what fate Adolf Hitler actually has locked up in his head for the democratic world! They simply can't bring themselves to believe that I really and truly intend to square accounts with that pack of swindlers! . . . Hess!" He embraced him. "Oh, Rudi! All of a sudden I feel so intoxicated . . . Here alone with you in this isolated house! So far from the world! And everything so quiet!"

"Ado! Do you really trust me again?"

"Silly!" He petted Hess's cheek. "You see, when I discovered my Will had been stolen, at first I felt—as if I had no skin . . . Can you understand that? For, mind you, not even such a friend as you knows my secret! Adolf Hitler has never confided it to anyone except his Will. All these years, I've been carrying it about with me!"

"What kind of secret?"

"The secret of why I'm so hated and so loved! What else could it be! The reason why I have to force all these picayune people of the earth to do nothing else, day and night, even in their dreams, but think and worry about me! Yes! Even while I'm sitting here talking with you, all the munitions factories in the world are running at full blast, cost what it may—and for no other purpose than to smash open this head of mine—! To pick my brains at last of the secret of my super-human successes! Ha-ha! It's quite true, when you and I were dancing around in a house just like this, twenty-five years ago, then—then, in-deed, this head of mine was just an ordinary soldier's ivory dome! Boy! dear boy! And what is it now? This same head with its same two ears is now the fountainhead of an entirely new faith! And even if that im-becile Dr. Sauerbruch tries to tell me: thoughts can penetrate the brain from the outside:—ha-ha!" He struck his hands together above his head, shrilling: "In *my* head—that's dead certain—not a single thing ever penetrated from outside! . . . You might just as well say: the chick enters the egg from outside! Ha-ha! I'll wager that scientific bigwig, Sauerbruch, suffered his first defeat, in conversation with me . . . Ah, Rudi! if I ever do actually make an alliance with those London bad boys!—they can trot out their high hocus-pocuses of Canterbury and St. Paul's and have them stand at attention—ha-ha!—while Adolf Hitler and his National Socialists—no matter how vege-tarian I'm supposed to be!—gobble up their Christian 'Lamb of God,' right down to the last bone, in the middle of Westminster Abbey!" Slapping his thighs, he laughed until the spit flew. Dumb with ad-miration, his Deputy Führer gazed at him. Suddenly he whispered:

"Ado—I adore you!"

"If it only wasn't so damn quiet here! Never mind! There'll soon be noise enough! Silence is, for me—negation! You know, I've recently had two kettledrums of the Third Bavarian Dragoons put in my bed-room. And when it gets so God-damned quiet in the night, like this, Rudi—then I pick up the drumsticks and beat such a tattoo that the flies on the wall turn round and look at me, wondering what's up! Ha-ha! . . . So! You love me? Do you, kitten? But that's far from being enough! I have to ask a great deal more than that of my Deputy Führer!" As Hess stared at him big-eyed, Hitler nodded. "Yes, yes, you black Eygptian! A great deal more than that! Sit down! Come—move over closer!"

"Listen! Wasn't that Douglo calling!"

"I don't hear anything."

"No! It's only the wind . . ."

"Hess!" Suddenly he felt of his own skull. "Darling! It's so mysterious—and so cozy here! And outside that window, somewhere out there, are the flickering lights of a great world capital. And here we sit —on this sofa? Here sits Adolf Hitler! And not a soul knows it! Yes— the very idea excites me!—There they are, out there, all those miserable democrats in their trumpery Christian beds with their ghetto sows, sound asleep! And not one of them knows that their bogey man, 'H-err-r-r-r H-ittler-r-r-r'—as Baron Jacques always whinnies when he sees me—that their hobgoblin, H-e-r-r-r H-ittler-r-r-r-, is keeping watch in this lonely villa, with his sword ready to rip open their bowels!" He giggled to himself. "I love that!"

Devoured by curiosity, Baldur pressed so hard against the banister that the wood creaked. Hitler looked up.

"Hello! That your Douglo at last?"

"Where?" Hess raised himself from the Führer's breast. "No! No! It's nobody! In his excitement at the prospect of meeting you, my good Douglo probably got thoroughly boiled! . . ."

"Rudi, I'm so excited! Just as if I were squiffed! Such a peculiar, fluttery feeling! My heart's racing! You know, Göbbels recently said to me, after a concert in the Reich Chancellery, he could never understand why music begins and why it stops again. Tell me, why do you suppose someone like me begins. Hm? Does someone like me—have to stop, too? . . . Wait! Where are you going?"

"I want to see if there's a telephone here."

"Are you insane?" Hitler recoiled, frightened. "You want to leave me here all alone?" Hess sat down again.

"Adol, you know what I think? It's just beginning to dawn on me— I'll bet that Ribbentrop—"

"Spiderwebs! Spiderwebs! Everywhere I go. Ah! Sometimes your Führer would do anything to get out of all this—even out of myself! God! if only *once* I could get outside this brain of mine!" He massaged his temples. "What is the use of it all? Pretty soon the whole habitable globe will belong to me, then I can go careering about it any place I like without a passport! But even if I can and do, no matter where I go, I'll still be sitting inside this brain of mine! If only once I could get out of myself—and drive past myself—and call out to myself 'Heil Hitler!' But all the time I have to sit next to these dull-witted chauffeurs! And always having to stare at their silver-laced uniforms, aped after the Kaiser's livery. Through Vienna! Prague! Warsaw! There I go, driving like a god! And all the time, locked up in this brain of mine! Rudilein, help me get outside myself! R-r-r-r-room! Sometimes, before the sun rises, my dog sees spooks, and then he runs to jump in

399

bed with me! That's when I'd like to be my dog! If only for one second to have Adolf Hitler as my Master! And then I crawl about in my pyjamas on all fours and bark!" Suddenly, he was on the floor and bit Hess in the calf of his leg. "Bow! Wow! Wow! Ha-ha! Is my Deputy Führer afraid of me? Bow! Wow!" His breath smelt of that peculiar smoke. "I suppose you think the way Roosevelt does, the way that cigar-slobberer in London does, that Hitler is a werewolf? They think he's got corpses in the cellar that he eats in winter! Wow! Wow!" He snapped at Hess's leg. "Wow! Wow! Ha-ha! Are you afraid I'll spread butter on your testicles and chew them off like corn on the cob! Wow! Wow!"

"Stop! What are you doing, Adolf?"

"Just pulling your boots off . . . Ha-ha!"

"Pulling my boots off?"

"That's what I said!" He put one of Hess's feet on the table and stroked his pedicured toes. The nails were red-enameled. "Wow! Wow!" And then he bit into it.

"Don't! you hurt! . . . Stop! . . . No!"

"Yes! Yes! Keep still! I know how to bite tenderly! Wait! Now I am going to bite you very tenderly on the sweet little nail on your dear little pinky!"

"He-hee! He-hee! He-hee!"

"How does that feel, Rudi? There! And now the big toe!"

"Let go!"

"Be still! Do you hear me! Do you want me to wash your stinking feet for you, like the Pope on Maundy Thursday? Well, to Adolf Hitler that's no ridiculous and empty ceremony! You know what I have in mind? As soon as I've finished conquering all these dumb peoples of the earth, then, before the world-wide Good Friday, there's going to be a Maundy Thursday. I'll pick out all the finest representatives of the different races and arrange them around me—in a circle . . . See what I mean? Bitt' schön—little girls—big girls—boys! Do you hear? Lots of slender Ariels. They'll all have to lie in a circle around me and present their naked toes. Sticking up in the air! Damnation! And I'll stand in the middle, like that cigar-slobberer of England! . . . So-o-o!" He yanked Hess's foot straight up. "And then—I'll set all their idiotic heads on fire, like cigars! And then I'll suck their toes! —and smoke! Like that damn Churchill! And bite them! Wow! Wow! And bite them!"

"Stop it!" Hess, terrified, tried to pull away.

"Haa-a! And when they begin to scream—yes, that'll really be some music! At all events, I'll know why it started!—and why it'll stop!" He let Hess's foot go. His features contorted in a lustful grimace, his teeth showing. Suddenly he tore off his own boots, grunting:

"Go and lie down on the sofa!" Hopping after him—"Wow, wow!" —he drove the soles of his feet flat against his friend's chest with such force that he finally lay at full length, with Hitler's feet in his face. The toes of the Deputy Führer to his lips, Hitler blew on them like a satyr on a panpipe. Then he bit them so tenderly that Hess, his eyes closed with ecstasy, sank backward into the cushions.

"Rudi! There's the look of the voluptuary in your face! You—by day the loving father and husband, dripping morality! Ha-ha!"

"Hold still. Hold still—"

"Hold still—" This from Baldur, upstairs in his hiding-place, unable to control his excitement any longer. But since Hess thought it was Hitler who had cried out, and Hitler thought it was his Hess—there they were all three gasping together.

"Yes! Simply dripping morality! But then—by night, my little Rudi-lein steals secretly out of his wife's chintz-hung bedroom. Eh? And sneaks away to such a lonely villa as this, eh? Party Comrade Hess!" Opening his collar and his shirt, Hitler flung his arms around and roared: "Tell me—weren't we going to have 'A New Order of All Moral Values'?"

"Yes—Adi! 'The Socialist Paradise on Earth!' "

"Bite me! Harder! Hess! Hess!" He squealed with delight. "Do you like it?"

"And you?"

"Heavenly! The closer it comes! Ha-ha! Yes! Bite me! Always closer to the time-fuse!" He whispered, his lips drooling. "And then, when the engine goes off the tracks at full speed—Rudi! Bite!—And the first six cars crash down into the abyss from the high trestle-bridge —Rudi! Rudi!—And the screams of pain screech through the winter night from the travelers torn to ribbons! Then down we'll dash to the scene of the catastrophe and mix in with the Red Cross personnel! What? And to all those screaming human beings we'll offer—bon-bons! Ha-ha! Hess!" He grabbed his friend's other foot.

"Ouch! Ouch!"

"Bite!" Hitler ordered. "Bite, I say!"

"Bite!" Hess suddenly cried out like a woman, and writhed on the sofa. "Bite! Bite! . . ."

There was the sound of heavy knocking on a door somewhere out-side.

CHAPTER THREE

HITLER AND HESS SAT UP SIMULTANEOUSLY.

"It's someone's knocking!" Hess murmured dazedly, pulling on his socks. "That must be he!"

"Yes, someone's knocking." Hitler turned.

"Quick! Put on your boots!"

The knocking came again—this time at the window shutters.

"Adi! That's Douglo! Who else could it be!" Hess had his boots on and snatched up the candles, setting them in the fireplace as far back as possible, behind the grate, so that it was almost dark in the hall. Tiptoeing to the window, he called "Hey! Dougi! Is that you? . . . No answer—perhaps it was a branch rattling! The wind's blowing up again. Must have been a branch falling down!"

"No!" Hitler was standing again, boots on. "No, Dr. Sauerbruch! Nothing knocks from outside. O-o-o-only here!" He pointed to his forehead. "Hess! That fact is, inside here is where the knocking came from—suddenly! Here—in the brain of your Führer! Do you understand? Yes, great Heavens!" With a running jump, he careered two or three times around the room, stood stock still, and his cheeks flecked with red spots, shouted:

"Sit down here! Quick! You can take shorthand? Have you got some paper? Sit down—damn it! Can't you hear how it's knocking here, inside my cranium? You thieves thought you'd gotten away not only with the Will of the Supreme Führer of the New Millennium, but with his intuition too? Forward! Sit down! The spirit is coming over me!" Getting the candles from the fireplace, he set them in front of Hess. "Go to it! Pen ready? All of a sudden—I can remember sentence for sentence! That's Divine Providence! No! You're not to leave your Adolf Hitler now!"

"Keep quiet! Somebody's knocking! Can't you hear?"

"I hear it—!"

"That's Douglo!"

"Douglo! Douglo! If that's your Scot, and he's kept the Supreme Führer of the Third Reich waiting until now!—he can knock till his noble fingers bleed. For the all-highest Lord of the Aryan world has found it again. What the Jewish world conspiracy stole from me, using the little Polish ballet dancer as cat's-paw! I have it! I've found it again!

402

Just one moment."

He crouched in the chair opposite the Deputy Führer, closing his eyes and pounding with his fist on the table until he could no longer hear the knocking outside.

"Write! Go to it! Got it?"

"What? What shall I write?"

"Go ahead and write! At once! Write down—: 'Page 23, Chapter 2, Paragraph A' . . . Yes, I've got it! Exactly! Word for word, the whole text. Hess!" he whispered, "it's just come to me, clear as ice: that band of thieves will naturally falsify and distort my Last Will! . . ."

"What do you mean?"

"Yes, of course, that's the only reason they hunted for it and hunted for it! With the one end in view of finding out my weak spot! And at that point they'd like to set to work on their dark deed of destruction! But since there isn't any weak spot in me!—since the entire international canaille of the Jewish world press couldn't sniffle out anything of use to them, in any phase of my existence—that's why they sent this dancer to me in my eagle's nest! . . . And, of course, the whole pack of Jews will now set up a howl of jubilation! But I'll spoil their soup for them! You know what I'll do, Hess? I'll just tell the entire universe that the stolen will is a brazen Jewish forgery. And I'll be just as brazen about it as the Jews were when they declared the Protocols of Zion to be a forgery!"

"Adi, you should never put anything down on paper! Such a great world Führer as you dare not! . . . But there's no use crying over spilt milk."

"Yes, Hess!—Unfortunately, there's one particular section of my Will that the ghetto rabble will most certainly twist to suit their own purposes and publish it with its meaning deliberately distorted."

"What section is that?"

"Bitt' schön—it's the part about the Jewish evil eye that tries to disintegrate us Aryans. While all the time the shrapnel is bursting in battle—there he stands staring and staring! But I've taken an oath to expose that Jewish evil eye. Otherwise, in the long run, these damn criminals will have falsified every heroic virtue. Until finally they'll be saying that such a one as I was found sitting behind an alder—with my pants down! . . . No, Hess! The fact is that when those cowardly kikes insist that *every* soldier must have been a coward at *least* once in battle, that in itself is just another one of their infamous, deliberate Jewish lies!"

"Sh-h-h-h! Somebody just knocked."

"Where? Who?" For an instant Hitler was silent. Abruptly he tugged at his friend's hair.

"Oh, Hess! You see what I mean? . . . . For it was precisely with that damned milk-toast expression of his that, after the war, the Jew did everything in his power—from the editorial desk—in his advocate's robes!—as theater director—as critic—to prevent the rebirth of our German victory!

"And ever since I've almost completely fumigated their black plague out of every nook and corner of Germany, the pestilence has moved westward, entrenching itself behind the skyscrapers of America! And those plague-carriers imagine that three thousand miles of water will prevent me from exterminating the whole damn pack of vultures, even if they settle down among the redskins! . . . Go on! Write, Hess. Ready?—'My Ambassadors report to me regularly how, after every new victory of Adolf Hitler's, this pack of vultures moves farther west and how they keep on asking themselves, fearfully: "Will we have to move on from here, too?" ' "

"Magnificent!" Hess cleaned his pen. "Go on—go on!"

" 'This flock of vultures has flapped its way out to the coast of California, believing that those few thousand miles of added Indians would prevent Adolf Hitler from turning up suddenly with his Gestapo in Los Angeles, to put things to rights!' . . . Got that? Go on now: 'Oh, you Hitler scouts! I can already see those rats and vultures scurrying out of their expensive villas in Beverly Hills, Santa Barbara, and Santa Monica, and boarding the fastest ships afloat to sail out, over the Pacific! . . . But what surprise and astonishment there will be when they find, upon going ashore in Shanghai, that my Heinrich Himmler is standing on the pier and calling out: "Clear the ship of Jews!" And then he'll settle the vultures down in the rice fields of China, where they won't find anything to sit at the hearth with but the yellow sun, the monotonous sandstorm, the bleached bones of their starved brats, and the favored guest, insanity—and there will be nothing to cook but their own dung, toasted for a frugal supper! . . . Yes! Göbbels'—that is Hitler's—hate encircles the globe! Just tell that to every Hebrew!' "

"Adolf!" Overcome, Hess kissed his Führer's hand. "Well I knew that you are great! But, that you could be *so* tremendous—"

"Bitt' schön! What the hell do you know!" Leaning back exhausted, Hitler stared into space. "Yes, what do any of you know of—*who* Adolf Hitler really is!" His expression became so hideous that Hess drew away, but the Führer came after him. "Darling, have *you* any

404

idea—who I am?" He held his breath, as if he himself could scarcely bear to make his final revelation. But suddenly his wild eyes bored into his friend's. "You!" he rumbled, "my astrologer told me that in the Apocrypha it says Christ prophesied that he would come again to dissolve the works of woman!"

Hess's eyes narrowed. Several seconds passed. Hitler moved closer.

"Party Comrade Rudi! Why do you start so? Perhaps you know now—*who* I am? Hm? As a matter of fact—apart from all you idiots—the whole of nature knows it—"

"Oh, dearest! Was not *I* the very first—who recognized you at once?"

"What's that you say?" All at once he pushed Hess down to his knees, pressing his shoulders lower and lower, raving on over him: "Yes! He is here! He of whom it was prophesied that he should come again in two thousand years—"

"What?" The Deputy Führer's head trembled, but as he could not bring himself to look his friend's madness in the face, he crouched down so that his forehead almost touched Hitler's boots.

"So you're shuddering, my sweet Saint John? . . . Yes, bitt' schön, you have to have been up there on Golgotha, gazing into yawning, infinite emptiness, before you can understand that there's no such thing for us human beings as an All-loving Father up in Heaven! That for us there is nothing but this earth, and our short span of life on this earth. Ha-ha! Tell me, how do you actually explain your Führer's magic? these unparalleled successes?—Darling"—he stooped down to Hess—"do you believe in me? You know, Marshal Keitel and the other Prussian swine—all they think of is how to increase their own fame by riding on my coat tails! But they don't *believe!* You must *believe!* From now on it must depend on your belief!"

"Yes, but what?" Hess grew more and more terrified.

"What must you believe? Believe that I am the son of merciless nature who likewise knows no pity. Who on a single tree produces millions of blossoms and, coldly smiling, let's all but *one* of them be trodden into the ground . . . You must believe that I have returned to this earth to make good my error and my madness on Golgotha. No! There is no Heaven! And I am going to destroy all these old-wives' imaginings. Do you believe that? Do you believe it?" His tongue clicked. He shook all over. Hess embraced his knees and whimpered:

"I believe it."

Hitler straightened his back, stretching every joint and sinew so that his height was visibly increased. Suddenly he twisted his mouth and

405

opened it like a hole. Then hideous sounds of triumph roared out of him.

There was another knock on the window. Hitler flinched. Hess sprang to his feet.

"Adolf!" Supporting him in his arms, he helped him to the sofa. As the knocking became more insistent, Hitler goggled at the window like a medium coming out of a trance:

"Somebody's knocking! . . ."

"I told you so . . . the whole time . . ."

"Hess!" His eyes darted here and there. "Somebody's knocking! Get out your revolver!"

"Haven't got one with me—"

"What?" He held a sofa cushion before his face. "Are you insane? You bring me out to this place—unarmed?"

"But Adolf—that's only Douglo!"

"Be quiet! Douse those candles! Idiot! To come out here without any weapons! Where it's simply teeming with refugees! Have you lost your mind? Be still! There you are! A fine pickle! Softly! Of course, some Jew must have been watching when I left the Embassy! Let them knock! Don't answer! Silence! Hear all those feet in the garden? Nothing but Jews! They've found out that I'm here!"

"Out of the question, Ado! That can only be Douglo!"

Outside the window, a voice called loudly:

"I am Nicodemus Latour!"

"What did he say? Who? Latour at last? Providence—"

"Latour? Then Ribbentrop sent him after us!"

"No! Providence! Hess, Hess!" He rose elastically. "And I was sure that my hour had come! Can't you see"—he giggled on—"it just demonstrates the utter idiocy of the Jews and freemasons. It's Latour —and not them. They didn't have any Heinrich Himmler—or they'd have known they could catch Adolf Hitler in this villa. Ha-ha!

"Hess, quick! Put the candles back on the table!"

"That's a dirty trick!" Hess shook his head. "Ribbentrop and his Abetz fixed it up together. But Adolf—Adolf—you promised me: Nothing against England!"

"Come—hurry up and let the Colonel in."

Reluctantly Hess went and opened the window.

CHAPTER FOUR

Through the open window, the lower part of his figure hidden by the sill, appeared a colonel of Spahis. His face, shadowed by the high French helmet, was unrecognizable. Fingers together, palm outward, he touched the blue steel and announced:

"Nicodemus Latour, First Aide-de-Camp of Marshal Pétain . . ."

"Come in! Come in!" Hitler was in high spirits. "Entrez, my dear Colonel!"

Gathering up the long, rust-red African cloak that hung from his shoulders in many folds, the Spahi climbed over the sill into the hall. He was wearing gold-embroidered, tasseled Turkish trousers.

Stretching out his right arm horizontally, the Führer bent it at the elbow, showing the palm of his hand in greeting. Then he introduced Hess: "My Deputy Führer!"

The Colonel's spurs jingled as he brought his heels together.

"Rudi, Rudi"—Hitler became more and more cheerful—"it's so gloomy in here! See if you can't find some more candles! Let's have lots of light! Oh, I feel so happy! I only regret that the necessity for strict secrecy compelled me to choose this out-of-the-way spot, my dear Latour. For Adolf Hitler has enemies! Paris is full of Jews! At any rate you're here now. Splendid! Bring the candles over here, Hess! Another one! And who brought you here? The officer on duty of my bodyguard?"

"Prince Ferdinand?" Hess asked. Finding an old, rusty lantern, he opened it, producing another candle stump, which he lit.

"Please be seated! Do sit down! Asseyez-vous, Monsieur! Yes, I've still got a few crumbs of French left over from the war. Delighted! Very pleased to stand face-to-face with the first adjutant of that brave marshal who, as my Under-Secretary of State Abetz tells me, when he was only Lieutenant Pétain, made heroic efforts during the shameless Dreyfus case, to throw into the scales the voice of 'secret', national France against the corrupt, international republic, ruled by Jewish females. Cher Colonel!" He wiped his nose and tried—not without difficulty—to suppress the joyous excitement which had been growing in him ever since his fear that he had been trapped here by his enemies had dropped from him.

"Something to drink? What can I offer you? . . . Oh! Croix de

Guerre? A front-line fighter, eh? Front-line fighter understands front-line fighter! . . . But damn it, why don't you sit down? Of course I have magnificent palaces in Berlin! Munich! Berchtesgaden! In Königsberg and Posen! mon cher! There I have every sort of pomp and luxury! But I like this better . . . Two front-line fighters! Or rather three! Friend Hess was also a front-line soldier! It's just as if we met in some temporary communications hut behind the lines! Not even any electric light! Yes, you probably imagined a more Napoleonic figure as the ruler of three-quarters of the world! But I am still the simple lance-corporal of the world war, just as I was then!"

The Spahi surveyed his surroundings. Out in the garden, the tree trunks groaned. Somewhere in the darkness an owl flew by, with heavy beat of velvet wings, and hooted.

"My Foreign Minister"—irritated by the unusual silence of his visitor, Hitler drifted into small talk—"His Excellency Ribbentrop has probably informed you as to the reason for my unexpected presence in Paris, hitherto,—thank God!—a strict secret? But won't you have a glass of wine?"

"Allow me—" Hess poured from the depleted bottle of Sauterne— "I believe there's still some left . . ."

"Have you brought your chief's proposals? My Chief of Staff Halder sent your Marshal my conditions over a week ago . . ."

"I am well aware," the Spahi began, "that this night's meeting is equivalent to a decision of world-shaking importance—"

"Decisions of world-shaking importance"—Hitler did not let him continue—"are always attained in the simplest manner. For instance, your General Bonaparte put an end to the Revolution simply by peppering grape-shot into the insolent advocates of the 'Rights of Man'! In our Berlin, a polite lieutenant in the Wilhelmstrasse captured the whole cowardly republican crew of the Weimar Jew Republic and held them captive in the Chancellery—without a single 'hero' having fired a shot in self-defense! Moreover, it was on a night like this that Marshal Pilsudski, with only two squadrons of dragoons, seized his position as President of Poland." Pushing the candles aside, Hitler fixed the Spahi with cunning eyes. "And whether it's called the 'White House' or the 'Red House'—you can o-o-o-only swing the thing according to the code of the 'Brown House'. Courage, Colonel! Believe me: all these democrats suddenly get 'brown-pants' when they look into the muzzle of a gun in the hands of a man! Ha-ha! . . . . How late is it now?"

"2:26 A.M., my Führer!" Hess replied.

"The very best time! People are sound asleep! There you are, Colonel! Into the saddle and off you go! You at the head of a few hundred cavalrymen! Dépêchez-vous! Off you go! While it's still dark! And then you simply load your trucks with whatever scum isn't already dead on the ground! You don't suppose my people would manage any differently in Washington? Courage, Colonel! In exactly one hour, at 3:36 A.M., on the basis of my experience, you can be master of the capital! . . . Precisely so the Duce became master of Rome! And I, Führer of Germany! Don't delay another instant! In a few hours it will be daylight! At the present moment, the republicans are still snoring . . . Courage! You won't be confronted with the blood of heroic warriors when, saber in hand, you suddenly enter their bedrooms! Oh, no! The red spots on the nightshirts of democratic ministers are simply from the lipstick of their women! So, courage! Why should the blood of brave soldiers flow in the plowed fields of battle? Let the Jews' blood flow instead!

"Colonel!" Pushing his chair closer, his expression that of a horse-thief, he muttered: "Latour! We've got four regiments of picked troops, scattered about your Place de la Concorde, disguised in civilian clothes—"

"But fully epuipped!" Now Hess too looked craftily at the Spahi. "Absolutely A-1!"

"So—off you go! Occupy all radio stations! Two regiments, I estimate, should suffice for the coup, and our Lehar can write an operetta all about it later! Ha-ha! A few hand grenades in the Salle des Miroirs —and your famous 'Liberté' will be losing its dinner!"

"Yes, yes!" Hess's cheeks were hot with excitement.

"Dearest Latour!" Hitler continued. "Sometimes when I go for a solitary stroll in my Bavarian Alps, and I feel how the broad Hand of Providence is laid upon my back, pushing me forward—then I ask myself: 'Can it really be true that I—the unknown soldier—have been called upon to restore justice to history? . . . That *I* alone shall really stand upon this globe, proudly holding out to Providence the hacked-off, imbecile Medusa head of the perverse and monstrous chaos of Bolshevism? That I at last shall be able to report to Providence that, for the next thousand years: "Orders have been carried out!"' "

Inasmuch as the Spahi, biting his lips, persisted in silence, Hess suggested to his Führer:

"But perhaps the Colonel is himself one of the heirs of the red revolution, and still believes in the 'rights of man'?"

"What? No! I can't believe that of an aide-de-camp of Marshal

Pétain's! Oh, no! I understand your silence, my dear Colonel: it is the mortified answer of a front-line soldier with nationalist convictions. Never mind, Colonel! Adolf Hitler's strong arm is at your disposal. Go! And make use of it so that no longer shall any Hebrew build his huts or dig his caves by the Seine, the Loire, the Garonne or whatever the rest of your Frankish rivers are called! Significant, isn't it, that the only body of water that Israel has to call its own is—what? The Dead Sea! Now, I'll tell you something else: On Adolf Hitler's map of the world, there's another spot especially reserved for the Israelites and it's called: 'The Dead People'!"

But then, somehow disturbed by the presence of this silent Spahi, as if beginning to sense some mystery about him, he leaned forward, staring at the many insects attracted from the night outside that now lay burned or stunned around the candle . . . Several minutes passed . . . The Spahi stood up. The blue trench helmet above the red cavalry cloak, reflecting the flickering candle flames seemed in Hitler's eyes to glitter with strange colors. Or was it still the effect of the opium?

He looked up. Hess, who thought that the outlandish uniform was beginning to annoy his friend, asked:

"Mein Führer—is that all that Colonel Latour has to say in answer to your glorious proposals? . . ."

The Colonel saluted: "Your Excellency—!"

"Ouch! Please do me the honor not to call me by that ridiculous title of the past century—"

"The fact is—"

"The fact is what? My good man, the fact is it's getting on for 3:00 A.M.! So vite! Get back to your squadrons!" Since, however, the Colonel remained obstinately standing, Hitler raked him from top to bottom with his Gestapo look and growled: "Go! Or have you any further orders?"

The red cloak parted down the middle. And, before Hitler could grasp the gesture, the Spahi had them covered, an army revolver in each hand.

"I have orders to shoot you!"

CHAPTER FIVE "WHA-A-A-AT? IS EVERYBODY DRUNK TODAY?" THE FÜHRER GAVE A CHOKED LAUGH AND WOULD HAVE made for the door, but the Spahi gestured with his revolvers

"Don't move!"

"Hess! Hess!" His eyes found the Deputy Führer, who stood there, blanched to the lips. "Hess!"

"Halt!" The Spahi barred the way with his revolvers.

"Bitt' schön. Then you're not—? Who the devil are you?" He squeezed along the wall behind the furniture to Hess, who had taken refuge in the shelter of the fireplace. But the Spahi followed, threatening:

"Come out of that! if you don't want your face-powdered Party Comrade to get hit too—!"

"I?" Hess ducked, his face chalk-white.

"Are you mad?" Hitler sprang out, picked up a candle, and ran to the window curtain, hoping to save himself by setting the place on fire.

The Spahi pulled the trigger—*bang!* The candle dropped to the floor. Hitler rushed back to the fireplace.

"Did he do anything to you, Adolf?"

"Bitt' schön—am I bleeding?"

Upstairs in the darkness, Baldur crept to the landing, reached out. And the next instant a heavy armchair flew through the air, smashing to the floor a few steps from the Spahi. He whirled round—"Who's there?"—and fired at the balcony. There was the sound of creaking boards, then silence.

A moment later the silence was broken by the heavy rattling of motor trucks on the highway. The villa trembled to its foundations. With wild and terrible vigor a chorus of husky voices was heard singing:

"Allons, enfants de la patrie . . . !"

"Mobilized troops?—already on their way to the border?" The Spahi shot an inquiring look through the window. Then for the first time he looked closely at Hitler.

Yes, there he stood. He . . . the one! . . . the only one! . . . At whose sole behest all those unknown men had to set out again. From here, there, and everywhere. From house and hearth! From plowed and

411

fallow fields! . . . From study and workshop! . . . And away down the long roads! Either as refugees—or with guns on their shoulders . . . To jam their rifle stocks against their cheeks and take aim at human beings—whenever this one man gave the order. He at whose sole command peaceful, fertile lands could be transformed by tank divisions into desolate wastes like nothing so much as the frozen craters of the moon! . . .

Abruptly the singing outside broke off, and the roar of the heavy trucks died away. Almost at once there was the sound of dry twigs crackling, as if under someone's approaching feet.

"Rudi!" Hitler huddled close to his kneeling friend, staring into the black night through the tall open window.

"Adi! Are we lost?" The curtain flapped. "Or was that only the wind?"

"So-o-o-o!" The Colonel sat down. Still keeping both revolvers aimed, he leaned back in the chair. Stretching out one leg, he extinguished the guttering candle on the floor with his boot. Then he drew the other candles closer, and pushed the trench helmet back on his forehead.—Uhle's face was completely changed. Cold hate distorted his usually kindly features. With biting irony he asked:

"So then—you are the unknown soldier of the world war?"

"Bitt' schön. Yes! Who are you?"

"I?" Uhle thrust forward his right shoulder; his eyes held him inescapably: "I am a German—a German to whom you have made the word 'German' nauseous!"

"A German?" Grinning nervously, the Führer mumbled something unintelligible. Uhle, however, turned brusquely on Hess:

"Hey, you Julius Streicher's boon companion! Go and untie that curtain cord there and hand it to your amico. In '34 in the Berlin Opera House this Brown rough-houser proclaimed to the assembled Nazi hordes: 'I, Adolf Hitler, am the one and only Supreme Justice, and against my judgment there is no appeal!' . . . Therefore I say that such a unique Supreme Justice can only be dispatched into the bottomless pit by his own just hand!"

His revolver poised, he followed Hess's every movement. Staggering, the Deputy Führer detached the heavy braided silk cord from the wooden knob, clumsily unknotted it, and, lurching back, handed it to his Führer.

"To the wall!" ordered Uhle—his voice growing every moment hoarser and more sinister: "Stand at attention! Hands at your sides! And don't make any false move, or I'll shoot you too. Understand?"

"Yes!" stammered Hess, moving quickly. "Yes, yes!"

"So now we'll proceed. A Hitler cannot but know how to go about it! The blood baths he has prescribed for 'minorities' must have taught him at least that! So, go ahead now! Begin!"

"Bitt' schön . . ." Hitler shuddered. "I certainly can't strangle myself!"

"No? Why can't you?" Uhle roared at him. "You can do it just as well as you can have an innocent dancer tortured to death . . . just as well as you can have countless other human beings strangled!"

"I can't do it. Bitt' schön . . . I can't do it!" Hitler stared at the cord in his hand. Suddenly he threw it down at Uhle's feet, showed his teeth—and produced sounds such as ring through the corridors of mad-houses.

Hess swayed against the wall. Only when Hitler barked at him did he revive from his faintness enough to gasp:

"When you're dead, Adolf—you can count on me!"

"When I'm dead! Ha-ha!"

"Pick up that cord and get on with it!"

"Bitt' schön! If you've never killed yourself, it takes a bit longer than shaving! Where's a mirror? At least, I want to see how it looks when Adolf Hitler can't breathe any more! . . ."

"Go on!"

"Now, look! Shouldn't I soap the cord first? My brave Buch always says it jerks tight better with kitchen soap."

"Do you want to wait until they come to lynch you?"

"Lynch me!" Hitler jumped up and leered into the garden. "Who's coming? Who wants to lynch me?"

But under Uhle's stormy, blazing eyes, he bent over the rope again, and muttered with chattering teeth: "Well, hanging may include some agreeable sensations."

"Get on with your hanging."

"Bitt' schön . . . under no circumstances will I be buried in Tannenberg alongside that tax-swindling swine, Hindenburg!—And Hess . . . when I'm really lying dead here, don't you dare close my eyes! I want to see what goes on afterward! What a pretty picture that will be! The way the dynastic sewer rats will pull out their crowns and coronets from behind their chamberpots and walk out again in the broad light of day! Bah! All the cousins of the plutocracy who have never yet lacked an Apostolic blessing! Phui!" He spat copiously.

"I'll bequeath the whole pack of dynasts to the White House. I hear that, every time I've kicked out some middle-aged, faded somebody and the damn stiff lands by clipper on La Guardia Field in New York, the White House suffers convulsions of the bowels! Ha-ha! Hess! Leave my eyes wide open! I want to look on while the Hebrews in New York and Paris light their seven-branched candlesticks and munch their mazzos and play oriental leap-frog round their fat roast geese—ha-ha!—all because the Bolsheviks have carried their red Star of Zion into Berlin in triumph!"

"I'll count up to three!" Uhle suddenly took aim: "One! . . ."

"Stop, stop! I simply cannot imagine it! How can I be dead? It's true, I have often walked along the narrow path to the cemetery when the east wind blew across the fields and the Bürgermeister and the priest would be coming down the walk from Braunau . . . Wait! Don't shoot!"

"Two . . ."

"Not yet . . . just a minute more! Shall I be able to get some sleep after this? . . . . without that fat slob Meissner sticking his chopped-up face in the door and drooling 'My Führer! Lord Halifax is here!' 'My Führer, the most exalted Duke of Windsor is just driving up with his most gracious, lovely consort!' . . . 'My Führer! The diplomatic corps of all nations and peoples, including America, is waiting downstairs in full regalia in the Brown Marble Hall, impatiently expecting your most gracious appearance!' . . . Yes—the Papal Nuncio, as the doyen of all these bedecorated, bestarred-and-gartered, totally superfluous chowder heads simply couldn't wait to wish me a blessed long life and good luck for New Year's in 1939! Ha-ha! When I am dead, shall I be rid of the whole tribe of Halifaxes? . . ."

"I repeat, two."

"All aboard!" The Führer blew an imaginary conductor's whistle. "Train leaving for Heaven! Ascension!" He looked for a hook on which to fix the rope. With the silk cord noosed around his neck like a badly tied necktie, he suddenly bellowed like a passenger who, just as the train starts pulling out, realizes that he has left something important behind:

"Hess! Hess! Hess! Be sure you stick 'Keep off the grass!' signs all over my Obersalzberg. Otherwise the Jews and Reds will come running in leather shorts, disguised as Tyrolians, and make a filthy picnic ground of all my mountains around Bayreuth! Hess! Beware! For, once I'm dead, the whole Venusberg amusement park will be thrown wide open again. And the next thing you know all those red-smeared females will have blond wigs made out of the hair of my wantonly butchered Hitler Youth, to wear over their black frizzly hair! And

414

when in the last act of the Passion Play at Oberammergau, they've finally hammered the long nails into the hands and feet of the accursed goy on the Cross—there'll be a bedlam of applause! . . . What?" He laughed raucously at the spectacle of his Deputy Führer, motionless, backed against the wall. "Rudichen! Doesn't even brush the flies off his nose! In such deadly earnest over the death-watch beside the future corpse of his 'Beloved Führer!' So-o-o! Now the only thing I need is my Cardinal Faulhaber in his blood-red silk robe to give me absolution! . . . Wait! Hess! Make a note of Adolf Hitler's very last thought for his Pan-Germany, before death sets in: Every night about 2:00 A.M. there's a death-watch beetle that ticks away in my night table. 'Tick! Tick!' And every time I put the chamber pot back again there's always a tiny heap of sawdust there. Are you listening, Hess? . . . And this is my command: The National Socialist Party shall guarantee its daily bread of charity to this faithful denizen of Obersalzberg! Because he always went 'tick-tick' before the clock went on! And I can never forget that . . . 'Tick-tick!' . . . Especially when it began to be so dark and dismal round my throat, and a pale face looked over the foot of my bed—"

But before Uhle's ever approaching revolver Hitler moved the cord lower on his Adam's apple, stepped up on a chest, and threw the cord over a window hook. Then he blinked with terror into Uhle's eyes. Their great light blinded him, like a single, strange brilliance.

Suddenly he felt that out of the air all around, millions of eyes were staring at him. Not the fish eyes he had dug out at the Embassy and flipped against the window, but all the terror-frozen eyes of his victims. White and dull, they looked at him out of the gas chambers and the mass graves. Millions of dead eyes, looking out of the terrifying silence of murdered bodies. Their stare was like the ineluctable beckoning of death.

Hitler gasped for breath as if the walls of his wind pipe had grown together. Suddenly he let himself fall. But under the weight of his body the hook pulled out and he thudded to the floor. There for some seconds he lay. Suddenly he leaped up, spun round on his heels, tottered, blue in the face, his spotted hyena eyes darting back and forth. And then, as if driven by the Furies, he reeled into an adjoining room.

CHAPTER SIX "**I**S HE DEAD?" UHLE—WITH A "BRING A CANDLE"—WAS QUICK BEHIND HESS. HESS HELD THE LIGHT HIGH, in the dead air of the room.

"There he is!" Hess set down the candle and bent over his Führer, who was lying by a rack full of billiard cues. He loosened the noose.

"Stand him up!"

"He's so heavy—"

"Stand him up!"

Hitler's eyes opened and blinked while Hess lugged him to the billiard table. Half lying on the green cloth, he stared at the smooth white ivory balls—which, with their long tapering shadows, lay there motionless like heavenly bodies whirled out of their orbits in the cosmos. Not until a huge black spider scurried across the table away from the candlelight, did he jerk back to his surroundings. He looked wonderingly around the bare, shadow-filled room. But at the sight of Uhle's cocked revolvers, life returned to his terror-whitewashed face.

"Bitt' schön," he whispered. "At your service"—but then his whole body began to quake so that the billiard table shook. For a full minute, Uhle kept him covered, then a tremor of disgust seized him.

"Go ahead! Hess! Take that cord and help that animal to make a quick jump out of the memory of man!"

"Who? I? Oh, no! no!" The tears ran down the Deputy Führer's cheeks. "No! I won't do it! No!" He threw himself on Hitler, clinging to his neck and kissing him. Dazedly, the Führer accepted the course of events. All at once, however, Hess grasped the curtain cord and exerted his powers of persuasion!

"Come! Adol! Come! You will live on in your people! . . . Come! I'll be very gentle! Let's show this inhuman being our National Socialist courage! . . . Come! You won't feel a thing!"

"What?" Hitler screamed, "what's that fat Adonis raving about? Hey! What are you going to pay my friend Hess for the head of the Supreme Reich Führer? Hey? Get the devil out of this!" He shoved Hess against the cue rack. "So! I'm going to live on in my people? And that's why you lured me out of the Embassy into this murderer's den? So that's your scheme—all cut and dried—eh? And *he* is your Douglo —eh? All so that Herr Hess can be Führer soon! Oh! What a dumb ox I am." He slapped his brow. "The one time in my life I'm guilty of a

416

stupidity! To come here unarmed! To trust a Rudolf Hess!"

The silence grew oppressive. The candle began to fail. Abruptly, seizing Hitler's black forelock Hess tugged and pulled at it, trying to force the noose down over his head again. At that, Hitler bit his wrist so hard that his friend let go, howling.

"Vorwärts!" Uhle pointed grimly at the stub of candle. "Before that burns down—"

"Listen! Give me one of your revolvers—and I'll fire it into my mouth! But don't torment me with that ridiculous curtain cord! It's so degrading! A green silk cord! Who ever heard of such a thing?"

"Yes!" Hess chimed in. "Shoot us both dead!"

"I'm not going to make martyrs or myths out of the two of you!"

"Oh, I simply can't stand this torture!"

"Hessel!"

"Oh, Adi!"

"Rudilein!"

"Oh, Adilein!"

They clung to each other, mussing each other's hair, and watching the dying candle flame grow ever smaller . . .

"I simply can't grasp it!"

"Nor I, Adola!"

"How is it possible? Just because that bloody gangster there has two filthy revolvers in his hands! Simply because of those blithering cartridges? And for no other reason, this perverse puppy dares— Just because a genius like me, for once makes a little mistake!" He licked the tears from his mustache. "Just because I haven't got a revolver with me! No! Stop! Bitt' schön—look here! Be nice! Just let us go out into the garden—just for one second!"

"Yes! Just for a breath of fresh air—!" Hess whimpered. "Fresh air—"

"Bitt' schön—just for a half a second—"

"Just for a half a second?" Uhle hesitated. Then he said icily: "Very well! Whichever one of you finishes off the other first—I'll let him go out for a last breath of fresh air."

"What's that?" They stared at each other.

"Yes! Whichever is the stronger of you two—can go out in the garden again—"

"Wh-a-a-a-t?"

And then—under the eyelashes of the two candidates for death— a dark fire began to flicker.

"Better make yourself scarce, Ado! You know I'm a little stronger than you! I warn you—!"

"So! You're getting that Bedouin glare in your eyes again?"

"Get out of my way! Look out now!"

"Don't bark at me, you jackal!"

"I warn you! Out of my way!"

"What? Even a greasy old hook-nose like Abraham didn't hesitate when God commanded him to take the knife to his Isaac! And you won't lay down your life on the altar of the National Socialist Party?"

"Out of my way! I tell you—Adi!"

"You won't die for me? When millions cheerfully immolate themselves for me? When there isn't a single person in the Pan-German Reich who wouldn't gladly be flayed alive for me! The Hitler females just lie down for me like cows in a stable—when I need fresh soldiers! My picture hangs over their beds instead of a saint! For me, life is procreated and life is destroyed. And my Rudolf Hess hesitates to die for me? When my Hitler Scouts—boys I've never even seen—shut themselves up inside torpedoes to be dropped as living bombs on the transport ships of all enemies of the Third Reich!"

"Out of the way! You know my muscles! Get away! Out! Out! You've lived your life! You've had all the intoxication of leadership! Out with you! *You* sacrifice yourself for your party! We party comrades have a right to demand that! Sacrifice *yourself!*"

"You Arab!" Hitler jumped on his shoulders from behind, bending his head back. But then Hess went mad:

"You miserable pipsqueak mock Christ, you!" And he snatched a billiard cue and went for Hitler. "So-o-o! How d'you like that! Maybe this'll fix you! You greedy goat, had enough, eh? You stinkpot!" Hess mopped his face with his pocket handkerchief. But as Hitler was still moving, he flew at him again:

"Are you going to be quiet, you rancid lecher? Hey? You drunken Messiah! Now!—if you want to resurrect yourself, there's nothing to stop you! But if you so much as budge—I'll show you the way to heaven, you stinker! You senile old man of fifty! Who stole the best years of my life? You! You! You!" He began hitting him with his fists.

"I gave you my all! . . . And you? All you were going to do was just finish me off! Simply to save *your* magnificent life! Well, I want to live too! Do you hear me? I'm not 'Fräulein Hess' any longer! You won't catch me pulling out the gray hairs on your breast any more! You can just turn on your shower yourself!" His cheek bones protruded, his tongue hung out dry and rough.

All at once Uhle cried out: "He's still alive!" And was about to give

Hitler the coup de grace when Hess, like a tigress protecting her young, threw himself in the way of the revolver.

"Kill me! . . . But not Adolf!" He flung himself on his friend's body, covering it with his own, clinging to him. "Adi! Can you hear me? Listen to me! It's me! . . . Stop! Stop!" he implored Uhle. "Don't shoot! Tremendous tasks before him! The housing problem for millions! Transformation of agrarian countries into industrial countries! Don't shoot! The very existence of Germany as a great power is at stake! Only Ado can protect Europe against brazen America and Asia! . . . Adi! Take my life! Adi! Even if I'll never be able to drive with you and Rommel across the Lion Bridge in Cairo—and we'll never drink chocolate together on the roof garden of the Hotel Semiramis—looking down on the Nile! Adi! I'll die for you! Even if I must give up my dream of sitting with you on top of the Pyramid of Cheops at sunset! Adi! Even if I shall never see your black-coated S.S. officers mixing with the red-coated British to celebrate the final victory over the Judocracies at a banquet in Sheppard's Hotel! . . . Adi! promise you'll think of me then—when you drive along the great Avenue of Acacias to Gizeh—even though I won't be able to button up your camel's-hair coat against the icy, desert night! Adi! Buy me a green silk scarf in the Arab bazaar! . . . gold-green like the grass on the banks of the Nile—when the round sun goes down in silent fire between the palms! And lay it on my grave! Du! . . . Du!"

CHAPTER SEVEN   FOR A MOMENT UHLE WAS CONFUSED BY THIS ABRUPT TRANSITION FROM THE OUTPOURINGS OF HATE TO a canine whining. But then his eyes began to flame:

"So *this* is how it looks when someone like you is confronted by the fact: death! You desecrator of the breath of life! You violator of the human body! . . . Do not you know that each single movement of the dancer you murdered was worth more than all you credit yourself with ever having achieved? Thousands of years have labored to evolve one such exquisite muscle—a muscle that in the dance annuls the very law of gravity! . . . And you proceed to destroy—not only that one miracle of creation—you murder human beings by the hundreds of thousands. Yes—cold-bloodedly extinguish the life of a whole

419

race with its thousand-year-old culture! But when it comes to ridding the world of yourself—something that any decent atheist, or even a disappointed Communist, is at any time prepared to do without much fuss—such a blasphemer and iconoclast as you hasn't even got the courage! Hey? A professional mass-murderer like yourself—and you haven't even the guts?"

While Uhle was speaking, Hitler, wriggling awkwardly, had freed himself from the arms of his Deputy Führer. He bared his teeth at Uhle.

"Bitt' schön . . . what do you expect? I am I! And everything else is just—not I! . . . And that's the only thing that matters!"

"I? I! So it all adds up to 'I'? Well—for once you've miscalculated!"

"Miscalculated? No! Bitt' schön! *My* reckoning is correct. No, you are not going to do anything to me! No! You're no murderer! Ergo, you won't *dare* shoot me."

Uhle, who had alternately turned red and pale during this speech, answered gratingly:

"You have left the unknown X out of your calculations. And to that unknown quantity I shall now surrender you—"

"Surrender me?" Hitler gave a start. "What does that mean?"

"And then you shall be passed from hand to hand. And die a hundred times over. Out there in the woods there are people waiting for a signal from me. People who have spent years working out a clear philosophy and an adequate technique—"

"Out there in the garden?" Hitler interjected, and stared through the open window. "What people? What kind of people?"

"There's one, for instance, who has spent weeks getting his hand in by plunging red-hot needles into the head of a wax doll fashioned in your likeness. There's a rabbi out there, too. And an Alsatian violin-maker. And Sorbonne professors. Refugees—whose entire kith and kin you have massacred. And now they know only one way of serving God—and that is to see that your last scream of torture on the rack shall be prolonged into infinity."

"What!" Hitler tore the noose off his neck. "Aha—a hireling of the Jews! So *this* is what you world-reformers look like! Think themselves so infinitely above the Reich Führer? And all the time they're waiting out there in the garden for nothing on earth except to torture me with my own Himmler's Gestapo tricks! While I, on the contrary—the Nazi leader you despise so much—*I* stand here all the time quietly waiting for the moral fire of all you superethical anti-National-Socialist Judocrats to touch my heart! Bitt' schön—waiting for the flame of your new world order to descend on such a poor devil as me—to warm my poor damned soul!"

His eyeballs protruding, he glared out into the wind-stirred darkness of the garden.

"The fire of the new world order"—Uhle stressed each word—"is already crackling through the building of your Third Reich, in all the high towers that you have built against God."

"You blackguard," Hitler flung at him. "A man who is what I am doesn't believe in a better world order, like you Judocrats! And that is the difference between you and me! No—I don't believe in mmmmankind!"

"No. *You* believe only in the beast in man!"

"If I had you in my power, as you have me in yours—you can be sure I'd prolong *your* last scream on the rack into infinity. That's what my Motz Street Barracks are for—ha-ha! So why don't you give your people outside the signal they're waiting for? It would actually be a pleasure to me to tell your Sorbonne professors to their faces how happy I am at last to have found out—definitely—that your whole Sermon-on-the-Mount imbecility that has been on tap in the churches and universities since Golgotha is definitely dead. Even in an ethocrat like you—! Yes, that makes it easier for me to leave this world!—to realize that your international-world-peace Sunday face and all the Nazarene's holiness-touting are finally and irrevocably dead in my adversaries! Yes, even in that mug of yours there isn't a spark now of him who once said, 'Bless them that curse you; do good to them that revile you, and despitefully use you!' Even *your* brain is straining itself trying to think up more and more horrible tortures for me—worse than the Catholic Inquisition and my General Buch. To be perfectly frank, that pleases me. It pleases me that you prize moral exemplars of Western civilization, when you get down to the business of exterminating an enemy, find you can't get anywhere with the Gospel of Love! That *you* use torture too! Tanks, bombers, and plenty of T.N.T.! That pleases me—as much as an Old-Testament Psalm of hate and revenge."

He laughed until Hess too caught the infection. And then the two of them yodeled their duet of mockery out into the dark garden together. As Uhle approached, Hitler suddenly roared at him like a gorged hyena:

"But I tell you—I tell you—even if you Judocrats should succeed in the West—bitt' schön—even if you hypocritical Lebanon lice could really egg my Americans into a war with the German race—I say, even if your goy-hating Morgenthau should manage to blast every good seed in the Indian West, until a great, industrious people with whom we Germans have no quarrel should at last, at Zion's order, turn their cannons against my movement—bitt' schön—one thing is sure: you may kill me, but you will not kill my hate. No, you Yankees! My hate will celebrate its most sublime orgies in your hate! For, supposing that the hate artificially injected by the Jews were actually finally to conquer my Third Reich—bitt' schön—would that be the victory of the Sermon on the Mount? NO!" His croaking shrilled over Uhle. "No, my esteemed Mr. President and churchgoers, it would be simply and solely the victory of *my hate!*—in you! Yes!" He looked straight into Uhle's horror-stricken eyes. "Because there's no escape from it. The law of hate is in me. And from me, hate passes over into others. And from them, it goes out into the world. The hate will be *in* you, you moralistic quacks—even if you shoot me down this minute. And it will burn on! Could anything be more magnificent!"

White-faced, Uhle stood before that mask of aboriginal hate of everything that would fain free itself from the animal sphere and become human. His mouth foamed with insane fury. For never before had the shame, the curse, with which the monster polluted the name not only of Germany but of all mankind—never before had it rankled in his blood as it did now. And he knew of no alternative but: either he would blow the monster's brain to atoms—or blow out his own in selfloathing. But as he took aim again at the flame-thrower of hate before him, he suddenly knew that he too was all on fire, that in his eyes there was now nothing but the blind white of mortal hate. In the anguish of that knowledge, he made a powerful effort to summon up before his darkening soul the quiet clear eyes of his Unknown Soldier. And the more he was successful, the more clearly he heard again the two voices, at his left ear and at his right, which he had heard whispering on the roof of the cathedral before the stone angel that afternoon:

"Shoot," one voice urged. "Do you want your mortal enemy to live? Dreamer!"

"Think!" warned the other. "For if you shoot him, will you be doing anything better than what he would do if he were in your place?"

"What was that?" came the whisper on the left. "You hesitate? Now —when you could satisfy your hatred of him! An eye for an eye! A tooth for a tooth!"

Then, as once before, the other voice asked:

"Has God chosen you to be his judge?"

Uhle groaned. For the very thought that the Creative Spirit—the

422

Spirit that separates Good and Evil—should have chosen him to represent Its Justice, crushed him. Slowly the muzzles of his revolvers sank.

Hitler was quick to notice it.

"What's this?" he triumphed in a whisper to Hess. "Isn't the assassin going to shoot? Bitt' schön, he has bullets in his firing chambers—and he doesn't shoot? He could spatter our brains against the wall—and he doesn't do it? That is stark staring madness!—Or the beginning . . . of . . . bitt' schön—of what?" He twitched. "This is worse than the plague, Hess—I'm his mortal enemy . . . and he is my mortal enemy! But if mortal enemies are no longer going to shoot at each other—then I ask you: what was gunpowder invented for?"

Suddenly he began to shake in every joint. Yet he went on babbling in an undertone to Hess, meanwhile staring into Uhle's face, which was steadily growing calmer and more inescapable:

"Bitt' schön, Rudi—there you are! Didn't the imbecile pioneer stand there just like that behind the alder that day, with his imbecile eyes popping out under his helmet, and try to make us doubt every national reality? Yes, those decadent types are always around wherever brave soldiers have been shooting at each other.—Hess! you see! He doesn't shoot. Can my astrologer have been right? Are the two thousand years accomplished? Has the goateed Bolshevik from Nazareth come back again?—Has the time really arrived when panzer divisions will have to put on their brakes before his cosmic gaze, and then stand around idiotically on the battlefield, their ammunition chests still full—because nobody wants to shoot any more!?" Suddenly he roared at Uhle, "I hate you! Because you too are nothing but another follower of the sandal-shuffling rabble-rouser from Galilee. But *I* am no centurion of Capernaum! Get me?"

He was continuing, but Uhle cut him off:

"Your pale pioneer," he began tensely—"at the coming world tribunal he will appear as state's witness against you. For he is here!—He who took part in battles, in hand-to-hand fighting, in patrols. He whose eyes saw countless tears, mass graves, horrors. He who, back there in No Man's Land, raised his hand with our clenched soldier's hands and swore: Never again! He whose ears, through the chaos of artillery fire, heard the cries of young soldiers calling to God, to mother, to sweetheart, to wife. He is here—he who closed the eyes of so many dying heroes . . . when out of the ice-cold fields of night no answer came to them but the bitter silence of nothingness. Yes! he is here! He has climbed the thirty-three steps from the lime pits into which our civilization, year after year, hunts its sons like rats. He is

423

here—the companion of sorrow—"

"The Judocrat?"

"The awakened! Dangerously has he risen—for the phrases of your Machiavellian soothsayer politics fill his mouth with loathing. State's witness will he be for that day when we millions of trench rats, on one side and the other, were so ready to forsake that empty volcanic landscape of mutual hate and insult . . . to reach our hardened hands to each other across all the double-dealing of cabinets, in a new, natural gesture. But who"—Uhle raised his voice as if he were before a world congress of future historians and had to account for the failure of his people—"I ask: Who among the powerful took the hand that we soldiers at the Front held out then? Oh, all you unknown soldiers! Bear witness! Who helped us then—when weary, fought out, we came back home? Who? There were plenty of hypocritical ministers and presidents and such-like everywhere, to stand with their hats off by the grave of the Unknown Soldier. But in that one minute of enforced silence, they did not hear the heartbeat of us *living* unknown soldiers! And the Devil saw it. And he sent his traveling salesmen to earth. And over the border he came, the Austrian bully boy. Sat down and drank beer in the Bräuhauskeller. Promised. Tempted. To him who had sixty marks a month, he promised sixty-five. To him whose business was going to the dogs, he promised Isaac's business across the street. And while our dream of a new world grew fainter and fainter, Satan's traveling salesman was busy—here, there, everywhere—throttling every throat that dared oppose him. And out of once courageous workers for peace, he made cowardly reactionaries and race-mad whelps. And since on this earth there are unfortunately always more cowards than brave men—the most cowardly soldier of the world war finally gathered the millions of other cowards behind him. But—already there is another around whom men are gathering! He whom they imprisoned thirty-three steps underground in Haudroumont Quarry! Yes, around him, the bravest soldier of the world war, men are gathering. Around him, who in the midst of the slaughter, dared to unmask your old military courage as cowardice! Who dared to recognize under the old military cowardice the first awakening of a new spirit of humanity!"

While Uhle was speaking, Hess had cautiously got on his hands and knees behind Hitler's back and then had crawled through the shadow of the billiard table. He reached the place where the candle stood. With sudden presence of mind, he blew it out. The room became totally dark. As Uhle groped for the candle, he heard a wild burst of mocking laughter. Then the steps of the two running away.

424

CHAPTER EIGHT

IN THE DARKNESS SEVERAL SHADOWY FIGURES CLIMBED IN THROUGH THE WINDOW, RUSTLING AND WHISPERING like a band of thieves.

"Oi-oi!" One of them, having with some difficulty struck a match, held it high. By its light we are able to recognize Krah and a group of habitués of the "Wailing Wall" café. In their hastily donned overcoats and mufflers they stood there for an instant like emissaries of the avenging Erinnyes materialized out of the night. Then they started a wild rush into the hall. But they came to a standstill almost immediately. Krah's match had burned out.

"Oi-oi!" Krah groped his way. "Here's an open door!"

"Look out!" warned the others. But Comrade Münzer shouldered forward:

"What's the matter? What are you afraid of? Forward!" He struck another match.

Krah's face, crisscrossed with adhesive plaster, jerked as if with St. Vitus' dance:

"Oi-oi!" Krah followed Münzer into what seemed to be an abandoned library. But suddenly, clutching Rabbi Wolff's arm, he cried out, "What's that by the cupboard? Isn't that someone lying there!"

"By God the Just!—Where do you see anything?" But since Münzer's match now went out and he was unsuccessful in striking another, Dr. Wolff stood stock-still until the violinmaker, Mathias Westermann, produced a cigarette-lighter and flicked it into action. The tiny blue benzine flame gave a ghostly effect.

"Look!" Münzer ran his hand over the wall. "Here's a door flush with the wallpaper!"

"Where? Where?"

"Damn! The handle's knocked off!" The Communist tried to open it. "Westermann! Lend me your pocket knife!" After some prying, he managed to break the lock.

"Oi-oi!" Krah craned his neck over the threshold. "Smells of red wine in here! Here's where the killers must have dined!"

To the left of the window the wallpaper was detached and curling, the bricks beneath it covered with mildew.

Krah goggled at the typically bourgeois dining room. Suddenly he discovered a strange still-life—a table invitingly set for two with choice

425

crystal and dishes.

"God! What gormandizers!" Krah ventured nearer. "Cauliflower!
. . . Whipped cream!" He quailed at the grotesque shadows cast by
the others on the wall.

"By God the Just! What is that?" The rabbi had picked up a white
satin evening gown from one of the chairs, and was sniffing at the
material. "Coty? That's the same perfume my niece Nadia uses!" he
groaned. But at the same moment Westermann cried out:

"There's someone under the table!"

"Under the table?" Münzer came running in his worn-out shoes,
snatched the lighter out of Westermann's hand, and, holding it at arm's
length, shone it down on the floor.

"Look, look!" he whispered. "There's someone there behind the
table—crouching on the carpet—"

They all crowded forward.

There, indeed, sat someone, his head leaning against the edge of a
chair, his legs hidden under the long, overhanging tablecloth. In his
right hand he held a pair of scissors with which he had apparently been
trying to clip off his mouse mustache.

"Oi-oi!" Shuddering, Krah shrank back against the door, and choked
sounds began to pour out of his throat: "Oi-oi! *Who* is it? That's what
Herr Krah wants to know! Who, who?"

The rabbi's thick spectacles glittered balefully. Suddenly he roared
like a wounded animal. The cigarette-lighter dropped from Comrade
Münzer's hand and blackness enveloped them.

An inextricable tangle of bodies swayed now this way, now that,
through the room. Chairs toppled over. Plates and glasses smashed. A
frenzy of cries went up, like the sounds in a lion house at feeding time.

CHAPTER NINE

OUTSIDE ON THE HIGHWAY POLICE
SIRENS SUDDENLY SHRILLED. THEN, ALL AROUND THE VILLA, VOICES CALLED
in French. Through the trees flashlights approached, their long beams
of light crossing in cubistic designs.

"Porca Madonna!" Accompanied by several sergeants, Commissioner
Armoni, with a sign to Sergeant-Major Grumbach, dashed through the
garden, jumped a hedge, and ran up the steps to the front door. "This

nust be the villa that Weidmann told us about in his confession."

The gendarme at his side tried several skeleton keys in the lock. This failing, they both tore back through boxwood and jasmine and acacia trees to the rear of the villa.

Meanwhile, Sergeant-Major Grumbach, accompanied by the heavy-set Sergeant Doriot, their weapons ready, did sentry duty in front.

"Damn it! If there's no more compassion and no more Kingdom of Heaven—then as far as I'm concerned, the whole kit and kaboodle can be pushing up the daisies by sun-up!" Hitching up the mourning band on his left arm, his expression that of a suffering man, he confided to his colleague: "I still can't take it in!—My cousin Klärchen is dead! . . . Only a few minutes ago warm, full-blooded—and now incontrovertibly dead! Already lying on her bier in the conservatory at the German Embassy!" He waved the muzzle of his revolver menacingly at the villa. "Those murderers! If I only had a starched shirt! We're invited to the funeral ceremonies—and my sister still has my best shirt soaking in the suds! . . ."

"Grumbach! Grumbach!" Armoni yelled through the trees: "Vite! Vite!"

"Chef!" The Sergeant-Major ran to meet Armoni at the hedge.

"Porca Madonna! Vite, vite—"

"Chef! Chef!" Another gendarme came up on the run. "In the cellar —we've discovered—corpses—women's bodies! . . . Found this brooch alongside one of them!"

"An American flag?" With a quick glance at the pin in his hand, Armoni shouted down the driveway: "Mr. Thomson! Mr. Thomson!"

A newspaperman who had been allowed to accompany the police climbed out of his Ford and hurried up. Then they all rushed round to the back of the villa and into the hall. Suddenly an ear-splitting shriek rose from the ground-floor room. It sounded as if hundreds of pigs were being slaughtered at once.

CHAPTER TEN "PORCA MADONNA!" COMMISSIONER ARMONI PUT HIS HANDS OVER HIS EARS TO SHUT OUT THE TERRIFIED crying, which began more and more to resemble the shrieking of a throttled rat. Several gendarmes dashed across the hall to the billiard

room, pounding so hard that the brass chandelier on its long chain fell
from the ceiling. Even Mr. Thomson momentarily stopped sending
out his clouds of honey-sweet tobacco.

"Et alors? . . . Et alors?" The gendarmes gathered around the
straw-hatted commissioner, staring at the door, and pushing back their
round metal helmets, adorned with little flaming silver grenades. Since
their breathless dash to the villa, they had not even had time to cool
their foreheads. Their black leather jackets gave off the penetrating
exhalation of moist tannin. The headlights on their motorcycles standing in the garden, together with the smaller beams from electric flashlights on the table, gave the villa—now occupied inside and out by the
Paris police—the typical appearance of some gangsters' hide-out a few
minutes after a raid.

About to follow his subordinates, Armoni was stopped by the headlong return of one of his gendarmes. His revolvers belted on over his
black leather jacket, his face tomato red, the man reported:

"Monsieur H-eet—lair!"

"Quoi?" Armoni pulled his head between his shoulderblades like a
June bug. "Quoi?"

"Mais oui, mon chef! H-err H-eet H-eet-lair!"

"You're crazy! Et alors?" Ripping off his straw hat, Armoni immediately put it on again, and glanced at the statement Uhle had just made
upon being rearrested. Neither Armoni nor his assistants had given the
slightest credence to Uhle's assertion that the Führer of the Third
Reich was present in the villa. They had not even thought it in con-
sonance with their dignity to check his statements.

"Porca Madonna!" Armoni pushed the two revolvers which had just
been taken away from Uhle, and also the red Spahi cloak, aside. With a
glance of almost idiotic consternation at the American reporter, he
started toward the uproar. But when he reached the door to the billiard room, he jumped, and then, taking off his hat, backed off as respectfully as if the President of the Republic were approaching. The
antiquarian, Laroche, and the Swiss verger, Xaver Grün, arrested outside the garden gates, stood stiffly at attention too.

On the threshold of the billiard room appeared Adolf Hitler, his
trousers unbuttoned. Supported under the armpits, right and left, by
two gendarmes sweating with fear, excitement, and servility, he was
dragged and somehow propelled forward, his knees at every step folding up and thumping against the floor.

Next, there was the shuffling of many feet. First the Rabbi. Behind
him, the other refugees, in a close pack, like a swarm of stirred-up

wasps, angrily humming, stings unsheathed.

"Damn it!" Sergeant-Major Grumbach poked his revolver into Krah's ribs and muttered, "damn it—taisez-vous!"

"Porca Madonna!" Armoni removed his straw hat in a wide arc, bowing, while his subordinates brought their heels together, polished boots gleaming below sky-blue trousers trimmed with broad bands of black braid. Palms outward, hands flew in salute to the brims of silver-and-gold braided caps.

"Monsieur H-eet-lair? . . . Porca Madonna—" he stammered.

He signed to the gendarmes to let go of the Führer. At once his knees buckled and he sank to the floor. Doriot, the fat sergeant, tiptoed around the Führer to Armoni and whispered excitedly:

"One of that pack of Jews was going to emasculate His Excellency the Reich Chancellor—we arrived just in time—"

"Quoi?" Armoni beckoned furiously to Professor Goldschmidt.

"Monsieur le Commissaire!" the doctor justified himself softly, "you had better order an ambulance at once, or I cannot assume any further responsibility! You see, in an insane asylum, when someone says: 'I am the Emperor of China!' we use the cold-water cure . . . Or, if he becomes violent, we use a strait-jacket. But if a madman says, 'I am the Supreme Führer of Europe!' . . . and that's what he actually is! . . . then, Monsieur le Commissaire, what are we going to do about it?"

"Taisez-vous!" Armoni flashed at him. "Taisez-vous!"

After the doctor had withdrawn, Armoni, gingerly approaching the Führer, again removed his straw hat with a profound bow: "Excusez, votre Excellence . . . !"

"Bitt' schön!" The Führer half opened his eyes. Münzer, seeing it, tried to push forward past the gendarmes.

"Let me at him!" he yelled. "I'll beat that skull of his to scrambled eggs!"

"Ça va! Ça va!" Doriot gave him a blow to the chest that sent him reeling against the wall.

"For goodness' sake!" Mr. Thomson laid his pipe on the table, inspected the figure on the floor, and assured the police:

"That's he! I was introduced to him once at a reception in the Berlin Opera House!"

Whereupon the gendarmes once more brought their heels together in resonant staccato. Shuddering with awe, they strained their chins over their collars.

"Son!" Sweating with ecstasy, Xaver Grün nudged the antiquarian. "Didn't I tell you so? . . . As soon as the Mercedes drove off from the

Embassy . . . didn't I tell you: 'Adolf Hitler's sitting in that car'?"

Armoni and Thomson helped the Reich Chancellor into a chair near the fireplace.

"Excusez, Excellence!" The Corsican put on his straw hat again and beat a flustered retreat to the sofa behind the table. "Votre Excellence!" His polka-dotted bow tie jerked up and down at Hitler, who sat as limp as a rag doll: "I've often admired you in countless photographs. I've even listened to many of your interesting radio addresses. But if the Holy Virgin had said to me: 'Armoni, you're going to see the world-famous Adolf Hitler face to face one of these nights, out in Neuilly in a lonely villa—' porca Madonna!" He giggled like a cackling goose. "Mais alors!"

Catching the infection, all the gendarmes relaxed their overstrained nerves in prolonged neighs. And as Hitler, as if awakening out of coma, his eyes half-opened, listened to this orchestra of diaphragms, the laughter became even louder. It was not until the dull blows of a pick-ax on stone, echoing from the cellar, were heard, that Armoni remembered his duties as a detective. He motioned to the refugees to come closer and was apparently about to resume his investigation. Instead—suddenly overcome with embarrassment in the presence of the master of the German police, he began introducing his colleagues, one by one. Each gendarme as his name was called stood at attention.

"Excusez, Excellence! You are the Führer of a mighty people, against whom many of us had the honor of fighting in the last war . . . Excusez! And had any of us ever dreamed that you, the all-powerful Führer, were out here in such a dubious locality . . . Excusez . . . I should certainly have closed off these woods and protected Your Excellency from any illegal attack upon your sovereign person!" He flashed lightnings at the refugees.

Hitler tried to say something, but his head sank against the back of the chair.

The blows of the pick-ax again resounded from the cellar below. Armoni began a voluble explanation:

"Down there, Your Excellency, in the presence of our police physician, a German we caught here is hacking away at the cement floor. And what do you think his pick-ax is turning up? Nothing but the corpses of young girls! Porca Madonna! . . . By a strange coincidence, the murderer Weidmann, just two hours before being guillotined, confessed that this villa is the headquarters for the entire organization of the Fifth Column in France . . ."

"Bitt' schön? . . ." The Reich Führer licked parched lips. "I'm

430

thirsty."

At a sign from Armoni, Sergeant-Major Grumbach poured a glass of water. Hitler drank, surreptitiously looking round to see if his Deputy Führer were visible anywhere. But in vain. . . . The gray-haired, sinewy sergeant whom we saw once before in conversation with Schleich, came down the wooden staircase. Placing several weapons on the table in front of Armoni, he reported:

"Chef! I found these things in the bathroom!"

While the Commissioner was examining the weapons, the elderly sergeant seemed suddenly to remember something. Removing his helmet, he stepped across to confront the Führer! "My name is Aubert. In 1870, my father fought against the Germans. In 1914, I spent four long years fighting the Germans in the Argonne. And now, my son is to be mobilized against you? You!! You!!!" He raised both fists. "By God, I'd like to eat every German alive! Tous les boches! Every last one of them! . . ."

"Help!" Hitler yelled, taking refuge behind his chair. "Protect me from this cannibal!"

"Protect you?" The refugees surged against him. "Beast! Reptile! Betrayer of the workers!"

"Arrêtez! Arrêtez!" Revolver drawn, Armoni sprang between them. Having finally succeeded in restoring order, he tipped his hat to the American reporter:

"Excusez, Mr. Thomson—but this must not appear in the papers. I'm sorry, but you'll have to go." The American rose, his parting greetings in the nature of a formula:

"Freedom! Liberty! Democracy!" He waved to the assemblage. About to pass in front of Hitler, he hesitated, not knowing what attitude to assume toward the man whom the American government had officially recognized as the head of the German nation six years previously. Unable to think of anything more appropriate in the circumstances, he said:

" 'I believe in the supreme worth of the individual and in his right to life, liberty, and the pursuit of happiness . . .' "

"By God the Just!" The Rabbi slowly took off his slouch hat.

" 'I believe' "—Thomson looked straight at Hitler—" 'that right can and will triumph over might!'—Lincoln! Good morning!" In a few athletic strides he was up on the chest, over the windowsill, and out in the garden, where he vanished in the darkness.

Hitler's eyes narrowed as he watched him go.

"Lincoln!" The Rabbi sobbed. And then with the other refugees, he cried that name out of the madness-laden room, like an S O S call. Longingly it followed the American:

"Lincoln! Lincoln!"

But above their voices, Hitler bellowed in the stentorian tones of a drill sergeant, so that the younger gendarmes involuntarily snapped to attention: "Damnation! Let me out of here, I am a sovereign! . . . Monsieur le Commissaire! Where's my coat? My coat!"

"Is this it?" Doriot helped him into his overcoat.

"Stop!" Armoni stood in his way. "I regret that until my superior has arrived, Your Excellency may not leave this villa."

"Not leave? Bitt' schön—"

"Quoi?" Doriot set his helmet at a provocative slant, and looked at Armoni challengingly:

"I at least—and my younger colleagues—intend to take every precaution that a sovereign on French soil—"

Further altercation was interrupted, however, by the appearance of Dr. Gunther, the Secretary of the Anciens Combattants, accompanied by several gendarmes. Managing his wooden leg skillfully, he made rapid progress. On the breast of his blue suit was pinned an imposing array of war medals, flanked by tricolor ribbons and a buttonhole of poppies and cornflowers. Above his ascetic features he wore an officer's cap showing the gilt bars of a commander.

CHAPTER ELEVEN "M ON COMMANDANT!" WITH A SIGH OF RELIEF, THE LITTLE CORSICAN RACED TO MEET HIM, AND THEN gave him some whispered information.

"Diable! Diable! Quoi . . . quoi?" As if fencing, Gunther made passes in the air with his cane. He then let himself be assisted in through the window. Grimly smiling, he measured Hitler from head to foot!

"Diable, Monsieur! If you're not his double, but, as Commissioner Armoni informs me, really the Chancellor of the Third Reich, then Madame Justitia has certainly crowned my juristic career with an inconceivable reward!" Saluting with his forefinger, he said dryly:

"Je suis le juge d'instruction."

"By God the Just! Did you hear that?" The Rabbi stepped on Westermann's foot. "It's the examining magistrate!"

432

Gunther's cheeks were ruddy with many purplish veins. His breath smelt of good wine.

"Monsieur!" He threw his cap on the table. "You know where I've just come from? From the Trocadéro—diable!—where four thousand delegates are assembled, representing the World War Veterans of all nations."

"Herr-r-r-r!" Hitler came storming in his direction. With a gesture of dignity, however, Gunther extended his wooden leg, and the Führer fell back. "Bitt' schön!" Faced with the cripple, he lost some of his self-assurance. "Kindly give orders that I am to be immediately conducted to my Embassy! Furthermore, I demand surrender of this clique of international murderers!"

"Sit down." The examining magistrate cut him short. Clenching and unclenching his hands deep in his pockets, Hitler sat down, at a loss. Abruptly he emitted a loud, braying yawn. With a mocking grin for Hitler, Aubert handed a sheet of paper to the examining magistrate. Gunther drew a chair to the table, sat down, and asked sternly:

"Votre nom?"

"Oi-oi!" Krah giggled out of the shadow. "Monsieur le Juge! Schickelgruber doesn't know French!"

"Bitt' schön!" The Reich Führer gazed slantwise at the stout Doriot. "What is this: an examination?"

"Votre nom?"

"Damnation—I am a sovereign in good standing in all countries!"

"Taisez-vous! Diable! What are you doing in this villa?"

"What?" Hitler swallowed. "Bitt' schön—a judge appointed by the French people, whom I hold in such high esteem, has the audacity to sit down in front of me with a notebook and fountain-pen! Just as if there were going to be another dictatorship of Versailles for the German people! No, the world is not going to see that a second time!"

"I asked you: What are you doing here?"

"What you're up to here! You betrayer of the workers!" Münzer clenched his fist.

"Taisez-vous!" Gunther whirled on him, then turned again to Hitler: "My police officers have surprised you in the villa of the murderer Weidmann! Diable! Répondez! What business have you out here in Neuilly at this time of night?"

"Oi-oi!" Krah interjected. "Such indiscreet questions, Monsieur le Juge! Heavens, how indiscreet!"

"Mais répondez donc!"

"Monsieur, kindly don't waste your doubtless valuable time asking me any more such imbecile questions!"

"Quoi?" Gunther gave him a long look. Abruptly, seized with horror of the vacuum in that face, he shuddered and, to conceal the repulsion he felt, began reading the document Aubert had handed him.

"Diable!" He banged his cane on the floor. "What's this? What is this name here?"

"Chef!" Armoni took off his hat. "The name is Uhle."

"Diable! You've arrested my friend, Uhle? Mais vous êtes fou! C'est une honte! Where is he?"

"Downstairs in the cellar, chef."

"In the cellar! Mais vous êtes fou!" He limped over to the trap door as fast as he could go. Aubert helped him down the stairs.

The younger gendarmes exchanged furtive glances, quite evidently of two minds about the whole affair. It was obvious that they were not at all reconciled to their superior's treating the Supreme Führer of a hundred thousand German policemen just as if he were an ordinary delinquent. Hitler, the trapper of human beings, sensed their attitude.

"Armoni! Armoni!" Gunther shouted from below.

"Chef!" The Corsican hurried down after him.

No sooner had he disappeared than, as if flung by the catapult of fate, the refugees threw themselves on the gendarmes who were guarding them. But Doriot blew his whistle. And, while he managed to get the Reich Führer to comparative safety behind the screen, the younger gendarmes drove the refugees back into the billiard room with their rubber truncheons. Armoni, his face apoplectic, raced up the cellar steps, thundering:

"Porca Madonna! Silence! Taisez-vous!"

"Chef," Aubert murmured in his ear, "you'd better put handcuffs on this animal before something happens. Some of our men are Laval adherents."

"Et alors?" After a moment's hesitation, Armoni shook his head. "Mais non! This 'animal' is a sovereign. He has his own accredited ambassador right here in Paris. He's the friend of the highest ministers. The President recently awarded him the Grand Cordon of our Légion d'Honneur!"

"Légion d'Honneur!?" squeaked Krah. "Oi-oi!" And with a burst of taunting laughter he and his fellow victims again attempted to get at Hitler. The Führer screeched with fear.

"Protect me! Otherwise, there'll be massacre between the Elbe and the Rhine!"

"Massacre?" The Rabbi tried to break through the police cordon.

434

'Nu! By God the Just! This monster thinks *he's* the only one who can chop off heads! No, no! Our Abimelech, five thousand years ago, slew he seventy sons of Jerubbaal on a single stone . . ."

"Silence—porca Madonna! Silence!"

"Herr Commissär"—Dr. Wolff persisted—"I don't mind a bit that his gentleman's Gestapo assassins charred my nostrils a while ago at ne German Travel Bureau! No! Why should I?" He grinned mockngly at Hitler. "Without pity for man or beast, our Samson drove the captive Philistines, tied together with burning foxes, out into the ields!"

"What's that black Samson talking about?" Hitler bellowed.

"The 'black Samson'! The fact is, our 'black Samson' had bright golden hair like the rays of the sun. I say—'the fact is.' And if by any chance an outhouse-painter like you ever heard of that giant among giants, Rembrandt, then you would know how *he* painted our Samson! By God the Just!" he yelled in the Führer's face. "Samson belongs to he Hercules-Siegfried saga! Ha-ha! Samson was unconquerable!"

"What?" Hitler nudged the stout Doriot. "This Caiaphas here thinks hat I don't know who Rembrandt was! Bitt' schön, meine Herren Gendarmen—when I was in Naples as a guest of Her Majesty, Queen Margherita, I remember her taking my arm as we walked through the gardens enjoying the fireworks arranged in my honor. There, in the presence of Vesuvius belching flames, Her Majesty was pleased to inspect a few water colors of mine, displayed on a multicolored marble table from the age of Tiberius. I had presented them to her through my friend, the Prince of Hesse, as an expression of my heartfelt thanks for the truly magnificent hospitality of that imposing sovereign. And Her Majesty, looking through her sparkling diamond lorgnette, enchanted, exclaimed: 'Rembrandt! Si—Si!' . . . Yes!" He bared his teeth at the refugees. " 'Rembrandt!' That's what Her Majesty said!" Then he began bawling so that his saliva sprayed:

"Yes! And all who were present—cardinals in their purple robes, princes, the American envoys, and all the representatives of all the conceivable courts of Europe—each and every one of them, in the presence of that spewing Vesuvius, smiled and repeated: 'Si! Si! . . . Rembrandt!' Yes, gentlemen of the police, there, in sight of the humming, singing 'sul mare lucida,' they all said 'Si . . . si . . . Rembrandt!' "

The gendarmes' whinnying laughter mingled with curses from the refugees.

In the midst of the uproar, the examining magistrate, his arm linked in Uhle's, reappeared from the cellar. Uhle's hair was wet and dis-

ordered; his shirt, open over his chest, was clammy with perspiratio
from his recent labors with the pick-ax. At sight of Hitler, alive as eve
and apparently under police protection, he came to an abrupt hal
With a groan of despair, he seized his head in both hands, lurche
across the room, and collapsed on the sofa.

Gunther, continually rapping out at Armoni "Mais vous êtes fou
Mais vous êtes fou!", anxiously tried to revive his friend with brandy
He was interrupted, however, by the return from the cellar of th
police physician, who handed him his report on the female bodies du
out from the cement.

"Quoi?" He skimmed through the memorandum while the other
stood in threatening silence. Then, with Sergeant Aubert at his side, h
advanced a few steps into the hall, banged on the floor with his woode
leg, and, his voice hard and cold, spoke into the silence:

"Monsieur H-eet—lair, in the name of the French Republic and i
the name of the rights of man, I arrest you!"

CHAPTER TWELVE W ITH SUCH SOLEMNITY HA
GUNTHER UTTERED THESE WORDS THAT EVEN HITLER STOOD FOR A MOMEN
as if paralyzed. The next instant, with the ineradicable instinct of th
cornered rat, his eyes darted here and there, seeking a way out. Hi
mouth dropped open on a:

"Wha-a-a-at? You want to what? Bitt' schön—wha-a-at?"

"Diable!" The examining magistrate signaled to the stout gendarme
"Allez! Arrest this man!"

"Arr-e-e-est!" Drawing himself up to his full height, Hitler glared a
Gunther, his eyes fixing on the cinnabar-red crown of the Command
er's gold-embroidered cap.

"You—talk of arresting *me*? Damnation! Man, that's a laugh for th
gods! An insignificant functionary like you has the colossal nerve—'

"Allez! Take him into custody!"

Inasmuch, however, as neither Doriot nor his younger colleague
could bring themselves to raise a finger against the head of the Germa
army, Gunther reiterated:

"Allez! Allez!"

"Bitt' schön"—Hitler looked about him—"you're not going to arres
me! *Me*—whom every New Year's, since 1933, the Pope has, throug

436

his Nuncio in Berlin, declared his accredited friend! Man! You should take time out to consider the different whereabouts of the cerebrum and the cerebellum!"

"Diable! Mais allez donc!"

"And by what right do you propose to have me arrested?"

"By the rights of all free peoples!" Krah interjected. "Oi-oi!"

"By what 'rights of free peoples'?" burst defiantly from Hitler. "Bitt' schön! Didn't your League of Nations drive out a sovereign who appealed expressly to the 'rights of free peoples'? Didn't you whistle down the white-robed Negus of Abyssinia when he came galloping to Geneva on his Lion of Judah? Didn't you hoot him out of the speaker's stand of the Plenary Session when he appealed to your 'rights of free peoples'?" With peasant cunning, he relished the suddenly changed expression of the examining magistrate. "Yes, Herr Monsieur, because of your glorious rights of all free peoples, I once spent many a sleepless night—"

"Sleepless nights? . . . Diable!"

"Yes! That's what I said! *But*—most fortunately, neither did America raise its powerful voice against the Italian campaign of spoliation, nor did any other awe-inspiring reality of Judocracy intervene! . . . So—what do you expect of me!"

"By God the Just, Monsieur le Juge, why don't you have him put behind bars?"

"Trap shut, you moldy Samson! Didn't your Chief Rabbi of Milan in 1935, in the name of all Italian Jews, address an enthusiastic telegram of congratulations to the Duce of Fascism, in his Palazzo Chigi, placing at his disposal every resource of the Jewish people in support of that neat little plunder raid of his against Ethiopia!"

"By God the Just! What did he say? 'A telegram of congratulations!' —to the Duce?—That gangster who stole everything from the Jews and then hunted them out of Italy into France—?"

"But not till 1937! Bitt' schön! Not till I met my great friend, up there on the Brenner Pass and opened his eyes to you pack of Sinai vultures! Not till then, bitt' schön! Not till then! Until that time he was your God! Your Caesar! Your Du-u-uce!"

"You beast, you!" The refugees shouted in unison.

"Or I ask you: except for Count Sforza, who raised his voice in protest in 1923 when my esteemed friend, Il Duce, had your socialist Matteotti cut to pieces outside of Rome—cut to pieces so that it was only after long searching in the sewers of the Via Appia that anyone was able to find the various portions of his Marxist anatomy? Who protested then, I ask you? Your Chief Rabbi of Milan?"

"You're going to let him talk like that, Monsieur le Juge?"

"Didn't everybody, definitely *dis*sociated from the international rights of free peoples, cuddle under his wings? Wasn't the Eternal City simply swarming with English aristocrats? Didn't Lady Chamberlain enthusiastically enroll in the Fascist Legion in Florence? Didn't all the princes and priests of the Church lick his boots? Didn't they smile with delight when his 'Balilla' clattered past their Eminences' windows in a wretched imitation of the Prussian guards' parade, imported from Potsdam? Ha-ha! Yes—did a single one of you Judocratic hypocrites want the international rights of free peoples *then?* . . . Internatiational *national* rights, yes! But Right itself?!"

"You dog!" Unable to contain himself, Münzer sprang into the air. "We're not talking about that bald-headed hero of women, Mussolini—"

"Calm down, calm down! . . . Bitt' schön, Herr Richter! Ha-ha!—in my lifetime I've fought many a case in court, coolly and objectively, without a trace of hysteria! So don't you listen to these emigrees. These profiteers of every revolution! Not one of them ever put his own head in danger of the guillotine! Each and every one of them is a shareholder in the general dung-heap of this epoch."

"That's the truth!" ejaculated the halberdier triumphantly.

"Yes! And just because I've unmasked the whole crew of them—that's why they hate me! Herr Richter—come on, now!—be nice!—come on and join the ranks in support of my cause! I'm the one who's determined to save all the little functionaries—such minor officials as you are, without bank accounts or priestly connections—and to lead them out of the decline of the Occident into the Promised Land, where—"

"Diable! Diable!" Gunther chewed his mustache. "Herr H-eet—lair. I warn you—the bars will soon clang shut behind you!"

Hitler recoiled before the sobriety and severity of the French veteran's words. A second later, however, he was raving again:

"Don't you dare touch me! It just so happens that now I'm alone! But tomorrow morning this impertinent judge of yours will be brought into court in my Europe! You hypocrites! No! Before I ever hear the bars clang shut behind me, I've still got a thing or two up my sleeve for you! Before that happens, I'll plank down my dossiers before your Judocratic Supreme Court!"

Impatient, but anxious to see if in this loquacious torrent of abuse, Hitler might not let fall something of interest to the security of

438

France, Gunther pushed the gendarmes aside and asked incisively:

"Quoi! What dossiers are you talking about?"

"Here!" Hitler tore some yellow envelopes out of his pocket and threw them at Gunther's feet.

"Quoi?" Gunther opened one of them. "This is a telegram!"

"Is it? Oh, yes, I forgot! That's the telegram his Majesty King George VI of Great Britain sent me on my fiftieth birthday."

"King George VI? Diable!"

"Yes—offering me his sincerest congratulations and best wishes for my future career!"

"And this?" Gunther picked up another envelope. "Is this a dossier?"

"Yes! It has been far more important to me than all the military statistics of my General Staff to find out what percentage of truth there is *behind* all your high-flown, mealy-mouthed phrase-making— that is, if there really is anything at all behind what you hypocrites say, that I should have to fear!"

"By God the Just! The monster actually said, 'to fear'!"

"Oi-oi!" Krah stared at the heap of yellow envelopes before the examining magistrate. "The animal is turning the indictment on his accusers!"

"Bitt' schön! There's the dossier of one of the most famous church-men . . . From his pulpit he called me 'The Beast from the Abyss'! Bitt' schön. There's *his* private life all written down! Enclosed is a letter from one of the women he seduced. Just help yourself! Would you like more, Herr Richter? Here's a noble Lord writing to the 'Times' to say they ought to shoot me down like a mad dog! . . . There! Perhaps you'd like to see the accounts of his arms factories with my Ministry of War! There you are! Bitt' schön, ever since 1922, he's been delivering me iron ore for German rearmament! Ha-ha! Against the menace of Bolshevism." He grinned fiendishly.

"So—supposing you do bolt the door behind Adolf Hitler—in that very instant, my Heinrich Himmler will open another door! We have in our possession a whole arsenal of such dossiers concerning you Judo-crats—hundreds of thousands of them all carefully card-indexed. We've got on file practically the whole stinking morass of your private lives! So, just try to lock me up, and you'll see such a Pompeii and Herculaneum of scandal pour down upon you Pharisees—"

"Oi-oi!" Krah fluted. "The animal is speculating on a bear market!"

"Mais oui!" Gunther tossed the envelopes onto the table. "You're speculating on the moral weakness of your fellow humans!"

"Yes—on what else, if you please, should I speculate? On your virtues? Ha-ha! No—I get a pretty good idea of them every time I go through the whole alphabet of your dossiers in my files with Himmler.—Bitt' schön, I pull one out! I turn the pages! And what do I find? Here's someone scolding me a 'tyrant'. I pull out his dossier, turn the pages, and what do I read? Divorced for cruelty by his wife in Reno, 1935! . . . Here's another calling me 'an exploiter of the workers'. I pull out his dossier, and what do I find? In 1938, his employees went on strike for the eleventh time because he wouldn't pay them minimum wages . . . Here's another who condemns me before 'the moral judgment of the world' because I consider hate more effective than love. And he himself can find no weapon against me but hate! Hate!" he hissed at Uhle. Uhle sprang to his feet, wanting to protest, but found that he could not utter a sound.

"Bitt' schön;" Hitler flung another bundle of yellow envelopes at Gunther's feet. "Herr Richter—go ahead and arrest me if you dare! There, in the dossiers of all your careers, I have found scarcely *one* per cent of the will to achieve a democracy, of the love of one's fellow men, of the love of liberty! Ha-ha! But I have found ninety-nine per cent of the will to power, of the lust of the flesh, of the love of money, of the greed for possessions! You hypocrites! Go on and arrest me if you dare!"

"What about your own dossier?" Krah's voice grated. "Oi-oi!"

"Yes, what about your own dossier?" The accusatory cries came from all sides.

"Bitt' schön!" He held his hands over his ears. "My dossier is in perfect order! I have no hypocritical pretenses at all. No! I'm quite ready at any time—in the presence of your Apostolic Chamberpots, your stinking Jenghiz Khans, and your newspaper whores—to cry out from the housetops at all times, 'My kingdom is of this world'!"

"Adolphus Magnus!" His eyes raised to heaven, the halberdier clasped his hairy hands, "Thy kingdom come!"

"Bitt' schön—I tell you, it's enough to make you tear your hair out, why *I*, and never anyone else, should always be dragged before the bar of justice! And now, once and for all, I demand that Secretary of the Treasury Morgenthau be called to the witness stand as an expert and asked what he would do if his President were one day, in all seriousness, to declare at the White House Press Conference: 'My kingdom is not of this world!' I'll bet anything the bank-realist would run away from there as fast as he could skedaddle for fear his Commander-in-Chief had been seized with an attack of the Higher Ethics!"

Amid the uproarious laughter of the younger gendarmes, Mathias

Westermann exclaimed:

"There he stands like incarnate original sin!"

"Original sin?" Hitler's mouth was distorted by a grimace of indescribable sweetness. "Bitt' schön! I was baptized a Christian!"

"You—baptized?" The examining magistrate looked at him appalled. "Quoi? You mean to tell us you received Christian baptism?"

"I should say so! My parents were Catholics. I'll have to admit that to this day I haven't been able to swallow the ubiquity of the Son of God in the Holy Sacrament! Bitt' schön!" He nudged the stout Doriot who had burst out laughing. "But I was baptized! Yes, you!" He looked at Westermann. "And by being baptized, I was freed from original sin! Ha-ha! Yes! My Uncle Alois wanted to have me baptized in Munich beer, but my pious Aunt Reserl found a verse from the Prophet Ezekiel that says God the Father demands pure water for the infant. And so they finally christened dear little Adolf in a manger full of Saint Ignatius' water. Right out of his chamberpot!"

Mathias Westermann, shaken with real horror, sighed: "This man is utterly without a soul! Right?"

"Soul!!!" Hitler broke into shrill laughter: "I've finally and forever done away with that millennial hypocrisy, the pretense of the existence of a soul! . . . Hands off!" He beat about him with his fists. "Keep your hands off! If you don't, I'll demand, before the jury of the World Court, an ice-clear answer to the dubious question: 'Has man a soul? or not?' . . . The further evolution of this entire millennium depends upon the answer to that question! For instance, if he has a soul, then my entire National Socialist program would be thrown on the dungheap! For if he has, then Monsieur Clemenceau must have had one, too! But if so, then how do you explain the Treaty of Versailles? My French comrades!" He turned to the younger gendarmes who, at every sentence, were ranging themselves about him like a bodyguard. "For instance, if the Negus, together with all his black Ethiopians, had a soul—bitt' schön—why did your Pope permit my friend, Mussi, whom I know perfectly well has no soul, to gas all those pickaninnies in Abyssinia? I demand a decision on this point from the Supreme Court before I'll ever permit your chef here to make sausage of me in his legal machine!"

"Adolphus Magnus!" Xaver Grün embraced Hitler's knees. "For the past twenty years, I've been carrying the halberd through the so-called main nave and cross naves of Notre Dame—quite apart from the side chapels—and I also know what is behind the high altar! I know where His Eminence likes to have the chamberpot placed during Mass—"

"Mais tu est ridicule, Xavier!" The antiquarian Laroche grabbed him by the collar and shoved him aside so vigorously that he fell, groaning, on the andirons in the fireplace.

"If all men have souls"—Hitler went on stirring them up—"why then do we see rich judges—and poor gendarmes? Gluttonous priests —and rubber-stamp laymen? If we all, all of us, have *souls*—then why did they let me go hungry? Why did Prince Eugene fight the Turks? Or why did England fight the freedom-loving Boers and Hindus?"

"Monsieur le Juge!" Krah dropped his monocle in his excitement "Oi-oi! Don't let this beast deliver a propaganda speech here!"

"If we all really have souls, bitt' schön, then why do hundreds and hundreds of fine ladies and gentlemen go streaming along Main Street in furs, in the dead of winter, past a poor fiddler, scraping his frost-bitten fingers raw—without one of them throwing so much as a pant's button in his cap? No—my worthy junior gendarmes! Going through the experiences of a lifetime crowned with triumph, and standing at the peak of my powers, I maintain: *Man has no soul! . . .*"

"No!" The halberdier extricated himself from the fireplace. "In this so-called corpus of Xaver Grün, there's nothing else but—nothing! It's true I've got rheumatism from the cold stones of Notre Dame! But the warmth of the soul has certainly never penetrated my bones by way of the so-called alms-bag! . . ."

"Vox populi!" Hitler grinned at him. "Yes! Bitt' schön! And what's more, since Cain and Abel, nobody has ever brought forward any proof to the contrary! For, Herr Richter, if Abel had a soul, then why did his brother Cain have *no* soul? I demand a decision from the court on that!"—Suddenly his voice was so hoarse that he could not go on. There was an interchange of searching and shamefaced glances among those present. His eyes closed, his cheek muscles twitching, Uhle murmured softly in the painful silence:

"Where, indeed, is there to be found a man who is good?—who is really good?"

"Bravo!" Hitler crowed. "Yes, bitt' schön, Herr Richter—Just show me one!"

"I say—where is there a man who is just?—who is really just?"

"Bravissimo! Yes—just show me one—and I'll abdicate."

Uhle looked around. "Where are the fighters for freedom who at the same time are free of the fetters of their own appetites? Where are the leaders into a better future for mankind who themselves are in their hearts free from the will to power? In very truth, if the justice of God were suddenly to lift the roofs from the houses of us anti-

442

Nazis, what would he find in our rooms? What, indeed, would he find in our offices—consulting rooms—banks—hotels—among our legal authorities—our writers—in the factories—Hollywood studios—and in all the radio stations—with everybody in the most democratic tones hammering on the same theme: The moral progress of humanity? I ask you: What would God's messenger find? Certainly not our 'better selves'!—Dear Gunther," Uhle laid his arm around the veteran's shoulders and seemed to be remembering his conversation with the Unknown Soldier in Notre Dame, "do you suppose for an instant that this Reich Führer whom every nation in the world has recognized could have become so appallingly powerful if we so-called 'better men' had been free of the vices on whose presence in us he counted for his success? Haven't you just heard it from his own mouth? It was *our* ambition that he unmasked, by pushing it to the point of pure wickedness. It was our cruelty that he used. It was upon our unscrupulous, animal lust, stirred from dawn to dark by every chance titillation, that he built his reign of shame. I tell you"—Uhle was shouting now—"he counted on our every evil instinct—on our frenzy of competition—on our rush for the food trough—on the beast in us! Yes, the beast that, deep inside ourselves, goes ever raging to fulfill its own particular lusts—it was on that that he counted!"

Through the angry buzzing of the refugees, Hitler measured him coldly and ironically.

"Bitt' schön!" he triumphed over them all—"you hypocrites! Just show me one! Just produce one of these wonderful beings of your democratic world! Just one who is worth more than the empty words of his mouth! Show him to me! Show him to me! Show me anyone who is better than I am!"

In the stifling, almost unbearable silence that followed this outburst, Uhle suddenly rose, like a herald who has a message to give.

"I can show the world one," he said, "one who is worth more than his word—" He pointed to the window. "He has come from the world of the trenches. An unknown soldier. His clear eyes will signify justice for us."

He ceased. Something like terror ran through them all. In the silence that followed, the wind outside could be heard, with now and then a forceful gust that rattled the windowpanes. From time to time a dead branch fell to the ground with a dull thud. Night birds called—like the death cries of wounded soldiers. Other sounds, too, came from the garden . . . as if shattered bodies with torn limbs were dragging themselves along trench floors to the nearest dugout.

443

CHAPTER THIRTEEN

THERE WAS A SUDDEN NOISE OF HURRYING FOOTSTEPS IN THE CELLAR. A GARDE MOBILE NONCOM CAME UP the stone stairs. When he saw the examining magistrate, he took off his padded helmet and reported:

"Chef—I tried to find you at the Trocadéro."

"Quoi?" Gunther started out of his abstraction. "What is it?"

"A communication from the Ministry of Justice—"

"For me? Diable!" Removing his glasses, Gunther read, with Armoni looking over his shoulder:

" 'Je suis désolé . . . But, to my great regret, my friend, His Excellency Herr Abetz, has requested me to refrain from paying my respects personally to Monsieur le Führer et Chancellier d'Allemagne, who is spending a few hours in Paris incognito . . . ' "

Gunther threw down the paper. But Sergeant Doriot picked it up and read on:

" . . . 'All police in the Department of the Seine are hereby notified that, wherever Herr Hitler may honor our capital with his presence, they are to place their services at his disposal with every mark of most honorable respect appertaining to such an eminent and supremely transcending personality, the Supreme Führer of our neighbor state, and to assist His Excellency in every possible way with our proverbial French courtesy—until the moment fixed for his departure, according to program, by plane at dawn of the—' . . . Signed: 'Marchandeau!' . . . Mais oui, Chef!" Doriot clicked his heels together.

While the refugees, staggering under this unexpected turn of events as if they had been bludgeoned, stared at Doriot, while the Rabbi flushed under his beard, Doriot wiped off the boots of the "Führer of the Gestapo," whose mouth expanded in a grin of malicious delight.

But as Gunther continued to stand wrapped in the impenetrable calm of his judicial office, Hitler slapped his resplendent Reich-Führer cap on his head so that its shiny lacquered visor shadowed the scornful triumph in his eyes. Only the point of his long nose caught the light.

"Bitt' schön!" He started walking. "Well—how much longer? You've had your orders, haven't you? Let me out of this! This is unbelievable!"

But the veteran commander slowly and deliberately put an un

lighted cigarette in the corner of his mouth. Then his eyes searched
the faces of the gendarmes. Armoni mopped his brow under the straw
hat. Sergeant Aubert nodded to his chief. Laroche sneezed and unbuttoned his frock coat. The younger gendarmes ostentatiously arranged themselves behind the thickset Doriot. Xaver Grün's red beard
shone with malignant joy, like scoured copper on Saturday night.

"Porca Madonna!" The little Corsican handed Gunther the minis-
terial letter. "There's a postscript to it, Chef!"

"What's this?" Gunther scanned the lines: " 'In regard to the missing
grand mutilé de guerre, responsible for the riot in front of Notre
Dame, arrested and thereafter erroneously released—every effort is to
be made to apprehend him at the earliest possible moment. He is immediately to be conveyed to an appropriate institution for incurable
invalids of the last war' . . . Signed: 'The Minister of Justice.' "

"Pardon!" Uhle seized Gunther's hand. "*Whom* does he want **you**
to arrest?"

But Gunther was tilting his cap off one ear, the better to **hear a**
whispered communication from the Garde Mobile noncom.

"Quoi?"

"Mais oui, Chef! We've already found him."

"Diable! You've got him?"

"Mais oui. We followed a trail of blood. Finally we found him—
wounded in the shoulder."

"Wounded?" Uhle started.

"Mais oui. He was sitting in the dark under one of the bridges, surrounded by tramps and bums, and he had no pass and no permis de
séjour. Voilà!" From one of his pockets he produced and laid before
Gunther a pair of compasses, the stump of a candle, a religious tract,
a reading glass, and a small cardboard box. "This is what we found on
him."

Gunther looked at the things one by one.

"Gunther," Uhle whispered, "it is my comrade from Verdun."

"The one you were sending to me at the Trocadéro? Diable!" He
turned back to the noncom. "And where is he now?"

"We left him at the police station in Neuilly."

"Why didn't you bring him along?"

"Too many nosey people around, Chef. . . . Mais oui!" the noncom stammered. "We even had to close the shutters—the rumor spread
like wildfire: A man who'd survived in a dugout for twenty long
years and now the police had arrested him!—Of course, everybody
is anxious to see him. There were even foreign reporters around."

445

"Eh bien!" Gunther clutched at his war medals. "You've heard the order of the Minister of Justice." He observed his gendarmes.

"C'est exact." The younger gendarmes looked at him provocatively and fingered their revolver holsters.

All at once, Gunther turned to Hitler: "Allez! I am going to confront you with this grand mutilé de guerre. And I sincerely hope that a man like you, who went through the war as a lance-corporal, will not be able to persist in your cynical answer to us Veterans from all over the world when you see the mutilated face of this fellow soldier . . . Allez!"

"Herr Richter," Hitler raised his fist and trembled with rage. "I warn you—you're risking your own head. If you weren't a cripple! Sakra! You've just received unmistakable orders as to how a sovereign like myself is to be treated—orders from your own Minister of Justice!"

Gunther hesitated for a moment but then he grasped his stick like a sword. "Allez! mais allez donc!" And then he whispered to Uhle, "I feel the moment of a world decision!"

"Back, there!" Hitler roared at Sergeant Aubert, who was preparing to lead him away. "Me—to change my mind? Not me! I am not the man to change his mind! And why should I? The road's clear! The final victory of Nazism is assured! . . . And besides, I can't do anything against the will of the stars!—I certainly can't defy the planets!—Hands off! I should submit to the wishes of four thousand World War Veterans? You want to confront me with a wounded soldier? What for? So that I should renounce the instrumentality of force, Herr Richter? What for, bitt' schön? Did you hypocrites by any chance set us the example at Versailles? No, you generation of vipers! On the contrary—in spite of your Judocratic 'milk of human kindness'—the instrumentality of force was actually your one remaining argument.—Let me out of here, I say!—Now, just when I've put Germany into a favorable position, you foreign Veterans begin setting up a howl—like tired sailors who would rather sit in a waterfront dive, drinking and gambling, than be sent out again to brave danger on the high seas . . . Movement, Herr Richter! That is exactly the entire meaning and sense of the whole idiotic universe . . . ! But of course you can never achieve that sort of thing by sitting cosily around a conference table and indulging in hypocritical drivel! . . ."

"No!" Uhle interrupted him, "it must be dead silent around the conference table! Yes, not until there's a cemetery stillness everywhere down below in the cellar . . . Not until they all lie there, side by side, in frozen cement, with no disturbing voice . . . Not until you

446

Nazis have stopped the mouths of all your victims with plaster . . .
Not until you've dulled the eyes of all who sought the light—and
planted them down there among the empty wine bottles and garden
hoses . . . Not until you've spattered their blood on all the walls . . .
Not until there is not a *single* thought left in all the brain-pans you've
smashed and shot!—Not a wisp of an idea to comprehend the glorious
harmony existing between the universe around us and each separate
blood corpuscle inside us, to say nothing of the dance of the atoms
under our skins . . . Not until you murderers have congealed the
miraculous blood streams in our bodies . . . Not until the bell-deep
tones of the heart in the breast are silent . . . Not until there is not
a single voice to defy you in your police state! . . . Not until *then*
is your promise redeemed! . . . And what is left, up above the murder
dungeons—your teeming hordes of gangsters, wearing your blood-
stained decorations on their brown shirts!—*that's* what you call your
movement, and you dare compare it with the cosmic movement!"

"Nu! By God the Just!" the Rabbi urged the examining magistrate,
"there is nothing to do with a werewolf but to kill it! Away with
him—"

"Hands off!" raged Hitler. "I say—hands off!"

"Allez, allez!"

"But even if you lock me up, Herr Richter—bitt' schön! My movement is under way! And all round the globe! And such an insignificant
functionary as you cannot stop it—by bolting a door—ha-ha! Back,
there! You should have gotten up much earlier—now it's too late!
Now, one pulls the other into the whirlwind across the globe! Bitt'
schön . . . Now, it has grown into a movement that rushes on and on!
Damnation!" . . . He made a face at the gendarmes, then stretching
himself to his full height:

"Back there—I say! . . . Have you any idea who I actually am?—
I am the purge in the bowels of the world! I have finally succeeded in
stirring up a movement in the stinking intestines of this carcass of
humanity after two thousand years of constipation! Once again the
brain and the glands of mankind are fresh as a morning in May—as
a jubilant chorus in cosmos! At last—when the intestinal gases demand
to be expelled! and want to radiate! Yes, radiate, Monsieur!—The fact
is, movement alone is the sense of the universe! Movement! . . . The
utmost possible movement! That is the aim of the glittering universe—
and only because of that—was it set going! . . . The stuff consumed
and burned by the rotation of planets, worlds, and suns! bitt' schön!
the droppings and slag and filth!—whether you learned men call it

447

'humus' or not—this crust from which the species of man was later evolved—this crust of the earth, comparatively no thicker than the skin under the shell of an egg—a cheese rind in which cheese mites have formed! Human cheese mites—which are absolutely nothing but a by-product, Herr Richter—and so why do you want to confront me with the pioneer? What do you expect will come of it?"

"That your conscience will wake up again in the presence of your mutilated front-line comrade! Diable!"

"Yes!" Uhle cried. "In the presence of a human being!"

"Human being! Human being!" Hitler mocked. "Man is nothing but a by-product of excretion!"

The air was still pregnant with his outburst when suddenly—from every corner of the hall—they moved up on him.

"Na, bitt' schön?" He fell back, step by step, before those who, step by step, were closing in on him.

For this time it was not the eyes of ghosts that stared at him, nor eyes gouged out of fish heads—but brown eyes, blue eyes, black eyes— the eyes of human beings—miraculously awake and quickened to remember that, once upon a time, in the beginning of things, they had emerged, out of the night of their existence—to light! . . . Remembering that once upon a time they had evolved out of their own urge toward light! Yes—that was the wordless message he read in them as they bore down upon him—no eyes of 'by-products', these—but the eyes of beings irresistibly determined to smash their way out of the dark dungeons conceived for humanity in his perverted, maniacal brain.

Gunther approached silently with the others. Nearer and nearer. But suddenly Uhle stopped. For something strange was happening. Out of the little box that the gendarme had put on the table—something was crawling. It looked like a strip of orange-peel. It made its way down the table leg to the floor like a caterpillar. And he saw that it was an orange-gold pupa about an inch and a half long.

Lured out of the box by the candlelight, it was moving along on its tiny elephant-clumsy feet—drawn by the urge to light. Uhle stared at it as if it were a living messenger from his comrade in the police station in Neuilly. He tried to read its message. Suddenly he called out to them all:

"Stop! Don't step on that caterpillar!"

"A caterpillar?" They all stopped, dumbfounded, and began to look for it on the floor. Even Hitler bent down.

448

CHAPTER FOURTEEN U HLE PICKED THE LITTLE CREA-
TURE UP AND CAREFULLY PUT IT BACK ON THE TABLE. THE REFUGEES,
raging over their interrupted vengeance, threatened him from behind
the gendarmes' bulky leather jackets. And not until, in utter bewilder-
ment, they saw that Hitler was staring at the caterpillar like a fascinated
schoolboy did they too gather around the table.

"Bitt' schön!" The blue nail of one numb finger moved erratically
around the insect as if his natural-history teacher in Braunau had just
brought it from the garden to give him a visible illustration of the
miracle of metamorphosis. "Bitt' schön. Look at that! You almost
stepped on it—the poor little thing! But it's still alive all right!"

"It's alive?" The halberdier pushed in front of Westermann, and
then, grinning broadly, asked: "Well, you Christians and Jews, would
you say that worm there has a soul? Because if souls exist, then there
must be one inside that worm too!"

With a gesture of disgust the rabbi looked at him. Uhle, who was
still trying to understand whether the caterpillar had a definite message
from his comrade for him, suddenly moved the candlestick so that all
around the table could see the bright-colored creature more distinctly.

"Here!" Uhle pointed to a golden-yellow glow, faintly shimmering
through the parchmentlike skin. "See them! There they are, quite
distinctly,—the future wings, formed already, inside the skin!"

"So they are!" Professor Goldschmidt pushed his glasses back on
his forehead. "Even to color and pattern! It seems that here we are
permitted a brief glance into the secret alchemy of life!"

"Into what—bitt' schön?" Hitler asked, with a face like a peasant boy
in front of a priest. "You mean . . . those wings in the worm . . .
represent its soul . . . ?"

"At all events they represent its future wings . . ." To protect the
little creature from the shoving crowd, Uhle put his hand over it. "Yes.
An obscure sense that it won't have to creep on the earth forever . . .
in fact . . . a secret presentiment . . . that out there—beyond its
creeping existence, is more—an unlimited possibility of life! That's it!
And it is that obscure presentiment that *formed* those wings."

"Gentlemen," interrupted Professor Goldschmidt, "it looks as if at
any moment now we may witness a very rarely observed phenomenon
—if I am not mistaken, we are going to see the birth of a butterfly!"

449

"What? Where? Where?"

Pushing excitedly, the crowd surged up behind the gendarmes. Only Dr. Wolff did not move. Everyone wanted to watch with his own eyes. Even the grounds of mortal hate that sprang from their mutually exclusive philosophies were for the moment apparently as much forgotten as the quarrels of children to be resumed later at recess in the school-yard.

"Careful!" Professor Goldschmidt pushed back the halberdier's clumsy hand. "Don't touch it!"

"Diable!" The examining magistrate tipped back his cap, and, strangely enough, in spite of the objections of some of the sergeants, tolerated this new delay—as if he were willing to grant Hitler a last chance.

"Porca Madonna! Chef, I've never seen anything like it before!"

"Damnation! Neither did I—you can see the wing already!" Münzer took a magnifying glass from his pocket and passed it from hand to hand. Like some gigantic antediluvian saurian, the pulsating, breathing creature loomed upon their awareness. Uhle too studied it through the glass.

"At all events those wings, already formed inside the creature in its present state, represent something that it can only use when it is no longer a caterpillar!"

"Nu!" The Rabbi snatched the glass away. "That's nothing new!"

"Certainly it's nothing new! Notwithstanding, it's just as astounding each time it happens."

"Just as astounding," Goldschmidt lectured as if he were in a class-room, "as, for example, the embryo in the mother's womb, in which eyes, nose, ears, hands, and feet are all formed—all of them organs which the embryo, locked in that close darkness, cannot possibly employ."

"By God the Just! We all know that!"

"Of course we all know that!" Uhle answered. "But one thing we don't know: What mysterious voice murmurs to the embryo: 'Create yourself eyes, ears, feet, and hands, so that after your birth—in the new state of existence awaiting you—you will not be a cripple but shall be able to hear, to see, to walk!'"

"Nu!" Dr. Wolff's eyes rolled behind his glasses. "We all know that. That's nothing new!"

"Mankind's dream of liberty—that is nothing new either, Doctor." Uhle said hotly. "And nevertheless, down to the present day, we have not succeeded in evolving such a wing for our dream of liberty!"

"Man!" Münzer joined in. "Liberty is a purely economic problem! What on earth has liberty to do with the soul?"

"Yes, by God the Just! What kind of talk is this, you goy! Anyhow, we're not insects. What's valid for the insect is not valid for us human beings!"

"Are you positive about that?"

"Absolutely. That's one thing I certainly am positive about!"

"And you . . ." Uhle suddenly addressed the insect as if it could understand him. "What are you positive about? Hm? The only thing you know is that you have to transmute your entire substance into wings, don't you? That's what you know—"

"By God the Just! But what it doesn't know is that we are bending over it, watching it—"

"No, you know nothing about that! Nothing whatever. And you have no idea that out there the stars will soon be paling . . . that somewhere out beyond the meadows there's a great metropolis glowing! You don't know that in Neuilly at the police station, an unknown soldier is waiting for us. No"—he nodded to Dr. Wolff—"certainly, of all those facts it knows nothing. Nor that we are watching how, true to its innate urge, it tries to burst the confines of its former creeping existence.—No, it knows nothing about all that . . . just as we know nothing about who is bending gigantically over *us*—perhaps is watching *us*"—suddenly he looked up—"After all, what do we know?"

The rabbi was going to answer. But suddenly the creature crept forward, in a state of tremulous excitement that contagiously affected the onlookers. It climbed the candlestick. Soon it was at the top. There it clung to a globule of wax. And now it began to be shaken by almost regular spasms.

"Those are labor pains!" Professor Goldschmidt exclaimed.

"What—bitt' schön?" Hitler took the magnifying glass again. "What's that?"

"Look—there, there!" Goldschmidt snatched away Krah's fountain pen, with which he was trying to tickle the creature. "Those are the birth throes! When I was a student and had to attend seven births before I could pass the state examination, it was always incomprehensible to me! Some little whore would be brought in—who until the very last minute had been tramping the streets, with no other language on her lips than the lowest jargon of the brothel—and at the moment of delivery her face would take on an expression more beautiful, more blissful than was ever painted on a Madonna!"

"Look! Look!" Hitler seemed excited. "Now you can actually see

451

the tips of the wings!"

"Oi-oi!" Krah peered from behind Grumbach's back. "Maybe it's a cabbage butterfly! Back in Prague, I used to spear cabbage butterflies on a needle! God, how I speared them!"

"Bitt' schön! Look! The soul is trying to get out! The soul wants to get out!"

Indeed, suddenly the creature jerked convulsively—as if determined no longer to remain enclosed. And, now, abruptly splitting the breast casing with ever more deliberate thrusts, it worked its way out.

"There—there—there!!"

"Yes—bitt' schön—there he is!"

And now everyone was shouting: "The butterfly is born!"

The scales on its infant wings were still moist. There it rested, numb and motionless. Suddenly something passed through the newborn insect as if some question of tremendous import were being weighed.

"What is it doing? What's it doing now? Bitt' schön!"

Uhle counted: "One second—four—sixteen! Attention! Now, now! There!" He looked at the others, as if only now had he grasped the entire meaning of the transformation. "There you are! Now the butterfly knows what he is destined to do in this enigmatic world of ours! *He* does not doubt any more!"

The wings opened once or twice—but the flying surfaces were still too wet. Suddenly the guttering candle began to send out circular waves of light—like the nimbuses sometimes seen around street lamps in a fog. As if moved from within, the haloes rippled out in ever-widening rainbow-tinted arcs.—Did the dying flame with its coronas of golden-green, orange-yellow, and electric-blue wish to greet the newborn guest?

Again the butterfly tried to rise. Again and again—but in vain. Now, however, the radiant fingers of light helped it from the candle. Tenderly they sustained its first flight, lifting it as often as it weakened. Ever and again! Until, at last, it was safe in its own flitting, light, exquisite strength . . .

"There! It's flying!" Hitler exclaimed, and tried to catch it.

"It's flying!" All their hands snatched after it. "There it goes!"

"You betrayer of the workers!" Münzer pushed his way from behind the gendarmes. Then he stared, now at Hitler, now at the butterfly. "Yes, *it* knows the meaning of it all. *It* doesn't question any more—whether there is a soul or not . . ."

"Bitt' schön! Where will it fly to—after all?"

"Into liberty!" The whole crowd stamped toward Hitler—but they

452

were driven back behind the table by the younger gendarmes.

Then Münzer, unable to hold in any longer, roared:

"Yes! You brown executioner, you! It is flying into freedom!"

The candleflame guttered out, in short puffs. And the orange-red wings of this youngest of all winged spirits, pursued by the beams of their flashlights, threw fantastic shadows.

"Freedom!" Uhle groaned, and watched the butterfly trying to find the way out. "Freedom! Thou art the eye in the light! Without thee, no seed would find its way out of the earth! No sapling would become a tree! No blossom would grow into an apple! Freedom! Oh, thou soul of humanity!"

In the sultry stillness of the hall, there was no further sound but the faint, fluttering wing beats of the butterfly as it bumped against the wall—then against the ceiling.

CHAPTER FIFTEEN

AFTER A TENSE SILENCE, UHLE'S VOICE WAS HEARD:

"In 1916, when I had to lead a replacement company from Beaumont village down into the Chauffour Gorge—to battle—I remember, they were all handsome boys of about seventeen. Their brand-new leather equipment rasped and squeaked at every step. Their thighs arched— they were lustily alive! The flowers that the women and girls had thrown to them at the railway station were still stuck under their shoulder straps. How gaily and cheerfully they sang the songs of the fatherland!—Suddenly, without warning—a crash! A heavy shell from the Fort de Tavanne! I was thrown sideways several yards—into a heap of leaves. When I looked around, of those two hundred young men nothing was left but tattered rags of uniforms out of which the flesh oozed like bloody rice. Only one of them survived for a few seconds. With great childlike eyes, he kept on crying: 'Come and help me! Oh God, oh God! Help!'—It seemed as if in a split second he had understood the sense and nonsense of it all! . . . a heavy presentiment in his eyes—as if he knew—he had not yet been able to form his wings! . . . He yearned to get out—out of his shattered human pupa! Into eternal freedom! But how could he?—There he lay, torn to pieces—and he had not yet developed organs for the other element.—How could he now ever?"

"How?" The violinmaker crossed himself, shaken. Then he murmured the consolation of his faith: "Only through Grace! Right?"

"Through Grace?" Uhle repeated. And then said firmly, "How can Grace still create a butterfly out of a crushed pupa?"

Mathias Westermann looked at him gloomily. Did a light dawn on him? Did he remember the boys he had seen crushed by artillery fire in fields and village roads? Lying there like worthless rags . . . and at night—loaded into carts, tumbled onto stretchers—carried to a mass grave?

Hitler too, brooded. All at once he pulled out a handkerchief, covered his face, and began sobbing so hard that Commander Gunther questioned the gendarmes with his eyes.

"Nu—by God the Just! . . . lead him away! Herr Richter! Take his hanky away from him—the monster!"

Meanwhile, exhausted from its first flight, the butterfly had lighted on a beam where it was out of sight. The examining magistrate nudged Uhle:

"Diable! Perhaps at last he will be shattered by the realization of what unatonable crimes he is committing every instant against life itself?"

"Yes!" Uhle looked at the Reich Führer. "Will it at last begin to dawn on him, that every one of those whom he has hung—tortured—and shot—had the possibility of evolving his own wings?"

"Every one?" Hitler pricked up his ears. "How so? Every one? You confuse me!"

"Once—behind the village of Merles—it had been snowing . . . For three days we had been in rest billets behind the front. The blue heights around Verdun were quaking under the bombardment—like the end of the world . . . Out there in the snow-covered fields we saw some crows sitting. Columns of half-frozen, tired soldiers and horses were waiting on the road that led to the wintry battlefield—column after column—waiting . . . All of a sudden, we made a tremendous discovery . . ."

"What tremendous discovery? Bitt' schön?!"

"We observed how the warm breath from the crows' bills—from our own mouths—from the horses' mouths—from all those sleepless and exhausted men before us!—how in the wintry morning air, all those breaths looked absolutely alike . . . wherever a living being breathed, there was the same whitish vapor. 'See that!' said a soldier. 'There you are! That's the "breath of life"—which God has breathed into all His creatures alike! Yes, there it is! the "breath of life!" the "hh . . ."'"

454

And now he exhaled a full, aspirated breath across the intervening space at Hitler. "Hh . . ."

The cobwebs fluttered.

"In very truth—if it was really God who breathed this breath into us all alike—then it certainly must originate from a reservoir to which everyone—and not alone the Nazi—has a right . . ."

The last words were taken up by everyone—in such a shout that Hitler fell to his knees on his leather coat.

"There! it's flying again!" He gesticulated to the gendarmes. "Bitt' schön—open the window for it! It wants to get out—out!"

"Yes—open up for it!" Münzer implored, as if he could no longer physically endure the sight of the butterfly looking for a way out.

"Damnation!" Hitler whimpered, "can't you see—it wants to get out! Only the other day when my Prince Ferdinand gave me a chaffinch, I let the birdie right out of its cage—"

"A chaffinch?" Krah's voice broke. "Oi-oi!"

"But not my brother! What?" Westermann groaned. "But not my brother in Dachau! Right?"

"And my little niece Nadia—nu, where is she?"

"And all the others in your ghettos and concentration camps—you betrayer of the workers! . . . What! the chaffinch is allowed to live —but we—we?"

"Bitt' schön—do open the window for it!"

"Stop!" Uhle threatened the stout gendarme—"stop—no one is to leave here—not even the butterfly!"

"No one!" the refugees joined in, as if they had taken leave of their senses—"No one—no one! We'd all rather rot—or be shot to death— than to live in such a world! A world in which only a chaffinch is allowed to be free!"

"Yes, shoot us!" roared Münzer—"shoot us! Leave nothing and no one alive!"

"What do you want of me?" Hitler jumped up and raised both his arms: "What do you want, all of you—of me? Bitt' schön! I simply can't stand it any longer! I am a prisoner myself! All around me—on all sides—nothing but Prussians—" Suddenly he moaned: "Open all the concentration camps! Open all the cages!"

"What's that he said?" Münzer's eyes were glowing in his ashen face like brown coals.

"What did he say?—Open all concentration camps?"

"Yes!" Hitler screeched so unbelievably loud that some of them ducked before the colossal power of his voice. "Open up Oranienburg!

Open up Dachau! Throw open all the concentration camps!"

"What? Open up Dachau and Oranienburg?"

Tumult ensued. Krah squeezed Goldschmidt's hand. Overcome by an upsurge of joy such as he had never experienced, Westermann embraced the Communist. Even the examining magistrate threw his cigarette away, limped over to Hitler, and said, his lips trembling:

"Mais, mon Führer!" Words failing him, he could only stammer, "Diable, diable!"

"Oi-oi!" Krah pinched the rabbi's cheeks. "Did you hear that? He's going to open Dachau! . . . That means that Uncle Theo will be set free!"

"By God the Just!" Dr. Wolff had detached himself from the seething mob and retired to the foot of the stairs. "Are you all crazy? 'Free?' Nu, who's going to be set free? No, no! The prison calendar on which they mark off the days in the Jewish dungeons of the goy prisons—I've long since, finally and forever, torn it down! . . . No, no! You'll never get me to believe in your 'Day of Liberation'! What? You trust that disgusting caricature there? Not me! Kicks and blows! Kicks and blows! Yes! . . . two thousand years long—I believe in them! Torture —by God the Just!—That I understand. But I won't believe in him— not in that beer-cellar squabbler! Never!" He retired a few steps further from the orgy of hope.

The blood rushed to Gunther's face—darkening it so that the silvery hair on his temples stood in high relief. Now he saluted:

"Your Excellency—would you be willing—to announce your decision—with your God-given oratorical powers—from the Eiffel Tower—personally over the ether waves—to the whole world that is trembling in uncertainty?"

"From the Eiffel Tower? Bitt' schön! In person?" Hitler put his hands on his hips.

Suddenly he looked tensely at Dr. Wolff. But then in a dull voice, like that of a convalescent who has just risen for the first time after a long illness, he said:

"If that Rabbi there asks me to, Herr Richter! The Rabbi must ask me to . . ."

CHAPTER SIXTEEN "Nu? . . ." DOCTOR WOLFF TURNED
HEAVILY AND LOOKED ABOUT—AS IF HE WERE NOT SURE HE HAD HEARD
correctly. Suddenly his body twitched, he took off his glasses, threw
himself on the sofa behind the table, and stared at the examining magistrate, shrugging his shoulders:

"Nu? . . . What is it that this non-man wants?"

"Diable! . . . Your Excellency, may I inform the authorities in
question at once? . . . So that all the necessary preparations can be
made . . ."

Without waiting for Hitler's answer, he beckoned to the gray-haired
sergeant. There was something like a smile of victory in his bold eyes.
"Aubert! Take your motorcycle! Vite! Vite! Dash down to the
Trocadéro! Report to the President of our congress what was promised
to us here, just now."

"Promised—what do you mean? Bitt' schön! Promised?"

But the sergeant was already out in the garden. Hitler started after
him, but Gunther raised his cane horizontally to stop him. Then he shut
the window, and when the noise of the motorcycle had died away, he
bowed:

"Pardon, Your Excellency—but in a moment a car will arrive from
the Elysée—to call for you—in proper style—as is fit for a person of
your high standing! You will be escorted by cavalry. Allow me!" And
with a chivalrous gesture he invited the Supreme Head of the Reich to
be seated in the big chair in front of the fireplace.

At once, Xaver Grün, Doriot, and the younger gendarmes stationed
themselves near him. Armoni lit a few more candles, scanned the faces
of the dumbfounded refugees, grinned, took off his straw hat, and carefully placed a silk cushion behind Hitler's back.

"Nu!" The Rabbi rose and mounted a few steps of the staircase.
"Monsieur le Juge! What has this monster to announce from the Eiffel
Tower to a 'trembling' world? By God the Just! Are we going to have
another pronunciamento like Clermont-Tonnerre's, who in 1791, during the French Revolution, cried out at a great meeting: 'To the Jews
as human beings, everything—to the Jews as a nation, nothing'?" He
glowered down on his fellow victims, all of them apparently blinded as
by a miracle.

"Oi-oi!" Sweating with excitement, Krah twisted his forelock. "For

5720 years we Jews, on the Day of Atonement, have been sending each other such nice little cards with the Star of David in silver and gold— Oi-oi! Dr. Wolff, maybe, we've really got there at last?"

"By God the Just, Herr Krah, you're a litterateur! What do you know about the Star of Zion?"

"My dear friend!" Professor Goldschmidt slipped behind the gendarmes up to the rabbi and whispered: "For heaven's sake, let's leave the hobgoblin of the Jewish question out of it!"

"Hobgoblin?" Dr. Wolff loomed gigantically on the staircase. "Nu —by God the Just! Not until the Jewish nation had been trampled underfoot was there any hobgoblin of a Jewish question! Not until then!"

"Diable!" The examining magistrate joined them. "Go on—ask him! He's waiting for it . . ."

"No, Monsieur le Juge! That monster! No! Even if he crams my people into more and more airless lodgings—even if we haven't another apple, not a leaf of lettuce—nothing but a crust of bread in our pockets —still we Jews will continue, on the highways and byways of this world, to dream our great dream . . ."

"Your great dream? You Jews!" Gunther knocked angrily on the floor with his stick. "Diable! When we were all sitting around the great horseshoe-shaped table this evening at the Trocadéro, in front of the carafes of Sauterne and Burgundy, not only were there Jews there, but Christians, Mohammedans, Hindus, Buddhists, Negroes, Quakers, everything you can think of. And yet we all were dreaming *one* great dream!"

"Nu, Monsieur—I tell you, if you're still talking about the dream of liberalism—that's one dream we've left off dreaming! As far as I'm concerned—now, I am a Jew—and nothing else!"

"Diable! When I went to the front, I was an atheist. I was fighting as a son of the Enlightment and the Revolution!"

"Mais oui, mon Commandant, mais oui . . ." A few of the gendarmes nodded.

"But as the captain of a company of men brave beyond praise, I had an opportunity, by studying the faces of my soldiers under fire, to determine to what extent the promises of the various religions were fulfilled. . . . Diable! When we were down there squashed in the shell holes, along with the sons of other mothers from all over the world, and we used to have to wedge the corpses of our comrades-in-arms, the minute they were shot down, into the parapet like sandbags, as some further protection against the hellish bombardment—diable!—then, in the midst of that annihilation, even such an atheist as I, was forced to ask himself what was the sense of the whole business? . . . And then I'd look about me, right and left, at my brave, God-fearing men and . . ."

"Mais oui, mon Commandant," Laroche agreed, "when a fellow found himself all alone under a barrage—and the only living creature that turned up evenings to visit him was a young and slender silver-gray rat, that would snuggle into the folds of his overcoat, seeking shelter from the shell splinters—and he'd share his crumbs of bread with her—mais oui!—then indeed, he used to ask himself: 'What's the sense of it all'?"

"Diable! Why—if there is such a thing as a God—why does He allow—?"

"Nu!" The Rabbi interrupted hurriedly. "In the sector where I was, the soldiers didn't ask themselves whether or not there was a God! What they wanted to know was: when they were going to get some better meat! . . ."

Several of the gendarmes grinned.

"By God the Just! . . . Goldschmidt—did the fellows in your company bother their heads about whether there was a God?"

"You mean, whether or not they were going to get some free beer!" Münzer laughed shortly.

"Nu, Monsieur le Juge, we certainly didn't get so melodramatic about things . . ."

"Diable! You mean to say that, in all those endless hours down there in the trenches with your comrades, you never once discussed the existence of God?"

"No! What for? Why should we? I already had my God! . . . By God the Just—he's the same one I picked out ten thousand years ago!"

"On Mount Sinai—right?"

"Yes, my dear Westermann! Ha-ha! Precisely! on Mount Sinai!"

"Diable! But we who did not have the benefit of seeing this much-prized and much-doubted God of yours on Sinai face to face—what about us, Doctor—?"

"Wolff is my name."

"Dr. Wolff! We who for four long years, in the slaughterhouse of battle, had nothing to do but think of how we could slaughter as many images of God as possible! Diable! We asked ourselves: Why, why exactly, did your God give His Ten Commandments up there on Sinai, if, after so many thousands of years, nobody has ever obeyed them? 'Thou shalt not kill!' Diable! So what? 'Thou shalt not commit adul-

459

tery!' So what?!"

"Oi-oi!" Krah made a face. "Long live Reno!"

" 'Thou shalt not covet thy neighbor's manservant, maidservant, nor his ox, nor his ass, nor anything that is his.' So what!"

"So what! So what!" Goldschmidt mumbled up to the rabbi.

"Nu! What! Just *because* we covet. And because what we chiefly covet is the things that belong to our neighbor.—That's why the law was given to us!"

"Diable! But if nobody has ever yet obeyed it?"

"Nu, Monsieur le Juge, we all are only—"

"Bourgeois!" the Communist interrupted, "you all still believe in the individual!"

"The individual?" Dr. Wolff felt that he was being surrounded. "Nu! Wasn't that the great achievement of Judaism! We, the Jews, were the first to elevate the individual out of the mass of collective termites! We awakened his conscience! We taught him to distinguish between good and evil! And that conscience—we then chose for our God!"

"And what change did that bring about? In all those thousands of years, nothing has changed at all! Right! Or have you Jews become better—than we?"

"Nu! You all look at me as if you expected us Jews to be a lot of immaculate angels? Oh, no! We have just as many failings as you!"

"Just as many failings?" asked Professor Goldschmidt perplexedly. "Then what did Moses awaken our consciences for?"

"What for? Oi-oi! Only to make us meshuga? Fine! So now we know what is good and what is evil—and then what?"

"By God the Just! We wrestle with the good just as Jacob wrestled with the angel!"

"Oi-oi! And how long is this wrestling match going to keep up?"

Laughter echoed through the room.

"Nu!" The rabbi ascended a few more steps. "You goys hate us just because we were the discoverers of God! Because we have given you God!"

"Given us God!" Xaver Grün stepped forward from the group around Hitler. "Son! We don't want any gifts from you—understand! Not even God! Particularly as he is only an invention! Or as His Eminence is always saying, 'The God of the Chosen People!' "

"Alias Moses!" mocked Hitler. "Alias Moses!"

"Nu—" The rabbi coughed through his beard into the silence that followed. "And I am to ask a favor of that Jew-baiter? I—Monsieur le

460

Juge? 'The vines still blossom and their yield is fragrant'. What goy has ever composed poetry like the Bible? I ask you—who of you—at night, when you cannot sleep, gets out of bed and climbs the stairs and gazes into the sky?!"

Gunther limped impatiently from one side of the room to the other with an almost regular rap of his wooden leg. In the meantime the air had become as brittle as glass—as it often does about four in the morning. Several gendarmes compared the time on their wrist watches nervously. All at once the examining magistrate stopped at the staircase, stroked his beard, and looked up at the rabbi.

"Yes, indeed! You gave us the Jewish God! C'est exact! Merci infiniment!—And you—" he looked at the violinmaker and the others —"you gave us the Christian God! Merci infiniment! And the sergeant there from Algiers—he prays to Mohammed! Merci infiniment!" He saluted them all and for the first time his voice rose above an ordinary tone:

"Diable! We soldiers from no man's land, at any rate, say: 'Thanks very much!' In the scum and slime of the trenches, everything failed!"

"By God the Just!" Dr. Wolff shook his fist above his head. "There is certainly *one thing* that has not failed!"

"What is it? What . . . ?"

"Nu! our belief in the nation!"

"Bravissimo!" Hitler clapped his approval.

"Oi-oi! That's nonsense!"

"Nu—no! Herr Krah! That's not nonsense! For, what centuries could not bring about—he could—" Raising his slouch hat, the rabbi gave a deep, ironical bow. "Thanks to the Herr Reich Chancellor and Führer, Judaism is at last awakened and united!"

"Come!—are the Jews the only people involved?" Westermann joined the group by the stairs.

"Quoi? More boundaries? One against the other again? Diable! *One* church against another church! *One* blessing against another! Buddha! The Bible! Allah!—Hélas! Has anybody in the past centuries been able to prevent the murderous slaughter of man by man? Monsieur! Who has ever been able to unite the religions or the nations?"

A heavy silence followed his question. Suddenly Uhle's voice came sternly:

"Who? No one! Except death! Only in a mass grave do they all lie peacefully, united. Blacks and whites. Christians and Jews. Germans and Russians. Tommies and Yanks."

He went to the window, sat down on the chest, and buried his head

461

in his hands. The rabbi looked at him balefully:

"By God the Just! What is the goy thinking about now?"

"What am I thinking?" Uhle looked up after a long pause. "I am trying to think whether there really is nothing that can unite us men in the short life that is ours? I say—while we're still alive."

There was a heavy silence. Suddenly Hitler thrust out his chin and winked covertly, as if he had found the formula:

"Bitt' schön, gentlemen. *I* know what could unite us all." He rose from his chair. "What we need is just all to be Jews together!"

"Oi-oi!"

And then there was laughter and shouting and cursing, through which Hitler gesticulated to the younger gendarmes:

"It would be the only way out—bitt' schön. For a Jew won't unite with anyone but a Jew!"

"Oh, oh, oh!" The rabbi descended one step through the increasing uproar, quivering to the tip of his beard. "Nu? And you Christians? You'll take that? You won't strike the beast down? By God the Just! But you Christians have always put up with the slaughterers of my people—for centuries. Nu, it is you that I accuse! The whole Christian world shall atone to me at last! Strike the beast down! I demand it as your moral atonement for all our sufferings! As your soul-cleansing atonement! As atonement, atonement—"

"Atonement?" Westermann made a powerful thrust forward. "He seems to think we Christians are responsible for Herr Schickelgruber there! No, Dr. Wolff! In fact—if we Christians wanted to let go—right?—if we Christians could play the propaganda game in the international press as you do—right?"

"Oi-oi! Here we stand then, like a man and wife in a ruined marriage—with nothing left but divorce! Oi-oi!"

"Exactly!" Uhle stepped behind the examining magistrate. "Just one careless word now, one bit of die-hard dogmatism, one wicked impulse—and we'll all be at each other's throats like mad dogs. Gunther," he said harshly, "what do you want that 'sovereign' to speak from the Eiffel Tower for? There is only one man who would have the right to do that—above all, the 'moral authority'."

"Nu, who?" The rabbi cut him off. "A new Messiah in sight, eh? No, no! The day is past when, every Friday night, like every Jew, I went out from Safed to the city gates to await the Messiah—"

"Await?" Westermann cried roughly. "Why wait? The Messiah has come—right? He came two thousand years ago."

"Nu," Dr. Wolff smiled sarcastically down to Comrade Münzer, "is our Catholic friend Westermann counting on poor humanity's taking flight back to Christianity for refuge?"

"Flight?" The violinmaker paled. "Flight?"

"Nu, if you don't like that word, you can say 'bankruptcy,' my dear Westermann. Yes, the Jew Jesus was a great prophet. But he watered down the wisdom of the Bible."

"Jew Jesus? Prophet? Watered?" The violinmaker boiled over.

"Nu, yes. I say: he watered down the lofty ethics of the Jews. For virtue, he substituted a reward in Heaven. And that we scorn."

"Blasphemy!" Westermann shouted.

"No. A reward in Heaven? That doesn't sound like the fulfilling of the prophecies!"

"Fulfilling of the prophecies? Reward in Heaven?" Uhle threw back his head. "Do you believe that if the Redeemer were to return, He would come back to earth as a fulfilling of Judaism or of Christianity? No!" He exchanged a glance with Gunther. "For us, He can only come back in those who fulfill His spirit of love!"

"Nu, then he will never come back—never!"

"On the contrary, Dr. Wolff. Because during our time in no man's land, He did already come back! There He was, in a filthy uniform—without decorations or stripes. With His haggered, unshaven face under a trench helmet. There—oh, how often—we met and recognized His brother spirit! I say—when just any soldier tried to rescue a wounded man from the barbed wire without thinking of his own life and got his own death wound for his pains—that was *His* spirit of love. Or when, in the awful fear that we all felt before battle, one soldier spoke comfort to a handful of his comrades cowering behind a trench parapet—when in the name of them all he cried up the question of the meaning of life, out of the death-filled air of the trenches, cried it up along his rifle barrel, as a religious question, to the Creator Vitae—"

"*Who* did that? Nu, who?"

"He—in whose eyes there was a certain light. He who heard our curses against the war. He who scribbled down the dying soldier's stammer of farewell to mother or sweetheart or wife—when the blood-stained lips had already begun to stiffen. He, Dr. Wolff, who never compromised with death or the Devil! He who has remained true to the spirit of the front in its demand for a new life. I say it in all truth"—he turned to Gunther—"the grand mutilé de guerre who is held in your police station at Neuilly was sent to us here out of the world conscience of the millions of unknown soldiers who lie under the grass. He has come up the thirty-three steps of Haudroumont Quarry, only to remind us that we were once united in our oath against this desecrator of the dignity of man!"

"Bravo, bravo!" Some of those behind the cordon of gendarmes shouted, and shook their fists at Hitler.

"Gunther," Uhle pleaded, "let us get out of this villa before your Minister of Justice—who of course always stands with his hat off under the Arc de Triomphe beside the grave of the *dead* unknown soldier—I say: before all the world's ministers of justice turn their police loose on the *living* unknown soldier and lock him up behind bars! Gunther, shan't we go and bring our comrade from Verdun back here?"

"Nu, like a 'sovereign' too, no doubt! In a state coach, with an escort of the Garde Mobile?"

"Let us grasp his hand!" Uhle cried. "Come! With him, let us form a first cell, a new movement, against the eternal profaner of life!"

"D'accord!" cried Münzer suddenly, and tore open a package of cigarettes. "Come on! To the police station at Neuilly!"

"Nu! And then?" The rabbi mocked the unanimous decision to set out. "And then?"

"Then?" The Communist beckoned to him. "Then every labor union will open its doors to him. Let's go!"

"No, by God the Just! *I* don't need your soldier. I have my seven-branched candlestick! I don't need anything else! The greatness of the inner Jewish world does not need anything else. . . . But tell me," he asked then, as though his vocal chords were bleeding: "When you've found your soldier in Neuilly, into what Land of Canaan will *he* lead you?"

"Where will he lead us?" Münzer puffed out. "He'll lead us where we don't have to work forever for others, but can work for ourselves—we workers!"

"Where a Christian like me can build a violin undisturbed, Dr. Wolff. Right?"

"Where we veterans"—Gunther grasped Uhle's hand—"shall have become a power against war!"

"Exactly!" Professor Goldschmidt nodded to the rabbi. "Where we won't just be allowed to *think* about truth but can put it into action!"

"Oh thou yellow, yellow River of Jordan!" the rabbi groaned. "Where—where is *my* home?"

"Dear fellow . . ." Goldschmidt went up the stairs to him. "Don't be the only one to stand apart from us!"

"The only one?" The rabbi rolled his eyes. "Since the days of

Esther, our story has been: 'There is a certain people scattered abroad and dispersed among the people; and their laws are diverse from all people.' "

"Doctor—" The violinmaker too went up the stairs to him. "Come with us! Right? When I was out there in the forest today—in the thunderstorm—there were all kinds of trees! Each one with its own law! Right? Each one standing just as alone as you are. Every tree trunk rooted in its own earth. Each one of them gave tongue, rustling and groaning after its own fashion—right? I say: each had its own law —by which it wanted nothing else but to grow and live! . . . Yet up above in the tree tops, through the topmost twigs and leaves, the storm-wind played and sang but a *single song!* The wind didn't ask 'Is this a poplar? An oak? A cedar, or a beech?'—It simply blew, and then the song rose—right?—one mighty song in which all jubilated together."

"In the name of all that's reasonable!" Uhle implored him, "you were at the front too! For those of us who know what that was like, there must be some sort of union possible between man and man . . . We have all in ourselves experienced this being—we have all known— the unknown soldier! Who helped us in the trenches. Who spoke to us when we could no longer bear up under the insanity of pure, sense-less slaughter. For whom no longer existed: Races! Distinctions! Who after the battle softly passed his hand over our bloody faces, took away the hate! The hate against each other! The hate!—Why cannot we unite finally with him? With him who could lead us out of this empty, loveless, senile age of hate and power! so that we might live on this earth simply, beside each other—like every little grass blade."

"Nu! And your soldier in Neuilly—*he* doesn't hate anyone?"

"No! He has kept alive in himself the spirit of love—and faith in love's future. Does any of you"—Uhle looked from one to the other round the room—"does any of you know another way out of our dark-ness of soul?"

Suddenly he turned back to the rabbi. " 'Let there be light!' That word of creation we can cry to one another—you and I—all of us— Christians, Jews, heathens!"

After a moment of mistrustful silence, Dr. Wolff started slowly down the stairs. But then Hitler caught his eye.

"Nu—no!" The rabbi stopped dead. "No! I'll work with a road gang cleaning out the swamps of Haifa! I'll load stones in barges with the navvies! Yes! I'll do any of those things! But no more mirages for me! By God the Just! No more Fata Morganas!"

All at once, Hitler sat up straight in his chair of state, stretched out

465

his arm, offering his hand to Dr. Wolff, and said oilily:

"Pax! Rabbuni, bitt' schön."

"Away! By the Almighty! Away! Blood! An ocean of blood is between us! No! No Pax Romana. No Pax Germana. Monsieur le Juge! As a priest of the Jews, I warn you . . . ! An oath-breaker remains an oath-breaker—a murderer remains a murderer! By God the Just," he blazed at his colleagues, "you are no Jews! You may be good doctors, good merchants, or good commentators! But you are no longer Jews! What! I should ask a favor of *him?* God, my God! Thou who didst smite Pharaoh and all his men. Why does the butcher of Thy chosen people stand there unscathed? Away from me! Can your soldier in Neuilly dry up the rivers of tears all over the world? Away from me—all of you!"

"Dear fellow!" Professor Goldschmidt took his arm. "Hasn't the time come to say: 'Credo quia absurdum'?"

"Credo! Credo? I'd sooner believe in the Devil! No! No!" And then, in the silence that followed, only the rabbi's weeping, like a brook in the distance, could be heard. Suddenly he lost his balance, swayed, and rolled down the last few stairs. Münzer and Goldschmidt hurried to help him—but he managed to stand up.

"Monsieur le Juge—" He wiped his wet beard and raised his fist— "God's word runs straight to the point: He who permits one guilty of bloodshed to escape, brings down the punishment upon himself! By God the Just! The Prophet expressly told King Ahab: 'Thou shalt die because thou hast pardoned a man guilty of bloodshed!' "

Before this scathing curse, Hitler retreated to the fireplace and tried to read the faces of the gendarmes who were whispering together there. Suddenly he started. Outside, the racket of an approaching motorcycle had become audible.

CHAPTER SEVENTEEN   Sergeant Aubert came tearing through the dark garden. "CHEF!" he panted from outside, "CHEF!"

"Have you been to the Trocadéro? Did you see the President of the Anciens Combattants?"

"Mais non, Chef! How could I? The workers wouldn't let me through. 'Hitler in Paris!' It has spread like wildfire. They're pouring

466

as far as my authority extends!—will do everything in my power so that from now on this representative of souls shall represent us at the League of Nations and at all future world conferences! . . . I don't give a damn for the whole ballyhoo of the gaudiest general staff with all their waxed boots! Bitt' schön! And I declare it to be nothing but an ordinary infamy of the Jewish world conspiracy to suppose *I* would ever again send my fine and brave front comrades along the highways again. No!" He made a face. "No! . . . and from the top of the Eiffel Tower I will swear it to his idiotic milk-toast face: Everybody shall have his quart of milk! Let me out! No war! I swear it to all the mothers in the world. Again and again and again . . . !"

"Swear to us that when our unknown soldier finally resolves your accursed 'sacred law of war' into the 'all-holy law of life', you will do nothing to prevent it?"

"I swear! Bitt' schön. I swear!"

But at the same moment with gangsterlike suddenness, and with his full weight behind his fist, Hitler delivered such a blow between Uhle's eyes that he fell backward into the garden.

The rabbi gave a scream that rang through the hall. The others stood as if paralyzed. And before they could utter a sound, Hitler, aided by the stout gendarme, had climbed out the window and vanished into the darkness.

A salvo of shots followed him, mingled with curses. Curses.

But outside there sounded—as if sung by the sacred mouth of Nature —as if it were the terrific music of the world conscience—the song of the now approaching masses of poor, unknown devils from all over the world:

> Allons enfants de la patrie!
> Le jour de l'homme est arrivé!

BOOK SIX

CHAPTER ONE "**H**ASN'T HE MOVED YET?" AC-
COMPANYING HIMMLER, GÖRING TIPTOED CAUTIOUSLY ACROSS THE THICK
Persian carpet to the tremendous bed in a room on the top floor of
the German Embassy. There lay the Führer, still unconscious, just as
he was on his arrival after his successful flight from Neuilly.

Göring listened anxiously at the window. Around the Embassy,
from moment to moment, more and more people gathered—and the
secretly planned departure of the Reich Führer to the airport of Le
Bourget became increasingly problematic.

Downstairs through the corridors flitted adjutants, spreading ever
more alarming rumors about the ever more menacing attitude of the
Paris workers. Their faces were pale with the careworn pallor of
underlings who fear for the life of their employer.

"What does Sauerbruch say?" The Air Marshal's question broke a
full minute's silence in which he had stared at the black mustache under
the pointed nose in high relief against a bloodless complexion. Now
he looked impatiently at the clock. But the Chief of the Gestapo, irritated by the dull roar of voices outside in the rue de Lille, gave no
answer but a mute shrug of the shoulders. Göring vented a hoarse
rattle from a fat-obstructed larynx, his thick fingers at the same time
mechanically counting over the many stars and medals on his uniform.
Behind the drawn curtains, the confusion of voices in the street broke
off for a moment, and then there was heard the gallop of many horses.
After satisfying himself that the squadrons of gendarmes were driving
the crowd off the Embassy sidewalk, Göring suddenly whispered:

"Himmler, where does he keep that document pertaining to his successor?"

"As far as I know, in Berlin, Herr Reich Marshal."

"Damnation! What's that you're giving him?"

"Caffeine . . ."

"Caffeine?" Göring bent over the silk bedspread so suddenly that

470

his many medals jingled. "Won't that revive him?"

"It will, indeed, Herr Reich Marshal!" Straightening up, Himmler
put away the hypodermic. "It should revive him . . . or"—he glanced
at Hermann with shutterlike rapidity over the rims of his glasses—
"should it not revive him?"

"Himmlerchen! Himmlerchen!" Göring broke into a sweat. With
infinite precaution he eased himself down onto the bed. The inner-
spring mattress showed such powers of resistance that it did not even
squeak. "Adolferich!" he puffed in the face of the comatose Führer.
"Can you see us? . . . No, Himmlerchen, he still doesn't see us!
Where do you suppose he's floating about now? Well, at all events"—
he again rose cautiously to his feet—"whatever happens, Himmlerchen,
I shall certainly retain you as Chief of the Gestapo! Agreed?"

With a sweeping gesture, Himmler removed the glasses from his
wrinkled face and said softly:

"Heil Göring!"

"S-s-sh! S-s-sh!" Terrified, the Reich Marshal hid behind the high
head of the bedstead. But, as Hitler did not move, he strutted out
again. Turning on a shaded lamp, his arms widespread, he drew the
Gestapo Chief to his bosom, embracing him as closely as his waistline
and glittering array of medals would permit. And then his emotions
began to melt within him like a thousand pounds of butter in the sun.

"Ah, Himmlerchen!" The tears rolled down his fat cheeks. "What
a miraculous turn of events through God's Providence!"

Replacing his glasses, the founder of the Gestapo murmured through
the alcoholic vapors emitted by the Reich Marshal:

"How delighted my little daughter will be! We had always supposed
the Herr Reich Marshal would, upon the demise of the irreplaceable
Führer, appoint the Deputy Führer, as Chief of the Gestapo. Oh, Your
Excellency! How happy my family will be!"

"My wife"—Göring clutched him tighter—"saw all this coming!
When my little Hedda was christened, our erstwhile Führer toyed so
cutely with her tiny pat-a-cake hands . . . And afterward Emmy said
to me, 'Hermännchen, just now, during the ceremony, there was the
gleam of eternity in the Führer's eyes. You watch! He won't live
long!' "

"Did Her Excellency really say that?"

"Yes, that's what she said. And on the very next afternoon at Karin
Hall, when my good friend Henderson and I had been out shooting
deer and the huntsmen were bringing in the quarry, Emmy said: 'You
know, Hermännchen, there was exactly the same spot of white light

in Adolf's eyes yesterday noon that there is in the eyes of those dead deer!' And it was precisely at that moment that His Eminence, Reich Bishop Müller, was blessing our darling baby in the name of the Father and of the Son and of the Holy Ghost! Amen!"

"Yes, my faithful Party Comrade and comrade-in-arms, my dear Göring! There are certain moments in life when it seems as if our kidneys were absolutely gelid! Not a damn thing functions."

"That's just the way it is! God! God! . . . Just look how he's lying there now! So peacefully! And only to think how the whole world of Judocrats wished for everything evil to befall him! What horrible deaths they've all prophesied for him—these Western witches of Endor! . . . Ah, Himmlerchen, you might well say, the whole world, untied by hate, had strained its perverse imagination to think up a fitting death for him. Ha! Didn't they want to flay him alive? Well, now there he lies, so blissfully! Yes, that smile of his seems to express the whole noble sincerity of complete harmony, of a perfect being! . . . And the assassin? Have you clapped the handcuffs on him?"

"I am sorry—not yet! The murder gang succeeded in escaping from Neuilly to St. Denis. But Baron Jacques guaranteed to deliver the villains to me as soon as they are caught by the French Police. The whole police force of the Seine Department has been mobilized. Ah, Your Excellency!—if only we were safely out of the Embassy!—"

"Ah, Himmlerchen, who can discern the dark design behind all this? My heart is constricted . . . Excuse me a moment, my right suspender is digging into my flesh! Thanks very much! That's fine. And did you express to the Chief of the French Police the heartfelt thanks of the Gestapo for helping us with such genuine National Socialist solidarity?"

"I wish I could put the whole filthy refugee lot of them through the third degree!"

"Ah!" Göring sighed. "If only we could think of some extraordinary deed to perform in honor of this dying German! But after all we are nothing but poor, weak human beings! What we should do now is to so castigate the flesh of the whole Judocratic world that their blood would spurt to the stars! . . . But, shan't we perhaps pull off his boots?"

"At your service, Your Excellency! No reason why we shouldn't pull his boots off!"

"Oh, no! Let's not bother! . . . After all, we're not embalmers, lemon in hand! . . . Please give me that bottle of eau de cologne, will ou? Thanks! What time do you suppose it is?"

"It's still pitch-dark."

"And to think that in all probability he'll never again be able to
ing 'Oh, Du mein holder Abendstern!' Himmlerchen, you mustn't
augh! For God's sake, let's keep straight faces! . . . You know, when,
n 1917, my best friend Richthofen was shot down in an air battle, I
ad an attack of hysterical laughter. True as I live! I laughed like a
kunk in a henhouse! They couldn't do anything to calm me. And not
intil I'd shot down my sixteenth Englishman out of the clouds—not
intil I saw him crash in flames—did I get back my normal straight
ace! . . . So let's proceed cautiously, Himmlerchen! . . . If I could
only think what kind of a show we ought to put on for the day of
national mourning in Munich? By the honor of my sword—!" He drew
he naked blade back and forth across his tongue. "Himmlerchen! If
only I had more imagination! What we need now is the imagination of
he Catholic Inquisition! All the cruelty we could possibly achieve
eems absolutely nothing! A flea—a pig—an elk—a man!—So what?
. . If only we could put the whole bloody lot to the knife simultaneously! These peace-belchers!" He sighed. "But—the net is much too
coarse! You drive and you hunt this scum of the earth, and what happens? They just slip through the meshes!"

"But not from me! My dear Party Comrade—not from me! . . .'

"Didn't you say the red villains had escaped from Neuilly to St.
Denis?"

"We shall catch them! We shall catch them!"

"Only recently a Jew writer had the gall to say I looked like a blood
ausage stuffed with the blood of all the minorities! . . ."

"Yes, the world is ungrateful, Herr Reich Marshal—"

With a loud, creaking snore, Hitler woke. Göring and Himmler
umbled backwards. Then a valet came rushing in from the dressing
oom and stared at him:

"You're alive . . . ?" He stood at the foot of the bed trembling.

"Yes, my good Hofer, the people in the arsenal of democracy are
wrong." He sat up on the bed, straight as a ramrod, yelling triumphantly: "I'm alive."

Immediately thereafter there was a running and slamming of doors.

"Yes, how do you like that?" He snickered and flung pillows at
Göring and Himmler. "I'm alive! And that's a whole lot more important than tolling the bells on Good Friday! Serves you right, you
murderers!" He thumbed his nose triumphantly in all directions. "I
am alive! . . . bitt' schön. How often I've said to the British Am-

473

bassador in Berlin, when he asked for a private audience: 'Mister, if I'm really such a monster that there's nothing to be done but finish me off, then—why don't *you* shoot me—bitt' schön? Or why doesn't Molotov —with whom I've so often drunk a friendly cup of tea?'—"

Suddenly he jumped off the bed, the pouches under his eyes as purple as boils. Slowly, portentously, he approached Himmler.

"So-o-o-o! . . . So, this is the way my Supreme Chief of the Gestapo protects me! You—my supreme factotum of police!"

He spat on Himmler's glasses, and, turning his back, ran into the bathroom, Hofer at his heels.

Göring poured himself a glass of water and drank it. Then he pressed Himmler's hand as if in mute condolence. The Gestapo Chief wiped his glasses. Then he whispered:

"Herr Reich Marshal—the strange fact is that the French Police arrested his astrologer in Neuilly in connection with the attempted murder."

"Milarespo?" Göring drew him away from the bathroom door. "His star-gazer?"

"His star-gazer, Your Excellency—under cross-examination by Buch's Murder Division—turned out to be a Tibetan from the Gobi Desert!"

"That shaky old man? You don't mean it!"

"I can't talk about it yet," Himmler whispered. "But I can give you some details: At first Stalin intended to have a midnight supper with him in the Kremlin, but then he thought better of it and drove him out to the house of some relatives in the suburbs. They had dinner in the kitchen—Siberian whitefish and—"

"Siberian whitefish?"

"After dinner Marshal Stalin took him into the next room—where several Soviet marshals were waiting."

"Go ahead! What happened next?"

"I'm afraid you won't believe me, Your Excellency!—First, Stalin breathed on the windowpane so that the frost flowers melted. After getting his pipe to draw properly, he gave this astrologer fellow the floor. Who spoke as follows: 'It's only a few centuries ago that Buddhism enjoyed its conquest over all other religions! . . .'"

"The victory of Buddhism?" Göring glared at the Gestapo Chief.

"Party Comrade!" As if to prove his statement, Himmler produced a glamorous ruby from his breast pocket. "There! Milarespo claims that he showed this ring to Stalin."

"Damnation!" Göring grabbed the blood-red stone from Himmler

474

But that's the same ring that Schleichopovski had on his Bolshevik nger!"

"This ring belonged to the Mongol conqueror, Genghis Khan!"

"Hell and damnation! Here's our swastika engraved in it!" The Air Marshal puffed out his cheeks.

"Your Excellency—in Mongolia there's an ancient legend to the ffect that the awakening of Pan-Asia can only begin when the worst man has been born here in Europe—"

"The worst man? Did the yellow lama tell you that?"

"Precisely! And among the innumerable horoscopes that they udied during our monk's time in the monastery, the Buddhist priests elected the boy Adolf Hitler's constellation to serve their plans for he aggrandizement of Buddhism. Authorized and commissioned by the iving Buddha, Milarespo journeyed to Braunau—"

"Himmlerchen—how many glasses of beer have you had?"

"Herr Reich Marshal, I am completely sober! And now follow me losely: The plan was set in motion and the work began. Disguised as German tramp, this Buddhist agent managed to scratch, scrawl, and aint the sign of the swastika everywhere—on walls, milestones, even n the doorsteps of the school in Braunau—so that the boy Hitler nould always have the symbol before his eyes—"

"Heinrich, I had no idea you could tell fairy tales!"

"Fairy tales! . . . Listen! The astrologer confessed: Their plan was, o distract his attention from the Crucifix—which, in his Catholic irthplace, was naturally displayed everywhere—and to fix it on this Mongolian symbol—to the end that, in time, Adolf Hitler should effect he total extermination, root and branch, of all the cardinal virtues of Christianity!"

Göring would have burst out laughing but he restrained himself at ight of the sheepish expression on Himmler's face.

"And in the vacuum resulting from the disappearance of Christian-ty, they foresaw the day when our continent would be transformed nto such a terrible desert that, in the hearts of the nobler Europeans, fanatic yearning after new values would arise . . ."

" 'After new values'?"

"Exactly! After new values! And this, said our Mongol Milarespo o Stalin, would be Asia's hour of destiny! . . . In that hour, Stalin vould be exalted as the new God of War to reconquer the Western World for the Asiatics . . ."

His sentence remained unfinished, for Hitler came storming into the oom, leaving behind the tumultuous sound of rushing water.

"Bitt' schön—Lady Mitford always used to say: 'If ever an assassi should really succeed in laying me out cold, the whole civilized worl would have to use artificial restoration on me—because only I coul master the chaos that would follow my death!' "

Reflections from the lights outside flickered on the ceiling. He wer to the window and peered out through the curtains. Before the hig wall of the Embassy, the rue de Lille was completely empty. But o the right and left, behind the police cordon, he became aware of a dar crowd in the street. With changed voice he turned to Göring an Himmler:

"Bitt' schön, gentlemen!—Let's postpone the audience until tomo row, when we are back home again.—Where is Colonel Engel? I war to know immediately how soon I can start. Go find him!" He sat dow on the windowsill. "My mind is just a little bit dull. Damn it! Hov exhausted I am!" He cocked his head like a dog listening to musi "What was that?"

"It sounds as though shooting were starting on the other side of th Seine."

"Shooting?" He picked up a chair and started at Himmler. "Go on I want to get to the airport! Quick! Quick! Order the cars! Go on!— Halt!" He grabbed the Gestapo Chief by the arm. "Heinrich! So—yo just calmly let assassins crawl around in my vicinity? Shame on you You idiotic Saxon policeman! Shut up! God only knows, there's plent of the Passion of Our Lord in me! Aunt Resi always used to say, if kept on this way, I'd turn out to be a regular second Therese vo Konnersreuth!! . . . Bitt' schön, and whenever I feel this itching— here! or here!—then she used to say—that was the Passion in me an it would soon come out in bloody, scabby wounds. Damn it! What ar you driveling party donkeys staring at me like that for? I have escape from the jaws of death all right! I only wish my Faulhaber were her so that he could see the way you're all tormenting me! And the jok of it is that, after three hundred years, of course, they will canoniz me as a saint. On his last New Year's visit to me in Berlin, the Nunci himself was telling me, 'His Holiness will never excommunicate You Excellency—because of the Consistorium—and because of your qualifi cations for the altar later on.' "

His tall Colonel Engel entered.

"My Führer," he reported, "the Police Prefect of Paris begs you i the interest of your personal security to postpone your departure t Le Bourget airport . . . until the road to Vincennes is cleared. Th communists have succeeded in advancing their columns of worker from St. Denis south through Aubervilliers as far as the road to Le Bourget. The Police Prefect himself has gone to the Ministry of War."

"Well—then let me get just a little more sleep! Hofer!" he called the valet. "When Lady Mitford's had her bath, tell her to put on her red panties when she comes in here . . . Tell her I used to have much pleasanter dreams when I wore my old nightshirt than in these silk doo-dads of hers. Yes!" He jumped up and pressed his temples. "You know—I have had terrible dreams—I dreamed—Halt!" But the Colonel was gone.—Hitler threw himself on the bed and yawned. Suddenly he said, "Hofer, have that big woman in the kitchen put on Major Engel's boots and come in naked.—Yes, Hermann!" He yawned at Göring. "Only recently, in my English garden, my Lady Mitford was asking me why there should be this amazing institution of nature: man and woman? Why all this dimorphism of the sexes? Yes, she's always asking me such things.—What are you going to say to such a fine lady? That's the way it is!" He slapped his thigh. "Male and female! Until the next Sodom and Gomorrah!—that's how it is. Sauerbruch thinks it's all on account of the production of eggs! The Duke of Bedford thinks it's really all because of the semen . . . but I say: In the last analysis, it's simply the principle of a just division of labor . . ." Squatting on his heels on a bearskin on the floor, he licked the tips of his fingers.

Suddenly he looked out of the corner of his eye at the Chief of the Gestapo. "Tell me. Was this assassin paid by the Jews?" For answer, Himmler bowed over his Führer's hands and kissed them with a resounding smack. Göring too gave him a cumbrous embrace.

"Bitt' schön, it's a dead certainty that Churchill gave him the brilliant idea of sneaking up on me disguised as a French colonel! It's just like one of his ideas—the puff-cheeked, septuagenarian embryo!"

Rising slowly to his feet, he stroked his hips, risked another look out of the window, and muttered: "These 'Leaders of Democracy!' They'd rather fraternize in the Kremlin with the mass-murderer of millions of bourgeois, Stalinsky, and flirt with the camera, than have the modesty to recognize that here, before them, stands, once and for all, one who is in fact *the* Superman! . . . Instead, they send an assassin after me! Me! My respected Mr. police donkey!—an assassin! . . . But just let me tell you something: neither of you will have a pleasant death! Now get out! And put steam behind the French police so that I can finally get away from here!"

No sooner were Göring and Himmler out of the room than the Führer collapsed on the rug. Hofer wrung his hands in despair and ran out. A few seconds later a concealed door opened softly. Freshly bathed, swathed in a sky-blue silk negligee trimmed with feathers, and surrounded by a cloud of perfume, Frau Göring entered. With a loud "Oh!" she recoiled at the sight of the Führer lying there so deathly still. She wheeled about, her enormous weight adroitly poised on red satin mules, and sought safety in flight. But then she stopped, reflected, and returned. Stooping over, she put her hands under his arms and tried to raise him. He blinked uncertainly at her.

"Don't talk . . . I'm so exhausted. And just when I was lying still—so blissfully! . . . I just want to stretch my legs out and do nothing but stare at the ceiling and dream . . . My fanny's heavy as lead . . ."

"Beloved Führer!" Emmy caressingly swept the strands of hair off his brow. "Wouldn't you rather lie down on the bed?"

"Now look, my sweet . . . Chamberlain was telling me, up there on the terrace of Bad Kreuznach, above the Rhine that . . . snails and slugs and crickets imbibe their secretions by night. Ha-ha! I told the woolen merchant: 'Mr. Chamberlain, you know, the main thing is esthetic nobility'! But"—he raised his head—"if this high-stepping England simply won't grasp that fact, then Churchill and his Roosevelt can lie down together on the psychoanalytical sofa and kindly leave me in peace with their 'Four Freedoms'! . . ."

"My glorious one!" she breathed, her face close to his. "You want to lie down on the sofa?"

But she could only manage to prop him up against her bosom. His head cozily pillowed, he remained silent. Suddenly he grinned:

"Yes—it must be very fine—to be a woman—Moo-oo! Moo-oo! And to have your butter churned for you . . . But then there's always the subterranean force of hate—from the worm up to man! It's forever the same old thing: the seminal spirit! . . . And in the midst of the sexual act—you mean to tell me, the drama suddenly ends for us men? No!" He raised himself against her. "That's where I go on strike!"

"Führer!" her voice rose in a falsetto of adulation. "What would we ever have done without you?—without you! . . . I'd like to go down on my knees in gratitude! My glorious one! . . . You're alive!"

"Yes"—he kneaded his fingers in her twisted Gretchen braids as if in a pan of dough—"only the other day, it was still May! And now it's autumn already. I'm always afraid of the calendar . . . Come Tuesday and they'll be driving the cows down from the mountain meadows . . . And then it's Christmas again! And the Madonna sits by the manger. And the donkey lies in the straw behind her . . . And Aunt Resi says: 'Go and kiss the Christ Child, Adolf!' . . . But then, there's

478

Joseph standing there so idiotically! . . . And the wind! . . . Look—always that ice-cold wind! . . . And Uncle Alois shuffles across the yard to the outhouse, going to the can—He's got the stomach-ache! . . . The supersensual principle got under his belt during the Christmas Mass . . . And ever since that time—I'm just scared!" He snuggled more closely against her. "Now look! Here—in the cerebellum—there sits the beast—waiting its chance to get out—Makes me scared . . . And when the priest preaches about the shepherds and their sheep in the fields—and how the angel up there in the clouds called out of the darkness: 'Fear not! For behold! I bring you good tidings of great joy! For unto you is born this day in the city of David a Saviour!' I just can't help it: I'm scared, that's all! . . . Now look—when this toe of mine itched so—and the icy wind played with the bed covers—and the Christ Child didn't bring any presents for me—I was just scared, that's all! . . . Ah, little woman!"—he put his arm around her neck—"fifty years ago I wasn't here! . . . And fifty years from now I won't be here! Bitt' schön—yes—isn't that enough to drive anybody crazy?"

Abruptly he pushed her over backward and rolled on top of her.

Göring appeared. As he cleared his throat, Hitler started back, roaring:

"Murderers! Assassins! . . . Nothing but assassins!"

"You? Hermännchen?" Her face flaming, his wife stood up and pulled her negligee together.

"My Führer," Göring reported, "the French Government extends to you its felicitations on your providential escape from the assassin."

"Fine!" Hitler rose. "And when can we go to Le Bourget?"

"Adolferich!" Göring glared at him. "Didn't you and I once take an oath together that we'd find the last happy couple on earth, even if we had to go to the ultimate Coral Island in the South Seas—and annihilate them? Here!" Tossing the giant ruby, wrested from Himmler, in his wife's lap, his head thrust forward pugnaciously, he muttered softly for Hitler's ear: "You are the worst man in the world! . . . But nevertheless and notwithstanding, the yellow men of Asia shall not prevail over us! . . . Heil!" Hitler was astonished into silence.

During this brief passage Frau Emmy had regained her composure and, nodding to Himmler, who had just entered, said, "I hear your little daughter goes strolling about Salzburg in red slacks. I'd never let my daughter do that."

"Your daughter, Your Excellency, is still far too young!"

"Ah!" She sighed, while the Führer's looks grew darker. "Lots of

479

children! That's the apex of happiness! I'm already longing to be home again! I yearn for the nursery—the hullaballoo . . . the teddy-bears! Everything so fresh and rosy! . . ."

"Emmy!" bawled Göring from the hall. "Emmy!"

She rustled out of the room.

" 'Lots of children'?"

Hofer entered with fresh linen, and the Führer unbuttoned his shirt. Still embarrassed by the fact that he had surprised his commander-in-chief with the wife of the Supreme Air Marshal, Himmler took a snapshot from his breast pocket. "Have you seen this new picture of my little daughter?"

"A man who copulates with a woman, Heinrich—he's not accomplishing anything! Man does not procreate in woman. The only thing he brings to birth is spermatozoa! . . . Yes—isn't that the absolute beginning of the whole insane business? . . . Himmler!" Picking up a silver-mounted comb from the bureau, he flourished it high above his head. "Man only procreates, sword in hand!"

Holding this pose for several seconds, he finally let his arm drop, sat down in front of the mirror, and ordered: "Shave me!" But Hofer whispered: "Herr Meissner respectfully suggests that you start for Le Bourget unshaved." Hitler yawned and let the valet dress him. When it was over, he turned a look surcharged with hate on Himmler:

"Bah! . . . You and your swinish Gestapo! I still live—it's true! But only because Providence protected me! But not you! You didn't do anything about it! You false Saxon!"

His glasses awry, Himmler swiftly made his exit. Then Hitler wandered up and down. Suddenly he stopped, and beckoned his valet.

"Look, Hofer! There's a spider! Didn't you dust the place at all while I was weekending in Neuilly? Ha-ha-ha! There! Look at that! How restlessly he roams around! Looking for his wife, eh?" Hofer handed him a pair of blue spectacles and he put them in his pocket. "Yes—when a couple of filthy Jews treacherously massacred German citizens in Almerigo, I simply had my battleship *Deutschland* steam up to within a mile of the Spanish coast and blast a couple of salvos from my twelve-centimeter guns into that pestilential, Bolshevik dungheap! And after that everything was all quiet." He tweaked Hofer's ear. "But when you have to do with a lot of lunatics who haven't the slightest notion how their brains are leaking! . . . My good Hofer, in that case, there's nothing left but to exterminate them! . . . Exterminate them!"

He ran out through the adjoining rooms.

CHAPTER TWO

He stopped only when he came to the long, low private sitting room of the ambassador's wife. Here he picked up a Siamese cat that was sitting there sphinxlike and looking at him out of its indifferent, turquoise-blue eyes. "Nice pussy! Tell me what this deceitful household has conspired against me in my absence?—" He raised his eyes.

Against the wall, at the foot of a short flight of wooden steps leading up to a tower room, stood Baldur Hermann. Unwashed—his yellow hair wild around his face. Smiling ironically, he stood there smoking a cigarette. At a jab in the ribs from General Buch, he ground the cigarette under his heel as the Reich Führer, his curiosity aroused, approached. Almost lackadaisically, Baldur raised his arm in salute.

"Bitt' schön"—Hitler was studying his face—"what's up? Who's this?"

"Your newly appointed bodyguard standard-bearer!" recited Himmler. "It was to him that Prince Ferdinand yesterday entrusted the personal safety of the Supreme Reich Führer during his stay at the German Embassy in Paris.—"

"Entrusted to you?" The Führer's eyes narrowed.

"My Führer," Buch continued, "he was arrested by the Paris police in the forest of Courbevoie, west of Neuilly. And it's only thanks to the very considerate treatment of the Minister of Justice that Party Comrade Hermann was not handed over to the Paris Judocratic authorities like his blood-group friend, Weidmann."

"Boy! You stink of alcohol!"

"Most honorable Führer—I admit—that I've been boozing! And what's more, not very elegantly."

"He claims," Himmler explained, "that he was in front of the prison when the executioner entered Party Comrade Weidmann's cell."

"That's correct," the blond answered. "The executioner went into his cell to dress him up for Madame Guillotine, and to offer him the traditional cigarette and glass of rum."

"You were there?" Hitler stared into the lamplight.

"Yes. I was standing in front of the huge black prison gate. The guillotine had already been set up in the square outside. There were some 120 sensation-seekers standing around the machine of death. In spite of the early morning hour, they had crawled out of their stinking holes to look on, while the authorities chopped off the head of a strapping blond Hitler Scout. They were mostly Jews. A few bankers in silk top-hats—"

"Jews?"

"Yes, my Führer. Several Aryan prostitutes from the Quartier Latin and some salon snakes from the Quai d'Orsai. In their long, diaphanous evening gowns and gilt slippers, they stood shivering and staring lustfully at the gigantic prison gate. One of the black-haired Esthers winked at me. 'Monsieur,' she said, 'I hear they're just shaving his neck —there where that lighted window is!' "

"Did the ghetto sow say that?"

"Yes, my Führer. At last Party Comrade Weidmann came out of the black gate, dragged along by two prison guards as strong as bulls. For a single instant his blond hair glistened in the lamplight. He wanted to cry out something, but there was no chance! Everything happened so damned fast! In no time, the Frogs had strapped him down on the board under the guillotine. Like a lightning flash, the blade hissed down! . . . That sound, my Führer, that sound! And the next thing you knew, they had swept his remains up from the sawdust and stuffed him into a long basket. The banker next to me took off his hat."

"Took off his hat? Ha-ha-ha!"

"And the other Jews, too, lifted their hats, and grinned. Their ugly mugs were masked with joy—"

"With joy? Because they'd chopped off the head of one of my Aryans? They grinned over that?" He pinched Baldur's ear harder and harder. "The foul Jews grinned? Yes—they hate us! But don't worry, boy. I'm not going to be your executioner. And when Adolf Hitler tells you something, you can believe it!"

"My Führer!" Himmler tried to find some way of stopping this chatter. "Large sums of foreign money were found on this man."

"Foreign money? . . . Do you belong to the Spy Section?"

"No, my noble Führer!"

"Then why didn't you surrender your foreign valuta?"

"I've never yet surrendered anything!" As Hitler grinned, Baldur continued, " 'It's up to you to enrich yourselves!' Weren't those your very words, my highly respected Führer, when you invited us body-guards to the festivities on your last birthday in the New Marble Hall?"

"Right! But what were you going to do with the money?"

"I intended to go abroad."

"Why?"

"Why?" Baldur hesitated for a second. But then he looked boldly into Hitler's face.—"Because I want to eat too, like your little midge on the alder leaf did in 1914—instead of being so idiotic as to be killed in the coming war!"

"Wha-a-at?" Hitler bared his teeth like a yawning horse.

Abruptly he threw the cat into Baldur's face. Then he walked up the stairs, shaking his head. Suddenly he stood still and shouted:

"General Buch!"

"Here!" The Chief of the Murder Division scurried up to him.

"Bitt' schön, old murderer, you're a regular Bible expert, aren't you? Well then, come on and give me a load of it. This is what I need to know—right now: What exactly is the philosophic basis of this imbecile Judo-Christianity?"

Just as the brand-new General was going to answer, Hofer appeared and whispered to Hitler:

"Party Comrade Baron Jacques is outside in the hall."

"Sakra! Then we can leave at last?"

"No. Party Comrade Baron Jacques has just left the Commissioner of Police and respectfully informs you that the bridges over the Seine are not yet cleared of the populace."

"Not yet cleared of the populace? Sakra! Then why doesn't he fire a few rounds into them? Sakra!"

As the valet made no answer, Hitler beckoned to the Chief of the Gestapo:

"Well—if the bridges aren't cleared, I'll talk to that drunken guardsman. Send him upstairs to me."

With heavy tread Baldur climbed the stairs. As soon as General Buch heard the oak door shut, he joined Himmler. The two police chiefs stood at the foot of the stairs, listening.

"When that rascal was transferred to my special division"—Buch winked at Himmler—"I said to him: 'So long as you're with me, just remember that religious instruction is not in our curriculum!' . . . But I had no idea he'd ever get out of hand like this, the smart aleck!" He ceased speaking, for at that instant even through the closed door Hitler's shouting became audible:

"What? . . . There I labored night after night, under the eternal stars, above the eternal snows, in my eagle's eyrie, formulating the fundamental, granite-hewn, ethical principles of the Super-Aryan race, to endure for the next ten thousand years. And then a drunken swine like you has the nerve to— Get out of here! If you don't you can eat dog-dung for six weeks in Dachau before I have you strung up by your imbecile ears in the latrine!"

The two police chiefs had leaped away from the staircase, and stood goggling. Himmler's glasses fogged over. Buch pulled out his Service Bible and began leafing through it.

"Your Excellency?" He turned to Himmler, who, expecting the worst, had sat down and was looking at snapshots of his little daughter. "Do *you* happen to know—what is the basis of Judo-Christianity?"

"Sorry! I'm no expert!" Himmler looked up. "But do you imagine that we could possibly have built up our Gestapo so cosily in Europe if there had really been any basis for Christianity?" He laughed harshly and slapped Buch on the back. "But as far as I know, the so-called Christ never even existed! As I heard once from a Jew: The whole insipid myth of Jesus was nothing but a sort of stock-market specula-tion trumped up in Jerusalem—they sold shares in the Kingdom of Heaven! Ha-ha! Reich Minister Göbbels on the other hand insists that this Nazarene really did exist. But the Roman military occupation authorities considered him insane, and had him taken down from the cross before he died, and then secretly put him in a lunatic asylum . . ."

A shrill outcry came from upstairs. With a swift exchange of glances the two police chiefs hurried away from the door. Hitler appeared. When he saw his police chiefs he rattled the balustrade. Then, pointing at Baldur, he roared: "Was I ever a coward in battle?—that's what this filthy guardsman wants to know! And there's the result of your Hitler Youth education—you oxen!" Then he turned and screeched at Baldur. "Was I a coward? You idiot! It was *I* who rounded up you blond youths from the asphalt of the vicious great cities—just in time! It was *I* who fished you out of the misery of unemployment! And you —you scum of the earth!—you dare—!"

"Most noble Führer—"

"Shut up, you Jew-bitten swine! It was *I* who saved you from the claws of the apocalyptic beast, Bolshevism! It was *I* who rescued you prodigal sons of the fallen heroes of the world war, abandoned as you were by this Jewish, so-called democracy! It was *I* who once again held up before your eyes, in the heavens of the Pan-German dominion, a tangible ideal! It was *I* who led you forth, out of the stifling labyrinth of Judo-Christian ideologies—into the ice-clear air of Aryan realism!"

"And in the name of that ice-clear realism," cried Baldur, "I ask you this ice-clear question: Were you a coward in the war?"

Both S.S. generals spontaneously grasped the hilts of their daggers, but Hitler signed to them to desist. Then he swung back into the upstairs room and called flatly: "You idiot! Come here!"

After the door closed, Himmler, confused, blinked at Buch, "Do you believe he'll turn us out now?"

"Believe!" grinned the other. "According to Hebrews eleven, verse one—'belief is the substance of things hoped for, the evidence of things not seen.'"

"Oh! Bravo! There you have the 'basis of Christianity' you were looking for! You hope! you don't see anything! and nevertheless you believe it! . . . Bravo!" He was about to continue when the door at the top of the stairs again opened.

Hitler descended arm-in-arm with his bodyguard standard-bearer, smiling with relief as if after a successful bowel movement.

"Sakra! You spies! What are you doing there at the keyhole? Get out of here!" He waited till they had both gone. Then he looked at Baldur: "The gray-headed donkeys! Bitt' schön! . . . I get along much better with my blond young people! We understand each other perfectly! Eh, Baldur? . . . I begin to feel young again myself! My standard-bearer, that you are an Aryan is going to be your world passport! Do you begin to catch a glimmer of why it was that your Führer, in 1914, at the crossing of the Meuse, incontestably *had* to remain alive? Hm? Does it begin to dawn on you? I knew absolutely that I should have to protect you blond Germanic youths from the lustful hate of the African Judocrats! Of course they hate you—because you still have your strength and virility! Because those enervated pacifists simply will not understand your great yearning—to be a man, and a ruler of men. Just like any English Lord—of whom certainly no one would ever dream of inquiring how many subhumans and jungle apes his Lordship had shot down out of the trees along the Jordan! Bitt' schön, Baldurchen, for just such fine specimens as you, your Führer has spent long, sleepless nights—thinking out a special reward—I'm going to build you the slickest speedways you've ever seen from Munich to Shanghai and back again by way of the equator! . . . Listen to me, Baldurchen"—he drew him close—"where did you say you'd hidden it?"

"What?"

"My Will—sakra!—the Will!"

"Where? All the bridges were barred." Baldur lied stutteringly. "I ran back into the Forest of Courbevoie. But suddenly I saw that I was surrounded by French police. So I put the papers into an old water-pipe—twenty paces from kilometer stone number 3, on the road to

Nanterre. And then I closed both ends of the pipe with stones."

"Fine! And you'll go and get it for me? Because it's the only authentic one. It's the only one that contains my merciless Race Code against those nation-poisoners—the Jews. As I said before, Baldurchen, you must bring it to me absolutely secretly. Is that clear?" He thumped the base of Baldur's skull affectionately with his fist. "Sakra! That white-blond hair of yours is just too wonderful. Yes, damn it—after all, to whom should this imbecile earth belong in the future if not to such a wonderful, glorious and (speaking purely from the architectonic point of view) such an A-1 specimen as you are! Sakra! Only for such as you is the thick, sweet-scented golden honey of the Volga steppes good enough! And the mineral waters of the imbecile Caucasus! Plus the tobacco fields by the Caspian Sea! Bitt' schön! For whom do you suppose divine Providence put all that oil and wood in Siberia? Plus the granaries and treasuries of the five continents? For the Jews? No—for you! They're yours for the taking! . . . Standard-bearer, does it begin to penetrate that thick German skull of yours—what it means that I, an Austrian, should have wandered across the Alps, to you Reich Germans? Solely and simply so that in the eyes of Divine Providence, I alone could be held accountable for all *your* National Socialist deeds!"

"For all our National Socialist deeds?" Baldur pricked up his ears.

"Of course! That's what I said! For all your deeds! Let them be upon my head! Indeed! Standard-bearer! Whatever any one of you has *had* to do in the name of the Aryan World Idea—I take it upon myself!" His voice dropped. "Everything—I take it upon myself! Everything!"

"Everything?" Baldur stared before him. "That's colossal! And frightful!"

"Of course! You child! The man of the new age has to be frightful!"

"Most noble Führer," Baldur stammered suddenly, toneless, "the fact is, I just happen to have bumped off my old lady."

"Whom?" Hitler let go his arm. "Your mother? Why?"

"Why?" The blond looked at him out of ice-cold eyes. "She happened to get in my way . . ."

"To get in your way?"

"Yes, Mummy was trying to read your papers."

"And that's why you killed her!" His face wreathed with ecstasy. All of a sudden Hitler ripped the Order-of-Blood medal off his own coat and pinned it on Baldur. "Folk Comrade!" In ceremonial tones he continued: "As of today I herewith appoint you Gauleiter of the Upper Mississippi region, including all local gasoline-stations!" And with that he fell back exhausted into an armchair.

486

There was a trace of anxiety in his gaze at the broad and towering form of his bodyguard standard-bearer. "Is that an actual fact? Your mother tried to read my Will? And that's why you finished her off?"

Baldur nodded vigorously. A yell of triumph burst from Hitler's curd-white face. He rose to his feet and shook his fists at the masses in front of the Embassy.

"My movement still lives! Movement! Movement! Come!" Grabbing the blond by the elbow, he dashed with him to the door, shouting: "To the airport at Le Bourget! Bitt' schön, Herr Gauleiter. And if anyone 'happens to get in our way'—we'll make short work of him!"

CHAPTER THREE BETWEEN ARM-STRETCHING CHAMBERMAIDS AND FOOTMEN HITLER AND BALDUR RAN THROUGH THE CORRIDOR, and then downstairs.

Below in the hall frightened adjutants tried to stop him from leaving the Embassy. But he pushed them away. Only in front of the enormous wooden door which gave onto the street, did Field Marshal Keitel succeed, with blunt warnings, in bringing him back inside. After a moment in the library, Keitel persuaded Hitler to follow him into the Embassy garden, where he was safe from the street mob.

After a wild curse at "this stupid fear of the Paris mob"—Hitler stopped in his tracks, listening. From the conservatory came the sound of a harmonium. He approached curiously. Out of a small forest of evergreens loomed an oaken coffin, decked with the swastika flag. On either side tall six-inch candles burned flickeringly. The air was heavy with the delicate smell of wax.

Hitler entered. Göring, the betrayed husband, kept his eyes on the sweat stain in the crown of his marshal's cap, held upside down before him like a chamberpot. When Baldur, holding the standard, stationed himself behind the Führer beside the coffin of his mother, whom he had murdered with his own hands, Göbbels and Ribbentrop gave him looks of sorrowful sympathy.

With measured tread, Dr. Gerhardus rustled forward through the dust-filmed laurel bushes. Laying swollen hands on the coffin, as if it were a reading desk, he began, as Göbbels had carefully instructed him, to stretch out his funeral speech:

"My Highly Respected Herr Reich Chancellor! My Führer and supreme initiator of all most exalted enterprises! With profound, National Socialist rejoicing we greet you, once again safe in our weeping midst after an insane attempt upon your most sacred person!

"It was our own prince of poets, Goethe, who said in 1810—However, it is more befitting solemn ceremonies such as this—But—What was I saying? . . . Ah, yes!" He pointed to the swastika. "This symbol of the movement is to be found everywhere—where there is movement! . . . Although it bedecks this beautiful sarcophagus, nevertheless all movement has, so to speak, ceased to be within these narrow oaken boards. That is to say: who can tell—perhaps it has only just begun? . . . I am of course, it goes without saying, not here referring to those movements in a dead body unhappily foreordained by nature, such as we, my highly respected mourners, commonly designate by the typically German words, 'decomposition' and 'decay' . . .

"Indeed, I very much doubt if any one of us here assembled will ever be spared the common fate of decay . . . It was Angelus Silesius, our own medieval National Socialist mystic, who said: 'Man! do thou become essential!' That is: 'of essence', 'of being' . . . It's true, he did not say: 'Man! do thou decay!'

"At all events, I hope that our great Führer, standing there, his hands folded in genuine German—yes, we could almost say Gothic devotion beside the corpse of the Leader of the Heidelberg Cultural Division . . . Ah! Who is there among us who, at the mention of the word Heidelberg, does not involuntarily think of Heidelberg? Alas, my fellow mourners! In this coffin there lies a mother! And what is more: a Reich mother! And what is still more: a dead Reich mother!" Hitler moved his head. Suddenly, with one echoing stride, he kicked the coffin so violently that it groaned like a packing case. Then he cried:

"Take away that corpse! . . . Get that corpse out of here! Sakra! I won't have any dead mothers around me! Get that corpse out of this conservatory, I said! I need *living* mothers! Mothers to bear me soldiers! No use for corpses! Sakra!"

Officers and servants were falling over each other in terrified haste, scrambling to lift the coffin from its three wooden trestles, stumbling out with it and dumping it in a rhododendron bush.

Ribbentrop—who, for the flight to the airport, had especially chosen to wear the broad blood-red silk ribbon of the grand cross of the Légion d'Honneur on his coat—smilingly approached his master. "The meteorological forecast from the Eiffel Tower just now announced that we may expect a heavy fog before sunrise in and around Paris.

488

The Police Prefect therefore recommends that you wait for this favorable condition before setting out for the airport."

"Fine! Fine!" Hitler leered out into the dark garden, and nodded to a few prominent faces. "Yes, my generals! There's one thing you've got to get firmly fixed in your minds: Whether you're commanding six men—or a company—or a million or so privates, artillerymen, and the rest of the sons-of-bitches—or still more—that's purely a matter of addition . . . My dear Bock-und-Pollach, do you understand me?" He pulled the other's mustache. "Mayer plus Mayer equals two Mayers! But Poland plus Russia adds up to something a great deal more! . . . Bitt' schön—take the earth as a whole, apart from those that are missing, and you've got quite a few people! Ha-ha! But you get used to it! At all events"—he stroked the nose of the handsome Colonel Engel, who was standing near him—"this America they talk so much about has become a rather pitiful small province alongside of what is called Asia, Russia, plus Europe. Yes, my Party Comrades—I want you to know that I intend to ask from the French Government, for this attempt upon my life by the international, criminal clique, a retribution such as the world has never seen."

His further utterance was drowned by a roar from behind the garden wall: "À bas Hitler! Down with Hitler! Nieder mit Hitler!" It shrilled through the wet dark morning. It grew more and more sinister and menacing, so that even the French police, arriving at full gallop, were apparently unable to control it. But like an answer from inside the wall, the bodyguard band struck up the Badenweiler March—with such a frenzied beating of drums, that the booming and thudding resounded as if giants were clubbing the skulls of the crowd outside—head by head—into the asphalt of the quai. And then on the ramp in the rear of the Embassy building could be heard the tramping of soldiers' boots in harsh, metallic marching rhythm . . .

"My Führer," Colonel Engel announced like one released from a spell, "the officers and men of your bodyguard and the Embassy guard are ready to march in review."

Thereupon Hitler, first zig-zag, then like a hunted man, ran through the trees, until he reached the tall French windows of the library. There he finally succeeded in regaining his composure.

Between rows of party members holding torches, the first squads of marching men emerged out of the darkness.

489

CHAPTER FOUR

L<small>IKE DEATH'S OWN BALLET DANCERS</small>

THEY CAME.

As they passed Hitler, all the slender young lieutenants and soldiers brought down the soles of their boots and flung their legs forward from the hip horizontally in such fanatic fashion that earth and gravel sprayed the back of his hand, outstretched in salute . . . Slowly the grains crusted his hand, like planetary fragments hurled into space, charged with a new destiny . . .

The field marshals, raising their batons to their foreheads and flinging them out in widespread salute, grinned at each other. The stones of the Embassy shook from the staccato tread of the drilled masses of men, drowning out the noise of the mob on the quai. As soon as the last soldier had marched by, Hitler ordered the officers to appear before him and receive the order of the day.

"Comrades! Don't let yourselves be flabbergasted by that horrible animal bawling of the mob outside. When—as you soon will—you storm ahead to attack this red Judocratic world—in every engagement, hold your revolvers conforming both to the shooting regulations and also all the other regulations! I alone will be responsible for tactics and strategy! Above all I now give to you as parole and supreme leitmotif for the coming Götterdämmerung this single word"—drawing a deep breath and stretching himself to his full height—"and that word is—Courage!"

The standard in Baldur's hand shook. He gripped it tighter.

"Yes! Courage!!" Hitler shrieked the word again. "And anyone who displays the least sign of cowardice is to be handed over at once to the military authorities! I tell you that I am going to make demands of you —so long as there's a single soldier left alive to carry a knapsack!—demands such as have never been made before! I tell you, you are going to have to accomplish prodigies of bravery! In our fight against the Bolshevik dragon, whoever thinks for a single instant of his *own* life will pay for it under martial law! His regimental insignia and medals will be torn off, and his only epitaph will be eternal shame! Yes! I shall give you commands that would have made your fathers tremble with terror! Germans! By the shining souls of our forefathers! By their fiery blue eyes! By their enormous bodies! By the neighing of the sacred steeds!—the Great Day is at hand! I have opened the book of a thousand years of history! With *your* blood shall I write its chapters of glorious deeds! And to bring about the victory of the National Socialist mission of salvation—I tell you that even twelve million such magnificent specimens of the German people, their blood as fresh and vigorous as those who have just marched past me, are not too great a price for me to pay! Providence be with you! Forward! And now—go on and prove to the cowardly Judocrats that the 'will to live' has no place in the mind of any German! Sieg Heil!"

The answering cries of "Sieg Heil!" became so vehement that the shouts of "Down with Hitler" around the Embassy broke off short.

CHAPTER FIVE

IN THAT MOMENT OF SILENCE, GENERAL JÜNGER AS IF IN AN OVERFLOW OF HIGH SPIRITS, SUDDENLY FIRED HIS revolver at the torso of the Christ of the Trenches, which had been thrown into a salvia bed by the footmen.

"Sakra!" Hitler jerked convulsively. But when he saw what had happened, he left the generals, walked across the ramp, and stared wonderingly on that bowed and tragic head, so full of blood and wounds.

General Jünger was about to make a flippant remark, but Hitler snatched the revolver out of his hand.

"Gentlemen!" He cleared his throat ceremoniously. "My Lady Mitford used to say that when the Jewess, Mary Magdalene, saw her dead lover on Easter morning, in the misty garden, she ran back to Jerusalem and told everybody far and wide that their Master, Jesus, had risen from the dead. And by so doing, she was responsible for the founding of Christianity. Is that correct?"

"In a certain sense, my Führer," grinned General Buch.

"So! For the past two thousand years the Christian dogma of the Resurrection has been based on the hysterical hallucination of a Jewess in love?"

"My Führer! In First Corinthians, fifteen, verse four, Paul says: 'But if there be no resurrection of the dead neither is Christ risen; and if Christ be not risen, then is our preaching in vain.'"

"Ergo: If only I had been alive then, I'd have stopped the jaw of this Mary Magdalene in time—eh, Himmler?—and we should have been spared two thousand years of insanity—" he bowed toward the wooden

Christ. The others laughed uproariously.

"It's incredible! In 722, just for the sake of that bearded Bethlehem Trotsky, along came this shameless Pope Boniface and chopped down the sacred Donar Oak, so venerated by our forefathers the Frisians. 'If your heathenish god Donar wants to stop me'—the insolent priest told our German ancestors—'let him send down his lightnings and strike me dead!' And he went on chopping away. There came no lightnings, and that millennial, marvelous oak crashed with a thunderous roar on the floor of the forest! Horrified that their god had not come to their aid, those poor, superstitious Germans instantly permitted themselves to be converted to Christianity.—Ah, if I had been alive then, I would have opened their eyes! Their god didn't answer—because there is no God. Shame on the German who ever kneels to the Jewish myth again! Shame! Sakra!" he turned to Jünger. "Is he made of bronze?"

"No, my Führer—of wood."

"Indeed? Of wood? Colonel Engel, if you please, take out your watch and hold it! And you," he motioned to another officer, "set that unshaven Judo-Christian God up on the balustrade here. I am now going to give him, precisely as Pope Boniface gave the German god, exactly five minutes to think it over!"

After the Christ of the Trenches had been set up like a target, Hitler addressed it mockingly: "If your Father in Heaven wants to send his lightning of vengeance down on my head, he has five minutes at his disposal! At the end of five minutes I shall shoot you down from that balustrade with my own hands. Do you understand me? And"—he turned grotesquely, like a circus clown ready to launch a joke—"I invite the whole visible and invisible Pauline-nonsense world to watch my target practice."

He had hardly finished speaking before, from all parts of the Embassy, poured a flood of footmen, chambermaids, cooks, actors, gardeners, directors, composers, politicians, and more and more officials and officers. The ramp was too small to hold them all.

"Herr Führer"—Colonel Engel looked at the second-hand of his watch—"the five minutes now begin!"

"Fine!" Hitler aimed at the head of the figure. "Did you hear that? You God of the Jews? You know: I don't joke! Very well, then! Turn on your thunder machine! Let your lightnings descend upon me! Sakra! I'm *not* joking! . . . And I repeat: I don't give a hoot in Hades whether the world hereafter calls me 'Devil' or not!"

"One minute gone!"

"Already? Ha-ha! Thus far your father Jehovah (alias Moses) hasn't made Himself noticeable! . . . And I very much doubt whether this entire Judocratic Punch-and-Judy show will be able to stand up against the shock of our arms—against me and you, Party Comrades and soldiers of my armies! No matter how many lemon-faced old maids offer themselves in the employment bureaus of London, Washington, or New York as governesses for the education of the German people!"

After a roar of applause Colonel Engel exclaimed, "The second minute is over!"

"Did you hear that? Sakra! You God of Isaac and Jakie: not forgetting Kohn! Ha-ha! Did the whole Three-in-One hear it?—the second minute is up! You sacrificial Lamb of Bethlehem," he screamed at the wooden figure, "I'm not joking!" And again he bellowed out his insane laughter—so that even Göbbels felt chills run up and down his spine.

Into the mad-house racket, a footman stepped—a man named Vogt, from Darmstadt, with tired, inflamed eyes. He brushed off his brown livery nervously and spoke with an effort in a thick Hessian dialect:

"Ei! Is it possible? Ei! I was a common soldier too—and I saw more dying than I wanted to. Ei—have you really forgotten it—all the blood on the uniforms? And how Maier's bowels hung out after that machine-gun attack? Ei? Try to remember how at Douaumont in 1916 the French artillery found us and we were all buried together? Ei— have you forgotten all about it? How our comrade with the Sunday face under his helmet dug us all out again one after the other? and we blinked in the sun like a lot of Lazaruses in the jaws of death? And then we were so happy because that time we'd escaped the casualty list. Ei— have you forgotten how, after saving our lives, he pulled his canteen from under his torn cloak and gave us all a drink? Have you forgotten his pale, unshaven face, and his cloak with no shoulder straps or insignia? And then, down in the dugout among the corpses, he talked to us so beautifully about life, that even our tough Minenwerfer gunner, who usually wouldn't sit down to his breakfast without first conquering Persia, grubbed a handful of earth and grass out of the trench parapet and plunked it down on a box of hand grenades, and said: 'If I ever get out of this mess with a whole skin, I won't need anything more than a handful of earth like this to be perfectly happy!' Don't you remember it? And now again—war? Ei—haven't you heard it—what those thousands of people outside the Embassy want? *They* don't want war! No! They want peace! We want peace! Peace!"

"Quiet!" Some of his liveried colleagues tried to pull him back, for they had observed that Hitler's eyes were assuming more and more that uncanny glazed expression of the eyes of stuffed birds of prey. Göring

493

too tried to quiet the footman:

"Our Führer, my good Vogt, is certainly the best-natured person on earth. But," he whispered, "at the same time he likes to eat people alive. And when he hears the bones crack, he loves it. So shut your mouth and make yourself scarce."

The bystanders laughed uneasily. But as if he could not hold them back, the footman's words poured on:

"Ei, have you forgotten it all, Herr Reich Marshal? Didn't every one of us say: Never again? Ei!" Suddenly he shook his fists at Hitler and his generals. "We have had enough of this eternal shooting! We've had enough of war! Ei, enough!"

There was complete silence. Baldur leaned the standard against a tree and cleared his throat. Some of the generals set their jaws. The footman looked from one to the other as if he were delirious. "Ei, have you really forgotten what a shudder went through us when we first saw all those blood-soaked rags? Have you forgotten that, all you officers? That horrible shudder at the first sight of butchered human beings?"

In his eyes there flickered for a moment that strange, dangerous, dark light that shines in the eyes of doomed soldiers.

For a single second the earth seemed to pause in its revolution. And if it be possible, as philosophers maintain, that the shifting of a tiniest grain of sand may suffice to give impetus to a new universe—then it may be truly said that in the moment of silence that followed Vogt's appeal there did exist the possibility, through some spontaneous decision, of clamping the brakes on the wheels of war's machinery so wantonly set in motion.

Hitler sensed the passing of this instant . . . Inasmuch, however, as there was no move among his fellow National Socialists, a smile of triumphant scorn played about his mouth.

At once some of his gauleiters rushed wildly at the poor, gray-haired old man, who was standing there dazed by what he had dared—rushed at him and beat him and kicked him until he lay in the grass like a trampled toad.

"Yes! Bitt' schön!" Hitler took a few steps toward the Christ of the Trenches. "Yes! This is *your* glorious work! Of course! In every company there were two such idiotic eyes that were forever trying to question everything—everything that is dear and true to the brave soldier! Yes!" He looked despisingly at the footman in the grass. "You used to stumble over the species in every trench and shell hole! Gentlemen!" He addressed his officers. "I myself remember how a certain pale-faced

494

soldier tried to break down my courage with his imbecile staring—with that look of 'brotherhood'!" He pointed to the wooden face of the Saviour. "German Folk Comrades! I impress it on your memories—that milk-toast face! For it will be that unshaven Bolshevik who, when the walls of our bombed cities are falling in ruins, will murmur to you again: 'Don't do anything! Throw down your arms! Stop fighting!' . . . In that hour when every single one of us will have to have nerves of iron—that white face will bob up—in the munitions factories!—in the breadlines!—in the trenches!—in the hospital trains! . . . Every way you turn, you'll see those imbecile eyes and hear him whispering: 'Don't do anything! Just stop fighting! Throw down your arms!' . . . And when, like the athlete on the point of dropping, you've just got your second wind and you need every last ounce of strength to pull through and hold out—then that creature there will go prowling about in the night and standing before your windows and knocking on your shop doors and whispering: 'Don't do anything! Throw away your arms! Give up fighting!' . . . But before that happens, I shall have made that face a thing of mockery to every German Folk Comrade. For if ever in the days to come I shall have earned fame, it can only be because I shall have definitely made an end of that creature there with his soap-bubble eyes and his gentian-blue look of complete insanity!"

"The five minutes are up!"

"The five minutes are up?" Hitler took aim. "Well, if you've still got something to gas about—I'll be generous and give you another ten seconds!" Taking Colonel Engel's watch, he stared at the hands.

Abruptly he took careful aim at the head of the Christ of the Trenches.

"Ping!" His first shot was a direct hit. And now, as if gone berserk, with lightning rapidity he emptied every chamber. When the last cartridge flipped out of the barrel, he screeched:

"Your revolvers!" As fast as they were handed to him, like a raving maniac he fired them, one after the other, at the face of the Saviour now smoking from powder vapor. With the final expenditure of all their ammunition, including that of General Tot's revolver, the wooden torso slumped from the balustrade and went tumbling down the slope in the darkness. For some time after, they heard its hollow bumping as it rolled.

Hitler spun round like a whirling dervish. Tossing the last weapon high in the air, he screeched:

"You!—my German Folk! Bitt' schön! I herewith declare that Christianity has come to an end! . . ."

The jubilance of his followers over the liquidation of the religion of Nazareth, seemingly so alien to their being, reverberated about the Führer again and again. Reveling in the tidal wave of their enthusiasm, minute after minute, Hitler preened himself. His intoxication was interrupted by Ribbentrop, who surreptitiously drew near and muttered something in his ear.

Hitler started. Field Marshal Keitel immediately joined them and asked: "What is the matter? Can we not get out of the Embassy?"

"No. All the bridges over the Seine are occupied by the mob."

"Sakra," bellowed Hitler, "and the Prefect of Police seems to be too cowardly to give the order to shoot!"

"My Führer!" whispered Ribbentrop, "there is only one way to get out of here."

"What is that?"

"There is a tunnel from one of the furnace rooms that leads to a place a few blocks away from the Gare d'Orsay. From there we can drive around the Cimetière de l'Est and then straight out to the airport."

"Sakra! Then quick! quick!"

CHAPTER SIX   AFTER DRIVING THREE QUARTERS OF AN HOUR, AT TOP SPEED, THROUGH THE STREETS OF AWAKENING PARIS, Hitler finally arrived unobserved with his party outside the metropolis on the boulevard Mortier. From here Colonel Engel directed the chauffeur of the first car forward past Romainville to Boisy, avoiding the suburb of Pantin which was reported to be full of workers. And from there across the canal to Robigny on the Drancy-Le Bourget highway. Then Colonel Engel turned to Hitler who, masked with blue eyeglasses and an enormous cap, sat cowering wordlessly beside Ribbentrop on the back seat.

"Only ten kilometers, my Führer. Then we'll be at the airport."

Hitler, his throat chilled by the morning fog, began to cough. When the attack was over, he nudged his Foreign Minister and asked him: "Sakra! Where's Hess?"

But Ribbentrop was too terrified to give any reasonable answer. His face frozen, he held onto the adjutant who sat in front of him. He was muttering to the driver:

"Forward! Forward! Chauffeur! Don't toot so loud, you donkey! Forward! For God's sake! Why does the donkey turn out for that old milk woman? Now he's waiting for all those bicycles to pass! Is he crazy? . . . Forward! You donkey! Quick! They say there are a thousand communists in Pantin. How fast is he driving? Forward! Step on it! Forward! Forward! And the devil take the hindmost!"

After another twenty minutes at high speed over an assortment of ducks and chickens, they finally arrived on the open highway. And now the chauffeur opened up. The four powerful Mercedes cars whizzed by the milestones so fast that the poplar trees rustled! But near Grosslay Farm they suddenly saw people across the highway in the fog, waving their flashlights, signaling them to stop.

Immediately Hitler's chauffeur put on the brakes and drove slowly up.

Gauleiter Baldur, accompanied by Baron Jacques, hurried to Colonel Engel and whispered seriously, "Better get out! I respectfully repeat: there are rumors that only two kilometers away from here some three thousand workers have broken the police cordon in Le Bourget and are coming across the meadows to the highway. So—everybody out! It is possible that the road to the left which leads to the airport is already occupied. Therefore I propose to try to reach Aulnay through the meadows to the right by going back to the canal without crossing the park. There I will wait for you with the car. And then we have only three kilometers to the airport."

Hitler, who had listened breathlessly, jumped from the car and shouted at Baron Jacques:

"Well—where are your lousy French police?! I thought the Prefect told us that this highway was free from the red swine!"

A shot rang out only a hundred yards behind the car. Hitler threw himself flat on the road. Then, before any explanation could be given, he leaped the ditch as if possessed, and ran in the direction suggested by Baldur, through the darkness of the foggy fields.

"My Führer! My Führer!" cried Ribbentrop behind him. But Hitler ran so quickly over the furrows, that even a champion runner could not have kept up with him.

Without noticing that the fog was coming up from the valley thicker and thicker, Hitler ran on. All at once he stood still and screamed: "Damnation! Where are you all? Ribbentrop!"

No one answered. Frantically he rushed forward, stopped again and listened. But only the soft cool noise of driving fog was all around him in the darkness.

497

With his handkerchief over his mouth, he peered around. Having no overcoat on, he shivered in the chill air . . . "What was that?" Behind him he seemed to hear a distant beating of drums and marching of feet. He turned and looked over his shoulder. It was like the noise that had so unnerved him that night in the lonely villa in Neuilly when he heard the rabble marching along the highway with the grand mutilé de guerre, chanting the "Marseillaise" . . . Nearer and nearer . . .

"Damnation! Buch! Buch!" No answer. "Sakra!" He could no longer see three paces before him. Fog . . . everywhere . . . fog . . . Suddenly he was seized with a grim and boundless terror. Here and there in the mist he thought he saw lights. Round and golden. Like will-o'-the-wisps.

"Sakra! Wasn't that somebody clearing his throat?" Looking harder, he thought he saw someone. But then it turned out to be only a grotesquely twisted willow tree. He clutched it—out of breath. A cloud of little moths flew from the bark . . . "Hawk moths. Seem to have the gout. Yes, it's been a damp summer . . . and the fodder is poor. Besides, there's this eternal wind . . ." Shuddering, he pulled his collar up about his ears. "Moths! Nothing but moths!"

He squashed one of them and smeared its juices on the willow. Suddenly he started back.

"Who's there?"

Only a few feet away a man suddenly rose out of the mist with the greeting:

"Well, boy! . . . Are you the judge advocate I've been looking for so long?"

"Bitt' schön?" Hitler staggered off the path into the wet grass.

"Permit me!" The stranger came up behind him, tugging at his coat. "Captain Hermann is my name!" Removing his field cap, with his sleeve he wiped the cold moisture from his stubbly face.

"I have an official statement to make to you. Those red-braided general-staff scoundrels back there on the highway tried to talk me into believing I was suffering from paranoia! Ha-ha! The facts are otherwise! . . . I'm sixty-three years of age. The gentlemen with the raincoats over their uniforms made me sick. But you are a member of the court martial, aren't you? . . . It wasn't easy to find you here in this pea-soup! I'm supposed to repeat my report to you and—"

"Bitt' schön!" Holding his arm over his eyes, Hitler stuttered so that it was with great difficulty that he finally said: "Aha! You must be—the commander of my subterranean poison-gas and artillery depot. I ordered him to come to me at the Embassy."

498

"No, boy. I'm the officer on guard duty, in charge of the Little Jew Jesus."

"Wh-a-a-at? . . ."

"At your service! I've just come from Haudroumont Quarry." He seemed to billow like a gray phantom as he came closer.

"Bitt' schön!" Hitler looked in vain for a weapon. He was unarmed. "What? You're not the commander of my munitions depot?"

"Boy—I dutifully repeat as follows: Although the underground shelter is reinforced with corrugated iron, earthen walls, and heavy stones—nevertheless and notwithstanding, the Little Jew Jesus has managed to escape!"

"The Little Jew Jesus?" repeated Hitler, rattling in his throat and staring, with his hair standing on end. "At all events, my Lady Mitford always says: If God needed seven times twenty-four hours to transform the raw material of chaos into the cosmos—bitt' schön—then I certainly would have done a better job! Sakra! Sakra!"

He made off as if pursued by a ghost. Stumbling, he yelled for General Buch, picked himself up and dashed on, erratically returning in his own tracks . . . Captain Hermann close behind him. Finally both brought up short, gasping for breath.

"Boy! What if the supreme military administration does try to hamstring me? What if they do suspend me from office? Amor fati! I am most obediently at their service!"

"Buch! Help! General Bu-u-u-u-ch! . . ." His yells were sopped up in the mist like water in cotton.

"Boy!" The other ran after him, hooking his fingers in Hitler's leather belt. "If every general who loses a battle is brought before a court martial, there soon won't be any more generals willing to take the job. My most obedient advice therefore runs as follows: Give me my legal pension—and enough said: No hell-raising about it! I've got thirty-eight years of service to my credit! Pay me annually 7800 bills of some valid currency—and release me from my onerous duties! Damnation! I've certainly done everything humanly possible! I was right at the heels of the pioneer, but all the rest of my dead subalterns followed me! . . . Emil, the Senegalese, was the first who tried to get out. I whammed him on his fuzzy black dome, and he caved in! But right behind him crowded the two pasty-faced poilus! And the Englishmen in their khaki! . . . According to regulations, I gave every one of them a crack on the noodle! They somersaulted down the whole thirty-three steps! . . . Yes, boy! I could hear their bones rattle quite plainly . . . But that was the cue for an alarm in the Cadaver Utilization Factory! Quick as a wink, I shoveled the earth away until I got outside. And then I galloped helter-skelter after my Little Jew Jesus. But with a long head start, he had already reached Beaumont."

"Man!" Hitler struggled to clear his throat, stifled by the fog. "I and I alone tore Pan-Germany out of the realm of myth and fiction. And now—?"

"I, at any rate, am no fiction nor maid-of-the-mist or anything-else fancy! However, the so-called organ of natural cognition is seated here!" He pointed at his hairy ears. "And whoever imagines that those voices by means of which I am in communication with the dead soldiers are fiction—well, he simply is ignorant of the fact that none the less, under the humus, humor still holds its ancient sway . . ."

"Man!" Hitler shook himself. "If you'll tell me why the Turkish crescent—is no full moon . . . and why the Star of Bethlehem has only five points—then I'm bound to answer you, faithfully—" His mouth snapped shut, and once again he went tearing off into the fog.

"Upsy-daisy!" Captain Hermann was right behind him. "Did you stumble?"

"Bitt' schön!" Hitler glared into the grass. "Who's that lying there? Somebody's lying there!"

"Yes, I know! I told you so: they're right after us!"

"Sakra! He's got hold of my feet! . . . Chop those ice-cold hands off my boots, I can't move a step! He's got me fast."

Bending over, the other hacked away with his sword, swishing through the mist around Hitler's boots. Obsessed with the delusion that five fingers still clutched at his heel, the Führer galloped off again.

"Boy!" his pursuer breathed in his ear. "I therefore most obediently take the liberty for the umpty-umpth time of calling the attention of the various Headquarters of the top-side world to the fact that Operational Divisions of the various Supreme General Staffs are none the less in error when they maintain that: Soldiers who have been shot dead are therefore necessarily—dead! No, Mr. Judge Advocate! Notwithstanding the fact that this assumption may have been the basis for rifle-shooting regulations hitherto, I nevertheless would propose the insertion of an appendix or a new paragraph . . . It's perfectly true that in 1916 I had to clean up the evidence of all those soldiers destined for the so-called Kingdom of Death, due to the ostensible operation of ballistic laws governing the trajectory of bullets! Despite the fact that I crammed and cemented them into niches, behind rococo mirrors, and in every conceivable inch of space in the walls of abandoned underground shelters, *yesterday* they simply picked up their fleshless bones

500

e crutches, and got under way! . . . Absolutely! And although I
verely admonished them, in no uncertain terms, that their conduct
as in direct defiance of rules and regulations—they just impudently
ent ahead anyhow! . . . I wish to report that: all those beneath the
ttlefields, no matter how peacefully they slept in the 'peace of the
ord,' suddenly and with horrible gallows humor made a total mockery
the entire code-of-war articles I had hammered into them—and
mply marched off after the aforesaid Little Jew Jesus! . . ." He
ointed dramatically into the mist:

"There! . . . There they are! . . . Now they're coming to a halt!
o you see them, boy? . . . Now they're drawing up in rank and
e! Evidently they're waiting for those other pallid columns of the
ead, down there, to march up! Damnation! . . . Do you see that?
. . Now they're shouldering their little wooden crosses! . . . Do you
ant to use my binoculars, boy? They magnify nine times! Just look
rough these! . . . Do you see them? There they are, all that gray
oming over the fields! . . . That's them! . . . Boy!" His talons dug
to Hitler's arm. "There they come! Yanks! Canadians! Germans!
egroes! All of them arm in arm with Frenchmen and Jews! . . . Just
if there were no longer any enmity between the opposing artillery
orps! . . ."

"Let go of me! Sakra!" Hitler tottered back, but the other only held
m faster.

"There they are! . . . There! . . . Look at that! That one in the
d wool shirt is my Emil, from Senegal! Now he's leading all the
olonial troops, black men and yellow men, out of the woods there!
. . Hark to that, boy! How insolently he beats the drum! He's evi-
ntly trying to whip some sort of military system into the dead!
sten to that! Did you hear that? Did you hear what he just yelled
ut:

" 'All the dead are free!'

"Stand still, boy! Don't move! There, in the middle of that field—do
ou see him? Standing there like an enigmatical element! . . . Mr.
udge Advocate, I propose that we sneak along this furrow to where he
ands . . . Halt! Now he's pacing the front—and bellowing some-
ing! Listen to him bellow!

" 'Comrades! Hereby we found the Party of all Unknown, Fallen
oldiers! We swear: Never again! Never again!'

"Would you look at that! Out of all those empty sleeves, they're
luting—like a forest of bleached bones! . . . Don't they look like
ousands of flagstaffs with no flags? Who-o-o! . . . that's some

501

drumming! Who-o-o! . . . How it whistles and rattles through t[h]
weeds! . . . Mr. Judge Advocate, I wish to include in my testimor[y]
what Oliver Cromwell is supposed to have said once:

" 'Oh! I have come out of the darkness!' "

"Who-o-o!" Hitler took up the cry, howling into the damp solitud[e]
"Who-o-o! Who-o-o!"

"Boy—There! One regiment after another, squad after squa[d]
Nothing but hairless skulls! Nothing but empty domes of all races a[nd]
peoples on earth! Boy! boy!" He pushed Hitler ahead into the whi[te]
wall of mist. "And there! Those coming down from the height[s]
They're the reserves! . . . Look—their army's become vaster a[nd]
vaster every second! Left! Right! Left! Right! . . . It rolls on like [a]
thunderstorm coming up! . . . Halt! Where do you think you'[re]
going? Marching off to the Moscow Institute for the Scientific Invest[i]
gation of Human Labor? . . ."

Hitler fled, and straggled here and there. At last he saw a light shinin[g]
through the fog: like a glowing spark, it grew larger and larger, un[til]
he was almost close upon it. He could not believe his eyes. In the mid[st]
of the empty field stood a brightly illuminated house.

"Boy!" came the voice at his ear: "Just look at that! There they [are]
sitting down around that long table! Nothing but a rag-bag of supe[r]
fluous human beings who apparently haven't even a notion of wh[y]
they've been shot dead!"

"Bitt' schön!" Hitler groped forward. "What do you suppose they'[re]
up to?"

"They're disputing among themselves! Listen to that! . . . The ta[ll]
fellow is telling them:

" 'We refuse any longer to have an army in which millions of [the]
soldiers get mowed down—but only a handful of generals ever g[et]
killed!' . . .

"Mr. Judge Advocate! Why don't you take the proper measures? A[s]
far as I can gather, they're demanding the creation of a Central Autho[r]
ity! . . . Boy—what do you say? Shall I shoot all the swine down '[en]
feu de file'?"

Hitler gnawed on his numbed fingers. At length he asked tonelessl[y]
"Who's that there—in the middle?"

"That's him! The Little Jew Jesus! Look at that! They've woun[d]
some rusty barbed wire around his trench helmet . . . Do you s[ee]
that? The way they're all grinning at him now, with their bleache[d]
jaws? . . ."

"What's that he's saying? Bitt' schön! What did he just say?"

502

"He says: 'We intend to do away with the common soldier!' "

" 'Do away with the common soldier!' "

"At your service! That's what he said! You'd better take steps now! ive 'em hell before it's too late! . . . There he goes steaming up all ose perfectly good-for-nothing dead soldiers over the mystical ob- ssion that everybody is suddenly a personality in his own right! . . . ems as though they're absolutely determined to find some logical undation for the inconceivable majesty of the Inconceivable! . . . 1, boy! The urge toward unity is the worst torment of humanity. ou'd better take steps now! I warn you! For if we don't instantly see it that the combined forces of reaction swiftly and promptly react, w, this moment, according to rifle-shooting regulations—then, in- ed, it's altogether possible that the sovereignty of the 'well-known ldier' may have to give way to the sovereignty of the 'unknown ldier'! . . ."

Hitler's eyes goggled into the spectral mist, and a deep groan was rn from him.

"Boy! I therefore now take the liberty of proposing to the Supreme ilitary Administration that they simply allow me to gas this whole deviled question! . . . Yes! I'm perfectly prepared—if the higher- s will benevolently and responsibly grant me permission—to hand in y resignation now—and to visit the necessary mineral springs and her national spas so that I can take a thorough cure for my ailments quired in the line of duty . . ."

"Mineral springs! National spas! My dear sir! Since I assumed the ins of government, I have not had three days of vacation! And you on raving about spas and mineral springs!" His voice rose to a sterical falsetto: "I need shells! Countless shells! Millions of shells!"

"That's *his* voice!" Prince Ferdinand came tearing through a clump birch trees, flashing his electric torch to and fro so that his party mrades by the canal would know that the Führer was found.

"Where? Where is he?" Göring came panting up behind him, calling t: "Adolf! Adolf!"

There was no echo. Nothing but ever-heavier masses of white mist. aning his heavy carcass on the young S.S. prince's shoulder, Göring tened like a hunter. From the opposite direction Himmler and Gen- al Buch came sloshing through the wet grass. Göring rattled off in e prince's ear:

"Your Highness! S-s-sh! Make yourself scarce! I understand that immler has just ordered your uncle August Wilhelm arrested! And me of the Embassy personnel too—"

503

"Damn it! Did the Kaiser get out of the cellar in time?"

"Yes. But your grandfather simply could not comprehend that I will never again ascend the throne of his fathers. He keeps on yammering: 'And to think that the Kaiser's hope and faith have always been with Thee, Lord God! And my entire Evangelical Church as well!'"

"That sounds like the man who lost the war, all right!"

"Go on! Go on! Make tracks! Here's Himmler!"

"Your Excellency!" The Chief of the Gestapo bore down on Göring out of the fog. "Didn't you hear voices?"

"Can he have lost his way?" Buch asked.

"No. The canal's on the right. How can he lose his way?"

"Ah, Your Excellency!" Himmler unbuttoned his overcoat shame-facedly. "I'm absolutely beside myself! Just before he was shot, Marespo told me that our agent Schleich is in the service of the Cheka and is an intimate friend of Stalin! . . . I'm at my wits' end!"

"Didn't I always tell you, Himmlerchen? But you wouldn't believe me! Have you had the red swine arrested?"

"Ah, Your Excellency—he's already escaped over the border at Eydkuhnen, with that actress Tchechova. But I hope we can catch him —before he gets to Moscow! . . ."

General Buch lit a cigar. "You know, I can't get that star-gazer's last words out of my mind—"

"What were his last words?" Göring took a swig of brandy from his field flask.

"He said: 'The Sphinx will smile when the ice melts . . . and the desert wanders north!'"

"Is that what he said?" Göring gaped at the mist. "Utter nonsense! Well, I'm certainly tickled to death that you've finally polished off that fakir . . . Just a while ago I was saying to Ribbentrop: You can't go making war north, south, east, and west! No! Damnation! My bombers only fly in one direction! And Bolshevism is, politically speaking, the backside of National Socialism . . . Damnation! You certainly have to have some place to put your backside when you take a seat—politically speaking . . . Well, I've got an idea! You two go down there, along the canal to the right until you see the road that branches off to Livry, and I'll go to the left here toward those houses.— What did he say? 'The Sphinx will smile?' Nonsense!"

No sooner had Göring disappeared out of the circle of light from Buch's flashlight than Hitler, his collar turned up around his neck, came down the slope from above.

"My Führer!" Buch waved his flashlight. "Here! Here we are!

We've all been searching for you the past half hour."

Hitler blinked in the light and wiped his dripping mustache.

Perceiving that Hitler was shivering, Buch pulled off his quilted leather coat, helped him into it, and buttoned it to the neck, not daring to ask any questions. The lantern light was reflected in the creases of wet leather as if in running water.

"What was that?" His Führer started.

"That's a horse neighing in the meadow."

"Wait a minute! Who's that whispering behind us?"

"Nothing but the willow branches, my Führer . . ."

"What! Can willow branches whisper like that? Ah, Buch," he sighed, gazing at the ground at his feet, "just look at that! Nothing but ants! Can you please tell me what rhyme or reason there is for the existence of such a little black ant? What purpose does it serve? What value has it? What kind of a life is that which is simply incapable of comprehending *me!* What good is such a tiny, raven-black brain if it simply cannot grasp such an exalted being as I am! Ah!" He sighed profoundly. "Can you believe it, my Party Comrades, when I tell you that this very thought often detracts from the enjoyment of my hate! The very idea that some raven-black Isaac is not even able to take in the gigantic grandeur of my hate! Himmler, I ask you: What's the use of living for such an ant? Is it worth the trouble of creation? Why go to all the pains of creating such a raven-black piece of carrion from Sinai and giving it eyes and ears and all the other senses if, with all those organs, it simply cannot comprehend *me?*—Adolf Hitler!— Buch, I've a longing for some camomile tea. There's camomile growing all around here. It's such a healing plant—it's pretty too, and it smells so like childhood. Ah, I wish I were back in my Berchtesgaden home, lying in my gentian-blue room upstairs—with the view of the lake, and that Maria-Theresa bed so cosily set in the alcove, and my cat purring on the pale-blue coverlet— It's so cold all around here. But soon"—he threw back his shoulders—"soon Warsaw shall go up in flames! Flames! Flames!" he shouted into the fog.

A voice answered from below, by the canal:

"Hello! Hello! It's Baldur! I'll be there in a moment!"

The blonde arrived breathless.

"Two kilometers from here is the headquarters of the column of workers that succeeded in breaking the police cordon south of Le Bourget. The whole gang of the red swine who raised the Paris mob are in a barn on Rougemont Farm—in a perfect position to be captured."

"To be captured?" cried Hitler. "Sakra! Then capture them!—Forward! capture the red swine!" Tense with joy he trampled upon the little black ants until not one was left alive.

CHAPTER SEVEN WHILE COMRADE MÜNZER ISSUED ONE ORDER AFTER ANOTHER, THE REST FOLLOWED ON A MAP BY THE YELLOW glow of a lantern the further advance of the proletarians in the suburbs. According to a dispatch just received, Column 3, heading north from Pantin, had broken through a police barricade east of the village of Drancy, to cut off Hitler's route to the airfield at that point.

A bicycle patrol shot up to the barn door and reported that the Reich Führer had left the German Embassy, and that the police escort which was to accompany him through the enraged masses would be so powerful that it would be next to impossible for anyone to approach his car.

A grim "Down with him!" swept through the barn. Then Münzer feverishly pointed out all the road forks where the advance patrols of his column must hold themselves in readiness. Workers armed with rifles hurried from the barn.

In spite of the swirling dust kicked up from the straw by the tramp of many boots Hyacinthe was visible in the dim lamplight. At the end of a table surrounded by excited, arguing workers, sitting before a typewriter, puffing one cigarette after another, she was typing away at a manifesto 'To the Workers of the World' which Münzer had just dictated. As she worked she hummed along with the whistled snatches of the "Marseillaise" that rose here and there in the crowd. But as some of the workers were dissatisfied with the manifesto, Münzer tore the paper out of the machine.

When Gunther suggested the title, "Avis au Peuple," a wild argument instantly flamed up among the international revolutionaries over the language in which the manifesto should be framed. Since for the moment repeated votes failed to produce any unanimous opinion, Münzer finally reached a general understanding on one point: That after Hitler had been disposed of and all the Nazi-Fascist governments of the world had been eliminated, they must present the masses with a "definite program."

506

For the third time Hyacinthe inserted a new sheet. Meanwhile farm girls in wooden shoes dragged in huge tin cans. Hot coffee was served and freshly baked bread. After Münzer had swallowed a couple of mugs he again began to dictate, with new emphasis and force:

"Workers! Your greatest moment is the message of freedom! We bring you that message. The plague-laden air which has breathed upon us so long from the Third Reich—is ended! Ended are the camps where prisoners were murdered on the rotting straw! Ended all the refinements of horror . . . the scenes of terror and cruelty! Now no man will be beaten, flogged, shamed! Or shot down in transports or gassed in cellars. We workers have beaten the Fascist-Nazi police wherever they opposed us. And it will not be long before this betrayer of the workers, this filthy rat, will be rendered impotent! Then we shall be free!"

At the word "free" several men threw their caps up and shouted: "Vive la liberté!"

"Yes, indeed!" Münzer bit into a crisp chunk of bread. "We are free from this nightmare of shame! Brother workers, in the darkness of this last August night and amid the gathering throng of all the working, exploited proletariat of the world—here, ten kilometers from Paris, a new dawn breaks for us all!"

"Stop!" Gunther wanted to get in a word. But Münzer went on dictating: "Wherever you find a picture of Hitler in your village, town, or city, in stores, homes, schools, or barracks—tear it to bits! Wherever you find his name written or printed—scratch it out! To the stake with 'Mein Kampf' and the 'Nuremberg Laws'!"

Fierce laughter broke out, cut short only when the sound of distant shots was heard. "That's our third column," cried Münzer, "south of the canal."

"Diable!" Gunther jumped. A few of the men stood up. "Is there a battle brewing?"

"Damn!" others shouted, as a windowpane clattered in the barn. "That sounds like artillery fire. The police must have called in the army to help them."

For a moment everyone looked worried. But Münzer laughed grimly:

"Army? All the better. What are you trembling for? Let the Nazis tremble! We others have nothing to lose today but our chains!"

A general cry of triumph answered him.

All at once, from the direction of the canal below, machine-gun fire could be heard. Münzer dashed to the door of the barn:

"Apparently the Nazi police are trying to smuggle the cars of those betrayers of the workers over the canal, somewhere east of Noneyilles Farm. But our people have occupied the whole park southeast of Aulnay. He can't get through there . . ." A renewed storm of "Hurrahs" was his answer. Then a motorcyclist thundered in from the direction of Pantin, stopped, dismounted, and reported:

"The mayor's office in Pantin has just heard by telephone from the Prefect of Police. The Governor of Paris has ordered the 7th and 12th Regiments of Chasseurs, together with tank brigades garrisoned in Paris, to clear the road to the airfield of all 'communist rabble.' "

"What?" Münzer's voice grated. "Perhaps these French fascists want to conduct the German gangster Führer to the airfield between the bayonets of their poilus?" As he sensed a moment of hesitation among the others he raised a pitchfork high in the air and shouted: "Comrades! It's an old experience—as old as the world. Man is worth only as much as the courage he possesses!"

"Death to the fascists!" resounded through the barn . . . "Death to all the dictators! Death to every Nazi!"

"Silence!" Suddenly Krah waved his fountain pen. "Oi-oi. A resolution has just been prepared to the effect—"

"A resolution? Listen, everybody!"

Krah rolled up his red shirt sleeves and read aloud:

"We have decided, in the name of all hard-working laborers engaged in hard work—"

"Herr Krah," Hyacinthe protested, giggling, "since when are you engaged in hard work?"

After a general laugh, she stood up and said: "Besides, friends, I believe it was agreed that we were to make no decisions that were not approved by our President!"

"By our President?" They looked at each other stupidly. And only now did those in the barn seem to remember again that a few hours earlier in Neuilly they had unanimously elected the grand mutilé de guerre, just freed from the police, to the presidency of all the oppressed and degraded.

He sat there on an earth-encrusted plow, supporting his head on his hand. His shoulder, wounded before Notre Dame, was conspicuously bandaged. Someone had tied a bit of rusty barbed wire around his filthy trench helmet. His eyes glowed from the dun-colored mask of a face, peaceful as stars at daybreak. They represented the only fixed pole in the restless, noisy crowd.

"Now then! Come here!" A man beckoned to him. "Didn't you

508

hear? Our program is to be formulated."

"Our program?" Münzer tore the pen from Krah's hand. "Our basic principle can only state: . . ."

"—No one shall go hungry any more—all over the world!" a working woman put in.

"All must work," cried others.

"Comrades!" Münzer made himself heard again. "On March 14, 1525, the German peasants formulated, in their 'Twelve Swabian Articles'—"

"German peasants, German peasants!" a black-haired machinist shouted. "I'm a Czech and I protest."

"Quiet!" Münzer climbed up on a bench. "I say: at that time the German peasants demanded: Freedom of the fisheries! Freedom of woods and waters! Freedom of light! Freedom of firewood and construction wood!—"

"Let our President come to the table," the machinist screamed, "and say whether a Czech like me—"

"Oi-oi! What is our President's nationality?"

"Comrades! We have no time for this squabbling! For if we do not act now with devastating speed— Quiet!! With my great namesake Thomas Münzer, I cry: Forward! Forward! Fall to—while the iron is hot. May our swords never stop dripping with the blood of our enemies. Forward!"

After further uproarious argument, most of them finally gathered around Münzer by the typewriter.

CHAPTER EIGHT KASPAR FRIEDRICH UHLE, WHO WAS SITTING APART ON A HEAP OF STRAW UNDER SOME SCYTHES AND FLAILS that hung from a beam, put away the little New Testament which he had been reading. He looked up into the shadowy beams and groaned softly. Ever since Hitler had struck him between the eyes with his fist, he had been trying to decide whether that blow had not been a warning to him from God.

While Hyacinthe, over at the table, was typing the manifesto paragraph by paragraph, as, after a series of fierce arguments, it was dictated to her, Uhle noticed that his soldier from Verdun was looking at him. But then the backs of several workers threw the soldier into shadow again. Uhle was going to get up and go to him. But he thought for a moment, and then took out of his pocket the letter which he had begun to write in the Hotel Balzac. Until now, he had had no chance to finish it.

"Irene!" he began writing where he had left off:

"So much has happened since I wrote to you yesterday about the soldier whom I found still alive in a dugout under the battlefield of Verdun. Now he is sitting across from me in a barn far outside Paris. The sun has not risen yet.—Oh, Irene! How strongly his eyes remind me of that other about whom I have often told you—the pioneer who once in 1916 came down into our dugout with a handful of anemones that he had picked in the snow under artillery fire. He laid them so carefully on our little table, made of box boards knocked together. And then he held up one of the red and white dotted flowers and suddenly said in a strange voice: 'Anemone nemorosa, the windflower'. And truly, Irene, I felt as if, in the midst of the brutal human slaughter, he had wanted to give me a sense of the subtlest meaning of creation. Windflower—the word made me tremble. A few days later I was ordered to Headquarters at Charleville. To raise the obviously sinking morale of the troops the General Staff had seen fit to order me to write something that would revive the martial spirit of the men. I went to the communications center of the High Command to talk to Major Nikolai, the head of 3-B. There I sat in his office, saber and shako in hand, trying to make it clear to the bald-headed major that up there in the front-line trenches, where companies of two hundred and fifty men had been mowed down to twenty-three, something very strange was happening to the soldiers on both sides. No one up there (I said to him) feels any hatred for the enemy now. On the contrary. An entirely new spirit of brotherhood, in fact, a brotherly love, comparable only to the love of the early Christians in the catacombs, was spreading from rifle to rifle, like an utterly new society. The simplest soldiers (so I told the major) often suddenly confess their most secret thought to each other—the thought that the soldiers on both sides could simply climb out of their trenches and shake each other's hard hands in a perfectly simple gesture, and from there proceed to begin a new life. Nicolai, puffing smoke rings, looked at me coldly. Then he polished his monocle. Suddenly he growled at me: 'Damn it all, you're talking pure communism!' 'No, Major!' I tried to control my excitement. 'Not communism. No—I have been telling you about a strange phenomenon—the development of a general spirit of brotherly love. A sort of *communionism* of front-line soldiers.' 'Nonsense!'

510

Nicolai turned purple. 'Communionism! Early Christians! Brotherly love! Utter nonsense! No—damn it—I know the boys up there better than that. They're happy when they can get to a field kitchen and fill their faces.'—Would you believe it, Irene? I still get hot in the face when I think of it.—I rose. An abyss opened.—I returned to my battle sector shaken. But as soon as I was back among my pale, unshaven comrades, as soon as I saw the battered trench helmets and the blood-spattered trenches, I took the stiff hand of one of the fallen and swore an oath. Do you remember the field postcard I wrote you then? That when we got home, everything should be lived anew! Everything! Every breath, utterly new and transformed. No more, in us, of the rotten hypocritical social system that had hunted its sons into this slaughter, into this world of barbed wire and rats and corpses. Oh, everything should be *new*. That I swore to my fallen comrade. New—in our very blood corpuscles. New, Irene, between man and woman too! A new 'fixed point of reference'! Above all, a new love!"

He stopped writing, for over at the table it seemed that the communists, the workers, and the refugees would come to blows at any moment over the question of wages and the right to strike.

"Irene," he returned to his letter:

"Was there not one who said, 'Man does not live by bread alone'? Ah, often I feel that, no matter where I turn, I am an outcast. I fall between two stools. When, before the war, as a young lieutenant, I resigned my commission, I hoped that, outside the walls of the barracks, I should find freedom. And for that my people called me a traitor! And just now I was sent away from the council table—I am mistrusted. Krah was almost on the point of saying that I was a Nazi! Simply because I dared to say that freedom was not exclusively a matter of politics—that there was another freedom. Simply because I reminded them of what He said on that windy night to Nicodemus—I mean, Christ's most profound question—his mysterious words about a rebirth by the spirit . . ."

He had to put away his letter, because, in a new struggle around the typewriter, one of the workers had knocked over the lantern. When it had been lighted again, Westermann spoke:

"Pardon me! . . . Pardon me! What should actually be the basis of this constitution?"

"What basis?"

"Oi-oi!" Krah again filled his pen. "I think the question here is the precise formulation of a new, more perfect idea of society!"

"Idea of society?" Münzer stamped. "I shit on ideas! Marx said:

'Ideas can accomplish nothing. For the execution of ideas we need men who command a practical power!' " He smashed his fist on the table top, so that the milk cans rattled. Krah wanted to retort but was shouted down from all sides.

"Comrades!" Münzer lighted a cigar. "We've grown out of the baby shoes of the proletariat! We—"

"Friends!" Hyacinthe stopped her typing to interrupt him. "Why is it that no one asks our President what the new basis of our constitution should be?"

"Our President?" A few glanced sidewise, ill-humoredly, toward the grand mutilé de guerre. "And has he the new basis in his pocket?"

After a long moment of waiting Münzer turned to the soldier.

"Comrade President, we who believe in the materialistic interpretation of history—we are absolutely opposed to any newly sprouting idealism! We of the working class reject all metaphysics! In our manifesto we only want to deal with the real man. For Lenin already led the fight . . ."

"I know, I know . . ." The soldier rose, and went over and sat beside Uhle. "Yes!" He straightened his mask and looked strangely at one after another of them. "For the sake of the 'real' man, outstanding geniuses have fought a courageous fight in these last decades. Yes! Great doctors have struggled to free humanity of cancer and other deadly diseases. I still remember very well the revolutionary enthusiasm that reigned in Berlin when Professor Koch first demonstrated the virus of tuberculosis before an international group of physicians—"

"What drivel is our President talking?" muttered a couple of iron workers. "We asked him about the new basis."

Münzer looked impatiently at his watch. All at once he asked harshly:

"If our President has any more preaching to do, he'd better hurry. Our manifesto must go to press before noon in St. Denis."

"During the long, endless hours of my twenty years of loneliness, I asked myself again and again . . ."

"What, for God's sake?"

"A doctor who stands before the horrible fact of an apparently incurable source of disease never allows himself to be satisfied with merely cutting away the growths which spring from it. Day in, day out, he works in his laboratory and does not rest until he has determined the activator of the source. And only when he knows that, does he begin the exact and methodical attempt to attack the tiny bacillus ruthlessly with every means that chemistry has at its disposal

512

". . . and to render the bacillus impotent . . ."

His voice held them. They listened in wondering curiosity.

"Why, then," he continued, "since we have already had this ravaging spectacle of the disease of Nazism in the body of mankind before us for so long, do we attempt to heal it again and again by cutting the outward growth away? By bloody revolutions do we attempt to master the virus, instead of deciding courageously, once and for all, like the Pasteurs, Virchows, and Ehrlichs, to make the effort to determine the moral source of the eternal plague?"

"Man!" Münzer's patience was exhausted. "Is this why we snatched you away from the gendarmes in Neuilly and carried you here like a banner? Is this why we mobilized thousands of working comrades in the factories, so that someone like you should teach us morals? Man! We have gathered here to rid the world of the plague of Nazism once and for all! Is that clear?"

"To rid the world of it?" the soldier asked earnestly. "And without even trying to find out the source of it?"

"Enough!" Münzer hammered on the table. "Damnation! We have clearly formulated our goal. And the time is ripe! Man, we class-conscious workers finally want power for ourselves! Power!"

"Bravo!" A thirsty roar went up. "Mais oui! La force! Power! Yes, we want power! Power shall at last be ours!" And now hardened fists grasped flails, clubs, and scythes.

The unknown soldier from Verdun waited until the racket died down. His wounded face gleamed through his mask.

"Comrades," he said. "Now you have yourselves shown the source of this evil. It could not be demonstrated more clearly. There it is! The bacillus that flourished in Caesar, in Augustus, in Herod! In the Borgias, in Machiavelli, in Loyola! From the House of Habsburg right up to the White House . . . and all the other lustful wolves in the capitol of power . . . Yes." He stood up. "To want to be more powerful than your neighbor, to think you are better than your neighbor, to want to lord it over the weak—that is the bacillus of Nazism—of all plagues—of all war—of the whole dance of death!"

"Stop!" Münzer shouted, and made a gesture to the others to be quiet. He came toward the soldier, his long arms hanging. "Listen, you from under the ground—you in your dirty cave! I don't give a damn about your Augustus! But if you, during your twenty years of unemployment down there in Haudroumont, had really understood anything about the lustful wolves in the capitol of power, then you'd know that we class-conscious workers are not going to let the wolves

513

snarl at us or tear us to bits another day or another hour. We want to do the snarling and the tearing ourselves now!"

After a hoarse laugh of applause Münzer scratched his head and grinned. "I hope that's all clear now, Comrade President. But if you should know a more effective remedy for overcoming the cause of this present-day brown fascist plague than to fight it—as we're going to do—please tell us the name of the serum."

Stimulated by louder and louder bursts of laughter he bowed.

"Comrade President, if you do not reveal to us this apparently still mysterious remedy, you will permit us to use the most effective remedy we know against these plague-spreading Hitlerite rats—to kill them wherever they show their filthy snouts! Or are the bosses to exploit us forever? Is England to rule the Indian people forever? Is Wall Street to have more power than we working proletarians forever?"

"No! No!" They all shouted. "We want power now! We! We!"

The crippled soldier remained silent, huddling in his Spahi cloak as if he were freezing. After a while Uhle answered for him:

"There is no other serum against this 'I and Power' plague than that we kill it in ourselves, down to the tiniest corpuscles of our blood . . . in the most microscopic cells of our desire, when one ego desires to overwhelm another. Day and night the bacillus is at work, like trichinosis, in our blood. It multiplies! It demands its satisfaction! No matter what the other must suffer. It wants to rule, even in the narrowest radius: in bed, in the apartment, in the office, it gives orders like any Nazi. Only within ourselves can we battle successfully against these myriad Hitlers. Only when the bacillus finds no more nourishment for itself in *us*—only then will the vampire die in ourselves. And then it will at last lie dried out and finished, like a jellyfish washed up on the beach from the deep sea slime to be destroyed in the rays of the sun."

Several of the older men became thoughtful. But they felt the impossibility of overcoming the acute crisis which had already set in in the sickroom of mankind, by such a prescription. Led by Münzer, all assembled around their red flag and began to leave the barn. But Hyacinthe, as though in a trance, stood up from her typewriter, walked past Uhle to the soldier, and said ecstatically:

"My musician! You who had played the organ so beautifully in Notre Dame—you messenger from the realm of souls, save us! Bring a miracle to pass and heal us from the horrible bacillus of power! Heal us!—for you can!"

After a moment of sneering puzzlement Münzer pulled her away by her red hair:

514

"Comrade! The struggle of the proletariat is deadly serious! Hysteria will never bring us to our goal!"

But some of the women ran to help her. Suddenly, as though impelled by the willingness of all their superstitious instincts, they fell on their knees before the soldier, raised their arms, and implored:

"Yes, you unknown soldier—achieve the miracle—the miracle!"

The hermit of Haudroumont drew back and stared into all their shining eyes. Suddenly words issued from his torn face—quietly, surely:

"Miracle is not truth—Truth is the miracle!"

"Truth? Oi-oi!" Krah leaped at him as if in a frenzy and hissed Pilate's old question into his ear—"What is truth?"

As the soldier answered, his eyes shone and he loaded each syllable with some magical potency:

"Your life—that is *truth!*"

"*Our* lives?" several of the women giggled, amazed and, as it were, scoffing at their own personal importance.

"Your life," the soldier repeated, "yes. Because for each one of us, from birth to death, *that* is the one great, irrefutable truth."

"Quite right," Münzer replied, unfurling his red flag. "And may all the ruling classes tremble before it!"

"Comrades," the soldier went on, "if we could succeed in recognizing that crystalline truth clearly, and making it active not only in us but in the brain of every dweller on this earth, the discovery of this perfectly simple truth would have the same physical force as the law of gravity, or the geometry of Euclid, or as Archimedes' discoveries in mechanics."

"Yes, away with the bonds of slavery!" Münzer shouted, looking around, his senses aglow with the intoxicating air of revolution.

"Yes!" The soldier threw back his cloak. "Away with the bonds of our slavery to our own senses! Only then shall we have found the lever with which to shake from its foundations the colossal empire of the beast! The strength with which to oppose all its marshals and generals, grown hollow-eyed in their millennial serving of death—who in the Capitol of Power—under the banner of Heaven or Hell, in the name of the East or the West, from right or from left—have but one aim: ruthlessly to rape, steal, corrupt, and deprave the only possession we have on this earth—our Life!"

His words were terrifying, but at the same time so strangely enticing that these people, making ready for their conquest of power, gaped at him as though he had spoken to them of something better, of some

515

secret treasure, which, though difficult to secure, was destined only for them.

Meanwhile they had not observed that, slipping behind the haystacks, a grinning horde of Paris fifth-columnists under Gauleiter Baldur's leadership had steadily made their way into every corner of the barn. Only when a dairymaid screamed the alarm, did Münzer, as if awakening from a trance, turn thunderstruck—and then the others. But it was already too late for any resistance. Their sticks and flails were torn out of their hands from behind. Then, at the point of revolvers, they were driven into the hay like a flock of sheep. Meanwhile others, boys scarcely sixteen years old, stood on guard at the barn door, watching every twitch and movement of the captives.

CHAPTER NINE "WELL, MY HIGHLY RESPECTABLE FRIENDS!" THE SON OF THE MURDERED CULTURAL LEADER SPOKE with heavy irony, a fat cigar in the corner of his mouth. Broadshouldered, his hands thrust deep into the pockets of his raincoat, he stepped forward. "We've come here in a purely comradely spirit to help you get your 'new basis of life' in working order. Particularly with the help of this reliable old lever of Archimedes here!" He held out his army revolver mockingly. Then he strode to the table and took possession of the papers he found there. "It is my privilege to inform you, my honored friends, that your honorable brothers and comrades have obediently returned to their respective factories. In St. Denis work is already progressing on full shifts. For it goes without saying that the fight at the canal ended victoriously for the power of the State—you boobs—and that more than one worker's corpse was left lying in the fog-soaked grass."

"And Hitler?" shrieked Krah suddenly, as if he had gone mad.

"The Führer," said Baldur contemptuously, pointing to a broken window, "who until now took part in your marvelous 'Front Populaire' assembly in deepest incognito behind that ladder, has unfortunately been compelled, by urgent Reich business and complications of a serious nature with Danzky-Polsky, to leave for the airport without being able to greet you!"

There was a general howl of rage. Then they surged toward the

516

barn door. But Baldur thundered: "Get back there, you red swine! You can't catch him now! No, he's safely on his way to the airport!"

"To Le Bourget!" yelled Münzer. "Impossible, there's treachery here, we are betrayed!"

"Hold your Marxist tongue, you stinking Bolshevik!" Baldur threw a stool at him and then seated himself comfortably at the table. "And now listen: The Prefect of Police of the Seine District has had the remarkable kindness to leave you all to the Chief of the Gestapo, Herr Himmler, for further consideration."

The women screamed.

"Écoutez—" Baldur inquired sarcastically, pushing back his cap— "there's supposed to be a French examining magistrate here, named Gunther. Where is he?"

"Present!" The cripple limped forward. "I'm Gunther. Diable!"

"Bon! You and any other French people here are being taken over by your French Minister of Justice! There's an armored car waiting outside. Shove off!"

The Secretary of the Anciens Combattants brushed at his cap. Suddenly a scream like that of a wounded animal escaped from his throat, and he hobbled, his cane raised menacingly, toward Baldur. But before he could reach him he was seized and, together with the representatives of the Paris labor groups, marched out of the barn.

Immediately there was an inarticulate confusion of such curses that Baldur covered his ears. Yet the clamor grew and grew, until it was an SOS call for help to all their comrades in the world outside. Then suddenly from the mass of stunned, huddled human beings, there rose —as in the wood in Neuilly—the workers' hymn—sung now with such reckless bravado and scoffing fearlessness that the Gauleiter promptly had the great barn door barred.

"I'll have you all bayoneted if you dare to open your mouths again!" he yelled, his neck arteries swollen and purple with rage.

As the singing nevertheless grew in strength and he felt himself powerless, he set fire to a bundle of straw. As the flame shot into the air he held it high:

"Now then, unless there is silence here instantly I'll set this whole, trumpery old shack on fire, and then you can sing as loud as you want to—as long as your breath holds out—just like the men in the fiery furnace—ha-ha!" and he held the torch close to one of the stacks of hay.

In terror of being burned alive, they broke off their singing, and Baldur, appeased, stamped out the burning torch.

"Come along now, Hänsel"—he beckoned to Hess's young adjutant who stood waiting in his raincoat—"have the pit in the forest, into which you dumped the other bodies, dug a bit wider—halt!—when you're finished notify me—you know that we've got to put all these swine underground before the fog lifts!"

Several S.S. youths disappeared.

"Herr Gauleiter", Hänsel puffed on his pipe, "in the meantime do you want to wring anything the Gestapo should know out of these front-populaire animals?"

"No, Hänsel. Their corrupt Judocratic train of thought is known to us. But where is that war cripple the French military authorities are looking for?"

The soldier of Verdun was brought forward.

"Aha!" Baldur gaped curiously at his artificial face. "So this is the famous milk-toast face—highly edifying! And those are the two insane eyes against which our Führer especially warned us? Well, brother, come here and sit down at the table. Come on!—so you've found yourself a cozy role here—playing the agent provocateur, eh?"

He turned the smoking wick of the barn lantern lower, drew out of his coat pocket a double-bellied glass bottle of sparkling colorless spirits, uncorked it, and smacked his lips:

"Here, Hänsel, have a whiff—real raspberry brandy. Here's looking at you!" He took a hearty slug. Then he lit a fresh cigar over the lamp chimney and blew a few smoke rings into the air. All at once he raised his eyebrows: "Well, brother, according to your cripple's view of things, the only irrefutable truth is—life?" He waited for an answer. Then, finally irritated by the other's profound silence, he pumped himself full of alcohol.

At that moment the piano-mover, who had come from the Embassy with them, rushed clumsily in, buttoned his raincoat over his swallow-tail, and reported:

"Herr Gauleiter, we have room now for the first twenty."

"Bon. Get along, Hänsel, count them off and then out with the red swine—and I hold you personally responsible that not one of these communistic pigs escapes."

The grand mutilé de guerre jerked back to his surroundings. Suddenly, as if to implore mercy for them, he strode to the barn door and stood in the way of the gruesome convoy. But Baldur had run after him and caught him by the cloak. He waited until the twenty doomed human beings had been escorted out of the barn. Then, at the point of his revolver, he forced the soldier back to the table. Then the grand

518

mutilé de guerre suddenly fell to his knees. His head sank onto a stool. And he began to pray aloud.

CHAPTER TEN

AMONG THOSE LEFT IN THE BARN WERE KRAH, WESTERMANN, RABBI WOLFF, PROFESSOR GOLDSCHMIDT, UHLE, and Münzer.

"Come on, now"—Baldur bent over the praying soldier—"tell me, why have you been making such fools of these poor, red swine—hm? Such an old-time war veteran as you surely knows that the gray-haired Communist back there was absolutely right when he admitted that the only truth in the desperate struggle for existence of man against man is power. The devil!" He stamped his foot and slouched over to the chained captives. "Or is there any other way of getting out of this continuous ideology swindle and reaching the food trough of reality? If so, tell me!" He stood, legs wide apart, before them. "You undoubtedly share my opinion when I assert that *only* he who has power over others really lives in the full juice of life. Am I right," he shouted, "you bow-legged Communist over there?"

Münzer turned red to the ears, nodded, and muttered something.

"Thank you!" Baldur jabbed a cigar into Münzer's mouth, which Münzer promptly spit out. "Yes, you world proletarians—at any rate, fellows like me are at least as excessively honest as you! We'll be just as sure to kick over any vaporous ideal as you are. Even when imported from holy Moscow—ha-ha!"

He slouched back to the table, took the piece of barbed wire from the soldier's helmet, held it up, and grinned:

"This rusty crown, I suppose, is meant to symbolize something particularly profound? Yes? Ha-ha! Yes, I'll admit that when you Marxist peasants were sitting around the long table here, I had to think of an engraving in our dining room at home. 'The Last Supper', it was called. Yes, in the picture there was a bearded president too—with his 'poor in spirit'—sitting at a long table like this one—he and his Easter rabbits —haggling over a new manifesto for all the 'poor in spirit' in the world, ha-ha!" His mocking laughter was taken up by his Gestapo comrades.

"Nu—such beasts!" the rabbi groaned, "such beasts!"

"Shut up!"—Baldur spat at Dr. Wolff, who was cursing on into his beard.

"Nu! Mass murderers! Utter beasts!"

"Beasts?" Baldur lunged toward him, in his fury devouring the cigar in his mouth. "Yes—but highly evolved beasts—get me? Honest beasts —get me? Yes—honest to excess! As for me, I'd rather be a heathen and humbly admit with our Nietzsche that I worship the 'blond beast' —than subscribe to the lying Ten Commandments of your arch-ancestor Moses! You old synagogue-cleaner! Anything rather than be a hypocrite from morning to night for seven thousand years! Hypocrisy! Hypocrisy!"

"Nu! What is he saying?" Dr. Wolff trembled in every limb. "He would rather profess the doctrine of the 'blond beast' than the Ten Commandments? You are a beast yourself! You will not recognize what such a one as Moses wrote on the tables of the law in the face of all the great ones of the earth—'Thou shalt not—' "

"Thou shalt not babble!" Baldur hit him on the cheek with his revolver butt.

"Nu!" Dr. Wolff staggered, streaming blood. "I'm done for!"

He fell. Uhle, who was standing near him, picked him up.

"Get him out of here," Baldur stormed.

The rabbi was dragged out of the barn.

"The lightning has struck," shrieked Baldur. "Don't you Judocrats realize yet that, with your hate-treaty of Versailles, you drove us Aryans into precisely the same political situation as the Romans once put you? For centuries you were gagged and prevented from rising to your own national greatness—and all the time you 'chosen people' had only *one* thought: how to free yourselves as quickly as possible from the yoke of the Roman army of occupation."

"Old wives' tales! Lies!" Uhle cried when none of the others spoke up. "No! God had stricken the sword from our hands, so that at last we—"

"Shut your damned pacifist mouth!"

"But the demon—the age-old demon of the sword, in his den in the Teutoburger Forest—he rose in wrath. He came, with the hellish face of the beast, with the smooth, false mask that is called 'national greatness'!"

"If that clodhopper doesn't keep quiet—" Baldur raved, and signed to the guards, who immediately knocked Uhle down into the hay.

Baldur released the safety catch of his revolver and half sat on the table:

"The false mask of national greatness? I maintain that the Messiah who had at that time been predicted and expected by all your awe-inspiring prophets represented in the sly little heads of all right-thinking Semites none other than the *national* hero and liberator! Or will you deny that, you Judocratic swine?" He lit a new cigar. "And just as Hitler, whom—thanks be!—you so devoutly hate, sat on that fateful day at the famous table in the Bräuhauskeller with his first disciples Hess, von der Epp, and Franck . . . and then—hocus-pocus—the three disciples grew to six, then a hundred! yes, millions . . . I say again, just exactly so your Jew Jesus of Nazareth gathered around him, if not at the beer table, then at the Sea of Galilee, *his* first disciples, Peter, Jacob, etc., until he had finally drummed up twelve. And then they went on a propaganda tour and the Semites flocked to him exactly as we Aryans rallied round our Hitler. And just as then, every national-minded Hebrew pointed the finger at Jesus saying, 'it is he who will free us from the Roman exploiters', just so every Aryan pointed at Hitler, saying, 'It is he who will free us from the Judocratic exploiters!' Ha-ha! Yes!"

He came to the middle of the barn and stared at the prisoners with alcohol-glazed eyes. "And just as uninterested as your Pharisees and Sadducees were then in the 'great mystery of the incarnation of the Son of God,' just as uninterested are we Aryans today in your whole international-brotherhood jabbering, including its demands for the re-awakening and regeneration of 'the moral personality through the Judocratic spirit'! We puke on it!!! Do you understand!? We are amoralists—understand?!"

"Oi-oi!" Krah's voice became audible. "But that is the only sympathetic thing about you! God—are you amoral!"

"Thanks," nodded Baldur, grinning and puffing smoke into the air. Then, raising the ring which he had meanwhile braided out of the barbed wire, he went on:

"Yes—and then the zero hour for Judah approached. The march on Jerusalem was decided on by the twelve gauleiters! His Excellency Peter—"

"Oi-oi!" panted Krah, and there was a burst of yowling laughter from the S.S. men.

"I repeat," Baldur grinned, "His Excellency Peter already felt the portfolio of Minister of Defense in his Maundy Thursday toga—ha-ha!"

"And His Excellency John?" shouted Hänsel. "He must have claimed the Ministry of Public Worship and Education for himself."

"That's it!" Baldur laughed, spurred on by the applause. "And Party Comrade Mark—what did he want? Banker Judas, like our tom-cat

Hjalmar Schacht, was certainly playing for the finances!"

"And Gauleiter Matthew?" Hänsel doubled over with glee. "What about Party Comrade Matthew?"

After salvos of wild laughter, Baldur struck an attitude.

"And now they all set out to hold their last Party conference at an extra-special little supper. They sat down at the table and awaited their Master's last commands. In memory of the first liberation of the 'Race of Rulers' from Egyptian slavery, they served up the Easter lamb, ceremonially decked out with spring flowers. Yes sir—but what did their elected President say then to all these fishermen and carpet-weavers who already felt themselves to be governors of the various provinces of Israel? Hm? Well—" he pointed with his cigar to the soldier from Verdun, who was still kneeling in prayer—"he said exactly such absurdly stupid, such deeply disappointing tom-fool drivel about the ideal of power as your elected President there—he said things that were in such striking contradiction to the national hope of the Jewish people that even the prudent, humdrum prospective Minister of Finance, His Excellency Iscariot, left the conference, in a hurry, shaking his beard—"

After renewed howls of laughter from his gang, Baldur tapped the kneeling soldier on the shoulder. "What! Now that we Aryans have definitely ejected this debilitated Judo-Christianity from our very marrow, out of the wilderness again comes a man like you? Do you really think that we Germans will allow you internationalist swine to smuggle the Judo-Christian Jesus of Bethlehem into our Pan-Aryan millennium? No!" He stood up. "No! not even in the dirty uniform of an unshaven war cripple! It's enough to make anybody puke! No! Those feeble words which the president of all vagabonds, publicans, and prostitutes is supposed to have said two thousand years ago to his Marshal Peter just before the march on Jerusalem when Peter tried to have a couple of Roman police spies protect him from capture: 'Put up again thy sword into his place, for all they that take the sword shall perish by the sword'—I say: such idiocy makes absolutely no impression nowadays. Not only on us Nazis! For, through that window there, I was delighted to observe that the Twelve Apostles couldn't have looked half as blank when that happened to them as you international Kremlin-followers did when *your* president tried to make your very understandable desire for power for the proletariat, loathsome to you! No, you poor red swine, let a man like me tell you once and for all that only he who does *not* take the sword will perish!"

Through the roar of applause from his party comrades, Baldur shouted at Uhle:

"And that goes for you more than any of the rest of them, you fool."

Uhle seemed to collect his thoughts for a moment, and then said steadily:

"Baldur, what do you know about the singer of the 'lilies of the field'? What do you know about all that was happening in the souls of us soldiers in 1914 when, advancing at night, we saw everywhere on the roads lighted by the glow of battle, *His* body, the crown of thorns on His bleeding brow, hanging from a crucifix?! What do you know of what awakened in us when we had to march ahead stumbling over the shattered skulls of our fallen comrades—and still keep on—tramping through curdled blood—along the highway? How can you know what we felt when, from blood-drenched fields everywhere, we saw the Crucified, with outstretched arms, coming toward us from his cross!"

"Propaganda!" the Nazis roared. "Propaganda!"

"Where were you when in the winter of 1916, before Verdun, the reviled Son of Man, here—there—everywhere, looked at us out of the face of any weary, unknown soldier so warningly, so meaningly, while the snow fell around us?"

"They were still dirtying their diapers," volunteered Münzer.

Westermann clenched his fist at the laughing Nazis. "We infantry men of the World War didn't go into battle as amoralists!"

"No," Uhle cried. "In 1914 we marched into our first engagements as believing Christians."

"As believing Christians?" Baldur slapped his thigh. "That explains everything." He exchanged angry looks with his gang.

Uhle was immediately seized, and they started to drag him out of the barn. In his violent efforts to resist, his little New Testament fell out of his pocket. Baldur picked it up and leafed through it delightedly:

"Say!—Before you're shot, would you like to look up the direct route to Heaven in your Jew guidebook here? Now"—he turned to his men—"is it clear to you why our fathers lost the war?"

"Herr Gauleiter!" Hänsel pointed to the first page of the little book. "It says that his great-grandfather carried this New Testament through the war of liberation against Napoleon, in 1813."

"Wonderful! And his grandfather too. What? Why, it says his father carried it too—when the guards stormed Saint-Privat in 1870."

"Yes!" Uhle turned fiercely on the mocking S.S. men. "And we their sons—I say, we soldiers of the first World War—we had something better before us than 'national greatness'! All alone in some shell crater under the solitary moon, among mountains of dead human beings, what we found in our hearts was not your Third or Fourth Reich."

"But what?" Baldur came toward him, his mouth twitching. But suddenly he changed his tune.

"Get going," he snarled. "I've had enough of these fresh Judocrats. Shoot the whole swinish herd of them!"

While Hänsel was fettering the victims, Uhle's eyes rested in a last, long look on his unknown soldier:

"Verily, you remain. To be our assurance that no one of us bled to death in no man's land in vain. That no one of us will bear torture here in vain . . . For you, in your endless solitude, behind the rococo mirror, discovered the *new* law for us all. I say: The dynamite of truth with which soon all the outcasts among men will blow to atoms the Reich of those who pray to death—the Reich that *looks* firm because it is criminally cemented with the blood of innocents—"

"Take him away!" Baldur foamed. "Take the whole gang of them out of my sight! Wait for me at the edge of the forest six kilometers from here. Halt!" He pulled back an S.S. man who was going to take along the praying soldier too. "Let that cripple alone. He stays here."

CHAPTER ELEVEN BALDUR WAITED UNTIL THE BARN WAS CLEARED. THEN, WHEN HE WAS CERTAIN THAT NO ONE WAS OBSERVING him, he tapped the soldier cautiously, almost curiously, on the back. He looked at the faded Moroccan cloak which dragged in long folds on the floor and gleamed rustily here and there in the lantern light.

"You kneel there like a bishop at the high altar at Whitsuntide.— Whom are you really praying to? Well—once upon a time little Baldur was just as religious and prayed to 'God the Father'. Let alone the Son and his Holy Ghost . . . In the evening, for instance, when Mummy came to my bedside—with her kerosene lamp, and the circle of light played so yellow on the ceiling. For God's sake—now lay off with your Paternosters. Say, are you praying against me, maybe? Because, really, I'm no long-tailed devil. I'm only honest. Yes, and excessively

524

honest. But because, as that Judocrat just said, you have discovered a truth that contains dynamite, I should like to learn from you now—just exactly what that truth is—"

He began to pace around the kneeling man like a wild beast certain of its prey. "You see—later, when we've laid you out cold, we can be definitely certain that—now you're dead as a doornail. But—damn it —how can I be certain that a man's alive? I haven't figured that out yet. Answer me, you grisly war veteran! Are you sabotaging me? Are you on strike? Don't you want to let me in on your 'truth'? I'm asking you, how do you recognize if a man's alive?"

"By his love."

"What did you say?" The blond jumped back, but then stood firm. "Lo-o-o-ve! Yes—the first time I was in love with a girl, I thought it was something pretty wonderful too. But later on, when you wake from a woman's arms in the darkness of some dead-end street, or in some dump of a hotel—what remains then of the dream? Two drops of blood on the sheets. I've always made out miserably with love. No! For me, this life is still a cross-word puzzle without a solution. Or what else is it then? The devil with it! What else is this lump of slime?"

"Substance . . ." answered the praying man, without looking up. "Holy substance."

"Holy substance?" Baldur made a face. "And what's someone like me supposed to do with that?"

"What does a sculptor do with his clay? He creates a work of art out of it—doesn't he?" The soldier raised his head and for the first time looked steadily through his mask at Baldur.

"Now, come on, brother." The gauleiter dropped his eyes. "Because if you can't do any better than that, you can just be on your way to our nice mass grave!"

The soldier turned his head, listening. Through the barn door commands could be heard, interrupted sometimes by shrieks. All at once he said:

"When the mass murderer Genghis Khan had a high wall built out of the innumerable skulls of fellow men he had murdered—just as he was going to march past it in triumph, he stopped for a second. An ant was scuttling out of his path—and he debated whether or not to let the little creature live. And because he nevertheless wantonly trod on it—according to a Mongol legend, he afterward became lame."

"Genghis Khan?" Baldur blinked. "Really? And just because of a little ant?"

"Yes. For in that moment the destroyer of life had for the first time sensed within himself the reality of the life of *another*. And because, *despite* that, he trod on the creature—"

"That's why he became lame?" The blond scratched his neck and tried to think up a joke. But the other continued implacably, with the full weight of his insight:

"Wantonly to tread down a living creature—to be sure, that is not difficult! There are plenty of opportunities! But, given the opportunity—then to *refrain* from doing it—" he fixed the gauleiter with his eyes. "Oh, whoever has felt that rapture! When a man restrains his hand, already raised to strike, and lifts himself above blind instinct and nature's urge to kill—lifts himself even to the creative joy of the Maker of all worlds—to feel His delight in the least of his creatures—I tell you: whoever leaves even an earthworm to *live* the life it was given— only he begins to approach the living thought of the Creator, and only he will be approached by HIM."

Angry and puzzled, Baldur gaped at him, rubbing the barrel of his revolver.

"Well, brother, either you're a visionary . . . or you're crazy—or you just don't understand the fundamental laws of life."

"But someone like you—" the cripple looked sidelong at Baldur's revolver—"*you*, of course, know the fundamental laws of life! Tell me —when you were going to kill someone, did you ever stop and think about the origin of the motion that signifies life? Do you know the methods of geometry and mechanics? Are you such a great mathematician that you can reckon and measure the strength and tension of the muscles you want to destroy? Do you know anything of the ramifications of the tiny hidden veins in our connective tissues? Have you ever been seized with astonishment at the wonder of the flow of our blood— the wonder of the dance of the atoms?"

"He's getting excited"— visibly embarrassed, Baldur took the cigar out of his mouth—"and all on account of such insects! And at a moment like this! when titanic forces in Moscow and Wall Street are arming against one another for the final struggle for the final power on this grisly planet! Now, when we are all going to be flung in like zeros, like chessmen on the board of global politics! Now you're getting excited? It just doesn't matter a hang, brother, whether or not an insect like Schulze or Maier is squashed in the machine-gun fire of the coming war for existence!"

After a heavy silence during which the gauleiter opened his raincoat, the other asked:

"If we are all zeros, and nothing but chessmen—if this life is really

526

as worthless as you say—then why did a certain Lance-Corporal Hitler in 1914, at the crossing of the Meuse, crouch with his pants down behind an alder, hiding, and fail to carry out an order clearly given him by his sergeant to replace the fallen Maier up at the machine gun . . . ?"

"What?" Baldur's jaw fell. He retreated to the stacks of hay.

"Why then did this certain lance-corporal envy a little midge (*Limnobio Korea*) which looked at him so clearly out of its light-red turban eyes—?"

"Stop!" Baldur shrieked. "What was that?" And the thought rushed through his brain:

"How does this soldier know anything about the Meuse crossing and the alder? How does this faceless fool know anything about the damned Will?"

"If life is really so worthless," his prisoner went on, speaking as calmly as ever, "why did that quite unknown lance-corporal admit to me that day that it seemed sheer insanity to him that the tiny midge on the alder leaf would be able to munch peacefully that afternoon, while he perhaps, hit by a machine-gun bullet on the hill, would be long since lying dead in the grass among the others—"

"Stop!" Baldur roared even louder, and aimed his revolver . . . "But before I extinguish you, I'd just like to give you this thought to ponder over in the mass grave where you are going. If—as you just stated—a certain lance-corporal really did fail to carry out an order given him in the face of the enemy—by God, it was because he already felt that decisive tickling in his big toe—"

"What decisive tickling?"

"It was because even then he already knew—*who* he is!"

"And you think that we other common soldiers—we workers, painters, socialists, musicians, artisans, and poets—you think we wouldn't have known then exactly *who* we were?"

"Impossible! Or you wouldn't all have been so stupid as to die like a lot of worthless insects—"

"So stupid?" With a jerk the soldier from Verdun rose from his knees. Stretched himself. And his shoulders grew broad so that he threw gigantic shadows all about him in the flickering lantern light—even up among the beams. It looked like an auditorium full of threatening figures—wafted in with the fog from invisible spheres, through every crack and crevice, to take part now in the dialogue. And then he whispered through his mask:

"Have you ever seen a brave soldier fall? And lie so shamelessly

527

abandoned on the field? Have you ever silently taken off your helmet before such a tragic reality? And then looked into the soldier's waxen face?"

After a long, thoughtful pause during which he blew smoke through his nostrils, Baldur suddenly flashed: "And you, brother, what were you doing behind the alder tree, in 1914 at the crossing of the Meuse?"

"I was in the Engineers. I was laying a telephone wire."

"You were laying a wire?"

"Yes, and while I was doing it, I happened to see an inscription over a soldier's grave—'Greater love hath no man than this, that he lay down his life for his brothers.'"

"Was that what it said?"

"But then, while I went on working, I asked myself: Has he not, perhaps, still greater love who *lives* his life for his brothers?"

"You asked yourself?"

"Yes, and then the plague-black detonations of shells bursting all around in the clear blue September afternoon looked like sulphurous little demon faces."

"Is that so?"

"And then suddenly I saw all the pretty flowers and beetles in the grass with new eyes. It seemed to me as though God had carried me away from the battle into his Paradise. And suddenly I understood why the grass grows so beautifully; why the chaffinch on the branch has such a sweet song in his throat. Yes, there in the battle, facing death, where no one can cheat any more—there I understood why the high heavens are so clear and the rays of the sun so warm. As though, according to some still unwritten but eternally valid law, whatever was not involved in the slaughter seemed so joyful within itself."

After a silence he went on:

"And then this happened to me! the old military courage turned into cowardice, and the old military cowardice was transformed into a new, unheard-of courage. And then I understood for *whom* all the still unharmed little farmhouses everywhere were waiting—along with the plow in the sod."

"You understood that? And what else?" Baldur stared at him impatiently.

"What else? I looked at my limbs, still whole, these arms, these hands, and then very simply I knew, we are born to live. To enjoy wheat and potatoes and the whole wide, beautiful world. All this, I felt, belongs to us. To us from everywhere. And this freedom too, and this breath of the spirit over the meadows, and the little lark there rising

528

from its nest, higher, higher, until it is lost to sight. Everything belongs to us—even the lark's song warbling jubilant gratitude somewhere in the blue sky. It was as if the first day of creation were beginning for us—"

"Brother!" Baldur cleared his throat. "Tell me the truth: He really didn't go up on the hill to the machine gun, did he?"

"No."

"And when the sergeant had gone, what did he do?"

"He laughed!"

Baldur looked up into the beams, where the circular gleam of the lantern played strangely. A gust of wind blew across the farm. The other waited until it was still again. Then he said:

"And after that new discovery, there were only two possible paths. The one led the rotten way back to the age-old, criminal law of war. But the other—the other led forward into the new, mystery-drenched divine law of life. He took the one path—"

"And you, the other?"

"Yes," the soldier from Verdun nodded. "Yes."

All at once his eyes began to sparkle greenly, like the eyes of an angry god:

"But let him not deceive himself! The erstwhile lance-corporal! For the revelation of the truth that came to us that day behind the alder, while our comrades fell like flies in the machine-gun fire on the hill— it was not meant for him or me alone! No! It belongs to all mankind!— even if he thinks he can exploit that awakening to life—that awakening out of the age-old, criminal law of war—for his own unscrupulous egotistic purpose! I say: This time, his mocking laughter over all those who have again been 'stupid' enough to die like flies, even though he sits behind no alder tree, but in a fine, tiled toilet in his highest head-quarters—east or west—this time his laughter will eat through his throat like a cancer!"

Baldur looked nervously about him as the soldier continued, louder and more menacingly:

"I tell you—in the new millennium, whoever has once been freed by an eye—even if it is only the eye of a midge, seen for an instant—from the ancient law of murder and enchanted into the mystery of living breath, breathed into us by the Creator—whoever, in spite of that throttles the divine breath in another—he is the most cowardly mur-derer since Cain killed his brother."

Baldur's forehead was flecked with sweat. Suddenly he straightened up and asked in a military manner—

"May I say something?"

"What is it?"

"Well—when I entered the Hitler Youth and was taken to camp—while the flag was being raised and the band played the Horst-Wessel song, Major Buch instructed us: 'Kids,' he said, 'the nineteenth century's challenge to the youth of the world was: Liberty! Equality! Fraternity! But the twentieth century's challenge to you Aryan youth is: Go to the toilet and shit the whole Judocratic mess, including the Ten Commandments of Mr. Moses, out your Pan-German pants as fast as you can.'"

Gusts of wind blew around the barn. The hermit of Haudroumont listened. After a time he gave the Hitler scout an ineffable look:

"Boy, did you really never feel something inside you—like the sound of eternity?"

"The sound of eternity?" Baldur gave him a wry stare. "Man, that almost sounds like music. Like something composed by Master Gluck —when you turn the music pages for your girl friend because she insists on plunging into the mournful adagio. The sound of eternity? That's terrific, marvelous! But I don't understand it."

"How can you understand it as long as you do not belong to yourself?"

"To myself?" Distractedly he kept buckling and unbuckling the belt of his coat. Suddenly he jerked. "Brother! I ask you now with the deadly seriousness of a man whose deeds my Führer has taken irrevocably on himself. I ask you as a German who would no longer shudder at any October fair, not even in the chamber of horrors if the wax figure of the bloody matricide Orestes glared at him like all the Furies! I ask you as one who has complete power over you: what is *your* idea of the challenge of the twentieth century to us, the youth of the world?"

"Become yourself."

"Become myself?"

"Or perhaps you are no longer able to make a decision by yourself?"

"Of course I can. But what shall I decide on?" He plucked excitedly at his necktie, and then suddenly muttered: "You know, brother, once when I entered a Jew's cell to shoot him—his eyes looked at me so gigantically in the . . . damn it! . . . the doggone light of Aurora."

"So gigantically?" the soldier asked. And, after a pause: "Did you shoot him?"

Baldur was silent. The soldier came a step nearer:

"Perhaps that day in the dawn light you felt the sound of eternity within you."

"What are you babbling about?" Baldur recoiled and tried to laugh. "In any case, brother, we can't help it, the steam-roller is on us."

"But at this dark turning," the cripple whispered close to his ear, "each one of us is alone—each one of us is dependent only on his better self."

"Brother, brother!" Baldur's voice rattled. "Lately I've been feeling such a pain here—all around my heart."

"The heart has its own center of gravity. Even though the world around us stands on its head . . ."

"The heart?" groaned Baldur. "The most superfluous organ in the body—as the Führer likes to call it! That blood pump! No, brother! And besides let me tell you—I was begotten under Mathias Grünewald's picture of the Crucifixion."

"There is a picture of the Resurrection, too."

"But not for me, brother. No—no longer for me!" His breath labored. "Oh, to hell with it!" he suddenly moaned. "What do you want of me? With my vacuum of a conscience I can't run into the arms of democracy at this late date! Hah!"

"In you is the will to the beast—in you is the will to God. As you decide—so it will be. Decide."

"The old stuff again— If someone hits you on the left cheek, turn him the right?"

"No. If someone strikes you on the left cheek, think to yourself: Whom have I struck on the right?"

"But, man," he shouted, "one can't just accept any stupid insult?"

"You are to accept nothing. Resist everything. Save the one thing—"

"What 'one thing'?"

"In everything that you do, always choose the higher decision."

"What 'higher decision'?"

"Resist the age-old temptation always to shift the responsibility for your deeds onto another. *You* are responsible to yourself—within yourself. For yourself."

Baldur's knees sagged. Then he asked in a whisper, as if pleading:

"Brother, what shall I do?"

"What? There is only one conquest, only one victory."

"Which?"

"Over yourself."

The other was silent for an eternity. Suddenly he said:

"*You* begin."

"I begin?"

"*You* become free."

"I become free?"

"Begin! You begin! You begin, *you* begin."

The blond collapsed. As the soldier did not hold him, he slumped down against the table. And now the unknown of Verdun stood before the armed gauleiter like a sorcerer. A man of might whose power did not even harm the grass on the ground under his feet. A ruler, but one who, thirty-three steps underground, had seen the quicksilver of the mirror of things from behind. The first cold morning light coming through the barndoor played about his figure with such magic that Baldur was maddened by this titleless majesty. He thrust two fingers into his mouth and whistled shrilly.

The Gestapo youths on sentry duty outside came running.

"Come on! Get him into the truck. And shake your legs! Get that idiot out of here!"

"Where are we to take him, Herr Gauleiter?"

"Where?" Baldur glowered across the highway in the increasing morning light. "Wherever you like, God damn it! It's all the same to me."

CHAPTER TWELVE

As soon as the armored truck was out of sight, Baldur made water in the highway ditch. Meanwhile he goggled over the endless, brown reaped fields, crossed here and there by brooks, and vanishing in hilly waves toward the foggy horizon. The church steeple of Drancy was hardly recognizable. But the bell, which was ringing for early mass, boomed like an organ tune through the landscape. Wind blew cool and fresh in the grass, and every silver-green blade seemed to sense the coming light. Such melancholy was in the air as sometimes follows when summer has fled. And yet, here and there in the new-sown fields, there was an odor like spring. Now and again a rabbit ran across the highway.

From the great city of Paris only a distant, dull roaring and humming was audible. It sounded like the murmur of the ocean.

Baldur started off at top speed and, followed by his S.S. sentries, ran in the direction of the Parc d'Aulnay.

Before long, he could see Hänsel, who had his prisoners drawn up at the edge of the wood and was showering them with unnecessary orders.

"Come on! Forward!" Baldur called. "Where have you got that long ope? Come on! Tie all those restless Judocrats together so they can't et away!" He looked at his watch. "Make it snappy! All ready?"

He slung two rifles over his shoulder, and turned to the section of ifth columnists commissioned to do the shooting. "You stay here!"

"Permit me, Herr Gauleiter!" A sergeant in civilian clothes pointed o a slip of paper in his hand. "General Buch gave me express orders—"

"Are you trying to tell me what to do, you camel! I don't need an nterpreter, now when the glorious end is in sight!"

"I'm not interpreting, Herr Gauleiter!"

"Then keep your mouth shut, you double-humped camel! Get out of ny sight! or I'll teach you to roll yourself with the blue globe through he morning air." He pushed the sergeant away. Then he gave Uhle kick in the knee, shouted, "Company—march!" and herded the risoners off. One behind the other, they disappeared to the left into he undergrowth of a cathedral-dusk forest.

"Herr Gauleiter!" The sergeant came running after Baldur. "It says ere quite plainly: 'The execution squad is to fire three salvos, and if ny of the prisoners still moves, the sergeant is to give him the coup de râce with his revolver . . .'"

"You camel! You purely sentimental interpreters make me vomit. ou are to stay on the highway with Party Comrade Hänsel. Get me? ou're there to see that no rabble from the surrounding villages follows s. Do you understand? Or don't you think I can liquidate a couple of udocrats all by myself!?"

The sergeant saluted and went back to his group of civilians.

Meanwhile the candidates for death marched among impenetrable lackberry thickets, pressing forward in single file through the dew-oaked grass. Overhead, the yellow, spotted autumn foliage let hardly ray of light through.

"Step up!" Baldur jabbed Krah with his rifle butt. "You black master f ceremonies from Mt. Sinai! Hop along! Keep going, all you damned k-slingers! Let's get this comedy over with! so that I can have my reakfast! Think I'll try the Café de la Paix! . . . Ha, ha!"

The silence of the forest solitude, shut off from the outside world by lose-ranked trees, gradually began to sound in the prisoners' ears. Like he harps of a freer world, toward which they were irrevocably triding. Soon there was light coming through the twigs. Pushing for-ward to the head of the line, Baldur commanded:

"Company—halt!"

They had debouched into a large rectangular clearing, and now

533

stood not far from an open trench, about ten yards long and six fee
wide. Out of it sprawled, grotesquely disjointed, the topmost layer o
the bodies of the workers who had been shot in the battle at the cana

"Get along!"

When Hyacinthe saw the mass grave which was to be their last rest
ing place, she gave a terrible cry, and, losing consciousness, sagge
from the rope between the violinmaker and Münzer.

"Keep moving, damn it! What did you pack of vultures think? W
were going to build you a snazzy, brand-new sarcophagus, out o
Carrara marble, with a gold coat-of-arms, like the one the Pope re
cently erected for his deceased predecessors? . . . $25,000 to be waste
on you scum of the earth? . . . Forward! Get on with it, damn you
Come on!" Seizing Uhle by the arm, he led him along the opposite sid
of the trench on a path about a foot wide—the others dragging afte
Along this path, he ranged his victims side by side—in a long row
their backs to the grave.

The prisoners now faced a wall of earth shoveled up from the trenc
which would act as a backstop for the bullets. Over the top of it the
could just see into the depths of the grotto-green, dark, silent fores
solitude.

"Everything ship-shape? . . . Anybody want to pray? Go ahead i
you like!" He took off his overcoat and laid the two rifles on a moss
bank. "Yes, my esteemed Judocrats! The key to unriddling the myster
of such great events as these I can hardly be expected to place in you
hands in these last few moments! The new man is frightful. Yes, frigh
ful! And the fact is, there are damned, tremendous things at stake fo
the future. So don't kick. For the moment, unfortunately, I can d
nothing more for you than to offer you the consolation of etern
night. Ha-ha!"

Picking up one of the rifles, he shot back the bolt with a metal-har
snap, counted out the cartridges, and got ready to shoot. The water ra
down Hyacinthe's legs. The sorry rank of the condemned stoo
hunched and silent, each completely absorbed in himself, awaiting th
volley.

"Oi-oi!" groaned Krah despairingly. "Like Danton on the scaffold,
say, 'Would that I had remained a simple fisherman!' Oi!"

"Don't be afraid!" whispered Münzer. "We shall be enshrined in th
great heart of the working class!"

"Fear?" The rabbi raised his head defiantly and smiled encouragingl
at Krah. "No! We Jews have been campaigning against death for th
past six thousand years! Ha! Let him shoot—the beast! From ou

534

:douin forefather Abraham, to Baruch Spinoza, Einstein, and me!—
ath has not yet been able to conquer us! . . ."

Mathias Westermann's lips murmured prayers. Uhle looked up into
e sky. Then suddenly he began to speak softly aloud, as if before the
d he wanted to establish a last connection with his Irene, across the
her waves:

"And Thursday when I got back to Verdun from the battlefields
ith my soldier—there, in front of a café on the deserted market place,
t a lieutenant in the khaki of the French Colonials. He had a prostitute
a red silk blouse on his knee. On the round iron table before them
ere was a bottle of green absinthe. Somewhere a phonograph was
aying the 'Merry Widow' . . ."

"Shut up!" Baldur thundered. "Who's that babbling?"

"We walked past," Uhle went on, "and then, through the old, nar-
w streets of burned, blackened houses up to the cathedral."

Professor Goldschmidt fell forward against the earthen wall, weep-
g:

"Why doesn't he shoot? why doesn't he shoot?"

". . . . To the right, about halfway up the hill, in a shop window
ft unshattered by the bombardment, there were the pink-silk bras-
res that had been put on display there twenty-three years ago. Light
air they looked—like so many balloons. Above our heads a plump
t ran across the street along a charred beam. Then we were at the top
the hill, standing in the square in front of the ruined cathedral. In
16, we had seen its two square black towers day after day, looming
er the snow-covered battlefield. But we had never reached them.
ow they were before us—colossal, towering up into the darkness. All
e doors and windows were boarded up, with posters everywhere:
)éfense d'entrer!' In a niche in one of the crumbling walls stood a
ladonna, holding the Christ Child in her arms—"

"Oi-oi!" Krah began to tremble. "I can't stand it any longer!"

"As we approached, the head of the Virgin fell to the ground with a
ud clump. I picked it up. It looked like you. Truly, Irene, it looked
ke you! . . . Behind the sacristy a Newfoundland dog was barking
d scratching at the rubble. We finally found a big shell-hole in the
all and crawled inside. The soldier walked cautiously to the high
tar. I followed him. On the altar there were still two bouquets of
ithered wild flowers in turquoise-blue glass vases. After all those years
ie night wind stirred dryly through them. And in the tall Gothic
indows on either side shattered fragments of stained glass tinkled in
eir lead fastenings whenever the wind stole through the ruins—"

535

"Go on!" Hyacinthe pleaded. "Go on!"

"Don't stop. He's not going to shoot! Right?" the violinmal whispered.

"Oi-oi! Why doesn't he shoot?"

". . . . Round about us, as far as we could see, to the horizo millions of little white wooden crosses shimmered—from Douaumo —from Hill 304—from l'Homme Mort—from the Bois de Fayette . So white!—The whole landscape seemed a gigantic, bony skelet hand, closing steadily on the fields, on the town, on everything! It w as if we were standing upon the last soil of Existence. . . ."

"Go on!" the others implored him. "Go on!"

"All of a sudden, Irene! there came a tone, high in the air, like t singing of angels! We climbed the ruinous staircase to the organ lo and listened. His red cloak fluttered in the wind. And he kept climbir higher and higher still, up into the tower! Mice scampered out of t way. But he followed the tone. Up over splintered stairs. Then v listened again. It sounded like a music never heard before. 'What c that be?' I asked. He held a finger to his lips. 'S-s-sh! It's the birds dreaming in the bell tower!' And then it seemed as if on all sides, t crosses, all the way to the horizon, began marching. Yes—on th came! All the unknown soldiers—nearer and nearer. They pressed th pale faces against the windows of the cathedral. Face after face, crow ing together, listening to the tone in the bell tower."

"Dreaming birds?" Hyacinthe asked. "What were they dreami of?"

"Of life!" Uhle's eyes shone. "Of life!—And then there was a moa ing all around Verdun: 'We all dream of life—we fallen soldiers!' "

There was silence. Suddenly, in his tobacco-hoarse voice, Bald began:

"So you're dreaming of life, are you? Come, do you Judocrats su pose I'm standing here feeling perfectly happy? No—damn it! I t sometimes have my ineffably lyrical moods! But what's the use of that! It does not necessarily follow that the world could be anythi but what it is! So—are you all steady on your pins again? What do y think you're looking at with those big fish eyes? Behind every one us there's your humble servant, Death, peeping over your shoulde But we ignore him! We ignore him! There! You prospective corpses He tossed them the bottle of raspberry brandy. "Have a last swi Don't say I let you appear before your All-Creator with empty belli Everybody's got to die at least once! But, anyhow, before the er you've still time for another snifter! One more deep draught of ple ure! At least that's some consolation for the pay-off on this cock-eyed farce! Bottoms up! Prost, sweetheart!" He toasted Hyacinthe. "Here's to your slender, rose-tinted amphora of the sparkling wine of life! Prost! It's better this way than just a drop every weekend! Why the hell shouldn't we shoot the whole works at once! . . . Prost! Come on, everybody, have a drink! God in Heaven! Can't some of you cheer up a little! . . . I feel like making some real whoopee!" Fishing a harmonica out of his pocket, he blew a few bars on it and burst into hoarse song:

> There he dangles—
> The late-lamented Jew!
> A bullet recochetted
> And pierced his heart through!
> His eyes to Heaven rolling!
> Thank God it isn't you!

"Come on! Everybody sing! Come on and sing! . . . 'His eyes to Heaven ro-o-o-lling! . . .'"

". . . ro-o-o-lling!" Krah shrieked as if he had gone mad.

"Stop!" roared Baldur. "Don't yell so! Can't you see that 'Aurora's light' is already glimmering on your long nose?" He turned to stare over his shoulder at the leaping streamers from the sun. "Damn . . . Is it sunrise already?" Backing off a few paces, he hunched his shoulders against the trunk of a fir and glowered on the handful of humanity, delivered over to his mercy, there in the forest clearing, breathing their last few minutes on earth.

"You drunken rabbits—for God's sake stand up straight. By the whole crazy world, it gives me the heebie-jeebies to think of you all going down into your mass grave loaded with superstition! It gives me goose-pimples! Well, what's become of your sound of eternity now? Ha-ha! Damned if I can hear it! You're nothing but a lot of imbecile May flies! Here! This is the only majesty that counts!" Tossing his rifle into the air, he caught it and shook it, vauntingly. "Only when you've got a gun like this in your hand, do you amount to anything! Damnation! And if you weren't all such a lot of imbecile May flies—then you'd all have to go down on your knees before me right now! You swine! For *I*, and I alone, now in your very last hour on earth, here represent the whole arsenal of Aryan might! And the glory of the blond Herrenvolk! Forever and ever, Amen!"

Discomposed by the stillness of his audience, he plunged forward, flourishing the rifle.

537

"Fall down and worship me! You Judocrats! You May flies! You May flies! . . . I said, fall down and worship me! . . . Down with you! Down!" He was close upon them, the breeze playing in his hair.

Through the topmost twigs of the pines, long oblique rays pierced like searchlights, bringing dawn to the night of the forest, washing the green darkness with transparent moonstone-blue.

Baldur caught at his throat. Without further warning he flashed up his rifle, jammed the stock against his cheek, and aimed. His hands shook so that he had to lower it again.

Like a bolt from the blue, a heavy bomber heading from Le Bourget swept into sight across the forest with such terrific velocity that the tree tops, thrashed by the air pressure, fanned out like waves.

"The Führer!" Baldur raised his rifle. He was going to say something more. But the blast of air caught him and the others and swept them back against the trees.

And then something happened. The maelstrom of air churned up by the four immense, potent propellers transformed the atmosphere into a conelike whirlwind . . . Every growing thing in the clearing below was sucked up by the roots into the typhoon funnel: blue larkspur! purple heather! yellow asters! crane's-bill! . . . even the still-sleeping butterflies! . . .

With increasing momentum the spheric vacuum caught up out of the mass grave blood-drenched caps, torn clothes, colored headscarfs, siphoning them with uncanny suction, up and up, into the slanting, spiraling rays of light.

Suddenly they seemed to form into countless spinning masks and faces—pallid and bloody and bearded and haggard! Some of them wreathed with waving locks of hair! More and more of them appeared, as if the depths of the earth had exposed the victims of the most secret crimes . . . Freed, like young herons with necks thrown back, longingly they flew upward crying—glided with cries of joy . . . As if the living breath of God were irresistibly liberated from their trampled, mishandled, and crushed ribs, liberated—and assembled somewhere high in the shining sphere. Then, like a colossal hurricane delivered from its bonds, it roared down again, and blew so tremendously that Baldur staggered, stumbled, overcome with terror. In vain he strove to hold fast to the ground . . . At last he grabbed his rifle, and fired every single shot intended for the prisoners—at those faces high in the light!

However, lifted beyond all earthly accessibility, their contours disappeared in the floating glamor—in the all-illuminating giant glory of

538

a new day.

At the sound of his firing, there was a confused running about by the condemned, each one thinking he had been hit. But Uhle saw Gauleiter Baldur Hermann fire the last bullet into his own mouth, and then with shattered skull, drop over backwards. Uhle sank down on the moss and exulted:

"They dreamed of life, Irene! Of life! of life!"

The others turned away. Fired by the rays of the now fully risen sun, the depth of the forest blazed before them like a storm of light. It led them on—in color like the cloak of the soldier from no man's land, in brightness like the love-longing of all the world's unknown, clad now in the festal garments of its arising from the buried depths of the soul.

But the smudge on the clear morning sky which was Hitler's airplane in headlong flight became—in obedience to the laws of perspective— smaller and smaller and smaller.

Uhle stood up. Raised his hand high in the air and repeated the oath of Verdun as with the lips of his soul:

"Never again!"

FINIS

Accustomed for a lifetime to present my thoughts and ideas as a dramatist on the European stage in the form of plays, of tragedies and comedies, I was deprived by the Hitler terror of every possibility of seeing my works performed and had to resort to the other form of art which is called the 'novel.'

The entire production in epic form of ten years of exile was lost in the turmoil of war in France. Having escaped from concentration camps, I fled for weeks from the Gestapo through France and Spain and stranded finally—rid of all personal belongings—here in the United States.

Without contacts, without the assistance of an organized group, I tried, all by myself, in my own way, to resume in America the struggle, begun in Europe, against the desecrators of human freedom. Without books or notes, relying exclusively on my memory and the 'furor anti-teutonicus,' I conceived this panorama of our apocalyptic age. I wrote down its dance of death in dramatic prose, and in doing so I isolated in the darkest recesses accessible to self-analysis the bacillus which is the cause of Nazism. Not only to exhibit it to others but to point out the possibility of its eradication—was the sense of this work.

New York, 1943.

F. v. U.

A number of American publishers and agents reacted with curiosity and amazement to this epic of dramatic inspiration. Its strangeness, however, prevented them from offering it their hospitality. Only a young editor's faith in this work and its special significance for our time made possible its final publication. To Dr. Alexander Gode of STORM PUBLISHERS belongs the author's deep-felt gratitude.

New York, 1946.

F. v. U.

540